WELCOME HOME

"Be prepared for anything," Mesh said to Kinta Jane and Dockery as the⸺ ⸺ ⸺ own toward the villa⸺ ⸺ngs, and three times ⸺er-son who commit⸺ ⸺ot always welcomed⸺

The first giants ⸺ Jane saw other than Mesh were children, who were nearly six feet tall but had the large eyes and energetic playful motions of youth. They stopped playing with hoops and balls and throwing javelins when the mastodon caravan passed, and fell into line behind the great beasts, singing.

At the first pair of painted poles, which seemed to indicate the border of the village, two Misaabe men waited. They wore overlapping sheets of leather riveted together and bearing large bronze discs, and they leaned on spears so long you could plant them and hang flags from their heights.

The taller Misaabe spoke first; he had long gray hair and a thick beard. "Prince Chu-Roto-Sha-Meshu, son of Shoru-Me-Rasha," he said, bowing. "Welcome home."

The second was even taller, and had hair so bright red it was nearly orange, and a jaw like a granite ridge. In addition to his spear, this giant carried a long ax. "Prince Chu-Roto-Sha-Meshu, son of Shoru-Me-Rasha," he said. "You are under arrest."

BAEN BOOKS by D.J. BUTLER

To purchase any of these titles in e-book form,
please go to www.baen.com.

SERPENT DAUGHTER

D.J. BUTLER

SERPENT DAUGHTER

This is a work of fiction. All the characters and events portrayed in this book are fictional, and any resemblance to real people or incidents is purely coincidental.

A Baen Books Original

Baen Publishing Enterprises
P.O. Box 1403
Riverdale, NY 10471
www.baen.com

ISBN: 978-1-9821-2575-2

Cover art by Dan dos Santos
Maps by Rhys Davies, Bryan McWhirter

First printing, November 2020
First mass market printing, November 2021

Distributed by Simon & Schuster
1230 Avenue of the Americas
New York, NY 10020

Library of Congress Control Number: 2020036503

Pages by Joy Freeman (www.pagesbyjoy.com)
Printed in the United States of America
10 9 8 7 6 5 4 3 2 1

This book is for Alex Moore and Chris DeBoe.
It's good to have friends.

CONTENTS

———◆———

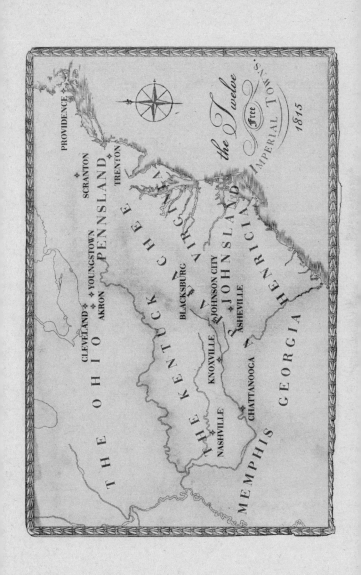

SERPENT DAUGHTER

My name is Maltres Korinn. I am Duke of Na'avu, a swamp blessed with many berry brambles on the northern borders of the land of Cahokia. I have been Regent-Minister of the Serpent Throne and Cahokia's Vizier. Now I am uncertain what titles, if any, I still hold.

By temperament, I would write only those things that I have seen. The events that I have seen include miracles sufficient to adorn the memoirs of any ten men. But the doings alone that I have witnessed will make little sense to any eventual reader of these words, so I must also write of events that have been told to me.

If this tale can be said to have a beginning, then it began in the Garden. There our first parents walked among the gods, and by some configuration of the Man, the Woman, the Serpent, and the Tree, contrived to end their blessed state split into two races of mankind: my race, the Firstborn or Children of Wisdom, mana-gifted and silver-cursed, possessed of an extra quantity of spirit, and the Children of Eve, always more numerous than us and always inclined to war.

In more recent memory, the Lion of Missouri, Kyres Elytharias, became King of Cahokia. He inherited a kingdom that had tried to reject its own goddess, the serpent Wisdom, and strove to return it to its former *path. He died half a failure, at least, murdered by one of his own men at his goddess's great sacred site, the Serpent Mound, at the confluence of the Ohio and the Mississippi. By his arcane arts, though, his wife, Hannah Penn, the Penn landholder and Empress, conceived three children.*

Hannah's brother Thomas, who had contrived Elytharias's murder, immured Hannah, taking both the Penn family wealth and the Imperial throne. Hannah bore her three children in secret, and sent them away to be hidden in corners of the empire remote from Philadelphia.

Following the death of Kyres Elytharias, Cahokia had no king. Her good and great sought, by counsel and consensus, as well as by rite and oracle, to replace him, and never succeeded. Cahokia suffered from kinglessness as well as from the Pacification of the Ohio, in which the Emperor Thomas turned all the machinery of his state to grind the wealth and spirit out of Cahokia and the other six Sister Kingdoms. He did this at the bidding of his secret dark master, the Necromancer Oliver Cromwell.

I was summoned from my bog and bramble to administer the city and to order the search for a new ruler.

Fifteen years passed from the death of Elytharias. Having learned from one of her servants of the birth and sequestration of Hannah's children, Thomas tortured his sister to death to unearth what he could of this threat to his wealth and power. Discovering from Hannah that one of the three had been hidden with the Elector and war hero Iron Andy Calhoun near Nashville, he sent his servants after the child.

Thus it was that Sarah Elytharias Penn, who knew herself only as Sarah Calhoun, came one day to the fair in Nashville town and was attacked by Imperial officers. The emperor's dragoon bodyguards, the Philadelphia Blues, and his chaplain-wizard, Ezekiel Angleton, attempted several times to kidnap her. Sarah escaped by her native wit and magical talent, and with the help of her father's confessor, a Cetean monk named Thalanes. Dodging Imperial pursuit, she and the monk and Calvin Calhoun, a grandson of Iron Andy, fled down the Natchez Trace to New Orleans. Their path was dogged not only by the Blues, but also by strange sorcerous creations of the Necromancer, and by his personal servants, the undead Lazars, led by the greatest of the Lazars, the Sorcerer Robert Hooke himself.

At this time, I received troubling embassies from the Heron King, informing me that Peter Plowshare was dead. I did not fully understand the message then, but I now know that the death of Peter Plowshare the father commences the reign of Simon Sword the son. Peter Plowshare blesses with abundance, peace, and stability, and Simon Sword brings judgment, destruction, and change. I rejected a call to submit to Simon Sword, and soon heard from Missouri and the Greenwood of the rampaging of the beastkind. Towns were leveled and fields destroyed. Refugees began to pour into the city, and we took them in. We took them all in.

In New Orleans, Sarah lost her companion Thalanes, but gained the service of William Johnston Lee, a Cavalier soldier who had been head of the Philadelphia Blues under Kyres Elytharias, and who had hidden Sarah's brother at his birth, and Cathy Filmer, a

Harvite healer and Lee's love. Sarah also witnessed the murder of the righteous and beloved Bishop of New Orleans, Chinwe Ukwu, by the same Imperial officers who had been pursuing her.

Sarah left New Orleans. At the Serpent Mound itself, she recovered the regalia of Cahokia: the Sevenfold Crown, the Orb of Etyles, and the Heronblade, a golden sword her father had carried into battle. Besieged by the Imperials and Lazars, by the gendarmes of New Orleans, and by beastkind under the personal command of Simon Sword, Sarah bargained with the destroyer. She exchanged the Heronblade for something no one knew existed—the Heronplow—and for command of a troop of beastmen. With those beastmen, she defeated the other two armies confronting her, and came away with a new follower: a man named Jacob Hop, in whose body Simon Sword had been manifesting himself. Sarah soon sent Hop east to Johnsland, looking for her brother Nathaniel, following information provided by William Lee. One of William's enemies, the wizard-priest Angleton, turned in the encounter on the Serpent Mound toward the personal service of the Necromancer, and also journeyed eastward.

After the death of Bishop Ukwu, his son Etienne, a crime lord and gambler, was ordained by the Synod to replace him as bishop. Following this strange turn of events, New Orleans has proceeded in ever more unexpected directions. The new bishop and the City Council fomented a tax revolt against the Chevalier of New Orleans that eventually led to the revolt of the city's gendarmes. The chevalier himself fled the city, and is now camped about it with an army of Spanish soldiers.

The bishop's other son, Chigozie Ukwu, a more conventional priest, exiled himself from New Orleans. Among the beastkind of Missouri, he became a prophet-like figure, the head of a congregation calling itself the Merciful. Compelled by enemies, the Merciful found themselves the custodian of a savage child of Simon Sword.

Sarah entered the city with her cousin, Alzbieta Torias. Sarah had bound the priestess Alzbieta by arcane means, forcing her to take an oath on the Sevenfold Crown. In the same encounter, she had outwitted Alzbieta's counselor Uras and knocked her wizard Sherem into a comatose state. Alzbieta was one of seven candidates I was preparing to present to the goddess for Her consideration as possible kings or queens of Cahokia, and for a time, Sarah appeared in our councils at her side.

The Imperial forces of the Pacification within our city then came under the command of Notwithstanding Schmidt, one of the Directors of the Imperial Ohio Company. With her came the hedge wizard, Luman Walters, a dabbler in esoteric traditions, a seeker of arcane lore, and her magical aide.

Seeing that Sarah sought her own ascension to her father's throne and would disrupt my labors, I foolishly raised my hand against her. The day before the winter solstice, when the seven candidates were due to appear before the goddess on Her Serpent Throne, I imprisoned Sarah and Calvin Calhoun to prevent them from interfering. I also allowed my wardens to be deployed alongside Company troops to pin Sarah's allies in the city within the house where they were staying, so they couldn't come to help her.

That same night, by no plan of mine, the beastkind of Simon Sword broke through the Treewall surrounding the city and fell upon my people.

But, by great fortune, Sarah was mightier than I, and perhaps she had already been chosen by the goddess. Despite hundreds of miles of separation, she came into contact with her brother. Nathaniel, plagued by voices and a falling sickness all his life, ascended into spirit realms with the assistance of an Anishinaabe guide named Ma'iingan.

This ascent gave Nathaniel healing powers. He raised Sherem, he turned the heart of Alzbieta toward serving Sarah out of love, and he showed Sarah a secret path to meeting with the goddess, away from the presentation ceremony I had arranged. This meeting was not to be at the Temple of the Sun atop the Great Mound, but at an older, nearly forgotten holy place, the Sunrise Mound.

I returned to the Temple of the Sun to gather up the regalia from where I had left them, on the seat of the throne. Calvin Calhoun came with me, and in the encounter, he was forced to fight and kill a man, one of the candidates, shedding blood on the Serpent Throne itself. For that blood-guilt, he was excluded from the vision of glory that followed: using the Heronplow, Sarah reconsecrated the Sunrise Mound, and within it found Unfallen Eden and the goddess Wisdom Herself, Unfallen Eve.

Alzbieta, Sherem, and I stood as three witnesses alongside an angelic host as the goddess declared Sarah to be Her Beloved.

Calvin fled, returning to Nashville.

With the Heronplow, Sarah healed the wounded

Treewall of Cahokia. William Lee and Sarah's beastkind retook the city, with my wardens at their side, and with the aid of some of the Imperials, who defected. Another defector to Sarah's cause in this battle was the hedge wizard Walters, who single-handedly defended the city's Basilica from a pack of beastkind.

Simultaneously with the battle at Cahokia, in distant Johnsland, Jacob Hop and the Anishinaabe Ma'iingan defended Nathaniel from an attack by Ezekiel Angleton, who had become one of the walking dead, a Lazar.

The Imperial Ohio Company, with militia and artillery and with hordes of shambling dead, quickly returned to surround and cut off Cahokia. Soon, they were joined by the Roundhead general Sayle and his famous apostolic cannons, and the walls of Cahokia shuddered.

Having been identified by the goddess as Her Beloved, Sarah was nevertheless not Queen of Cahokia. One obstacle in her way was the city's Metropolitan Zadok Tarami, who returned from pilgrimage after the battle and was admitted by the besieging Imperials. Tarami was a partisan of the reformers in Sarah's grandfather's time, the men who sought to cast the goddess as a demon and the Serpent Throne as a monument to Her defeat. Though Tarami did not ally with the Imperials, he stood in Sarah's way as she struggled to feed and unite the city. His entrenched reformers and the worshippers of the goddess struggled over burials and other rites notwithstanding Sarah's inclusion of the Metropolitan in her councils, and her giving him a role in her anointing as queen in the Basilica. Despite being crowned as the political queen of the city, the Serpent Throne and its power remained inaccessible to Sarah, and the city's defenses grew weaker. Sarah consecrated the Temple of the Sun and closed the veil over the Serpent Throne, but then found that she could not enter.

The smuggler and pirate Montserrat Ferrer i Quintana sneaked into the city, bearing a message from the Chevalier of New Orleans—that he had captured Margaret, the third child of Kyres Elytharias, and would trade her for Sarah's hand in marriage. Trusting in her brother to rescue Margaret, Sarah took Ferrer i Quintana and the hedge wizard Walters to the Serpent Mound at the confluence of the rivers, where Sarah—aided by her brother, with his strange abilities to enter and travel in spirit realms—consulted with the shade of Kyres Elytharias.

We learned of the fall of Zomas, the eighth kingdom of the Firstborn in the New World, and the only one on the western shore of the Mississippi. We began to receive a trickle of Zoman refugees mixed in with the flood of Missourians.

Following the battle in Cahokia and Johnsland, Nathaniel and Hop had turned northward, finding Margaret imprisoned in the Hudson River Republic and on her way to being sold, perhaps to her uncle Thomas, though that is but one possibility. In rescuing Margaret from her bonds, they crossed paths with a man called Isaiah Wilkes, once apprenticed to Benjamin Franklin as a printer's devil, then later a lieutenant to the Lightning Bishop in his secret Conventicle, then later still the bishop's successor as the Conventicle's head, its "Franklin." Wilkes and one of his co-conspirators, a woman named Kinta Jane Embry, were traveling to Acadia in pursuit of allies to fulfill the Conventicle's raison d'être, to stand against Simon Sword.

Sarah formed a council to guide her in an attempt to reconstruct a forgotten enthronement ritual and seat herself upon the Serpent Throne. Her advisors included Luman Walters, Isaiah Wilkes, and Jacob Hop: the latter two already dead men, Wilkes having drowned in a canoe accident and Hop having been murdered by Emperor Thomas's machiavel, the grandson of the Lightning Bishop, Temple Franklin. Sarah and the three men were connected by Nathaniel and his abilities, but when the Imperials broke through the Treewall, Sarah lost patience and entered the Temple of the Sun.

At the same time, Oliver Cromwell and Robert Hooke transgressed the temple's sanctity by crossing its threshold, as well.

Though Wilkes was dead, his colleague Kinta Jane Embry continued the Conventicle's quest. In Acadia, she and her guide, a frontiersman named Timothy Dockery, were taken captive by one of the Anakim, Chu-Roto-Sha-Meshu, an exiled prince, who is called Mesh among the Children of Adam.

With the aid of her council, interpreting clues buried in Franklin's New World Tarock, Sarah ascended the Serpent Throne. I do not know what she experienced, but I know that she encountered some energy of Simon Sword within, and I know that she and Luman Walters were buried in a grave by the Necromancer and his Lazar, who interrupted the rite at its climax. I know also that Sarah solved a riddle that overcame her undead foes, burning away their bodies with the power of life, and that she solved the riddle with the help of the young Bishop of New Orleans, the former crime lord, Etienne Ukwu. I have been told that at the last moment, she left Luman Walters behind and went on alone, and then...

And then, I do not know anymore.

Light and life burst from the Temple of the Sun. The shambling dead crumbled to the earth, and the Imperials fled.

But they were not gone. They regrouped in the Ohio, drawing reinforcements from the east and the south. And in the meantime, the beastkind continued to rage across the Mississippi; the reign of Simon Sword was not over.

Perhaps it had not even truly begun.

And Sarah had not emerged from behind the veil.

*"Kanawha is lost. What makes you
think you can find it?"*

CHAPTER ONE

A week's journey from Montreal, with the valleys of
Quebec behind them and surrounded by rocky, snow-
capped peaks, the giant Chu-Roto-Sha-Meshu, son of
Shoru-Me-Rasha, let Tim Dockery go.

The eight-foot-tall redheaded man, known to both
his prisoners as *Mesh*, stood at the edge of the light
thrown by their tiny fire, leaning against the flank
of one of his mastodons and stroking it with his left
hand as he stared through thick pines at the darkness
below and behind them. "Very good, Dockery," he
boomed. "You can leave now."

Dockery was startled from his reverie. He'd been
contemplating escape. He and Kinta Jane Embry had
been contacted in Montreal by the giant, and had
taken him for an ally, until the giant had killed the
third member of their party and taken them prisoner.

"Go where?" Dockery spat tobacco juice. "We're in
the hinterland of Acadia now, there ain't a settlement
within days of walking."

The giant grinned, his enormous teeth shining in a

horizontal line that nearly split his head open. "There are settlements in the Outaouais. Even a tracker as poor as myself should be able to locate a hunting party within a few hours, and possibly a village."

Mesh pointed his spear at Dockery. Taking that to be a command, Dockery stood. He shrugged, adjusting the wool pullover frock on his shoulders to center it and straightening the badger pelt on his head. "You . . . hungry?"

The giant squinted, the firelight flickering around the clay-colored skin of his face and making his eye sockets look cavernous. "I have had enough of you. You are no longer welcome at my fire."

Kinta Jane stood, alarm on her face. Mesh whistled sharply and both his dogs, each the size of a small pony, lunged forward to seize Kinta Jane's match coat in their teeth and pull her back to the ground. They did this without uttering a sound; dogs couldn't bark at all in Kinta Jane's presence—she claimed that she had a dog's tongue in her mouth, and Dockery hadn't pressed for more explanation.

"Why?" Kinta Jane demanded.

Mesh pointed his spear head at the woman, but turned his eyes to Dockery. "I will not explain myself to either of you. Dockery, leave now, or I kill Kinta Jane."

Dockery choked. "No," he said. "No, I'm going." Mesh was right. Dockery would be able to survive in the cold, even if he might not immediately find a hunting party. Kinta Jane was from New Orleans, and suffered from the winter weather.

"Take your rifle." Mesh smiled.

Dockery scooped up the long weapon—his Missouri

war ax and knife were still on his belt—and stumbled into the cold darkness.

He owed Kinta Jane no debt of love, though she was, practically at least, his superior in the Conventicle. Thinking of her receiving a spear wound filled his heart with too many dreadful images: Gert Visser, dying impaled by that same spear on a tree; Julia Stuyvesant, once Dockery's lover, carrying Dockery's unborn child to a wedding with the Emperor Thomas Penn, and the horrifying void that was all Dockery could call to mind when he tried to imagine that child's eventual fate.

In moments, the yellow light of the fire was gone, and Dockery was plunged into moonless darkness.

The snow was thick and crusted with a thin shell of ice, no new flakes having fallen in two days. While he gathered his thoughts, he marched quickly and kept to their trail—the mastodons, or *shu-shu*, as Mesh called them, cleared a broad and manageable trail with their bodies, and since they had zigzagged up a steep incline to reach their camp, retracing their steps had the added virtue of quickly putting Dockery out of Mesh's line of sight, in case the giant decided to shoot him in the back with his enormous bow.

What was Mesh doing? He had held them prisoner by their own fear of violence rather than by any explicit threat, and claimed to be taking them to his people. Dockery and Kinta Jane had gone along out of fear, looking for an escape opportunity that had not yet materialized. They had also gone along because they had been looking for an ancient ally among the giants, someone or some group called Brother Anak. Mesh knew about Brother Anak and the secret alliance, so traveling with Mesh, they seemed to be at least close to being on the right track.

But why cast Dockery out now?

Surely, Mesh wanted Kinta Jane to himself.

To offer her a secret bargain? To beat information out of her about the Conventicle, or about its great enemy, Simon Sword?

To eat her?

Dockery stopped. He shivered from the cold creeping up under his pullover frock and around the edges of his badger-pelt hat.

He had to rescue Kinta Jane. This was the opportunity they had been waiting for, or at least, Dockery could turn it into that opportunity. With fingers growing stiffer by the moment, he checked the firing pan of his rifle and then turned to look back up the hill. The fire was a distant twinkle, a mere Biblical jot.

He could leave her. Dockery had the skills to return to Montreal on his own. He'd been raised by hill folk outside Pittsburgh, counterfeiters who preferred making their own trails to taking William Penn's tollways, and he'd lived for years with Wild Algonks. He owed Kinta Jane Embry a duty by their mutual association with the Conventicle, but that was all.

Surely, that shouldn't be enough duty to hold him.

And yet his feet didn't go anywhere.

She was a woman, and in danger.

"Dammit, Dockery," he growled.

"Do not move," an unknown voice behind him whispered. "Or I will kill you." At the same moment, a razor-thin wedge-end of cold metal touched Dockery's neck.

Best to believe the voice.

"If you snuck up on me and I didn't hear you," Dockery said, "you're an Indian. Up here, I'm going to guess some kind of Algonk. Cree? Or could be, what, Mi'kmaq or Mohawk?"

"Lay down the musket," the voice said.

"Your English is good, anyway. Méti?" Dockery obeyed, pushing the butt of his musket down into the snow and leaning the barrel against the nearest pine trunk. "I'm friendly. Out here on a matter relating to three brothers." He was holding his breath.

The other man hesitated. Was that surprise? Confusion? "I have two brothers," Dockery's new captor finally said. "We each came from a different mother and father."

Dockery let out a sigh of relief. "Such brothers would be a marvel to remember until the end of days." He turned, but the grin that had been forming on his face melted—the other man was indeed an Algonk; he wore a fringed shirt and leggings much like Dockery's, and he still held a long knife to Dockery's neck. In his other hand he held a short carbine, barrel now pointed at Dockery's belly. A blanket over his shoulders might have been dyed gray and red, but it was hard to be sure, in the darkness.

The Algonk had his head cocked to one side and his eyes narrowed.

"I ain't saying I expect hospitality," Dockery said, "but this is starting to feel downright hostile."

"Shh."

Silence. Dockery smelled pine and some animal musk he couldn't identify.

The Algonk pursed his lips and whistled two notes, following them with a *tut-tut* clicking of tongue against teeth.

The Algonk wasn't alone. Whoever he was signaling, though, made no response.

"Listen," Dockery said. "We're being held prisoner—"

An enormous spear appeared suddenly, as if it had sprouted in the center of the Algonk's throat. Blood spurted in all directions, a hot whip of it slashing across Dockery's cheek. At the same moment, a dark mass crashed from the pines. It knocked Dockery aside and threw the Algonk into the snow, and then it pounded into a screen of pine trees on the other side.

Dockery heard a gunshot, and the twang of a bowstring, and then cursing in Algonk. "Skanak!" "Skunagoose!" Another man in a fringed leather shirt and pants took three long steps forward out of the trees, a musket clutched in both hands, but no head on his shoulders. At the end of the three paces, the man stopped, stood on tippy-toes and raised his hands as if trying to place the musket on a high shelf. A single jet of blood lanced upward from the short stump of a neck that remained, and then he fell forward into the snow, disappearing into the bank beside Dockery.

More screaming kept Dockery from staring too long—he grabbed his musket and knelt, watching the trees. Silver starlight danced on dark green boughs as they shook from violence hidden by the trees for a few more seconds, and then were still again.

Dockery heard chopping and tearing sounds, and then Mesh emerged from the trees. He dragged a man with one hand around the fellow's throat; the prisoner was taller than Dockery, but he dangled like a puppet in the giant's grip. The captured man wore leathers, and in a splash of starlight, Dockery saw paint on his cheeks and a topknot of long black hair.

Dockery aimed his musket at the giant's chest and pulled back the hammer. "That's our friend." His hand trembled, but only slightly.

"Hmm." Mesh scratched his chin with his free hand. Where were the dogs? Keeping Kinta Jane pinned? "He's my prisoner now."

"And us?" Dockery asked. "Are we your prisoners, too?"

Mesh chuckled softly. "Do we have to say these heavy words, Dockery? Even a worm of such lowly intelligence as I am can sometimes understand a thing without speaking it."

"Kinta Jane and I are leaving," Dockery said.

"No." Mesh stepped forward—

Dockery aimed at the center of the looming giant's chest and squeezed the trigger—

click.

Mesh punched him in the face, bowling him into the snow. Ears ringing, blood rushing to his face, breath coming in ragged gasps, Dockery heard the giant mutter, "I urinated into the barrel of your musket this morning. If you didn't notice *that*, all I can think is that you must have an even poorer sense of smell than *I* do."

Dockery lost track of the world for a time. When he had mastered his senses and pulled himself up into a sitting position, he was shuddering violently from cold and pain. Mesh stood looking at him; the captive Indian was tied hand and wrist and slung over one shoulder, and Mesh held his spear in his hand, tip aimed generally in Dockery's direction.

A large sack was tied to Mesh's belt.

"Come," Mesh said. "Pick up your gun and return to camp."

"You pissed into my gun." Dockery hurt. His body felt far away.

"It's a stupid weapon."

It took Dockery three tries to stand, and longer to find his firearm where it had fallen in the snow. "Maybe you'd just like to kill me, right here and now."

"I don't want you to die," Mesh said.

Dockery took his first stumbling steps back up the hill. "If you thought we were being followed, you could have asked my help. You didn't have to trick me into being bait."

"I didn't *think* we were being followed," the giant said. "I *knew*. And I didn't *trick* you, I just didn't *tell* you what you were doing."

And what he had been doing was luring their pursuers into the open so that Mesh could deal with them. And those pursuers included men who had given Dockery at least the initial watchwords of brothers of the Conventicle.

Perhaps they were the men he and Kinta Jane had been trying to contact.

Perhaps the Algonks, the forces of Brother Odishkwa, had come to rescue them.

Dockery's blood froze in his veins as he lurched up the slope.

He felt as if the bones in his legs might shatter as he stepped back into the small yellow ring of warmth, fenced in by thin pines and sunk into a slight depression in the side of the hill. Mesh's two enormous dogs sat staring at Kinta Jane. The giant had tied her hands and feet all together behind her back and bound a rag into her mouth, so she lay on her side with a blanket tossed over her.

To hell with the giant, Mesh could kill them at any time. Dockery knelt and removed Kinta Jane's gag, then untied her.

"I would have yelled," she told him when her mouth was freed.

"I guess he figured as much."

Mesh appeared between two trees that were only slightly shorter than he was. Stooping, he rolled the Algonk onto a snowbank on his back. The man's eyes were open, and he stared at the Talligewi furiously.

The giant sat on a large stone, as tall as Dockery's chest height. He wrapped both fists around his spear and leaned on it thoughtfully, staring back and forth at his prisoners. "Perhaps," he rumbled, "this is a puzzle that will require a greater intellect than my own to solve."

"Let us go," Dockery said.

The Algonk looked back and forth between the others and said nothing.

The giant teased at the inside of one ear with a finger. "I feel that a more clever man than I would be able to resolve this with a single question. You may perhaps be familiar with the sorts of question I have in mind—you, Algonk, what would Dockery say if I asked him about so and so. And the cleverness of the question would lie in eliciting an answer that would show me which of you to trust, if any."

"Who are you?" the Algonk asked.

"Me?" Mesh seemed surprised. "I am just a poor hunter, really. A Misaabe is what your people call me, I believe. Talligewi. Anak. A poor hunter of no account, with inadequate brains."

"Let us go," Dockery said.

Mesh ignored him. "I suppose," the giant said to

the Indian prisoner, "we had better begin by dispelling any false notions you might have of rescue."

A light flashed in the Algonk's eyes.

"Yes, there it is. You came with companions, and you are convinced that some of them will storm the camp at night, or perhaps that they will go for aid. You are not alone, are you? Others among your people are part of your . . . conspiracy?"

"Others know of . . . the matter relating to three brothers," the Algonk said.

Mesh snorted and waved a hand. "We are past that now. What I must know is . . . well, wiser men than I have told me I must take all things in their proper order. So first, about rescue."

"Let us go," Dockery said.

"Your people have from time to time taken the scalps of their enemies," Mesh said to the Indian. "For various purposes."

"And had our own taken," the Algonk said.

"Yes," Mesh agreed. "For the medicine, for the power, that is in the scalps. And to mark territory. And to terrify an enemy."

"Yes." The Indian's face was impassive.

"And to count. Though with hands as large and ungainly as mine, it is difficult to take only the hair." Mesh reached into the large sack hanging from his belt and produced a man's head. He raised it by its long black topknot, allowing blood to drip from the cleanly severed neck to the trampled snow. "I count one."

Kinta Jane vomited. Dockery's own stomach turned, but he held it in check. The Algonk's face was impassive.

"One is not very impressive," Mesh said. "If you had come here as a pair, like a Wandering Johnny and his hired porter, the sight of your companion's head would let you know that you were alone. But you did not come here in a pair, did you?"

The Algonk said nothing.

"No," Mesh said, "you don't need to tell me. I raided your camp, and I tracked you in Quebec, and I've been watching you for days. You didn't come here in a pair." He set the severed head neatly on the earth, upright, eyes facing his prisoners. "You didn't come here in three, either."

He pulled a second head from his bag. "This fellow's name is Segenam. He loved to suck on dried meat, never chewed it, just sucked on it for hours on end, didn't he? Mind you, a lowly barbarian such as I has no comment to offer on another man's eating habits. I am merely sharing what I observed. Oh, and I forgot to introduce your first companion. He was called Chogan. Chogan loved horses; he always lingered to look whenever he encountered one. But then, you know both their names, don't you, Etchemin?"

Cree names.

The Algonk still kept a calm expression on his face. "You know my name too, giant. What of it? Do you threaten me?"

Mesh shrugged. "I merely wish you to appreciate your situation."

"I am not afraid."

Dockery, though, felt a thin cold lance of fear stabbing up through his belly and along his spine.

"What names do you know of my people, I wonder?" Mesh reached out with his spear butt and tapped Etchemin on the forehead. "Do you know *my* name? Do you know the names of any of my kin?"

The Cree said nothing.

"Why are you following me?" the giant asked.

"You kidnapped these people," Etchemin said.

"And you are rescuers?" Mesh frowned. "Rangers sent by Champlain?"

"You know we are not."

Mesh nodded. "I know. And I grow weary of counting." He stretched the drawstrings of the bag and overturned it. Three more heads bounced onto the earth. One rolled so close to the fire that its topknot fell across the coals, and the stink of scorched hair filled Dockery's nostrils.

Kinta Jane vomited again.

"Mukki," the giant said. "Wematin. Hassun."

For the first time, Etchemin looked nervous.

"Yes," the giant said. "You came in six. Don't waste time either denying or confirming it, you and I both know it's true. One thing you should know about me is that I have little imagination. Poetry is wasted on me, and so is bluffing."

"I'm not afraid to die," Etchemin said.

"I didn't say I planned to kill you."

The Cree's eyes narrowed. "What then?"

Mesh stood. "I have killed my own cousins, Algonk. I have killed the very uncle who initiated me into the ways of manhood and I have killed my brother, and I have done these things to be able to take the places of those men. I would seize the power of Kanawha and restore my people to their ancestral lands and might."

Something like a smile crept over Etchemin's face.

"What do you say, Cree?" the giant asked. "You were willing to be my uncle's ally? Will you be mine instead?"

"Yes," the Algonk said.

"What the hell are you doing, Mesh?" Dockery blurted out.

The giant ignored Dockery. Taking a long knife from his belt, he stooped to cut the Indian's bonds with it. Then he tossed the blade to the ground beside the Algonk and resumed his position leaning against the boulder, hands wrapped around his spear.

"These two southerners are faithful to the vision of William Penn," he said to the Indian. "Kill them, and you and I will plot how we shall share power."

Kinta Jane lurched to her feet. Vomit was still splashed on her lips, but she was faster than Dockery, who was rising to his knees as she stood. The Cree, though, was faster than both of them. He snatched up the blade and sprang into the air, hurling himself at Dockery—

but Mesh swung the butt of his spear and caught Etchemin midair, cracking him in the forehead with the heavy wood.

The Algonk dropped to his back beside the tumble of severed heads, all the air leaving his lungs in a single *whoosh*, and then the giant fell upon him, driving his spear downward with both hands, through the dead center of the man's belly. Dockery heard the wet tearing of flesh and the crack of Etchemin's spinal column and finally the muted *thud* of the earth receiving the spearhead, all rolled into a single split second of sickening sound.

This time, Dockery vomited.

"What are you doing?" Kinta Jane brandished her stiletto. It was a ridiculously tiny weapon.

Mesh left his spear pinning the dead man to the

ground and withdrew a pace, leaning again against the stone. "This man was your enemy and mine. All these men were."

"You couldn't just tell us that?" Dockery asked. "You had to stage all this...theater?"

"You wanted to test them," Kinta Jane said.

"No," Mesh said. "I had been stalking them for weeks, and I knew their mettle."

"You wanted to test *us*," Dockery guessed. "You wanted to see if we were in league with them. I was bait to lure them out of physical hiding, but they were bait to see if I would come out of...another kind of hiding."

Mesh nodded.

"I wasn't hiding," Dockery said.

"Did we...pass?" Kinta Jane asked.

"You are alive," Mesh said.

"Did you really kill your uncle, and those others?" Dockery felt sweat cooling on the back of his neck.

Mesh nodded. "I did not wish to, but when I learned the evil they were attempting, I had no choice. Even a worm such as I must from time to time straighten as if it had a spine, and take righteous action."

"Now what?" Kinta Jane asked. "Now do you tell us what all that meant, about Kanawha? And why did you kill your uncle? And who are you really, and what are we doing here?"

"First, you may leave if you wish." Mesh gestured at the two shu-shu. "Take Uchu or Shash if you like, either one. I think they'll obey you now, and I know Dockery is enough of a woodsman to get you safely back to Montreal. I am not your captor any longer. I apologize for holding you as I did, I beg your forgiveness, and I give you your freedom."

Dockery frowned. "Do you want us to leave?"

"No." The giant's voice was firm. "I want you to stay. I need allies. And I will tell you why, but only if you choose to remain with me." He smiled, but somehow the sight of his horselike teeth was less frightening now. "As friends."

"You killed Gert Visser," Kinta Jane said.

The giant frowned. "That was an error of judgment. When he sneaked into my camp, I believed I had been outwitted. I jumped to the conclusion that he, and you, were my enemies. I know now that I was mistaken."

"That was no error," Dockery muttered. "Bastard deserved it."

Kinta Jane ignored his comment. "What is Kanawha?"

"I have many things to tell you," Mesh said, "if we are friends and allies. If you are merely going to leave me, then you must direct your questions to a book-cadger."

"You aren't Brother Anak," Kinta Jane said. "You lied when you said that you were."

"I never said that I was Brother Anak," Mesh said. "Groveling and mealymouthed worm that I am, I *did* intend to mislead you on that point. But what should be more interesting from your point of view is that I can *become* Brother Anak."

"I guess you better explain that," Dockery said.

"The three brothers have failed." Mesh leaned forward to pluck his spear from Etchemin's belly, wiping blood from the blade in the snow. "Onas has become too interested in his own power. Anak and Odishkwa have formed an unholy alliance to abandon their oaths and join with the monster Simon Sword, rather than to resist him."

"Join with him?" The word sprang from Dockery's startled lips without his bidding. "How do you join with a force of nature?"

"You offer him aid and sacrifice, in exchange for things you want. Just as you join with any other sort of power."

"But would Simon Sword honor such a bargain?" Kinta Jane asked. "*Could* he honor such a bargain?"

Mesh rubbed his large chin. "When I was a boy, I believe my uncle would have told me no. He would have said that Simon Sword does not have a will as you or I, he rushes with all his force and rage along the path that lies before him. But my uncle became corrupted, and his men, including my cousins, came to believe that they could regain Kanawha by making a bargain with the destructive demon of the Ohio."

"And with Odishkwa," Dockery said.

Mesh nodded slowly. "And I believe the men carrying on the Algonk tradition of the three brothers must have become similarly corrupted. It is easy to imagine how—in exchange for, say, the wealth of Pennsland, many men would change alliances, or sell their country's honor."

"You know the story of the three brothers," Kinta Jane said, "because it was taught to you."

"My family knew the secret," Mesh said. "My grand-fathers met with William Penn, and his son, and his son's son. When I was a boy, my uncle met with Hannah, when she was Sister Onas and I was newly initiated."

"And when did you learn that your family had lost its way?" Dockery asked.

Mesh's face darkened. "Last year. My two cousins, whose short names were Kush and Toru, took me down to the shores of the Michi-Gami, as your Ojibwe cousins call the sea on which my people live. They told me that I had gained in wisdom and stature, and that it was time to tell me the true nature of our tradition, which was that it was a plan to retake our lost land of Kanawha, and that with our Algonk allies, we would destroy Brother Onas and share his land."

Kinta Jane looked stunned. Dockery felt dizzy.

"How did you react?" Kinta Jane asked.

"Kush and Toru are bad liars." Mesh's face was impassive. "I killed them both, and I buried them in the dirt, touching no stone."

"And you brought your uncle to justice," Dockery suggested.

"My uncle accused me of secret murder," Mesh said. "His men bore false witness, and I was cast out. But it is true what I have told you of myself—I am a hunter. I lay in wait on the fringes of my people's lands, watching my uncle's movements and the movements of his men, until it was clear that they were coming to meet with Brother Odishkwa and Brother Onas, and then I followed them."

"The larger snowshoes you had," Dockery murmured.

Mesh continued his story as if uninterrupted. "I killed my uncle, but he has many allies who yet live. I thought I had killed their Algonk allies, but other men followed me—tonight, you yourself have seen those men die."

"And you thought perhaps you could not trust us, either," Dockery said.

"I did not know," Mesh admitted.

"Does that mean the end of the three brothers?" Kinta Jane asked.

Mesh shrugged. "Are there more Talligewi or more

Algonks who know the story, and carry on the tradition?"
He shrugged again.

"Are we part of the same organization?" Dockery
wondered out loud. "Somewhere, are there children
of Adam and Misaabe who know each other and who
jointly pass down the story of the three brothers? Are
there members of the Conventicle who are Misaabe and
Algonk? Are there cells of the Conventicle prepared to
intervene in the case of the failure of Brother Anak?"

"I do not think your Bishop Franklin had influence
among my people," the giant said. "I believe that he
feared the failure of Brother Onas, and prepared a
remedy. John Penn must have told him the watchwords."

"The Franklin might have known the answers to
these questions," Kinta Jane said. She didn't look at
Dockery, quite conspicuously, but he felt her words
like a dagger to his heart.

It was his fault that the Franklin had died.

"Maybe John Penn feared his son Thomas," Dockery
suggested. "After all, he made his daughter Hannah
the landholder, and Sister Onas."

Kinta Jane sat silently a moment before answering.
"Maybe we will one day know the answers to these
mysteries. But if you intend to become Brother Anak,
Mesh, and lead your people to stand against Simon
Sword, then I am with you. It is for this end that my
brother René brought me into the Conventicle. I have
seen Franklin's Vision, and I have taken his oath."

Dockery saw in his mind's eye, for just a moment,
an image of the face of Julia Stuyvesant. In his mind's
eye, she was screaming, not in fear or from a wound,
but in the moment of giving birth. Julia screaming, and
then Julia handing a child to her husband. To Dockery.

And the child was beautiful.

Then his heart tumbled. If there ever was such a birth, if such a child were ever permitted to come into the world, it would never know Dockery as its father.

"I'm with you, too," Dockery said. "I've severed all my ties."

"I said nothing about leading," Mesh clarified. "A poor near-imbecile such as myself, with modest talents at hunting and warfare, can scarcely hope to lead a nation as mighty as the one I with great temerity claim as my own. At most, I can hope to beg some small amount of assistance. Indeed, I think the most likely outcome is that I return to my home and am executed on sight, for the deaths of my cousins and my uncle, or for the new killings with which I have more recently bloodied my hands."

"Well, *now* I feel cheerful," Dockery said.

"You should know the risks."

"What is Kanawha?" Kinta Jane asked.

The giant's expression flattened instantly, into something that looked like reverence, or maybe awe. "Ah," he said. He pulled a wide-bladed copper knife from his belt, a blade Dockery had never seen before, and began to examine it.

"You called it a land," Kinta Jane continued. "I've heard stories that the Ohio was once inhabited by giants."

Mesh nodded. The dagger's blade was pocked with lines of dots, forged into the metal. "So long ago that *many years* fails as a description. We were lords of the Ohio so long ago that the stars were different. The children of the Serpent had not yet come to the Ohio when my people ruled it."

Dockery frowned. "They came in the Serpentwar,

didn't they? Richelieu and Wallenstein and Adela Podebradas?"

"Wallenstein led an exodus from the Old World," Mesh said, "but long before him, a sorcerer-king named Onandagos came. My people tell that it was against him that they fought and lost, though they name him Ona-Tagu in the ballads."

"And is Kanawha your people's name for the Ohio, then?" Kinta Jane asked.

Dockery shook his head. If Mesh wanted to dominate the entire Ohio, how did that make him any different from the uncle and cousins he claimed to have defeated? Besides, the name Kanawha struck him as familiar.

"No," Mesh said. "Kanawha is a river, and the land it flows through, and perhaps also the mountain where the river has its head. It is an old name and its meaning is shrouded in mystery. It may mean the *greatest waters*, but it may also mean the *river of evil spirits*, in the same way that the greater land surrounding Kanawha bears a name that may mean *land of tomorrow*, or *cane and turkey lands*, or *the dark and bloody ground*."

"The Kentuck," Dockery said. "Holy shit. Kanawha is in the Kentuck?"

Mesh nodded.

"That's ghost country," Dockery said. "I don't mean ghost country like 'my cousin knew a fellow who told him that he saw a ghost,' I mean that I've seen 'em myself. Three separate occasions, and none that I'd especially like to talk about. The Kentuck is haunted."

He squinted, trying to force out of his mind images that angrily crowded in: a weeping woman gliding across the water of a beaver pond, holding in her arms a child whose arms and legs had been severed; an angry face shouting from the hollow of a dead tree; and five dead Indians whose paint and dress he'd been unable to puzzle out, who had followed him wordlessly, day and night, across that entire blasted land, spoiling his appetite and his sleep alike.

"The land is full of ghosts because it was the site of a mighty war," Mesh said. "There were Indian allies on our side and on the side of Ona-Tagu and his usurping warriors. The songs say that each captain fell with his ten thousand at his side."

"Ten thousand is a lot of men," Dockery said.

Mesh cracked a faint smile. "Perhaps we can allow for a little exaggeration, or for a poetic use of the number. But many died, over many years, as Ona-Tagu and our war-queen, Eru-Jay, daughter of Chaku-Me-Setu-Ro, drove each other back and forth across the land. Ona-Tagu was a mighty wizard, but Eru-Jay was invincible with her fighting staves. She was said to stride the land three miles to a step, and to swing batons made of whole tree trunks, and if our people have no wizards, as you know them, we have always had mighty Spirit Riders. Alongside Eru-Jay fought Nika Pe-Shu-Re, who was said to have as her spirit guides the rivers themselves, so that with each attack of Eru-Jay's wands, the Ohio itself drove home the blow."

Dockery whistled. "You're saying this is the side that *lost*?"

"The final battle took place at Kanawha," Mesh said. "Thousands fell, bloodlines were exterminated. Merely in the deaths of the singers who fell at Kanawha, we lost thousands of years of remembered history. We had gods once, until Kanawha."

"What do you mean?" Kinta Jane asked.

Mesh's face was expressionless, and nearly perfectly still. "People generally say that so many priests and priestesses died in that battle that we forgot how to serve our gods, and they therefore forgot how to care for us. But I have had it whispered to me, in a secret chamber upon the waters of the Michi-Gami, that the truth is darker still, that in those dark days, when sacrifices were required, we slew not only Eru-Jay and Nika, but indeed our very gods."

Dockery's mouth was too dry to curse.

"We were forced to the dread acts by our enemy," Mesh continued. "Or rather by his new ally, for in the final battle Eru-Jay had the river turn against her. Ona-Tagu had made a sacrifice to the Ohio River, and the Ohio River rode to war in his retinue. When the Heron King took the field for the Firstborn, Nika Pe-Shu-Re's arts failed her, and Eru-Jay's mighty thews turned to brittle sticks. We fled, but we left behind our mightiest on the field."

"They made your retreat possible?" Kinta Jane stared into the darkness.

"The sacrifice was terrible," Mesh said, "but we lived. We lost, but we also survived, and a smaller nation, guided by fewer chieftains and protected by fewer Spirit Riders, fled north, to make our homes upon poles on the great inland seas. Before Kanawha, we dwelt upon the land, like ordinary men."

"You live on water because of Kanawha?" Dockery asked.

Kinta Jane struggled with the same idea. "You live on the water because . . . because being on a different body of water gives you protection against the Heron King, who is your enemy."

"It gives us *some* protection." Mesh nodded.

Dockery took a deep breath. "Why do you want Kanawha back? Pride? Are you looking to recover the graves of your ancestors?"

"All of those things." Mesh looked at the dead Algonk, suddenly reticent. "And . . . one thing more."

Dockery found himself intensely curious, but also hesitant to provoke the giant.

"We can help each other best if we understand each other's aims," Kinta Jane said softly.

"The lost genealogies." Mesh looked up. "The forgotten gods, with their liturgies and their strictures and their theologies. Our ancestral laws. Our uncorrupted language, before our tongues were broken. The secrets which once made our Spirit Riders the greatest magicians on the face of this continent. They are written down, and the book is buried at Kanawha."

"If all of that is located at some mountain in the Kentuck," Dockery said, "and has been there for thousands of years, just waiting, why haven't your people gone after it?"

"Fear of the Heron King?" Kinta Jane asked.

"Do not dismiss that fear," the giant said. "But nevertheless, over the centuries, many of our bravest have tried. They have failed because of the Heron King and his agents, or they have failed because the ghosts of the Kentuck have misled them or killed them or driven them mad, or they have failed because they could not find Kanawha, and returned with empty hands and wrecked ambitions."

"You forgot the way," Kinta Jane said. "You forgot the road to Kanawha."

Mesh blinked slowly. "Along with everything else, yes."

"So you're willing to stand against the Heron King," Dockery said, "and in order to do that, you want to return to this ancestral land and recover a lost book that no one has ever been able to find. That book will let you stand against the Heron King, and maybe also you think that writing should be your reward for standing against the Heron King."

"Correct," Mesh said. "Both."

"But Kanawha is lost," Kinta Jane said. "What makes you think you can find it?"

The giant Chu-Roto-Sha-Meshu, son of Shoru-Me-Rasha, smiled. He put the knife away in its sheath. "Because I have been there."

*"Then we must go to Philadelphia,
and perfect the world."*

CHAPTER TWO

Sarah looked upon the veil of her goddess's temple
and *saw*.

She looked from the inside, a vantage point she
had held for weeks. She sat on the goddess's Serpent
Throne, with its seven lamps—through Sarah's Eye
of Eden, they appeared as seven salamanders, or the
seven visible planets—or she stood before the veil.
The throne sustained Sarah. She slept on it, and
awoke mostly rested. She reclined on it, and did not
hunger. Though her only exercise was to stand before
the veil and gaze upon it, or pace the few steps it
took to cross the goddess's sanctum in any direction,
her body did not wither.

She hadn't left the sanctum for weeks, not since
the day she had successfully ascended through magical, sacred space to take the Serpent Throne, as her
father never had, during an Imperial siege of her
father's city, Cahokia.

She itched to get out, to breathe fresh air and feel
warm sunshine on her skin, but she was afraid she

might not be able to leave. Before the ascent, the magic Sarah had worked in the short months since leaving her childhood home in Appalachee had left her stretched and exhausted, unable to sleep anywhere but in the goddess's temple, and from time to time even bleeding.

She found respite on the throne, but the throne didn't heal her.

You cannot escape me.

She was also afraid of the door in the corner of the sanctum. It was framed by pillars that looked like vine-wrapped tree trunks, with a gnarled vine-like lintel across the top. With its vegetable stylings, the door resembled the front entrance of the goddess's home, the Temple of the Sun, but through the door lay darkness that Sarah's eye could not penetrate, and from the door came distant screaming, and from time to time, a voice like the piercing cry of a hunting bird.

The priestesses who tended to Sarah could not see the door, and they did not hear the voices.

You and I are bound. And I shall be master.

She hadn't heard the voice immediately upon her ascent to the Serpent Throne, but it had come to her in the days shortly after. It was the voice of Simon Sword. Whether it was the Heron King himself speaking, or some echo from her own mind, or something else still, was a question Sarah wasn't sure she could answer.

Sarah ignored the voice and gazed upon the veil. Since the blow of a clay-made Mocker had dislodged from her eye socket the acorn by which her father had transmitted to her mother his dying blood, allowing her to conceive three children, Sarah had had gifts of vision. She saw ley lines and could both draw mana from them and transmit her vision along them. Since the land's great rivers, the Mississippi and the Ohio and the Missouri and the others, were all mighty ley channels, Sarah by her own power had a wide-ranging view of the Ohio Valley.

The veil let her see farther.

What she saw looked something like the magic lantern she had seen in a Nashville tent show as a child. Despite the name, the lantern had nothing of gramarye or hexing about it; in a dark tent, a man calling himself the "projectionist" had charged two pennies a head and talked up the marvels of what he was about to display until he had packed his tent, children (including Sarah) sitting on the dirt up front, then those willing to pay an extra penny sitting on two rows of folding wooden chairs, and then everyone else standing behind. The projectionist himself had stood at a wooden box on three metal legs, with a steel snout poking out the front, and a rotating steel cylinder in the middle, and at the back a powerful mirrored light. The "magic lantern" had cast still, colored images onto a hanging white sheet: angels, bogies, romantic vistas.

But those images had been still. The images Sarah saw on the veil moved, shadows that seemed to be cast by the throne's salamanders. By force of will, she could find places she knew, and people she had connection with, and observe them. Instinctively, though it didn't seem necessary, she moved her hands in front of her face as she watched, gripping images to draw them closer to herself or push them farther away, and sliding images from side to side and up and down as she sought the visions she wanted.

From the towers of my land, you can see the entire world.

"You ain't got no land!" Sarah snapped. "You're a usurper and a thief!"

I am the truest king there could be. I am inevitable. I am the one who always returns, by right as well as by nature. My people all welcomed me. Did yours welcome you?

"The goddess chose me!" Sarah barked. The words cost her physical effort, but they silenced the voice that cried through the door, at least for a time.

She had tried her arcane arts to shut the portal, and to stifle the sounds, and had failed to accomplish either.

With the veil, she could see, if not the world, then at least the empire. And Sarah didn't need to look for people and places within Cahokia's Treewall. Instead, she felt and heard and saw Cahokia, all at once, all the time. She *experienced* the city of the goddess. She *was* the city, and knew herself. The veil was how she looked outward.

Knowledge and vision flowed through her constantly.

She looked for her brother and sister most often. All three of them had been raised separately as foster children, unaware that their mother was Mad Hannah Penn, the empress sequestered by her brother Thomas Penn on the grounds of insanity, and their father was Kyres Elytharias, the Lion of Missouri, the wizard-king of Cahokia, greatest of the Moundbuilder kingdoms of the Ohio, or, as Sarah had learned to call them, the Seven Sister Kingdoms. Only when Thomas had learned of the existence of the three children and set out to kill them had Sarah discovered her identity, and then helped rescue and unite her siblings.

As she had many times before, Sarah watched the images of Nathaniel and Margaret, tramping along a muddy forest track, and wished the veil allowed her to see across time as well. She longed to see her mother and father before death had divided them, her brother as a foster child called Nathaniel Chapel in the care of the Earl of Johnsland, her sister as Margarida, the ward of the smuggler and pirate, Montserrat Ferrer i Quintana.

Sarah followed the line of the trail they were walking and frowned. Where were Nathaniel and Margaret going? Thomas wished all three of them dead, so Sarah wanted Nathaniel and Margaret to join her in Cahokia. Cahokia was not safe for them—no place was safe for them—but it must surely be one of the least dangerous places they could be.

Instead, Sarah's sister and brother followed a path that joined larger and larger trails, flowing toward Philadelphia. Once their mother's capital, now Thomas's. She must reach out and urge them to take a better road.

Sarah and Nathaniel communicated easily across distance. As she had a gift of sight, bestowed by her father's acorn in her eye, he had a gift of hearing, acquired from an acorn that had been wrapped inside one furled ear at birth. The voices young Nathaniel heard had left him fragile and shattered until, with the aid of an Ojibwe visionary guided by his personal spirit, Nathaniel had been healed. Sarah did not fully understand how that had happened, but Nathaniel was able to enter the realm of spirits, and had the ability to speak with some spirits of the dead. Of the dead who stayed close to this earth, perhaps.

Also, when Sarah wanted him to hear her, he could.

Margaret's gift from their father was a brutal strength and a heroic capacity to shake off blows, both of which were only available to her when she was angry or afraid.

You think yourself a queen. You shall be a slave, chained to my throne.

"I've got one," Sarah said. "Don't require a second. Thanks, though."

And her uncle Thomas?

Sarah found him quickly. She could not always see what he was doing, and she wasn't sure why her mother's brother sometimes disappeared from her vision. Was he shielded from view when in the presence of his dark lord, the Necromancer Oliver Cromwell? Sometimes he seemed to disappear when putting on certain articles of clothing, or entering certain places—Philadelphia's College of Magic, for instance.

She saw him now, growling at a man who resembled Benjamin Franklin, the old Lightning Bishop. That would be Franklin's grandson, Temple Franklin, who was the emperor's counselor and errand boy. Nathaniel had crossed paths with Franklin, and the result had been the death of one of Sarah's most prized servants, a Dutchman named Jacob Hop.

Franklin looked resolute, though not daunted, and Sarah followed the machiavel from the scene. The man left Horse Hall, the Imperial palace, and walked Philadelphia streets shaded by tall elms until he came to a hotel. Sarah watched, not hearing any sound at all, as Franklin pleaded with a burly Dutch woman in the lobby for half an hour before finally stomping away.

What errand had Thomas so furious, and his aide so thwarted?

Sarah and her people—but mostly Sarah's goddess, *the* goddess, the Mother of All Living, who was Wisdom and the Serpent and Eve—had defeated Imperial artillery and a besieging force of Imperial Ohio Company men and Imperial militia on the spring equinox, a month earlier. That victory had earned them breathing room; the Imperials had retreated a short distance eastward, where they were rebuilding their forces.

Sarah looked for and found Calvin Calhoun in a brick building in Philadelphia, lodgings he shared with the Elector Charlie Donelsen and the Cahokian soldier Olanthes Kuta and a man who appeared to be a lawyer. After her siblings, the person Sarah most watched was Cal. They had been childhood playmates and Sarah was still in love with him, though her rejection had driven him away.

And she would never see him face to face again.

Cal and those with him met in smoky rooms, and huddled in the corners of restaurants, and in basement chambers accessible only via secret passages. At the instruction of his grandpa, Sarah's foster father, the Elector Iron Andy Calhoun, Calvin was leading the charge to remove Thomas Penn as Elector and Emperor under the Philadelphia Compact of 1784.

Did Calvin ever think of her?

She hoped he succeeded, though she thought the odds were long. Under the compact, he needed a two-thirds vote, and many of the Electors were on Thomas's side of the issue. Some resisted out of conservatism, and a desire not to be too hasty; others resisted Thomas's removal because they were beholden to him, for land or cash or preferment or other favors; others still might in better circumstances have voted against Thomas, but required his help now because they wanted Thomas's soldiers to defend their lands again the rampaging beastkind of Simon Sword, the vengeful face of the Heron King, god of the Mississippi and Ohio Rivers.

So Calvin talked and collected testimony and presented motions, but Thomas was still emperor.

Cahokia itself had a right to send an Elector. Sarah was legally entitled to be Cahokia's Elector, under the Compact, but Sarah hadn't gone to Philadelphia and she hadn't given anyone her proxy. She was afraid that if she sent anyone, Thomas would have the person hanged.

I will sacrifice you and I will drink your blood. Whatever threat you think you represent to me shall end when I swallow your heart, witch.

"My grandpa always told me that iffen a feller knew how to do somethin'," Sarah grunted, "he ne'er had to waste his breath certifyin' it to other folks. 'A wind bag is an empty bag,' he'd say."

Sarah fell to the floor of the sanctum, pain shooting through her arms and legs where she struck the floor. She heard a thousand screams. Her body shook, like the spasm of a violent fever. Reflexively, she looked back at the door in the corner, but it remained dark.

She heard a long laugh, in the tones of Simon Sword.

The screaming had come from outside the Temple of the Sun. It had come from Cahokia, from her city. Sarah's city was shuddering, buildings collapsing, fires springing up from the ruins. She felt it all. The sound of collapse and terror was enormous.

Sarah ran.

She didn't stop to think about her fears that she couldn't live beyond the veil, that she was being sustained only by the power of the goddess. The veil was heavy, but it parted for her, and she rushed down the steps into the temple nave.

Through her earthly eye, Sarah saw the long narrow hall rush past her, its mosaics of earthly paradise below, and astral imagery above, illuminated by the daylight flooding through the open doors. Through her Eye of Eden, she saw angel ministers and glowing salamanders and a passage as long as the entire world. At the same time, she knew that buildings were collapsing, trapping and killing her people inside, and homes were bursting into flame.

Just inside the temple's doors, she rushed past the oathbound Podebradan, Yedera. Yedera had sworn herself to defend and advance the interests of all Firstborn generally, but in particular, the interests of Sarah's family. She pivoted to follow Sarah.

Sarah burst from the doors to find the world shaking. Three priestesses knelt on the flat, cultivated top of the mound; they had been weeding the goddess's furrows, but now they looked up in terror, eyes traveling westward.

Across the Mississippi River, storm clouds roiled.

And Sarah could see the earth rolling toward her, like a sheet shaken over a bed before being allowed to drift into place. Waves from the river slammed across Cahokia's docks, already shattered by war, and swept trees from both banks. The living Treewall surrounding the city rippled and danced. Cahokia shuddered as the earth tossed beneath it.

Simon Sword. This came from him. What terrible new phase of the reign of Simon Sword did this herald?

Simon Sword's power was her fault, and she must stop him.

"*Terram confirmo!*" she shouted, pushing her soul and her will down through her words into her feet and into the earth.

The Treewall stopped moving. The ground continued to shudder, but, as if a heavy blanket had been thrown across the entire city to weigh down the jumping of the earth, the ripples were subdued and slower.

Sarah's breath left her and she fell.

Yedera tried to catch her, but missed. Sarah crashed to the ground and lay on cold, wet grass. Her face felt wet and warm. The ground trembled still, so she murmured again, "*Terram confirmo,*" wishing she had brought with her the Orb of Etyles, which would have channeled more power into her act of gramarye, even as the power she channeled threatened to burn her to ash.

The earth shook one final time and then stopped.

Sarah touched her lips, and when she looked at her fingers they were covered in blood. Her ears rang, and Sarah began to vomit.

Far away, she heard the priestesses screaming again.

And beyond that, she heard the laughter of Simon Sword.

"Butterfly, butterfly, show me where to go." Ma'iingan opened his eyes.

His twin sons, Ayaabe and Miigiwewin, had both vanished. Ma'iingan saw their tracks plainly in the disturbed earth and leaves of the forest floor; when they were older, he would follow such marks directly to them, and teach them to hide the indications of their passage. But his sons were scarcely more than a year old, and today he would reward them for finding good hiding places and keeping silent.

He had to keep silent, too. That was the game. So, quiet as a butterfly, Ma'iingan ignored the marks on the ground and stalked through the forest.

His sons were both healthy. Ayaabe had thrived from birth, but his son Miigiwewin had been born in a ritual fault, and had not prospered, until Ma'iingan had traveled deep into Zhaaganaashii lands and brought him a healer. In the months since, Miigiwewin—who also had the second name Giimoodaapi, given to him in an act of rebellion by his uncle—had shot up in height, though he remained quite thin.

"Baabaa!" Father. That was Ayaabe, who could not contain his excitement. Ma'iingan pretended not to have heard, looking inside a hollow tree and lifting a rock to look beneath before Ayaabe's repeated calls to be noticed became so much that he had to find his son.

"Ingozis!" he cried, scooping up his son and kissing him on the forehead. *My son*! "Now, do not tell me where your brother is."

"Gaawiin ingikendansii," the boy said. *I do not know.*

Miigiwewin, whose second name meant *he laughs in secret*, was a good hider, because he was very quiet. Ayaabe wanted to be heard by his father at all times, and now followed close at his heels as Ma'iingan crept through the forest, but Miigiwewin had yet to speak a word in his life.

After ten minutes of searching and listening, Ma'iingan gave up and resorted to tracking his second son. The boy's footprints led directly away from the glade in which they had been playing, in a straight line. Ma'iingan and Ayaabe followed the footprints, Ma'iingan singing a song to his son to keep him amused even as his own heart beat faster and his fears of wild animals and other dangers grew.

When he found Miigiwewin, he nearly ran the boy over. His son stood perfectly still in the center of a small clearing.

Ma'iingan laughed and picked up both his boys. "Miigiwewin! I have found you, and now it is your turn to look for us!"

"The man with wolf ears just left," Miigiwewin said. They were his first words, and Ma'iingan nearly dropped his son in astonishment. "Wolf ears?" he asked. Ma'iingan's name meant *wolf*, and his manidoo, the several times Ma'iingan had seen it, had taken the form of a shining man with a wolf's ears.

"He said he has been calling you, but you have not heard him. You are too distracted. He said you might listen to me instead."

Ma'iingan set his boys down. He smiled, though his limbs shook. "Listen to you say what, Miigiwewin?"

"I am Giimoodaapi, Father. A second messenger is coming, and you must not miss this one. For the good of all of us, you will have to leave."

Rememberest thou this place? the Lord Protector asked.

Oliver Cromwell, the Necromancer, inhabited the body of a child. It was a vehicle he had taken during the recent Imperial attempt to take the city of Cahokia. The child stood pale and naked, with white, empty eyes, beside the stone wall encircling a church outside Boston.

Lucy is buried here, Ezekiel said. His betrothed. Dead in a carriage accident years ago.

Both men spoke without using their tongues. In Ezekiel's case, his tongue had rotted away as his body had grown cold. Nathaniel Penn and his Indian ally had called Ezekiel a wiindigoo, an ice cannibal.

Ezekiel had resisted the description, but it was apt. His muscles were cold as ice, and he ate the flesh of men. He traveled at night, or avoided roads, or veiled his face. A man whose appearance was as terrifying as he knew his now was could stand scrutiny if traveling with an armed company—as the Lazar Robert Hooke had done through the streets of New Orleans—but risked being attacked if caught alone.

Ezekiel had followed the summons of his master Cromwell, heard in his dreams and in quiet moments in his thoughts, to this church by traveling at night, and now the two stood side by side in darkness.

I have told thee a partial truth, the Necromancer continued. *I am here to tell thee the higher truth, and to offer thee a choice.*

Ezekiel Angleton, once a priest of the order of St. Martin Luther and now a walking corpse, knelt before his master.

Upon the Mississippi, I told thee that I was no haunt. That was a partial truth, my son.

Yaas, My Lord, Ezekiel said.

I have had the first resurrection, Cromwell said. *And upon the Mississippi, I administered the same resurrection to thee, as thou hast since given it unto others.*

Yaas, My Lord.

The second resurrection awaits us still. In that resurrection, our flesh will be restored to perfection, and escape the rot of this world. It is to this end that we wrap our fingers around the Firstborn throat, and it is to this end that Thomas Penn serves us.

Yaas, My Lord.

Cromwell paused briefly, as if to let Ezekiel consider. *If thou wish it, I shall administer the first resurrection to Lucy Winthrop.*

Ezekiel trembled. Did he dare hope for so much? He raised his hands in supplication to his master—and then saw his own dead, white flesh.

My Lord . . . will Lucy be but bones, after these long years?

Cromwell rested a cold child's hand on Ezekiel's shoulder. *I can give her flesh. But she will not be as thou rememberest her. She will be as I am, and as thou art.*

Ezekiel thought of Lucy sitting beside the Winthrop hearth, rosy cheek and fair ear pressed against the bell-shaped end of the courting stick. He remembered the warmth of her body in his bed, separated and yet bound together by the bundling board. He had never before or since slept in a bed so warm.

Or, Cromwell continued, *we may await the time when we may administer the second resurrection to her directly.*

Ezekiel heard the soft plop of drops of liquid falling into the grass. He touched his face and, in the light of the stars, found that tears moistened his fingertips.

Black tears.

No, My Lord. His body shook and he touched the earth with a hand to steady himself. *The time is not ready for her. If we are to bring Lucy Winthrop back into this earth, I would bring her into a perfected world.*

Cromwell nodded. *Then we must go to Philadelphia, and perfect the world.*

~You should think of this as an act of healing,~ Isaiah Wilkes said.

Wilkes was dead.

~Yes, that's definitely what you should think. Rescue is healing, isn't it?~ Jacob Hop countered. *~We are rescuing the land from the scourge of Simon Sword, and perhaps also rescuing Kinta Jane Embry.~*

Hop was also dead.

~We are healing the land,~ Wilkes added.

Nathaniel and his two familiar spirits—living men who had died and chosen to stay in Nathaniel's service—rode a horse that was also a drum across a rolling plain beneath the starry sky. Nathaniel was alive, but had the ability to enter this land of the spirits and the dead, and to travel within it. He rode now to fulfill a promise.

In life, Isaiah Wilkes had been the head of a secret society called the Conventicle. The Conventicle had been founded by old Benjamin Franklin himself, and it existed to be the secret glue keeping together three allies who had sworn to stand against Simon Sword at his return. The alliance had fallen apart, and he had been killed in his efforts to reassemble it. An agent of his, a woman named Kinta Jane Embry, had survived to continue the mission. Nathaniel had promised Wilkes he would find Kinta Jane, and try to help her if he could.

~Are you listening?~ he asked.

~Yes,~ Wilkes said. *~Is this Montreal?~*

They descended toward a pond, in the center of which stood an island with three buildings.

~Yes,~ Nathaniel told him. ~Things look different in this place.~

~Hold still, so I don't have to listen over the drumbeats.~

Nathaniel paused, stroking the neck of his horse, smelling sweat and leather. He'd been raised among the people of Johnsland, who were riders, so the transition to this world of riding across infinite grass was not unpleasant.

Jacob Hop had not been a member of the Conventicle. He had been a deaf-mute turnkey, and Simon Sword had inhabited his body for a few weeks. When the Heron King had left Hop, the Dutchman had found himself possessed of an astonishing capacity to learn and a fierce loyalty to Sarah Elytharias Penn. He had helped rescue Nathaniel from the grasp of the emperor's servant Ezekiel Penn, and then been killed by another Imperial servant, Temple Franklin.

Nathaniel suspected that Wilkes stayed with him in order to continue to carry out his mission, and Hop stayed with him to help Sarah.

~How do you feel?~ Hop whispered to Nathaniel.

He asked because he knew that Nathaniel's ability to travel in this place, and do all he could do here, had been given to him in order to be a healer. When Nathaniel attempted to do other things with his gifts, he was ill.

Nathaniel nodded.

~Over there!~ Wilkes pointed at the far side of the pond, where the land rose slightly and was capped with sheets of ice.

Over the rise, they found a trio surrounding a small fire. Nathaniel saw the largest first, and immediately turned his horse aside, pulling back from an encounter.

The man was a giant.

Nathaniel had never seen one in real life, but he had heard stories about them, in Acadia or in Algonk lands. The man was half again Nathaniel's height and had red hair; he leaned on a long spear, as if it were a walking staff. Of the three, he was the only one standing, and he looked away from the flames, turning his head left and right and watching.

The other two were a man and a woman, both huddled around the flames and wrapped in wool blankets. He wore a badger-pelt hat, making him look as if he had an animal lying over his forehead; she had a dog's tail.

~*That's her!*~ Wilkes said.

~*The beastwife?*~ Nathaniel asked.

Isaiah Wilkes chuckled. ~*She's not beastkind. Whatever mark of animal you are seeing on her is her tongue. She had had her tongue removed, but I needed her to witness to Brother Onas . . . to Thomas Penn . . . so I arranged for a hexenmeistres to give her a new one.*~

~*From a dog?*~ Hop asked.

~*Should I have cut out a man's tongue to use instead?*~

~*Are you afraid of dying, Dockery?*~ the woman asked.

Badger Hat shook his head. ~*I'll keep my oath. Even if it means that Thomas Penn kills my son, when I could have rescued him.*~

Were they the giant's prisoners? Nathaniel couldn't tell.

~*This is far.*~ Nathaniel looked at the ice sheets and shook his head.

~*We have to help them,*~ Wilkes said. ~*I left them alone, and they've lost their way.*~

~They're far,~ Nathaniel said. *~And there's something else I must do, something much closer to hand. Can you do anything to help them without me?~*

Wilkes shook his head, defeated.

Nathaniel considered. *~Then we will have to involve someone else. I believe I know the right person.~*

Maltres Korinn was meeting the general in the Hall of Onandagos when the earthquake struck. The building shook and he heard cries of surprise, but Maltres's ancestors had built well, and the hall didn't fall.

The hall was a sacred building, but Cahokia knew gradations of sacredness. The Hall of Onandagos was less sacred than any of the precincts of the Temple of the Sun, less sacred than the city's Basilica, perhaps less sacred than its graveyards. The hall was where the city's kings and queens met in council, received foreign dignitaries, and hosted state occasions.

Since Her Majesty Queen Sarah Elytharias Penn did not leave the Great Mound, the Hall of Onandagos was the domain of her Vizier, Maltres Korinn. Maltres was the Duke of Na'avu by inheritance, and had been invited to be Regent-Minister of the Serpent Throne during its vacancy by the great and good of the city, and then appointed Vizier by Sarah as she had come to power. By preference, Maltres would be at home in the north, on the border of the German Duchies, tending to his farms.

Instead, he was discussing sources of silver with the Cavalier, Sir William Johnston Lee. Lee was a former Imperial officer who had been instrumental in saving Hannah Penn's children from her brother Thomas, and was now general of Cahokia's armies, which were steadily taking shape under his hand. Lee was a big man, solidly built. His hair and mustache were going white, but still streaked with gray, and his eyes were a piercing green.

They sat in Maltres's office, which was furnished with three chairs, a large but simple desk, and abundant shelves. The earthquake shook the hall, casting papers from the shelves onto the floors, and nearly knocking Maltres from his seat. Repositioning himself, he levered his weight by gripping his staff of office, which lay against the desk beside him.

The tall black staff, capped with an iron horse's head, was known as the Earthshaker's Rod. Maltres wrinkled the corner of his mouth at the irony.

"I would like to have considerably more silver than we at present have access to, suh," Lee said.

"Our iron coins are readily accepted by every partner with whom we trade, General," Maltres said. "From Chicago to New Orleans. Is there some market you believe we are not accessing, for our lack of silver?"

"Heaven's chamber pot, no." The general grunted, adjusting himself in the wooden seat on the other side of Maltres's desk. "I know nothing of trade, and would like to know less. What worries me, Korinn, is the return of the Imperials. They will come in larger numbers next time, and I fear what black sorcery Cromwell and his allies have yet to throw at us. I want silver *bullets*, and, if possible, silver *cannonballs*."

"For that quantity of silver, we'd need to be trading with the Lord of Potosí," Maltres said. "Or the silver miners of Georgia. Or, of course, Thomas Penn."

"Quite." Sir William shifted again in his chair.

"Your legs hurt," Maltres said. That winter, William

Lee had been injured several times in succession in his thighs.

Sir William nodded. "So long as my queen needs me, I am choosing not to dull the pain."

During the siege, the Cavalier had several times seemed distracted or lethargic.

"Your wedding approaches," Maltres reminded the other man. "That, too, should keep you from wishing to blunt your sensations."

Sir William smiled and was opening his mouth to say something when the door was thrown wide.

"The Great Mound!" a boy in a gray and gold messenger's tunic yelped. Wet hair was plastered to his head, and water streamed down his face. "The queen is ill!"

Maltres sprang to his feet, and was astonished to see that the general did the same. Maltres leaned on the Earthshaker's Rod, Lee gripped the heads of two sturdy walking sticks.

"Tell the priestesses." Maltres rushed through the door. Lee followed, the messenger now hurrying to keep up.

"They know!" The boy's face was distraught and his voice strained; Maltres stopped for a moment to pat the young man on his shoulder.

"Perhaps Cathy may attend the queen," Lee suggested. "She is a healer, and now a member of the queen's order, so she can treat the queen in her . . . abode."

Lee touched upon an interesting question: What kind of healer could treat Sarah, if she never left her goddess's holy of holies? And a related question was: What kind of healer could do any more for Sarah than she could do for herself, if she was ill? She was the most powerful magician in Cahokia.

"The queen isn't in her abode," the boy chirped. "She fell down outside, during the tremor."

"Outside?" Maltres ran, and Lee ran with him.

The Hall of Onandagos was not far from the Great Mound; the greatest effort in running from one to the other lay not in the distance, but in the descent down the first mound and especially in climbing up the second, made worse by the fact that rain slashed across Maltres's body and slicked the earth under his feet. Still, they were only minutes apart. The messenger must have come running immediately after the earthquake had ceased.

Even focused as he was on reaching the Temple of the Sun, Maltres saw that the tremors had caused more damage than he would have guessed. Climbing the mound, he saw several houses burning, despite the rain, and several more flattened. He would need to see to the relief of the occupants.

In the streets below the mounds, and again rushing up the Great Mound, Maltres dodged among trees. The city had always had trees within its walls, but they grew in neat rows to provide shade to avenues, or in small fruit-bearing groves. At the end of the Siege of Cahokia, trees had sprouted throughout the city.

They had sprouted wherever one of the Imperial draug had stood, or lain defeated, at the final moment when Sarah and the goddess had worked their great act of gramarye to drive the Imperials out.

Maltres barely beat Lee to the top of the mound, despite the other man's greater age and his injuries. There he found a swarm of eunuchs and several priestesses laboring over Sarah, raising a stretcher upon which she lay. The Podebradan Yedera stood to one side, her scimitar in her hand. Her face held a fierce scowl, but if anything, she looked helpless. What did her oath, her sword, her armor, and all her martial skill, avail her, when her queen simply fell to the earth, broken?

Sarah was swathed in the white linen she had worn since entering the sanctum. Now she also had linen bandages over both her eyes. There was dark brown blood crusted around her nostrils and at the corners of her mouth, and seeping red blood soaked through the bandages.

"Her eyes," William Lee groaned. "Great god of heaven, she's bleeding from her *eyes.*"

Sarah moaned and stretched out a finger weakly. Lee reached to grasp it and was barely able to touch his queen's fingertips before a tall priestess with an angular face thrust herself into his path and raised a warning finger.

"Lady Alena," Lee gasped. "I've sent for Mrs. Filmer to come see to the queen."

A second figure intruded upon the space between Lee and his queen. It was a man this time, broad hipped and shaved bald, and with snakes tattooed on his face, converging in blue spirals upon his open mouth. The man was a eunuch, and Lady Alena's voice.

"Mrs. Filmer will not be allowed to see the queen!" the eunuch hissed. "Mrs. Filmer is corruption!"

"Easy, Bill," Maltres said, using the familiar form of the general's name to get his attention.

Sarah groaned and the eunuchs carried her within the temple and out of sight.

"You understand," William Lee said slowly to the eunuch, "that I have killed more men than you have plucked hairs from your greased chest?"

The eunuch trembled, but stood his ground.

"I have killed men because it was my job, suh," Lee said. "I have killed men for honor. I have killed men in anger, and with a calm heart. I have killed men of every nation I know, and I have killed men whose nations were a mystery to me. I have killed enemies, and I have killed men who had been my friends. I have killed by day and by night, at land and on sea, mounted and on foot, with sword and with gun and even with my bare hands." He took a deep breath. "Now tell me again, slowly this time so that there is no mistake, what you just said about my *betrothed*."

Lee's hand rested easily on his belt, but his voice was iron.

"Bill," Maltres said again, in a low murmur.

"The queen," a new speaker said, "where is she?" The voice had an imperious tone to it, and an urgency that would not be denied.

Maltres, Bill, the Lady Alena, and her eunuch all turned to look at the new arrival.

The speaker was tall and thin. His eyebrows were white, though his long hair, high above the forehead and long upon the shoulder, was still an iron-gray. He wore a long Ohioan tunic, gathered by leather wristbands on each arm and a slender belt, but his feet were bare. On his head he wore a thin gold circlet, but no entourage followed him.

The Lady Alena bowed deeply and her eunuch knelt.

William Lee squinted. "I have seen you before, suh, but I am struggling to remember where and when."

"You rode with the Lion." The newcomer smiled, a taut and impatient expression.

"This is His Majesty Kodam Dolindas." Maltres bowed. "The King of Tawa."

"The spirit of understanding," the King of Tawa said.

"Have you come to help my queen, suh?" Lee asked.

"I have. And I see that I come just in time to meet the storm." The King of Tawa swept into the Temple of the Sun. Yedera marched in on his heels.

The eunuch rose to his feet and William Lee punched the man in the face. The eunuch dropped to the earth, bouncing and falling into one of the muddy furrows that covered the top of the Great Mound.

"Do not speak that way of Cathy Filmer again," Lee growled. "In my hearing or out of it."

Thou hast asked for a demonstration of my intent. Oliver Cromwell's voice rang in Thomas's ears like shattering glass, though Cromwell's lips didn't move.

Only it wasn't just Oliver Cromwell. It was Cromwell, and it was also in some way William Penn, Thomas's own ancestor. Cromwell had escaped final destruction at the hands of the zealot John Churchill by traveling to the new world in the breast of William Penn, to whom he had granted Pennsland.

Cromwell had anointed Penn king of the granted lands, and he had anointed Thomas in the same fashion, in a secret ceremony in Shackamaxon Hall. He had shared with Thomas his vision of an eternal commonwealth, with Thomas at its head as the man who had finally vanquished death.

Now Cromwell, in the child's body he wore, and Thomas Penn, and Temple Franklin stood in a warehouse a short distance from the Port of Philadelphia. A fourth man sat tied in a chair against the wall. Tall windows in all the walls stretched toward a high ceiling, allowing in a flood of early summer light; beneath the windows stood worktables laden with carpentry tools, potter's wheels, lumber, and raw clay. Thomas gazed on two man-shaped replicas.

One was a wooden puppet. It lay on a table, but if it were to stand it would be six feet tall, or perhaps slightly taller. Its body was planed smooth but was only approximately the shape of a man; its head had been finely carved and painted, and resembled Thomas Penn. A younger Thomas Penn, as he looked when he had ridden to war against the Spanish.

The second was made of clay. It sat on a wooden chair, head slumped forward almost to its chest; the features of this replica were very approximate, and it smelled of wet earth.

"I've browbeaten the Electors into raising taxes," Thomas said. "Then I borrowed against future tax receipts to be able to spend the money now, and I am recruiting the army which I shall use to raze Cahokia to the flat plain of the Cahokian Bottom. But you said that if I got you bodies, Grandfather, you could make soldiers of them. Here are two bodies, and as we agreed, more are being produced in Pittsburgh and Youngstown."

"Thousands more," Temple Franklin said. "Of various scales."

"I would understand this army you speak of, Grandfather," Thomas said. "I would *see*."

The naked child Cromwell nodded. *And thou hast brought this live man, too.*

"I assume you intend a sacrifice," Franklin said. "This fellow is a pickpocket and a cutpurse. He won't be missed."

"None of us will be missed," Thomas murmured,

"save for a few moments, and excepting only those of us who build things of eternal worth."

Cromwell nodded. *Help me lay these creatures upon the floor.*

Franklin hesitated, but Thomas did not. Urging on his advisor, he stretched the wooden mannequin out upon the hard floor, then laid the second figure out as well, so the two rested side by side, separated by two feet of open floor. The gray wet clay stuck to his hands as he worked, and he wiped them off on a dry rag sitting on one of the tables.

The man tied to the chair struggled. He was blond, young and hale, with big shoulders and strong arms. By rights a man with that physique should be working or fighting, not stealing coins in the street. Thomas scowled at the shirker. The blond man strained at his ropes and groaned, stretching his head toward Thomas like a dog asking to be scratched behind the ears.

How literal a sacrifice did Cromwell and Franklin mean?

While he had been distracted, Cromwell had drawn a large circle on the floor with chalk, enclosing himself and both models within it.

No, not quite. There was a small gap in the circle still.

Before I finish the seal, Cromwell said, *lay the sacrifice in the middle.*

"What's his name?" Thomas asked.

"Benjamin Trumbull," Franklin said.

Thomas raised an eyebrow at him and nodded his head.

"Good," Franklin said. "If we are going to take the life of a man, we should know his name. Benjamin

Trumbull. Former apprentice blacksmith, but broke his articles and took to thievery as a way to live. Also pandering, allegedly, and maybe even a little road-agenting."

Trumbull groaned.

Excellent, Cromwell said. *Thou hast spoken truly, Franklin, son of Franklin.*

Franklin snorted contentedly and grabbed Trumbull's ankles. Thomas put his hands under the man's armpits, and together they hoisted him into position, between the two models.

Trumbull wriggled, but couldn't escape.

Thomas stepped back and stood at ease, hands clasped behind his back. Franklin sat.

Cromwell chanted. Thomas knew more languages than most, but still could neither understand the words nor even identify the tongue. The Necromancer closed his circle and then added numerous additional markings—Thomas recognized astrological signs and seals along with Hebrew characters, but couldn't add any of it up into a coherent sum.

With a start, he realized that the light was gone.

Stepping to the window, he looked through the glass and saw hints of the city street outside: the outline of a tree, the silhouette of a man, the steady back and forth of things floating in the harbor. But he saw no light and no sun. The street looked as if the sun had simply been taken away.

A thick gurgling sound made Thomas turn again. Trumbull lay between the two models still, thrashing in his bonds. Blood sprayed in jets from his throat with the dying beats of his heart, spraying the mannequin, spraying the clay man, spraying Cromwell.

Franklin pulled his eyes from the spectacle to look coolly at Thomas, then returned to watching.

Thomas made himself watch, too. He had seen death before, on the field and in the hospital. He'd killed his own sister, after torturing her into giving away the location of her daughter Sarah.

He wasn't repulsed by Trumbull's death, he was ... bored?

Cromwell was speaking again, and he addressed a shadow that hovered over the corpse. Squinting to focus, Thomas saw that the shadow resembled nothing so much as a squid. The extremities that dangled down toward the dead man at first made it appear that the smoky shadow-squid had emerged from Trumbull's slit throat, but as he looked closer, Thomas saw that the dangling protrusions weren't tentacles, but tongues, dangling from something that resembled a levitating skull.

The tongues dangled into Trumbull's mortal wound, and were drinking from it.

Cromwell's address rose in pitch and volume. Franklin's breath hissed in and out between his teeth.

A second shadow appeared, of the same shape as the first. Thomas forced himself not to step backward. Cromwell raised his hands, scattered chalk dust though the dusky shapes, and for a brief moment, they appeared solid.

They were not red. Thomas had imagined that demons would be red, but instead they were a bright pink, the pink of the lips and tongue of a newborn baby, an obscene pink that would be unsurprising as the color of some internal organ. They were covered with eyes, whose visible sockets drooped as if they were melting, and whose lidless gaze stared in all directions. From the outside of their bell-shaped hulks, a viscous white slime dripped, raising acrid smoke where it dropped onto the wood of the floor.

In the split second during which it was visible, one of the monsters emitted a sound like a purring cat.

Trumbull was still trembling.

"Delightful," Franklin murmured.

Thomas only smiled.

Then the chalk dust dissipated and the creatures became darkness again.

And sank into the models.

Thomas had the distinct impression that the clay model's mouth yawned open to receive the creature being put into it, but it had to have been a trick of the light, because when he blinked, the sculpture appeared unchanged.

Trumbull lay still.

Cromwell stepped back. Thomas had grown accustomed to seeing his Mentor, his guardian spirit, in the body of this child, but the sight of the naked youth with blood covering its arms up the elbows, and chalk caked into that blood, struck him in the moment as bizarre.

"Is it finished?" Thomas asked.

Rise, Cromwell said.

The models stood. The wooden puppet rattled as it moved, but the creature of clay was virtually silent. If anything, Thomas imaged he could hear a very faint squishing sound as the creature's limbs worked.

"These will fight, I take it?" Franklin nodded satisfaction.

They can be made to answer the orders of any

battlefield commander, or relentlessly pursue any objective. They will not fire a gun with any skill, but they will swing a sword or stab with a pike.

"This fellow, though." Thomas grinned, tapping the wooden model on the chest as if he were a private who had earned special recognition during inspection. "Don't make him look too much like me. It wouldn't do for my commanders to start taking their orders from a blockhead."

He chuckled drily at his own joke.

Cromwell laughed along, a dry rasp. *No, it wouldn't. But the greater threat of that is from the other. This automaton of clay is sometimes called a Mocker.*

"Surely I have a stronger jaw than the clay man," Thomas joked, but his attempt at a smile fell completely flat; the Mocker's face was changing.

So were its limbs, and its proportions. It took nearly a minute for the entire transformation to be completed, but when it was done, a tall, blond, muscular man stood before him. Benjamin Trumbull.

Thomas checked; Trumbull lay dead on the ground before him, and Trumbull stood in his presence, a ready grin on his face.

"He still smells like mud," Franklin said.

"This will do," Thomas said. "This will do nicely."

"Doesn't Cahokia have doctors?"

CHAPTER THREE

At Sarah's insistence, Cathy Filmer had been made one of the Ladies of Tendance, the seven women who were permitted to pass through the veil of the Temple of the Sun and enter into the presence of the Serpent Throne. One had to be clothed and anointed to enter—otherwise, the eunuchs and the other Ladies had warned Cathy repeatedly, the Serpent Herself would strike Cathy dead on the spot. Therefore, generally speaking, a Lady only entered the Holy of Holies when it was her day to do so, to refill oil lamps, to clean and polish with the special implements designed for the purpose, and, on festal days, to clothe the goddess.

Which meant clothing Sarah in sacred garb.

Cathy's day was Sunday, but when she heard Sarah was injured, she quickly had herself clothed and oiled to enter Sarah's presence and provide whatever support she could. Sarah lay murmuring in deliriums on the throne, so Cathy stood in the corner, hands folded and heart heavy.

The other Ladies of Tendance had had the same

response, and all seven stood crowded about the sanctuary, or the upper end of the temple nave.

Three of them, of course, perfectly keeping their vows of silence.

Kodam Dolindas, the King of Tawa, also waited on Sarah. Kings, one of the eunuchs gave Cathy cattily to know, were allowed to pass through the veil at will. The King of Tawa wore no shoes, which Cathy took to be a sacred geas. Perhaps his being subject to such taboos was connected with his ability to pass into sacred space.

He also stepped into the sanctum as if he belonged there. When the Ladies of Tendance entered, they knelt first and touched their foreheads to the floor.

The King of Tawa was a magician. With Cathy and other Ladies watching, he stood beside the Serpent Throne for hours, singing songs with strange melodies over Sarah, resting his fingers gently on her bandaged eyes, and twice hushing her when her sleeping murmurs crossed into whimpering. During this time, the Ladies brought him wine and water as requested, and burned the incenses he asked for, and twice joined him in song, the three with vows of silence humming along.

The rain on the temple roof and the distant thunder, rolling in along the nave, provided an unsettling accompaniment.

A physician was sanctified at the door by lesser priestesses, attended by eunuchs, and brought forward. Not a Circulator, but a man Cathy had seen during the siege, a man who had studied physick in Memphis. He couldn't pass through the veil, and the King of Tawa wouldn't send Sarah out, so the healer stood on the steps outside and spoke with the king, whispering back and forth information about Sarah's condition.

With a baffled and frightened expression on his face, the physician eventually retired.

Then the King of Tawa withdrew from the sanctum. He asked one of the Ladies—the youngest and freshest—to remain on watch, and invited the others to come with him. As he parted the veil so that he and the Ladies could leave, the seven flames of the Serpent Throne dimmed.

The Cathy Filmer of six months earlier would have felt dread at the sight of the throne acting of its volition. Cathy Filmer, Handmaid of the Virgin, Lady of Tendance of the Serpent Throne, bowed her head to acknowledge and revere the goddess's act.

At the King's request, Maltres Korinn convened a meeting in the council chamber of the Hall of Onandagos. Also at the King's urging, Maltres invited the Ladies of Tendance.

Cathy sat with five other Ladies around a table, beneath a stained-glass window depicting the goddess's tree of life, now awash with rain. Bill stood behind her, which made her feel more than a match for the Lady Alena and her cadre of eunuchs and her acolytes. Cathy was so distracted by Sarah's illness that she almost forgot the fear and uncertainty that gnawed at her own heart.

She carried a letter, against her skin. The Earl of Johnsland had written it and sealed it, and it had been delivered by the earl's emissary, Landon Chapel. The letter informed Cathy that Landon was her son, and that Landon himself did not know the fact, and gave it into her discretion to inform him or leave him in the dark, as she saw fit.

When she looked at the young man, she wasn't

surprised in the least; he resembled Cathy, with a little of the earl thrown in. She wasn't fearful of Landon's reaction, but she was terribly afraid to tell Bill. If she told him about her child, what else would she have to tell him? And would he cast her aside when she did?

Also standing were the Metropolitan Zadok Tarami, with his fierce white eyebrows; the wizard Luman Walters, with dark, curly hair and spectacles; and the dark-skinned princeling of the plains, Gazelem Zomas. Maltres Korinn stood at the head of the table, leaning on his staff of office, with its iron horse's head; tall, with cheeks pocked with childhood scars, and dressed in his habital black, he brooded above them like a vulture. Beside Korinn stood the king.

"The queen is dying," Kodam Dolindas said.

Zadok Tarami leaned forward, his face stricken with grief, and mumbled a prayer.

"Do not discount my queen yet, suh," Bill said. "I have seen her defeat greater odds than any mere illness. She faced down the Chevalier of New Orleans, the Sorcerer Robert Hooke, and Simon Sword in a single encounter."

Good, loyal Bill. Cathy's knight, and Sarah's.

The king nodded. "I do not discount her. I am astonished that she is alive at all, and I attribute it to personal reserves and sheer resilience. But she has broken her own body with her efforts."

"What do you mean?" Cathy asked.

Dolindas smiled gently. "I can give you metaphors. She has burned her candle too fast, at both ends simultaneously and perhaps also in the middle. She has drawn too much water from the well. She had mined too deep and too fast."

"A good metaphor clarifies," Cathy said. "I don't understand what you're telling me."

"Are you saying my queen has used up all her ability to perform magic?" Bill asked.

The king looked up at the circle of tree imagery above him; the light filtering through seemed to come to rest like a bird on the king's face. "I mean that it is easy to think of magic as a spiritual and intellectual act, drawing on spiritual reserves," he said, "and such a concept is not false. A spiritually rooted person makes a strong magician. And it is also true that the spirit and the mind and the body are connected, so that the energy channeled through the mind and spirit also marks its course across the body. The performance of magic brings fatigue, and can leave the magician ill. It weakens tissues and drains vitality, physically as well as spiritually."

"Sarah has harmed herself," Luman Walters said. "The acts she performed to save the rest of us—the ascent to the throne, the miracles of fertility, the sign of the flowering staff, the consecration of the Sunrise Mound, the flying rowboat, the confrontations with Cromwell, the opening of the gate of Eden—all of it. It was harming her all along, and now it is killing her."

"This is bad news for the city and the kingdom," Tarami said.

"And the empire," Gazelem murmured.

"Harming her *body*, yes," the king said. "Whether it is fair to say she harmed her *self* is an interesting question."

"I am not interested in the philosophy of it," Maltres Korinn said. "You have convened us because there is something that we can do for her."

"Do not be so quick to disdain philosophy," the King of Tawa said. "If we are to heal a thing, we must first properly identify and understand It. I do not know that there is a way to heal the queen's body, but I believe that her self can be saved. And healed, and even exalted."

"What of the earthquake?" Cathy asked.

Dolindas directed a penetrating gaze at her. "What of it?"

Cathy wasn't entirely sure how to articulate her thought. And what would Sarah want, or permit, her to say? "Since her ascent, Her Majesty has strongly... identified with...the city. She is aware of what happens in the city, she feels the city as she feels her own body. Is it not possible that it is the earthquake that has injured her?"

"Perhaps it is a factor," the King of Tawa said. "Perhaps her injury caused the earthquake, and her exaltation will prevent further quakes."

Gazelem Zomas frowned.

"I am trying to be patient," Bill growled, "but what you are saying sounds dangerously close to theology."

"It's not *close* to theology," the king said. "It *is* theology. Sarah Penn will die. But the Queen of Cahokia may be raised to an angelic state, in which she may continue to give us guidance and assistance."

Stunned silence.

"There is an anointing to the purpose," the king said. "It is royal lore, part of the patrimony of the Ohioan kingdoms. You may have heard it by its name, the Serpent Daughter Anointing."

The Lady Alena's face tightened, giving her the appearance of deep concentration.

"What does this ritual entail?" Cathy asked. If there

truly was some ritual that she, or the king, or the seven Ladies, could perform, then she was in favor.

"It is an ancient practice." The king knit his fingers together and stared into them. "Not done in this century, or the last. But once, the goddess ruled on earth through a king or queen, and through the Angel of the Throne. The Angel Metathronos, in some ancient texts."

Korinn looked as if he would fall over, and leaned more heavily on his staff. "Is the Angel of the Throne not a way to talk about the monarch as an anointed person, the monarch as agent for the gods?"

"Yes," Tarami said quickly.

"Yes," Dolindas agreed. "But not always."

"'Give heed to the Angel of the Throne, for he is as a god unto you,'" Tarami recited. "That's in *The Law of the Way*, and it is Onandagos, instructing his people to obey their duly-appointed monarch."

"It is," Dolindas agreed. "But the exact same words appear in a poem called *The Wisdom of the Dead*, which is in the Onandagan Florilegium. In *The Wisdom of the Dead*, the words are spoken by a dying king to his daughter, who is to rule after him. If the queen is to *hearken* to the Angel of the Throne, then the queen cannot *be* the Angel."

"Those texts are not in my breviary," Tarami said. Was he resisting? Admitting defeat? Or simply acknowledging his own lack of expertise?

"I know," Dolindas said. "But Saul was not condemned for seeking the advice of Samuel. And when Solomon sat upon a throne, he set his mother upon a throne beside him. And her name was Bath-Sheba, the Daughter of Seven."

Tarami said nothing.

"There may be other options," Walters said.

"Waste no time," Dolindas urged. "If we are to raise Sarah to become the Angel of the Throne, we must convene all the Kings of the Ohio. It is the kings who will perform the anointing, along with Sarah herself. Oil and perfumes must be made according to recipes that have been safely guarded, but not used, for many years. Garments of light must be prepared, according to patterns that were given from the beginning, and kept secret by the queens and kings of the Firstborn."

The Lady Alena shifted repeatedly in her seat. The Lady's fidgeting made Cathy, if anything, more conscious of her own body, and she was careful to keep her poise. Was Alena distressed? Anxious? Enthusiastic?

Her eunuch said nothing.

"Is it merely luck that brings you to us now?" Bill asked the king.

Kodam Dolindas smiled. "In a time of crisis, the man who himself does not *need* help must become one who *gives* help. Perhaps it is bad luck that I have come as late as I have."

"We will not delay." Maltres Korinn tapped his staff on the floor. "I'll send messengers to summon the other five kings."

"The empire has begun to issue trustworthiness certificates and passports," Bill growled, "which are aimed to restrict travel. We may find we are *smuggling* five kings, rather than *summoning* them."

"Then we shall send smugglers to do the work," Korinn said.

"I will add my messages to yours," Dolindas offered.

"The Hansa," Walters suggested. "If we could have their assistance with this, it might greatly forward the labor. Or perhaps Chicagoans, to ferry the kings across the Great Lakes, rather than bringing them overland."

"The Swords of Wisdom," Bill growled. "They are in all the Seven Sister Kingdoms."

"I take my leave," the king said. "To write to my fellow kings and also to my own people."

He departed with a determined stride.

"Those bare feet must be uncomfortable in winter," Bill murmured.

"A taboo that is easy is no taboo at all," Cathy told her betrothed.

"Ladies," Maltres Korinn said, looking at the Lady Alena, "please resume watching over Her Majesty. Let me know immediately of any change." He shifted his gaze. "Mrs. Filmer, if you would please remain for a moment."

The Lady Alena stared darts at Cathy before she left, the other Ladies and the eunuchs in her wake.

"You have said nothing, Gazelem," Korinn said.

"I have nothing to say about the Angel of the Throne," Gazelem Zomas said. "It is a new idea to me."

"But you look deep in thought."

"I am considering whether I know any other remedy for the queen," Zomas said. "And I am also . . . thinking of another matter."

Korinn didn't even look curious about the unspecified other matter. "Luman," he said, "what alternatives are you talking about?"

"Nathaniel Penn," Walters said. "He is a healer of great power. I do not know his limitations, but he may be able to help."

"How would you contact him?"

"The queen seemed to be able to do so with ease,"

the former Imperial wizard said. "I shall attempt with what means I have. And I shall do so immediately."

Korinn nodded, then was silent for a moment. "Do we have any other options?"

Silence.

"Forgive this question," Zadok Tarami said. "I know that, coming from me, of all people, it could be misunderstood, but I must nevertheless ask. If the queen dies...who succeeds? Will we be returned to the chaos we struggled through before her arrival?"

"If the queen dies," Maltres Korinn said, "chaos will be the best we can hope for."

Nathaniel was returning across the starlit plain with his two familiar spirits on the back of his horse when he heard a voice.

~Medicum quaeso,~ it called. *~Medicum Nathanielem quaeso.~*

Nathaniel knew no Latin, but the call felt as if it were directed at him. He changed course, heading westward. They rode, hearing the voice calling still and feeling the thudding of the horse's hooves like a drumbeat pattern on the horse's back, until they arrived at Cahokia. Nathaniel had never seen his father's city in the flesh, but he recognized it in this place easily.

On flat ground between two mounds, Luman Walters sat on a wooden chair beside a wooden table. On the table, two candles flickered; the man rubbed a plain brown stone between his fingers and stared into it.

~Medicum quaeso,~ he said again.

~I'm here,~ Nathaniel said.

~Medicum Nathanielem quaeso,~ Walters said again, staring into his egg-shaped stone.

~He's saying 'I seek the healer Nathaniel,'~ Jacob Hop said. *~I think he's casting a spell.~*

~Do you know Latin now?~ Nathaniel asked.

~When you're not here, he studies languages,~ Wilkes explained.

A germ of an idea sprouted in the back of Nathaniel's mind, and he tucked it away for consideration later. *~I'm here!~* he shouted.

Luman hesitated, cocking an ear.

Nathaniel reached out and fluttered the fingers of one hand through a candle flame, causing the flame to dance.

~Ah ha!~ Luman Walters leaped to his feet. *~Nathaniel, thank you! We have a catastrophe here!~* The wizard raised the brown stone to his eye as if to look through it, and turned his face toward Nathaniel. *~There you are!~*

~What do you need, Luman?~

Luman smiled, a soft grin that was rueful and even a little sad. *~Sarah is ill. Can you heal her?~*

~Sarah!~ Nathaniel called. *~Sarah!~*

Luman Walters winced at the sudden cry, but there was no answer from Sarah.

~Where is she?~ Nathaniel asked.

~On the Great Mound,~ the wizard said. *~In the Temple of the Sun. In its sanctum sanctorum, if that matters.~*

Nathaniel galloped to the only mound that could be the one Luman was referring to. It was the tallest mound in starlit Cahokia, and it had strange trees growing on its slopes. Trees with faces, trees that seemed to watch as Nathaniel and his two spirit companions raced up the slopes of the pyramid—

only to find no one at the top.

Atop the pyramid sat a small garden, neatly furrowed, planted with beans and squash and corn and tomatoes. But there was no sign of a gardener, and no sign of Sarah.

He turned to race back, and found Luman Walters standing right behind him, staring through the brown stone.

~*Do you see her?*~ Luman asked. ~*Can you heal her?*~

Nathaniel shook his head. ~*Wherever she is, she's beyond my reach. What's wrong?*~

~*She's dying,*~ Luman said. ~*Burned herself out with gramarye.*~

~*Doesn't Cahokia have doctors?*~

~*Yes. They can do nothing for her. Only perhaps, there may be a Firstborn solution.*~

~*What does that mean?*~

~*It means we're going to try to make Sarah into an angel,*~ Luman said.

The Heron King's child grew rapidly.

Within a week, he stood five feet tall. Within a month of his birth, he towered over Chigozie.

The child looked like the Heron King—well muscled, covered with fine white feathers that shone with iridescence when the light struck them just right, and possessing the large head, elongated neck and sharp beak of a river heron. His first meal was a mouthful of flesh torn out of his mother's warm corpse, and thereafter Ferpa, who took special care of him, fed him fish from the Missouri river.

He refused grain and milk and roots and vegetables. He refused fish that had been cooked. Within a week, he refused fish that wasn't brought to him live, and then he took to hunting on the river for his own meals.

In addition to fish, he learned that he could eat snake.

Ferpa took special care of the boy, and Kort watched over Ferpa. Chigozie noticed the large bison-headed beastman watching the cow-headed beastwife who was his counterpart whenever she was in the child's presence.

Worried he might harm her?

The child needed a name. At eight days of age, which seemed propitious to Chigozie, he, Kort and Ferpa carried the heron-headed child down into the Still Waters, into a pool deep enough that Chigozie was submerged up to his waist. Long discussion the night before with the Merciful and with the Zoman outrider Naares Stoach had ended with no conclusion, so as Chigozie stepped into his place in the pool, he was still considering possibilities. *Benjamin*, son of the right hand. *Daniel*, who did not resist, but went peaceably into the lions' den. *Matthew*, who recorded Jesus' commandment to turn the other cheek. Like a wheel of fortune in his brother's casino, the names rolled past his eyes in sequence.

The discussion had, though, dwelled at length on the child's need for baptism. Seeing the Heron King's child eat the flesh of his own mother had shocked Chigozie, and what felt like the appropriate remedy was to baptize the child, asking for aid from the powers of Heaven in restraining the child's innate wickedness and violence. To be baptized, Chigozie had explained to Kort and the others sitting with him, was to die and rise again, a new creation. It was to enter the waters of chaos and emerge remade, free of former guilts and clean and ready for a new life.

"The river," Kort said. "The river and the dry land."

Chigozie had nothing to say to that, so he merely smiled.

Kort, looking across the ravine at Ferpa, rocking the child to sleep, asked why *he* was not baptized, and Chigozie had no good answer. In his heart, he feared the answer was somewhere in the space bounded by several sentiments, not all equally noble. First, he had a feeling, never verbalized, that the Merciful were not quite the same as the children of Adam. In the same way that he would have felt uncomfortable baptizing a dog, he did not feel at ease baptizing a man with a dog's face. Second, perhaps more flatteringly, he found that on some level he didn't feel the beastkind needed baptism. They seemed more like children to him, like innocents. On the other hand, he knew some of the things Kort had done, and he knew that if Kort were a child of Adam, Chigozie would enjoin not only baptism, but serious repentance, upon him. Third, to his shame, the idea simply hadn't occurred to him.

He had promised he would baptize Kort.

Within minutes, he had had to promise that he would baptize any of the Merciful who desired it. This proved to be all of them. Stoach, when urged earnestly that he, too, should consider baptism, had waved a hand to dismiss the idea. "I've done my god time. It was good while it lasted, and it was enough for me."

Chigozie briefly met Stoach's gaze as he stepped into the water. Stoach looked away.

God of Heaven, Chigozie prayed. *Give me a good name for this dangerous child. And redeem the child from its nature.*

Kort and Ferpa joined him in the pool, holding the Heron King's child between them. The bird eyes looked at Chigozie, reflecting his own image back at him in glittering black pools.

"By the authority vested in me by this community," Chigozie intoned, "I christen thee Absalom."

Absalom.

The name hadn't even been among the possibilities he'd discussed with the Merciful. Was it an ill omen? A good one? It meant *father of peace*, or perhaps *my father is peace*, and Chigozie certainly liked the idea that peace was part of the name of the Heron King's son. An assertion, contrary to fact, that the child's father was peace might act as a shield against the fact that the child's father in fact appeared to be war and destruction incarnate.

Kort and Ferpa bowed their heads.

"I baptize you," Chigozie said, "in the name of the Father, and of the Son, and of the Holy Spirit."

He cupped his hands and filled them with the warm, sulphurous water. Raising them together, he poured water over Absalom's head.

Absalom shrieked, a strangled sound of hideous rage, and attacked Chigozie.

A single thrust with his beak struck Chigozie in the shoulder. He fell back, blood mingling with the warm waters that closed over his head.

He kicked, his feet striking nothing, and then hands grabbed his shoulders, dragging him from the water. The cold air on his skin shocked him, but he still couldn't breathe. With dry air on his face, he felt himself drowning—

and then the person who had pulled him from the water turned him and struck his back. Chigozie coughed water from his lungs, sucking air back into them in its place. The Zoman outrider held him and continued to thump him between the shoulders, but Chigozie couldn't tear his eyes away from the pool.

Absalom hurled Kort from the pool. The big beast-man was four times the size of the Heron King's son and it didn't matter; he bounced off the steep ravine wall, tumbled down onto rocks, and lay dazed.

Ferpa seized Absalom from behind. She seemed to have hooked a leg behind the child's leg, because he was off-balance and shaky. She bore down on him from above, leaning her weight across both his shoulders and pushing him down . . . down . . .

Trying to force him into the waters of creation.

"No," Chigozie said, but the sound was weak because his lungs still held water. He tried to stand, but Kort rose before he could, and leaped back into the pool.

The Merciful stood staring, in distress and fascination.

At the last moment, when it appeared that Absalom was about to break the surface of the water, he twisted, and pushed Ferpa under instead. He slashed with his beak, aiming for her throat—

and Kort caught the blow.

He wrapped the fingers of one enormous hand around Absalom's beak, squeezing it shut. Absalom hissed in rage, twisted his body, yanked his head back, and tried to open his maw, to no avail. Finally, he grabbed Kort's fingers and thumb with his own hands, trying to pry open the beastman's grip.

Kort bellowed in anger, but Absalom didn't flinch.

Kort grabbed the beak with his second hand, wrapping his fingers around Absalom's fingers and squeezing. Ferpa emerged from the waters shaking her head and bellowing. She made sounds that sounded like squeals of protest, but there were no words in them that Chigozie could understand.

Chigozie coughed up more water and managed to stand. "Peace!" he cried. "Blessed are the merciful!"

If Kort heard him, he gave no indication.

The Heron King's son ripped one hand free. As Kort maneuvered the bird-headed boy into the deepest part of the pond, Absalom punched Kort, twice in the belly, and then in the loins. Kort flinched, flinched again, and then roared in anger.

Just when Chigozie though Kort might force the boy underwater—and Chigozie was considering whether it made sense to recite a baptismal prayer, whether it would mean anything to God or anyone else in these circumstances—Kort headbutted Absalom. He cracked his thick bison forehead down on the crested heron skull. The contact made a noise that Chigozie felt in his bones, and then the beastman hurled the boy from the pool.

Absalom rattled across the boulders at the edge of the water, then drew himself up into a crouch at the base of a cliff. He bled from several wounds, and so did Kort. They stared at each other for long seconds, and then Kort turned to Chigozie.

"Baptize me," the big beastman said, and knelt in the center of the pool.

"This is madness," Naares Stoach said.

Chigozie tottered into the pool, limbs shaking. Again, he cupped water in his hands. "I baptize you in the name of the Father, and of the Son, and of the Holy Spirit." He poured the water over Kort's head.

Kort rose, eyes gleaming, and he gripped Chigozie in an embrace.

Absalom emitted a sullen chirp and didn't move.

"Now me." Ferpa entered the pool.

One by one, the Merciful entered the pool, and one by one, Chigozie administered baptism to them.

When he was finished, the Zoman outrider was gone.

Absalom, though, remained. When the last of the Merciful emerged from the Still Waters, Chigozie stood and looked up at the Heron King's son. Absalom stood, straightening to his full height, and stared down at the wet priest.

"The water is warm." Chigozie extended a hand. It was a ridiculous gesture to make to a monster who had attacked him as well as the beastkind who nurtured him.

Absalom stared at Chigozie with cold, glittering eyes, for nearly a minute. Then he opened his mouth and spoke, with a voice that was shrill as the war cry of an eagle and pierced Chigozie to his core.

"You may place your Adam-name upon me, priest, but that is all that you shall do. I shall not be remade, not by you, and not by anyone else of your kind."

Then Absalom fell silent, crouched, and didn't speak for weeks.

When Chigozie next looked for him, Naares Stoach was gone.

Charlie Donelsen spat tobacco juice through one of the many gaps in his teeth. His aim was true and his shot was long, as they sang of the Lion of Missouri, and he launched the brown gob across the wooden trestle table and hit the roots of an azalea bush in violet bloom.

"I heard tell as Gaspard le Moyne has jest up

sticks and left." The Donelsen Elector's voice was so high-pitched, he probably had to drop it an octave if he wanted to sing.

A band, with hurdy-gurdy, banjo, and snare drum, rollicked through a long foot-tapper while the preacher, a long-haired young man with a sweaty face who stared at the ceiling of the tent every time he opened his mouth, sang the lead. Cal clapped along with the music, politely, but not too loud.

He and Donelsen stood in a Sunday tent meeting, near the back of the hot part of the crowd, the part that danced and sang and felt the spirit, and therefore made a lot of noise. The cooler New Light enthusiasts clustered around the punch and cookies tables at the back of the large tent. They met here because the noise would cover their conversation, and because it ought to make any spies the emperor sent after them stand out like bulls in a herd of sheep.

Olanthes Kuta stood by the tent entrance, holding a glass of punch but not drinking from it. He looked every bit the Ohioan foreigner in his long tunic, leggings, and high boots, to say nothing of his pale complexion and the straight sword hanging at his belt. On the other side of the tent door stood one of Charlie Donelsen's boys, a young man named John, who had a long knife in each boot and two pistols at his waist.

> You'll need a lawyer at the judgment,
> > hallelujah
> You'll need a lawyer at the judgment,
> > hallelujah
> Don't matter who you are, you'll need Jesus
> > at the bar

You'll need a lawyer at the judgment,
    hallelujah

A woman in gingham, with a chin that poked out past the tip of her nose, cried "Jesus, represent me!" and swooned into the arms of her neighbors. Barton Stone followers made up part of this New Light crowd, and they expected this sort of thing.

"I been in that palace," Cal said. "That's a lot of sticks to move."

"I expect he left the palace behind," Donelsen reckoned. "New Orleans had become an inhospitable locale for him."

Cal had heard of Le Moyne's departure—the Philadelphia news-papers had been full of it. "Treason, I guess. Impeaching him ought to be a cakewalk."

"Problem is they's too many places to send my boys to." Donelsen spat again. "Got some of 'em watchin' out for me here, some of 'em watchin' the family, but where else do I send 'em?"

"Sarah Calhoun's still fightin' the beastkind on the west bank of the Mississippi," Cal said. "Not to mention the emperor's armies massin' in the Ohio. Lord hates a man as won't help his kin afore he goes a-helpin' strangers."

Logan Rupp joined them, mouth full of cookies and a glass of punch in each hand. He beamed. His blocky physique and the powdered sugar in his abundant jaw whiskers made him look like Father Christmas.

Donelsen nodded enthusiastically. "That's a true sayin', and Sarah's closer kin to me'n Tommy Penn, that's for sure. She's closer kin to me'n the Memphites, or Kimoni Machogu, or either of them fellers as is runnin' the show down in New Orleans. But sometimes, you got to deploy your forces in a manner that ain't obvious. Indirect force. Where do I send my boys so as to do the most good for Sarah, not to mention the Donelsen family, and the empire in general?"

"I met that feller in New Orleans," Cal said.

"Bailey?"

"The other one. The bishop. Only he wasn't bishop then, he was a gangster."

Donelsen laughed. "I expect he still is. Hell, if they wasn't always a fine line between a bishop and a gangster, they wouldn't be no New Light."

Logan Rupp swallowed his mouthful of cookie. "Ah, it makes me feel right at home, hearing the word *feller.*"

Charlie Donelsen's eyes flashed irritation. "I thought you's a Philadelphia lawyer as got lost and accidentally wound up among the honest folk of Nashville."

Cal chuckled. "No, Charlie, he's tellin' us he's a Jew."

> *You'll need a friend in Jesus, hallelujah*
> *You'll need a friend in Jesus, hallelujah*
> *Come the day you die, you'll meet Jesus in*
> *   the sky*
> *You'll need a friend in Jesus, hallelujah*

Rupp frowned and took a deep drink of punch. "I have nothing against any honest member of the Israelite nation, as I have nothing against any honest member of any other kindred. But I have no notion of how you can have arrived at such an erroneous conclusion, or, if I may be permitted to employ a common colloquialism of my adopted hometown, Nashville: How do you reckon that, Cal?"

Cal shrugged. "Simple. The word *feller* makes you feel at home. *Feller* is a biblical word. Who wrote the bible, Logan? Mebbe it ain't written in your law books this way, but in Sunday School they taught me as it was the Jews."

Logan Rupp snorted. "*Feller* is not a biblical word."

"Bet you ten shillin's it is."

"Just because you heard one of your Kissing Campbells talk about *what a feller ought to do to gain the Kingdom of Heaven* from the preaching stump does not mean that the word *feller* is in the bible."

"I ain't much of a reader," Cal admitted. "Ain't really read but the one book. Still, I remember it pretty well. I bet you *twenty* shillin's the word *feller* is in the bible."

Rupp glowered.

"What you got to lose?" Charlie Donelsen barked. "You got your room and board with Cal, don't you? You're gittin' paid, ain't you? Hell, you might win twenty shillin's. Iffen you're worried Cal ain't good for it, I'll stand guarantor."

"The word *feller* is not in the bible." Rupp spoke deliberately, carefully enunciating each word. "I'll take your bet."

Cal spit into his palm. Reluctantly, Rupp did the same, and they shook hands.

"Well?" Rupp asked.

"Isaiah fourteen," Cal said. "Since thou art laid down, no feller is come up against us."

Logan Rupp's eyes bulged out and he slowly turned purple.

"Easy there, Rupp," Donelsen said. "You're a young man yet to die of a burst blood vessel."

You'll need someone to back you, hallelujah
You'll need someone to back you, hallelujah
Your soul is deep in pawn, you'll need Him
   to go your bond
You'll need someone to back you, hallelujah

"I didn't mean *that* kind of *feller*," Rupp rumbled.

Cal shrugged. "Jerusalem, then you should a said so. You ain't got to pay me now, Rupp, tomorrow'll do. Iffen you're feelin' tight for cash, I'll jest take it off your bill."

Logan Rupp ground his teeth. "I feel . . . pleased to have such a cunning client."

"I ain't your client," Cal said, "Iron Andy is. And I wouldn't call him clever so much as terrifyin'. But what're you doin' here, Rupp? I didn't figure you for a churchgoer."

"Speaking of Andrew Calhoun . . ." Rupp reached inside his jacket and produced a folded sheet of paper. It was battered and yellow, and some of the ink on it had bled, as if the paper had been exposed to rain. "We've received a message from him."

"What, by post?" Cal frowned. "That seems odd."

"It was some Calhoun I don't know." Rupp shook his head. "He left the letter for you, but he wouldn't stay. He said he had to get back urgently to Calhoun Mountain. I gather big things are happening, so I came right here with the letter."

"You ain't read it, then?"

Logan shook his head.

Cal took the letter and turned about slowly, looking for unfamiliar eyes on him. He saw more swooners, and dancers, and the sweaty young preacher rattling through another verse. He unfolded the letter and read it.

Calvin Calhoun

I have information to communicate to you about your aunt, which may also affect your bill of particulars in the Assembly. Meet me on the Feast of the Ascension in Youngstown, at a tavern called the Blue Goose.

                              Andrew Calhoun, Elector

He'd never received a letter from his grandpa before, but Lord hates a man as can't adapt to the times. Being New Light, Cal didn't always have the strongest grip on saints' days and feast days, and he didn't rightly remember when the Feast of the Ascension was.

"Charlie," he said. "Remember me a bit of calendar. Feast of the Ascension, that's what, forty days after Easter?"

Charlie Donelsen nodded. "May twenty-fourth this year."

"A good omen." Rupp nodded. "Ascent into heaven after the forty-day ministry."

"Good to know you ain't totally godless, Rupp." Cal grinned, but he was distracted.

"What happens on the Feast of the Ascension?" Rupp asked.

"You and I got a meetin'," Cal said. "You and I and Olanthes Kuta." He beckoned to the Firstborn warrior, who discreetly checked the tent door and then walked his direction.

"The Elector's coming to Philadelphia?" Rupp frowned. "But I thought the whole point of his proxy was that you would do the work here."

"We'll meet him in Youngstown," Cal said. "Which don't leave us much time. Better git packed."

One of Eggbert Bailey's great keys to what success he had achieved so far in life was that he needed very little sleep.

A man who could sleep three hours a night and feel fully rested could drive his men to work hard when they had slept only five. A man who was awake until after midnight and up again well before dawn could easily handle the necessary administrative tasks, answering logistical questions, solving disciplinary riddles, and dashing off required correspondence, without cutting into the time he needed to drill his men, command, and strategize. And a man who was alert for over twenty hours a day, every single day, had time to explore his commandeered headquarters while most of his men slept.

Technically, the commandeered Palais that had belonged to the Chevalier of New Orleans was shared between Eggbert Bailey, commanding New Orleans's gendarmes, and Bishop Etienne Ukwu, its . . . complicated . . . spiritual head. Ukwu, the son of a saintly Christian cleric, was not only an ordained Christian priest, but also a houngan asogwe of the Société de Mars Vengeur—Eggbert knew this last, because he himself had seen the bishop invoking Papa Legba before a congregation of swaying worshippers.

Some of the Igbo of the city, including the bishop's bodyguard Achebe Chibundu, seemed to regard Ukwu as something more than a priest. His ally, the Igbo hôtelière Onyinye Diokpo, if anything, encouraged the whispers.

It was easy to share power with the bishop, because his desires and Eggbert's seemed aligned. Ukwu remained hell-bent on destroying the chevalier, who was now camped with the armies of New Spain on the other side of the river. Ukwu expressed gratitude for the protective wall of the Mississippi River, but also frustration that the same river—and the hissing, hovering hedge of basilisks that infested its lower reaches, the worst infestation of the creatures in decades—stopped Bailey from sending raiding parties.

Or assassins, which is what Ukwu really wanted.

So the bishop helped the city's teeming hordes find various forms of spiritual comfort, and pushed Bailey to find ways across the river, and worked his arcane rituals in secret.

What Eggbert Bailey wanted was mysterious even to Eggbert himself. He had joined the bishop's revolt against the chevalier, secretly organizing dissatisfied, underpaid, overdisciplined gendarmes into a hard-fighting corps at the center of a larger army of raw recruits and men who simply worked for salary. That army had, so far, held the river against the Spanish in the west, and the northern walls against a pack of violence-maddened beastkind that had crashed against New Orleans the same night that its chevalier had betrayed his trust and marched against it with a foreign army.

Before he'd become a gendarme keeping the peace for the chevalier, Eggbert had been a sergeant in an army that had invaded, briefly taken, and then lost the city. He'd turned his coat in the retreat, after Jackson's execution, to survive, but until that moment he'd been a believer in Andrew Jackson—Old King

Andy, as the ballads called him now. He had marched on his birth city of New Orleans expecting to take it and live under the King of the Mississippi, who would distribute the wealth of the city's banks and traders to his soldiers, as well as to the poor.

But now . . . he felt incomplete. Eggbert Bailey had turned his coat back around and driven out the chevalier who had killed his former commander. Did that recover his honor? And even if so, to what end?

Should he make himself King Eggbert Bailey? That didn't feel right.

What would Andrew Jackson have done? He wasn't sure, and as he stalked the Palais and the streets of New Orleans at night, in his surplus hours, he asked himself the question over and over.

Late one night, on the second floor of the Palais, he found the bishop's Creole accountant, Monsieur Bondí, sitting at a desk and reading correspondence ledgers.

The Creole sweated at any temperature, and the stains made the sleeves of his shirt look yellow in the lamplight. He was a short man, chubby, with skin the color of cinnamon and wavy hair that seemed to sweat right along with his skin.

Eggbert threw himself into a wooden chair before the desk. Eggbert's appearance was in stark contrast with the accountant's—he was tall, broad shouldered, and muscular, with a head and mane like a lion, as well as sharply chiseled facial features several shades darker than the Creole's. He wore a blue uniform coat, though without insignia of rank—his men knew him by his height and hair and rolling bass voice. But the Creole, looking up, showed no sign of intimidation in the warrior's presence.

"Have you had enough of drills and mess?" Bondí asked in French. "I could use an assistant, if you are bored. Or are you looking for firewood? I can spare the desk, but none of the papers."

Eggbert laughed. "You work long hours."

Bondí shrugged. "I work."

"Looking for money the chevalier might have hidden away?"

"We already knew the chevalier was low on cash. I'm auditing his assets, preparing formal accounts and tracking where . . . some of the money came from. And I'm also looking for anything I can sell."

"I believe the Spanish have cash," Eggbert suggested. "They might be willing to send us this year's treasure fleet, if we gave them the city. Call in the Lafittes and their navy, spike the guns in the river forts, and the Spanish will come calling promptly."

"His Grace already offered them the city," Monsieur Bondí said, "though I believe it was in exchange for the head of Gaspard Le Moyne."

"They said no?"

The Creole nodded. "But they thought about it. Next time we offer . . . perhaps they'll think about it longer."

Eggbert looked around the room. The walls were lined with shelves, groaning under the weight of ledger books. "What is this room? The chevalier's archive?"

"I believe it belonged to his intendant," the accountant said. "Or his seneschal, is what I believe you Jamaicans would have called him."

"René du Plessis," Eggbert said. "A man with his fingers in many pies."

The Creole gestured expansively at the shelves.

"And Jackson?" Eggbert said impulsively.

The Creole's casual, welcoming smile didn't change, but his eyes tightened slightly. "Are you looking for your own service records?"

"If my name were on a list of Jackson's soldiers in the chevalier's possession, I never would have survived five years in the chevalier's employ. I'm looking . . . I don't know what I'm looking for."

Meaning? Direction?

"You're right, I haven't found anything like muster lists or payroll." The Creole pointed to a bookcase in the corner. "There are a few half-empty ledgers over there, with correspondence from the Jackson days. No treasure maps or manifestos, I'm afraid, and definitely no paternal blessing directed at you."

Eggbert looked at the shelves and steepled his fingers, trying not to look too anxious. "Have you read them?"

"I read them first, actually." Bondí ran his fingers through his hair. "For the short time he ruled the city, I thought Jackson might have found himself in exactly the same situation we're in, looking for cash."

Eggbert nodded. "Anything interesting?"

"Jackson wanted silver. If the correspondence in those books is a complete record, then he was obsessed with it. I knew he hated banks—and accountants—but I never realized how much. The man sent letters to Potosí, to the Viceroy of New Spain, to the Georgia Jews, and even to the Old World, all asking for silver, and offering to trade cotton and tobacco and even land at a huge premium."

"You need cash to pay men." Eggbert thought of the whippings, pillories, and beatings that had kept the gendarmes more or less in line for the payless month before the revolt.

The Creole shrugged. "You can pay soldiers in any medium of exchange that whores, taverns, and greengrocers will accept. Paper money usually works just fine, and gold is *always* sufficient."

Eggbert Bailey frowned. "You're saying that Jackson wanted *silver*. Not cash, not money, but specifically the metal silver."

The Creole nodded. "He preferred it in bullion form, if possible. When you stamp silver into a use-able coin, it goes up in value—it costs more. Jackson wanted as much silver as he could get, as cheaply as he could get it."

"Hmm."

"I thought you knew," Bondí said.

"As a younger man," Eggbert said, "I was mostly a doer of deeds. Only recently am I beginning to become a man who has to understand things."

"He even reached out to the Emperor Thomas," Bondí added. "Jackson discovered certain secret payments the emperor had been making to Le Moyne, and wrote to suggest that they should be continued. I believe that letter is likely what caused the Imperial troops in the region to be sent down here and turned against Jackson."

Eggbert Bailey stood slowly. Across the hall from the room where Bondí worked was a window, and through it he could look across the city, over the western walls of New Orleans the Mississippi River, and see the spangle of yellow sparks that made up the campfires of the armies of New Spain.

What would Jackson have wanted with silver?

"The truly ambitious man raises his fellows."

CHAPTER FOUR

Kinta Jane Embry had become accustomed to riding mastodons. The first few days had been the worst, until she learned to rise and fall with the beast's rhythms rather than be battered by them.

From Montreal, the St. Lawrence led south and west toward the Sea of Ontario, and the Ottawa flowed closer to due west, toward other cities and farmlands of Acadia. Both rivers were followed by footpaths and trafficked by boats of many sizes—the St. Lawrence, from Kinta Jane's brief views of it in Montreal, seemed particularly traveled by Ophidians.

Mesh followed neither river. Instead, he led their shu-shu caravan north, into mountains that were still thick with snow and rivers still choked with ice. He referred to the mountains, or to the land through which they rode, as Outaouais, but he couldn't explain the name's origin. "Algonk, perhaps," he suggested. "But a person of such mean instruction as I am cannot be expected to know such things with any confidence."

"Maybe that's where Ottawa comes from," Dockery suggested. "That'd be Algonk, all right."

"If we're being followed by Algonks," Kinta Jane suggested, "maybe we shouldn't travel right in their homeland."

"I am a fool and I make poor decisions." Mesh nodded, his head bobbing in a thick, snow-laden wind like the top of a young spruce. "But I don't believe the lion looks for prey in her own den."

"Yeah," Dockery muttered, "but what about when the lion comes home and the prey ain't left yet?"

They rode north, then west, then south. They rode into snowstorms, the mastodons plodding along without complaint even as Kinta Jane felt she might freeze to death without being noticed, and get knocked off by an overhanging tree branch. The mountains were old mountains, worn down by time, but they still possessed peaks, cliffs, and rugged ridges enough to make travel dangerous.

And there were always the dogs, watching. Within fifty feet or so of Kinta Jane, they fell silent, but she came to find that silence ominous, though her own enchanted tongue was the cause. She listened for the dogs' footfalls, and turned deliberately to face them, to let them know she knew they were there.

As the snow became cold spring storms, they turned west, tracing valleys muddy with rain and rivers swollen with chunks of ice. Mesh relaxed—was he confident they had lost any pursuit? Kinta Jane no longer saw shadows outside the circle of campfire at night. Mesh took to singing, his rumbling bass with round vowels frightening birds out of many trees as he passed.

I'm going down to New Orleans
I'll tell you what it's for
I'm going down to New Orleans
To try to end this war

Dockery joined in at the chorus. To Kinta Jane's surprise, he harmonized.

Get along home, Cindy, Cindy
Get along home
Get along home, Cindy, Cindy
I'll marry you one day

Finally, as the cold rainstorms drifted into the gentler, warmer rains of spring, they turned south. Mesh began to strip off his furs, and Dockery bundled up his wool pullover frock.

At a palisaded trading-post town called Sault Sainte Marie, Acadian leatherstockings and trappers walked the streets alongside several different kinds of Algonks, like a small New Orleans in the wilderness. Mesh procured passage on a ferry.

Dropped off by the relentlessly cursing ferryman on a pine-bristling shore, they crossed a narrow neck of land in one long afternoon and then were ferried across a body of water that seemed like the slender arm of an inland sea. Kinta Jane tried to remember the names of the great Eldritch seas some called the Great Lakes and couldn't. *Michigan* was one of them.

On the far side, Mesh turned left and followed the sea. "There is copper up here," he said. "It attracts people from your empire. Other than the copper and furs, your Pennslanders and Germans and Acadians find little of value up in this land. They leave it to us and the Algonks."

"Copper," Dockery said, "like that knife you have at your belt."

The giant glared, his face dropping abruptly into a mask of menace and anger that nearly knocked Kinta Jane from her perch on the shu-shu. Then he seemed to remember himself, and smiled to show all his teeth.

They passed a village of Algonks that Mesh identified as *Zhaabonigan*. "I think it might mean 'the sewing needle,'" Mesh explained, "though an ignoramus like myself is not to be trusted. But the village borrowed the name from the river."

Kinta Jane had lost track of the days, but nearly a season had passed when she and Dockery and Mesh, on the backs of gigantic, hairy shu-shus, rode into a Misaabe village. Kinta Jane had never seen its like—she saw the village coming from a mile away, because a row of wooden poles, broad and tall as enormous tree trunks and each carved and painted with a colorful stack of fanciful creatures, stood along the seashore facing outward. The poles were set into the land, but the Talligewi houses stood on shorter poles, resting directly on the water—the houses were made of wood, thatched, and painted brightly with some of the same characters and creatures that adorned the poles.

"Be prepared for anything," Mesh said to Kinta Jane and Dockery as they rode a narrow trail down toward the village of perhaps a hundred buildings, and three times as many decorative poles. "A person who commits such vile deeds as I have is not always welcomed when coming home."

The first giants Kinta Jane saw other than Mesh

were children, who were nearly six feet tall but had the large eyes and energetic playful motions of youth. They stopped playing with hoops and balls and throwing javelins when the shu-shu caravan passed, and fell into line behind the great beasts, singing.

At the first pair of painted poles, which seemed to indicate the border of the village, two Misaabe men waited. They wore overlapping sheets of leather riveted together and bearing large bronze discs, and they leaned on spears so long you could plant them and hang flags from their heights.

The taller Misaabe spoke first; he had long gray hair and a thick beard. "Prince Chu-Roto-Sha-Meshu, son of Shoru-Me-Rasha," he said, bowing. "Welcome home."

The second was even taller, and had hair so bright red it was nearly orange, and a jaw like a granite ridge. In addition to his spear, this giant carried a long ax. "Prince Chu-Roto-Sha-Meshu, son of Shoru-Me-Rasha," he said. "You are under arrest."

Montserrat Ferrer i Quintana stood in the prow of a keelboat, booted foot resting on the gunwale as she watched the dark western shore of the Mississippi under heavy rain. The boat had lanterns, but they weren't lit—flames on a dark night such as this would only make the boat a visible target. The keelboatmen stood at rest, a light anchor holding the craft in place against the muddy river's tug; the Eldritch riflemen held their weapons wrapped and plugged against the rain, resting them on the gunwale or on the boat's narrow roof.

If the rain persisted, the river would begin to flood. Would that make the city's defense easier? If anything, the beastkind were better swimmers than the children of Adam.

Miquel stood among the riflemen. He was a good shot, and accustomed to firing at men, though not at close range, and mostly at men wearing the uniform either of the Imperial Revenue Men or the customs officials of the Chevalier of New Orleans. He moved easily among the Cahokian musketeers, pushing jokes through the clogged stream of his poor English and clasping arms, and now he sighted along his own rifle, standing beside them.

This was not a vessel Montse was used to; it worked more like a ship's boat than like her beloved *Verge Caníbal*. She preferred to raise her flag in her sailing vessel, inherited from her mother and therefore very dear to her, but it served her well to set foot in as many of the keelboats, shallops, bateaux, and Memphite barges as she could. It meant her men could see her, be exposed to her competence, feel her affection, and give her their trust. It also meant she could better understand the capacities and weaknesses of the various kinds of craft she was using to defend the shores of Cahokia.

Beastkind who came to the eastern shore could be shot, if they came by day. Many still did so, their rampaging depriving them of ordinary sense, but the greater challenge for the Cahokian navy was to detect and shoot them at night, and shoot the swimming beastmen who crossed the Mississippi.

This keelboat was one of many ships patrolling the river this night, and Montse's visit was completely routine.

"Capità," called the keelboat's captain. "Are those

men?" He pointed, his arm a line of shadow in the darkness.

Formally, Montse's title was *admiral*. Following the example of Josep and the crew of the *Verge*, most of the navy simply called her by the Catalan word *Capità*. This suited her just fine.

She looked through her spyglass; at first, she saw nothing.

Then she spotted a woman. She wore a tattered cloak that had once been dark red but now looked closer to black, and she scrambled down a steep bank toward the river. She was too far away to be audible, but Montse could see that her face was red and streaked, suggesting tears.

As if she had realized Montse was watching her—which was not impossible, given the waxing moon—the woman started waving one arm.

Only one, because, Montse realized, she held something in her other arm. She trained her eyeglass on the bundle and focused. The woman turned left and right, sloshed her way up and down the mudbank, waving at the river.

She couldn't see them. She was waving to people she *hoped* were out there.

"Captain," she said. "Bring us to shore. That looks like a refugee, and we're going to pick her up."

"Yes, Capità."

The anchor came up quickly, and the keelboatmen sprang to their work. Montse continued to watch the woman, and when she turned again, Montse got a clear look at the bundle—it was a baby.

The woman turned because she was waving at someone unseen, high up on the bank over her head.

Moments later, more people emerged and began to creep down the thick mud slope toward the water's edge.

"Faster, Captain," she said. "And signal for assistance."

The keelboatmen ran a banner up the keelboat's pole. Montse checked her pistols, refreshing the firing pans. In a more well-ordered navy, it might appear peculiar that its senior officer dressed and was armed in such a piratical fashion; as head of what might be termed a *mob* of keelboatmen, merchantmen, former Hansa traders, and hunters in canoes, Montse wasn't even close to the most colorful person.

Montse checked the refugees through the glass again. She made them thirty—far too many for her keelboat to carry. Pivoting and looking out over the river, she saw two more keelboats, a wide shallup, and several large canoes following her to shore. It might be enough.

Miqui and the riflemen with him were focused on the approaching shoreline with deadly calm.

Then she turned back to look at the shore and saw changing shadows. At the top of the slope, the silhouettes of what might be more men, but looked too bulky and misshapen. She examined the moving figures under the moon's gray light, looking for the indications she feared she'd find.

There—a pair of horns.

There—wings, like a bat's, but larger than an eagle's.

There—a thing with two heads, and a forest of tentacles sprouting from its chest.

Beastkind.

They were close enough to shore that she could hear the shouting refugees. There were English cries, mixed in with French and Ophidian. She had thought Missouri had already been scraped empty of its population— where were these people coming from?

"Captain," she said. "The hill behind these people swarms with beastkind. Prepare to fire, and to put ashore as many fighters as possible, so we can carry away the largest number of refugees. Signal our intentions to the others."

The captain, a man with a large forehead, curly red hair, and tiny eyes set deep into his head, nodded. "Aye aye." He turned and bellowed orders to his sailors, who checked their muskets and pistols and took aim at the shadowy bank. Every man on the ship was either poling, or prepared to shoot. Even the captain took a carbine into his hands.

If only she had a few cannons. A single ball, even a small three-pounder, bouncing through several ranks of an enemy, made a big impression.

Montse looked through the glass. The beastkind were hard to see, shadowed, hidden by trees and tall grass. The refugees didn't see them, and were screaming and signaling to the ships on the river.

"Aim over the heads of those refugees!" the captain called.

The shore drew closer.

Canoes and other vessels of the Cahokian river-navy were a couple of minutes farther out. How long would it take them to reach the shore?

The beastkind charged.

At first their motion was a mere ripple, a shadow that shifted upward and then settled back into place, but Montse saw the outlines picked out against the hill change with that ripple, and then change again.

Beastkind were charging, and more beastkind were taking their place.

There could be thousands of them.

The captain saw it too. "Fire!" he yelled.

In the darkness, the volley of musket and pistol fire erupted red. The wall of smoke was quickly battered flat by the rain.

Yelling turned to screams.

Montse had pulled both pistols, but she didn't fire with Miqui and the others. Instead, she took one in each hand. As the keelboat's shallow bottom bumped from hitting river bottom, she jumped out of the boat. The sudden shock of cold water from the waist down was an old friend to Montse.

She sloshed up onto dry ground and found herself face to face with the first woman she'd seen through the spyglass. Meeting her face to face, she saw that she hadn't realized the woman's age earlier—she was young. So young, the baby might be her sibling, or if it was her child, it was her first.

With her were other women, children, and old men. No warriors, and no visible weapons.

There were dogs, though. A line of mastiffs at the back of the refugees slowed the beastkind advance, biting hands and heels. But hoof and spear were gradually crushing the dogs, small bodies being cast aside.

"Cahokia and Elytharias!" Montse shouted. A beastman with the head of a goat and a third eye, set into its forehead, trampled over the corpse of a hound dog and lunged for the young woman with the baby.

Bang!

All three of its eyes closed forever, and the beastman

fell onto his back. Montse realized she was weeping, and she wasn't sure why.

Did she miss Margarida?

A beastwife with horse's hooves and a turtle's shell charged. *Bang!* Montse's shot took her in the center of her chest and she dropped.

She heard the splash of the keelboat's riflemen jumping into the water to join her on the shore. More beastkind ran in her direction, so there was no time to reload. Montse barely had the time to sling the two firearms back into her belt and arm herself with her saber before a third beastman fell on her and the young woman.

Was it that defending this young woman with a child felt so much like defending Sarah?

Montse forced aside a spear tip, stepping boldly closer to its beastman wielder with heavy jaws and long fangs, and then grabbed him by the horns, forcing his face down into the water.

"Behind me!" she yelled to the young woman.

Carrying her baby and sloshing awkwardly through the muddy water, the young woman complied.

As two more beastkind charged Montse, the one face-down in the Mississippi stopped struggling, and she was able to let him go. One spear, though, was difficult to defend against. Two was nearly impossible, especially if one had noncombatants to defend.

Montse parried the first attack, and prepared to take the second attack in her own body.

Her tears, she thought, came from her failure to save Hannah. She had failed Hannah, Hannah had been imprisoned and died, and Montserrat had only ever been able to save one of her children.

But *this* young woman, and *this* child...she could save them.

Even if it killed her.

She braced her teeth to take the blow—

bang!

The sudden musket shot at her side left her with ringing ears, but it cut one of the beastmen down, reducing it in one second from a raging, berserk man-beast to a corpse floating on the river's muddy breast.

And then Miquel charged past her with bayonet fixed to the end of his musket. Bayonet against spear might be an even match, but Montse saw no reason to leave her young crewman fighting even matches. She joined him, and together they killed this beastman, Miqui delivering the *coup de grâce* with a slash of a bayonet across a throat that looked like an alpaca's.

Montse immediately sheathed her saber and began loading her pistols. "As many as can get on the boat, go now!" She turned to face the young woman and pushed her in the right direction with her own shoulder. "You first. You and your baby. Go!"

Half the keelboatmen pulled in their poles. While their colleagues held the boat in place, they pulled aboard refugees. At the captain's direction, small children came aboard first, but soon panic overcame order and women and men came aboard without differentiation until the captain stopped them and the keelboat poled away. It rode low now, the water lapping nearly over its sides, but the keelboatmen had strong arms and knew how to exert leverage with their instruments, and the boat was soon away from the shore.

The next nearest boat was still a minute out, and it was a canoe.

Montse turned to face the oncoming beastkind. Her pistols were loaded, and she stood side to side with Miquel and a handful of Cahokian marines. "Load!" she shouted.

"Aye, aye, Capità!" A few of the marines followed her instruction—the others aimed already-loaded weapons forward.

Maybe as many as twenty people huddled in the water behind Montse and her men. An old man holding a hayfork pressed himself to her side and stationed himself with his fork pointing at the beastmen.

"Where are you from?" Montse asked. "Missouri?"

"Beyond Missouri." His voice cracked with fatigue. "Zomas."

Montse had a much better idea of the geography of places that bordered the sea, or major rivers, than of landlocked cities. She had heard of Zomas, mostly in connection with the slave trade. "That's an Eldritch city? Inland?"

He nodded. "Destroyed eight weeks ago, by the Heron King. Her people have been fleeing on foot, first through the snow, and now in the mud. We have been hunted by the beastkind at every step, and our numbers have been reduced from the population of a mighty capital to enough people to fill, perhaps, a town. We are dispossessed, starving, and desperate. And we are but the first."

Montse nodded grimly. "Welcome to Cahokia."

The beastkind charged.

"Fire!"

Etienne Ukwu found himself thinking of the Appalachee Queen of Cahokia often.

It seemed clear that she was indeed the queen. He'd received her messengers to that effect, a week after the rising of the basilisks over Bishopsbridge. He'd sent her congratulations and had notice of the fact published in both the *Picayune Gazette* and the *Pontchartrain Herald*. In those notices, he had been careful to refer to himself as the Bishop of New Orleans, and not to claim the title of chevalier.

Additional verses to "Le Sou de l'Evêque" had sprouted out of the Mississippi mud the very date of the announcements, verses in which Sarah made war alongside Etienne. There was even a verse about the basilisks, although it left out all the most astonishing parts of that encounter—the Brides, Etienne's mother, the strange space underground with Sarah and her magician—and reduced the event to a joint spell to summon flying snakes.

Eggbert Bailey also made no attempt to claim the title of chevalier; he called himself General, the title, Etienne knew, that Andrew Jackson had used when he had laid siege unsuccessfully to New Orleans. His men called Bailey the Midnight Captain, for his habit of prowling the city at all hours, or sometimes, less respectfully, the Midnight Creeper.

New Orleans had no chevalier.

Etienne didn't know the Philadelphia Compact well, but he had learned his Elector Songs as a boy, and he thought that the empire had no right to interfere in deciding who the Electors were, other than in the case of barring them for misbehavior, or other extreme possibilities. It was up to Louisiana to decide who the Chevalier of New Orleans was, and for that person to present himself to the Electoral Assembly.

But that Appalachee rube Etienne had met in his casino had commenced impeachment proceedings against both the Emperor Thomas and the chevalier. Monsieur Bondí had been summoned to Philadelphia to confer with Electors. In theory, he might be called to testify, over his repeated objection that he would never in this life do such a thing. However, he was willing to tell Electors how to find the evidence of malfeasance they were looking for.

As a result, Bondí was away from New Orleans. Therefore, Etienne spent more time with the City Council, that now included him and Eggbert, along with Onyinye Diokpo, Renan DuBois, Holahta Hopaii, and Eoin Kennedie. Eggbert headed the city's military and law enforcement operations, the others administered the city as, in theory, they should have been doing under the Chevalier le Moyne, and Etienne, in name, was the city's spiritual prince. He preached and administered mass in the Place d'Armes, in sight of the new cathedral just beginning to rise on the foundations of the old one.

In fact, Etienne gave all the others leadership, and sometimes command.

The entire city of New Orleans was now, whether it knew it or not, bent on avenging the murder of Bishop Chinwe Philippe Ukwu. Though so far, Etienne's nocturnal invocations of the mystères had not, as far as he could tell, struck down his enemy.

Really, Etienne should have been chevalier. In practice, maybe now he was. But he had followed the paths that had been laid out before him, and they had made him bishop instead. He had become bishop to undertake to avenge his father's murder on the Chevalier le Moyne.

He must now defeat the Spanish in the field to complete that vengeance.

And then . . . Thomas Penn? But Penn seemed far away, and embroiled in his own struggles. Including a struggle with Sarah Elytharias, Queen of Cahokia, and Etienne's strangest and also most sympathetic ally.

Etienne and Eggbert rode to Bishopsbridge to examine the city's defenses. It was not routine—Etienne avoided routine because he feared assassins—but the Mississippi was a key defense that kept the Spanish out of New Orleans, and Bishopsbridge one of the key vulnerabilities.

Achebe Chibundu, the Igbo fighter who sometimes wrestled under the name Lusipher Charpile, rode silently with them. He had become expert at maintaining an invisible station just out of Etienne's sight, and at leaping to intervene at the slightest threat.

Attack by sea was also a possibility. Jean and Pierre Lafitte and a naval militia of Catalan and Igbo smugglers gave Etienne and Eggbert regular reports on their activities sinking Spanish ships, and setting fire to Spanish ships in ports that were too close to New Orleans. The occasional Spanish ship that slipped past the Lafittes was blasted to pieces by the guns of Fort St. Philip and Fort St. Henri. Fort St. Henri, on the far shore of the Mississippi, was protected from Spanish investment by its swamps, which not only bogged down approach and rendered the work of sappers impossible, but also swarmed with basilisks. The small garrison in Fort St. Henri could only be supplied by small unmanned boats, dragged across the river from her sister fort by means of pulleys.

Upstream of the two forts, a pair of chain booms

stretched across the Mississippi and anchored to sunken hulks provided an additional line of defense, one that had not yet even been reached.

The basilisks had not returned to sleep. They had hatched in astonishing numbers and awakened early and were far more active than usual, rendering the lower Mississippi more dangerous than it had been in decades, more dangerous than it had been since the original le Moyne and de Bienville leadership of the city had come down to the river with smoke and fire, and smothered or burned every winged serpent they could find. Stories from that time spoke of the stench of scorched and rotting flesh, and a jungle that bloomed the following spring on the nurturing flesh of the basilisks.

And now the serpents defended the city. They ignored Etienne, but any other person, friend or foe to New Orleans, was in grave danger if he attempted to cross the river.

And when winter came, and the snakes returned to their long sleep?

After the rising of the basilisks, at Etienne's direction, Bishopsbridge had been converted into a fortress, with a thick-walled wooden barbican at the near end. Eggbert's forces manned the fortress, keeping an eye on movement on the western shore as well as on the river itself.

The general and the bishop surveyed the men—a motley assortment of New Orleans inhabitants, men of all nations and fiercely loyal to each other and to their adopted city—confirmed their morale, and checked their supply of food and ammunition. Etienne pronounced a blessing over them.

Then the two men rose halfway across Bishopsbridge, Achebe Chibundu at their shoulders. Before them, the swarm of snakes parted, given passage.

"Jackson was your leader and your hero," Etienne said to Eggbert. "What were you to Jackson?"

"An aide-de-camp," the Midnight Captain said. "Nothing more."

"Would you have been made a Prince of the Mississippi, when Jackson had himself crowned?" The words were strange and slightly ludicrous, but Etienne meant the question seriously, and tried not to smile. "Or the Baron of Baton Rouge, or something?"

"I don't think so," Eggbert Bailey said. "Jackson never promised me such things, and I rarely felt I truly understood his actions."

"I can understand his actions easily enough," Etienne said. "Ambition, lust for power, lust for the flesh and for wealth, a desire to grind the faces of your fellow man, pride—these are the ordinary accouterments of the soul. It is the exceptional man who, having the opportunity, would choose *not* to conquer New Orleans."

They rode back toward the city walls.

Bailey shook his big, shaggy head. "No, that's not it. Jackson was ambitious, but his faithfulness was bigger than his ambition, and he knew the most important thing about ambition."

Etienne looked and Bailey and smiled. "Tell me the most important thing about ambition."

Eggbert chuckled. "You laugh, because you're thinking, this fellow showed no ambition at all until my accountant found him, deemed him corruptible, and used him to organize a revolt."

"I laugh because I find wisdom in unexpected places,"

Etienne said. "It's a laugh of delight. I don't believe you are corruptible, Eggbert Bailey—I believe you were biding your time until the right opportunity came along."

"That is correct."

"So tell me the most important thing one should know about ambition."

Eggbert Bailey drew himself up straight in his saddle and threw back his chest. He was resplendent in his uniform, which was still the uniform of the chevalier, blue with the gold fleur-de-lis, repurposed to be the livery of the city rather than the livery of its former nobleman. Bailey's stature added weight to his words, which he spoke slowly and for dramatic effect. "To be ambitious is a correct principle. To seek to better one's self is desirable. But the only true way to better one's self is to better those around you. The truly ambitious man raises his fellows, so that in doing so, his own influence becomes greater over a kingdom that is more powerful and more extensive. And the first and most constant pursuit of power in which such an ambitious man must engage, is the pursuit of power over one's self. Self-discipline, generosity, and ambition—properly understood—ride farthest when they ride hand in hand."

Etienne stared.

"You cannot persuade me otherwise," Bailey said. "I have thought long on this subject."

"I do not wish to persuade you otherwise," Etienne said. "I am considering whether I should make this the subject of my next sermon, or invite you to speak on the subject yourself. You have impressive charisma."

"Surely, there are better things to think on than *my* thoughts." Bailey shrank to normal size as he spoke.

"As bishop, I have to speak often. Ambition would be far from the most trivial thing I have spoken about."

The walls of the city were in view, rising above the Spanish moss-draped oaks and the cypress trees.

"Jackson was ambitious, and disciplined," Eggbert Bailey said, "and he did not come here to make himself a despot."

"What, then?" Etienne asked.

"I do not know." Eggbert frowned and shook his head. "Only that a great crisis is coming. He spoke often of *Franklin's dream*, as if that were somehow key to this crisis, or perhaps was a dream of the crisis itself. And somehow, New Orleans was key to the coming events, and had to be taken from the chevalier."

"Could he not have asked the chevalier to cooperate in managing the coming disaster?" Etienne asked. "Or paid the man? If you seek a corruptible person, you'll find few more despicable examples than Gaspard le Moyne."

"I believe Jackson did approach him, and was rebuffed." Eggbert Bailey shrugged.

"And you don't know what the crisis is?" Etienne asked. "The invasion of the Spanish? The rampaging of the beastkind? Perhaps even the rise of the basilisks?"

"I do not know," Eggbert Bailey said.

They rode into the city of New Orleans, Etienne deep in thought.

General William Lee gazed at the muddy ribbon of the Wabash River from the low height of an old mound, surrounded by water on three sides. His horse muttered a protest against the uncertain footing of the rain-hammered slope, and Bill eased the animal back a length. "Tell me again what they call this place, suh," he said to Landon Chapel.

Bill tried to remain mounted as much as he possibly could; his shattered legs would hold him only with pain, leaving him able to run a very short distance, or stand with walking canes. But mounted, he was the man he had always been.

Chapel fidgeted, even mounted. He was brave enough, and could ride and shoot, but the man fidgeted. He was handsome, with long brown hair that required no perruque to hide it and reminded Bill of someone, though he could not have said who; but Landon was also young. Bill hoped his own son Charles had more self-possession. Charles would be older. Charles must be riding with the Earl, defending the borders of Johnsland. Bill had written letters to inquire after Charles's health, but after years of writing similar letters and never receiving a single answer, he was accustomed to silence.

More than once, he had wanted to ask his three hundred Johnsland riders if any of them knew Charles, but it seemed indecorous. In time, he would learn how Charles fared.

"Waayaah-tenonki is the Indian name," Chapel said. "I think the French call it Ouiatenon. I do not know whether the Wigglies have their own name for it."

Bill nodded and watched the trees on the far side. The sound of shooting was distant. The bulk of Bill's forces were at his back, but a raiding party of riders, including most of the men from Johnsland, chased Imperials to drive them back.

"Send someone to the village up the road," Bill ordered. "I'll want to use the *Firstborn* name of the place in my report to Her Majesty."

"Yes, General." There was a brief silence. "Will we be defending the Wabash?"

Bill felt happy to receive the question. At Cathy's urging, he had appointed the young man to be his aide, though Chapel had expressed several times a preference to be fighting. Bill would like to be teaching his protégé something worthwhile, but found he had no head for saying anything systematic about war and its prosecution. A question from Chapel gave him the chance to say something discreet, and hopefully wise.

"It is a mistake to conceive of a river as a wall," Bill said. "Unless your opponent is fashioned from crêpe paper and therefore unable to swim and terrified to board a boat, it is much more clarifying to regard a river as a highway. We may make some desultory defense at places such as this, which are easy fords for Tommy Penn's conscripts, but the empire can easily fell some of those trees on the west bank and fashion rafts or bridges anyplace along this river it wishes." Bill frowned, unsettled at the thought. "It bears remembering that our enemy's commander, or at least one of them, is a Director of the Imperial Ohio Company who has spent her entire adult life in a canoe."

Chapel looked up at the iron-gray storm clouds. "If it rains enough, the rivers may become more effective barriers. At least to artillery."

"If it rains enough, you and I shall become superfluous, and the navies shall enter the valley to fight." Bill barked at his own jest.

"It's a shame we have no high ground to defend," Chapel offered.

"True," Bill acknowledged. "Her Majesty's kingdom

may be the flattest land on this continent. Nevertheless, that is the land that we shall defend, when the Imperials receive enough reinforcements to turn around and march in our direction again, as they must inevitably do. As we have no wall, we must consider alternatives."

"Mounted raiders," Landon said immediately. "Horsemen who can strike the sides and rear of the advancing army."

"Spoken like a true man of Johnsland." Bill smiled his approval. "Yes. Horsemen and any other rapid skirmishers we can field." He wished he still had his platoon of beastkind—for all their noisy, stinking peculiarities, they had been fierce, fast, and loyal.

Only in their death had Oliver Cromwell turned them.

"If the river is a road, then we must control it," Landon Chapel added. "If we do, then we can land skirmishers at the Imperials' backs."

Bill nodded. "And if we do not, then they may choke us off from our sources of food. Our Chicago Germans may prove to be vital in this regard, though I also find myself quite glad of our Catalan admiral. In a land as flat as this, movement will be key. And our lines of supply."

"Perhaps we can fortify some of the . . . Firstborn . . . towns," Landon suggested. "With artillery and cavalry, a fortified town at an important crossroads might significantly delay the Imperial forces. Many of the Moundbuilder towns are surrounded by banks of earth, which are already a good beginning to fortifications."

"You make excellent suggestions, suh." Bill's legs ached, and he wanted to dose himself with the Paracelsian Tincture that the Zoman princeling Gazelem supplied him with. He must be careful, though—he knew that each time he used the drops, the tincture itself would whisper to him, suggesting that he shorten the period that passed before his next dose. He limited himself to one dose daily, after he had eaten his afternoon meal. "In every case, the particularities of the battle and the terrain shall govern. We shall attempt to choose the place and time of battle, and always outnumber our foe, and take him by surprise."

"General." Landon's voice dropped in pitch and slowed down. "General Lee, you know that I am a man of Johnsland."

"As am I." Bill nodded proudly. Was Landon Chapel now going to tell him about his son Charles?

Landon was silent.

"Am I correct to think that you were raised alongside Her Majesty's brother, Nathaniel?" Bill prodded the younger man.

"You are." Landon gulped and nodded. "And it was you who saved him at birth from the Emperor Thomas, carrying him to the Earl. I saw the miraculous milk rag from which the boy nursed—the earl had kept it ever since."

"I don't know that the rag is miraculous," Bill said, "so much as magical. My old friend Thalanes was a hell of a *magician*, including in a pitched battle, but even he would balk to think of himself as a *saint*."

The thought of Thalanes's face painted onto votive candles or tiled into a mosaic behind a devotional altar, though, made Bill smile. Perhaps one day he would endow a chapel, and at least place therein a monument to his friend.

"And also…" Landon hesitated. "And also, I know that you fought a duel with the Earl's son."

"Richard." Bill sighed. "Hell's bells. I did not want to kill him."

"You had to choose between two loyalties," Landon said. "It was a knightly dilemma, and you had to either serve Kyres Elytharias or respect the Earl. You chose Kyres. Earl Isham respects that, however many years of... discomfiture it caused him."

"Say *madness*, rather. A soldier should speak clearly."

"Yes, General, he was mad. We were a laughing stock." Landon Chapel's face twisted into a grimace. Chapel was the surname of a bastard—whose child was Landon Chapel? It would be someone of worth in Johnsland. Chapel himself might know, but it was not polite to ask. "At the hearing of a cuckoo's cry, my ears fill with the hateful ballads that were sung of him. But Nathaniel Chapel... that is, Nathaniel Penn... healed him. Completely. You might say magically, but I would not hesitate to pronounce it a miracle." Chapel's face shone.

"Yes. I would like to meet Her Majesty's brother again." Bill frowned. Sarah hadn't been able to heal Bill's legs completely—would Nathaniel be able to accomplish such a feat? But a man who could heal madness might be fundamentally different from a physician who could straighten shattered legs. "Perhaps I acted out of loyalty. But also, I acted out of fear. Perhaps with a wiser head, I might have been able to serve both my lords, and avoid an unnecessary death. Instead, I killed a young man who did not deserve it, and I spent fifteen years—sixteen, now—separated from my wife Sally, my two daughters, and my son."

"I should tell you, suh," Landon said, "that Sally is no more."

"No?" Bill found himself surprisingly affected, perhaps because he was already in the grip of emotion. "Tell me, how did she die?"

"Illness, I think, some years ago. As a child, I knew who she was."

Bill sighed. "I thank you. You have relieved me of a significant burden. I feared I might be about to make myself a bigamist, whatever the lawyers say. And my children?"

"I believe that at least one of your daughters has married and moved away."

"And Charles?"

Landon hesitated. "Charles . . . had his commission."

"Of course, he did." Bill's chest ached. "And is a damned fine officer, I'd wager my soul."

Tears pooled in Bill's eyes. It seemed manlier to him to let them run down his face than to dab at them like a lady, so he allowed them to flow.

After a minute of silence, Landon Chapel cleared this throat. "I'll look into the name of the town, then, General." Were there tears in his voice, too?

"Yes, suh," Bill said.

Landon Chapel rode away into the wind and rain, and Bill found himself thinking of the young man as a son.

Gazelem became aware that he was being followed when he was crossing one of Cahokia's great plazas.

All his life, he'd lived with the possibility of assassins and spies. As a young man, he'd developed habits that had protected him since: he made his own food, he didn't drink from open bottles of wine, and he carried various purgatives and antidotes on his person; he'd become an expert in the effects of plant and mineral decoctions that healed and harmed, he never walked the same route twice, he deliberately circled back on his own tracks at least once on any journey, and more.

Who would be following Gazelem now? The wardens of Maltres Korinn again?

But no, he thought the Vizier had learned to trust him, and besides, the Vizier and his men were too busy finding homes for refugees and bringing food to those who had suffered from earthquakes. •

The wind and lightning had let up, though the air was still damp with drizzling rain, and brown water pooled in every depression of the city. Circling back on his own tracks in a plaza now, he saw that he was being followed. The other man might be Zoman, with bright blond hair, dusky skin, and a broad nose that together suggested some sort of Creole origin. Also, he wore the wooden breastplate lacquered red, along with a steel sallet helmet, and Gazelem came up behind him as the man was trying to follow Gazelem through an elbow created by the shop tents of a couple of German provisioners.

He noted the sword hanging in its scabbard from the man's belt, and then he pressed the point of his long, thin dagger against the man's black tunic, angling its blade to reach up and underneath the breastplate. At the same time, he put his left hand on the other man's shoulder, to hold him in place to get leverage if he needed to take.

"Hey, hetar," he whispered. "You must be just about the clumsiest assassin that's ever come after me. You're so awkward, I'd feel bad killing you, so let's walk down to the river together, and put you on a boat."

"Going where?" the other man asked, in Zoman-accented Ophidian.

"Home, I assume," Gazelem said. "But really, I don't care."

"Home is gone," the man said.

Gazelem wiped water from his face. "Zomas?"

"Gone. Its people dead or refugees. Some of them must be here."

Gazelem had seen refugees from his homeland. He'd done what he could to help them, but none of them had said that his city, his fathers' city, had been destroyed. "When?"

"Two months ago. More. I saw it fall."

"And didn't die defending it?" Gazelem sat. "Once, Zomas had warriors worthy of her."

"I saw it from afar. I was returning from a . . . raid General Varem had sent me on."

"You're not here to kill me?"

The blond man turned slowly. The black-crowned cuckoo painted on his breastplate was scratched and grooved, but not obliterated. The man bore wounds on his face and his arms that hadn't yet healed, and had the lines of a thousand miles in his face. He smiled, then knelt. "Gazelem Zomas," he said. "I am Captain Naares Stoach. I served the Lord of the White Towers while they stood, and I swear on all my dead that I haven't come to harm you. To my knowledge, you're the last surviving member of the royal house of Zomas. You might be the last surviving descendant of Onandagos through the male line. I have come to serve you."

Gazelem stepped back and put away his knife.

"There is nothing left to serve," he said. "If Zomas

is gone, perhaps we can gather her people. If we can bring all the survivors here under the nose of the rampaging Simon Sword, then perhaps we can persuade Queen Sarah Elytharias to take them all in. I have lost friends and good servants in the recent siege, so there is room in my household if you would join me. Perhaps we can at least build a memorial of Zomas here, that will do her honor."

Naares Stoach nodded. "And what if there were a power that could be turned against Simon Sword?"

Gazelem frowned. Had Stoach been reading his thoughts? "What kind of power would that be?"

"A power that comes from the Heron King himself. The only power to which Simon Sword is truly vulnerable." Naares Stoach smiled. "The son of the Heron King has been born."

"I cannot decide if you are the empire's
best bootlicker, or its worst."

CHAPTER FIVE

"Virgo rises in the spring, yes," Temple Franklin said. "But Virgo rises every spring. Surely, with the influence of Mars collected to your benefit..."

"Shut up, Franklin," Thomas Penn said.

"Am I mistaken?"

"Virgo rises with the equinox, Temple. The equinox was six weeks ago. She is risen, so to speak. Shall I now wait until the next equinox, to see her setting?"

"I defer to Your Imperial Majesty." Temple doffed his hat, a tall affair with a brim that curved up over Franklin's ears. "You are Philadelphia's great astrologer."

"Now you're being obsequious. And what is that godawful hat you're wearing?"

The two men rode horseback to the Walnut Street Prison. Temple had suggested a coach, one built of thick oak, reinforced by spells of the wizards of the College. Thomas had insisted on being more visible to his people, and he waved to them now.

Someone in the crowd sang as Thomas and his Machiavel rode past.

Lord Tom went a-courtin', he did ride
Sing-song, Mississippi, Ohio
With a sword and a pistol by his side
Sing-song, Mississippi, Ohio

Princesses came, one, two, three
To the lord of Philadelphi-ee
And the chairman of the Dutch Company
Sing-song, Mississippi, Ohio

Others joined in. The song was a novelty, having sprung up in Philadelphia taverns the day after Thomas's engagement to Julia Stuyvesant was announced. Thomas had been pleased until Temple Franklin admitted to having paid a poet to compose the song himself.

"Just don't have the man killed to keep the secret," Thomas had grumbled, and had thereafter pretended to be displeased. As he rode now, though, he tapped his own thigh in time with the music.

He rode 'til he reached the Hudson's shore
Sing-song, Mississippi, Ohio
And he swore that he would ride no more
Sing-song, Mississippi, Ohio

Julia was the daughter fair
Sing-song, Mississippi, Ohio
Of the very wealthiest Dutch meneer
Sing-song, Mississippi, Ohio

The singers sang the name *Julia* as if the girl had been named by Pennslanders, rather than the *YOO-lia* of the Hudson River Republic. And Adriaan Stuyvesant was far from the wealthiest citizen of the Hudson River Republic, but his colleagues of the Dutch Ohio Company had been motivated enough by the thought of trade peace with Thomas's Imperial Ohio Company to come up with a staggeringly good dowry.

"It's a postilion hat, Thomas," Franklin said.

"You look liked a damned coachman."

"Yes, that's why they call it a *postilion hat*. Postilions wore them once, but the gentle classes are wearing them now, as well. The hat is very au courant, I assure you."

"And I suppose you must also wear the stock tie and the white gloves?"

The Lightning Bishop's dissolute grandson smiled. "It is the height of fashion for a successful professional man in Philadelphia, or a man of landed wealth, to dress in a fashion indistinguishable from the fellow who drives his coach."

"This is why you wished to ride in the carriage—so that the conveyance would complement your hat?" Thomas guffawed. "You planned to ride up front and crack the whip, did you?"

Miss Julia wore her dancing shoes
Sing-song, Mississippi, Ohio
She'd dance whatever tune he'd choose
Sing-song, Mississippi, Ohio

"Let the barrel organ and the squeeze-box
    play!"
Sing-song, Mississippi, Ohio
"We'll dance until the break of day!"
Sing-song, Mississippi, Ohio

The details of the song were picaresque and charming. Thomas resolved to dance with Julia as soon as possible.

Temple Franklin smiled softly. "Your Majesty has advantages of personal beauty and grace that I, alas, do not. I am only attempting to make myself sufficiently presentable so as not to undercut the splendor of Your Majesty's presence."

"I cannot decide if you are the empire's best bootlicker," Thomas said, "or its worst. You are certainly its most incorrigible."

"I am thoroughly committed to all my duties. But I was saying, I have taken steps to gather all the influence of Mercury that I can—"

"And I was telling you to shut up. Any man who has read his *Picatrix* knows that the faster planet produces the weaker effect. Therefore, Mars and Venus when applicable, yes, but Jupiter at all times." Thomas cleared his throat. "Jupiter at all times."

A black windowless coach waited a few lengths up the street from the prison's steps. Despite the cool, moist air of the May morning, Thomas smelled a fetor when he came within fifty feet of the coach. Atop the coach hunched a tall man in a peaked black hat, maggot-white skin showing through multiple holes in his tattered brown cloak.

That was Ezekiel Angleton, or it was the Lazar that had once been Ezekiel.

Within the coach would be Oliver Cromwell, in his child body, stolen from one of the College's Parletts. The Lord Protector still seemed to be able to hear everything said in the presence of any of the still-living Parlett brothers, here or in the Ohio, with Director

Schmidt. Ezekiel had taken to acting like Cromwell's body servant, driver, and personal guard.

Thomas had asked Angleton to invite the Lord Protector to join them here.

The warden was a thin man who stood curved forward like a question mark on the steps of the prison, wrapped in nankeen knee breeches and waistcoat under a coat of black velveteen that had been worn to a high polish. He wore a neat white perruque, a short and unelaborated nod to fashion. His solitary presence boded ill, Thomas feared. It meant the damned fellow was likely to want to talk.

"Captain," Thomas said, "you and your men will wait here with the horses."

The crowd around the prison was thick—families who had heard that the Emperor Thomas would be releasing prisoners today, as acts of clemency for his imminent wedding. The Philadelphia Blues, the reconstituted company of dragoons who acted as Thomas's bodyguard, pushed the crowd back from the steps and the front wall of Walnut Street. Thomas handed the captain his reins and approached the steps.

"Your Imperial Majesty." The warden bowed low. His high forehead was bald over a hawklike nose, and iron-gray hair falling down three sides of his skull was gathered into a green ribbon at the nape of his neck.

Thomas had to make an effort to remember the man's name. "Mr. Cavendish."

"Lord Thomas," the warden continued, "I have come to beg you, in the name of the memory of your illustrious ancestor William Penn, to remember the great traditions of this prison."

Thomas nodded and tried to show patience with

a smile. "Sleeping naked in a common room? Solitary confinement for the lucky few? Flogging for the obstinate?"

"The first Landholder abhorred executions," Cavendish said. "Your grandfather built this prison to honor that sentiment and continue the Penn tradition of mercy."

"*Thy* grandfather," Thomas said, chiding the warden for his slip.

"*Thy* grandfather." Cavendish blushed.

"Yes." Thomas waved to the crowd of people waiting beyond the cordon of dragoons; they cheered. "I am here to continue the Penn tradition of mercy, myself. I shall be pardoning and releasing prisoners, and the people of Philadelphia know it."

"Prisoners who have sufficient wealth," Temple Franklin murmured.

"But thou hast also instructed me to build gallows," Cavendish said.

Thomas nodded, letting his face grow solemn. "I shall be emptying out your prison today, warden."

Angleton arrived. He moved with long, lurching steps, and black worms writhed in black gel around his eyes, which had gone completely white. Thomas nodded at the Lazar who had been his friend and servant at Harvard.

What dark path have you walked since, my Roundhead friend?

He didn't have the stomach to ask what dark path he himself might be on.

Behind Ezekiel came Cromwell, in the pale dead flesh of a young boy.

The warden frowned. "You've come to free them

all?" Then realization spread across his face like a sudden dawn. "No. Those you don't free, you will hang."

Yaas. As a first step.

Ezekiel Angleton's voice broke into Thomas's mind like the crackle of dried leaves, or the snapping of an autumn bonfire.

The warden straightened his back, rising from a question mark into an exclamation point. "Then I must tender my resignation immediately."

"You didn't build the gallows, I take it," Franklin said.

Never mind, Ezekiel said.

Would the Lord Protector insist that the designated men die? And if so, would he insist that Thomas himself do the deed?

"But you have arranged the wagons?" Thomas asked Franklin.

"Naturally." Franklin smiled.

"A canal would be convenient," Thomas said. "Once we've finished the sewers, we should think about building canals to send boat traffic west."

"Noted." Franklin bowed.

"You may resign," Thomas said to the warden, "but do not leave. When I am done here, the Walnut Street Prison will have at least one occupant."

Cavendish's pale complexion grew gray, but he bowed and said nothing.

"Surely," Franklin said, "the good warden has assembled the prisoners who are to be released. As an act of mercy."

The warden nodded. "They stand waiting within the doors." He hesitated. "Shall I bring them out?"

Temple Franklin adjusted his absurd hat and smiled

at Thomas. "Perhaps the emperor would like to address the rejoicing families."

"Fewer words are better in these situations, I think," Thomas said.

Franklin bowed his head. "The magnanimity of the deed will speak almost entirely for itself. Almost."

"I'll release the men when you're ready," Cavendish said.

Temple Franklin smiled blandly. "The ninety-seven men. I'll be counting them carefully."

Thomas climbed the steps halfway and turned to face the crowd. Behind and above him rose the prison's bell tower with its narrow cupola. To either side of him, stone guardhouses framed the steps and connected them with the walled-in prison yard below. The crowd had grown during the course of his ride, and the dragoons held back perhaps as many as a thousand Philadelphia burghers, along with their wives and children, along Walnut Street. Smoke drifted across the mass of people, bearing with it the smell of bread and bacon, and a low sun in the east cast long shadows.

He heard Ezekiel's voice again in his mind: *Ani magbir et hakol.* Since no one else reacted, Thomas guessed the words were only for him. Since they were in a language other than English—and in good Roundhead tradition, he had always known Ezekiel to perform his castings in Hebrew—he assumed Ezekiel was performing some act of gramarye.

He smiled at his former fellow student. Ezekiel smiled back, revealing teeth that were long, yellow, and pointed, like the teeth of a hound, sprouting from gums so red that his mouth appeared to be full of blood. The Yankee had pinched a corner of his cloak into a cone, and was holding the cone near his mouth.

Thomas managed not to shudder, and addressed the crowd.

"Neighbors," he said, and his voice boomed at an unnaturally loud volume. Ezekiel's work? "Citizens of the Empire of the New World. Fellow dwellers on the great Penn Land Grant, and beneficiaries of the broad-minded generosity of William Penn."

The crowd cheered. Too many words already, but Thomas felt he had to officially give a reason for his largesse.

"I am to be wed." More cheering. "In consideration of my nuptials, I am today releasing ninety-seven inmates of Walnut Street Prison. Every man released is pardoned of all prior crimes. Let us welcome them back into our society with open arms."

The crowd cheered a final, sustained time, and some of them broke out into more verses of the wedding ballad:

> *The fairies raised an urchin queen*
> *Sing-song, Mississippi, Ohio*
> *The ugliest you've ever seen*
> *Sing-song, Mississippi, Ohio*
>
> *The beastkind rampage in the west*
> *Sing-song, Mississippi, Ohio*
> *With all that racket, Tom can't rest*
> *Sing-song, Mississippi, Ohio*

Cavendish had retreated to the double doors at the top of the stairs. He now opened them, and men emerged. Cavendish had at least followed Thomas's instruction that the men were to be fed well for the three days prior to their release, and bathed this morning. They blinked at their freedom, and some walked as if they were drunk, but they rushed forward, deloused and scrubbed, into the arms of women and children. The sound of joyous weeping warmed Thomas's heart—this was why the empire needed a strong ruler, so that freedom and health, not to mention functioning sewers and canals, could be rained down upon its deserving peoples.

Thomas retreated from the crowd without ceremony, into the prison, and found Cromwell, Angleton, Franklin, and the warden waiting for him. "There is a gate in the back, I presume," he said to Cavendish. "I would hate to disrupt the celebrating families with the sight of less-fortunate prisoners being sent off to a different fate."

"There is." Cavendish's voice was bitter. Crossing through the central hall of the prison building, he pointed out through the yard. The prison was shaped like the letter *U*, surrounding a central yard on three sides. On the fourth side, opposite the prison's front door, was a high stone wall. Set into the center of the wall, piercing it through a thick barbican tower, was a gateway.

"The wagons are ready when you are," Franklin said.

"Have you segregated out the Children of Eve?" Thomas asked.

Cavendish's shoulders slumped. "I have done everything you . . . thou asked, except build the gallows."

Cromwell laughed, a sound like crockery exploding.

"*Commanded*," Thomas said. "I did not *ask* anything, I *commanded* it."

Cavendish nodded.

"Give your signals," Thomas said, gesturing to both Cavendish and Franklin.

He stood watching the yard below through a wide glass window. The gate opened and thirteen long prison wagons rolled in, driven and accompanied by keepers in Imperial blue. The prison's staff brought out a long line of prisoners, who were loaded into the wagons, where they leaned against iron bars or huddled on straw that would soon become filthy. Many gazed up at Thomas, but few looked at him for long.

He, on the other hand, forced himself to stare at them. These were sacrifices he was making, and they would not be the only sacrifices. He must make them—he had no choice—but the honest way, the noble way to make sacrifices was to acknowledge and accept the cost.

He tried to look at each face separately, for at least a moment.

When the wagons were full and locked, Thomas and his retinue descended into the yard. The morning sun was fully in the sky now, turning the moist air into a thick, unpleasant stew, rich with the scent of sweat and tooth decay. The Walnut Street jailors stood in disarray around the wagons, slouching, picking their teeth, and grinning.

"Do we need these men?" Thomas asked the Lord Protector. The jailors stared in awe at the sight of their emperor talking with a naked boy.

We do not.

Thomas nodded. "Men," he said, "the Walnut Street Prison is closed, at least for now. If you lack employment, I invite you to seek it with the Imperial Army, or with the Imperial Ohio Company, both of whom need experienced, hard workers to carry out the Pacification of the Ohio, as well as the continued struggle against the Cahokian upstart. But whatever you do, you must leave the prison grounds. *Now.*"

They left.

Cavendish remained. "I assume I am not dismissed."

"You are *not*." Thomas turned to the Lord Protector. "There is no gallows." He wanted to suggest waiting, but he doubted Cromwell would accept that suggestions. "I am, however, wearing my sword."

The strange child-man body that carried the Lord Protector within it looked frail and short, but the voice that came out was an aural attack. *Thou shalt not require thy sword, my son. I have a wedding gift for thee.*

Thomas nodded, unsure whether he should feel dread or relief. "Direct me."

Kneel. Give me thy hands.

Thomas did as instructed. Cavendish stepped back, breathing hard. Temple Franklin showed admirable self-control, but he watched closely. Ezekiel Angleton grinned like a wolf.

The Lord Protector took Thomas's hands. He pressed his thumbs into the center of Thomas's palms, and the pressure went immediately from firm to painful. Thomas gritted his teeth and didn't cry out.

I give thee first this warning, my son. Thy banns are published, thy bride cometh. Thou mayest touch her to lie with her. Do not touch her otherwise.

Thomas bowed his head, stunned. He felt no loss at the instruction not to touch Julia Stuyvesant—his wedding was a political and financial arrangement, and not a love match—but he felt confusion. What was happening?

Thy touch shall be death, the Lord Protector continued. *To all. From this moment on.*

The Lord Protector's forefingers and thumbs abruptly pierced Thomas's hands, sinking physically into his flesh. Thomas grunted, feeling a sensation of burning or acid, but didn't move. When Cromwell stepped back, there was a small hole, half an inch across and blackened all around the edges, drilled through each of Thomas's palms. Thomas could see the gravel of the prison yard through his own hands.

He rose to his feet. Feeling that his will was forced, but feeling no despair in that, he turned to face the prison's warden.

Cavendish dropped in turn to his knees. "Your Imperial Majesty," he said. "Lord Thomas. Please. Please, I beg thee."

The men in the prison wagons, and the men in Imperial uniform who were to drive them west, stared.

Thomas reached forward with a trembling hand. He felt as if he were reaching forward to touch the consecrated host, or perhaps extending his hand to grip a lightning rod in the middle of an electrical storm, and his hand shook.

He wrapped his fingers around Cavendish's throat and squeezed.

The flesh where he grabbed the prison warden immediately turned black. Spidery lines of black, like cracks, or veins, spread out from where Thomas touched the man, and all his color seemed to be drawn into those black lines and then disappear. As the last color drained from the warden's face, his eyes turned milky white and his body slumped in death.

And Thomas felt alive.

Alive and *strong*.

An awed silence fell over the yard. Thomas broke it by casting Cavendish's corpse to the ground with a *thud*.

"If Cavendish had family," he said to Temple Franklin, "let's give his widow a pension."

Franklin nodded. "I will have it done."

"After all, we are cash-rich again. And I'm going to need to borrow those gloves of yours." Thomas turned to face Oliver Cromwell. "First, I shall deal with all the Children of the Serpent who are still in the prison."

You will find them delicious and nourishing, the Lord Protector said into his mind. *And so will I.*

The Treewall flourished. This was no surprise; it had sprouted into verdant growth again on the day of the equinox, when Sarah Elytharias had entered the walled city of Eden in that strange space that was and also was not within the Temple of the Sun atop Cahokia's Great Mound, and Luman Walters had almost entered with her.

Almost.

He did not regret his choice to remain outside. Something—he believed it was Cahokia's goddess—had given Luman the gift of gramarye that day. He believed that he would not have received the gift, if he had tried to enter Eden without an invitation.

He took the gramarye as a gift, and as a message.

You too, Luman, can be approved by the powers of Heaven. You are imperfect, and you are not yet standing in the center.

But you can be approved.

The Treewall had survived the earthquake on the day of the queen's collapse, and two further earthquakes since. Each quake cracked the wall, but the wall knit itself together again afterward.

A mighty enough tremor, it was clear, might shatter the wall entirely.

In addition to the Treewall, the Gun Trees flourished. There were twelve of them, arrayed in a semicircle on

Cahokia's landward side, and each held an enormous cannon high above the ground, gripped within its very trunk. The guns had each been named after one of the apostles, and the trees had acquired the names of the guns in turn. A week after the repulsion of the Imperial besiegers, the first intrepid pair of Cahokian lovers had picnicked in the branches of the apostolic cannon trees.

A third set of trees had sprouted, not on the morning of the equinox, but late that same day, and they were scattered around the city. Some had grown up within the holes pounded through the Treewall by Imperial cannons, and Luman—and others—had at first taken them to be the Treewall's attempt to repair itself. And indeed those trees had sprouted, and within days the regrowing Treewall itself, weaving into the branches of the new growth, filled in the gaps in the Treewall as if they had never existed.

But the new trees sprouting elsewhere around the city did not grow into the Treewall, or come to resemble it. Instead, they sprouted separately and grew within days into full-sized trees. They were strange trees in appearance, with white bark and leaves of such pale green that the leaves, too, appeared white from a distance. Their trunks were thin, and remained smooth and branchless until seven or eight feet above the ground, at which point they sprouted broad, leafy branches that reminded Luman of nothing so much as palm branches. The Cahokians had named them *Ashtares*.

They smelled sweet, of citrus and cinnamon.

The thickest stands of Ashtares grew about the height of the Great Mound itself.

He stood on a wet morning in May beside one particular Ashtar. It grew in an avenue, between a spot where Imperial guns had breached the Treewall, and the Great Mound. Luman could think of no reason why the spot should be significant, and no reason why this tree in particular should speak to him.

But it did.

He brushed the smooth, wet bole with his fingertips. He knew no braucher or Memphite incantation that would tell him anything, but he had brought a dowsing rod with him. He'd carved his name into the split hazel rod and sung appropriate psalms over it as he'd created the instrument, and now he was prepared to ask it questions.

Foot traffic passed, and donkeys, and the occasional cart, sloshing through puddles. He didn't love the idea of someone eavesdropping, but then again, he didn't love the idea of creeping out at night to attempt this divination. It seemed too much like skullduggery, and he wanted to be done with that sort of trade.

And he definitely wanted to attempt this divination in the presence of the Ashtar in question.

He pressed his divining rod gently against the tree's trunk, massaging both bits of wood up and down until he couldn't feel the difference, and the two seemed to have become a single tree. He incanted the rodsman's psalms over them as he did so.

For good measure, he essayed a bit of gramarye at the same time: "*Virgam facio,*" he murmured over the rod. "*Virgam ex arbore facio.*"

Curious how similar the words *virga*, rod, and *virgo*, virgin, were.

He walked in a circle around the tree, and then he began to ask the rod questions.

"Am I Sarah Calhoun?"

Nothing.

"Is this the month of December?"

Nothing.

"Is my name Luman Walters?"

The rod bobbed.

"Is this particular Ashtar connected with me some-how?"

The rod bobbed, but that was such a broad question that it was nearly useless. All it confirmed was that Luman wasn't imagining things.

"Did I plant this Ashtar?"

Nothing.

"Did this Ashtar grow here because of some deed of mine? Was this Ashtar caused to grow by some object I once owned? Did a spell of mine cause this Ashtar to grow?"

Nothing.

Luman hesitated. "Does the serpent goddess want me to do something with this Ashtar?"

Nothing.

Luman shook his head in frustration. What could it be?

"Have I seen this Ashtar in some other form?"

The rod bobbed.

"Did I see its seed? Did I see its fruit? Did I see its planting?"

Nothing.

Luman looked down along the avenue, at the scattered arrangement of the Ashtares. He looked up the other way, toward the Great Mound, and saw its pale green mantle of newly sprouted trees, shrouded in the rain and in the low clouds. Running from the former location of the breach in the wall up to the mound where the Imperials had finally assaulted Sarah—and

Oliver Cromwell and the Lazar Robert Hooke had broken through into the Temple of the Sun and attempted to assault its goddess—the trees reminded Luman of nothing so much as an invading army.

"Did I see this tree when it was a person?"

The rod bobbed.

A chill ran up Luman's back.

"Was this tree a child of Adam before it became a tree?"

The rod bobbed.

Luman Walters tried not to think about the strangeness of that answer. He focused instead on whom he might know, who could have become a tree. One of Cahokia's defenders? One of its assailants?

"Was this Ashtar once Notwithstanding Schmidt? Sherem…" he couldn't remember a surname, "Sherem the Polite? Alzbieta Torias? Robert Hooke?"

Nothing.

He tried to think of stranger possibilities. "Was this tree once Sarah Elytharias?"

Nothing.

"Was this tree once… Luman Walters?"

Nothing.

He heaved a sigh of relief.

"Hey, hetar," a voice called, "what are you doing?"

Hetar was an Ophidian word. It meant something like *friend*, and was informal. Luman turned around and found he was being watched by a group of young Firstborn, none of them older than fifteen. They wore broad hats that kept the rain off their heads, and a combination of oilpaper slickers and wool cloaks.

"I'm trying to figure out something about this tree." He smiled, then pointed at his dowsing rod. "This is an old technique for getting answers. It's called a dowsing rod, or a Mosaical rod, because Moses and Aaron had rods in the Bible."

"Dowsing rods find water." The young woman who said this looked like she could have been Sarah's cousin, pale skinned and blotchy, with stringy black hair and eyes full of curiosity. She lacked Sarah's hard edge, though. "Are you trying to find out whether there's water in this tree?"

Luman shook his head. "I feel drawn to this tree. I feel as if, well, it's embarrassing to say because it makes me feel a bit silly, but I feel as if this tree wants to talk to me. I don't suppose you know anything about this tree, do you?"

They all shrugged and shook their heads.

"You should start a college of magic," the girl with stringy hair said. "Cahokia doesn't have one."

"If I did," Luman said, smiling, "would you sign up?"

"Yes," she said immediately.

"Really? Even though I'm not Cahokian myself?"

"You're Queen Sarah's wizard," the girl said. "If you taught classes on how to use a dowsing rod, I'd go."

"Queen Sarah made the trees grow," one youth said.

"They sprouted the night the Imperials got through," another added.

"Do you live near here?" he asked them. "Were you here on this avenue on the night the Imperials got through the walls?"

They all nodded.

"What happened here, that night?" Luman smiled at the children. He wished he had candy or something to offer them, though they looked too old to be bribed with sweets.

"There was the wagon with the sick people," a red-haired girl volunteered.

A child with a thick growth of freckles in a saddle across her nose pointed at the wall. "There was the Spaniard lady. She threw the cannon down off the wall and smashed the draug. And then she came over here and killed another draugar."

Several of the children nodded.

"The Indian draugar," the freckled child clarified.

Luman frowned. "Indian? What kind of Indian?"

The children all shrugged.

Luman felt a growing suspicion like a tickling sensation in the pit of his stomach. "Was he wearing a tall hat? A tall hat and a red blanket?"

The freckled child nodded.

Luman took a deep breath and exhaled slowly. Then he stepped back to make room for the operation of the rod, gripped its fork with his two hands, and pointed its shaft out, parallel with the ground. "Was this Ashtar once a Haudenosaunee named Dadgayadoh?"

The rod bobbed.

Luman felt light-headed. Dadgayadoh had been a good trader, an ambitious Company man from the Ohio Forks. He had become a draug . . . and then a tree.

Luman wanted to sit down. He almost wanted a drink to steady himself, but he had sworn off alcohol to his Memphite initiator, years earlier.

"So?" the girl who resembled Sarah asked. "Are you going to start a college of magic?"

Luman laughed at the incongruity, and then smiled. "You know what? Maybe I will."

❖   ❖   ❖

"I have not felt at home in many years," Bill said.

"I regret that I was not able to make New Orleans a more accommodating place for you." Cathy smiled at her betrothed. "I did *try*."

They rode horses through the streets of Cahokia, he would not say to where. They crossed many-sided plazas and passed building after building in a state of partial construction; many had been shattered or burned by the Imperials or the beastkind, and more had been knocked flat by earthquakes. Cathy shielded herself from the rain with a baleen-framed umbrella that Bill had given her, while Bill relied on his coat and hat.

Bill laughed. "My lady, but for you, New Orleans was a hell on earth. But that is not what I mean. I am a soldier, and a cavalryman, and my life has been lived in saddle, tent, and hotel room. I am a man of Johnsland, but it is many years since I spent any significant time there. I need a home."

He stopped his horse and Cathy stopped beside him. She reached out to touch his hand, big and muscular, and wet with cold rain. "I have felt the same."

Bill nodded and took her hand. "I hoped you would say that. I hoped you might feel that *this* could become our home."

She smiled at him. "Cahokia *is* our home, Bill. But truthfully, I would spend another twenty years in tent and saddle, so long as I could be with you."

"Heaven's finials, Cathy, I am so tickled at your words that I can scarcely bring myself to point out that you misunderstand me."

Cathy's heart skipped a beat, but her long practice at concealing uncertainty served her well, and her smile remained in place. "Whatever can you mean, my knight?"

"This." Bill released her hand and gestured, and for the first time, Cathy really noticed the building beside which they had stopped. It was a low mound, of the Cahokian residential style—its first floor was half-sunk in the earth, with additional stories built atop it. Only this mound was wrecked and burned, its timbers askew in the mud and its thatch only vaguely remembered in tufts of scorched straw lying here and there. "I had hoped *this* could become our home."

Cathy gasped. She tried to say something elegant, and couldn't find words.

"I want roots again," Bill said. "I want them to be with you. And Sarah gave me... gave *us* this house. I shall have to build, but for you I will build, even if it means building a mound. For you, I will build a thousand mounds."

Should she tell him about Landon Chapel?

Cathy looked at the ruined house and saw possibilities. She saw timbers raised and a thatched roof above them, or perhaps a flat roof for stargazing. She looked at the nearby houses and saw neighbors and shops. She saw children, flashing across a puddled street, and imagined that they were hers.

She should tell Bill.

But not yet.

"It is perfect, my love," she said.

Achebe Chibundu asked for the Eze-Nri's blessing before he left. He waited until they were alone, in the Palais.

The Eze-Nri, whose god within had demonstrated

itself mightier than the god within the city's old chevalier, immediately understood. "You wish to undertake something dangerous, Achebe?"

"I wish to avenge the death of your father." Achebe knelt before Etienne Ukwu. "With your god and my god assisting me in a righteous cause, surely nothing can be dangerous. But first, I need to get past the serpents."

Ukwu smiled solemnly. "My god has been working to find a means to avenge my father's death."

"My god and I accept."

The Eze-Nri took a small powder horn from his belt and sifted grains of gunpowder into Achebe's hair. Then he rested a hand on the wrestler's brow. "Maitre Carrefour," the Bishop of New Orleans said softly, "go with this man. Bring the Rainbow Serpent to ward him against the basilisks of the Mississippi and against all venomous things. Choose his paths for him so that he may find what he seeks and may find his way of return. Open every door before him, and shatter every manacle that binds. Make him truly Lucifer, the Adversary and the Morning Star, the venomous fang of justice."

Achebe nodded his agreement and rose. "I do not do this to rob you of your vengeance. I do this to *be* your vengeance."

The Eze-Nri nodded. "Go."

Achebe carried nothing with him; he was going to an army, and would find what he needed when he arrived. He wore a loincloth and a short tunic. He walked, singing songs of revenge and justice.

He walked to Bishopsbridge, though he had no intention of using the bridge itself; that would only attract attention. Instead, once the Barbican rose into sight above the oaks above the river, Achebe turned right and walked ten more minutes. Then he dropped down the bank, onto the mud of the river.

A serpentine body slithered across his upper arm, and he felt feathery wings slap his face. "Serpent," he said in his native tongue, "I am your brother. I shall fly like you, and move unseen as you move, and like you I shall kill with one bite."

The basilisk left him alone.

Achebe's heart beat faster. Another basilisk bumped into his thigh and a third struck him in the back, but he did not fear.

"Maitre Carrefour," Achebe murmured. "Chukwu, and all other gods who may hear the Bishop of New Orleans, go with me now."

He did not pray to his own god, his *chi*. *Onye kwe, Chi ya ekwe*, his father had told him many times—if a man agreed to a thing, his chi agreed to it as well, and a man's destiny was in the care of his personal guardian god. The chi connected a man to Chukwu, the sun.

Achebe waded into the cold waters.

Other things slithered across his legs as his toes squelched mud between them, but he did not fear. Once he was waist-deep, he dove neatly forward into the water and swam.

He didn't worry that the water might wash away the gunpowder anointing he had received; the power of the Eze-Nri was in Achebe now, not in the grains of powder. He could feel the power in his limbs as they swam, and in his lungs as they inhaled the warm, humid night air, and then blew it out underneath the water in great bursts of bubbles.

Without meaning to, he took the long parade steps of the first minutes of a wrestling match up the bank of the river. He inhaled deeply, watching starlight shimmer off the scales of the swarming basilisks, and flexed the muscles of his chest, arms, and shoulders. With those muscles, he had lifted horses off the ground and broken men's legs.

He walked through the forest toward the Spanish camp.

The Spanish army was impossible to miss. Their fires and torches ran parallel to the river for several miles, but set back far enough so that their sentries wouldn't be bitten by the basilisks, and the force was vast.

Lusipher stalked his prey silently through the woods. He looked for the silhouettes of men, listened for breathing, searched for the glint of starlight on a metal helmet. Finally, he smelled tobacco.

Guards.

"*Buenos días,*" he said in a loud voice. "*Buenos días. Etufuola m okporo uzo.*" *I have lost my way.*

"*Quien va allá?*" A sentry loomed closer in the darkness, grabbing Achebe by the shoulder and shoving a pistol against his belly.

"*Buenos días! Etufuola m okporo uzo!*"

A second man detached himself from the shadow of an oak tree; this one held a musket, and sucked the stump of a cigarette. "*No ves que es uno de los africanos?*"

"*Si, ahora lo veo.*"

"*Tiene armas?*"

"*No. Es casi nudo.*" The first Spaniard shook Achebe. "*Qué haces aquí?* What you do here? *Qu'est-ce que tu fais ici?*"

"Buenos días! Etufuola m okporo uzo!" Achebe said again. *"Agua! Agua!"* If he gave any indication that he really understood Castilian, he'd only have to tell more complex lies.

"Dónde está su acampamento, los africanos?" Pistol asked Smoker.

"Están por allá." Smoker waved an arm. *"Distante, pero. Al lado de los japoneses."*

"Allá!" Pistol mimicked the gesture, waving his weapon. *"Me oyes? Allá! Distante!"*

Achebe bobbed his head up and down. *"Buenos días!"* he cried one last time, and then he walked in the direction indicated.

He had no interest in finding *los africanos*, of course. He preferred not to talk to anyone who could interrogate him. He stole a pair of trousers and a long white shirt from a laundry line at the periphery, and then walked into the camps.

His hopes for a place to hide were quickly dashed. If he had understood the rhythms of this army—why and when men were driven from their beds to stand watch or drill, and what the patterns of traffic were—then he might have been able to situate himself somewhere unseen, and with a strong vantage point. As it was, he feared that at any moment, if he stopped moving, someone would challenge him or try to assign him a task.

He passed a sleeping unit of Mexican warriors with stone flakes set into their clubs and a banner made of a jaguar pelt. He passed lancers sleeping very close to their horses, each man lying alongside his barbed lance. He passed pale-faced men he thought might be Germans, with large blond mustaches and short, wide-mouthed guns.

He was passing a quartermaster's wagon, laden with dried meat and beans, when he noticed the messengers.

A steady trickle of men moved about among the units, dressed in white and wearing white caps. They carried papers, and Achebe slowed his pace to watch one deliver a paper to a man at the quartermaster's wagon, and then stand and wait as a reply was written out.

When the man turned and jogged the other direction clutching his new message, Achebe followed.

"Will his taste ever turn to the flesh of men?"

———◆———

CHAPTER SIX

"Tell me who you are," Maltres Korinn said to the second Zoman.

He sat in his office, facing Gazelem Zomas across his desk. At Gazelem's side sat another Zoman, blond and broad featured, and wearing lacquered wooden armor bearing the emblem of the Lost Sister: black cuckoo and crown on a red field.

The fourth person in the room was Cathy Filmer. Maltres included her because, in the process of becoming Queen of Cahokia, Sarah had taken Cathy as her special confidant. Elevating the woman to the priesthood suggested that Sarah intended to continue favoring Cathy, so Maltres included Cathy in his private councils.

Gazelem had asked for a meeting, and hadn't balked at Cathy's inclusion.

"I'm Captain Naares Stoach. I was an outrider of Zomas, while she stood."

"I grieve for the loss." Some Cahokians would have sneered at the fall of Zomas, but Maltres was sincere.

In the best of circumstances, the news of the fall of a great city would at least mean the deaths of men. In the situation in which he found himself, he would have greatly preferred to have Zomas standing and an ally, or at least standing and an irritant in the Heron King's flank.

Also, he had now spent many hours among the city's Zoman refugees, personally negotiating accommodation and other living arrangements. He very much regretted the fall of the city that had shattered these people and thrust them into his care.

Gazelem looked at Cathy. "Is Her Majesty suffering because of the earthquakes?"

Cathy didn't bat an eye. "It's possible. She is intimately connected with this city. It would not surprise me if an injury to the city would also do harm to her."

"What are you thinking?" Maltres asked Gazelem.

"I worry," Gazelem said slowly, "that what the King of Tawa undertakes may avail us nothing. If he transforms Sarah into this . . . angel, but she remains connected to the city, then earthquakes might continue to wound her."

"If they are wounding her now," Cathy said. "I am only speculating."

"Are you saying you have some means to stop the tremors?" Maltres asked.

"I believe I know what is causing them," the Zoman princeling said. "And I believe it may be an attack upon us. And yes, perhaps, I know what we can do to defend ourselves . . . to defend *Sarah* . . . against the attacks."

"Enough preliminaries," Maltres said. "Tell me."

Gazelem nodded at the Earthshaker's Rod, leaning

against the desk. "Tell me what you know about that staff you bear."

"The queen gave it to me to function as a staff of office, but properly, the Earthshaker's Rod belongs to the office of King or Queen of Cahokia. We have it from Onandagos, who led such a mighty exodus of peoples that he was called the Earthshaker in his time; the earth shook under his people's feet. The wood is ancient, of a tree that we do not any longer grow and whose name we have forgotten. Onandagos brought the staff with him from the Old World."

"And the horses?"

"They represent the sacrifices the king once made, from his own herds. Some dark stories say, rather than the sons that the kings of our most distant ancestors sacrificed."

"Gods become gentler." Gazelem frowned. "At least, some do. Let me tell you some things about that rod that you may not know."

Maltres arched his eyebrows and waited. Cathy leaned forward in her seat.

"The head and the ferrule indeed come from the Old World," Gazelem said. "They were brought by Onandagos along with the Orb of Etyles and the Sevenfold Crown, as the original regalia of his kingship. The staff upon which they used to fit had shattered in the magical contest that led to the sinking of our people's ancient homeland, the Drowned Lands. As had the staff's twin."

"There were two?" Maltres asked.

"There *are* two." Gazelem took a deep breath.

Naares Stoach ran fingers through his hair and sighed.

"Where does this wood come from, then?" Cathy asked.

"Before he could settle in the Ohio, Onandagos had to drive out its original inhabitants. In this he was opposed by his eldest son, Zomas, but Zomas was overruled, and did not at that time rebel against his father. So the Firstborn, and some of their allies, made war upon the Talligewi who lived here before them, and upon the allies of the Talligewi."

"The Talligewi are the giants," Cathy said. "The Anakim."

Gazelem smiled. "You are from warm Virginia, so the giants of this land may be but a rumor to you. But my ancestors battled them, and drove them out, and they resettled in the north, on the Great Lakes."

"The Eldritch Seas," Cathy said. "I am aware of the giants. I understand they are never more than ten feet tall at the most."

"Tall enough," Maltres murmured.

"The last great leader of the Anakim was a warrior named Eru-Jay," Gazelem said. "She fought with a staff in each hand, said to be thick and strong and deadly, of a wood now lost to our knowledge, but appearing as slender wands in her mighty hands. After defeating her, Onandagos placed the ferrules and horse heads of the Earthshaker's Rods upon Eru-Jay's staffs and simply claimed them for himself and his successors."

"I knew it as an ancient part of the regalia, a part that predated the inclusion of the Heronblade, and perhaps had been replaced by the Heronblade. It was the only part of the regalia that remained in Cahokia after Kyres's death, so I used it as Regent-Minister, with the consent of Notaries, to remind others of the obligations I had assumed." Maltres looked at the Earthshaker's Rod. "This is a war trophy."

"And there is a second," Cathy said. "That must be the principal point of this story."

"There is a second," Stoach the outrider agreed.

"You believe that the Earthshaker's Rod can be used...to shake the earth," Maltres said.

"*Earthshaker* was a title of our monarchs before we left the Old World," Gazelem said. "We fought the rivers and the seas, and our magic was so powerful, it shook the earth. And when my ancestor Zomas, eldest son of Onandagos, was denied his rightful inheritance—do not look at me with that reproachful eye, Korinn, I know that this is not how your people tell the story, but *I* am talking now."

"And I am listening."

"When Zomas left the other Firstborn, or was cast out, the one piece of the regalia he was able to take with him was one of the Earthshaker's Rods."

Maltres frowned, puzzled. "I was unaware Zomas had regalia."

"The Earthshaker's Rod is not used by the King of Zomas in public," Gazelem said. "It is...it *was*... used privately, to prevent tremors from destroying the lands of Zomas, and in war. Onandagos and his successors in Cahokia did the same thing with their rod—the Ohio is a land of many tremors, only most are so faint that they are unnoticed, or are dampened by the rod."

"If the rod requires conscious use, it has not had it," Maltres said. "At least since the death of Kyres Elytharias, and likely longer. Why have we not been destroyed by earthquakes these last sixteen years?"

"Two reasons," Gazelem said. "First, Zomas is not far away, and Turim Zomas the second, Lord of the White Towers, continued to use his Earthshaker's Rod even as you did not. And second, Peter Plowshare, during his reign, performs many acts of benevolence. When Peter Plowshare is king, disease is suppressed, crops are bountiful, herd beasts are fecund . . . and the Ohio doesn't suffer earthquakes."

"So because Peter Plowshare is no longer protecting us," Maltres said, "now we shall suffer tremors?"

"It's worse than that," Stoach said. "Simon Sword has the other Earthshaker's Rod, and he's using it against you."

Maltres absorbed that suggestion in silence.

"I believe this is why Simon Sword attacked Zomas first," Gazelem said. "Her Majesty empowered him by giving him the Heronblade, and he used it to level the White Towers and take the Earthshaker's Rod."

"So what do we do about it?" Cathy Filmer's eyes were fixed on the rod. "If you're right, then Simon Sword may be using the other rod deliberately to attack Sarah's person."

"We must learn to use the rod we have," Maltres said.

Gazelem nodded. "And also, we must take away the other rod from the Heron King."

Maltres sat stunned at the thought. "How do we do either of those things?"

"I do not believe that anyone alive has the necessary knowledge," Gazelem said. "However, I believe that the ability to acquire that knowledge may reside within the Treewall. Specifically, I hope that it may be found among the Zoman refugees."

❖　　❖　　❖

In a grove of trees on the outskirts of Philadelphia, Nathaniel settled into a cross-legged sitting position and pulled his drum into his lap. Margaret gripped a low-hanging dead limb of one of the elm trees and yanked it off. With efficient motions, she stripped the limb down to a heavy, spiky club, and swung it once around her head.

"Will you leave your shadow-bear?" she asked.

At the sight of his sister, Nathaniel felt a warm feeling in his chest. He had come a long way from being the neglected foster child of the Earl of Johnsland—the voices he heard no longer tortured him, the constant shriek of the world had resolved into the harmony of the spheres, his falling sickness had completely stopped, and he had gained extraordinary powers of travel and healing. He had also lost his ability to hold knives and ride flesh and blood horses, and his hat now only fit backward, while his hand-me-down coat only fit inside out.

But most of all, Nathaniel had gained a family.

"Shadow-bear, I like that." He smiled. "I don't really control Makwa—when I go to the starlit plain, Makwa comes here."

Margaret frowned. "Does that mean that while you're here, he's on the starlit plain?"

Nathaniel laughed, delighted. "I guess maybe it does. I don't know."

Margaret—his sister spoke with a Catalan accent, but had accepted the English version of her name—swung her club again. She smiled, but it was a ferocious expression, all teeth.

Nathaniel sang:

I ride upon four horses, to heaven I ride
To seek to heal my uncle, I must learn to hide
From my familiar spirits, down deep inside
I seek the land of spirits, to heaven I ride

He rose up the seven steps to the plain, where he found himself seated upon his horse-drum beneath a wheeling night sky of great beauty, smelling unearthly, fruited spices on a warm breeze.

He listened first, for the sound of the ally he had sent northward. Hearing the steady tread of the man's walk, and a song under his breath, he turned to the task at hand.

He rode west. The paths under the night sky were never familiar, but the directions were, and Nathaniel's horse rode like the wind. He flew over mountain ranges and along rivers, past fields of weeping spirits and tar pits that wanted to suck him and his horse in.

He reached the place where his two familiar spirits waited. It was the starlit-plain version of a building he'd never seen in real life, a library at a country palace called Irra-Zostim, that belonged to his father's family. Cahokians—his father's people—called their libraries *palaces of life*, and Nathaniel had taken to calling this structure on the starlit plain his Palace of Spirit.

Nathaniel dismounted at the door of the Palace of Spirit, and his horse became the drum slung across his shoulder. Isaiah Wilkes and Jacob Hop stood in the door, smiling.

~*I heard you.*~ Isaiah Wilkes looked as he had in life, a tall man with long dark hair and gray eyes, with a physique that was rangy and athletic. Wilkes was a master of the tools of spies—secret ciphers, occult networks, and, importantly, disguise. *~The practice is paying off, I could hear you rise to the plain. It gave me time to return.~*

~I heard your hoofbeats.~ Jacob Hop was short, blond haired and blue eyed. In death as in life, Hop was constantly fiddling with a pack of Franklin's Tarocks. *~This is getting easier.~*

~It is,~ Nathaniel agreed. *~Thank you for meeting me here.~*

~I was watching the Heron King,~ Wilkes said. *~He has smashed Zomas, and his marauders pursue the tattered remnants of Zomas's people across the Missouri and out into the Great Plains.~*

~I was in New Orleans,~ Hop offered. *~Your sister's gift of the basilisks keeps New Orleans free of the chevalier and his Spanish allies, for now. Though beastkind rage against the city's northern walls, and bereaved Zomans will soon be knocking at her doors. Also, I was learning Welsh.~*

Nathaniel nodded. Sarah likely knew these things—she saw events far from her throne in Cahokia—but he would visit to mention them to her.

~I need help,~ he said to Wilkes. *~I want to disguise myself and Margaret.~*

~You should disguise her as twenty armed men and a nine-pound cannon,~ Jacob Hop said. *~That way, when she goes into combat and completely devastates the enemy, her victory will not disrupt her deception.~*

Isaiah Wilkes looked thoughtful. *~How can we help?~*

~I've been pondering this,~ Nathaniel said. *~At first, I thought you might teach me how to put disguises on myself and on Margaret. But I think I have*

*a better way. I think I want you to ride back with
me on my horse.~*

~*Will that work?*~ Wilkes asked.

Nathaniel shrugged.

~*I will mind the store,*~ Hop said. ~*Hold down
the fort. What do you say about a library? I will
straighten the books? Only there are no books, merely
writing on the floor. I will read the letters, then.~*

~*I hope you are coming with me,*~ Nathaniel said.
~*I think it will help my disguise if I'm not speaking
English.~*

Hop's face brightened. ~*What shall we speak, then?
Deutsch? Français? Igbo? Cymraeg?~*

~*You speak Igbo?~*

~*I can learn it.~*

~*I think Dutch, for now. It will be easiest to try
this with you both at your most comfortable. And
Julia Stuyvesant has come to Philadelphia with an
entourage, everyone is talking about that for miles
around the city, so there are many Dutch-speaking
people around the emperor's palace. Plus, Margaret
already speaks really good Dutch.~*

~*Horse Hall?~* Wilkes's interest sharpened visibly.
~*What are you trying to do?~*

~*Find Lord Thomas,*~ Nathaniel said. ~*At first.~*

~*And kill the bastard?~* Wilkes asked.

~*Heal him,*~ Hop said. ~*Nathaniel is a great healer.~*
Wilkes nodded.

Nathaniel grinned. ~*Are you ready?~*

Both spirits nodded. Nathaniel struck his drum—
which instantly leapt from the palace and became
a horse, pulling him along with it—

and he in turn pulled both familiar spirits with

him. They all fit, comfortably, and Nathaniel rode back across the starlit plain, singing:

> *I ride upon four horses, through heaven*
> *   I ride*
> *I bear two noble allies, whose skills I've*
> *   tried*
> *We'll share a single bone-hoard, a single*
> *   hide*
> *I seek the land of mortals, through heaven*
> *   I ride*

He descended the seven steps in a single bound, the fourfold horse that was his mount slamming back into its physical form in the mortal world, a drum made of horsehide. He had descended from his ecstatic state many times now; he had also risen to the plain pulling another person with him. What he did differently this time was wrap an arm around both men and hug them tight as he descended, pulling them with him, drawing their chests into his chest, their faces into his face, their limbs into his limbs.

Then he opened his eyes and saw Margaret scowling at him.

"Something's different about you," she said.

"Did you have to defend me against many foes while I was unconscious?" Nathaniel asked.

Margaret shrugged. "Three. Made short work of them. Then there was a talking animal that called itself *Der Wunderbär,* but your friend Makwa taught it to fly, only it was a trick, because he didn't teach it to stop. *Der Wunderbär* took off, couldn't stop, and flew right out of here. Easy enough."

Nathaniel laughed. "Hold on one moment."

He listened. With his gifted ear, he heard the quivering tones of the cosmos, and also voices.

~May my saplings grow in peace to be mighty elms.~

~Water cools, water cools.~

~I am always alone.~

The earth was full of spirits: spirits of the dead, spirits of animals and plants and the natural world, spirits Nathaniel couldn't always identify. With his gifted ear, the one cosmic ogres had pounded an acorn-shaped bit of quartz into, Nathaniel could hear them.

That sense of hearing was the source, ultimately, of all his abilities.

He shut out the sounds of brook and elm and listened deeper. He listened within himself.

~I'm here, Nathaniel,~ he heard Isaiah Wilkes say.

~Ik ook,~ Jacob Hop said. *~That means me too.~*

Nathaniel smiled at his sister. "I'm the same, I think. But I've brought back friends."

"Jacob Hop?"

Nathaniel stepped aside within his soul, giving space to the Dutchman. "*Ja natuurlijk,*" his own mouth said. "*Hoe gaat het met jouw, Margarida?*"

"Margaret," she said back. "*Het gaat goed.*"

~Your experiment worked,~ Isaiah Wilkes said inside Nathaniel.

"I do feel your presence," Nathaniel said to the two men. He stood up, shifting his drum to his shoulder, and took several steps. "I feel your weight. I wouldn't want to carry you like this all the time."

Margaret stared in fascination. There was a shadow of a second expression on her face . . . what was it? Annoyance? Envy? Anger?

~Time to get you two into good disguises,~ Isaiah Wilkes said.

Temple Franklin rode west atop the foremost of the thirteen wagons that left the Walnut Street Prison. Thirteen wagons, one for each of his grandfather's virtues, though Temple could remember what the virtues were only with difficulty. His postilion hat turned out to be extremely fitting, as he sat on a wide bench beside a pimple-faced, unshaven turnkey with lank hair and one milky eye, who drove the wagon. At stops, the turnkey and his other colleagues—two per wagon—fed the prisoners gruel and bread so cheap it had twigs in it.

Some of the men in the wagons knew who Franklin was, or perhaps they guessed, because of his resemblance to his grandfather. Before the first day was over, they begged him for release whenever he was in sight.

He reassured them that of course they were being transferred. He told some of them in confidence that they were being sent to an experimental prison, one without walls and with great personal luxury. He told others in confidence they were being freed to join the Imperial Ohio Company Militia and participate in the Pacification. He told others still, and always in great confidence, that they were being freed, so that the Walnut Street Prison could be converted into an army barracks, but the condition of their freedom was exile, so he was escorting them to the western bounds of the empire.

These were all lies. He scarcely dared think what was actually going to happen to the men, and he certainly had no intention of saying it out loud.

He rode with one of the surviving Parlett boys, eyes always open, head shaved, dressed in an unmarked uniform of Imperial blue. The other was in the camp of Notwithstanding Schmidt, whither he was bound. A third Parlett survived, if only technically; the Lord Protector Oliver Cromwell inhabited the third brother's body. The link that bound all the Parletts together now included Cromwell, so when Temple spoke with Thomas through the Parletts, he heard Thomas's responses in an imitation of Cromwell's voice, whereas Schmidt's communication was passed on in an imitation of the Imperial Ohio Company's Sole Director.

Could Cromwell see through the other Parletts, or hear what they heard? Did Temple in fact ride west with a spy constantly transmitting all events to Cromwell, as they happened?

Temple assumed that that was the case, and behaved accordingly.

Originally, there had been five of the psychically joined boys. The other two Parletts had died at March's failed Siege of Cahokia.

Imperial soldiers, veterans, rode to accompany and protect the wagons. Though Temple had heard through his network that the Swords of Wisdom were active in the Ohio, he did not expect trouble; the prisoners carried in the wagon were children of Eve, and should not excite the sympathy of the Firstborn militia.

The third person who traveled with Temple was the emperor's body servant, Gottlieb. The square-faced man who kept his perruque impeccably powdered, his stock tie neat, and his frock coat free of dirt, was there to take care of the Parlett boy and keep an eye on him, but he also made himself useful to Temple, shifting his trunk in and out of the stations they stayed at along the road, cooking meals, and procuring acceptable wine at the small towns of Pennsland. Gottlieb made himself useful enough that Temple forgave the man his jaundiced eyes and his sly expressions, as if he were the upstart servant in some cheap opera, looking for his own advantage in every situation. Gottlieb still limped from having his leg impaled by the Masonic actor and prophet, Wilkes.

Gottlieb did make rather more small talk than his station in life should have permitted. Temple Franklin did not have democratic feelings, but after three days of rattling his tailbone against an oak plank that was not at all disguised by the presence of a cushion so thin it might as well have been a handkerchief, taking snuff to try to cloak the growing fetor of the human sacrifices crowding the movable hold beneath him, Temple began to talk back.

"It's certainly not a problem to travel indefinitely," Gottlieb was saying. "I have spent weeks at a time traveling with His Imperial Majesty. It's simply a matter of knowing how to procure the services of a laundrywoman at the right intervals and for a reasonable price. In the emperor's company, that turns out to be effortless—it might surprise you what lengths people are willing to go to in order to impress the emperor. Gifts of horses, sometimes. Cloaks, room and board, wine. But even without his additional, shall we say, ability to command, it's basically just a matter of reading a map."

"A map?" Temple asked, curious.

Gottlieb looked surprised to be answered, and it took him a moment to gather his thoughts. "Yes! Well, and knowing the contents of your trunk."

"How much clothing I'm carrying," Temple said.

"Correct. And ideally, you would tell me what you planned to wear and when, if there were, for instance, dinners of state or meetings with Electors you had planned, so I could make certain I had the right clothes cleaned. Planning is everything, you see. And then I would look at the map, or ideally, a gazetteer of some kind, such as Morse's."

"Morse's *Gazetteer* does not identify the presence of laundrywomen."

"Ah ha!" Gottlieb laughed. "No, but a map, you see, just indicates the presence of a town. The *Gazetteer* tells you how big the towns are, and from that you can guess where the best places are to find a laundrywoman."

"You're offering to do my laundry," Temple said.

"Well, no. That is, I'm just thinking out loud, I wasn't trying to offer my services. But if you need to have laundry done, I can certainly undertake the task."

Temple considered. "I believe my first meeting of any significance will be in the western Ohio, and specifically, at the camp of the Imperial Ohio Company, with the Company's Sole Director, Notwithstanding Schmidt. Until then, I do not give a fig, nay, not half a fig, for whether my stockings are white or my nails are clean."

"Of course." Gottlieb bobbed his head. "As you wish, and at your service. This boy is easy to mind—he's old enough to feed himself, all I need to do is draw him a bath every few days and pick the rocks out of his bread."

"When we get closer," Temple said, "I'll ask you—I'll *pay* you—to clean my clothing."

"No need to pay, happy to do it, His Imperial

Majesty pays me more than enough, and in addition, I am recompensed by the thought of my glorious station. I am but a little planet, but I have the honor of orbiting closely to a radiant sun."

"Surely, Thomas doesn't approve of your use of astronomical figures."

Gottlieb hung his head. "I have poor luck with the emperor and astrology."

"As do I." Temple took a pinch of snuff off the back of his hand. "I continue to try because my effort lets him know I am interested. And frankly, it's well for me that I do not exceed his lore. Let us both remember Signor Mocenigo."

Gottlieb crossed himself.

Temple found himself liking the little man with the square head. "Perhaps I could do with more fastidiousness. We'll reach Youngstown soon enough—do you believe you could find an appropriately skilled and devoted laundrywoman there?"

"Without a doubt."

"Then I look forward to wearing clean clothing after that. And I shall pay you, Mister . . ."

"Gottlieb, Mister Franklin. I'm a body servant, and we are called by our first names."

"I shall pay you, Gottlieb. I shall certainly pay the laundryman's fee, and a gratuity on top of that. I only ask—no, I *instruct*—that you not clean this coat that I am wearing."

"Understood. Lucky coat?"

"Yes, indeed."

The Parlett boy said nothing, but watched with large eyes.

✧　　✧　　✧

Eventually, Notwithstanding Schmidt would have to throw the might of the Company against Cahokia again. She prepared herself, swelling her ranks with militia recruits and pressing men from local jails wherever her forces moved, as authorized and instructed by the emperor.

The forces of the Heron King prowled the western shores of the Mississippi, not only hemming Cahokia in but also eroding her defenses and other resources. Refugees from the west ate her food. Cahokia was swollen to bursting with people. More came, and she turned none away.

In the wake of the failed siege, when the emperor's greatest guns, the Twelve Apostles, had been hoisted into the air by miraculous trees sprouting directly beneath them, allies had come to reinforce Cahokia. They served in motley companies under the city's Cavalier general, some from Johnsland, others from Appalachee, Germans from the north, and more—but not in large numbers. The tension within the empire, over the course of the Pacification, over the response to be made to the rampaging of the beastkind on the lower Mississippi, and over the attempt by certain Electors—encouraged and sustained by the brat Queen of Cahokia—to impeach Lord Thomas and remove him from office, meant that none of the powers of the empire could spare anything like its full force.

They sent tokens.

If it came to another battle, the queen would be assailed on two sides, and defended by an army of tokens.

The thought that one of Cahokia's enemies was Simon Sword, the legendary bugbear of the Mississippi, continued to strike Schmidt as extraordinary.

And Cromwell? He and his lieutenant Robert Hooke had entered Cahokia and very nearly entered its sanctuary, before the golden light emerging from the temple had blown them to dust. But surely, he couldn't be gone.

In the meantime, Thomas Penn's instructions were clear: choke Cahokia's trade. Raid its farms, stop inbound merchants, don't let it build up a store. Cahokia could live on its abundant fruits and grains for the summer, but without trade, and with more and more mouths to feed, it would starve, come winter.

Armies were on their way.

So Schmidt blockaded the Mississippi River, just above the confluence with the Ohio. The heaviness of the spring rains meant that the river was widening, and the blockade required more and more of the boats at her disposal as time passed. Traffic between Youngstown and New Orleans could continue as usual—subject to increased taxes—but traffic north was not permitted. She similarly blocked the roads in the Ohio itself, so no traders overland could reach the Eldritch city.

She didn't have the reach to block the Mississippi river to the north, either by sailing past Cahokia or by marching to the river overland. Her men took potshots at the Chicago German ships that sailed down, but the river was too wide for them to do much damage, so Chicago wheat and corn flowed into Cahokia.

She couldn't stop traffic on the far side of the river, either, but there wasn't much. Simon Sword had taken care of that.

Onacona Mohuntubby stepped into her tent, wet from the rain. At her request, the emperor had reassigned Mohuntubby from the Imperial Army to the Ohio Company, and specifically to her. He was a long-limbed

Cherokee soldier with a high forehead and thick eyebrows. He was ambitious—she couldn't prove it, but Schmidt believed he had killed the artillery commander assigned to besiege Cahokia at her side, a general named Sayle.

Sayle's death had been convenient for Schmidt.

Now Mohuntubby saluted. "The Parletts are speaking."

Schmidt set down the accounts book she was working at and stood. A communication through the Parletts meant a message from the emperor. She brushed past Mohuntubby to take the lead and crossed a short confusion of rain and wind to reach the Parlett's tent. As she entered, the young man spoke, with a voice like windows shattering around a brick.

"DIRECTOR SCHMIDT."

She took a seat on a lightweight camp bench, brushing water from her shoulders. Mohuntubby ordered out the two men under his watch who were standing guard, then stood in the doorway.

"Is My Lord President there?" she asked.

"I AM." The voice coming from the boy continued to be the horrible shattered voice of Oliver Cromwell.

Schmidt and Mohuntubby met each other's gaze and they both frowned. This was not how the Parletts' communication link had previously functioned; in the past, the local Parlett had always imitated the voice and even the face of the distant person speaking. Unless Oliver Cromwell was pretending to be Thomas Penn, something had changed. "My Lord President, are you well?" Schmidt asked slowly. "You sound different."

There was a hesitation, and then a laugh. "FASCINATING. I AM NO LONGER SPEAKING THROUGH THE...UNINHABITED PARLETT. INDEED, THAT

YOUNG MAN IS ON HIS WAY TO YOU. LORD CROMWELL ASSURED ME THAT WE WOULD BE ABLE TO CONTINUE TO COMMUNICATE, HOWEVER, AND THAT APPEARS TO BE TRUE."

Uninhabited Parlett?

"Who . . . is one of the Parletts inhabited?" she asked.

"THIS IS THE LORD PROTECTOR SPEAKING NOW. AFTER THE DESTRUCTION OF THE BODY I HAD TAKEN IN THE OHIO, I PLACED MYSELF INSIDE ONE OF THE PARLETT BODIES IN PHIL-ADELPHIA."

"So where is the . . . second uninhabited Parlett?" Schmidt asked.

"THOMAS AGAIN. I'VE SENT HIM TO YOU. TEMPLE FRANKLIN IS BRINGING HIM, ALONG WITH SEVERAL WAGONS OF PRISONERS."

"More soldiers?"

"NO. FRANKLIN WILL EXPLAIN HIS MIS-SION. YOU'RE TO HELP HIM, AS BEST YOU CAN, WITHOUT RELEASING YOUR FIST FROM THE THROAT OF CAHOKIA."

"Do you not wish to explain to me now?"

"I BELIEVE WE HAVE BEEN SPIED UPON IN THESE COMMUNICATIONS."

Schmidt rocked back in her seat. Spied upon by whom? "By the witch of Cahokia? She is said to have extraordinary vision."

"PERHAPS. AND PERHAPS ALSO BY THE SER-VANT WHO TENDED THE PARLETTS. AND PER-HAPS BY OTHERS."

Schmidt tried to remember who tended the Parletts at the Philadelphia end. "It was your valet, wasn't it? A man with a German name? Gunther?"

"HIS NAME IS GOTTLIEB."

"You've had him imprisoned, I take it. Or executed."

"GOTTLIEB IS MAKING HIMSELF USEFUL ONE LAST TIME. WHEN HE REACHES YOU, I WANT YOU TO INTERROGATE HIM AND THEN DISPATCH HIM."

This was what it was to be Sole Director of the Imperial Ohio Company. "I'll make certain word doesn't get back to anyone else at Horse Hall about his fate."

"I'M GLAD WE UNDERSTAND EACH OTHER, DIRECTOR SCHMIDT."

The Parlett's chin collapsed onto his sternum, as if the effort of speaking had exhausted him. The conversation was over.

The child Absalom grew.

After the failed attempt to baptize him, he didn't again attack Chigozie. The Merciful mostly avoided him.

Was it merciful on their part to avoid him, to lessen conflict?

Or was it an exquisite cruelty?

Either Kort or Ferpa was with Absalom nearly at all times, fishing and hunting to feed a hunger that seemed constant and insatiable. At one month old, Absalom took to eating the flesh of beasts. Woodchucks and gophers, wild dogs, bobcats, and birds of all kinds fell to his appetite.

"Will his taste ever turn to the flesh of men?" Chigozie whispered to Kort one day, watching the adolescent twelve-week-old who was seven feet tall tearing a deer to shreds with his hands and his beak.

"Children of Adam, like you?" Kort asked. "Children of the angels, like me?"

Chigozie put a hand on the big beastman's arm. "You are as much a man as I am."

"I fear his taste already turns to the blood of men," Kort said. "I fear that his thoughts dwell on how men taste, and whether we forbid him the flesh of men because it is sweet, and he is not to be allowed this grace because we do not love him."

Chigozie groaned.

"I fear to tell him this," Kort continued, "because I do not believe he trusts me. I have tried to be a father to him, but I do not know how a father should behave, and neither does he. He fears me, perhaps, a little. I do not think he respects me. Nor does he respect Ferpa. I fear that if I forbid him the flesh of men, he will only desire to seek it out the more."

Chigozie put his face into his hands.

"You say I am as much a man as you," Kort rumbled. "Tell me something about the man that you are."

Ferpa sat on the rocks above Absalom, watching him. She had helped him find the deer, but now she eyed him carefully, club in her hand. Did Absalom feel cared for, or caged?

"I have no secrets," Chigozie said.

"Tell me about marriage."

Chigozie looked at Kort's face and found him gazing at Ferpa. The sight gave him a ridiculous amount of joy. "I am not married. But I approve of marriage, with all my heart."

"With all your heart?"

"Yes. It is commitment for life to another person, as well as to something that is larger than either one of you. To the combination the two of you make." Chigozie found himself remembering his father, in the last days of his life, but then also his mother, lying on her deathbed, and all the hours Etienne had spent at her side as she breathed her last. "And to the children you produce together, if you are so blessed."

"The children," Kort rumbled.

"And marital love is a mighty..." Chigozie searched for the right word, "a laboratory, a workshop..."

Kort frowned.

"A hunting ground," Chigozie tried, "a field to labor in. The work a person does in marriage is discipleship that refines the soul."

"Marriage can bring you closer to God."

"Yes."

"God approves it?"

"If done with an honest heart, I believe so. We understand that Adam and Eve were married."

"And if I wished to be married to Ferpa?" Kort continued.

"Have you asked her?" Chigozie said.

"I am asking you first." Kort looked at Chigozie and the expression on his big, shaggy head might have been bashful. "I need the Shepherd to tell me what is permitted."

"Yes," Chigozie said. "I will gladly marry you. Now go ask Ferpa."

"Was Hannah reckless, or was she bold?"

——◆◆——

CHAPTER SEVEN

Calvin Calhoun was packed to leave in three minutes. It was easy enough—rifle, powder, shot and accouterments; a second set of clothing, rolled up in a bedroll; done.

Logan Rupp, on the other hand, took hours.

"Come on, Logan!" Cal bellowed from the entry hall of their rented Philadelphia house. "Jerusalem, iffen you can't git a little pepper in your step, we're gonna miss the Feast of the Ascension and have to wait for the actual resurrection!"

There was no one to laugh at his joke, the Donelsen boys all being out with Charlie Donelsen. The Electors of the Ascendancy who were in town met often to eat, and generally in taverns in the seediest parts of Philadelphia, which required them to bring along armed kinsmen.

Cal went ahead and laughed by himself. Lord hates a man as can't appreciate the humor of a good joke, no matter who tells it.

Rupp bellowed down the stairs, voice echoing off

the peeling blue wallpaper in the stairwell. "If I only had to bring a coonskip cap and a pair of moccasins, I'd be ready too!"

Coonskin cap? "I ain't e'er worn nor owned a coonskip cap!" Cal called up the stairs. "You callin' me a chawbacon?"

"I'm only saying I have books to pack!"

"You plannin' on appearin' in a Youngstown court?" Cal snorted. "No one cares what you're wearin', Rupp, and we're a-comin' back!"

"My formbooks!" Rupp called. "If the Elector wants a legal document drawn up, I'd rather not have to rent a form from some local practitioner."

Cal blew a raspberry and retired to the drawing room. This was a spare room next to the bottom of the staircase, furnished only with three high-backed chairs that had all sprung leaks and were slowly losing their cotton batting.

Cal was being careful with the Elector's money— Iron Andy and Charlie Donelsen split the rent on this house. Cal knew how far a shilling would go, and how hard it was to rustle a heifer and get her to market, and how many Calhoun mouths there were to feed.

He threw himself into one of the soft chairs and sat watching the street through cotton curtains. A breath of air lifted the curtains, bringing in the leafy smells of spring along with the earthy reek of horse droppings, to mingle with the odors of sweat and tobacco that were deeply impregnated in the rented house's wood.

He was ruminating on what the Elector might want from him and on the general direction of the impeachment proceedings when a man climbed the wooden front steps of the house. Cal had been distracted by his own thoughts and had missed the opportunity to get a close look at his face, and then there was a knock at the door.

If the Donelsens had been there, one of the boys would have answered the door. In the event of mischief, three or four big-knuckled Donelsens always stood between Charlie and danger, which meant that they often stood between *Cal* and danger.

Cal decided to be careful.

He took his rifle with him and slipped out the back. That took him through the blocky parlor and then the rectangular kitchen, and then he lifted the latch on the kitchen's door.

The visitor knocked a second time as Cal let the white-painted door carefully shut.

He vaulted over a wooden handrailing to drop off the porch into the thick green grass, dark green with the flush of spring rain, and then crept around the side of the house.

He checked his firing pan but then shifted the long rifle into his left hand, taking his tomahawk into his right.

Peering around the front of the house, he saw the lightly trafficked street, with its elms, cherries, and dogwoods. A mule cart with three large barrels marched slowly along the street, and a portly, dark-skinned man stood at the door. Irritation and curiosity showed on the man's face as he knocked again—he was short and tended to the rotund, with a black vest and white sleeves, stained with sweat. Sweat stood out on his temple, and as Calvin looked at him, he had the feeling he'd seen the man before.

He didn't look armed, and he didn't look like a Polite. Still, it never hurt to make a good impression.

Cal threw the tomahawk.

He sank it neatly in the flaking white paint and dry wood of the handrailing, and at the same time raised the rifle. He didn't quite point it at the stranger, but he didn't really point it *away* from him, either.

"Evenin'," Cal said.

The stranger laughed. "I see that New Orleans has nothing on Philadelphia for danger!"

"Do I know you?" Cal asked. "We got business?"

"We met in a casino." The man's accent was thick and French. "You were with Sarah, queen of the Eldritch. You came to see my boss, Etienne Ukwu."

Cal frowned. "You're the accountant."

The man grinned, his teeth shiny white. "Monsieur Bondí. I hold the proxy of the Bishop of New Orleans. And I am also prepared to give testimony."

Cal lowered the rifle. "I expect I might have to leave the lawyer here with you, then."

Ahmed Abd al-Wahid spent weeks observing the Mississippi. He watched the basilisks rolling in the warm mud, slithering over each other, and zipping through the air.

He requisitioned cattle from the chevalier and his Spanish allies and drove them to the river, watching the big beasts die slowly as Abd al-Wahid tried to count how many basilisks were sinking their teeth in. He saw that a snake that bit could bite again and again, its fangs apparently venomous each time, with no reduced potency.

He noted that there was no time of day or night that was free from the possibility of encountering one of the bad-tempered, highly venomous creatures, but that they were more active at night. They hunted at night, killing the little rodents, frogs, and bats that lived along the shore of the river. A basilisk that killed then swallowed its prey whole and sank itself into the mud to digest. The basilisks flew as high as the bats did; Abd al-Wahid saw bats snatched a hundred feet above the river.

He experimented with temperature, covering a calf with cold mud and sending it down to the water's edge to see whether the mud would conceal the calf from the snakes; it didn't, and the calf died in horrible spasms of pain, foaming at the mouth. He experimented with scents, and they all failed to camouflage creatures from the snakes. He experimented with noise, borrowing a three-pound cannon and firing it very close to trees where he knew the flying snakes nested—individual snakes fled their sleep-place and a few even came to investigate the source of the sound, causing the mameluke to take shelter behind a lightning-shattered oak, but by and large the serpents were unfazed.

He watched for alligators and wild cats and other venomous snakes, and noted that basilisks seemed to be the only killer on this stretch of the river. Perhaps the serpents ate the other predators' food, causing them to leave. Or perhaps they had driven the other predators entirely into the bayous and the Pontchartrain Sea, which made these flying snakes the deadliest and fiercest predator of all.

The bishop had chosen his defenders well.

Finally, Ahmed Abd al-Wahid resolved upon a plan. It might fail, but as the Prophet said: *No disaster strikes except by permission of God. And whoever believes in God—He will guide his heart.* Ahmed

Abd al-Wahid let God—as filtered through his own wit and science—guide his heart, and if what God led Abd al-Wahid to was lethal, it could only mean that God wanted the mameluke dead.

For a week, he paid bored Texians to collect vermin for him. Bats were hard, but mice were easy to catch, and frogs were easier still. The Texians relished a good contest, and something they called *bragging rights*—the right of a contest winner to boast—so he offered to pay them by the creature, as well as a barrel of whisky for the winning platoon.

For a week, they brought him *critters* and *varmints*. He kept them alive with insects he paid the Tonkawa and Comanche to bring to him, and with grain.

He reported his findings to the Chevalier of New Orleans, who was amused by the contrast between Ahmed Abd al-Wahid's effort to think through the challenge of the basilisks, and the Spanish approach. The Spanish, apparently, were building a bridge up the river, and they were doing it at a staggering cost of life, and forcing the builders to cooperate by using slaves and by killing those who refused to work. It was the difference, the chevalier said, between the caress of a lover's bare fingertips and a punch to the face from a gauntleted fist.

Abd al-Wahid demurred that at times, it was the fist that was needed, and left.

He built a small trebuchet. This was medieval learning, but it was part of the science of war, and he had studied it along with the tactics of Salah ad-Din and Richard the Lion. He built it a hundred feet back from the river's edge, which was fifty feet farther from the water than he had seen any cow standing as it was bitten. He threw stones with the trebuchet, and if he couldn't throw them all the way across the river, he could throw them about half the distance.

He paid three Texians to help him build it and to help him fire it. They were fascinated, averring at first that it couldn't possibly work, and then hooting and slapping their broad-brimmed hats against their knees when it did.

It was not a perfect solution. He would require courage, and the help of God.

He wished he still had the assistance of his former colleagues, and he cursed the upstart bishop in his heart.

It was a May morning when he put his plan into action. He denied the Texians liquor the night before, to be certain they would be present and sober. Having watched the flying snakes gorge all night long, when the dawn came there were few enough of them flying over the river that he was willing to make the attempt.

One bite was all it took to kill a man, so a modest number of aggressive basilisks still made the river an impenetrable barrier.

But the snakes weren't standing watch, as men would do; it was simply the case that there were still snakes alert, bellies empty and looking for food.

Abd al-Wahid released a basket full of mice. Some had died, and lay still at his feet, but most rushed toward the river. The snakes fell upon them.

Abd al-Wahid released more mice, and frogs with them. As the gray and green creatures scurried and hopped toward the water, he launched others into the air. He threw mice and frogs, over and over, into the trees. Many of them passed through the spring foliage and fell into the river, but many were snatched midair and eaten.

He loaded basket after basket of mice and frogs into the trebuchet and fired them across the river. He didn't fasten the lids tightly, so each basket became a cloud of flying edibles that fell short of the snakes' habitats on the other side ... but came close enough to lure out the basilisks.

The snakes ate frogs and mice in midair. They also plucked them, swimming, from the surface of the river to eat them, and they even dove beneath the water.

When he no longer saw snakes, Abd al-Wahid sent a couple of calves down to the water's edge. The beasts made it to the waters of the Mississippi and began to drink—and no snake appeared to bite them.

For good measure, he fired the last of his baskets of rodents and amphibians upstream and down, to give any basilisk approaching a bounteous meal to eat before it got anywhere near Ahmed Abd al-Wahid.

Then he stripped down to his loincloth and walked to the water's edge. He carried his pourpoint and his scimitar in a small bundle.

He prayed as he walked, wordlessly, but with a solemn feeling of supplication in his heart. God had guided his heart to this moment, or God would kill him now.

At the water's edge, he saw the fat iridescent coil of a gorged basilisk, slowly turning over in the shallows. He ignored it, passed the cattle, watched his footsteps to avoid treading on any other irascible creature, especially any creature that was both irascible and venomous, and then lowered himself into the water and swam.

The water was cool, a welcome relief from the

heat, which in May already began to be oppressive. Unlike the Nile, the Mississippi filled the air with its humidity and choked off Abd al-Wahid's will to move, but once submerged within its waters, he felt good.

The water stank, and he was very careful not to take any of it into his mouth.

He swam with long, measured strokes. His belly, facing the bottom of the river, felt bare and vulnerable. Basilisks were a risk, but there were other venomous snakes—cottonmouths and coral snakes and others. And there were also alligators, smaller than the crocodile of the Nile, but still deadly to a naked man taken by surprise. And just because Abd al-Wahid didn't see any alligators, didn't mean they weren't there, waiting and hungry.

In the center of the river was a muddy sandbar. As Abd al-Wahid approached, the mud shifted, something beneath it slithering into motion. Gorged basilisks? Hungry basilisks? An alligator, teased into full appetite with a couple of frogs and now ready for larger meat?

But Abd al-Wahid was committed. There was no way to turn back, and no weapon, and nothing to do but hope, pray, and if an alligator came, try to seize its jaws and hold them shut.

He fixed his eye on the shore ahead and swam.

He bumped into swimming frogs and mice, as well as the corpses of drowned mice or frogs who died on impact with the water, or from the sheer acceleration of being flung into the air. Snakes slithered across his skin.

None bit him.

And none had wings.

Something under the water touched his leg. He

started, curling into a ball, but there was no second contact.

He approached the eastern shore. He would feel more comfortable if he had been able to hurl frogs and mice this far, but the Mississippi was simply too wide. The corpses of frogs and mice became more scarce, and then disappeared entirely. He was gambling that basilisks nesting in the trees or in the mud on this side of the river would all have seen the feast mid-river and gorged themselves into a stupor of sleep, but the eastern shore was too far from the western shore for him to have actually seen snakes feeding, and he might well be mistaken.

He lengthened his stroke, swimming more eagerly.

Whether it was conquest or death, he was swimming toward what God chose for him.

And, insha'allah, closer to the death of the gangster bishop who had killed so many of his comrades.

His foot struck mud, and then his knee, and then Ahmed Abd al-Wahid stood and ran. The cold Mississippi sucked at his feet and ankles, trying to drag him back in—

and then something sharp pricked his heel.

Blackness filled his heart.

It came to this, years of war and service, and he would die bitten by a snake in a jungle river in a land cursed by God.

He slowed, slightly, but continued.

If he was going to die, at least he'd die standing on solid ground.

He marched across sandy soil, held together with tall, thin grass, and then climbed up under gnarled and muscular oak trees.

Turning, he raised his arms above his head and faced the western shore. He had crossed the mighty Mississippi, at least, piercing the serpentine armor of the sorcerer-bishop, and if his dagger had failed to find the man's throat, it had at least come close.

But the fire in his veins and the chilling of his thoughts that he expected to kill him didn't come. He sat, puzzled, and looked at his foot.

A single puncture mark marred his heel. Not two, which would be the mark left behind by the bite of a serpent, but one.

His foot had struck a nail or a thorn, or something else in the Mississippi's cold mud that could sting, but delivered no venom.

He stood again, and laughed. He stretched his arms wide to embrace the perilous world of the Mississippi, then turned eastward again. A few miles away, the stone wall enclosing New Orleans was visible as a cold gray line.

Exultant, Ahmed Abd al-Wahid broke into a run.

He was nearly naked, barefoot, covered in mud, and armed only with his scimitar. And he had a bishop to kill.

"Cal," Sarah said.

She had murmured for two weeks; this was the first clear word she said.

Cathy took her hand gently. "Calvin's not here, Your Majesty. This is Cathy Filmer."

"Are we alone?" Sarah's voice trembled.

"We are."

Cathy stood beside the Serpent Throne upon which Sarah lay. The nearest other people would be Yedera, one of the lesser priestesses, and the messenger boy, all standing in the front entrance. Incense dictated by the King of Tawa burned in the nave, on the other side of the temple veil; piles of crushed herbs lay to either side of Sarah's head.

"Then call me Sarah, dammit."

"I'm here, Sarah."

"I'm blind, Cathy. What happened?"

"Your eyes are bound. You haven't been well."

With pale, trembling fingers, Sarah worried at the bandage around her eyes.

"That might not be wise," Cathy said.

Sarah pulled aside the strip of cloth. Both whites were bloodshot, and there was crusted blood and pus in both corners of both eyes, but when she fixed her gaze on Cathy, she heaved a sigh of relief.

"You can see," Cathy said.

"Jest tell me I ain't missed the weddin'."

Cathy laughed softly. "You have not. May I get you a glass of wine? There's a bottle here with herbs in it, chosen by a healer."

"Water," Sarah said. "Nothing doctored."

Cathy brought a cup of water to the throne. While Sarah nursed it, she asked the messenger boy to fetch the Vizier. She also took a moment to inform the Podebradan that Sarah was awake; Yedera said nothing, but stood straighter and smiled. By the time the water was gone—Sarah used the last of the liquid to dab crusted blood from her eyes—Korinn had arrived. The Vizier stood outside the veil, at the top of the steps by which one accessed the sanctum; Cathy knew from experience that he would only see the luminescent, golden silhouette of the throne itself from his vantage. Luman Walters had come with him.

"Your Majesty?" Korinn called.

"What happened?" she asked. "And remember, I can tell when you're lying."

"Only if you can see me, Your Majesty."

"Oh, if there's anything I can do for sure, it's *see*."

Cathy heard Korinn and Walters share a sigh of relief.

Then slowly, one event at a time, the Vizier recounted what had happened: Sarah's collapse, the arrival of the King of Tawa, the sending of messages to the other five kings of the Ohio, their meeting with Gazelem, the earthquakes that had continued to rattle the city. As he spoke, Sarah raised her arms and seemed to reach them toward the veil. She moved her fingers up and down, not touching the veil but reacting as if she were seeing something through her hands—something that was changing, because Sarah's expressions changed in response. Cathy watched, fascinated.

"Your Majesty?"

Cathy realized that the Vizier had been silent for a minute or more.

"We're here," Cathy called. "Sarah is just . . . seeing."

"I do not understand," Korinn said.

"It's the veil," Sarah said. "I can see with it. And who's that new fellow with Gazelem?"

"You're watching Gazelem Zomas?" Korinn asked.

"No. But I can see him anyway, because he's within the Treewall. We're drowning, we're soaked. Are people swimming house to house? But I'm looking eastward, at the roads."

"For the Sister Kings?"

"Yes. I see two of them, almost here. But there are two who can't leave. They're trapped inside their cities. I guess that'd be Adena and Koweta."

"Along the Ohio River," Luman said.

"They're trapped by Imperial forces," Sarah continued. "Sweet Jesus, what are those things?"

"We do not see what you see, Sarah," Cathy murmured.

"Wooden soldiers," Sarah said. "And clay men, but I know what those are, they're Mockers. In large numbers, walking through the woods. And also surrounding Koweta. At least I think so—does Koweta have a wall around it?"

"Koweta has a wall," Korinn said.

"So the King of Tawa wants to turn me into an angel," Sarah said. "I'm game, but it ain't gonna happen iffen we don't git those two kings here. And Oranbega, I guess. He ain't imprisoned, but he ain't goin' anywhere, either."

"I will see to it...Sarah," Luman Walters said.

"You have a plan?"

"I have an idea, if the Vizier can lend me resources. I know that some of the Hansa that Director Schmidt corrupted have broken their pact with her, so they may be willing to help us smuggle two kings along the river."

"I'll get you whatever you need," Korinn said.

"And take Yedera. She won't admit it, but I'd bet a year of kisses she's bored. I'll keep an eye on you both," Sarah said. "Mebbe help you as you go."

"Perhaps you had better not," Cathy suggested. "If gramarye is what is making you ill—"

"Then I guess the best thing I can use my gramarye for is to expedite the cure, wouldn't you say?" Sarah snapped. "In any case, I'll be the judge. I was a fool to step outside the veil, I just did it out of sheer surprise. The throne will sustain me. But what's Gazelem looking for? He and that blond fellow are talking to folks huddled in the Basilica. Zadok is feeding them, good for him."

"Feeding them your corn, Sarah," Korinn said. "Good for *you*."

"Good for us all, then."

"He didn't tell us exactly what he was looking for," Korinn said. "Which makes me think he is looking for a Ghostmaster."

"Enlighten me," Sarah said.

"Zomas is...*was*...a haunted place. Zomans summon the spirits of the dead to seek information. It is not a common practice in Cahokia, and he may believe—rightly, I think—that some Cahokians would frown on it."

"Do you frown on it, Maltres?" Sarah asked.

"It's beyond my ken," he said. "But I have been operating beyond my ken for a long time now. If a Zoman cunning woman can connect us with someone who can help us retrieve the Earthshaker's Rod in Simon Sword's possession, I would gladly pay her all my wealth."

"Looks like a little corn might be enough," Sarah murmured.

"Speaking of the Earthshaker's Rod," Walters said, "we should consider the other possibility coming out of Gazelem Zomas's revelations."

"Yeah," she said. "Bring me the rod, and I'll examine it."

"I have it here," Korinn said. "Should I pass it through, or...?"

"Stay there." Cathy stepped through the veil to

take the staff offered by the Vizier. He was a man whose facial expression tended toward the grave, and he now wore such a look of relief that Cathy almost kissed him. Instead, she took the Earthshaker's Rod and let the veil slide shut again.

Sarah made no move to take the staff, so Cathy held it.

"Only, Sarah," Luman said, "whatever it is that you think needs to be done with the staff, please let me be the one who does it."

"Champing at the bit, eh, Luman? Kind of fun to be a gramarist, ain't it?"

Walters chuckled. "I admit, it is. But no, I wish to spare you the effort. You should conserve your mana, and save the strain for when you really need to act. I am not the accomplished magician that you are, but—"

"Shut up, Luman," Sarah said. "I'll let you try."

"Your Majesty," Korinn said.

"Uh-oh," Sarah shot back. "We're switchin' to *Your Majesty*. Here come the kid gloves."

"I had hoped to spare you all this administration of war. Perhaps we could do something less strenuous, something a little more enjoyable."

"What do you have in mind, Korinn? A pull toy? A kitten?"

"We could finalize the honors list," he said. "Medals and titles to be awarded for actions during the siege. Also land grants. Your Majesty's holdings in the city doubled with the addition of the traitor Voldrich's parcels, and we were paring down a list of people and institutions to whom you intended to grant land."

"I remember," Sarah said. "Only we got hung up on all that peppercorn-for-a-year nonsense, and I said we needed to get back to the idea of just owning land. What did you call it, that lawyer phrase you used?"

"Fee simple absolute," Korinn said. "Yes, I have the statute drafted. I'll bring it to you to review, and then I think we can easily find Notaries to sign."

Sarah laughed out loud. "Look at me, getting drawn into the technicalities! You trickster, Maltres, distracting me. Fine, bring me your statute and your lists. Or give them to Cathy—she and I can edit them while you deal with the refugees and the beastkind and the Imperials."

"Sir William keeps the Imperials at a healthy distance these days," Luman said. "He trains our own troops to become something resembling an army, and in the meantime we are assisted by allies."

Sarah sobered. "Yeah, well, in a few weeks those wooden men are going to be here, and three guesses what they'll want. Time to shore up defenses, get all the soldiers in here we can, bring in the food, and be ready. Any refugees who can't hold a spear or fire a rifle, it might be best if we can get them shipped upriver to Chicago. After Gazelem has had a crack at them, I suppose."

"Understood," Korinn said.

"Get Sir William in here so I can tell him what I see coming our way. Maybe we can get raiders out there to slow them down or stop them."

"Yes," Korinn said.

Sarah reached for the Earthshaker's Rod and Cathy handed it to her. "Apparently, this thing can be put to offensive uses. Let me take a good look at it while you two go get organized."

Cathy heard the footsteps of the men as they retreated along the nave, and murmured words shared with Yedera at the entrance.

Sarah gazed deeply at the staff in her hands. "With the orb, I got sort of a hint from Simon Sword himself. I don't think he intended to tip me off, but he mentioned my *magnet*, and that helped me puzzle out what I was carrying. And from my conversations with Thalanes, I had a pretty good idea what the crown had to do, and I ciphered out the plow from things Alzbieta had said about Eden. But damned if I can remember anyone telling me anything about this staff."

"Your grandfather sent you on the road with a replica of it," Cathy pointed out.

"He said it would be good against evil spirits. And it was, but I reckon that was the white ash wood. And there was that song Alzbieta said she heard my father singing. *Breaker of horses, bane of the river.* Is an earthquake the bane of the river? Maybe. I expect an earthquake that was big enough could shove a river to one side or the other, change its course. *Keeper of the crown of two kingdoms* sounds like it might have to do with this rod, if this is the only regalia Zomas ever had. Or rather, the song is about someone who holds the staff. My father, I guess. Me."

"What else did the song say?" Cathy asked.

"Just about nothing. Alzbieta only knew one verse, and my father sang it in his delirium, so it might have been nonsense, anyway. Now that I think of it, it had another line about being *anointed of seven*."

"I am hesitant to suggest that Your Majesty use her Eye of Eden—"

"My eye's open," Sarah said. "I don't have to make any effort to use it, I can't *not* use it, unless I shut my eye. Yeah, I'm looking at the rod, but it doesn't have an aura, not like the Heronplow."

She puffed, winced, and handed the staff back to Cathy.

"Maybe I should stick with what I know," she said.

"I don't believe I've seen you do that once, Sarah."

Sarah laughed once, then laughed again, and then couldn't stop laughing until she gasped in pain. "Ain't that the truth? I've been ducking and diving since the first day of creation, I reckon. But what I meant was, maybe I could do something with the Heronplow. It marks off space that is safer, more civilized. It calms beastkind—maybe it will calm the shaking earth, too."

As her words ended, the earth shook, and Sarah cried out in pain.

"I think you had better conserve your mana for the anointing, Your Majesty," Cathy suggested.

"Dammit," Sarah said. "I hate to say it, but you're right."

Informed by a runner, Maltres Korinn stood at the Ohio Gate to receive two of the Sister Kings, or kings of the Sister Kingdoms: Talamatan and Talega. Standing without the Earthshaker's Rod, he felt unprepared, unqualified for his office, and unsure what to do with his hands.

He settled on standing with his feet shoulder width apart, hands clasped behind his back. Rain soaked his hair and streamed down the shoulders of his black cloak.

Thunder rolled. Around Maltres stood soldiers in uniform and a few city officers. At his side stood Cathy Filmer. Uninvited by him, the Lady Alena and two other Ladies of Tendance stood on the far side of the avenue, together with their eunuchs and mouthpieces and acolytes; altogether, they numbered over twenty souls. Maltres was wary of mobs, but the priestesses stood with dignity and in silence.

"My Lord Duke," a man said to Maltres's side. Turning, he saw that the man stood with a second man and a woman. They were sunken-cheeked and hollow-eyed, and they wore simple match coats and leggings, frayed at the edges; Missourians? Zomans? The two men might have been brothers, long haired and tall; they held hats in their hands. The woman curtsied when Maltres looked at her, face nearly hidden within a thick bonnet.

"Put your hats on, it's pouring." Maltres took the men by the hand. "Do you have food?"

All three nodded. "The Metropolitan and his priests have been very prompt to get us corn," the woman said. "We wanted to thank you."

"I will thank Her Majesty," Maltres said.

"Is she ill?" The woman's face was creased by a sudden frown.

"She lives," Maltres said. "The gods willing, she will continue to live." Smiling, he ushered them away from the path just as the two kings approached.

They must have met on the road, or perhaps had agreed to come together, because the two kings drew near side by side. The King of Talega, whose kingdom was famously populated by as many Lenni Lenape as by Firstborn, looked as if he might be one of the people the Algonks called the "grandfathers"—he had dark hair, but his features were more square than most Eldritch, and his skin was dusky despite the rainy spring. He rode with his long purple cape hitched up and across his lap and he wore a garland of rain-crushed flowers on his head.

The King of Talamatan wore blue cort-du-roi breeches and a pale green shirt, decorated with paisleys and puffed in the sleeves, under a dark green coat. On his head, he wore a dark green Tyrolean hat with a neat yellow feather on one side. His mustache drooped like William Lee's, but was longer. He might have been German, but a German with fine features, milk-white complexion, and dark eyes.

The kings rode side by side, and behind each man came a short column of retainers in single file. At the back came guardsmen, the sight of whom made Maltres almost as happy as the sight of the kings. He wanted every defensive gun and sword he could get.

He bowed to the two kings as they passed into Cahokia. "Gentlemen," he said. "I am Maltres Korinn, Vizier of Cahokia."

"The spirit of knowledge," the King of Talega said in a warm bass.

"We are grateful for thy lore." Maltres felt his face coloring slightly. Was he a participant in some ritual dialog of which he was ignorant? Had the process of preparing for Sarah's anointing already begun? If there was a script, he wished someone had shown it to him in advance.

The King of Talega smiled.

"The spirit of the fear of the Lord," the King of Talamatan said. His voice was stern and sharp, but his eyes were merry. "And we know thee well, Duke of Na'avu. Push the border of our kingdoms a few miles to the south, and thou wouldst be a member of my court. Though that corner of my land has more Germans than Firstborn."

Maltres bowed again.

"Cathy Filmer." Cathy curtseyed. "Handmaid to the Mother of All Living and Lady of Tendance."

"And betrothed to General William Lee," the King of Talega said. "We have heard of thee, too."

Cathy smiled.

The kings dismounted. At Maltres's directions, soldiers took their reins. "We have prepared accommodations for you."

"Perhaps our retinues might be sheltered from the storm," the King of Talamatan said. "And the horses brushed and fed. I, for one, have been longing to meet this daughter of Kyres Elytharias."

"I have heard she has Hannah's recklessness," the King of Talega said.

"Was Hannah reckless, or was she bold?" the King of Talamatan countered. "Oh, see, our chaplains are being welcomed by the Handmaids of the goddess."

Maltres turned to see the Lady Alena's eunuch bowing deeply and making elaborate gestures with his hands as he spoke to the priests in the kings' companies. "Excellent," he said. "I will allow the Handmaids to carry on the burden of hospitality, while Mrs. Filmer and I conduct you to our queen."

Cathy said nothing, but the slightly rigid set of her jawline suggested to Maltres that she was unhappy about something.

Two bodyguards followed each king.

"Your hat is quite stylish, Your Majesty," Maltres said as they began to climb the Great Mound.

"Call me Roland," the King of Talamatan said. "Roland Gyanthes. My wife tells me it makes me look too much like a democrat. She would like me to wear a military uniform whenever I'm in public."

Roland extended a friendly hand to Maltres, who took it and found himself joined in a masonic grip. He nodded deferentially.

"My wife would be very happy for me to dress as a democrat and never wear either a crown or a military uniform ever again," the King of Talega said. "She sees the kingship as a burden." He offered a more conventional handshake.

"She is not wrong," Maltres said.

As they reached the top of the mound, he looked back past the following guards to see the disposition of the kings' parties. His own officials and the kings' retainers had disappeared, taking shelter from the weather; the Ladies of Tendance and the visiting chaplains moved south down one of Cahokia's boulevards.

"Do you have any guesses where they're going?" he asked Cathy.

The Cavalier priestess shook her head. "Perhaps a tour of the city's sights. The Sunrise Mound lies in that quarter." Her voice was hard, and Maltres was reminded that the Lady Alena's eunuch had said that Cathy was "corruption."

Had William reported that to Cathy, or was the eunuch's statement a reflection of a larger conflict of which Cathy was well aware?

Yedera stood guard at her customary spot just within the doors. Her eyes flickered, barely showing recognition as the kings walked past. Oathbound Podebradans ignored all social distinctions and taboos other than their own vows. Podebradans walked freely on sacred ground, failed to salute, wore what they want, and ate without regards to mores.

They all stopped briefly while the priestess waiting

with Yedera anointed Maltres and Cathy both. No one suggested that the kings required anointing.

"Will you be joining us within the veil?" Roland asked pleasantly as they walked down the long nave of the Temple of the Sun.

The question caught Maltres up short. Of course, he would not be.

"I will accompany you if you wish," Cathy said, "though I must take a few minutes to prepare. Or you may simply enter; you will find Her Majesty Sarah Elytharias Penn fully capable of presenting herself and recounting her own tale."

The two kings laughed as they passed through the veil and into the presence of the Serpent Throne.

"Whole thing's jest gone to stupid."

———◆———

CHAPTER EIGHT

Two men joined Sarah in the sanctum. One had long dark hair and mustache and wore a stylish German hat; the other was darker skinned, maybe an Indian, and wore a crown of flowers.

She held the Earthshaker's Rod across her lap. She had given up trying to look into it with her Eye of Eden; however much she might try to put on a brave face for Cathy and her counsellors, she felt sick and exhausted. Her eyes ached, and the vision of her ordinary eye was dim. The effort of looking through the veil had left her with vertigo and nausea. Now she just squinted at the staff, running her fingers over the iron horse's head and the iron ferrule and the dark wood in between, hoping that something would come to her.

"Your Majesty." They bowed.

"Let's skip past the thee and thou bit," Sarah said. "Apparently, I'm dying, and I don't want to waste my time. You walked in here, easy as pie, so I figure that makes you Ladies of Tendance, oathbound Podebradans, or Firstborn kings. I can see that you're Eldritch, but if you're Ladies of Tendance, the order's requirements for physical loveliness are seriously slipping."

"I'm Roland Gyanthes," said the one with the German hat. "I'm your neighbor, the King of Talamatan. My friend here is Ordres Zondering, and he's the King of Talega."

"The German and the Lenni Lenape, according to the song," Sarah said. "I'm Sarah, which you might have guessed. Are you mixed bloods, then, like I am?"

"I am," Ordres said.

"I am not," Roland said. "But I do like schnitzel."

"I guess I met the King of Tawa already," Sarah said. "I was unconscious at the time."

Your friends will avail you nothing. A harsh scream punctuated the words of Simon Sword. *I am not a power you can resist. I am the inevitable turning of the world.*

Ordres gestured at the Earthshaker's Rod. "I had heard you were an accomplished wizard. I hadn't realized that the earthquakes were your doing. No wonder you're exhausted. Why are you shaking the earth—is it part of your war against the Imperials?"

Sarah laughed out loud. "Hell, Ordres, I wish it *was* me. If I was making the earth shake, I could stop it, too. Every time Cahokia trembles, I feel it in my bones, and these tremors *hurt.*"

Roland looked at the Heronplow, the Orb of Etyles, and the Sevenfold Crown, all lying scattered across the twisting serpents that comprised the arms of the throne. "I assume these objects are all with you because you have nowhere else safe to place them."

"No one you trust." The half-Lenni Lenape king looked sad.

You are alone.

"No, I trust my people," Sarah said. "Only these are *working* regalia, and I'm the only one who can use the plow and the orb and the crown. As for the staff, as far as I can tell, none of us knows how to use it, so I'm just sitting here, having a good, hard ponder on the matter." She laughed again. "I've got my own Thinking Shed, now."

"The staffs are used at the crosses of the earth," Ordres said.

"Not exclusively," Roland countered.

"I don't know what a magician might do with them," Ordres said. "'Cause earthquakes, I imagine. But I'm thinking of that passage in the *Reconciliations*."

"Yes." Roland stroked his long mustaches. "'And when the giants had departed, the land still shook with their footsteps. And in its shaking, the land shattered hill and ditch, palace and temple. And great fires and pollutions were across the land. And Onandagos raised the staffs of the giants upon the crosses of the earth and prayed to the Mother of All Living to still her unease. And one year and a day from the departure of the giants, the shaking of the land ceased.'"

"You think the staffs of the giants are the Earth-shaker's Rods?" Ordres asked.

"That's how my mother explained it to me," Roland said. "But since one of the rods is broken, I don't know whether the other rod, all by itself, will work."

"Broken?" Sarah asked.

"Or whether maybe the point of the story isn't the rods at all, but the prayers to the goddess," Ordres added.

"And then again," Roland said, "the book doesn't

say that the rods stopped the earthquakes. It just says that they stopped. Maybe the giants cast a departing spell that lasted a year and a day."

"Suspiciously neat time frame, that." Ordres nodded. "Although perhaps we're meant to understand that Onandagos raised the staffs a year and a day after the giants' departure, and they worked immediately."

"Wait," Sarah said. "This anointing you want to give me…is it based on the same kind of guesswork, maybe this and maybe that, but what about the other thing?"

Ordres chuckled. "Don't you find life is generally that way?"

"Shh." Roland elbowed his fellow king. "You're eroding her confidence. And nothing is more important than her faith in the anointing."

"It will work," Ordres said.

"What exactly are the crosses of the earth?" Sarah asked. Something rang a bell in her memory.

"There are two." Roland folded his arms over his chest. "They are popularly thought to have been built by Onandagos, but as they are described in the *Reconciliations*, they simply appear in the narrative, with no account of anyone building them. This suggests to me that they predate Onandagos, and were merely used by him."

"She doesn't care who *made* them," Ordres said.

"It seems relevant to me," Roland shot back. "This might be craft of the Anakim, or Peter Plowshare we're talking about. Properly speaking, it isn't royal lore, and we should be careful not to pretend to understand too much. Anyway, there are two of them, and one of them is on the borders of your land and mine, Sarah. Where Cahokia, Talamatan, Koweta, and

Tawa come together in a single point on the Kaskaskia River, the earth is thought to cross. Four kingdoms touch in a single point, and there is a monument that marks the spot."

"Zadok!" Sarah snapped her fingers.

"Excuse me?" Roland furrowed his brow.

"Zadok Tarami. My Metropolitan. I heard him say something about lying quartered on the crosses of the earth."

Ordres nodded. "He must have walked the Onandagos Road. The pilgrimage trail touches on both crosses. Pilgrims lie with one limb in each of the four kingdoms and say a prayer. It is believed to connect the pilgrim with the four corners of the earth, which is to say the entire cosmos, and Christ at the same time."

"So the second cross of the earth is on the Onandagos Road, too," Sarah said. "And it must be more east." She closed her eyes and tried to remember the maps she had seen of the Seven Sister Kingdoms. "Talega must touch that one. Along with Oranbega, Adena, and . . . Koweta?"

Roland nodded. "It's a source of great pride for Koweta that their lands touch both crosses of the earth."

"Maybe they should hold the rods," Sarah said.

Ordres shrugged. "And yet they never have. Cahokia was always Onandagos's own kingdom, after all."

"Cahokia is exceptional, even among the Seven Sisters." Roland nodded. "For instance, my city has a sanctuary of the goddess as well, but in my sanctum there is no back door."

Sarah's breath caught. "You see it?"

Ordres nodded. "I see it, too."

"Then it has something to do with the throne and

kingship," Sarah said. "It's not because of my eye that I see it, it's because I'm queen. But what is it?"

Both kings shrugged.

"As I said," Roland told her, "Cahokia is exceptional."

"And do you hear . . . a voice?" Sarah ventured.

"No," the King of Talamatan said.

The King of Talega shook his head.

Sarah shook her own head to clear it. Why were answers to her questions always so partial, so full of guesswork? "I have heard a story, that one of the rods was taken to Zomas."

"Did your father tell you that one?" Roland asked. "He was often in conflict with the men of Zomas, especially over their trade in slaves."

"I heard this story from a Zoman prince," Sarah said, "and he told it to me as a story of Zoman inheritance."

Ordres shrugged. "Who can say what is true?"

"I'll tell you who can," Roland said. "The man—or woman—who takes that rod and this one and uses them at the crosses of the earth to try to still tremors."

Ordres laughed.

"When you say 'uses them,'" Sarah probed, "do you have any idea how to do that?"

Roland shrugged.

Ordres shook his head. "The *Reconciliations* says it was a prayer."

"Funny thing," Sarah said, "it seems to me I'm constantly getting by on a prayer. And I suppose you're also telling me that, to find out what's behind that door . . . or *who* . . . I'm going to have to go through it someday."

"On the contrary," Ordres said, "*you're* the one telling *us*."

✧   ✧   ✧

The Franklin was dead. Or if not dead, then he wasn't answering any of Gottlieb Voigt's signals to him; not the note in the dead drop in the Walnut Street Theater, not the colored smoke from the chimney of Horse Hall, not the advertisement in the news-paper advertising an estate sale at a nonexistent address in Cambry.

Gottlieb had done his duty. He had taken wounds for the Conventicle, both to his pride, which he had had to mortify repeatedly and constantly over his years of service to Thomas Penn, and to his body, as when the Franklin himself had impaled Gottlieb, in order to make good his escape. Gottlieb still limped, though only slightly.

He also had cash. The Conventicle didn't pay—one served the Conventicle because one had had Franklin's vision, which Gottlieb had done as a young man, fresh out of the Comenian School. Working as Thomas's body servant didn't pay, either. But slowly stealing Thomas's surplus silverware over time and stashing the money in a bank account under a false name had left Gottlieb enough money to travel to any corner of the world he could imagine. That cash was mostly in the form of bank notes, tucked into a money belt on Gottlieb's person.

He had two things on his person that he hoped might prove more important than cash. He had them by theft as well, only in this case, theft from the Conventicle, thefts he had been able to carry out because he had had the good fortune to be in the service of Thomas Penn, and therefore he had quickly come into contact with Isaiah Wilkes. He had only realized late that Wilkes was the Franklin himself, but he had known from the beginning that the man was highly ranked. Gottlieb was a believer in Franklin's vision, but he had a dim view of other men, and he had long feared there might come a day when he was abandoned to his fate. Against that day, he had stolen two things from Isaiah Wilkes. One was a thick bead of the green paste that induced hallucinations. Not stolen, but learned, were the words to be recited and sung into the ears of one who took the paste; without the words and the melody, the vision might not result.

Gottlieb had been able to both steal the paste and learn the chant because his long trustworthiness had eventually resulted in his being chosen to help administer the vision to new recruits. And Gottlieb also had a list of names, stolen from an initiation meeting he'd attended. The names were code names, but they came with cities, and Gottlieb had recognized some of the faces at the meetings, so he'd deciphered a significant number of their identities.

What would he do with it? Blackmail seemed a possibility. Or could he sell the list? He didn't think Thomas would spare Gottlieb's life for the list—Thomas was not a merciful man—but perhaps if Gottlieb were out of his reach, the emperor would be willing to pay for the names.

Gottlieb had to flee, not because he had been caught stealing, but because he had been discovered. He had killed the Parlett boy—it was unpleasant and messy, and all the training the Conventicle had given him with dagger, pistol, poison, and garotte hadn't made it any less so. He'd done it because he had heard Thomas and Temple Franklin discussing sending one of the Parletts to the Missouri, to speak with the Heron King, and he had hoped that killing one of the boys would result in all their deaths. Then he'd bloodied his own nose and lain on the floor to make himself appear one of the victims of an attack.

But then the dead Parlett boy had reappeared at Thomas's side, talking, apparently hosting the ghost of either William Penn or Oliver Cromwell or both. And Thomas, who had certainly never been affectionate with Gottlieb, had grown cold.

And now Thomas was sending Gottlieb to the frontier. It could only be to kill Gottlieb, but to do so away from Horse Hall and Philadelphia. Thomas knew he had killed the Parlett boy—did Franklin know? Was Franklin going to kill him? Why not arrest Gottlieb and torture him instead? Did Thomas suspect that Gottlieb was a member of the Conventicle? From his interactions with the Franklin, he must surely understand that the Conventicle existed.

In addition to worrying about an executioner sent by Thomas, Gottlieb realized that he was also a liability to the Conventicle. Because Thomas might arrest and torture Gottlieb, the Conventicle could not afford to let Gottlieb live.

Which was why Gottlieb had repeatedly tried to contact the Franklin. He had wanted to negotiate, to make an offer to retire permanently. He would leave Christendom entirely, flee to Istanbul or Paris or some Africk port. But to no avail.

Or was the Franklin alive, and just ignoring Gottlieb?

But he didn't think so. Isaiah Wilkes was a man who responded. He was, moreover, a man who liked to use his own hands and be involved in resolving any crisis. If he was not answering, it was because he *could* not answer.

But if Wilkes was dead—or in a dungeon in Philadelphia, or gone—then there was another alternative to flight and death.

Gottlieb did not know the full structure of the Conventicle. He believed Wilkes did, or had, and possibly Wilkes alone. How to discover the levers of power, and put himself in a position to *become* the Franklin?

As head of the Conventicle, he could be hidden from Thomas, and as safe as a person could be, who was still in the New World. And as the Franklin, he could continue to serve the cause he still believed in, the defeat of Simon Sword. And taking leadership of the Conventicle would mean not only survival, but also power and influence, and the ability to enjoy some of the wealth he had stolen from Thomas.

Gottlieb smiled on the ride west atop the prison wagon, fingering his dagger and his strangling cord and his poison tablets, and considering the possibilities.

He was in Koweta lands, at a town called Dayton, in a bend in the Miami River, when one of the muleskinners told Gottlieb a friend was looking for him.

"What's my friend's name?" He and the driver were unloading trunks from the top of the prison wagon. The prisoners would sleep in the wagon, under rat-eaten wool blankets and huddling together for warmth, but Temple Franklin and Gottlieb and some of the drivers would sleep in beds.

The muleskinner, a rail-thin man with a scar that split one cheek and nostril with a bright pink cleft, shrugged. "Tall feller, some kinda uniform."

A soldier? A lawman of some sort? "Is there anything else you can tell me?"

"Might a been Cherokee. Dark, high forehead." The muleskinner jerked a thumb in the direction of the tavern behind him, which bore on its signboard an image of George Washington, crucified. "He was in the common room, there."

The Parlett boy in his care stared at Gottlieb with wide eyes. Was someone watching through another Parlett, in the western Ohio or in Philadelphia? Had this boy himself possibly told Thomas, intentionally or in his idiot-magician manner, of Gottlieb's guilt?

If Gottlieb acted, he would have to assume that Thomas saw everything he did, if not through the Parlett boy, then through the reporting of Temple Franklin. Any act now that was inconsistent with his duties as Thomas's body servant—likely even anything as simple as walking away from the Parlett child to find this person who was looking for him—was irrevocable.

Was he prepared to make his leap?

"Mr. Franklin," he called.

Temple Franklin groaned as he levered himself down from the top of a prison wagon. He gripped iron-bar handles set into the sides of the vehicle, and hissed at a prisoner who stretched a dirty hand with ragged nails toward him.

"I am not yet interested in having my coat cleaned, Gottlieb," Franklin grunted, striking the ground with both feet. "Rest assured, I will tell you when I am, and I will also credit you this evening with another round of very flattering groveling."

"Forgive me, I was hoping you could watch the Parlett boy for a moment. I have an urgent matter of hygiene to attend to."

"Do not mistake fashionable neatness for what is

necessary for the organism," Franklin grumbled. "There are no ladies present."

Gottlieb laughed. In other circumstances, he'd have fawned upon Franklin at greater length, but he imagined vividly that he could feel the point of a dagger pressing into his back, so he abandoned his trunk and scurried around the side of the inn.

A leaning outhouse stood in the mud behind the building, a few steps from the forest, but Gottlieb ignored it and pressed himself against the inn's wall. Creeping to the lone glass window, scattering a line of ducks as he went, he peered inside, and saw the man the muleskinner had referenced—he was tall, dressed like a soldier, and armed, with saber, pistol, and rifle. If it came to an open fight, the other man had the advantages of better weapons and a longer reach.

Gottlieb could not let it come to an open fight.

He could grab a horse from the stable and flee, but Gottlieb was no great rider. Best to seize the initiative here and now.

He opened the back door to the common room and entered. The other man was fixed on watching through the windows, and didn't hear Gottlieb approach, stepping softly among the farmers and herdsmen and muleskinners who were settling in to a tankard of beer and a tin plate of beef stew.

"Are you looking for three brothers, by any chance?" Gottlieb murmured.

The man jerked about, and Gottlieb saw that he had his hand on the hilt of a long belt knife. The surprise on the man's face quickly smoothed over. "I have two brothers. We each came from a different mother and father."

Lying, two-faced brother. He had come to kill Gottlieb. Gottlieb smiled warmly; years of licking Thomas's boots was better training than any the Conventicle provided for being false-faced. "Such brothers would be a marvel to remember until the end of days."

They clasped hands.

"I have important intelligence," Gottlieb whispered. The man had come to kill him, so Gottlieb must do whatever he could to push back the moment of reckoning and create space in which he could act. "I had intended to use a dead drop in Talamatan, but this is urgent. Did you notice the young man I am traveling with?"

The taller man glanced out the window at the Parlett boy. "Is he someone of importance?"

Gottlieb nodded. "Is it safe to talk here?"

The other man's eyes darted about the inn's common room. "Clearly not. There's a small wood outside."

Gottlieb led the way. He deliberately turned his back on the other man. It would avoid arousing suspicion; at the same time, if Gottlieb had successfully aroused the other fellow's curiosity, he wouldn't stab Gottlieb in the back. Still, Gottlieb felt sweat trickle down his spine as he walked out into the cool, humid evening again.

"Not too close to the outhouse," the other man said. "Someone might be in there."

"Do you take me for a fool?" Gottlieb asked in his most vacuous voice. "My name is Gottlieb Voigt."

"Onacona Mohuntubby."

Gottlieb stalked through mud to a tangle of redbud and butternut trees, still dotted with a few fading pink and yellow blossoms. "The thing about that young man," he said over his shoulder, "is that he's an arcane communication device."

Across the river, he saw lights. But he heard and saw no one who could possibly witness what he was about to do.

"What's it doing out here in the Ohio?" Mohuntubby asked.

What's it doing out here in the Ohio?

Why would Mohuntubby wonder that the Parlett boy should be in Ohio, unless he had reason to believe the boy was elsewhere?

Mohuntubby knew exactly what the Parlett boy was, and was surprised to see him not at Horse Hall. Mohuntubby was playing stupid, he knew more than he was saying. Mohuntubby was trying to trick Gottlieb.

"The emperor." Gottlieb kept walking. "Horse Hall has another such device, but this is going—"

He deliberately stepped toe down, driving the point of his own shoe into the mud. This made it easy for him to stagger and slip onto one knee.

"Mist!" he cursed, and slipped a dagger into his right hand. He raised his left, as if trying to get his balance. Onacona Mohuntubby grabbed Gottlieb's left arm to steady him. Gottlieb stood, firm and balanced on his left foot but dragging his right to make a loud sucking noise as he turned—

and slashed Mohuntubby across the belly.

Mohuntubby fell to the ground. In the evening shadow, Gottlieb could still make out the astonished expression on the fellow's face, but then the Conventicle man pulled his pistol and aimed it at Gottlieb.

"Slippery bastard," Mohuntubby hissed.

"Two-faced liar," Gottlieb spat. "You came here to kill me."

"You were discovered. I came here to give you the opportunity to kill yourself. That was your oath, Voigt."

"What if I can serve the Conventicle and Franklin's vision better by living?"

"That's not your decision to make." Mohuntubby shuddered. The bloodstain spreading across his stomach and chest was dark and enormous.

"You recognized the Parletts," Gottlieb said. "You've come from the camp of Notwithstanding Schmidt."

"Go to hell." Mohuntubby raised his pistol.

"If you shoot me, we're both exposed." Gottlieb smiled.

Mohuntubby's pistole wobbled.

"You're dying," Gottlieb said. "If you die, I bury you. The Conventicle has lost one man, doubtless a good man, but that is all. If we both die out here, questions get asked. Why did an Imperial soldier, assigned to the bodyguard of Imperial Ohio Company Director Schmidt, fight a duel to the mutual death with the body servant of the Emperor Thomas?"

"Or," Onacona Mohuntubby said, "I kill you and I live." He pointed his pistol at Gottlieb's chest and squeezed the trigger.

Click.

"Mud in your firing pan, I expect," Gottlieb said. "Bad luck. Do you want to try again?"

Click.

"That's it, then." Gottlieb smiled his condolences. "Would you like me to stand here and watch as you bleed out, or shall I end it for you?"

Mohuntubby grabbed for his knife. Gottlieb stepped forward in the same moment and stomped with the wooden heel of his shoe on the inside of the other man's elbow. Mohuntubby gasped, and with his left hand he grabbed Gottlieb, nails clawing, fingers groping for the body servant's eyes.

Gottlieb dropped to one knee again, this time cracking Mohuntubby's sternum with his weight, and then stabbing his dagger into the other man's throat.

Mohuntubby died twitching and gurgling.

When his opponent was finally still, Gottlieb stood up. His own arms shook—he'd killed the Parlett boy in Horse Hall, but that young man had barely been able to resist. It had been a long time since Gottlieb Voigt had fought someone capable of striking back. He looked around; the inn continued its previous soft bustle. In the quiet of the evening, he could hear the moaning of prisoners in the wagons on the far side of the building.

Gottlieb didn't want to draw attention to the Conventicle. He stripped off Mohuntubby's army coat, too big for Gottlieb, but warm, and set it aside. He took the man's pistol and shooting accouterments, and knife as well, and his boots. Then he dragged Onacona Mohuntubby's body to the latrine; lifting the neatly hinged seat, he slid the body slowly inside.

Mohuntubby's boots fit better than his coat did. Gottlieb filled his new coat pockets with his new pistol and knife, checked to be sure that his money belt was in position, cleaned and sheathed his dagger, and then turned and walked away from the inn in a straight line.

Cal rode the coach without companions. Charlie Donelsen was meeting with Rupp and Bondí, organizing Bondí's testimony before the Assembly. The Creole accountant had brought with him from New Orleans ledgers indicating regular cash infusions to the Chevalier of New Orleans, which he claimed came from the Emperor Thomas Penn. Unfortunately, there was nothing like a signed receipt, and Bondí's own knowledge of the source of the cash came from his involvement with Etienne Ukwu's war against the chevalier. Apparently, what Bondí and Etienne had done was not a violation of Imperial law, and Bondí was prepared to testify, even anxious to testify, but Donelsen and Rupp were trying to sculpt what Bondí actually said and gauge in advance how the Electors would receive such testimony. Similarly, Olanthes Kuta was preparing to give his testimony, as a witness to the Siege of Cahokia.

That left Cal to answer the summons alone.

Cal didn't own a coach and didn't want to waste money renting an entire coach, so it was a public conveyance and he held a single ticket. Women and men boarded and disembarked at every stop, across Pennsland and into the Ohio.

At the border, between Pittsburgh and Youngstown, in the middle of the afternoon, the coach stopped. A bristle-faced Imperial officer, some sort of revenuer, poked his head and shoulders into the coach and asked Cal for his passport. Cal provided the document—Logan Rupp had secured it for him before Cal had left Philadelphia—and the Revenue Man noted Cal's name and details in a notebook.

Two women on the same coach, a Firstborn who had been traveling to see her daughter outside Youngstown, and a German who identified herself as a lay preacher for the Ministerium, failed to produce passports, and were ordered by the revenuer to get off the coach.

Cal listened.

"Fräulein, you will have to return to Pennsland by the next coach," the revenuer was saying in a shrill, nasal voice that reminded Cal vaguely of Ezekiel Angleton. "And you, *hetara*, will need to produce a trustworthiness certificate."

"I'm not your hetara. And I've never heard of a trustworthiness certificate."

"You won't need one in Pennsland. But due to the insurrectionist activities of the Swords of Wisdom and others, you won't be allowed to travel between towns in the Ohio. And that includes a complete prohibition on entering any Free Imperial Town."

"I don't understand," the woman said. "Who has these trustworthiness certificates? I've never broken the law, and no one told me I had to have a certificate to travel!"

"Since you are in the Ohio now," the revenuer said, "and on the Imperial highway, and you don't have a certificate, you are breaking Imperial law at this moment."

"Can *you* issue me a certificate?"

"I don't know if you're trustworthy, do I?"

"Maybe I can pay," the woman suggested. "Can I pay? I have a shilling here, it was going to pay my return ticket, but perhaps my daughter's husband can pay for the ticket. Or I can walk home. But I need to see her, please, she's close to giving birth and it's a difficult pregnancy."

"Are you trying to bribe me? You're bribing me."

There was a pause.

"Officer," she said, "I just need to see my daughter. Please tell me whom to pay and how much so that I can do that."

"That's it! I'm taking you to see the magistrate, to swear out a complaint for attempted bribery of an Imperial officer."

"Let go of me!"

Cal jumped from the coach. Standing on the strip of gravel alongside the Youngstown Pike, he stretched to his full height and let his right hand dangle by his side—near, but not too near, his tomahawk. In the crook of his left arm, he gently carried a long rifle. A few steps distant was a little wooden shack with only three walls, and a desk and chairs inside. A second Revenue Man watched from the desk, pen in hand and sitting next to an accounts book.

The German woman was gone. The Firstborn struggled to yank her arm from the two-handed grip of the Imperial tax collector. He was a head taller than she was and burly where she was slight, and he wore a leather jerkin and a steel bonnet.

The woman was dark and slight, and looked a little like Sarah.

"Unhand that woman!" Cal bellowed his best imitation of William Lee, barking commands to the drilling beastkind, and very nearly fell into a Cavalier accent.

The Revenue Man jumped, but then sneered at Cal. "On whose say-so, Reuben? Just because you have a passport, that don't give you the right to order me around."

"On the authority of the Elector Calhoun." Cal unfolded the proxy letter, which he carried close to his skin, and showed it to the officer. "You can leave this woman alone, or you can come to the Assembly and explain to all the Electors why not."

"You ain't the Elector Calhoun," the officer said, but he was shaking.

"No," Cal said. "I'm his grandson. Iffen I's the Elector, you'd be dead already."

The revenuer took several steps back, toward the little shelter, and hooked his thumbs into his belt. "We can let her by this one time, I suppose. On account of the law is new, and she hasn't had time to get her certificate. And a passport, which she ain't got, either."

"She's travelin' with me into Youngstown," Cal said. "She'll be travelin' back, too, and iffen she's on her own then, and not with me, I'll expect you to show her the same consideration. Understood?"

The revenuer nodded and cleared his throat. "Get on then," he called up to the coachman.

Cal held the door for the Firstborn woman and then boarded himself.

"I did not know," she said. "I'm so sorry to have troubled you."

"Only reason I knew was because I been livin' with a lawyer," Cal said. "It's plumb stupid. Whole thing's jest gone to stupid."

"How will I get back?" She looked like Sarah, with dark, unruly hair and skin pale as china. Only this woman had two good eyes, both of them gray.

"Mebbe your daughter and your son-in-law can help," Cal said. "Try taking a road that ain't an Imperial Pike. Iffen you can't find one, try writin' me at this address." He gave her the street and number in Philadelphia.

Two stops later, at a village whose name Cal didn't catch, the woman disembarked.

Free Imperial Youngstown lay within its stone walls on the Mahoning River, embraced by the broad green arms of the Mahoning Valley. Calvin arrived in the middle of the night, alone on his coach but for the driver on top, and he saw the long, gentle ridges and walls and towers all alike as black shadows.

After a quick hailing and identification, the guardsmen at the wall allowed the coach in. Cal was prepared to show his passport again, but no one asked him, and moments later, the coach was rattling toward the town center.

The *Blue Goose* was a hotel two streets from the river. It was three stories tall, made of white boards, and had four chimneys. Balconies wrapped around three sides of the building, reminding Cal a little bit of his short time in New Orleans. The goose painted on the inn's signboard had ears like a hound dog and hooves like a horse and looked altogether like the production of someone who had never seen a bird at all. The paint looked fresh.

In the common room stood several stuffed chairs, each holding a scruffy-looking man. They had holes in their coats and knives on their belts and Cal could smell them from across the room. They read newspapers and books by the light of oil lanterns; against one wall was a bookcase containing other reading material, and in a corner stood a table with glasses and a bottle of whisky. A woman with rounded corners and a smile like two cherries greeted Cal from a desk near the door.

"Would you like a room?"

"I would," he admitted. "One night. Name's Calhoun. Calvin Calhoun. Lessen you can tell me, is they a Mr. Andrew Calhoun here yet? I's supposed to meet him."

One of the scruffy men, a black-haired, big-eared fellow poring over a news-paper called *The Vindicator*, looked up from his reading and blinked. Cal nodded slightly, and Big Ears went back to his news.

Iron Andy Calhoun was famous well beyond Appalachee, and Youngstown was basically Appalachee, anyway.

"Mr. Andrew is indeed here," the hostess said. "He has already reserved your room, which is number eight, upstairs. His room is number nine." She handed him a key.

"Is he in?"

"I believe so."

"Thank you."

Cal climbed the stairs, rifle in one hand and small carpetbag in the other. Was it his imagination, or did Big Ears watch him climb? All four men in the parlor looked like frontier types, with muddy boots or moccasins, long knives, and pistols.

At the top of the stairs, Cal reached a carpeted landing. He could see the numbers 7, 8, and 9 nailed to doors down one side of the hall and 10, 11, and 12 on the opposite side, but before moving any farther, he quickly loaded his rifle. He listened as he did, and heard the creaking of boards in the parlor below, and then a whistle out in the street.

Might be nothing.

He took the lariat from his carpetbag and set the bag aside. Tying the lariat to his belt where it would be ready to use, he took the tomahawk into his right hand, and then tapped with his knuckle on door number nine.

He was going to feel silly if his grandpa opened it.

But there was no answer.

Cal moved silently to door number eight. This was

his room, and he looked long and hard at the iron key. Did he trust the room?

At the end of the hall was a large window, pushed open to admit the evening breeze. Below, the street was a wash of muddy yellow and black, and the wraparound balcony Cal was hoping to see was not there.

That left door number seven. Cal knocked with a knuckle and listened; silence.

He was going to feel silly if he was wrong, and he was going to owe the innkeeper, but he felt he had no choice. Cal wrapped the doorknob to number seven in a spare shirt, and then smashed the knob off in one blow. The noise of the wood splintering wasn't too loud, and the shirt muffled the sound of metal striking metal. Cal pulled off the ruined doorknob and pushed the door open.

Room seven had no guest. There were a bed and a dresser and a wardrobe, a mirror and a washbasin.

And a door to the balcony outside.

Cal unlocked this door and eased onto the balcony. The timbers below his feet were settled, and didn't creak, as he crept to his right, along the balcony, past the windows from room seven to the windows where number eight began.

There he stopped and let his eyesight adjust to the light. He kept his gaze from the lights below and focused on the windows to rooms eight and nine, both of which were dark. When he could see well enough to see the grain of the wood in the window frames, he peeked into room eight.

Three men stood with their backs to the balcony. One stood to either side of the door, looking at the door, each man holding a long knife. A third man stood with his back to Cal and his arms crossed; Cal saw the butts of two pistols poking out of his coat pockets. Cal tried the handle of the door that connected room eight and the balcony, and it turned.

This was an ambush.

Most likely, his grandpa wasn't here at all. But Cal felt a deep sense of foreboding in his gut, so he slipped past room eight and peeked into room nine.

At first, he thought it was empty. But after a few moments of peering, his eyes adjusted further, and he saw two bodies, each lying on one of the two beds in the room.

He wrapped the handle of this door and knocked it off, holding back a terrible flood of emotion. His worst fears came true, and in one heartrending moment, Calvin Calhoun's life was turned upside down. On one bed lay his grandpa; on the other was his cousin Caleb. Both men were still and cold, multiple bullet holes in their chests and stomachs.

A paper lay pinned to Andy Calhoun's linsey-woolsey shirt. Pulling away the pin, Cal brought the paper up to the window so he could puzzle out the words by the light of the street below. He found he recognized what was written there: *As holder of the proxy of Andrew Calhoun, and at his direction, I hereby offer the following motions of impeachment.*

It was the beginning of a speech Cal had given, his first to the Electoral Assembly, and the one in which he'd presented the motion to remove Thomas Penn from office. This sheet was the reprinting of it in a news-paper.

Thomas Penn. Penn had tricked Cal into coming out to Youngstown, and he must have tricked Iron Andy, too. But how?

And to what end? To blame Cal for his grandfather's death? It seemed unlikely anyone would believe that. But maybe Iron Andy's death would warn other Electors away from the impeachment.

"Ashes to ashes, dust to dust," Cal mumbled over his grandpa and his cousin. But since those words weren't in the Bible, and he wanted to say something that was, he added, "The Lord is my shepherd; I shall not want. He maketh me to lie down in green pastures: he leadeth me beside the still waters. He restoreth my soul: he leadeth me in the paths of righteousness for his name's sake. Yea, though I walk through the valley of the shadow of death, I will fear no evil: for thou art with me; thy rod and thy staff they comfort me."

By the time he finished, he found there were tears running down his cheeks. "Thou art with me, Grandpa. Thy rod and thy staff. In the presence of my enemies. Lord hates a man as lets an injustice stand."

In the silence that followed, he thought he heard his grandfather say, *Amen.*

Cal stepped quietly onto the balcony, beside one of the windows, reckoned the distances, and formulated his plan. Taking his rifle in his left hand and his tomahawk in his right, Cal raised the war ax and smashed the window.

As the three men turned, Cal threw the ax. His judgment and his aim were true, and the blade struck the man with the two pistols right between the eyes, splitting open his skull. Cal then raised the rifle and fired into the center of a second man's chest.

Bang! Cal's target staggered and fell.

Cal being tall, he could almost step right through the windows. He swung one leg up over the sill, bringing his rifle up to parry the cudgel that came swinging for his head. Cal deflected the club, though he heard a loud *snap!* as he did so—he might have smashed the hammer from his weapon.

Swinging his other leg up, Cal eased forward into the room, and pushed the man with the cudgel back. Stooping, he plucked a pistol from the pocket of the dead man, and as Cudgel came bounding back for a second attack, Cal let him have a bullet in the stomach. *Bang!*

Shouting downstairs meant that Cal had little time. The two men he'd shot were both wounded and whimpering. He would have liked to hang all three men, like the criminals they were, with his lariat. Instead, he retrieved his ax.

Both men tried to plead with him, but Cal didn't hear their words. He heard a rushing noise in his ears like the wind of judgment, or like a river running over the rapids, and with swift, efficient motions, he cut off both their heads.

He heard banging and cursing at the door. Picking up the dead pistoleer's second weapon, Cal fired it through the wood, and was rewarded with more cursing.

He left the rifle; he could get another. Running quietly as he could down the balcony, he found the end that stood above a muddy alley, away from the main street. With quick, sure motions, he let himself down, then ran off into Youngstown, leaving shouts of dismay and cussing behind.

The town watch was soon rushing through the streets, but Cal climbed the town wall and headed south. He'd go back to Philadelphia, but first there was something he had to do in Nashville.

"Sleep, little creature. Sleep and dream no more."

———◆———

CHAPTER NINE

"Therefore," Zadok Tarami said, "one must not marry frivolously or with a double mind, but as a solemn, if joyous, act of will."

The priest stood at the top of three steps in the Basilica of Cahokia, wrapped in his clerical plumage. Bill wore a new coat of Cahokian gray. It was neatly pressed, its buttons glittered, and the newly dyed gray shone like Bill's blacked boots. Bill would have had a hard time saying what Cathy was wearing; he couldn't take his eyes from her face. How was it that she only looked younger, while he was falling apart?

He stood without a cane, and both legs ached.

"I do hope you know," Bill mumbled to the officiating priest, "that my doubts about you are long resolved. And I hope that you, too, can let bygones be bygones."

"Shhh, Bill," Cathy murmured.

The Basilica was full, as Cathy deserved. In addition to the priestesses of her sept, rows of soldiers sat straight-backed in dress uniform in the pews. Jaleta

Zorales, commander of Cahokia's artillery, was there. Maltres Korinn was in attendance as well, and Gazelem Zomas and Luman Walters and two Firstborn kings. Yedera the Podebradan had declined to leave her position of door guard at the Temple of the Sun. Sarah could not leave the throne, but had promised Cathy that she would be watching, anyway. Ambassadors attended from Chicago and Memphis and Appalachee and the Gulf coast, making Bill feel slightly self-conscious. Even the Earl of Johnsland was represented by young Landon Chapel, somewhere in the nave. Bill's exile had been lifted; but for his responsibilities in Cahokia, he could be in his Johnsland home.

A faint smile crept onto the Metropolitan's face. "William Johnston Lee and Catherine Filmer now come to be joined in holy matrimony. If any here can show just cause why they may not be married, speak now; or else for ever hold your peace."

Bill heard a muffled cry from the back. Turning in the shoulders, he looked for the source of the disturbance and could see nothing.

Tarami gazed for another few moments at the seated crowd, his face never losing its dignity. Then he turned to Bill and Cathy. "I charge you both, before this throne, from which no secret can be hid, that if either of you knows any reason why you may not be lawfully married, you now confess it."

"I know of none," Bill said. He was grateful to Landon Chapel for removing the one doubt that had plagued him. Bill's daughters still lived; he would like to bring Cathy with him when he went to Johnsland to look for them.

"None." Cathy smiled.

Zadok Tarami nodded. "William, do you take this woman to be your wife, to love, honor, comfort and keep, in sickness and in health, forsaking all others, as long as you both shall live?"

"I do."

"Catherine, do you take this man to be your husband, to love, honor, comfort and keep, in sickness and in health, forsaking all others, as long as you both shall live?"

"I do."

There was more ceremony, with prayers and a brief lecture, but from the moment Cathy Filmer said "I do," Bill lost track of time. An angel choir might have burst through the ceiling to sing his name with trumpets, and he would have missed it. He looked on Cathy's face and thought of the many hours they'd spent together in New Orleans, and on the road, and in Cahokia. He had felt bonded to this woman long before he had felt free to admit it, and shouldering the bond of matrimony felt to Bill more like casting off a shackle, of doubt and uncertainty and cowardice.

It felt like a homecoming.

Then he was stumbling out into the stormy gray light. Perhaps even Simon Sword assented to his marriage, he thought with numb humor; though the clouds roiled above, the rain had paused.

He shook hands and Cathy kissed cheeks. Somehow, they transferred to the Hall of Onandagos, into its reception chamber. There Bill and Cathy danced the circle, danced the square, and even, somewhat scandalously, danced the waltz, her chest pressed against his and her sweet breath in his nostrils.

When the entire company had dissolved into dance,

lubricated by casks of cider and the pumpkin moonshine the Firstborn called *shikaram*, Bill begged to be excused for a moment. Cathy squeezed his hand and let him go; she was engrossed in a conversation with the King of Talamatan about the king's struggles with Chicago.

Bill's thighs hurt. He felt as if he were being shot in both legs simultaneously, with each step. He had been very disciplined, limiting himself to sips from his laudanum-tinged cherry cordial only when absolutely necessary, but now a sip, or several sips, felt necessary. He slipped out the doors of the chamber, and then out of the Hall of Onandagos.

He stood at the top of the mound, looking down at the city lights below. The rain had started again, and its windy smell crashed into Bill's nostrils, driving out the odors of pumpkin and perfume. He took a gulp from his cordial and put the bottle back in his pocket, beside the smaller glass bottle of laudanum; merely anticipating the imminent relief gave its own solace, and he took a deep breath.

Landon Chapel crashed into him. He stank of shikaram and whisky, and he wrapped his arms around Bill's shoulder as if he were clinging to a rock to avoid drowning.

"Hell's bells, Landon," Bill said. "It is early for you to be this drunk."

"I started this morning." Landon vomited, but Bill managed to swivel the young man's head away from him in time to avoid soiling Bill's new uniform.

"Well, suh," Bill drawled, "inasmuch as it is the traditional service of a wedding celebrant to become inebriated so as to express joy with the bride and groom, I thank you for your signal gift."

"Captain," Landon said. "General."

"I'll appoint a detail to take you back to your quarters."

"I killed him."

Bill would have ignored Landon's words as the ordinary rambling of a man in his cups, but Landon stared at Bill with desperate fire in his eyes.

He wrapped his arm around Landon's chest to steady him. "Whom did you kill?"

Landon sobbed. "Charles."

Bill's heart froze. He took a shaky breath. "Charles? Charles who?"

"I tried to tell you. I tried to tell you before."

Bill threw Landon to the ground. "Charles *who*, damn your eyes?" he roared.

Lightning flashed. A crowd had gathered in the doorway, staring. Soldiers in gray, and other guests in finery. Were they not interfering because of Bill's rank, or because he was the bridegroom? Good, let them stand back. Bill scowled at the crowd.

"Your son," Landon sobbed, dragging himself up onto all fours. "Your son Charles Lee."

Bill stopped in his tracks and struggled for breath.

"He was my friend," Landon said.

"Don't tell me he was your friend!" Bill bellowed. "Tell me about his death, you worm!"

"I shot him." Landon bowed his head and covered his face with his hands.

"Faster, damn you! Was it in a duel? Was it an accident?"

"Bill." The voice was so soft, Bill almost didn't hear it. "Bill, this might be a conversation better held elsewhere."

Bill turned to see Luman Walters and Maltres Korinn. They approached him with their arms wide, palms forward. It was a placating gesture, as if he were a child throwing a fit.

"Go to hell!" he spat. His vision spun.

Landon stood. He held his sword in his hands, in front of him, still in its scabbard. "He challenged me to a duel. Because... because I had hurt someone. And I knew that I couldn't beat him, and I was scared."

"Scared?" Bill shook. "You were *scared*?"

"So I shot him in the head. Before the duel."

Bill's fists were curled so tight that he felt his nails break the skin of his palms. For years he had imagined Charles winning his commission, riding in parades, leading charges, winning the hearts of women, having sons of his own to carry on the mighty Lee name.

Bill would see none of that.

And Bill's name would die with him.

"I didn't plan it," Landon gasped. "It all happened so fast, and I made a terrible mistake. I've been trying to tell you."

Bill felt as if he were a tiny rider, perched atop a raging beast he could not control. "A mistake, suh? A mistake is when you use your salad fork to eat your beef. A mistake is when you address a bishop as *Your Excellency* instead of *Your Grace*. A mistake is when you tie your horse with two half hitches rather than a clove."

Landon stood, his head still bowed.

"You have murdered my son!"

Landon held out his sword, hilt pointed toward Bill. "I owe you my life," the younger man blubbered. "Take it."

"Oh, *hell* no," Bill growled. "Not like *that*. No instant relief from pain for you. I will kill you, Landon Chapel. I will kill you as my son Charles would have killed you. We duel tomorrow at dawn. Do you have a second, suh?"

Landon spat in the mud, a stream of phlegm and tears. "No." He sniffed.

"Nor do I. Your choice of weapon, suh?"

"Bill!" A new voice pierced Bill's consciousness, but it was far away. "Bill, please do not do this. Bill, I must tell you something!"

It was Cathy. Bill tried to reassure her with a smile—he might be old, but he was an experienced duelist, and could not lose, especially if Landon chose pistols. In his trembling rage and pain, he feared that his smile likely appeared more as a grimace.

Oh, Charles.

"Pistols." Landon straightened his back.

"Pistols it is," Bill purred.

"Bill, please do not do this." Cathy gripped Bill by the arm.

Bill glowered. "I do the young man a favor. I could kill him where he stands, having made that confession, and no one would think me in the wrong. He would die in shame, a criminal, a secret murderer. Instead, he atones for his wrong and he regains his honor, if not his innocence."

Cathy was weeping. She tried to speak, and couldn't.

"Do not fear for me, my thornless rose," Bill said. He tried to use a gentle voice, but his words were halting and his breath short. "I cannot lose."

"Bill," she finally managed to say. "Landon is my son."

Bill stared.

"Landon Chapel is my son."

Bill stared.

"Bill, do you hear me? He's my son, Bill. Please do not do this."

Some part of Bill knew that he was surrounded by a crowd, and discussing matters that were deeply personal. But he felt too much pain and rage to think about that—pain and rage at Landon's revelation, and now a sharp sense of betrayal at Cathy's. He couldn't think clearly. Had she wronged him?

"How?" he asked.

"He's Earl Isham's son," Cathy said between shuddering cascades of tears. "I was young and foolish, and he was a dashing cavalry hero. The earl promised he would raise Landon and see him established, but I had to leave."

"Your schoolteacher," Bill mumbled. "Your first husband."

"He was a tenant deeply in debt to the earl. He agreed to marry me and take me west, in exchange for the cancellation of his debts."

Bill felt sick, and cold, and alone. Landon Chapel—Cathy's son Landon—stared at his feet in the mud.

Good God, Bill's son Landon, now.

Who had killed his son Charles.

Bill vomited.

In front of hundreds of staring eyes, he took his flask of cherry brandy from his pocket and took a drink. He felt as if he were standing outside of his body.

"There's more, Bill."

"More." Bill laughed, and longed for numbness. "How can there be any *more*?"

"I killed him," she said.

"Killed him?" Bill tried to focus. "Killed whom? Charles?"

"I killed my husband. He resented his fate and blamed it on me, so he beat me, and I killed him for it."

Bill laughed out loud. "Hell's bells, I care not a fig for your dead husband. Do you have any idea how many men *I* have killed? Because I do not!"

"You just married me." Cathy sniffed. She was soaked, and her white dress was wrapped to her body like wet news-paper, her face as pink as a possum's. "You're not bothered that I killed my first husband?"

Bill looked from Cathy to Landon and back. "At this moment, I would welcome death."

Cathy again burst into tears.

"None of this is her fault," Landon said. "You are angry with me." It was a gallant thing to say, and in another moment, Bill might have respected it.

"Shut up," Bill said.

Could he still shoot Landon Chapel? Was the man really his son?

He felt that Landon *was* his son.

And he wanted to kill the man.

"You need sleep and quiet," Luman Walters said. "You'll think more clearly in the morning. Let me help you get some rest." The wizard put his hand on Bill's shoulder.

Bill shoved the wizard hard, hand in the center of the man's chest. Walters staggered back and fell to the mud.

"Bill!" Maltres Korinn seized Bill's left arm.

Bill punched him in the nose. The Vizier of Cahokia flew back and sprawled on the ground.

Bill turned and roared at the crowd. He wanted them to jeer at him, wanted them to strike him, and throw him down the mound. Instead, they stared at him. He couldn't see their eyes. What were they thinking of him?

He roared again, with no words.

And then Sarah was standing before him.

She seemed indistinct. She stood in a cloud of golden light, and at the edges she seemed to bleed into the light herself. She was bandaged and disheveled, her black hair was tangled in a ball on her head, but she wore the Sevenfold Crown.

"Your Majesty," Bill croaked. He fell to his knees.

"Bill." Her voice sounded far away. "You're wounded."

"Hell's bells, we are all wounded."

"Bill, I cannot have you like this."

"I resign my commission." He felt numb.

"I refuse your resignation. I have no one else."

Bill looked up at the faces staring down at him. Maltres Korinn had stood; his nose bled freely down his chin in the rain. Luman Walters continued to watch Bill warily from his seated position. The others mostly watched in shock and horror, as far as he could see; he was glad that the light was behind them, so he could not see their faces better.

"I understand, Your Majesty." Bill stood.

"I need you whole, Sir William."

"I believe I may no longer be Sir William," he said.

"I need you, General." A spot of blood appeared in the corner of Sarah's eye, and then she disappeared. Where she had been standing, Bill now looked on the calm visage and the flower crown of the King of Talega.

Bill turned and walked down the mound. No one followed.

He trudged through the mud to the home where he'd been staying, the former city palace of Alzbieta Torias. Torias was a Cahokian priestess who had opposed Sarah, but then come around to serving her. *How fitting*, Bill thought as he saddled a horse. *I once served her, and now am cast out as unfit.*

He rode out through the Ohio Gate without a plan.

Cathy was in the sanctum with the kings of Talega and Talamatan when the King of Tawa arrived, hair soaked from his journey. It was the middle of the night, but she had come here after her wedding, because she had seen the phantom of Sarah bleed, and she needed to know how Sarah fared.

Was Cathy still married?

After the wedding, Bill had disappeared. He certainly had grounds for an annulment, if he wanted one. Or he could simply stay gone for years, as he had been forced to do to his wife Sally.

Had Sarah meant to cast him out? This was the other question Cathy urgently wanted answered, the other reason why she had rushed into the Temple. Having to dress and be anointed, she had arrived to find Ordres and Roland standing beside the Serpent Throne. Sarah lay unconscious.

"She strained herself," Ordres had said. "Foolish."

"But understandable," Roland had answered.

Cathy had held back sobs then, and continued to hold them back, though she knew her face was red and she feared from moment to moment that a stray comment might set off her shattered emotions again. The ground shook beneath her feet, and she couldn't be certain that she wasn't just perceiving her own collapse.

Kodam Dolindas came through the veil and immediately took Sarah's wrist in his hands, feeling for a heartbeat.

"I find myself with three kings and a sleeping child," Cathy joked. "She lies on gold; where are the frankincense and myrrh?"

It was an impious joke, but Cathy was struggling with her sorrow and pain. Ordres and Kodam ignored her; Roland shot her a tiny smile of compassion.

"She has strained herself," Dolindas said. "How did you allow it?"

"Have you *met* the Queen of Cahokia?" Roland asked. "No one *allows* her to do anything."

"She acted in the heat of the moment," Ordres said.

Kodam raised a hand. "I have heard."

"How go the other preparations?" Roland asked.

"I have the robes. The oils and incense are being prepared. We must send for Adena and Koweta now. And Oranbega wants persuading."

"He wants flattery is what you mean." Roland snorted. "The spirit of the Lord, indeed."

"Then I will speak with Korinn, and we will organize the most flattering embassy that we can send. If we do not . . ."

Ordres nodded. "We are virtually in open warfare with the emperor now, all of us. We cannot lose this champion."

"To say nothing of the storms from Missouri," Roland added.

Kodam Dolindas turned to Cathy. "I heard your tale, from several witnesses."

"My current tale?" she asked ruefully. "Or the tale of how I came to be here?"

"Both," he said. "I refer to the death of your first husband. This . . . creates a problem."

"I am not worthy," Cathy said.

Dolindas smiled slightly. "This is not for me to say. It is a decision for the goddess, who will act through Sarah, once Sarah is awake. But until then, I must ask you to step down from your position, tending to the throne."

An icicle stabbed Cathy in her heart. "Why?"

"Don't worry," Roland said, "we'll take good care of her."

"Because for this rite to work, those associated with it must be in an advanced state of purity," Dolindas said. "Until the goddess absolves you, someone else must take your role."

"I know a good woman," Cathy said.

"The other Ladies of Tendance will choose who completes their quorum," Ordres said.

"I'm sure this is temporary," Roland added.

"But it will be . . . the Lady Alena will dictate."

"The Ladies of Tendance will choose," Ordres said again. "This is simply not something that you must worry about. There are more important problems."

Cathy took a deep breath. The Lady Alena didn't agree with Cathy, or with Sarah, on many things, but Sarah had seen fit to retain the woman, and had reinstituted her vow of silence when she had asked. Cathy nodded. "Perhaps I may be part of the embassy to Oranbega."

Dolindas nodded. "I was thinking Zadok Tarami might be a good choice, too."

"Best send the Podebradan along as well," Roland suggested. "If she stands out there grieving any longer, she may turn into salt."

The hotel had once been called the *Sir Christopher Wren*. At Thomas's direction, before his fiancée Julia Stuyvesant arrived, it had changed its name to honor its celebrated occupants. Thomas had not commanded the name change, but he had invited it, and he had also offered to pay for the remodeling of the hotel's lobby. He had never told the owner, an unctuous man named Skids who bobbed his head from side to side as he spoke, that the remodeling was dependent upon the name change.

He hadn't had to.

Skids himself had proposed a list of five possible replacement names. Skids had favored the *Pieter Post* on the grounds that Pieter Post had been an architect like Christopher Wren, but Thomas had pointed out that it made the hotel sound like an office of the mails. *Jacob de Wit* seemed to be an effort to be comic; *Abraham Blauvelt* sounded Jewish, which did not bother Thomas but might annoy Julia; and, worst of all, *Jan Steen*, pronounced in the Republican manner, sounded like *yon stain*. That left the *Huig de Groot*, which Thomas found perfect, since de Groot had apparently been a lawyer, and his impending marriage was nothing if not a product of the law.

Thomas entered the *Huig de Groot* with a distinct lack of patience.

He knew the room number because Franklin had obtained it for him. Until his departure for the Ohio, Franklin's creatures had been observing Julia's movements and, through Franklin, giving Thomas daily reports. Thomas didn't care where Julia shopped or what she ate, nor with whom she spoke or which theaters she attended. He wanted four things of her.

First, the riches that would come as her dowry, and those that would flow in afterward as a result of the combination of the two Dutch companies. Both events were contingent upon the actual performance of the marriage, or, not to put too fine a point on it, the consummation thereof. Julia was young and by all accounts pretty, but Thomas had little actual interest in making love to her for her beauty, any more than he was interested in conversing with her about current affairs and the governance of the empire. He would consummate the marriage for the money, and to produce heirs.

Heirs were the second thing he wanted, so it was good that Julia was young. Thomas had fought hard against the other Electors and his own family—was still fighting hard—and it would all be for naught if he left the Shackamaxon Throne vacant at his death.

The third thing that Thomas wanted from Julia was the easiest. She must be beautiful, and most especially, she must be beautiful on their wedding day. Her radiant beauty, made more radiant in the works of the cartoonists, balladeers, and news-paper-men, would redound to Thomas's honor. He needed honor now; it would help him fight his pesky war against the Electors, and against the Firstborn.

But finally, and most importantly, what Thomas needed Julia to do was not to shame him. All the good she did in the form of cash receipts or sycophantic news-paper accounts of what dresses she wore to the balls would evaporate and be replaced by bloody, smoking wounds in Thomas's side if she did anything to humiliate him.

This was why he had her watched.

This was also why he was going to see her now. She had rebuffed his every attempt to be seen in public with her, and Thomas had this week received two questions from news-paper-men as to why that might be the case. So this Friday, the Imperial Players would be performing, at Thomas's direction, *Henry V*. From the Imperial box, Thomas had already informed the news-paper-men, would be watching the emperor and his betrothed, the Lady Julia Stuyvesant.

Thomas rapped on the door number 25, his kid-leather gloves slightly dampening the sound. He had chosen the room himself; 25 was Julia's age, but it was also the date of their impending marriage, June 25, which was the date of the new moon. The best dates for marriage were the day of the new moon, or a day seven, fourteen, or twenty-one days following the new moon—no one needed an almanack to know that. Twenty-five was an altogether auspicious number for their wedding.

The peeping slot opened with the scrape of metal, revealing in an area two inches tall by six inches wide of the face of a mevrouw who had better not be Julia; she had crow's-feet around her eyes, and skin the texture of an Italian whey cheese.

"*Oh, Meneer Thomas*," the woman said through the door. "*Je kan niet binnenkomen.*"

"I wish to be polite," Thomas said. "Please open the door."

"*Je kan niet binnenkomen*," the attendant said again.

"I can very well *binnenkomen*," he snapped, "and

you bloody well know it. I paid for this room, I pay for your food and drink, and I even paid for the bride!" He realized that his voice had grown into a shout, so he stopped and took a deep breath. "I am here to invite her to the theater."

"Meneer," the woman said, "Julia is indisposed."

"Dispose her," Thomas said coldly. "I enter in ten seconds, will you or nil you."

He had counted down to three when the door opened.

Julia sat in a chaise longue beneath the window. A mound of fabric lay heaped upon her lap; she had a thimble on her left thumb and in her right hand she held a threaded needle. The thread ran through the pile of fabrics that nearly concealed her.

"My Lord." She smiled, and she *was* beautiful. Her features were fine to the point of being elfin, with an upturned nose and rosy cheeks, and hair bright as gold bouncing off her shoulders. She smiled with full lips and milk-white teeth; her neck was long and slender. "Forgive me. I have been difficult to find."

"You have been very easy to find," Thomas said irascibly. "You have simply been unwilling to see me."

The attendant, who was twenty years older than Julia but looked forty years older, scurried to one side and stood in a corner of the room.

"Do you not worry that it is bad luck to see the bride before the wedding?" Julia smiled.

"Some feel it is"—Thomas clasped his hands behind his back—"*on the day of the wedding.* We have weeks yet. And do not tell me that this is a Dutch superstition; I have known too many Dutchmen to believe such a thing."

"To the contrary, I had heard that *you* worried about such considerations, My Lord."

Thomas snorted. "Nonsense. And if you have heard that I have mathematical sensibilities, which is to say, that I am concerned for the motions of the planets, why that is another thing entirely. That is *science*, my lady."

Julia looked down at her sewing. "You are right, My Lord. May I confess a foolish thing to you?"

Thomas furrowed his brow. "Of course."

"I believe that I have simply been trying to prolong my maidenhood. To be married is a solemn thing, and to be married to the greatest man in all the land... to one of the great men of the world... is a heavy responsibility. I have been avoiding your company, and I believe it is merely that I have wished to continue being a girl for as long as I may."

He nodded. "Allow me to reassure you that as a wealthy lady of Philadelphia, you will still have time to frolic. The museums and the cafes and the shops will be grateful, indeed, to have your patronage."

"Thank you, My Lord."

"But the time has come that you must begin to be seen with me. Fear not, I will not bore you with the trivia of government. Nor am I the sort of boor who insists upon outshining the woman in his company. You will find me pleasant, and we shall attend public entertainments that are exquisite."

"Yes, My Lord." Julia bowed her head.

"Beginning Friday," Thomas said. "I have a box—that is, *we* have a box at the Walnut Street Theater. Friday evening, the Imperial Players will perform *Henry V*. It is well known to be my favorite play, and they shall dedicate it to you as their muse. We shall watch the play from the box, and afterward shall dine at the home of one of Philadelphia's wealthiest families, where you shall be the guest of honor."

Julia's eyes grew wide for a moment. Anticipation? Anxiety?

Could her expression possibly be *fear*?

"My Lord, I may not be ready by Friday."

"You may return to frolicking on Saturday morning."

"And yet..." Julia shook her head.

"How are you unready?" Thomas asked. "You have a mouth that speaks; I assume it must eat as well, no? I see feet beneath that mound of silk, I assume there must be legs connecting them to your torso."

"Such crude words!" The attendant rushed forward to interpose herself. "My lady is unwell."

"You said *indisposed* before," Thomas grunted. "It was a lie then. What is it now?"

"There is sewing to do," the attendant blurted.

"Sewing?" Thomas looked at the work in Julia's lap. "What are you making? A dress? Not your wedding dress, with those colors."

"Yes, a dress," Julia said. "I am making a dress for Lieke here." Her hands, Thomas realized, hadn't moved the entire time they had been talking, but had hung poised over the work.

"It is excellent that you sew," Thomas said. "I respect the work, and the creation. And when you are empress, it would be strange for you to sew dresses for your servants, but wondrous if you were to make clothing for the poor of Philadelphia. My people so soon forget the gifts of cash, but they remember images. They will remember the sight of my wife, stitching clothing at a poorhouse."

"Yes, My Lord."

"But there is nothing, let me be clear, nothing in this world, *not one damned thing*, the sewing of which is so urgent that you are unable to attend entertainments with me this Friday night."

"No, My Lord." Julia's face looked stricken.

"Have patience with us, My Lord," Lieke said.

Julia's hands continued to sit still.

"Let me see you sew," Thomas said.

Julia laughed, but the sound was hollow. "Oh, My Lord, I am so fatigued of sewing now. I shall put it aside, and Lieke and I shall consider what dress I may wear on Friday. Perhaps I should pick out two dresses, one for the play and the second for the dinner."

"One will be sufficient," Thomas said. "I am no parer of cheese, but a reasonable frugality is a virtue, even in an emperor. Sew."

"Oh, My Lord, I have not the will for it now. It offends you so, indeed, I may give it up entirely."

"It offends me that you do not sew," Thomas said slowly. "Make a stitch. *Now.*"

Julia nodded and pushed the needle through the fabric, pulling the needle out the other side. Even at three paces, Thomas could see that her stitch was larger and clumsier than the stitches that were already in the garment, and not in the same straight line.

"You have lost your gift for the needle," he said.

She exhaled sharply, setting down the thimble and needle upon the cloth. "Indeed, My Lord, I am all out of sorts from speaking with you. I can only hope I shall be recovered by Friday."

Thomas nodded. "Stand."

"She is unwell!" the attendant cried.

"If you wish to live, Lieke," Thomas said slowly, "then I solemnly charge you to shut your mouth." To Julia Stuyvesant, he said, "Stand."

She smiled, but her nostrils flared and her breath came quicker. Julia swiveled on the chaise longue, set the fabric and sewing tools down on the raised part of the seat, and stood.

She was thick around the waist.

Thomas gazed upon his fiancée and counted slowly to five in his mind. "Does your father know?" he asked.

"Know what, My Lord?"

"That you are great with child."

Julia touched her belly and forced a laugh. "My Lord, this is due to the delicious creamed cheese that you make in Philadelphia. So difficult to cut a thin slice when the cheese is a pudding!"

"Do not mock me," Thomas said. "You are slender in the neck and in the fingers and in the ankles. I may admire a pregnant woman and a plump woman equally, but I certainly recognize the difference when I see it. Now I will ask one more time, and, listen to me, you must be done with the lies. Your life is in the balance."

Julia swallowed and nodded.

"Does your father know?"

"No."

He believed her, and that was a relief. If Adriaan Stuyvesant had connived to humiliate Thomas, that would have undermined their deal, and all Thomas's plans. If Julia had simply connived to humiliate her father, and Adriaan didn't know about it . . . *that* was a problem Thomas could fix.

He removed the glove from his right hand.

"Tell me who the father is," he said.

"No one of importance," she said. "One of my father's men. Certainly, someone I'll never see again."

If the father was one of Adriaan's men, it was certain that she *would* see him again. Thomas nodded. "Tell me his name."

"Gert Visser."

Thomas looked to Lieke, who shuddered in the corner. "Does anyone else know?"

"No, My Lord," Lieke said.

Julia shook her head.

"What was your plan?" Thomas asked. "What were you thinking? Were you hoping the nuptials would be delayed? That I would not notice, and would accept a lie that a child born four months after my wedding was my son? That I would be humiliated into cooperating with the lie?"

"You are harsh, My Lord," Lieke said.

"But not unjust." Tears flowed down Julia's cheeks. "My Lord, I hoped for a time that my father would cancel the wedding."

"That is honest," Thomas said. "Let me say an honest thing in turn to you. Your father cares more for his money than for his daughter."

Julia hesitated. "My father has many responsibilities, and cannot always accommodate me as he would wish."

"So you have had a taste of how power works. And are you still hoping today that your father will withdraw from our agreement?"

Julia looked down. "I know that he will not."

"So you have no plan."

"I took an herb that Lieke procured. It had no effect."

"I see." Thomas felt a thrill run along his spine. "I will solve this problem for you."

Julia sucked in a breath and stepped back, bumping against the chaise.

"I think this will hurt," Thomas said. "But I believe you will live. Hold still."

He knelt before Julia.

"My Lord," she whimpered. "Please."

"Do not pretend to me that you are some bashful maiden," he growled. "And do not speak again until I have finished."

He reached under her skirt, but not to please her or himself. He raised his ungloved hand beneath the fabric until he could lay it on her belly, skin to skin. He was not certain he could do this without killing Julia as well, in which case he would certainly have to kill Lieke, and would have to offer Adrian some sort of reparation. But he thought he could control his power.

He visualized the child in Julia's womb. Small, concealed, hidden, an interloper. A thief of his dreams, an assassin sent against his authority and his honor. He felt with his fingers, knowing that it was far too soon for him to find a cranium or a foot through the mother's belly, but imagining that he could wrap his fingers around such a cranium.

Or around a throat.

"Sleep, little creature," he murmured. "Sleep and dream no more."

He heard a soft, wet *slap*, and smelled blood.

Thomas removed his hand and stood up. The veins in his wrist and in the back of his right hand were black, rather than blue; he flexed his fingers and stared.

Julia cried out and then sat down. A stain spread from the middle of her skirt; where Thomas might have expected a dark red mark, the stain was black. A lump of black tissue lay on the floor at her feet, trembling like an aspic struck with a fork.

Thomas raised his hand, showing it to the servant. "My spies watch you at all times, Lieke. If I ever have reason to think that you have spoken of what you have seen today, to *anyone at all*, or if you tell anyone at all that the Lady Julia Stuyvesant *ever* carried a child that wasn't mine . . . I shall wrap my fingers around your neck and laugh while you die screaming."

Lieke covered her mouth and wept, nodding.

Thomas replaced his glove. "The play begins at seven o'clock," he said. "I shall pick you up at six. And from now on, you will be available to attend any and all public entertainments I choose. Is that understood?"

He left without waiting for an answer.

"Ah, good. A witty man."

CHAPTER TEN

Kinta Jane and Dockery were thrown into a stilt-mounted hut. Of all the huts, it stood farthest out over the lake, connected to land across several sets of wooden catwalks, and past several other huts affixed to poles.

Their weapons were taken from them but they were not chained. The hut wasn't locked, and indeed, wasn't capable of being locked; it had a doorway, but no door. The hut's roof was of thick straw, its walls of boards, and its furnishings within were several heaps of animal furs.

Three large dogs, of the same wolflike breed as Mesh's beasts, lay watching from the catwalk or padded up and down its length, on guard. Beyond, the first hut to which their platform connected housed guards—the hut had a roof but no walls, a fire that was never out, and a periodically changing set of four armed men.

Four armed Anakim, with bow and spear and long, broad sword.

"We could swim," Dockery murmured to Kinta Jane as soon as they were left alone, "but those dogs will swim faster. Not to mention, the men will shoot us before we can get to shore. If we head out to sea, we'd drown before we can get across, and they'd likely follow us in boats while we tried."

"You've given up already," Kinta Jane said.

"Just thinking out our options. The most natural way out of any prison is to bribe the guards. Sadly, I don't think we'll be able to bribe those dogs."

"Maybe we can try bribing the men."

Dockery tipped his head from side to side to show that he was unpersuaded. "If we could hide and make them think we had escaped, maybe they'd abandon the guard post and we could sneak out. Hiding on the roof seems too obvious."

"Hiding under the furs seems even more obvious," Kinta Jane said.

"I was thinking maybe we could somehow dangle ourselves underneath the platform," Dockery whispered. "Or really, to stay out of sight, we'd have to strap ourselves tight against the underside of the floor. I'm thinking maybe, just maybe, I could cut my shirt into enough rope to strap both of us."

"How can you be sure you could cut your shirt into rope before you actually went ahead and tried?" Kinta Jane asked. "And once you try, you're committed."

Dockery nodded. "I'm studying on it. My other immediate thought is, what would happen if we contrived to light this platform on fire?"

"Keep studying."

They whispered other possibilities after dark, eating bowls of fish stew their Anakim captors provided. They had come to no resolutions by dawn, when two iron-faced warriors roared them out of their hut.

The village was entirely over the water, a large array of pole-mounted buildings, connected by walkways. On land stood the decorative poles—were they defensive totems? Or was their purpose to communicate, or to frighten away enemies, or were they meant simply as objects of beauty?

The poles were not of equal height, resulting in a village, or really a town, of three levels, in some cases the huts of one level being built directly above the huts below. Also, there were buildings two and even three stories high, though in all cases standing on stilts resting in the water.

Kinta Jane couldn't see an organizing principle behind the village's layout. All the catwalks seemed to be narrow, and they were not laid down in a grid, nor in a spiral, nor in a spoke-and-wheel pattern. As they left behind their prison hut and marched, they saw more and more Anakim, standing and watching. They were mostly red haired or fair, and they were all wrapped in furs. Kinta Jane saw many weapons, but not a single firearm.

"I think that one's a child," Dockery murmured, nodding toward a hulking blond boy. "He's taller than I am."

Their guards marched Kinta Jane and Dockery down to the lowest level, where the waves of the lake slapped against the wood. Here the buildings had the thickest walls, made of solid pine trunks, and the buildings were fewest.

A jagged boulder protruded from the churning water of the lake, like a single canine tooth. A platform surrounded the rock, but at ten to twenty feet of distance, leaving waves crashing against the gray stone. Here, and here alone, as far as Kinta Jane could see, the platform was wider than a mere gangplank, and a cluster of Anakim stood, a few paces back from the water's edge, staring at the stone.

A hundred feet from the water stood a building. The space between the water and the structure was a single broad platform, like a wooden plaza; it was the only platform of its size that Kinta Jane could see. The front of the building was entirely made of the decorative poles Kinta Jane saw on the shore, a wall of bulging-eyed, open-mouthed, sharp-clawed demons of judgment staring down at Kinta Jane Embry.

Between the cluster and the water stood two giants. One was young, with a pair of swords strapped across his back in an X pattern and copper armbands long enough to encase Kinta Jane's legs running from wrist to elbow. The other was a woman, and older, with hair gray as iron and deep frown lines.

Bound to the rock was Mesh.

He was naked and his skin was so pale it was almost blue. The cords were short, and kept his arms spread apart, stretching him between two iron pegs driven into the stone. His bare heels rested on a narrow shelf. The waves rose to splash against his chest and shoulders. How was he even alive, in the cold water? And how long had he been there?

But Mesh was laughing.

Kinta Jane and Dockery were pushed to stand at the edge of the platform. Water crashed into the wood just below Kinta Jane's feet, and the cluster of Anakim stared at her. There were men and women among them, and she noticed that where she saw metallic flashes—in rings, neck torcs, armbands, earrings, buckles, and weapons—she saw mostly the reddish glow of copper.

The man with swords across his back smiled at Kinta Jane and Dockery. "Welcome. My apologies for the rough manner in which we have treated you. This man is a criminal, and we were uncertain whether you were his accomplices, or his prisoners, or merely his fellow travelers on the road. Now we understand that you had no part in his crimes."

Mesh laughed again.

"I am unaware of any crimes committed by Chu-Roto-Sha-Meshu, son of Shoru-Me-Rasha," Kinta Jane said. It wasn't exactly a lie, in that she wasn't sure whether the killing of Gert Visser and the virtual kidnapping of Kinta Jane herself would constitute a crime in any court, since they had happened in the hinterlands of Acadia, and possibly in wild Algonk land. "I certainly have committed no crimes with him."

"Thank you." The swordsman nodded. "I am Prince Rusha-Ba-Chotu, son of Shoru-Me-Shila. I am commonly called Prince Chotu, by the English speakers who have difficulty remembering our longer names. Mesh is my cousin, and killed my father."

"I did not see him kill any Anakim," Kinta Jane said. Would it be safe to use the passwords relating to three brothers here? Or would that possibly result in her being condemned along with Mesh?

"Killed a passel of Algonks, though." Dockery spat tobacco juice into the lake. "They were trying to sneak into our camp and kill us, and Mesh there got them first. Wasn't really a fair fight, since he outnumbered them one to six. I don't suppose you're part Algonk?"

"My cousin Mesh," Prince Chotu continued, ignoring what might have been a taunt from Dockery, "in addition to being a murderer, is a thief. He stole from our nation something important."

Kinta Jane shrugged. "Unless it was the spear or the bow or the sword he had on his person when you arrested us, I can't imagine what that would even be." Or possibly Mesh's copper knife with dots forged into the blade in a large pattern?

Prince Chotu frowned. "He would have hidden it, in a place that he calls Kanawha. Has he ever mentioned to you such a place, or how to arrive there?"

"I don't know where Kanawha is," Kinta Jane said truthfully.

"Ain't that one of the Praying Towns?" Butter would have melted in Dockery's mouth, he looked so innocent. "In the Covenant Tract?"

Prince Chotu tried to suppress a look of disgust on his face. "I apologize for keeping you so long. We will release you immediately."

"We met him," Kinta Jane said, "because we were in Montreal, on a matter relating to three brothers."

"Oh?" Prince Chotu stared.

"No!" Mesh shouted.

The prince had not responded with the countersign. On the other hand, Mesh was visibly distressed, arching his back and yanking at the pegs anchoring his bonds. Had Kinta Jane made a mistake? But how bad could the mistake be, when nothing seemed to have happened?

The woman with frown lines stepped forward. "I have two brothers," she said. "We each came from a different mother and father."

The crowd behind her was visibly baffled. The woman stepped in closer still, leaning down to look Kinta Jane in the eye. Kinta Jane had pushed herself deeper—she wasn't about to be released now. But was what her next move?

She decided to press forward. "Such brothers would be a marvel to remember until the end of days."

The old woman nodded. "Tell me how you come to be traveling with my nephew."

Nephew? Did that mean that Mesh had killed this woman's husband, and her sons? Had Kinta Jane made a mistake? "My name is Kinta Jane Embry, and I am a follower of Benjamin Franklin."

"I am aware of the Lightning Bishop," the old woman said. "Tell me what he has to do with three brothers of different mothers."

The Anaks all stared. Did they understand English? To speak of these things openly made Kinta Jane's head spin, it went against all her training. But she wasn't sure what her other choices were. "Bishop Franklin knew of the three brothers, and he knew of the nature of the Heron King. As he built the Lightning Cathedral to protect Philadelphia from the storm of Simon Sword, he built another kind of machine to protect the people of the Ohio from the possibility that the three brothers might... fail."

"To protect the people of the Ohio?" the old woman asked. "Or to compel them to make the choice that he wanted them to make?"

Kinta Jane's stomach fell.

"Why should Brother Anak shed his blood to protect the Serpentborn and the Germans and Dutchmen in their little boats," the woman with frown lines continued, "when those people walk and sleep and eat and rut upon land that was stolen from Brother Anak centuries ago?"

"Simon Sword would gladly kill you all," Dockery said. "You know that."

"Simon Sword cannot touch us," the woman said. "We are not upon his rivers. We are not on land that drains into his rivers. We are beyond his reach. But his reach does touch the land of Kanawha. You know what that is. Mesh has told you."

Kinta Jane nodded. "You want your ancestral lands."

"And power," the woman said. "And our gods. And who can give them to us?"

"Why not ally with Brother Onas against Simon Sword, then?" Kinta Jane asked. "He is the most powerful man in the empire. He may own Kanawha and be able to give it to you."

"I do not think Brother Onas stands against Simon Sword," the old woman said. "If he did, I do not think you would be here, follower of Bishop Franklin. Or did you mean to ask, why not ally with Brother Onas, on the side of Simon Sword?"

"Because he is destruction to us all!" Mesh howled. "You cannot ally with the beast! You can only throw yourselves into his maw!"

"We may throw ourselves." The old woman shrugged. "We may throw others. And we may recover our lands and our memories and our selves."

"You're the biggest people on this continent," Tim Dockery said, "and you got the tiniest brains."

Prince Chotu struck him in the face, knocking him to the ground. A dissatisfied murmur arose from the watching congregation, and he turned to scowl at them.

"Simon Sword is the reaver!" Kinta Jane cried. "I have seen Franklin's vision—the destroying son makes nothing! He brings only death!" She felt desperation rising in her throat, like vomit seeking an exit.

"She speaks the truth!" Mesh cried.

Dockery stood. He spat again, and this time the brown tobacco juice was red with blood. He glared at Prince Chotu.

"I do not care whether she does," Prince Chotu snarled. He picked up a spear that leaned against a pine log that sprouted up through the center of the platform, supporting a catwalk above, and hefted it as if he were planning to throw it at Mesh.

"A destroyer may be all we need," the old woman said. "If a destroyer will remove those who stand now on our lands, we can take them back."

"And then what?" Kinta Jane asked. "Stand forever in the storm? Fight forever against his beastkind? Fear forever that the destroyer will tire of other prey and turn on you? We all need Peter Plowshare, the beneficent river. We all need peace. I have seen it in a vision!"

"She has seen a vision!" Mesh howled. "Try her!" *Try her?*

An uncertain murmur arose in the ground. One man tapped the butt of his spear on the wood, and then a second.

"There is nothing to try." Prince Chotu shook his head.

"We must try her in order to find out whether there is something!" Mesh craned his face forward, neck muscles bulging. "Try her!"

"But does she wish to be tried?" the old woman asked, a hint of a cackle in her voice.

"Very well," Prince Chotu said. "We will put it to her." He strode across the wood and stopped, feet shoulder width apart, facing Kinta Jane. She had to look up, or stare into his sternum. "Kinta Jane, you may leave if you wish. And if you stay, we will put you and your vision to trial. Understand that you may not survive the trial. Which do you choose?"

Mesh fell silent. He looked at Kinta Jane, and she met his eyes. Certainty shone therein, and passion, but also other lights that Kinta Jane could not identify. Cunning? Hope? Madness?

Mesh himself had offered her a chance to leave. Perhaps she should have taken his offer then. Perhaps she should take Prince Chotu's offer to leave. She and Dockery could look for members of the Conventicle elsewhere.

Or simply flee. She could live as the Anakim had, somewhere outside the reach of Simon Sword. New Amsterdam, for instance, or Paris. But her brother René had given his life. And if Simon Sword's reign was not shortened, many, many more would do the same.

More of the Anakim pounded spear butts against the wood. "Trial!" they shouted, and, "Try her vision!"

"I will take your trial," she murmured.

A grin crept across the old woman's face.

"Very well." Prince Chotu nodded. "Then you must choose. Trial by copper, trial by water, or trial by fang."

Kinta Jane's heart raced, and she struggled to steady her breathing. Trial by copper sounded like trial by combat; many of the Anakim had copper axes or copper swords. "May I choose a champion?" she asked.

Dockery wiped blood from his lip with the back of his hand. "I'll do it."

"Did a champion have your vision?" the old woman asked. "You may not."

Trial by water didn't sound good; Kinta Jane couldn't swim.

But trial by fang? Would that be a fight with an animal? Or a beastman? Or would the giants themselves bite her?

"I choose trial by fang," she said, voice as loud and clear as she could make it.

The number of spear pounders doubled instantly. The rhythm jumped from Kinta Jane's ears into the soles of her feet. "Trial! Trial! Trial by fang!" the crowd shouted.

Mesh collapsed back against the rock. He was shivering, and his skin looked blue, but he had a smile on his face.

"Come this way." The old woman beckoned, ushering Kinta Jane and Dockery back, away from the water's edge.

Other Anakim came forward with copper chains, snapping them onto copper rings, two parallel rows of nine rings and chains, forming a glittering red alley that ran from twenty feet from Kinta Jane's feet to twenty feet from the crowd of giants that continued to thump the wood at their own feet.

Snarling dogs appeared, led forward on short chains. Eighteen dogs, each the size of a pony, each looking like a crazed and angry wolf, and the Anakim snapped the copper chains to the spiked collars on the dogs' throats.

The dogs snarled and barked, leaping toward Kinta Jane, restrained by their chains.

"Copper," Kinta Jane said.

"It is the ancient metal, the metal that gives life,"

the old woman said. "It is the metal of our ancestors, who have mined it from the islands and shores of these northern seas for thousands of years. We mined it and smelted it into axes and spearheads and swords before your people showed up, before we had ever heard of the Serpentborn. We shall be mining it after you and they are gone. Eternal things, and things of the spirit, are things of copper."

"Ain't that nice," Dockery murmured. "We get a little sermon before they tear us to bits." He raised his voice. "I'll run this."

"You cannot," Prince Chotu said.

"I've run a gauntlet of Foxes, once," Dockery said. "I expect I can run a gauntlet of dogs." He tried to step forward, but Chotu pushed him back.

"If I must strike you again, it will be with my blade," the Anak growled. "You cannot, because we are trying the vision of the woman. If her vision was sent by true spirits, then our ancestors—and hers—will allow her to live."

Kinta Jane took a deep breath and nodded. "This is my trial. And if I pass, will you release Mesh?"

"No," the old woman said. "He will die on that rock where he now lies. But we will consider seriously what you have told us of your vision."

Kinta Jane looked at Mesh; the trembling of his limbs said that he was still alive, but he lay pressed back against the stone now, face turned up the sky. Was it even possible for him to survive, at this point?

But if she could live, perhaps the Anakim would listen to her, in any case. And perhaps then there was an opportunity to restore the alliance of the three brothers. She stepped forward.

Mesh's dogs, Chak and 'Uutz, had grown used to the effect Kinta Jane had on dogs, and had become willing to hold her down and bare their teeth at her. But in her first encounter with them, she had cowed them. She could only hope to do the same with these beasts.

But if she ran too fast, they would simply bite her before noticing anything amiss. And if she walked too slow, the dogs at the back might have the courage to attack her, notwithstanding whatever happened with the first rows of the beasts.

The dogs growled and snapped, straining at their chains.

Thump! Thump! Thump! went the spears.

"Trial by fang! Trial by fang!"

If she died now, she did not regret her life. Kinta Jane took another step.

The dogs growled and leaped.

"Trial by fang! Trial by fang!"

If I die, will I meet Isaiah Wilkes again? Or René?

She took another step.

The first two dogs fell silent. They leaped forward, snapping with their teeth, once, and then cringed, puzzled and defeated looks on their faces.

Kinta Jane accelerated, bearing down on the second pair of dogs. They, too, barked and leaped and then fell silent, and slunk away. The third pair parted before she reached them, whimpering until her presence took their voices away.

The thumping faltered. The Anakim stared.

Kinta Jane continued. It would only take one of the beasts changing its mind and leaping on her to show the rest of the pack that she was vulnerable, and then she would be overrun. She lengthened her stride, scowling.

Behind her, the dogs remained mute, or whined.

The Anakim crowded forward. Above her and around her, the giants watching from other platforms rushed forward for a better look. As she reached the final pair of beasts, Kinta Jane couldn't help grinning. Her heart pounded, but she felt triumphant and almost playful, so at the last moment, she broke into a run, scattering the final dogs.

Beyond the gauntlet of dogs, she stood now facing the cluster of giants. It had grown, from a party the size of a jury to a gathering the size of a mob. They collapsed around her, blocking out her view with their imposing stature. Kinta Jane stood before them and raised her arms over her head in victory.

"Behold the three wounds of William Penn!" She was consciously mimicking the Franklin's performance in Horse Hall. It was not a performance anyone had ever taught her. She slapped herself in her chest with her right hand, wishing she had stage blood to spill. With her left, she slapped her thigh, and then with her right again, she slapped herself in the forehead. "Behold, Brother Onas!"

The Anakim stared. Several turned to their neighbors to whisper.

"I do not know what you understand!" she cried. "I am not your enemy. I am the enemy of Simon Sword, and I am here gathering allies. I have seen the god of the Mississippi, and he is terrible. He is an eater of men and a wrecker of worlds, and if you are beyond his reach here, many thousands of people are in his path and within his grasp and do not know he is coming."

She had grown accustomed to speaking English, because of her time with Wilkes and then with Dockery, but as she spoke, it occurred to her that the Anakim, close as they were to Acadia, might speak better French. She repeated herself in that tongue, and was rewarded with more smiles and nods of understanding, or possibly agreement.

"*Voulez-vous vous allier avec nous?*" she ended her exhortation. She wasn't entirely sure who the *nous* was—Kinta Jane and Dockery? The Conventicle? But it had no troops, and Kinta Jane had little idea how to contact other members. Perhaps Adriaan Stuyvesant could help, though Wilkes had feared that his daughter's marriage to the emperor would corrupt him.

Then she lowered her arms and stood silent. She heard Dockery's footfalls as the trapper walked, skirting the gauntlet of dogs, to stand by her side.

The Anakim stared at her. She didn't know how to read their faces. Were they curious? Amused? Puzzled?

But none raised a voice or a hand to volunteer.

Heavier footfalls plodded on the wood behind her, and Prince Chotu joined Kinta Jane, standing on her other side. "I do not know whether I should feel shocked or tricked," he rumbled. "You are a sorceress?"

"I'm no hexer," Kinta Jane told him.

He nodded slowly. "Well, then, you have survived your trial by fang. I hope you live to a full old age and can tell many grandchildren, as you dandle them on your knee, how you ran the gauntlet of Misaabe fighting dogs and lived."

"Will you do nothing for me?" Kinta Jane asked.

"What should I do?" Prince Chotu smiled. "This village and the surrounding homesteads can muster a hundred fighting men. With all our extended kin, we could muster a thousand. Given a month to send out messengers, and a compelling message, perhaps I could collect ten thousand. If the Heron King is as terrible as you say, if he is half as terrible as our stories tell us he is, then all I would accomplish is the throwing away of ten thousand important lives."

"We could...find Brother Odishkwa," Kinta Jane said. "The Algonquin peoples are many and mighty."

"And have they stood to fight Simon Sword, in their great and mighty numbers?" Prince Chotu shook his head.

The woman with frown lines joined them; the creases on her face were so deep now, she looked as if her face might split open. "You have survived the trial by fang. Your vision is proved true. But your plan...is madness. Go now. In peace...but go."

Kinta Jane's shoulders drooped. René's death, and Wilkes's loss, were to be in vain. "Our things?"

"They have been brought for you. Here." Prince Chotu gestured with his arm, showing Kinta one of the guards from their prison hut. The burly Anak stood holding a bundle of furs in both arms, and wearing a stunned expression on his face.

The crowd backed away, allowing the guard to come forward. A hush prevailed over the scene, until there came a sudden cry.

The Anakim all turned to look at the water, and the toothlike stone that rose from it. Mesh was gone.

Prince Chotu seized Kinta Jane by the neck. "Where is he?"

"I don't know!" she cried.

"We didn't free him," Dockery said.

The prince lifted Kinta Jane by her neck until her feet dangled above the wooden floor. She choked, gasping for air.

"Let her go," the old woman said. "She passed the trial."

"But *Mesh*," Prince Chotu snarled.

"Let her go." The old woman pointed at the building with its wall of painted gargoyles and lowered her voice. "They are watching you, Chotu-shish. The whole village is watching you."

Prince Chotu dropped Kinta Jane. She wasted no time, crossing to the giant who held her possessions and taking them back. The giant stared, and twice opened his mouth as if to speak, but then didn't. Dockery also grabbed his tools, which were more numerous, and then Kinta Jane marched toward the shore.

"Sound the alarm!" Prince Chotu bellowed. "Release the dogs!"

Kinta Jane and Tim Dockery fled into the woods to the thundering sound of drums.

Ma'iingan left his home at the request of God-Has-Given, whose secret name was Makwa, the Zhaaga-naashii healer who was his friend. This was the second messenger his son had told him to expect. He had told Waabigwan the messenger was coming, and so had Giimoodaapi. She had not protested at all, though with the arrival of summer, a man might have been expected to spend extra time with his family, including teaching his two young sons the beginning of their skills as members of the people: hunting, fishing, gathering wild rice, which berries were edible and which were not.

Ma'iingan had taken his bow and gun, knife and tomahawk, and a canoe, and had set out into the land of many waters.

From time to time after his departure, Nathaniel appeared to him in dreams. This struck Ma'iingan as natural—the world of dreams was very close to the world of spirits, and maybe was the same place. A man's manidoo could appear to him in dreams much more easily than in a waking state. Nathaniel was a healer because he could travel the world of spirits, and had taken Ma'iingan there with him. Nathaniel didn't appear alone now, but with two spirits, a beaver and a gray fox, both of whom had the hands of men.

He gave Ma'iingan directions that led him through the German lands. Something dark was happening with the Germans—Ma'iingan had heard old stories about their ancestors shedding the blood of men as sacrifices, but he had never before seen it. But now, as he slipped past on his light canoe or padded through the forest, he saw men hanged and swaying in the summer breeze over planted fields, sometimes impaled with spears. He chose to avoid meeting other living men on his journey through German lands.

On the Michi-Gami, Nathaniel guided him north-ward. It was easy traveling, with some rain, but without the furious ice storms that made the water dangerous in winter. And then one night, Nathaniel and his two animal companions came to Ma'iingan in his dream and showed him a village of the Misaabe. It stood on poles on the water, and there, in two separate huts, they saw prisoners. One prisoner lay alone, and was a Misaabe. The other two were an Indian woman and a Zhaaganaashii man, lying together in a hut.

~These two~, Nathaniel said. *~Can you find your way here and save them?~*

~My canoe is small,~ Ma'iingan said. *~But they look skinny. You want the giant also, na?~*

~Yes,~ the fox said.

~Do you believe that is Brother Anak?~ the beaver asked. The beaver was shuffling playing cards in its hands, and seemed familiar.

~I thought they were his prisoners at first,~ the fox said. *~But now they seem to be prisoners together.~*

~Rescue them all, if you can,~ God-Had-Given said. *~And if you must, rescue the man and the woman from the giant.~*

~They are named Kinta Jane and Dockery,~ the fox said.

~Zhaaganaashii names are always so strange,~ Ma'iingan said. *~What is the giant's name?~*

Nathaniel and his two spirits all shrugged.

~How will they know I have come to help?~ Ma'iingan asked.

~Tell them that the Franklin sent you,~ the Fox said. *~Tell them that the Franklin's name was Isaiah Wilkes.~*

Ma'iingan rose the next morning well before dawn and went to scout out the Misaabe village. It was easy; the Misaabe had men standing watch on land, and even men standing at the corners of their village to watch the lake, but their sentries on the water were bundled in furs and sleepy, and Ma'iingan paddled silently past them.

He found the huts where the prisoners lay and was considering how he might effect a rescue when the giant prisoner was removed from his cell. The other Misaabe took the man down to the bottom of the village and tied him to a rock in the water. Ma'iingan watched from only a few feet away, bobbing up and down beneath one of the village's wooden platforms, lying low so as not to crack his skull when the waves tossed his canoe toward the wood.

He watched as Kinta Jane and Dockery confronted the Misaabe chieftain and his witch, and then was condemned to run the gauntlet of war dogs.

Should he leap out and snatch Kinta Jane away? There seemed to be nothing he could do, against so many. On the other hand, as all the Misaabe huddled around to watch Kinta Jane, it was easy for Ma'iingan to rescue the giant. He slipped across the few necessary feet to put him close to the man, cut the two rawhide thongs that held him, and then took him into the canoe. Mercifully, the giant was conscious enough to help get himself into the canoe, and nimble enough that his efforts didn't capsize the little vessel. –

Then he paddled straight out into the lake.

He threw his own sleeping fur over the Misaabe. "You will live, na?"

"With a wretched constitution such as I have," the giant said, "it is a wonder that I have lived to this day."

"Ah, good," Ma'iingan said. "A witty man."

From far out on the Michi-Gami, he heard the village pound its drums, and then he saw Misaabe swarm onto the land.

"Kinta Jane will live," the giant said. "She has a special way with dogs, and after she passes the trial, the people will insist that she be freed. And then Chotu will throw her out of the village."

"Good," Ma'iingan said.

✦   ✦   ✦

Dockery thought of himself as a man who could walk long distances. As a child, he'd more than once walked fifty continuous miles, even before his time among the Algonks. But he had nothing on Kinta Jane Embry. She walked as if her limbs were made of iron, and her feet could feel no pain.

And walking out of the Misaabe village, she walked fast.

Misaabe hunters passed them going south, and then passed them again coming north, hounds straining on their chains. Dockery smiled at the big-mouthed giants, but they didn't smile back. Some of them did bow, slightly, to Kinta Jane.

"I guess you're a prophet now," Dockery said as they forded a stream in the dying light.

"You had the same vision I did," Kinta Jane said.

"Yeah, but being a prophet is more than the vision, ain't it? It's the standing up to power, and bearing important messages, and also the queer, symbolic actions. All the stuff Wilkes loved. And now you're doing it. Three wounds."

"I would have been just as happy for you to run the gauntlet."

Dockery laughed again. "Yeah, only it might not have turned out so well. I'm not complaining, I'm impressed."

They made their camp in a tight stand of basswood trees beside a spring, whose waters flowed across the deer trail they had been following. No more Anakim passed them, and an hour after sunset, a man stepped into view on the path. He carried a long rifle crooked unthreateningly in his arms, with a tomahawk on his belt and a bow over his back. He wore leggings and a breechclout, his chest was bare, and he had two feathers plaited into long black hair.

Appearing as he did, either the man had no woodcraft at all, or he wanted to be certain Dockery saw him. Dockery stood up from the tiny flames he was trying to nurse into a small fire, making himself visible and showing that his hands held no weapons.

"Good evening," the stranger said. "You speak English, na? My French is terrible and I speak no German at all."

"*Indojibwem*," Dockery said.

The Indian grinned. "Your friend also speaks the language of the People, na?"

"No," Dockery said. "Maybe we'd better stick to English."

"My name is Ma'iingan, and I have two things to tell you. The first is that the Franklin sent me, and his name is Isaiah Wilkes."

Dockery was so astonished, he nearly sat down. Kinta Jane, who had been grinding dried beef and berries into a mash that would become a stew, leaped to her feet.

"When did he send you?" she asked.

"I will tell you," Ma'iingan said, "but it might sound a little strange."

Dockery laughed, and once he was laughing, he had a hard time stopping. Finally getting control of himself, he said, "I just escaped from a village of giants because dogs fall silent in the presence of my companion, and the Misaabe took that as a sign of her prophetic gifts."

"Lucky you," Ma'iingan said. "Dogs bark louder when I'm near, though sometimes it seems that's because the Zhaaganaashii train them to do that."

"When did Wilkes send you?" Kinta Jane pressed.

"I saw him last night," Ma'iingan said. "My friend, who is a great healer, came to me in my dreams. Franklin was with him, though he appeared as a gray fox with the hands of a man. The fox told me to say that to you. I believe it was as a sign that I am a friend."

"You got our attention, all right," Dockery said. "What's the second thing you wanted to tell us?"

"I rescued your Misaabe companion, the one who calls himself Mesh. Is he your friend? If so, I can bring him to you. And if not, we should discuss how to deal with him."

"He's our friend," Kinta Jane said immediately.

The Ojibwe disappeared back into the woods, and returned minutes later leading Mesh. The big Anak was wrapped in a single fur. Meeting Dockery's gaze, he scowled fiercely—but then his face relented, assuming a milder expression. Kinta Jane seated him beside the fire, in the most sheltered corner of the thicket, where he couldn't be seen from the path.

"What do we do now?" Dockery asked as they gulped a few mouthfuls each of the beef and berry tea.

"I will seek Kanawha," Mesh said. "If I can find it again, and capture its power, then I can return to my people and they will all follow me, ignoble worm though I am. Then we can stand against Simon Sword, now and in the future, and return to the land of our inheritance."

"What did you steal from your people?" Kinta Jane asked.

"Nothing." Mesh didn't react. "That was a lie, an effort to turn you against me."

Dockery looked at Kinta Jane. "I don't know what else there is for us to do. Go back to Montreal? Go to Stuyvesant? Figure out who's the Franklin now? Maybe it's Adriaan. Maybe it's you. Maybe it's still Wilkes, and he's just a spirit."

Kinta Jane stared into the fire. "Maybe the best thing we can do is help Mesh on his quest. Maybe this is the way to awaken Brother Anak."

"You're looking for allies, na?" the Ojibwe asked. "Warriors to stand against Simon Sword, na?"

"Are you going to tell us you're Brother Odishkwa?" Dockery said.

"No, I don't know what is. But my friend the healer is a foe of Simon Sword, he and all his family. They are strange, but they are powerful, in their way. His sister is the Queen of Cahokia."

Kinta Jane's head snapped up. "Go on."

"It may be interesting to have guidance from him," Ma'iingan said. "Perhaps Cahokia will be the ally you seek. Or perhaps in Cahokia, they know where this Kanawha is located."

"They ought to," Mesh said, "since they took it from us."

"How can we contact this healer?" Kinta Jane asked.

"He comes to me in my sleep," Ma'iingan said. "Since last night he helped me to find you, I think tonight he is likely to visit."

"What are you waiting for, then?" Dockery asked. "Go to sleep!"

The Indian stretched himself out beside the fire and was soon breathing deeply. Signaling that he would take the first watch, Dockery stood and stepped a few paces away, taking his rifle with him. Mesh also lay down, in a tangle of green grass and other matted vegetation, and Kinta Jane sat upright, watching Ma'iingan's face.

Dockery watched too, keeping one eye on the Ojibwe and the other on the forest.

They didn't have to wait long. Short minutes later, Ma'iingan's eyes opened and he spoke, in a voice that sounded clanky, like the imitation of a voice. "Kinta Jane Embry," he said. "Dockery. Queen Sarah Elytharias can help you find Kanawha. Go to Cahokia."

"The next time we meet, I shall have to kill you."

CHAPTER ELEVEN

Kinta Jane Embry was shaken awake under a gray morning sky. Dockery and Ma'iingan crouched over her, each man holding a rifle.

"Misaabe," the Ojibwe said.

"When did they get here?" Kinta Jane asked.

"I am unsure. They are stealthy."

Dockery held a shushing finger to his lips.

Kinta Jane rolled over onto her hands and knees and peered through the lattice of leaves. At first, she saw nothing, but then Ma'iingan brushed back a thick branch and Dockery pointed, and she saw a giant head, covered with thick red hair, and a copper spear head at the top of a stout beam.

The giant was facing away from them.

"Maybe he hasn't seen us," she whispered.

Dockery nodded. "Maybe *they* haven't seen us." He pointed in a different direction, a ninety-degree arc away, and Kinta Jane saw the back of another giant head, with bright red hair falling in two braids, suspended eight feet off the ground.

"Awful damn lucky they're just looking the wrong direction," Dockery murmured.

"You worry about a possible trap," Ma'iingan murmured.

"We should have set a watch farther away from our camp."

Mesh was awake and crouching at the far end of the thicket. He was naked, and without his clothes, Kinta Jane felt she wasn't even looking at a man. He was so huge, she felt as if a giant hunting beast was sheltering in the brambles. Contributing to the generally monstrous appearance, the skin of his legs was covered from ankle to midthigh in swirling tattoos. The creatures inked into his legs were furry, with long tusks and enormous fangs and wild eyes, but they roiled together like a clutch of serpents and their eyes seemed to follow Kinta Jane.

The giant held a club in one hand, and he pointed along a line that passed away from the deer trail, the spring, and the thicket, toward a gray, lichen-mottled spur of rock.

They left their sleeping gear, taking only weapons with them. Ma'iingan went first, war ax in his hand, with Kinta Jane right behind him. They crept with their torsos bent over, parallel to the ground. Kinta Jane was careful not to step on any visible twigs, and winced at the soft squishing sound her feet made as they depressed the carpet of rotting leaves beneath them. She kept her head craned to the right, eye fixed on one of the giants.

The red head was very still.

Ma'iingan reached the spur of rock first, and he and Kinta Jane crept around it together, the other two men close behind.

Standing behind the spur was another giant.

His hair was a dull yellow and a ragged beard clung to his chin. Through mismatched patches of leather and furs gleamed a copper breastplate and greaves covering his calves. He held a sheathed sword and a spear, and when Kinta Jane rounded the edge of the rock, she ran right into him, nearly banging her nose on his chest.

Ma'iingan leaped between her and the giant, raising his tomahawk. "Let us pass, Misaabe!"

"Keep your voices down," the giant whispered. "I don't know that pursuit has given up yet."

Mesh emerged from the forest and emitted a cry of joy. He and the copper-clad giant embraced, and then the newcomer handed the sword and spear to Mesh. "We hoped you were alive." He indicated a bundle wrapped in rough cloth, leaning in the lee of the rock. "Don't worry, I also have your clothing."

"Chak?" Mesh asked. "'Uutz?"

"And also your shu-shu," the blond giant said. "We could not bring the shu-shu effectively through these woods, so they wait on a road to the west of here, with both dogs. They would not let anyone else touch them."

"That is how they are raised." Mesh turned to his companions. "This is . . . his short name is Udu. He is a friend, though I know it is upsetting to contemplate the possibility that a wretch as lowly as I should have friends."

"I am a believer," Udu said. "And I have another twenty believers with me."

"Meaning that the other nine hundred eighty Anaks are with Prince Chotu," Kinta Jane asked, "looking to make an alliance with Simon Sword?"

"I am not a believer only in my prince," Udu told her. "I am also a believer in you. In the vision you related."

"Better nine hundred eighty," Mesh said, "than a thousand."

"Maybe not all nine hundred eighty," Udu said. "Maybe some of them will say they are undecided, and choose not to fight. Or they will wait for more information, or for a better sign."

"I hate to sound like a grumpy old man," Dockery said, "but you could put your breeches on now."

"Where are you bound?" Udu asked. Other Anakim stepped from the woods. They were half again Kinta Jane's height, so when they crowded around her the forest disappeared.

"Cahokia," Mesh said. "To ally with the serpent queen, and also in the hopes that she will help us find and reach Kanawha."

A rumble of approval passed through the ranks of the giants.

"No, really," Dockery said. "Your trousers."

"But I thought you knew where it was," Kinta Jane said. "You said you had been there."

"I have been there," Mesh said. "But I traveled in a strange place—perhaps the same place where friend Ma'iingan traveled with his healer."

"You're a healer, too?" Ma'iingan asked.

Mesh shook his head. "As a child, I was very sick. My legs did not work at all, and would grow no muscle. I was carried everywhere I went, by shu-shu or in my father's arms. My mother took me to the family's Spirit Rider, who was my uncle. And when he tried all the usual methods of healing, they did not work.

Even when he rode alone in the land of spirits, he came back without healing for me."

"So he took you to Kanawha?" Kinta Jane asked.

"My uncle had been taken there as a child," Mesh said. "Not in the flesh, but in the land of spirits. His own uncle, who gave him his drum, took him there to see. This was a great secret that was passed down among the Spirit Riders of my family, and my uncle was told that great power was available within the spirit chamber of Kanawha, but that it was dangerous to enter that place, and that the power should only be sought in times of extreme need."

"A Talligewi who cannot walk is a case of extreme need," Udu said. "Such a person cannot hunt or fish or fight."

"He took you there and healed you?" Dockery asked.

"He took me there and the guardians of the spirit chamber killed him," Mesh said. "But when I awoke, my legs bore these markings on them, and I could walk."

"Had he no successor Spirit Rider?" Kinta Jane asked. "Is there no one else who might take us there? Even in the world of the spirits?"

"Nathaniel Penn is a powerful magician," Ma'iingan said. "Perhaps if your Spirit Rider could take him there, or tell him how to get there, he could defeat the guardians of your spirit chamber."

"When my uncle died, his successor as a Spirit Rider, his daughter, was still a child." Mesh hung his head. "No one knows how to get there. Not even I, who have been there, in a manner of speaking, but then—"

"But then you are a lowly worm," Dockery said. "We know that part."

"So perhaps the Queen of Cahokia can help us," Kinta Jane said. "Or her brother, the Spirit Rider Nathaniel. Find Kanawha, and then we persuade the other Talligewi to join us in fighting Simon Sword. Whatever that means." She had thought that her errand with Wilkes was to speak to the leaders of the empire and rally them to send armies against the Heron King. Now it seemed she might rally an army from outside the borders of the empire, and she might herself have to march with it.

"And also find Kanawha, and use the power of Kanawha itself against the Heron King." Mesh smiled. "An easy task, for a party as mighty as we are."

"Mesh," Dockery said. "There's a lady present. Put on your damn pants."

It was a simple spell, using a lock of the girl's hair.

In other times, the spell was simple enough that Etienne would have smoked a cigarette as he cast it. When he needed the Brides, Etienne wanted Ezili Freda and Ezili Danto and their power of compelling lust to be a raging storm, so he fed them hot peppers, including hot, pickled peppers. But at other times, that storm could be inconvenient, and Etienne kept its power tamped down with tobacco smoke.

He did not now need the Brides to cast the spell, but he did worry for his safety, walking the streets of New Orleans alone. The Chevalier of New Orleans and the armies of New Spain were not far away, beyond the walls and across the river, and Etienne had enemies within the walls as well. If Eoin Kennedie decided to break with his ally the bishop, or an old rival wanted to take a shot at the gangster and moneylender, or even if some ordinary common New Orleans criminal wanted to rob Etienne for money, he would be prepared.

The Brides also enhanced his pulpit oratory, and, as Bishop of New Orleans, Etienne wanted to be ready to climb onto a box and deliver a sermon on very short notice.

The spell he followed was simply a bit of black hair lying along a steel needle. The needle lay on the feathered leaf of a bald cypress tree, floating in a wooden bowl full of water. Etienne had stroked the needle against his own hair, laid it on the leaf, and then covered it with the girl's hair. Then he had invoked Papa Legba, asking him to help Etienne find the girl's nearest kin—the needle had promptly swung around, indicating the direction Etienne should go.

The hair had come from the head of a girl named Marie. Marie had been a mambo asogwe, an initiated Vodun priestess, who had taken the side of the Chevalier of New Orleans against Etienne, because, she had told him, her loa permitted it. And then, accompanied by a squad of French mamelukes, she had ridden away northward.

Etienne believed she was now dead, because the Brides seemed to say as much, and also because, when he used this lock of her hair to try to find her, his craft remained inert. But he wished to discover why she had taken to war against him in the first place, and whether her grievance against Etienne Ukwu might be shared by others. If she had, say, a cadre of sorcerer sisters who all wanted him dead, Etienne would have to act.

He walked through the Vieux Carré, the Quarter, after dark. The district might have been safer during the day, but Etienne had lived many years in the carousing vice of the Quarter, and was not afraid. Also, at night, either darkness or drunkenness was likely to keep anyone from noticing that Etienne walked staring down into his cupped hands.

The needle was carrying him beyond the Quarter, across the tree-lined Esplanade and into the Faubourg Marigny. This was the ugly sister of the Quarter, a neighborhood with all the Quarter's roughness and criminality, but without the casinos and the dance halls. The Faubourg was a neighborhood where chickens and even children could disappear without eliciting public comment. As a place for a mambo to have her roots, the Faubourg could not be exceeded.

Etienne checked his weapons: the knives were in place, as were the two loaded pistols. One was loaded with a silver ball—as he was seeking the family of a witch, he faced the possibility of encountering hexes or monsters, and he wished to be prepared.

His compass brought him finally to a front door. He looked up, expecting to see a decadent old Spanish building, or the colorful indications in the windows that the cool loa were worshipped in this place. Instead, he saw a two-story plaster home, with iron railings and jasmine on the second-story balcony. The walls were whitewashed and the steps in front of the wide door were clean. It seemed the home of a respectable merchant or artisan, and not the lair of a witch.

He walked around the house, finding access to an alley behind it to confirm that his needle was pointing at the building, rather than at something beyond. Then he plucked the needle and hair from his compass, tucking them both into a pocket of his waistcoat, and cast the water and leaf aside. The wooden bowl was too large for any of his pockets, so he held it in his hands.

Thanking Maitre Carrefour, the Brides, and above all, his gede loa, he knocked at the door. As he waited, he felt his mother's locket tremble; touching it, he heard her voice: *You do not need absolution, my son. You did not kill the mambo.*

"I do not seek absolution, Mother," he murmured under his breath. "I seek answers. And I seek to protect myself and my plans."

Sometimes the thing itself is its own answer.

"Riddles, Mother?"

Not every hatred arises in response to an ancient wrong.

The door opened, and a man appeared. His skin was dark brown, his short gray hair curled tightly to his scalp. He wore a butternut waistcoat and white shirt and breeches, and he looked at Etienne through round spectacles. He smelled of sawdust.

"May I help you?"

"You're a carpenter?" Etienne asked.

"A cooper." The man smiled. "But with the Spanish siege and blockade, trade is slowed, and I do not sell as many barrels as I used to. I would take on carpentry work, if you have any."

Etienne hesitated. Did this man have reason to hate him, such that his daughter would undertake an act of vengeance? Had he ever wronged a cooper? It was likely enough that the man could have a son, or a brother, who had lost money in Etienne's casino, or failed to repay a loan and had his legs broken. "Do you have a daughter? Named Marie?"

The cooper's face brightened. "I do. Have you seen her? I have not heard from her in several months. Not since before the city was attacked, and our chevalier betrayed us."

"Nor I," Etienne said. "I worried for her family." It was not, strictly speaking, a lie.

Looking into Etienne's face, the cooper's eyes suddenly opened wide. "Your Grace!"

Etienne nodded. He looked around the dirty street, hoping the old man didn't make too much noise. "I am sad that you have no news of her, either, and more sad that I have no word to ease your mind. But it pleases me that you are a man who works in wood."

"Your Grace?"

"You must know that the cathedral is being rebuilt," Etienne said. "As of yet, no one is contracted to make the pews. Do you feel that is a work you could do?"

"For the cathedral's sake, I would undertake any challenge." The cooper smiled. "Pews will be easy. I make all our furniture in the house, including benches."

A woman appeared in the doorway, pressing herself against the cooper's side. She had a fair complexion, skin weathered by the sun, and her hair was dyed a slightly unnatural red. "Is this gentleman asking about Marie?"

"This gentleman is the bishop," the old man said. "And yes, he came about Marie."

The woman curtseyed. "I am Elsa Nwozuzu."

"Ah, forgive me." The cooper struck himself in the forehead. "I am Solomon Nwozuzu."

"You gave your daughter a French name?"

"She gave that to herself," Elsa said. "We called her Adaku."

"I knew your father," Solomon said.

Etienne felt as if an icicle had been stabbed into his back. "As a parishioner?"

"No." Solomon laughed, embarrassed. "I'm a twice-a-year Christian at best, I'm afraid."

"I was an infrequent attender myself for many years." Etienne smiled.

"I knew your father as a boy," Solomon said. "We came from the same village outside Montgomery, and then we were briefly students together. But then life took us in different directions. I saw him when he was bishop, a few times, but we never spoke."

"Marie never knew my father?"

Solomon shook his head. "She might have heard that I knew him as a boy."

"And my father ... owed you no debts?" Etienne asked. "You never quarreled?"

"Who could quarrel with Chinwe Philippe Ukwu?" Solomon laughed. "He turned both cheeks before you could even strike the first one!"

The Chevalier of New Orleans had been able to quarrel with Bishop Ukwu.

Perhaps envy. Perhaps greed. Perhaps inborn malice.

"These are strange questions," Elsa said. "Is something troubling you, Your Grace? Would you care to come in and talk?"

"Ah, no, thank you." Etienne reached into a waistcoat pocket and found a small purse, which he handed to Solomon Nwoẓuzu. "There are twenty Louis d'Or in there—will that do for a deposit?"

"Your Grace." Solomon reached for Etienne's hand, trying to kiss it.

Etienne grabbed the cooper's hand in a firm handshake instead. "Please. My father is the true bishop.

I am merely the bad son, doing his best in the surprising circumstances in which he finds himself. I will
let the foreman know you are coming—you will want
to take measurements at the building site, and send
me your invoices."

Elsa laughed with delight and squeezed Solomon
around the shoulders. "If you are the bad son, Your
Grace, the good son must be truly astonishing."

"He is, indeed."

And where is Chigozie now?

Had that been his mother, his gede loa, or his
own thoughts? Etienne bowed slightly and wished the
Nwozuzu family a pleasant evening.

Had the mambo Marie hated Etienne for no reason at all?

Did he, too, hate without a reason?

The door shut and Etienne stepped away into the
night.

It was rarely difficult to find the bishop; he governed the city now, and he had to do the work of
ruler. He was often out and about, and he left from
and returned to the chevalier's Palais, so that even
if he disappeared into a crowd, he emerged again,
predictably.

But Ahmed Abd al-Wahid was looking for a good
opportunity to take the bishop when his defenses were
down. Ahmed was alone now; he wasn't afraid to fight
the bishop in single combat, but he didn't want to
have to fight the soldier, Eggbert Bailey, or a platoon
of gendarmes. He also remembered well how devilish
sorcery had enlisted the women of the cathedral to
the bishop's defense, and the strange feelings that his

former comrade Ravi had identified as the work of Astarte, an ancient goddess.

A false goddess, served in secret by this false bishop.

But the falseness of the pagan goddess didn't take away the fact that the bishop had power, and especially over women. Abd al-Wahid therefore wished to catch the bishop alone.

He stood in the Faubourg Marigny, in the shadow of a high-walled wagon whose wheels had been removed. Its axles sat on stacks of bricks and its bulk created a shadowed pocket on the street corner, in which the mameluke could wait, unobserved. Even people walking on the boardwalk nearly bumped into him, and then rushed away, hissing.

Abd al-Wahid wore his pourpoint, but to disguise himself he wore a match coat over it, and a wide-brimmed, low-crowned hat. He hid his face, as was his preference, but rather than a silk scarf, he wore a blue cotton bandanna, printed with paisleys. Under all the protecting and concealing layers of fabric, he sweated profusely. His right hand rested on the hilt of the scimitar at his belt, and his eyes were fixed on the Bishop of New Orleans.

The bishop stood before the open doorway of a house, speaking to two people within: an old man and an old woman. Were they agents of the bishop? Informers?

Parishioners?

Etienne Ukwu handed the old man something, and Abd al-Wahid considered waiting where he was, and then breaking down the old couple's door, demanding to see what the bishop had given them. But it was likely nothing—alms from the bishopric, or a payment

from the crime lord—and he didn't want to lose his
chance for a shot at the bishop.

He noted the address; he could return.

The bishop turned from the door and walked into
the Faubourg Marigny. Abd al-Wahid followed.

The bishop moved with a hurried pace toward the
Esplanade, the grand tree-lined avenue that incon-
gruously separated the riotous Vieux Carré from the
sordid Faubourg Marigny. Abd al-Wahid was forced
nearly to run to keep up, despite the length of his
legs. He freed the scimitar from its sheath, the match
coat hiding the soft sound the blade made as it was
unveiled. He held the weapon beside his right leg,
point out with his wrist turned slightly, to be able
to leap forward and attack with minimal preparation.
The scimitar was a slashing weapon, and more than
once, Abd al-Wahid had managed to take the head
off a foeman with a single clean sweep. With his left
hand, he drew a straight dagger—if by some miracle,
the bishop parried or ducked the scimitar attack, he
would find the short blade in his belly.

"Does not the poet say," he murmured, "'our death
is but a wedding with eternity'?"

Abruptly, the bishop turned. Rather than moving
forward toward the trees and the light, he stepped
down an alley to his right. This was better—the alley
was empty of other men, and only dimly illuminated
by one second-story window.

Mud sucked at the bishop's shoes, the loud sound
hopefully concealing the softer sound of the same
mud, clinging to Abd al-Wahid's boots. The bishop
pressed against the right wall as he walked; the alley
was narrow, and Abd al-Wahid doubted he would be

able to swing his scimitar in a wide enough arc to cut off the man's head. The scimitar had a point, but it was not especially sharp.

Abd al-Wahid adjusted his grip on the scimitar, turning the blade up and outward, parallel to his arm. He'd have to step in much closer to make his attack, and it would be a slash across the back of the neck, or the belly, but he had the advantage of surprise—

the bishop spun to face the mameluke.

He stood beneath the lit window, and in his hands he held two pistols. Something fell to the mud—a bowl?

Abd al-Wahid froze. "*Me menacez-vous, monsieur? Je ne vous souhaite aucun mal.*"

"*Vous me suivez.*"

"*Par chance. Par accident.*" With his changed grip, the scimitar rested behind the mameluke's body and out of the bishop's sight.

"*Menteur. Vous êtes le mamelouk.*"

Abd al-Wahid leaped to the attack, his only chance to regain the initiative. He hurled himself at the bishop's face, raising his forearm with the weapon tight against it, blade out, slashing toward the man's unarmored neck.

Bang!

Abd al-Wahid felt the ball strike him in the shoulder. He lost his grip on the scimitar and it fell in the mud as he stumbled, catching himself by throwing his weight against the wall. The noise of the Faubourg continued unabated.

The bishop stepped back. He lowered one pistol, but kept the other trained on the mameluke. "I have shot you with the silver ball," he said, continuing in French.

"If you are offering to pay me, one silver ball is not enough."

"I admire your bravado. You are the commander, are you not?"

"I am the prince-capitaine."

The bishop smiled. "And I am a prince of the church. What an elegant court we hold. Do you have any men remaining, Prince-Capitaine?"

"I do not need men."

"I tell you that I shot you with silver so that you know that any arcane defenses you may have had are now gone. Surely, your mameluke science of war includes the knowledge that silver undoes a magic spell."

Abd al-Wahid stepped away from the wall, straightening himself. His right arm hung useless at his side, but he still held the dagger in his left hand.

"I am a good shot, Prince-Capitaine. I *chose* to shoot you in the shoulder. The second ball is mere lead, but I shall place it in the center of your head, and you will not survive."

"You would not talk so much if you could kill me as you say," Abd al-Wahid said. "You would simply shoot me."

The bishop frowned. "I find myself in a strange mood tonight. Not forgiving, quite, but . . . reflective. Do you have anything personal against me, Prince-Capitaine?"

"You killed my men."

"You have tried to assassinate me multiple times. The deaths of those men may be on the conscience of someone, Prince-Capitaine, but they are not on mine."

Abd al-Wahid adjusted his grip on the dagger, preparing to stab. Sweat stung his eyes. He would lurch forward as if falling, and stab directly through the match coat. He felt woozy from loss of blood, and his vision blurred in his right eye. He stepped forward—

bang!

The second shot took the mameluke not in the head, as threatened, but in his other shoulder. He spun a quarter turn, and when he tried to tighten his grip on the dagger, he found that he couldn't.

His fingers were numb.

Then the dagger fell from his hand and plopped into the mud without dignity.

"Your timing is fortunate, Prince-Capitaine. I will not kill you tonight. I think if you were to simply leave and return to Paris, the chevalier would never know you had gone. He would assume I had killed you. You could waive any claim to revenge for the death of your men, as I could waive my claims to justice, and we could both walk away."

Abd al-Wahid laughed. "Part as friends?"

"Part as enemies," the bishop said. "But part."

"I will not do that," Abd al-Wahid said.

The bishop nodded. "A man of principle. Good-bye, Prince-Capitaine. The next time we meet, I shall have to kill you."

Abd al-Wahid wanted to throw the bishop's threat back into his teeth with a retort of steel. Instead, the bishop picked up his bowl and walked away unanswered, while Abd al-Wahid fell to the mud.

Olanthes suspected the lawyer.

In the first place, he was suspicious of everyone, by training. Olanthes Kuta was one of the Swords of Wisdom, a patriot, a rebel, and member of a secret knighthood that existed in defiance of Imperial edict, a Freemasonry of cloak, dagger, and pistol ball. As he concealed, he expected others to do the same.

He was also suspicious of the very idea of a lawyer in private practice. A man whose only loyalty was to get the best result for his client, regardless of the right and wrong of a situation, was dubious to begin with. It might work, it seemed to him, but only if the lawyer was a person of unquestioned personal integrity, or governed by ironclad rules.

But he was particularly suspicious of *this* lawyer, Logan Rupp. Rupp was not a man of unquestioned personal integrity, he was a bankrupt and a fugitive from justice. But he had been Andy Calhoun's lawyer for years, and so Calhoun had sent Rupp off to Philadelphia with young Calvin Calhoun to represent him in the effort to impeach the emperor.

Rupp had worked long hours, duly drafting the motions and interrogatories and the writs *sub poenas duces tecum*, preparing the Electors and proxyholders allying themselves with Andy Calhoun's motion to ask and answer questions in the well of the Assembly, and even running such minor errands as purchasing new quires of paper when the old were exhausted. Olanthes's unease with the man had begun to slumber.

But then Calvin Calhoun had received a message from his grandfather Andy, out of the blue sky. It had seemed out of character for Andy Calhoun to send such a message, Olanthes thought, and to arrange a meeting in Firstborn territory. Perhaps, he had told himself to quiet his concerns, the Elector had been on his way to Philadelphia, to join the trial in person, and wanted to discuss strategy with Calvin on the road.

But Calvin had not come back, and Andy had not appeared.

And from the moment that Cal had ridden away in a coach along the Imperial pike, Rupp had changed. It wasn't that he stopped working, or was less effective—if anything, Logan Rupp began to work harder. But he also began disappearing in the middle of the day and in the morning, sometimes for hours. He made up for his absences by working late into the night, consuming ever more coffee in the form of whole black pots and ever more tobacco in the form of thick rolled cigars.

Something bothered Logan Rupp, and that bothered Olanthes Kuta.

So when an envelope was shoved under the door with the name *Logan Rupp* scrawled onto it, and Logan was out, Olanthes snatched up the envelope and peered through the parlor curtains to see who had left it. A clean-shaven man with a brown coat, white cravat, and black tricorn hat strolled away from the door, looking very much like any Philadelphia gentleman at his ease. Olanthes noted the sandy blond hair, the red ribbon in the fellow's queue, the filthy hands, and the sagging yellow stockings, and then he slipped out the back door.

In some cities among the eastern powers of the empire—for instance, in New Amsterdam, or in Miami—Olanthes would appear very much out of place. He was Firstborn and looked it, with fair skin, slender features, and long dark hair. He dressed in the fashion of his people, too, with a long tunic, colored Cahokian gray, high boots, and leather armbands. He carried a long sword at his side, but he also carried a brace of pistols in his belt.

In Philadelphia, he was less obvious. The Ohio was not so very far away, and the presence here of the Assembly meant that Firstborn roamed the streets because they were members of the bodyguards or entourages of the seven Ohio Electors or their proxy-holders, or in the families of such men, or because they were merchants who catered to those people.

Still, to be safe, Olanthes grabbed a rigid black Pennslander hat, belonging to Logan Rupp himself, and pulled on a long coat. On close inspection, he might look ridiculous. At a casual glance, the hat and coat might make him go unnoticed.

As he exited the building's rear door, Olanthes tore open the envelope—it was smudged with ink at three of its corners, and left a black smudge on Olanthes's palm—and read the note inside:

> Esteemed Mr. Logan Rupp, Esq.
>
> I find that you owe me, after all, another hundred pounds. You know how to pay me.
>
> F.

He pocketed the note. He could seal it into a new envelope, if he needed to, but dread and anger both rose in his gorge, and his immediate thought was that he would find Logan Rupp and shove the letter down the lawyer's throat, demanding an explanation.

The debt in question could be innocent. Perhaps it was a debt for stationery. Perhaps it was a bill for food or wine, which were delivered in large quantities to the house where Olanthes, Cal, Rupp, the Creole accountant Bondí, and multiple Donelsens all stayed.

Perhaps, less innocently, it was the reminder of some past debt, come back to haunt the bankrupt. Such a claim might make Rupp vulnerable, and his vulnerability could put the entire impeachment at risk. If the hundred pounds was an old Pennsland debt come back to haunt the lawyer, Olanthes would be angry.

But it could also be something worse.

On the street, he found the man in the brown coat and yellow stockings easily. He sauntered after him straight down the cobblestones toward the Market Street Wharf, whistling past streetlamps designed by the old Lightning Bishop himself. And then Yellow Stockings stopped, abruptly, beside a news-paper seller.

The man hawking papers yelled his top news stories in a loud voice, and in rhyme, apparently to attract interest. Perhaps for the same reason, he also wore a powdered white perruque, distinctly at odds with his sagging britches and scuffed shoes. "The chevalier refuses to appear!" he cried. "Lord Thomas's wedding draws very near! The Lightning Cathedral fix is dear!"

Yellow Stockings produced a penny and took a newspaper. Olanthes looked the other way and walked past. He tried to watch from the corner of his eye, and for a moment was able to see the man standing in place, surveying the street over the top of his cheap news sheet. The man was checking to see whether he was being followed.

Olanthes turned right at the next corner. When he was out of sight he stopped, sitting on a bench underneath a spreading sugar maple, and waited for Yellow Stockings to reappear.

He didn't.

Cursing under his breath, Olanthes rushed back the

other way. If only he had the gift of gramarye Queen Sarah had, he would transmute his face into something unrecognizable and follow the man with confidence.

He reached the news-paper-man, and saw no sign of Yellow Stockings.

He quickly searched the street; there were buildings here the man might have entered, including a print shop (likely where the news-paper was printed), a dressmaker's shop, a bookseller, an ironmonger, and an apothecary. Scanning the windows, Olanthes saw the man in none of them.

Across the street, though, a brick lane ran perpendicular away from the avenue, between the ironmonger and a private residence. Olanthes strode purposefully, and as quickly as he could, across the street and down that lane. He passed a stable and a kennel, both surrounded by other buildings and without presence on a main street; he passed the back side of two brick tenement houses, nearly windowless and four stories tall, and then a warehouse.

When he emerged out the other end of the lane, he stood on a different street, beside a fishmonger, and across from a butcher and a baker. The street was narrow and crooked, and Olanthes couldn't see farther than a hundred feet in either direction, but he did see the mouths of at least three more alleyways.

And no sign of Yellow Stockings.

He ran. It surrendered any advantage of stealth he might have, but he rushed to the opening of each alley to look down it, and then into each of the shops, and a few hundred feet up the street in both directions, all to no avail.

"Cotton price is high!" A man waving a news-paper

in his hands bellowed. "Storms in the western sky! Wedding bells are nigh!"

Olanthes snorted. The news-paper-man, a heavyset fellow with a black patch over one eye and filthy hands, snorted back at him.

Olanthes turned to go past the stables and kennels to the house. He'd need to find a stationer to replace the envelope he'd torn open; whatever the right and wrong of it was, he didn't want Logan Rupp to know he'd torn the envelope off Logan's letter.

The filthy envelope.

That had stained Olanthes's hand with ink.

He dug a penny from his pocket and went back to the news-paper-man crying about cotton prices.

"Not too good for me after all, eh?" The news-seller grunted. He held out a news-paper. "Just for you being saucy, this will be tuppence."

Olanthes looked at the man's hand. It wasn't dirty, it was stained with ink smudges. The paper, too, had smudged ink—perhaps the sellers took the papers down from their drying racks too eagerly, before the ink had dried.

"In that case," Olanthes said, "never mind."

The news-paper-man grunted a retraction and a reaffirmed one-penny price and something that might have been close to an apology, but it was too late— Olanthes was charging back up the alleyway down which he'd come.

He found the first news-paper-man, standing and bellowing about the cost of renovations to the Lightning Cathedral. He stood, as Olanthes had correctly remembered, in front of a printer's shop.

Olanthes drew his sword and entered.

"Whoa, whoa!" A wide-bellied, droop-faced man setting type on a rectangular lead case stepped back from his work and raised both hands over his head. "If you're upset with something we said about you, sir, may I suggest an action for libel? Or even a formal duel under the code would be better than mayhem."

"Shut your mouth." Olanthes surveyed the room. One man wrote at a desk on blue-lined paper. Another set more type. A third seemed to be carving a woodcut blank. He didn't see Yellow Stockings. He didn't see the actual printing press, either. "Where is your press?"

"Sir," the man standing beside his type begged, "please. The sword."

Olanthes saw stairs leading down at the back of the shop. "The press is downstairs?" He pointed with his weapon.

"Please don't break the press," the man begged. "We just replaced it."

Olanthes switched his sword into his left hand and drew his pistol with his right. Really, neither was his preferred weapon; as a soldier, he was trained to fight with a spear, but carrying a pike around Philadelphia definitely would have attracted too much attention.

He descended the stairs, pistol first.

A large basement lay beneath the printer's shop, and here squatted the press itself, a great wooden loom with a handle that raised and lowered the pressing block down onto a tray of set type, and many overhead wires from which hung drying papers.

At the press stood Yellow Stockings, his back to Olanthes. As Olanthes crept up behind him, he finished painting ink over the tray of letters and then set the brush back into the pot. He lay a large sheet of paper over the type—

and Olanthes shoved him down onto the paper with his elbow.

Olanthes set down his pistol, grabbed the handle of the press, and pressed the weight down on Yellow Stockings's head.

Yellow Stockings screamed and flailed about. He grabbed the pistol Olanthes had set down and tried to aim it at Olanthes—

bang!

His shot went wide. Above, on the ground floor, Olanthes heard a scream.

"Good," Olanthes said grimly, "now I am fighting in self-defense." He raised the printing block again, and then dropped it on Yellow Stockings's head.

"What do you want?" Yellow Stockings hollered.

"Are you F.?" Olanthes switched his sword to his right hand and pressed the blade against the man's neck, keeping pressure on with the press.

"My name is Perkins! Get that off my head!"

Olanthes slapped the intercepted letter down onto the press in Perkins's sight. "Tell me why Logan Rupp owes you a hundred pounds, and I'll let you stand up!"

"Nothing! I don't know anything!"

Olanthes put some of his weight onto the press, carefully; he was afraid of cracking the man's skull.

"Yes, fine! I wrote him a letter! I wrote for him!"

Olanthes raised the press and hurled Yellow Stockings to the floor. He stood over the man with his naked sword in his hand. "Logan Rupp knows how to write for himself."

Yellow Stockings grunted and looked away.

"No one would pay a hundred pounds for a mere scribe," Olanthes continued. "Even if that scribe were learned, and, say translating, or composing. A hundred pounds is a fortune."

Yellow Stockings cast a sour eye on Olanthes and spat on the floor.

"A hundred pounds is blackmail money," Olanthes guessed. "You wrote a letter for him, but it wasn't as his amanuensis. *F. stands for forger.*"

"Will they care, if their dividends go up?"

CHAPTER TWELVE

Becoming one of the messengers of the Spanish army had been easy. Achebe had simply put himself in a line of messengers at a dispatch tent and received a message and directions to find its recipient. Then he had come back and taken a second message.

The third time he had picked up a message to deliver, the block-shouldered dispatcher with tiny hands had lambasted him for being out of uniform. Achebe had hemmed and hawed, the dispatcher had guessed that Achebe had lost his uniform, and then he'd given Achebe a white shirt, trousers, and cap.

Food and water were not a problem. On his errands, he was frequently standing beside full pots, laden messes, or quartermaster's wagons, and no one objected if he took a slice of bread or a bit of broiled fish or a ladleful of water. He couldn't eat a proper meal, but he could eat small amounts all day, and it was enough.

Sleeping was a small challenge. Not having a unit or a tent of his own, Achebe had to lie down wherever and whenever he could, to nap. He was frequently taken for a shirker, and many captains and sergeants bellowed or beat him to wakefulness, sending him back on his presumed way. He would have liked to creep away from the army and lie down in the forest, but he didn't want to be taken for a deserter—on his second day, he'd seen the army hang three deserters, sallow-faced men with their hair in topknots who had tried to get into a boat and paddle back to Mexica lands. He also didn't want to be eaten by alligators.

He wasn't on payroll, but otherwise, Achebe had effectively joined the Spanish army.

He learned quickly how to find the command tents. The army was a conglomeration of many nationalities—Aztecs, Jamaicans, Haitians, Spanish, Apaches, Pueblo, Celestials, Germans, French, and more—and each unit had to be commanded in its own language. A cluster of tents housing captains and advisors, standard bearers and musicians, was inevitably to be found somewhere near each nation's troops, and generally at the edge of their encampment, along the *carriles*. The *carriles* were lanes that the Spanish had laid out on a grid, packing them down with gravel or straw to create a network of paths by which commanders, as well as messengers like Achebe, could quickly move from any one part of the massive encampment to any other.

The chevalier had a tent, and it was with the command tents of a French brigade. Achebe was not sure where the Frenchmen came from—some sounded from their accent as if they might be Acadian mercenaries, some sounded as if they might be fighters from the Caliphate, and some spoke with a Louisiana accent, so it was possible that the brigade had been scraped together from various oddments. The French unit was camped near the center of the massed forces, a short walk from where the Spanish general had his tent and the tents of his adjutants and heralds. That meant that the area around the chevalier was always swarming with soldiers, French and Spanish alike. The chevalier was also accompanied everywhere he went by a squad of six gendarmes, burly New Orleans fighters with scarred hands and faces.

The more he got to know this massive army, the more astonishing Achebe Chibundu found the magic of the Eze-Nri. New Orleans's priest-king had summoned a curtain of flying serpents, and they held back whole nations of warriors. Somewhere to the north, Achebe heard soldiers and messengers say, the Spanish were building a bridge across the Mississippi. No man wanted to volunteer for the task of building; they said that on average a man could make three trips down to the river to throw in a stone or set a timber before he was bitten, and those who were bitten all died.

Corpses floated regularly down the Mississippi.

In addition to the basilisks, there were snipers on the eastern bank. Eggbert Bailey kept roving scouts moving among the trees, and they would shoot builders and their military guards alike. Still, the Spanish put up wooden screens and purchased slaves from the Comanches to do the labor and die, and continued to work, and slowly, a bridge was rising.

Achebe tried to get himself assigned messages for the chevalier by casually demonstrating his language abilities. He spoke French in front of the dispatcher whenever he could. Unfortunately, the dispatcher learned of Achebe's ability with Spanish even before he learned that Achebe could speak French, and there were many more messages that needed to be carried to Spanish speakers. Also, his proximity to the general's tents meant that the chevalier was in direct communication with overall command, and received few messengers.

On a morning of scattered rain, the opportunity came.

"*Para el caballero di Luisiana*," the dispatcher said, handing Achebe a sealed envelope. "*Atención, Lucifer, que esté es un hombre soberbio, y no da propinas.*"

Achebe took the message and ran.

His plan was simple. He would contrive to get into the chevalier's presence, and then he would break the man's neck. This would be no wrestling match, with posturing beforehand and rules to restrain the fighters' moves. He would attack without warning, and he would kill the man. After that, whether Achebe lived or died did not matter.

He would do it for the Eze-Nri, and all the good the man and his mighty gods had done for the city, and Achebe's chi approved his destiny.

He ran the *carriles* quickly until he came in view of the French encampment. Then he slowed down and watched closely as he approached. It would be a waste of an opportunity if the chevalier was away from his tent, and some underling insisted on receiving the envelope in his place. But the Chevalier of New Orleans stood in front of his assembled men. They stood at rest and focused on him, laughing as he spoke, in good humor despite the rain.

Achebe ran past the French command tents. He lapped a Spanish unit and a German artillery corps,

whose role so far in this assault had been to keep
their long guns oiled and underneath tarpaulins so
they didn't rust. He reached the French camp again
in time to see the chevalier pulling aside the white
canvas flap to enter his tent.

Achebe slowed to a quick walk and approached
the tent. Two of the chevalier's six bodyguards stood
at attention, one on either side of the entrance. They
glared at Achebe with indifference; unarmed, he did
not appear to be a threat. He raised the envelope and
risked a phrase the dispatcher had not said to him.

"*Pour les yeux du chevalier.*"

The two guards didn't so much as grunt an acknowledgement, but neither did they try to stop Achebe.
He lifted the flap and passed into the tent.

The chevalier stood over a folding wooden table.
On the table lay a map, which might be New Orleans,
since it showed a city with water on two sides. The
chevalier leaned over the chart with a pencil in his
hand, annotating a section of the map. No one else
was in the tent; a second table held unlit lanterns, a
telescope, rolled-up charts, and a large block of cheese.

"*Pour vous, monsieur,*" Achebe said. He lay the
letter down on the table and stepped aside, putting
himself nearly in the corner of the tent.

"*Attend-il une réponse?*" the chevalier asked.

"*Je crois que oui.*"

The chevalier turned his back on Achebe and picked
up the letter.

Achebe attacked. He reached forward to grab the
chevalier's head in both hands, but at the last moment,
the chevalier stepped backward. Achebe's hands were too
low to do what he wanted; instead, he snaked his arms

under the Frenchman's shoulders and then reached up to interlace his fingers behind the man's head.

"*Assassin!*" the chevalier cried. "*Je suis trahi!*"

When Achebe's skin touched the chevalier's garment, he burned. The coat did not change in color, and no flames were visible, but Achebe felt as if flaming oil had been sprayed across his chest and arms, and also onto his chin, where it was pressed into the fine wool of the coat.

He pushed the chevalier's head forward, trying to snap the man's neck that way, but the chevalier had strong neck and shoulder muscles, and he resisted. So Achebe pushed with his legs, leaping forward and up in order to bring his weight all crashing down—

smacking the chevalier's face into the table.

The tent flap was thrown open and men were rushing inside. There were the scarred bodyguards, but there were other men as well, men Achebe didn't recognize.

The Frenchman avoided losing an eye to an inkpot sitting on the map, and then both men fell to the dirt floor. Grunting in pain, the chevalier rolled to one side, getting Achebe underneath him.

Some of the men coming in looked like priests, or wizards.

Achebe let go of the chevalier's neck with his left hand. He reached around to claw out the chevalier's eyes—

"*Dormi!*" one of the priests shouted.

Achebe and his chi resisted. A wave of fatigue washed over him, but he blazed with energy and he was needled with pain, and he fought off the urge to sleep. He missed the chevalier's eye and dug his fingernails into the skin of the man's face.

Gaspard le Moyne shrieked in rage as Achebe tore bloody furrows down his cheek and jaw. Achebe laughed defiantly.

"*Dormi!*" the priest shouted again.

Achebe collapsed.

"You believe this is a place we can find help?" Montse asked.

The Catalan smuggler queen had confided the defense of Cahokia's Mississippi flank to other captains and insisted on coming. With the river rising and nothing but occasional beastkind swimming across, defending the city's western side was mere police action, and her skills might be necessary in the Ohio. She had left her flamboyant hat and coat in Cahokia, and was dressed as a keelboatman, her copper hair tied behind her head. She still wore a fighting knife on her hip, but her saber and pistols lay under a stretch of canvas.

Luman was also dressed as a keelboatman, in baggy cotton shirt and canvas pants, with light sandals on his feet. His magician's coat, in which he kept his ritual athame, his peep-stone, and all the accouterments he had used to practice magic before the goddess had given him the greater gift of gramarye, lay under the same canvas with Montse's weapons. Luman, he himself believed, was a particularly unconvincing keelboatman, but he had also felt his muscles harden in their days of poling down the Mississippi and up the Ohio.

They pulled the keelboat up to a Parkersburg dock and tied it in place. Miqui was the only other Catalan on board—it wouldn't do to look like smugglers—and the other boatmen were Ohio Germans, warriors borrowed from the entourage of the King of Talamatan. They had the muscles to be boatmen, and handled the poles well, but didn't sing hearty German songs as Luman expected real keelboatmen would.

The Imperial and Dutch Ohio Company boats that had stopped them hadn't noticed the singing. Instead, both boats had inspected Luman's forged bill of lading— forged with the aid of his gramarye, and claiming that their boat had come from New Orleans—and all their forged passports, poked through the cotton cargo, examined the crew for the presence of Firstborn by pressing a shiny Imperial shilling into each person's cheek, charged an on-the-spot tariff, and let them go.

"This is a Hansa town," Luman said.

"You are not Hansa." This was a conversation they had had twice before already, nearly word for word.

"I have met the Hansard in charge of this town," Luman said. "And I have reason to believe he can be persuaded to help us. If he doesn't try to kill me instead, that is."

"You don't want to simply put the kings under our bales of cotton and push off?"

"We have to get to the kings first. I think the Hansa can help us do that."

Parkersburg was a chaotic merchant town; the section close to the docks consisted entirely of warehouses and office buildings. Luman remembered where he had been on his previous visit, and walked toward the office of Reuben Clay. Montse came at his side, and they stepped out of the mud onto the boardwalk together.

Notwithstanding Schmidt had knocked once and entered without waiting. Luman knocked and stood back, hands clasped before him.

"You are certain you don't want to be armed?" Montse asked.

"I'm *not* certain," Luman admitted. "But on balance, I think it's the best idea."

Reuben Clay opened the door. He looked unchanged, bull neck and receding hairline combining to give him the general appearance of a burly thumb. He took one look at Luman and laughed. "Oh, it's the bat-killer. Remind me your name. Truman? Schumann?"

"Luman Walters."

"Walters. Have you come back to show me that you've moved on to kittens now?"

"That's reasonable," Luman admitted. "I want you to know, first off, that I am no longer with the Imperial Ohio Company."

"Imperial and Dutch Ohio Company," Clay said. "They're operating together, pending completion of the merger, the day after the emperor's wedding. Don't you read the news-papers? Mind you, once Thomas has all their money, he'll change the name right back to the Imperial Ohio, and the Dutch will realize they've given up everything. Stupid Dutch."

"Will they care, if their dividends go up?" Luman asked.

Clay shrugged. "How long will they get dividends? And if you think your friend Schmidt can't figure out five hundred ways to benefit Thomas Penn without actually paying out a dividend to all the shareholders, you're still wet behind the ears. I give 'em eighteen months at most before they're back in court."

Montse spat on the boardwalk. "This is why I prefer to work alone."

"Well, as I said, I'm not with the company," Luman

said. "And really, I was never master of the talk of dividends and margins, in any case."

"You looking for a job, wizard?" Reuben Clay fixed him with a rivet-like stare. "Parkersburg's already got a wizard, and anyway, if I told people what happened last time you and I met, I'd have to string you up."

"I won't call *that* fair," Luman said. "But I believe it."

"I'm not done yet," Clay said. "Why don't you introduce your friend, and I'll show you something?"

"I am no one special," Montse said.

Clay squinted. "Well, for starters, from your accent I'm guessing that in your head you said *ningú especial*. You're a long way from the Gulf, *senyora*."

Montse inclined her head. "My name is Montserrat Ferrer i Quintana, and of late, I have made my home in the Ohio."

Reuben Clay whistled. "Are you telling me the *Verge Caníbal* is docked at Parkersburg?"

"I did not think I was so famous."

"Among smugglers, you are. What are you doing with this wizard, then?"

"We are both in the service of the Queen of Cahokia," Montse said. "The daughter of Hannah Penn."

"Ah." Clay's eyes widened and he nodded. "Well, step inside. Before we do any business, there's something I have to show you, to make the terms of our engagement absolutely clear."

Luman felt queasy, but he entered, and Montse followed. The office looked unchanged, except that a wardrobe stood in the back corner of the room. It was easily eight feet tall and five feet wide, with no visible drawers at the bottom and double doors in the front, both shut.

"Last time you were here," Clay said, "you threatened me."

Luman wanted to object that technically, Director Schmidt had done all the threatening, but he didn't think it would help. He kept a serious face and paid attention.

"You also bribed me," Clay continued. "I was to starve the Adenans, and therefore also pick the pockets of my own traders, but in return I was to get some douceurs from all my bottom-dollar sales to the empire. Is that how you recall the deal, Walters?"

"Yes," Luman admitted.

"And you left a fellow behind to keep an eye on me, didn't you?" Clay grinned. "A fellow who was a hell of a knife fighter."

"I think his name was Oldham." Luman felt sick. "Ira Oldham."

"Ira Oldham," Reuben Clay said. "That's right."

He opened the wardrobe door. Inside stood the body of Ira Oldham. It was immediately apparent that this was the corpse, and not the living man, because it stood still and its skin had gone a shade of gray. Its arms and legs were lumpy. Luman smelled formaldehyde—an odor he knew well, having encountered it in more than one magician's laboratory. Ira Oldham's eyelids were sewn shut, and long straws poked out between his lashes.

Luman's gorge rose in his throat.

"*Bonic*," Montse said. "*Heu après dels espanyols, o dels musulmans?*"

"I'm afraid I don't actually speak the patois, Quintana." Clay grinned.

Montse turned a chair around to face the wardrobe

and sat. "So we see you are serious. If we cross you, you will have us stuffed."

Clay nodded.

"Do you wish us to prove that *we* are serious, also?" she asked.

"I believe you are serious, Capità. And if Luman Walters was willing to walk in here unarmed, and able to bring you with him . . . I suppose that means he's serious, too." Reuben Clay crossed the room and lowered himself into the chair behind his desk. Montse turned her chair, and Luman sat. "Now I expect you'd better tell me what it is we're all being so serious *about*."

"The kings of Adena and Koweta are trapped," Luman said. "We need to get them out."

Reuben Clay shook his head. "You're talking to the wrong fellow. If you need to win a fight on the docks, or to break down a warehouse, I can gather up the kind of men needed to do that. I don't have an army."

"We don't need to raise any sieges," Montse explained. "We need to bring the kings out, and bring them to Cahokia."

"Do they want to be brought out?" Clay took a toothpick from a cup standing on the corner of his desktop and began to probe beneath the molars on the right side of his mouth. "Or are we talking about kidnapping?"

"Something in between, perhaps," Luman said. "We've had no answer to our messages, so we think the messages never arrived. We need to get to the kings and then persuade them to come with us."

"And if they don't want to come?" Clay asked.

Luman looked at Montse and saw resolve in her eyes. "I suppose I'd be up for a little kidnapping."

The smuggler queen nodded.

Clay leaned back in his chair and picked at his teeth while he thought. "You're in luck," he finally said. "It so happens that after Mr. Oldham and I disagreed on contract terms and I ended our arrangement, I came to an arrangement with some other customers. They are . . . Adenan patriots, and I supply them food."

"Adena has cash to pay you?" Montse asked.

"Adena has resources with which to *get* cash."

"Can you put us in touch with these patriots?" Luman asked. "Obviously, this is risky, and we expect to pay for your services."

Reuben Clay smiled. "Oh, you'll pay."

Cathy Filmer had volunteered for this journey, hoping it would take her mind off her marriage. She had also hoped that it would take her mind off the Lady Alena, and the fact that four of the seven Ladies of Tendance were aligned in a phalanx that was opposed to Cathy's presence, and had described her as "corruption." Likely, that meant that four of the seven septs were being purged of Handmaids with any sympathy for Cathy. Would she ever be able to return?

If Sarah recovered, she would. Sarah had always been unequivocally on Cathy's side, had brought her into her council meetings when she had no official portfolio, as Sarah's personal counselor, and had commanded her ordination to the priesthood of the goddess once she ascended. The seven Ladies of Tendance were, doctrinally speaking, peers, each ruling the needs of the day to which she was assigned, but in practice, as the holder of Sarah's ear, Cathy had held much sway.

She would hold such sway again. When Sarah recovered, she would restore Cathy, and Lady Alena's partisans, with their supernumerary vows, their obsession with blood, and their practice of being served by eunuchs, could recede back into their ordinary position as one of a number of different groups and views that were woven together to make Cahokia's sacred tapestry.

The only thing Cathy could do was complete her undertaken mission—persuade the King of Oranbega to come to Cahokia. And still, she could not stop thinking about the Lady Alena.

And Bill. Sweet Jesus, Bill.

Was her lover—now her husband—William Lee somewhere out here in the Ohio? He'd ridden out the city's eastern gate, but he could easily have turned north or south. Still, she dreamed of encountering him on the road, dreamed that he would forgive her and then she would forgive him.

And Landon?

The rains of spring had not given way to summer sun. Rain continued to fall, and to race across the countryside propelled by gales and accented by lightning bolts. Frequently, Cathy and her party passed the signs of recent fires, ignited by lightning storms that raged back and forth across the Ohio. The great mercy of the rain was that it put out the fires.

The earth continued to shake, the tremors not diminishing as they rode away from Cahokia. Regularly, at least twice but as often as four or five times a day, the ground rattled from its bed, sometimes knocking over trees and houses.

Given the devastation caused by the storms and

the earthquakes, it was difficult at times to spot the impact of the Pacification ... but it was there. Cathy saw it in burned and abandoned buildings, and in fields trampled by Imperial troops and cropped to the ground by Imperial horses. She heard it in the voices of refugees, who claimed that in the east—but coming this direction—the empire had fielded strange creatures, troops out of legend, walking men made of wood or clay or the corpses of the dead.

Cathy and her party—Zadok Tarami and the Podebradan Yedera—carried passports, but Luman Walters had forged them. Rather than rely on their false documents, they hoped never to meet any Imperial official who would ask to see them. To that end, they planned to stay off the Imperial pikes and away from the Free Imperial Towns, and they therefore rode east on the Onandagos Road. It was straight enough for their purposes, running generally north and west across the Ohio toward the border of Talega and Oranbega, where the city of Oranbega stood, on the shores of Lake Erie.

It also had the virtues that it was too small a path to accommodate a military force of any size, which meant the empire's troops shouldn't be marching on it. Further, its smooth circular paving stones held up well against the mud and the rain.

"Mrs. Lee," Zadok Tarami said quietly. "We have reached the first of the crosses of the earth."

For a moment, Cathy didn't realize that Zadok was talking to her. Then she was grateful that the rain, her broad-brimmed Pennslander hat, and the woolen scarf around her face conspired to conceal her blush.

"Perhaps it is best to call me Mrs. Filmer for now."

She felt the weight of the dead man's name as she never had before, an anchor chained to her hopes and to her soul. "Or Cathy, even better."

"Cathy," Zadok said.

"What river is this?" she asked. The watercourse in question was gray-brown and dimpled with rain; it was clearly far over its ordinary depth, because Cathy could see the tops of trees emerging from what appeared to be the middle of the river. More poignantly, on the other side of the flood, she saw two rooftops protruding from the dark waters. One was a thatched roof similar to many she'd seen in Cahokia, and the other appeared to be a shingled barn.

"The Kaskaskia," Zadok said. "It is an old Illiniwek name, and we shall have to cross the river imminently. But first, behold the cross."

Cathy turned and saw what he wished her to look at: beside them rose a hill. As once before at Irra-Zostim, what at first glance appeared to her to be the work of nature, a hill covered in green grass, with trees climbing halfway up its height, quickly resolved itself into a work of artifice. The hill was too steep, too conical, and too regular to be natural.

"The cross is at its peak?" Cathy asked.

Zadok nodded.

Cathy spurred her horse up the side of the mound. She wore Turkish pantaloons for the journey—they might not accord with the fashion for women, in Cahokia or elsewhere in the empire, but they allowed her to grip her mount with her knees. She had a brocaded dress packed in her traveling back, but she intended to wear it only for the event of her presentation to the King and Queen of Oranbega.

The ascent was difficult. Weeks of rain had loosened the sod, so the horse's hooves sometimes found purchase, but sometimes gouged out long, muddy troughs, the sudden appearance of which sent the beast sliding back downhill, neighing its disconcertion. Cathy was a Virginian, and though her father had had only small holdings of land, he had raised horses. She kept the saddle, and the beast stayed upright, and after several tries, she reached the top of the mound.

Lightning flashed, falling to ground below her and far away as if she had thrust herself up into the storm itself. The storm hung like a skillet, black as iron where not illuminated by electric flashes, immediately over Cathy's head. The wildness, the elemental fury of the storm, whipped Cathy's breath away.

It whipped her hat with her breath. The black hat's broad brim caught the wind like a sail and went flying out over the woods below. Yedera, wearing scale mail under a heavy cloak, urged her horse toward the knot of trees into which the hat had disappeared. Zadok struggled to help, but he had all the horsemanship skills of a one-eyed rooster, and his mount carried him away to a stand of elms for shelter.

The wind whipped something else from Cathy, though she couldn't have said what. It felt as if she might be scoured away, or struck by lightning, and in that moment, those fears made her feel *young* and *simple*.

She laughed.

In the center of the flat top of the mound, a cross was carved into the earth. Its arms and legs were of equal length, each six feet long, which made it appear mathematical rather than Christian, and it was white. The turf that was cut away revealed a layer beneath that was made of chalk, or perhaps someone filled the cross-shaped indentation with chalk. In the storm the chalk cross was nearly full of water, becoming a giant whitish-brown puddle.

Zadok Tarami's pilgrimage had involved lying in this indentation. Was there some prayer one said, or some story about Onandagos such a pilgrim was supposed to recite?

And what would one do in this spot, with the Earthshaker's Rod, that would still the rumbling of the earth?

She pulled a riding glove from one hand to feel the wet wind. The sensation sent shivers down her spine, leaving her feeling alive.

Yedera appeared at the top of the mound, on her horse, holding Cathy's hat in her hand. "You serve our queen poorly if you die of pneumonia before you ever reach Oranbega, Cathy." The Podebradan handed Cathy her hat.

Cathy covered her head, thinking of Bill's battered old dragoon hat, which he still wore. Somewhere in this rain, that shapeless bundle of felt was keeping water off Bill's head. "You're right," she agreed. "Let's get back on the road."

At the edge of the hill, though, she stopped. On the eastern horizon she saw fires. Moving among the fires, she saw tiny black dots.

"Why does that fire seem to crawl with ants?" she asked.

"That is no lightning strike." Yedera's voice trembled. "You see two burning towns. The movement may belong to the soldiers who burn them, or perhaps to the inhabitants, who flee."

They descended quickly, both horses neighing in near-panic as they skidded nearly a third the length of the mound. Resuming the muddy trail—where it emerged from beneath the cover of forest canopy, the Onandagos Road was a waterlogged track—they wound their way to the bank of the river.

Zadok Tarami stood up to his knees in water, in what must usually be a cornfield, speaking with the occupant of a flatboat. The boat had a single sail on a short mast, but it was tightly furled. In addition to the man Zadok spoke with, who was thin and white-haired and wore denim, two brawny young fellows in Firstborn tunics and wool pullover frocks stood at the back of the boat, leaning on poles.

"These men will give us passage," Zadok said.

The horses didn't board the boat calmly, but they boarded, and the boatmen began to pole. Zadok in particular struggled with his animal, and as the horse grew more agitated, the boat began to rock.

"Cover its eyes!" Cathy called. She wrapped her own scarf around her horse's eyes, whispering comforting words to the creature. Zadok tried, but his mount was too nervous, and drove him away with flashing hooves. Zadok stumbled and sat down on the flatboat's gunwale.

Cathy handed her reins to Yedera. "Easy," she called to Zadok's horse. "Rest easy, we'll have you on solid ground again in just a few minutes." The horse whinnied a protest, and Cathy shucked off her riding cloak. With soft protests from the horse, she wrapped its eyes, stroking its nose and chin and whispering to it as she did so.

Handling the horse led her mind inevitably and by

a very short road back to Bill. He was a horseman, a Cavalier like she was. He had spooked, like this horse had done.

But no, Bill had much more severe reason to bolt than the horse did.

Would she ever see him again?

A chicken coop floated past as Cathy was calming Zadok's mount. Swept right off its poles by the flooding river, the coop now drifted along on the brown water. One wall of the coop was propped up with a locking timber, and a dozen hens clucked anxiously within as they passed.

Finally, the beast relaxed. The slight twitching of its legs told Cathy it remained a bit nervous, but it stood still until they reached the far side of the flood.

Zadok took his horse's reins back as Cathy squeezed rain out of her cloak. "Thank you," the priest said. "One great advantage of undertaking the pilgrimage of the Onandagos. Road on foot is that one never has to worry about an agitated mount."

Cahokia had not had slums before the arrival of the refugees from Missouri, beginning six months earlier. It had been a small and orderly city within its Treewall, dotted with wells and parks and private orchards and gardens.

During the winter, the Missourians had taken refuge in buildings. The Basilica, the city's great royal chapel, had become a mass shelter, with the Missourians not even turned out during services, thanks to the expansive Christian heart of the Metropolitan. Great homes and some shops had provided similar service. Pavilions in some parks had had boards nailed to their sides to make them into improvised buildings, sometimes with earth heaped up around the walls and over the rooftop, in what seemed a caricature of the Ohio's characteristic style of architecture. Trellises had been woven through with withies or rope, to similar effect.

By spring, the city had seemed to reach an equilibrium. Deaths during the siege, and evacuations immediately afterward—many who had family in Appalachee or the Kentuck or Pennsland fled, hoping for a new life with their kin—had relieved some of the pressure, and Maltres Korinn had turned many parcels of public land into multifamily dwellings. Empty palaces were divided into apartments, pavilion mounds were given rows of neighbors, and Missourians threw up their own buildings, often in Appalachee fashion—heaps of rocks with boards over the top, maybe with turves laid over the timbers.

But then a second wave of refugees had arrived, a wave that had not yet ceased to strike. These new refugees had piled into the same parks and churches and private homes and new tenements that the old refugees were in. The Missourians and the Zomans had been awkward neighbors at best before, when each group occupied its own land, but now they fought for the same sleeping spaces and food and water, and the competition had led to bloodshed more than once.

Zomas had fallen under the personal attack of the Heron King. Gazelem Zomas—to his knowledge, the last surviving member of the city's great royal family, descended from the oldest son of Onandagos himself—had heard the story of the city's fall from multiple tongues, and only most recently from the Zoman outrider Naares Stoach.

The other tale that Stoach told was more horrifying still. The Heron King had a son who had lived, a son born to him of a New Orleans witch, a monstrous son who had eaten the flesh of his mother, and was being raised by a mad prophet to the beastmen, somewhere along the Missouri River.

Stoach had suggested that the Heron King's son (called Absalom, and not Peter Plowshare) should be in the control of Gazelem Zomas. That if Gazelem could master that creature, he could use it to gain power in Cahokia, and to restore his native land.

But Gazelem had no idea how to master the beast Absalom, and no desire to gain power in Cahokia.

Instead, he and Stoach were crawling the new slums of Cahokia.

Specifically, they were in a part of the city that was beginning to be called Riverside. This was an elegant name for an inelegant place; the Treewall had been damaged by assaulting beastkind on that side of the city, who had then poured through the gaps. In their savagery, they had flattened or burned many buildings. Close to the river as they were, they had been the warehouses and taverns and net-menders and carpenters who serviced the river trade. That trade was struggling to recover, given the flooding of the Mississippi, the constant lightning storms, and the Imperial restrictions on the Ohio, so refugees had moved in.

"She's called Auntie Bisha," the Zoman said. He was toothless despite being a young man, and his left arm ended in a stump just below his elbow. "You'll find her in there." He gestured with the stump toward a long heap of board, shingle, and turves, pierced here and there with dark openings.

"Thank you," Stoach said.

The night was dark with rain. The occasional lightning flashes gave illumination to the Zomans' feet; the rain and wind were too strong for most lanterns.

"A coin or a crust, hetar?" the one-handed man asked. Gazelem gave him an iron coin, and the Zoman slipped away, toward buildings that remained standing, and a tavern called *Mimir's Well*.

As they approached the ramshackle building, Gazelem saw dim orange gleams peeping through the nearest opening. He checked his knives to reassure himself, and then ducked into the tottering pile.

Immediately, he smelled the sour stink of an unwashed body and the rank odor of rotten teeth. A man grabbed him by the front of his tunic and brandished a knife, waving it back and forth. "This squat belongs to the Dirty Cutters!"

Beyond the Dirty Cutter stretched a narrow hallway, with ramshackle doors exiting on both sides at uneven intervals. Rain thumped on the shingles just over Gazelem's head and the floor was mud. An orange fire somewhere back in the labyrinth threw out oscillating glows and unpredictable shadows.

"I'm not interested in your street gang," Gazelem hissed. "Unhand me!"

"Or what?" the thug wanted to know.

Naares Stoach exploded over Gazelem's shoulder. He punched the gangster in the throat, the stomach, and the nose, before finally landing a blow between the eyes. The Dirty Cutter dropped his knife to the mud and sank to his knees. Stoach drew a knife.

"Don't kill him, Captain," Gazelem said. "He may be able to tell us what we need to know."

"Ngh . . . ngh?" the Dirty Cutter warbled.

"Auntie Bisha," Gazelem said.

The thug pointed to a doorway down the hall. Stoach pushed him, and he fell over.

Two more men appeared in darkened doorways, each with a short cudgel in hand. At the sight of Naares Stoach stomping up the hallway in his lacquered red wooden armor, they faded quickly back into the shadow. Stoach peered into the indicated door, then stepped aside, drawing his sword.

"I'll stand guard," the outrider said.

Gazelem had to stoop to enter this room. Inside, a short, fat tallow flickered, sitting on a clay dish in a high angle of the room. Its uncertain light revealed a sofa, with one leg missing and the sofa leaning instead on a boulder the size of a man's head. Gazelem couldn't be sure of the sofa's color, but he thought it might be green. On a single plank that served as a shelf sat various oddments of the sort an occult practitioner might use—a shrunken head, organs in a jar, colored powders.

On the sofa lay a woman. She was bone thin, small, and frail looking, with deep bags of wrinkled surplus skin on her elbows, cheeks, and neck. Her hair was white, other than a black streak running back from her left temple, and she had the tattoos around her lips that were the sign of her profession. She murmured, as if talking in a dream. In her hands she clutched a jug—Gazelem could smell the cheap corn liquor. Corn alcohol was not a Zoman craft, but it was common enough in Missouri.

Better that the two tribes of refugees trade with each other than fight over territory.

He pulled a sack from his belt that he had brought for the purpose and scooped all the Ghostmaster's visible possessions into it, including the jug, which he carefully stoppered using a cork he found on the floor. Kneeling, he tried to wake Auntie Bisha.

"Leave me alone," she murmured. "I only want peace."

He hoisted her over his shoulder; she was light, but carrying her forced Gazelem to shuffle out the doorway with his knees nearly touching the mud. He got turned around in the hall and walked past several chambers before he could find an exit from the building. He saw a cooking pot, and could barely smell squash and venison over the stink of unwashed men and women. He saw a string of three men with slave collars on, staring up at him through filthy faces—but whose slaves were they? The law of Zomas was that only the king owned slaves, but Zomas had fallen. Would these Zomans say the slaves belonged to Queen Sarah? To the building and its occupants? To individual owners, in the Cahokian fashion?

To Gazelem, as rightful king of Zomas?

He felt relief when he staggered from the heap and was able to inhale rain-scented fresh air. The Ghostmaster shrieked as water struck her, and then Stoach threw his cloak over her.

"What's that?" Gazelem asked the outrider. With his left arm he held the Ghostmaster pinned to his shoulder; with his right hand, he pointed to a light that bobbed and skittered through the darkness, running down toward the Memphis Gate.

"It might have nothing to do with us," Stoach said. Gazelem nodded, trying to find words to explain why he cared. "Captain," he finally said, "my family's city has fallen. Its lands are filled with monsters. If there is a Zomas still, it can only be in these people."

"These people, like the Dirty Cutters."

"Yes. And so Zomas only survives because Cahokia and its walls still stand."

"You're worried that someone running with a light to the gate in the middle of the night might signify treason."

"I'm *curious.*" Ghostmaster still on his shoulder, Gazelem followed the light. He heard Stoach take a deep breath and then follow.

They followed the light south through the city, and right to the edge of the Treewall. At Sarah's insistence, her soldiers had kept a band of earthy fifty feet wide inside the wall free of any construction, no matter what the needs of the refugees—this gave soldiers a space to maneuver in, when the wall needed to be reinforced.

And in this spot, that band of clear earth encompassed an old, worn mound, crowned by seven crooked stones.

A cluster of figures stood on the mound. As Gazelem arrived, the light was snuffed out. Gazelem and Stoach hid behind the corner of the nearest building, somewhat protected from the hammering of the rain by a long thatch overhang. The silhouettes, some ten or twelve of them, sang a wordless melody, and then he heard the panicked cries of birds.

"This is a sacrifice," Stoach said.

"I can smell the blood," Gazelem agreed.

"Let's get out of here."

Gazelem let himself be led back toward his house.

His mind raced, thinking about the questions he needed to ask the Ghostmaster, the furtive sacrifice he had almost witnessed, and the fact that the light, just before it had been put out, had clearly illuminated to him the face of the Lady Alena.

"They are to be eaten."

———◆———

CHAPTER THIRTEEN

Ferpa woke Chigozie. The Still Waters became very dark at night under the best of circumstances, but the relentless rain crashing through the narrow slit of sky left the ravine pitch black, except for occasional lightning flashes. Chigozie recognized Ferpa primarily by her bovine smell.

"Shepherd," she murmured. "Shepherd, Absalom is gone."

Chigozie forced himself up and out of the void in which he had been drifting. The humid air of the Still Waters made sleep comfortable and languorous, so to bring himself to full wakefulness he stood, slapping his own cheeks.

Several of the beastkind waited behind Ferpa, making small sounds of agitation: snorting, hoofs pawing at the wet earth, uneasy whinnying.

"Where's Kort?" Chigozie asked.

"Following Absalom."

Chigozie scooped up his hat and furs. "Take me."

He had no answer to the challenge of Absalom. He

had prayed, he had conferred with the Merciful, and the best answers always seemed to be that they must either kill the Heron King's child or they must continue to live with Absalom, in fear, doing their best to teach him patience, kindness, and mercy. If they cast him out, they feared, he would surely become wild, and wreak a bloody trail through some settlement of mankind.

Ferpa took Chigozie down to the Missouri. In flashes of lightning, she showed him the remains of a camp on a wet, forested slab of earth rising above the water—a small fire hidden behind large stones and in a thicket, scraps of discarded food, fresh wood chips from someone's whittling.

"I see Kort's tracks," Chigozie said. "And Absalom's. They go downriver. But I don't see more tracks of the men."

"They were in boats," Ferpa told him. "They stopped here late last night, and we kept an eye on them. When Absalom slipped free of us, Kort ran to warn them."

"Perhaps the warning arrived in time," Chigozie said.

"Perhaps." Ferpa didn't sound convinced.

They followed the tracks, the rain slapping Chigozie's cheeks and his hands. They tried to stay above the river, for ground that was firm, if not dry. The Missouri was flooding, and the slopes leading down into it were slippery and treacherous.

Was Chigozie mistaken, after all, about Absalom? Did Absalom have a nature that was unredeemable, savage and bloody without exception?

Chigozie feared that possibility, though he wasn't entirely sure why. Perhaps because, if Absalom was in truth only a wild animal, despite his powers of speech, then maybe Kort and Ferpa and all the others were also in truth nothing more than beasts. The thought made Chigozie look over his shoulder at the beastkind following him, and shudder.

Bang! A gunshot shattered Chigozie's thoughts, followed by a scream.

He tried to run, but the ground sucked at his boots and slowed him. Ferpa scooped him up into her arms, and sprinted into the storm. Chigozie heard further gunshots as Ferpa raced into a stand of trees along the river's edge, and a bellow that told him that Kort was charging to the attack, and then Ferpa set him down.

He could see nothing. "Absalom! Absalom, stop!"

He heard an immense *crack*. Lightning flashed, and he saw Kort and Absalom clearly illuminated. The big beastman had the Heron King's son in a wrestler's grip, head to head and shoulder to shoulder, his arms wrapped around Absalom and trying to draw him in closer.

Absalom's beak and talons were red with blood.

Darkness fell and Kort roared in rage and pain.

Bang! In a brief gunpowder flash, Chigozie saw a man in a long leather coat, with a long, thick black beard, firing his pistol at Absalom and Kort. Then *bang!*, he fired a second pistol. Kort was on his knees, and Absalom savagely struck the bison-headed beastman in the shoulder with his beak.

"Stop shooting!" Chigozie tried to run toward the gunman, but in the darkness and the mud he slipped, falling onto his face.

Beastkind rushed past Chigozie. He heard Ferpa's mooing and then a wild screech of protest from Absalom. The squelching thuds of running in all directions, and then Chigozie heard splashing.

"Kort?" Chigozie found he was crying.

"I am here." The big beastman's voice was a pained grunt.

"The others?"

"They pursue Absalom. They will not catch him. He has become too fast for us."

"Who are you?" a third voice demanded. It was a man, and from his accent he sounded New Muscovite.

"Don't shoot anymore," Chigozie pleaded. "We came to try to protect you."

"Protect me?" Muttered curses. "Boris? Mikhail? Alexei?"

Silence.

"I have a lamp. If you are as friendly as you say, then stay where you are while I light it."

Chigozie stood. He shivered from the cold mud that had gotten inside his furs and from the rain that pelted his face. In a flash of lightning, he saw the bearded man working the shutter on a storm lantern, and then the light came on.

The New Muscovite shouted something unintelligible and drew a long knife with a talon point. "The beast is still here, beware!" he shouted to Chigozie.

"No!" Chigozie sloshed through the mud to put himself between the bearded man and Kort. "This is my friend. He saved you."

Kort sagged on his knees, chin slumped to his chest, blood spilling from his shoulder.

The New Muscovite frowned. He looked about him, and Chigozie saw now four canoes, each laden with a long bundle wrapped in gray oilcloth. He also saw three dead men, all bearded and wearing long coats. One had large gashes in his chest, the second was headless, and the third had been torn limb from limb, so thoroughly destroyed that Chigozie was only certain there was a third dead man because he could see six boots on dead feet.

"*Pizdá*," the New Muscovite muttered. "What was that monster?"

"Do you have a bandage?" Chigozie asked. "My friend is bleeding."

The bearded man kicked open an oilcloth bundle and tossed Chigozie two shirts. "Friend? You have beastman friends? And was that beastman who attacked me also your friend, then?"

"I am friends with the Merciful," Chigozie said. "Kort here was among the first of the Merciful. And the . . . creature . . . who attacked you was no beastman." It wounded him to say *creature*, rather than *person*. "That was the son of the Heron King."

"*Pizdá*." The New Muscovite shook his head, then gently kicked the decapitated corpse. "Damn you, Boris, I would have happily cheated you out of your share of the profits, but I never wanted to see you go this way."

Chigozie wrapped Kort's wounds, which were more numerous than he had been able to see before. Once he had a bandage around the largest of the gashes, he applied direct pressure with his hand. "You're a merchant?"

"Yes. My name is Yevgeny Bykov. Bykov, ha, it means the bull! Like your merciful friend here. And thank you, Mr. Merciful. For saving me, I am grateful."

"Kort," Kort murmured.

"Mr. Kort."

"Are the people of New Muscovy not aware of the rampaging of the beastkind?" Chigozie asked. "The Missouri River is unsafe."

"Except for you, huh? But yes, we have seen the

beastkind rampage, as you say. That is why we expected large profits from this voyage."

"What are you selling?" Chigozie nodded at the nearest oilcloth bundle.

"Ah, you want to be cut in for a share, do you?" Yevgeny licked his lips. "Well, I'm not as hopeless as I may appear. I could hide some of my goods here, and make multiple trips. Or I could pull three canoes behind me, like a mule train, so you see, I have possibilities. And also, I have accomplished most of the journey at this point, so if you were to join me, I could only reasonably offer you a very small portion of the profits. Say, a twentieth share."

Kort snorted. "And when Absalom returns to you?"

"The monster is named Absalom, huh?" Yevgeny rubbed his hands together. "Well, you make a good point. What do you say to a tenth share? It is a short journey from here to Cahokia, and if I cannot sell there, then upriver to Chicago is not so far. If we have to go to Chicago, then a one-eighth share."

"No. We are not merchants," Chigozie said.

"Huh. Then what do you say to accompanying me as friends?"

"What are you selling?" Kort asked.

The Muscovite trader's eyes sparkled. "What do people under attack need? What do they need so much, that they will pay extra, enough to compensate me for the costs and risks of a long and dangerous voyage? What would keep without spoiling for the entire trip from New Muscovy to Chicago?"

"Guns," Chigozie said.

Yevgeny spread his arms wide, nodded, and then clapped his hands together.

Ferpa entered the circle of yellow lantern light. She was soaked, but not injured. Behind her, Chigozie saw the shadowy outlines of the other Merciful.

"Absalom escaped," Kort said.

Ferpa nodded.

"We must follow him and bring him home," Chigozie said.

"We must follow him." Kort put a hand over his wound and stood. "I do not know whether it is wise to bring him home. Perhaps it is wise to give him the mercy of death. Perhaps this will be mercy to all he would otherwise encounter."

Chigozie refused to let himself make that decision yet. "In any case, we must follow him."

"One-third share," Yevgeny said. "Really, this is as high as I can go." He gestured at the three corpses. "You see how I already have to care for three widows, not to mention the orphans. Alexei alone had nine children, by three different women, the rotten bastard."

"If we ... deal with ... Absalom," Chigozie said, "we will come try to find you and be certain of your safety. I'm sorry, that's all we can do."

"And if this Absalom deals with you instead? What then, huh?"

Chigozie could only nod. "Before we go, we will help you bury your friends."

Nathaniel heard his sister Sarah's voice, from far away. "I must find a place to ... *ride*," he told Margaret. He needed better words for describing what he did when he left his body to travel the starlit plain.

Margaret scowled. "So I'm to be left again."

"Makwa is here if you need him."

"Are you going to be attacked?" Margaret's question was fierce and pointed. "Do I have to risk my life again, and kill again, to save you?"

"It's Sarah," Nathaniel murmured. "She sounds unwell."

Margaret kicked at a cobblestone and her nostrils flared, but she didn't object.

They left the plaza in front of Horse Hall, where Nathaniel had been examining the building and thinking about how to approach his uncle Thomas, and returned to their tiny rented room over a cobbler's.

Nathaniel lay on one of the two straw-tick mattresses in the corner, while Margaret threw her hat onto a tiny table and poured herself water from a pitcher. Nathaniel drummed himself up onto the starlit plain, and then rode toward the sound of his other sister's voice.

She sounded faint, and weak.

He followed the voice to the mounds of Cahokia, and up the tallest of the mounds. There he found a mosaic, set into grass; the image showed a golden serpent, wound around a tree with seven branches, against a blue background.

Sarah was nowhere in sight.

~*Sarah?*~ he called.

~*I'm here,*~ she said. ~*I can see you, though faintly.*~

~*Where is here?*~ he asked. ~*I don't see you at all.*~

~*I'm behind the veil,*~ she said. ~*I can't come out, and maybe that's why you don't see me. But I see you, standing on the other side of the curtain.*~

Nathaniel giggled. ~*This just gets stranger all the time.*~

~*That's what I been saying to myself, jest about every day. Nathaniel, I'm dying.*~

Nathaniel nearly fell over. ~What?~

~Don't write my epitaph yet,~ Sarah's disembodied voice said. ~They're trying to give me something called the Serpent Daughter Anointing, which I guess is expected to save my life... or something. But in the meantime, I can't go out, and I sleep a lot, and magic hurts like hell.~

Nathaniel felt a pit of fear in his stomach. ~How are we talking now? How did you call me?~

~Magic, you ninny. I can do it, it just hurts. Now listen up. What are you doing, and can it wait?~

~I want to heal our uncle.~

Sarah was silent for a moment. ~Heal him of what?~

~His hatred, I suppose. Whatever it is that makes him want to kill us. His fear?~

He expected her to react angrily; that was why he hadn't communicated his intentions to her until now.

~I hope you can do it,~ she said. ~It sounds difficult. How can I help?~

~You can't.~ The last thing he wanted was to kill his sister while trying to turn his uncle's heart. ~I'm just figuring out how to go about it. I think it will have to be when he's outside his palace, because that's protected.~

~By a spell, you mean?~

~I suppose it must be a spell. I see it as a high wall that I can't get over. And when he leaves the palace, he wears armor.~

~What, like King Arthur? Chain mail?~

~It looks like that to me, but I'm beginning to think it might be his coat. So I think I need to reach him when he's out, but not dressed to be out.~

~You got any clever ideas about that?~

~I'm thinking we'll try to follow him on his honeymoon.~

~That should be lovely,~ Sarah said. *~Where do you think he'll go? London? Paris? New Amsterdam?~*

~I don't know. I'm still thinking about how to get myself inside as a servant. But why did you reach out to me, Sarah?~ The thought that she was in pain grieved him.

He heard his sister sob. It was a heartbreaking sound, that rolled across the spectral Cahokia in which he stood, and then traveled out across the starlit plain. It came back to him in a keening echo that sounded like thunder almost as much as it did like weeping.

~What is it?~ he asked.

~It's Calvin,~ she said. *~You don't know him. He's the red-headed feller who was in the gaol with me, when you set me free.~*

~He seemed sweet on you.~

~He is. And dammit, I'm sweet on him. But my foster father is dead—that's Cal's grandfather, and Cal is hightailing it back to Nashville.~

~He didn't seem like a coward to me.~

~He ain't, not the slightest bit. But I reckon he knows that, with the Elector dead, there's gonna be a scrap to determine who'll be the next Elector. I expect he's heading home to warn people, and mebbe get 'em prepared.~

~Or maybe to rally support for himself in the scrap?~ Nathaniel suggested. He didn't know the Appalachee well, but he understood that their leaders were generally the ones who could fight their way to the top of the heap, rather than people who inherited

position. *~Do you need me to try to help him? I'm really only a healer.~*

~Can you be a messenger?~ she asked.

~I'll take Calvin your message.~

~Not to him,~ she said.

Margaret was staring at the walls.

Again.

She was grateful to Nathaniel for rescuing her from her kidnappers. She was thoroughly convinced that he was her brother, and that they had a third sibling, this Queen of Cahokia, who provoked strong reactions from everyone.

But she was also alone a lot.

And when she was alone, she thought of the men she had killed. Cracked skulls, sunken ships, broken limbs. She regretted none of it. She had been a victim, she had been attacked, she had been a prisoner. Her hand had always been forced. Every man who had attacked her and died had deserved it. No court of law could possibly fault her.

So why did her hands tremble when she remembered their faces?

And why did she see their dying expressions, over and over, whenever Nathaniel left her alone?

Screaming, she hurled the pitcher against the wall. It shattered, and the tinkle and the crunch of the pitcher's eruption calmed her nerves. Slightly.

She stood against the wall and touched the wet spot with the palm of her hand. Its coolness reminded her of the sea, and the *Verge Caníbal*, and Tia Montse. She didn't want to go back to her old life, not exactly. She knew she couldn't go back.

But she wanted to stop feeling rage.

"Do you want to go meet some people?" Nathaniel sat up on the straw pallet, awake.

"I broke the pitcher," she told him.

"That's the second one this week."

"Does this mean you've finally got a plan?"

"I'm starting to get one. But Sarah asked me to carry a bit of news, and it's to people who are close to here."

Margaret put on her hat, and led the way out of the building.

Nathaniel slung his drum over his shoulder and took the lead, then, down two alleys and across two avenues, until he stopped at a three-story brick building, with brick front steps and curtains blowing through the open windows.

"Maybe you should knock," he told her. "People sometimes don't know what to make of me."

"You just dress funny." Margaret rapped the brass knocker against the black-painted wood of the door.

"You know I don't choose to dress this way, right?"

"That's what you told me," Margaret said.

A man in a long gray tunic answered the door. He wore high boots to match his Ohioan tunic, and he had the pale skin and dark hair of a Firstborn. He wore a longsword at his hip, which made him look medieval.

"Are you Olanthes Kuta?" Nathaniel asked.

The expression on the Eldritch man's face was one part recognition, one part suspicion, and one part bafflement. "If the printer sent you to ask about Perkins," he said, "I still have no idea where he is."

"I'm here with a message for you," Nathaniel said.

"Though Sarah said I could also give it to Charlie Donelsen."

"Sarah Elytharias?"

Nathaniel nodded. Margaret fought down an urge to kick the wall.

"She's our sister."

Olanthes Kuta peered back over his shoulder and then stepped into the street, closing the door behind him. "Listen, there's someone here who can't be trusted, so why don't you give me Sarah's message elsewhere. There's a coffeeshop down the street."

"I like coffee," Margaret said, and Nathaniel shrugged.

The coffeeshop was called *Markoe's*, and Olanthes steered them to a round table in the back. He sat with his shoulders facing the corner, and his eyes on the door. While they waited for their three coffees, Nathaniel delivered the message.

"Sarah says that her grandfather is dead. The Elector Andrew Calhoun."

"Is she sure?" Olanthes asked.

"She has seen his body in a Youngstown hotel. Full of bullet holes, she said."

"And Calvin, who went to meet him?"

"Calvin lives, but he's not coming this direction. He's rushing back to Appalachee, likely to find out who the new Elector is."

"The new Elector might withdraw the proxy." Olanthes covered his face with his hands. "This is bad."

"Murder is terrible," Nathaniel said.

Margaret ground her teeth.

"Cal must fear that if he isn't in Nashville, the new Elector won't be someone who supports the impeachment. Or maybe Thomas will spend money to try to influence who becomes the Elector."

"I don't think it works that way," Nathaniel said, "but maybe."

"So that's bad," Olanthes said. "But there's another problem. Thomas Penn—or rather, the Memphite Electors, who are doing his bidding, have brought a cloture motion."

"That sounds like a bad thing," Nathaniel said.

"If the motion passes, then we vote on the impeachment now. And we've only just begun to show evidence, and we haven't even got the accountant onto the witness stand yet."

"You think the emperor will win. That he won't be removed from being emperor."

"Or from being Elector. Yes, I think the cloture vote is very close, and that's only a majority vote. If cloture passes, there's no way the Assembly removes Thomas from office."

Nathaniel looked far away, lost in his thoughts.

"Do you think you can persuade more Electors, if you have more time?" Margaret asked.

"We hope so," Olanthes Kuta said.

Onacona Mohuntubby's disappearance irked Notwithstanding Schmidt, and raised questions in her mind. He had seemed a sober and cunning careerist, of the sort who was willing to expose his machinations to a potential superior—Schmidt—turning full disclosure into the ultimate tool for manipulation and getting what he wanted. Schmidt could respect such a mentality; more to the point, she could work with it, and Mohuntubby had done her the favor of getting rid of

Theophilus Sayle, the Roundhead artillery commander who had briefly been her rival.

Mohuntubby's disappearance without explanation made Schmidt think that his disclosure had not been full, that her own assessment of the man had been incomplete. What mysterious errand had taken him away from her?

Had he some other loyalty than to his own career?

Schmidt had no wizard to ask. Luman Walters, whom she had rescued from irate Haudenosaunee, had briefly been her Balaam, to be replaced even more briefly by the arrogant and dangerous Robert Hooke, the Lazar sorcerer in the service of Oliver Cromwell. If she still had Luman, he might cast pinpricks across a card and tell her what they suggested. Who knew what Robert Hooke would do to divine the location of the missing captain? Probably something that involved murdering innocent children.

She stood above a map of the Ohio, examining the course of the roads that led to Cahokia. Reinforcements were coming, and a simultaneous advance along every Imperial highway and major Eldritch track—which the emperor had assured her would be possible—should shatter the Firstborn kingdoms' morale and force them to submit. A show of power should also break the resistance to Thomas among the Electors, and cause the rebels to drop their impeachment suit.

After the split forces separately reached the Mississippi River, they could converge from three directions on solitary Cahokia. She expected imminently the arrival of Temple Franklin, who was supposed to have more information on the nature of the reinforcements that were coming Schmidt's way.

"Madam Director." Schäfer stood in the door of her tent. The Youngstown German had survived Luman's defection, Mohuntubby's disappearance, and the death and undead resurrection and final evaporation of Dadgayadoh, his partner. He was useful. "There's someone here to see you. He says he has a message from Mohuntubby."

Schmidt frowned. "Naturally, he has insisted it can be given only to me, and that it is confidential. Tell me what he looks like."

Schäfer shook his head. "He looks more like a prancing milord than like a courier. Or like the toady to a prancing milord. Only his boots and his cloak are too big for him, and look like a soldier's."

"He must not have given you his name."

"He has not. He speaks German, and his accent is Pennslander."

Schmidt considered. "Strip him of all weapons. Be thorough. Then bring him in here, and position yourself behind the tent flap, with pistols ready. If I say the word *opportunity*, that is my signal that you are dismissed."

Schäfer stalked out into the storm, his departure accompanied by a blast of wind and rain across the tent flap.

Schmidt rolled up the map, tied it with a ribbon, and placed it in the cabinet. Since Sayle's death, she had forced herself to consider, not just the logistics of keeping her company men and militia in the field, but also tactics and strategy. She had done this while fighting constant minor guerilla battles against a First-born masonic militia calling itself, according to her informants, the "Swords of Wisdom." Whoever the Swords were, and it seemed they were dispersed in the general population, meeting at night like a vigilance committee rather than bivouacked like a proper military force, they didn't strike at the empire directly. They holed boats and broke axles and occasionally hanged an Imperial scout or two. Above all, they stole food.

Which suggested to Schmidt that the Pacification was working. Not all the Hansa she had corrupted stayed corrupt, but many did, and her own principal tool for feeding her own militia, especially those who had recently been released from Imperial prisons, was to turn them loose with license to take what they needed from the Ohio itself, but not to harm planted fields or orchards.

Additional troops from the emperor, if they truly were enough to march along three roads to the Mississippi, might seriously strain Notwithstanding Schmidt's ability to keep them fed. She was considering methods for protecting the harvest and requisitioning it entirely.

Schäfer returned. "The courier, Madam Director."

The courier came in from the storm. He had a blocky head and soft features, and Schäfer had been right about his clothing—over elegant waistcoat and breeches, he wore a heavy army coat that was too long and boots that were too big.

And Schmidt knew him.

"You're Thomas's servant."

Schäfer excused himself.

"Madam Director," the man said, "let me come directly to the point. My name is Gottlieb Voigt. I am Thomas's former body servant, and I believe that you have received instructions to kill me. I am yours to dispose of, but if you spare me, I can give you great power."

This was the very man Thomas had instructed her to kill. A loyal servant to Thomas would kill the man on the spot. How much had Schäfer heard? Gottlieb had blurted out his offer so quickly, Schäfer likely had not been in position.

"How was your road here?" she asked Gottlieb.

Gottlieb frowned, puzzled. "Madam Director, I don't know why—"

"How was your road here?" She stared him down.

Gottlieb cleared his throat and shifted from foot to foot. "Wet, Madam Director. My road here was wet, and long, and it took some rather unexpected turns."

Schmidt nodded slowly, trying to give Schäfer the time he needed. "That sounds like a very interesting opportunity." She spoke loudly and clearly.

"Yes, Madam Director." Gottlieb looked thoroughly confused.

Schmidt held up a finger, urging the emperor's body servant to wait. She counted a slow ten, then stood and looked behind the tent flap where she had directed Schäfer to stand—there was no sign of him.

"Come with me, Mr. Voigt." Notwithstanding Schmidt threw a thick wool rain cloak over her shoulders and a broad-brimmed hat onto her head. Grabbing Gottlieb by an upper arm, she propelled him before her into the wind.

"You are going to hear my offer." Gottlieb beamed.

"That doesn't mean I'm going to take it." Schmidt marched Gottlieb up onto a knob of earth that rose above her tent. It wasn't tall enough to be useful for lookouts, and it was completely unsheltered from the wind, so the storm slammed them both as they climbed. At the height of the knob, they would also be visible to anyone who chanced to look their direction. On the other hand, no one could eavesdrop.

What game was she playing? Was she really willing to betray Thomas Penn for this underling?

It depended on his offer. And whether she took his offer or not, she could always kill him later, and explain any delay as her judiciously trying to protect her shareholder's interests. But the fact that this man had discovered he was to be killed, and, rather than fleeing, had come with an offer to the very person who was supposed to assassinate him, intrigued her.

It suggested courage.

And possibly insanity.

"Very well, Gottlieb Voigt." She spoke in low tones, despite the fact that no one could overhear them. "I was instructed to have you killed. And I most likely will still carry out my instruction. You are three steps from the grave, at best. But this moment, right now, is your opportunity to save yourself. What power are you talking about?"

"Madam Director, I am a member of the Franklin Conventicle."

Schmidt snorted. "You are *two* steps from the grave. Nonsense will not save you."

"Thomas Penn wants me killed because he has learned that, as a member of the Conventicle, I worked against him. I killed one of his Parletts, and I helped the head of the Conventicle escape Thomas's wrath."

"You are *one* step from the grave. Thomas is a famous believer in nonsense."

"I carry with me the initiation secrets of the Conventicle, and a list of many senior members. I can help you seize control of the Lightning Bishop's secret organization." Gottlieb's voice rose in pitch to the end of his words, and when he had finished speaking, he cringed.

Schmidt considered. "Tell me what I can do with this organization."

Gottlieb straightened, slightly. "The network collects information. It could bring you news about harvests and yields, which you could use to trade."

"My factors already bring me such information."

"And personal knowledge, dark secrets. Opportunities for blackmail."

"Are you suggesting that I am *underhanded*, Gottlieb?"

Gottlieb's eyes grew wide. "Or assassination!" he spluttered.

She took a wild guess. "As you assassinated Onacona Mohuntubby?"

Gottlieb gasped, tried to speak, and gasped again.

"I do expect answers," Schmidt said.

"Yes! Yes, I killed him, because he came to kill me!"

"Mohuntubby was a member of your Conventicle."

"Yes!"

"Hmm," Schmidt said.

"Madam Director," Gottlieb said, falling to his knees in the mud, "please."

Beyond Voigt, emerging from the shrouds of rain, a form Schmidt knew well came marching toward the knob of earth. Schäfer.

"What apparatus would you require?" she asked.

"None," Voigt gasped. "None!"

"Get up right now, damn your eyes," Schmidt muttered, "or you're a dead man."

She grabbed Gottlieb's arm and hoisted him to his feet.

Schäfer trundled doggedly to the top of the small hill. "Madam Director," he said. "Temple Franklin has arrived. At the head of a procession of prison wagons, only he insists the prisoners are not to be freed to join the militia."

"He wishes to speak to me."

"Everyone wishes to speak to you." Schäfer nodded. "What shall I do with this one?"

"*This one* is named *Bauer*," Schmidt said, pushing Voigt into Schäfer's arms. "Georg Bauer. He's a defrocked preacher from the Ministerium, and he and I still have business to conduct. Put him under watch in a tent alone. I want you to supervise in person. And since there's a cloud of scandal following him... I want you to keep your mouth shut about it, and keep him from seeing anyone. Bring him his food and empty his chamber pot. If he tries to talk to anyone, including you, shoot him."

Schäfer nodded, then took Voigt by the elbow and led him away. Schmidt turned and slogged through the mud toward the road.

She would have this initiation and she would see Gottlieb Voigt's list. Then she would probably kill him.

Unless she could find some other use for the man.

A line of wagons sat on a wooden mat beside the road. The mat was Schmidt's idea; it kept a wagon from sinking into the mud, in this storm, and she had had it built long enough to accommodate ten large quartermaster's wagons. Counting the wagons that squatted there now, she lost track in the sheets of rain. At least ten.

And these wagons were enormous, wide and heavy. They were tall, as well, like circus wagons. Oilcloths hung from three sides, obscuring the wagons themselves. Muleskinners swarmed to tie down the cloth where it flapped, set blocks under the wheels, and pass hot coffee hand to hand. Schmidt walked toward a loose flap at the corner of one wagon, to peer at the wagon's contents. She reached for the flap to pull it back—

and a muleskinner seized the oilcloth, yanking it away from her and pushing it flat against the wagon.

Schmidt heard groaning sounds, and smelled ordure.

"These wagons belong to the emperor," the muleskinner said. He had a scraggly brown beard and eyes that looked in different directions, but he was young and his teeth were still all in his head.

"I am Notwithstanding Schmidt. I am the Sole Director of the Imperial Ohio Company, and I command here. You can move your hand or lose it. Your choice."

The muleskinner stumbled away.

Schmidt raised the flap. Behind the oilcloth were iron bars, stretching from the flat bed of the wagon up to a heavy wooden roof. Within the cage, crouched, slumped, lying flat, or leaning against each other, were men. Certainly twenty, maybe thirty or more.

"Good afternoon, Madam Director."

Schmidt turned and found herself talking to Temple Franklin, the emperor's personal devil. "Nothing good about it. I am waiting for reinforcements from the emperor, but I have been told that these men are not to be mine. Do they not fit in uniform, Franklin?"

Franklin smoothed the oilcloth back into place and stepped away from the wagon. His smile was polite and knowing, and Schmidt allowed herself to be led a few paces away, underneath a canvas awning that bellowed like a drum under the rain.

"I am taking these men across the Ohio and into

Missouri," Franklin said. "To the kingdom of Simon Sword. I have one of the Parletts with me, though the valet who was to be caring for him disappeared."

"That's quite the embassy you have." Schmidt planted her feet shoulder width apart. "These men aren't your bodyguard, though."

"I understand they're to be a gift to Simon Sword," Franklin said.

"To fight for him?" Schmidt sniffed. "They look like rabble."

"As I understand it," Temple Franklin said, "they are to fight for no one. They are to be eaten."

> *"I have the same power that any
> man with a gun has."*

CHAPTER FOURTEEN

On the starlit plain, by listening, Nathaniel found Julia Stuyvesant. There was something wrong with her; she sat, stone-faced and still, staring out the window of what appeared to be a hotel room. On the plain, it appeared as a sofa within four walls, the Dutch-orange wallpaper peeling off the walls to reveal beneath a layer of Imperial blue and gold.

~*Is she an idiot?*~ Nathaniel asked. Wilkes and Hop were both with him.

~*I never met her,*~ Wilkes said. ~*That doesn't seem likely, though, does it? In the emperor's bride?*~

In the starlit-plain hotel room, Nathaniel listened carefully. He heard: a colicky horse complaining in a stable; a sly scullion telling a pretty maid outrageous lies; the creaking bones in the back of the concierge; the hum of fruit flies in the trees in the carriage yard.

Then he descended into physical Philadelphia, dragging both Wilkes and Hop along with him, and he and Margaret set out looking ... or rather, listening ... for that same combination of sounds.

Margaret walked by his side, swinging a stick at trees and passing dogs. When they barked at her, she growled back, chasing off more than one stray. She had left her coat at the rented garret, of course, but Nathaniel wore his.

Coat inside out, and hat backward, as always, with his drum slung over his shoulder.

The creaking bones of the concierge grew louder, the kitchen boy stopped talking to take an offered kiss, and there was the hotel. The *Huig de Groot*.

~This is never going to work with you dressed like that,~ Jacob Hop said.

"We're going to try something," Nathaniel told him.

"What are we going to try?" Margaret asked.

"Ah, I was talking to Hop."

Margaret struck her stick against an elm trunk with such force that the stick snapped.

"We're going to try a disguise," Nathaniel continued. "You speak Dutch, so no problem. Jake speaks Dutch, so no problem. And Wilkes is an actor, who wears many costumes."

Margaret folded her arms across her chest. "Do we need to go hide?"

"I don't think so." Taking a deep breath, Nathaniel stepped aside to make room for his familiar spirits. *"Kan ik nederlands spreken?"* they asked together.

"Ja, je kan," she said.

"This is it, Wilkes," he said. "Time to put on a disguise."

Together, Isaiah Wilkes and Nathaniel Penn took off their coat and hat.

Nathaniel felt strange, naked without his coat and hat. He also felt burdened by the two spirits he carried with him, so his steps were bowlegged and hesitant. But with Wilkes taking some of the guidance of his limbs, he found it was possible to be without his strange dress.

"It worked!" he cried.

A passing man wearing a brown tricorn over brown hair frowned at him, but kept walking.

"Next time, try riding a horse or using a knife," Margaret said.

"One step at a time." Nathaniel hung his coat, still inside out, over one arm and drum. He held his hat in his hand. "Let's go see Julia."

He navigated by sound again, climbing stairs to get the right amount of distance between himself and the kitchen, and between himself and the carriage yard, so that the buzzing of the flies and the boy's whispers and the creaking bones all faded into the correct relative volumes. When they sounded exactly right, he stopped, and found that he was standing before a door bearing the number 25.

Margaret knocked.

A slot in the door opened, Nathaniel saw a woman's eyes stare briefly at him, and then the peephole closed again. "*Ga weg!*" the woman cried.

"*Mevrouw,*" Nathaniel said, and continued in Dutch, "I've come from the Lady Julia's father, Adriaan Stuyvesant."

The peephole opened again. "What does Meneer Stuyvesant want?"

"He worries that his daughter doesn't have enough servants," Nathaniel said.

The woman behind the door snorted. "She has *me*, and the staff of the hotel is very accommodating."

"Yes," Nathaniel said, "but I believe Meneer Stuyvesant wants to be certain that Julia is *seen* to be served."

The woman chuckled. "Oh ho, is that how it is? Can't put on a poor show in front of Philadelphia and all of Thomas's friends, can he? What the lady Julia really needs is—"

The woman cut herself off. There were tears in her eyes.

"I'm Jacob," Nathaniel said. "This is my sister Margarida."

"Hallo," Margaret said.

"I'm Lieke," the woman said. "Are you musicians?"

"I only have the drum. May we come in and pay our respects?" Nathaniel asked. "Maybe what Lady Julia could use is the company of someone closer to her age. We could play a few games of toepen."

Lieke hesitated, then nodded. She opened the door, and Nathaniel and Margaret entered. Lieke herself was a woman in middle age, wearing a simple brown dress. Behind the door was a parlor, with two tables, four sofas, and a pianoforte in the corner. A large window opened above the street—a warm breeze ruffled long white curtains, and smell of elm trees and horses drifted in, mingling with the scents of two different bouquets of flowers in the room, and an expensive toilet water.

A young woman sat in a wooden chair, staring out the window. Nathaniel had seen her on the starlit plain; she wore a dress that was bright yellow and plain, but new and clean. She held her hands in her lap and sat still and silent.

"Hello, Lady Julia," Nathaniel said. "We rejoice with you for your impending wedding!"

Julia didn't stir.

"I don't know," Margaret said. "I think a woman getting married has things to mourn, too."

Nathaniel shot his sister a scowl.

Julia turned her head slightly and looked at Margaret, then returned to gazing out the window.

~Something is wrong,~ Wilkes said.

~Perhaps the joyful imminence of her wedding has driven her mad,~ Jake suggested.

~No, she grieves for something. My God, the baby.~

"What baby?" Nathaniel asked.

Lieke stared at him, and then tightened her face into an angry mask.

~She carried a child,~ Wilkes said. *~Not Thomas's. Can you tell whether she is still pregnant?~*

Nathaniel listened, but heard nothing of a child in Julia's womb.

"I do not know what baby you are talking about!" Lieke snapped. Then her expression melted into fear. "Did Thomas send you?"

"No," Nathaniel said to both Lieke and Wilkes.

"Who are you?" Lieke asked.

"Adriaan Stuyvesant didn't send me, either," Nathaniel admitted.

"Get out!" Lieke shouted.

"I am a healer," Nathaniel said. "Not a medical doctor, but a..." He didn't have any good words to describe what he was. "A magician?"

"Een tovenaar?" Lieke was barely breathing.

"Only for healing," Nathaniel said. "It's all I can do. And this really is my sister."

"You've come to heal Julia?" Hope flashed in Lieke's eyes. "Can you heal her heart, too, *tovenaar*? Can you heal her mind?"

"Maybe," Nathaniel said. "I can try."

The woman's excitement slipped into suspicion. "But who are you? And what brought you here, to heal Julia?"

"I can hear . . . some kinds of wounds, and some kinds of illnesses," Nathaniel said. "Even from far away. It's difficult to explain, there aren't any good words for what I do. But before I came here, I heard Julia's sorrow. I didn't understand it until I came here, but now, I think she has lost a baby."

"She has lost a baby." Lieke nodded. "How did you know?"

"There are spirits who talk to me," Nathaniel said. "One of them knew, and told me."

Lieke's hands were clasped in front of her in a gesture of prayer. "You can heal her?"

"I don't think I can give her her baby back," Nathaniel said. "But I may be able to do something about her broken heart."

"She must rise up from this sadness." Lieke turned to look at Julia. "Lord Thomas will take her to the theater tomorrow night, and I fear that if she cannot smile and be pretty on his arm, then he will kill her. But I must ask her first." The woman then set a chair close to Julia's and sat with the curtains blowing over her shoulders. "Julia, my little one," she said, her voice rising to a pitch that sounded like baby talk. "There is a doctor here. He knows about the baby, and he's come to try to help you feel better."

Julia didn't move.

"Julia, I think he is a good person, and I want to let him try. May he attempt to help?"

Nothing.

"Since you're not telling me no, I'm going to ask the doctor to help you." Lieke waited a moment, and then stood. "What do you need?" she asked Nathaniel. "Will you let blood?"

"All I need is space on the floor." Nathaniel climbed into his coat, inside out, and put on his hat, backward. "Margarida will be here—she is a mighty warrior, and she will protect you and me and Julia, there is nothing to fear. You will see a bear, but the bear will not harm you. He is only part of the magic."

"A bear?" Lieke's eyebrows climbed her forehead.

~*I'm astonished she's letting us do this,*~ Jake said.

~*She's desperate,*~ Wilkes replied.

~*Who was the father?*~ Jake asked.

~*The man Ma'iingan rescued from the Anakim. Dockery. I don't know what happened to the baby.*~

~*Perhaps Thomas Penn did something to it,*~ Jake suggested. ~*Lieke certainly fears him.*~

Nathaniel lay on carpet so rich, it was more comfortable than many beds he'd slept on. He had become so familiar with entering the starlit plain that it took just a rapid slap of the fingers against the skin of his drum, and he was leaping up, on horseback, ascending the seven stairs that led to the plain. Jacob Hop and Isaiah Wilkes rode the horse behind him—leaving his body and riding his drum made the weight of carrying two additional spirits immediately disappear.

Nathaniel looked down and saw Lieke, sitting abruptly, with an astonished look on her face. Makwa the bear settled like a shadow over Nathaniel's body, and Margaret poured herself water from a pitcher.

~*Don't break anything,*~ Nathaniel urged her, knowing she wouldn't hear.

~*She's angry,*~ Jake said.

~*Yes, but why? She's can't be angry at me, I didn't kidnap her or make her go into hiding or keep her from her family. All I did was rescue her!*~

~*You could ask her,*~ Jake suggested.

~*Perhaps she, too, needs healing,*~ Wilkes added.

~*Later,*~ Nathaniel said. ~*We have other things to deal with first.*~

He turned to look at Julia Stuyvesant, in the hotel room on the starlit plain.

She sat still and alone; there was no sign of Lieke here.

He knelt beside Julia and pressed his ear against her belly. He heard nothing. ~*There is no child in here.*~

~*If Thomas learned about the child, he would have killed it,*~ Wilkes said. ~*He has a powerful wrath.*~

~*Or perhaps she killed the child so that Thomas would not find out about it,*~ Jake countered. ~*I think for me to kill a baby, I would have to feel trapped.*~

~*Julia Stuyvesant was definitely trapped,*~ Wilkes agreed.

~*Shhh.*~ Nathaniel listened harder.

He heard a heartbeat. He didn't hear it from within Julia's womb, but he heard it *through* her womb. He stood and followed the sound.

His two spirits followed.

He walked for what seemed an hour. When he looked about him, he was no longer in Philadelphia, but in some starlit plain mirror-place he didn't know. Above him, the stars were familiar, but everything else was strange. The plain was larger than usual, or perhaps it had always been larger than he thought.

He listened. He could still hear the heart beating, but it sounded no closer than before.

~Get on the horse,~ he said to Wilkes and Hop.
~We have a long road to go.~

They mounted and rode.

He listened, and over the sound of the hoofbeats, he could hear the heart. He urged his drum-mount to faster and faster speeds, and the heartbeat began to grow louder. The plain fell away behind him, and he was riding through mountains.

What were these mountains? He had always ridden across the empire before as a plain, and Nathaniel had assumed that, in its spirit-mirror version, the entire world was a plain. And yet here were hills, then peaks, then mighty crags.

Long, pale faces howled at him from behind rocks. Overhead, the shadow of something circling blocked out the stars. Nathaniel felt weak and hungry, and suddenly afraid. Where was he?

Guided by his ear, he rode to the top of a mountain peak. At its height, a river flowed. The water sparkled silver and red, and ran in a mighty ribbon across the rocks and into the sky. Beside the river stood a giant—not a seven- or eight-foot-tall man, as the Talligewi were said to be, or as the giants had been who had torn Nathaniel apart and reassembled him to give him this gift of travel in the sky, but a giant hundreds of feet tall, holding a bow that was even taller. At his feet, two hounds that were bigger than Nathaniel, his horse, and his two familiar spirits combined, chased a hare in and out of the mighty river.

Although Nathaniel had thought he was at the top of the mountain, he saw now that a further cliff rose up behind the giant, gleaming silver. The cliff was sheer and seemed, at first glance, impossible to climb.

Nathaniel pulled his horse sideways, and it leaped out of the path of one of the hounds. He listened for the heartbeat, and could hear it, beyond this sheer cliff.

~*Giant!*~ Nathaniel called.

The giant looked down at his feet. ~*Mouse!*~ he bellowed back.

~*I am no mouse, but a healer!*~

~*I am not sick!*~ The giant laughed. ~*I stand forever, guarding the river of souls and the gates of ascent and descent.*~

~*Is that a riddle?*~ Nathaniel asked.

~*If you like.*~

~*I am not an expert on giants,*~ Jake said.

~*Nor I,*~ Wilkes added. ~*I was on my way to try to meet giants when I drowned.*~

~*What giants were you going to meet?*~ Nathaniel asked.

~*A giant, or giants, named Brother Anak,*~ Wilkes said. ~*I think perhaps Kinta Jane and Dockery found him.*~

~*Is it worth guessing?*~

Both familiar spirits shrugged.

Nathaniel turned back to the giant. ~*You are Brother Anak!*~

The giant bellowed, his laughter rocking the mountain on which he stood. ~*Ah, you children of Adam have forgotten so much! The greater your cities and kingdoms become, the more you are cut off from your past. And if you do not remember your ancestors, can you even say you are the same race as they were? No! I am not Brother Anak!*~

Nathaniel huddled with his allies to confer. ~*Other guesses?*~

~The giant Atlas holds up the end of the earth, doesn't he?~ Jake said.

~What about Adam?~ Wilkes suggested.

~Adam?~ Nathaniel was puzzled.

~There's an old story that Adam was a giant,~ Wilkes said. *~Nine hundred feet tall is the way I heard it, from a Philadelphia rabbi. Maybe that's what he means by his talk about our ancestors, and us not being the same species as they are.~*

~Well?~ the giant rumbled.

~You're Adam!~ Nathaniel cried.

~Wrong!~

~Atlas!~

~Wrong!~

~Goliath? Gogmagog? Bran the Blessed?~

The giant laughed. *~All wrong, and now I can give you no more guesses.~*

~Is there no other way to pass you?~

~Of course, there is,~ the giant said. *~You can die.~*

~There must be still other ways,~ Nathaniel insisted. *~I am a healer, and I have come a long way.~*

~Those being born and those leaving these lands pass through these gates,~ the giant said. *~If you are not prepared to die, perhaps you are prepared to be born.~*

~I am,~ Nathaniel said.

The giant raised his bow and shot Nathaniel.

Nathaniel had a memory of screaming, afterward. He remembered screaming for a long time, and falling into an abyss that had no bottom. But in the moment, he experienced none of that. An arrow the size of a tree slammed into him, flattening him and knocking him and his horse and his two companions down off the mountain—

and then he was again mounted, and standing at the feet of the giant.

~*I am born again,*~ Nathaniel said. ~*Will you give me a new name?*~

~*You will have to find this name for yourself.*~ Then the giant stepped aside, and beyond where the giant had been standing, rising up the lower flanks of the cliff, Nathaniel saw a silver thread of a path.

Nathaniel climbed. He was halfway up the cliff face when he realized that Isaiah Wilkes and Jacob Hop were gone. Had the giant destroyed them? Was this the price of being born again, that he must lose his familiar spirits?

If so, then it was all the more important that he make the gain worth the sacrifice. He would heal Julia Stuyvesant of her pain. He pressed on.

He ached by the time he reached top of the cliff...

Only he found, at the top, that he was stepping down off the bottom of an immense rock face. Startled, he looked up, and saw the cliff face ascend and ascend, marked by a threadlike silver path...

Until it reached a plain in the sky. Dimly, he saw a giant, upside down, standing at the height of the cliff. At the giant's feet played two hounds and a rabbit. If Wilkes and Hop were there, they were too far away to be visible. Nathaniel listened for his friends, and couldn't hear them.

But in listening for his familiars, he heard again the heartbeat.

And it was loud.

Nathaniel looked about him. The plain was overhead. He stood among the stars.

And the stars danced.

The pattern was not recognizable to Nathaniel. Individual stars ranged in size from so tiny that he thought he could put several under his hat, and still have room, to so vast that Nathaniel could only comprehend them as flat surfaces. He seemed to see all things and to see *through* all things, so that he could at the same time understand the enormous star before him, and the dusting of tiny stars circling on the far side of their larger fellow, and also the pattern in which they spun, and the larger pattern of which their pattern was a part.

He danced with them, swept away in the eternal cosmic moment.

He danced along a current of stars, and began to see that their patterns were not abstract. The stars whirled together and apart again and again, ephemerally forming centaurs, leviathans, scorpions, long-necked giraffes, sailing ships, horrific monsters, and maidens of heartbreaking beauty. Or were the patterns, after all, in Nathaniel's mind? Did he only imagine them, and in his absence, would this place be chaos, without form and void?

Then the stars about formed into the face of a child, and he heard the child's heart beating.

Nathaniel stopped dancing. The child's face also came to a stop, facing him. Behind the face raced currents of stars and within the face, countless points of light spun and dipped and continued to dance, their patterns nevertheless all combining into the whole of the child's face. Nathaniel had no sense whether the child was a girl or a boy, or that it even had a sex at all. But it was a child, and it was beautiful.

And the heartbeat sounded like a waterfall.

~My name is Nathaniel,~ he said.

The child-face smiled, eyes twinkling.

~Your mother was to be a woman named Julia,~ Nathaniel continued. *~She grieves your loss.~*

The child's lips moved. They seemed to mouth the word *mother.*

~I am a faithful messenger,~ Nathaniel said. *~What token may I bring her from you?~*

The child's eyes turned a warm, compassionate yellow as stars whirled into and out of place. Pursing its lips, the child-face blew a kiss.

Nathaniel felt love.

Within the kiss, he saw something bright. Nathaniel reached his hand in between the child's lips and felt petals, and leaves, and stalks. Putting in his second hand as well, he grasped a bouquet of flowers and drew it forth.

The bouquet was not wrapped in paper and was not planted in a vase, and yet it was alive. The stalks of the flowers, shimmering emerald green, wrapped themselves lovingly about Nathaniel's forearms. The flowers, which were bright yellow and a deep, soulful blue, craned toward him as if seeking an embrace. He could not have said what scent rose from the blossoms, except that it reminded him of peace and joy.

~Thank you,~ Nathaniel said.

Mother, the lips mouthed again.

And then the child's face dissipated into cosmic mist and rejoined the dance.

Nathaniel turned to retrace his steps—

and found he did not know which direction to go.

There was no path across the stars. There was no up and down. There seemed to be no time, so that

Nathaniel saw, for a terrifying, glorious moment, visions of himself spinning out in all directions among the stars. He stood with flowers in his hand, he danced with the stars, he reached into the mouth of a giant face.

Was the face smiling, or leering at him?

Nathaniel listened for the sounds of the starlit plain. ~Wilkes!~ he called out. ~Jake! Makwa!~

He heard no answer.

He listened for the sound of the giant with no name, and heard nothing. He could not hear the giant's hounds, or the hare. He listened for the sounds of his sisters, and heard nothing.

He sang:

> *I seek the starlit grasslands, to heaven I ride*
> *I bear the gift of angels, and peace inside*
> *I've danced among the stars and all along*
> > *the cosmos wide*
> *I seek the grief-marred mother, to heaven*
> > *I ride*

Nothing happened.

Was this how he was to end? In a sea of dancing stars, death by impossible beauty, an eternal end with no pain. Some would desire it.

But Julia Stuyvesant would continue to grieve. Thomas might kill her, and Thomas himself would not be healed.

What else could Nathaniel do? How else to find his way back?

He took a deep breath, inhaling and exhaling stars the size of mites. Or had Nathaniel now become a giant, and were all the stars the size of mites?

He closed his eyes. His horse. The drum made of

horse's skins that was his constant companion and that was also his steed on the starlit plain. It had not come with him; it was still with the giant.

Unless the giant had killed it.

Nathaniel listened for his horse. As first he heard only the burning and the leaping and the dancing of the stars, along with the child's heartbeat, drifting slowly away from him in the sea of motion and brilliance. He tried to shut out those sounds. His horse.

He drummed a pattern on his own thigh with his fingertips, the same quick pattern he used to summon his horses and leap into the sky.

Across the sea of stars, he heard an answering tattoo.

Uncertain of the direction, he drummed again. Again, an answer came.

Nathaniel kept his eyes closed. He walked, knowing that he walked on nothing, and he followed the sound, knowing that he was in a place of no directions, a place where perhaps there was no such thing as place.

He drummed and followed, trusting his horse and trusting his ear.

When his feet touched rock, he opened his eyes. He stood at the bottom, or at the top, of the silver-threaded cliff. He looked up and saw the top of the giant's head, and the hills rolling down onto the seemingly infinite grass of the starlit plain.

He climbed the cliff until he descended it, eyes open now, and regained the mountain peak beside the flowing river. Away at the river's edge, the two hounds continued to chase the hare. The giant gripped his bow with both hands like a walking staff and leaned toward Nathaniel. *~Ah, here is a newborn thing. Did you find what you sought, little infant?~*

~*I think so,*~ Nathaniel said.

The giant nodded. ~*Get along, then. Time to be born.*~

Wilkes and Jake waited astride Nathaniel's horse, which neighed a constant sound like a beating drum, like a child's heart, like a horse's own hooves in full gallop.

~*The giant killed you,*~ Wilkes said. ~*He shot you with his bow and you fell right into the river and drowned.*~

~*Or he gave me birth.*~ Nathaniel sprang onto the back of his horse. ~*If you thought I was dead, why didn't you leave?*~

~*You seem like the sort who would come back,*~ Jacob Hop said.

Nathaniel placed the blue and yellow flowers into his hat and cradled the hat in the crook of his left arm, as if holding a baby. His one hand was sufficient to hold the reins, if not of an earthly horse, then at least of this starlit mount. Listening for the sound of Lieke weeping, he turned the horse's nose downhill and raced toward Philadelphia.

As he raced, the stars overhead seemed to cheer him on. More than once, he thought he saw them swerve out of their predetermined rotation and swirl together to form the face of a child, gazing down at him.

When they reached the grieving, still form of Julia Stuyvesant, sitting all alone on her chair, surrounded by peeling wallpaper, Nathaniel stopped and dismounted. He replaced the hat on his head and took the flowers in both hands. What to do with them?

He knelt before Julia, and held out the flowers.

She continued to stare through drifting white curtains.

He placed the flowers in her lap, and she failed to notice them.

Isaiah Wilkes and Jacob Hop watched.

Nathaniel held the flowers in Julia's lap with one hand and with his free hand took one of hers, trying to raise it to touch the flowers.

Nothing.

Nathaniel held the flowers up to Julia's nose. To him, they still smelled of peace and joy. She stirred slightly, and blinked.

~*Where did you find the flowers?*~ Wilkes asked. ~*Were they growing on top of that cliff?*~

Nathaniel sat back on his heels. Julia stared out the window, eyes not moving. He gripped her jaw with his left hand and pulled it down, opening her mouth. Inside, he saw no tongue, but only a black void.

He sang.

> *I come with gift of healing, from heaven*
>   *I ride*
> *I bear the gift of angels, with joy inside*
> *These flowers come from the mountain that*
>   *all the worlds divides*
> *To heal the grief-marred mother, from*
>   *heaven I ride*

Julia Stuyvesant stirred, and her jaw relaxed. Nathaniel pulled it down, her mouth gaping wider than it should have been able to, so wide it would have snapped her jaw off completely if he had done the same thing to her physical person, so wide that Nathaniel thought he saw, for just a moment, the glitter of stars, somewhere deep inside the blackness within Julia.

He reached inside her mouth and placed the flowers there.

Then he stepped back.

Julia closed her mouth and swallowed. Several long seconds passed, and then she smiled. She turned her head, saw Nathaniel, the horse, and the familiar spirits, and smiled again.

And then her smile erupted into weeping.

Nathaniel stepped forward as Julia surged to her feet and opened his arms. She embraced him and he could feel heat flowing from his spirit-body into hers. She wept and she laughed and she wept again.

"Thank you," she said.

Then she sat down and disappeared.

~I have had many jobs in my life and in my... whatever this is,~ Jacob Hop said. ~I was a ship's boy, and a muleskinner, and a cook, and a gaoler. I remember, or rather, I remember remembering lives in which I was a king, a high priest, a conqueror, and a god. But this is the best job I've ever had.~

~Are you willing to come down with me again now?~ Nathaniel asked.

~Do you need us?~ Wilkes asked.

~Well, I still don't speak Dutch.~

Both Nathaniel's spirit guides came with him. He wrapped his arms around the two men and leapt downward on his horse—

then sat up on the carpet of the hotel room, clutching his drum.

Lieke and Julia stood by the window and wept, clinging to each other. Margaret stood by the door. Nathaniel grinned at her, and got a scowl in return.

He stood, and the two women turned toward him.

Julia smiled, and he thought he saw recognition in her eyes. Did she remember him? Might she have, for instance, dreamed the same thing he had just experienced on the starlit plain? Might she have dreamed all of it?

"Lady Julia," he said, Jacob Hop finding the right words for him in Dutch. "I have come from a far-distant place, and I bring you a message."

"From my child?" Julia asked.

Nathaniel nodded.

"What is the message?" she asked.

"Love," he said. "Only love."

Grief and joy, isolation and fulfilment, anger and peace all warred for control of Julia Stuyvesant's expression. She wept and embraced Nathaniel, and thanked him again as she had on the starlit plain.

"This *tovenaar* wishes to be your servant," Lieke said, smiling.

"I must tell you the full truth," Nathaniel said. "I have come to heal Emperor Thomas."

"The emperor!" Lieke frowned. "That's not what you said!"

"I am unarmed. I have no weapons. I cannot fight." Nathaniel turned his hands palm up. "I cannot hide, because the spirits force me to dress like this, so I am always noticed." Should he explain his connection to Thomas? "I am only a healer."

Julia nodded, tears in her eyes.

"Lady Julia, I am Thomas's nephew. My sister Margarida is his niece. He knows us, or he knows of us, and he believes we are a threat. We are not. I wish to heal Thomas. Something gnaws at him, something brings him to do evil. I wish to lift that burden from him."

"I understand."

"I think that if we can be your servants and accompany you on your honeymoon, I will be able to reach Thomas when he is not so surrounded by his defenses, and I will be able to help him."

Julia was silent for a long time, looking at Nathaniel.

Perhaps he had guessed wrong. Perhaps she didn't want to help Thomas. Perhaps the thought of Thomas feeling at peace made her angry or resentful. Would she summon the watch and have him arrested?

"I am happy to have you pretend to be my servants," she finally said. "For as long as you need to do so."

"Oh, I won't pretend." Nathaniel said. "I was raised as a foster child in Johnsland. I can black boots and rub down horses and chop wood and cook as well as anyone, I expect."

"I will be pretending," Margaret said. "I do not do any of those things. But if you need someone to tie a bowline or shorten a mainsail, I can help. And I do know many entertaining games, if you have a deck of cards."

"What shall I call you?" Julia asked.

"Jacob," Nathaniel said again. There was no reason Thomas should know that name. He might need Wilkes to help him stay in disguise whenever the emperor was likely to be around.

Margaret shrugged. "Margarida."

Nathaniel wanted to suggest something else, something that wasn't just another version of the name Margaret. Thomas might know his niece's name, and if he heard the name, he might realize how very Firstborn Margaret's complexion and features were. But if he objected now, he would only draw attention to the name.

"Probably most of the time," he suggested, "you should refer to us as 'my servants,' and address us as 'hey, you.'"

"You should stay with me. Or rather, near me. I will go with Thomas to the play tonight, and I will tell him I need a second suite at the hotel for a couple of servants my father sent me." Julia smiled a melancholy smile. "I will purse my lips and be pretty, and he will not begrudge it to me."

"We'll come back in the morning," Nathaniel said. "Is there anything we can do for you in the meantime?"

She shook her head. "Thank you," she said, and hugged Nathaniel again. Then she embraced Margaret, too. Margaret blushed and pulled away, but only slightly.

"May I offer you something?" Lieke asked. "Water, at least?" She held the pitcher in her hands, and gestured at two glasses on one of the tables.

Margaret took a glass of water.

Nathaniel stared at the pitcher and struggled. He wanted to say yes, but he found that he could not.

He could not any longer drink water, any more than he could wear his coat right side out or use a knife. He wanted to explain himself, but he found he couldn't do that, either.

"No, I cannot," he said. "I'm sorry, that is a terrible thing for a servant to say. Thank you. I will get my own drink, on the way home. I'm not thirsty."

Julia smiled graciously, though Lieke simply looked puzzled.

"We'll come back in the morning," Nathaniel repeated, taking his leave, and while he was bowing, he heard the door behind him shut. Margaret had already left.

He raced down the hotel hall to catch up with his sister.

"Isn't it about time you told me what's wrong?" he said.

"Nothing's wrong," she said. "Everything is perfect."

"No, it's not. Everything is terrifying and scary, and I never know what I'm doing and I think from moment to moment I'm going to fail and die, and our sister is in fact dying right now and our uncle wants to kill us."

At the top of the stairs leading down to the hotel lobby, Margaret stopped. She took a deep breath, exhaled, and then smiled at Nathaniel. "That's all true. And also, you have an extraordinary power, Nathaniel. I have no idea how you did what you did back there, but I saw the result."

"You have an amazing power, too."

"I have the same power that any man with a gun has." Margaret started down the stairs.

"I'll take you with me, if you like," Nathaniel said. "I can do that. I just like having you to protect me. It makes me feel safe, to be with you."

Margaret glared.

"Can we get some coffee or beer?" Nathaniel asked. "Or wine? I'm terribly thirsty."

"I hid them well. We might have until noon."

------◆------

CHAPTER FIFTEEN

Reuben Clay made a single introduction, in a Parkersburg inn called the *Jolly Piper*, presenting Luman and Montse to a man named Ritter. Ritter was tall, with long, thin limbs, and the distending belly of an active man just beginning to leave middle age. His hair was still dark, though, and his brown eyes keen.

"Ritter," he said, "is a Sword."

Then he stood and left.

"Your name isn't Ritter," Luman said.

"It's a name I use. We know you, Luman Walters. We know your errand. We will get you into Adena, and also into Koweta."

"Are you like Podebradans?" Luman asked. "You do this for a vow?"

"Podebradans are solitary," Ritter said. "They can be eccentric, even quixotic. Sometimes a Podebradan is merely a poet, imagining himself in love with a long-dead queen. We take vows, but it makes more sense to think of us like Savoyard Knights."

"Only instead of resisting the Caliphate," Montse said, "you resist the Pacification."

"For now," Ritter said. "More generally, we serve the goddess and all her people."

"I attended a funeral at which Swords of Wisdom were the honor guard," Luman said.

"At Cahokia." Ritter nodded. "In room three of this inn, there is a change of clothing for each of you. Leave your old clothing behind, and I will see that it is sent back with your boatmen. There is also hair dye for you, *Capità*. Black."

"We are to pass as Firstborn." Luman smiled.

In room three, Luman changed into a long tunic and high boots while Montserrat dyed her hair over a basin of water. He would have to leave his coat, which was a loss, as its many pockets contained wax, thread, chalk, stones, ink, paper, and all manner of other objects he had used as a hedge wizard to practice magic.

Leaving them, he would have to rely on his new gift of gramarye.

He took with him his ritual dagger, the athame, and his peep-stone. He also took his spectacles, and then he went out into the street to meet Ritter. Expecting horses or a carriage, Luman was surprised to find the Sword of Wisdom standing in the street with a bedroll over his shoulder, and two more at his feet.

"Will we ride canoes?" Luman asked.

"We'll walk," Ritter said. "It is my people's preferred mode of travel."

"Our people," Luman said. "Do I choose a name for myself, or will you give me one?"

"You are Zytes Polog, a medical doctor."

"I have small skill at healing."

"We know."

Luman wasn't sure whether he found it comforting or upsetting that the Sword of Wisdom referred to himself in the plural. "Your name means *rider*."

"It's a joke."

They waited an hour, Ritter saying little and Luman not pressing, and then Montse joined them. Her hair remained curly, which was unusual in one of the Firstborn, but it was now black and tied behind her head. She wore the Ohioan long tunic and boots like Luman did; his was brown and hers was a forest green.

Ritter gave her her Ophidian name: Nemia Polog, Luman's sister. "Don't worry," he reassured them, "Children of Eve will see only your clothing and your dark hair."

He produced a passport and a trustworthiness certificate for each of them.

A ferry took them across the river, Ritter paying the ferryman and no one talking. Then it was as simple as a two-day walk, and they arrived at Adena.

En route, they saw no Imperials. Ritter led them on small paths, and frequently stopped to consult with people by the wayside: peddlers, shopkeepers, farmers. The first time he did it, Luman felt impatient, but often after such a conversation, Ritter changed path, and Luman came to realize that he was conferring with watchmen and lookouts.

They saw evidence of Imperials, in burned barns, orchards, and homes. And they saw evidence of something else, too, something Luman struggled to understand. Swathes of vegetation, from grass to oak trees, lay shattered in long ribbons. Crossing one such trail, Luman looked in both directions and could see no end.

"It is as if the world's largest circus rolled through,

smashing everything in its path," he said. "What would do such a thing? Are the sleeping giants of the north on the warpath again? Or have the oversized beasts of Missouri, the aurochs and the ground sloth and the dire wolf, ridden eastward in a pack?"

"I think you will see, before we are done," Ritter said.

Adena was not a city on the scale of Cahokia. It was a smallish town, surrounded by a belt of farmland that was luxuriant with wheat and corn, and was in turn surrounded by Imperial soldiers. Their flag suggested that they were from Scranton in Pennsland, and they looked like raw recruits, their tents not yet weathered by long campaigns.

"These are the troops imprisoning the King of Adena?" Luman asked.

"They are imprisoning the food," Ritter said. "They'll take most of the crop when it's ready to harvest. The king is imprisoned by his compassion."

Adena was surrounded by a log palisade. It had Pennslander-style block houses at regular intervals along the walls, and two of them over the town's main gate.

The gate was open. Within, a Pennslander so young he had a line of pimples down each side of his mouth stood at a relaxed guard. "You're not from here," he said, taking their papers and looking at all three of them.

"Just coming to visit kin," Ritter said.

Pimple Mouth squinted at him. "Who's your family?"

"Koiles Delet is my brother," Ritter told him. "He owns the dry goods store, the *Giant of Adena*, his wife is Alia. These are my niece and nephew, Zytes and Nemia."

"Koiles is what to you?" the watchman asked. His boots looked new, and his musket looked so recently from the factory that Luman fancied he could smell sawdust. "Your father?"

"Uncle," Montse said, giving the rehearsed answer.

The young soldier gave them back their papers. "The gate shuts at night. We've had trouble with raiders."

Ritter scowled his disapproval of raiding, and they entered the town.

"We can see the king," he said. "We'll go see him right now. The problem is that the king cannot leave."

"He's not trapped here by an army," Luman said. "What keeps him?"

"Hostages," Montse suggested.

Ritter nodded.

The roads of Adena were laid out like the spokes of a wheel. At the center of town was a circular plaza made of the same smooth, round white stones Luman had seen atop Wisdom's Bluff. Within the plaza stood two buildings, one a wooden-walled square building atop a low mound, likely concealing within it a second, lower story, and a rectangular stone building with two trees growing on the two sides of its entrance, their branches interlacing above.

Ritter led them into the square building, descending short steps to the entrance. A Firstborn page took their names at the door, and then led them inside, under the watchful eyes of two Adenan warriors with spears. Within, from a lobby, a door opened into a large hall with a raised dais and a seat at the far end. Another door was shut, and stairs led up.

A voice behind the door sang as they approached:

I'll sing you one, O
Green grow the rushes, O
What is your one, O?
The spirit of the Lord's fear
And it ever more shall be so

I'll sing you two, O
Green grow the rushes, O
What are your two, O?
The spirit of knowledge
And it ever more shall be so

I'll sing you three, O
Green grow the rushes, O
What are your three, O?
The spirit of the Lady's might
And it ever more shall be so

I'll sing you four, O
Green grow the rushes, O
What are your four, O?
The spirit of Great Counsel
And it ever more shall be so

I'll sing you five, O
Green grow the rushes, O
What are your five, O?
The spirit of the understanding son
And it ever more shall be so

I'll sing you six, O
Green grow the rushes, O
What are your six, O?

The spirit of Wisdom
And it ever more shall be so

I'll sing you seven, O
Green grow the rushes, O
What are your seven, O?
The spirit of the Lord
And it ever more shall be so

The page knocked at the door. The singing stopped.

Moments later, the door opened and the King of Adena appeared. He was short and slender, and his hair was white. He dressed in a simple blue tunic and leggings, but he wore a thin gold circlet on his head.

"Come into my office," he said. He shut the door behind them, leaving the Adenan warriors and the king's page outside. "And please, no need for thees and thous. It only agitates the Imperials to hear me addressed that way."

The office was simple. Its walls were lined with books, and in the center of the room stood a wide desk on which sat more books. The king stood close to Luman and Montse and lowered his voice.

"You come from Queen Sarah?" he asked.

"Yes."

"I wish to help her," he said. "It is an honor even to be asked to administer the Serpent Daughter Anointing. I confess I had to look up the procedure in my books. But if I leave this building, Thomas Penn will kill my two sons."

Luman frowned. "They're in Philadelphia?"

"They are at school," the king said. "When the motion for impeachment was presented, Thomas assigned them minders. They are followed everywhere now, and I believe that one of the minders is a magician. I have also been given to understand that if I vote for Thomas's removal, my sons will be killed."

"This comes of not having your kin with you at all times," Montse said.

"It is always thus; the reward for the peaceful man is wounds. And it was always thus for Adena, standing on the borders of William Penn's kingdom."

"We could rescue your sons," Montse said, her eyes fierce.

"Do we have time?" Luman wondered. "Sarah is dying."

"Do we have enough men?" Ritter asked. "Thomas would try to take the child back, and the involvement of a magician would make everything harder."

"Well, one response would be to involve a wizard on our side, as well," Luman murmured.

"I mean no offense," Ritter said, "but aren't you a braucher? Thomas employs university-trained gramarists."

"I was a braucher," Luman said, "after a fashion. The goddess has given me a higher gift."

"If we were to seize my children," the king pointed out, "it would be an open act of insurrection. We could expect more sequestrations of food and more retaliatory murders. And to make up the greater deficit by purchasing from the Hansa, I shall have to sell more of my kingdom's land to the speculation companies."

Luman nodded. This was how Adena was eating.

"Speculation companies?" Montse asked.

"Companies formed in Pennsland," the king explained, "and in the Free Imperial Towns, Akron, Youngstown, and especially Cleveland. They buy land now when war depresses the price, hoping that peace will raise the price before they want to sell. Or that Thomas will utterly destroy the Seven Sisters, and then pay homesteading subsidies to anyone willing to come resettle our ghost-haunted farms and pastures."

"Subsidies would allow them to sell the land at inflated prices," Ritter said. "But at any price, it is a crime. We are forced to sell our land to avoid starving, but without land, how shall we feed ourselves in the future? And where shall we live?"

"Perhaps we shall live elsewhere," the king murmured. "Perhaps in Cahokia. And I have been told that there are other Seven Sister Kingdoms, in the west, in a land where the sun bakes clay hard in a single day."

"Everyone believes in a magic land somewhere, free of trouble," Montse said. "That land is always far away."

"What if we leave your sons in Philadelphia?" Luman asked. "And we take you with us, but in a way that leaves the Imperials believing you're still here."

"I am watched. Theoretically, I may leave, but practically, I may not. Several times a day, a soldier comes to confirm my continued presence. Most days, I work in here, writing my histories, except at sunrise and sunset, when I briefly adjourn to the shrine to offer a sacrifice of my broken heart." The king frowned. "You must be suggesting a magical solution."

"I am," Luman said. "Your Majesty, you were singing a song as we approached."

"Yes, your queen has been much on my mind."

"I thought I heard 'Green Grow the Rushes, O,' only I did not know half the words."

The King of Adena nodded. "These are the older words, or the current pronunciation of the older words, before the English undertook to rewrite the verses endlessly. It is the song of the Serpent Daughter Anointing."

"Some of it sounded like Isaiah chapter eleven," Luman said. "The spirit of the Lord shall rest upon him, the spirit of wisdom and understanding, and so forth."

"Yes." The King of Adena smiled. "Also that."

Luman explained that he wanted a substitute for the king, and Ritter promptly left Adena to find the required person. Luman seemed to think he had planned a great joke, so Montse let him enjoy his wit.

The substitute was Firstborn, and he came in through the gates later that afternoon, his passport and his trustworthiness certificate in order. After making a conspicuous stop at a tavern called the *Raven's Cup*, he made his way to the dry goods store.

In the back room of the dry goods store was a museum. Koiles Delet, a balding man who leaned forward to support the weight of a slack belly, led them to it and shut them in with the skeleton that had to have been eight feet tall, posed sitting on a chair made of stones cemented together, and holding a copper ax across his knees. "Don't worry," Delet said. "I'll turn any travelers away. If anyone in an Imperial uniform asks to see the giant, I'll knock and you can exit by the back door."

Luman turned to explain his plan to Montse and the substitute, whose name, according to his papers, was James Goram. "We will sneak unobserved into the shrine. When the king comes in to worship, in an hour or so, we will simply switch your places. You will wear his clothes out and he will wear yours. He will leave Adena—temporarily, you understand—and you will wait for him in the palace, pretending to be the king."

"I don't look like the king," James said. He was young, with curled brown hair, and though he had the pale Firstborn complexion, he had bull-like shoulders and thick features. "You will weave some enchantment?"

"Exactly. You'll understand that you have to stay in the palace until our return? It might be a few weeks."

"I came prepared to die," James said. "I am certainly prepared to wait a few weeks in the best library in the kingdom."

"And then we will simply walk away with the king," Montse said.

"I'll watch from the store," Ritter said. "I can intervene if there's trouble."

Luman cast his first spell on them, standing right there in the one-room museum. He paced at length before he could do it, muttering and patting himself down as if searching for nonexistent pockets. Montse looked at the walls while he did so, enjoying a map of the location where the giant had been found, as well as a neatly handwritten note explaining that a farmer had been plowing his field when the tooth of the plow had turned up a stone barrow, within which had been located this giant skeleton, sitting on a stone seat.

Finally, Luman took an egg-shaped brown stone from his pocket and held it up to his eye. Looking first at Montse and then at the Sword with his vision blocked, he muttered a short Latin phrase: "*Nos ipsos abscondo.*"

Both men disappeared from Montse's sight.

"We'll walk out the back of the shop. I'll talk, you two can follow me by the sound of my voice."

"We should hold hands," Montse said. "Much easier. Talk only when necessary."

"I'm glad to be invisible," Luman said. "You can't see me blushing with embarrassment."

Holding hands, they sneaked out the back door of the dry goods shop. A short walk between two houses led them to the plaza, empty but for a handful of sheep, cropping the grass sprouting up between stones. With Luman in front and Montse in the middle, they crossed the plaza and crept to the door of the temple, between the two trees. There Luman stopped.

"This is consecrated space," Luman whispered. The sun was orange on the western horizon.

"Don't you worship Sarah's goddess?" Montse asked.

"I suppose I do. I have a gift from her. But wait just one moment." Luman's hand tugged slightly downward, as if he were crouching, and then a gold coin appeared on the ground in the doorway. Luman stood again. "*Divina domina, accipe nos qui servi tui sumus.*"

"Was that an incantation of gramarye," Montse asked, "or a prayer?"

"Yes." Luman led them inside.

The shrine of Adena was not on the same scale as the Temple of the Sun on the Great Mound of Cahokia, but it was built to a similar layout. A nave rolled out before Montse, and at its far end a wooden ladder climbed to a cubical niche in the wall, big enough to be a small room, small enough that a man could barely stand in it.

The floor was of white stone; the walls were plastered

with a landscape in stucco, that started as forest and then turned into wasteland, and then became a river or a chasm just before the ladder ascended to the inner sanctum. No veil covered the inner sanctum, and no throne sat within it; a small iron altar was the only furnishing.

Torches set into brackets in the nave provided light. Luman dropped his spell, and he and the substitute both came into view.

"There is nowhere to hide, should someone other than the king enter," Montse noted.

Luman nodded. "But I must preserve my strength for the larger spell I am to cast shortly. If anyone comes in...we stepped inside to pay our respects to the goddess, and no one stopped us."

"Which is, after all, true," James Goram said. Facing the niche and its altar, he knelt and clasped his hands before him.

A quarter of an hour later, the King of Adena entered. He carried a long staff with a serpent carved into the head, and he wore a linen tunic that fell almost to his ankles.

"Can you bear to wait five minutes?" he asked them.

Montse wanted to tell him no, but Luman was already nodding. "After all, it is this same goddess in whose name you will be anointing Sarah. It won't do to anger Her."

The king's five minutes felt like fifteen or twenty, as he ambulated about the nave three times, climbed into the niche to light incense, and then knelt on the stone floor of the nave facing the niche to sing a modal tune in some Eldritch tongue. Then he returned to Luman, and James stood.

"I am ready," the king said. "Shall we exchange clothing?"

"Wait one moment." Luman turned to the volunteer. "I cannot be certain how long this will last," he said. "But I intend it to endure until the king returns. Avoid silver. Avoid the windows, and being seen, if you can. Wear the king's clothing at all times, read at his table, sleep in his bed."

"Do not worry," the king said, "I'm a widower."

"I know, Your Majesty." James bowed his head.

Luman touched both men, one hand on the shoulder of each. Montse looked out the window; the sky was clouded, but the town of Adena itself cast a kind of constellation out the windows of its home and stores.

Someone had entered the plaza and was ambling in this direction.

She wanted to urge Luman to be quick, but also didn't want to interrupt his concentration. She had left her saber and pistols in Parkersburg, but she still had a knife, and she drew it now.

"*Commutate corpora,*" he said. "*Commutate corpora. Regis faciam tibi do.*"

Luman's eyes were shut. "Exchange clothing, gentlemen," he murmured.

The king easily shucked off his linen tunic and handed it to James. The volunteer had slightly more complicated clothing, but set about stripping it off with due expedition, boots, then breeches, then tunic.

Montse watched the plaza. The man approaching stopped in the middle of the open space to yawn and look around. He wore a blue Imperial uniform; it wasn't Pimple Face himself, but one of the men of his troop.

The substitute took the king's white tunic and slipped it on over his head.

"*Commutate*," Luman murmured again.

When the tunic dropped around James's shoulders, he had the face and hair of the King of Adena.

The Imperial looked toward the doorway of the shrine. Had he heard Luman, or had he seen some hint of movement? He stared at the building and walked directly toward it.

"A soldier's coming," Montse hissed. "Does your plan still work if we leave a body on the floor? And how will your goddess feel about that?"

She had to worry about Ritter, too. They hadn't agreed very specifically at what point he would intervene, and he might rush out prematurely and cause a scene.

Luman was still deep in conversation. Montse grabbed him by his tunic and dragged him into the corner. Still pulling clothing on, the king followed them. He pressed himself into the angle of the two walls to prop himself up while he pulled on the substitute's tall boots. The king was a shorter man than James Goram, so the boots tended to ruck up about the ankles, and the tunic fell about a handspan longer than was generally stylish.

Montse pressed herself against the wall and held her knife ready.

The substitute king stepped into the doorway. "Good evening."

"Ah, Adena, it's you," the guard said. Montse had no special regard for titles and forms of address, and for certain titles she even felt disdain, but this soldier's familiarity with the King of Adena was vulgar. "I thought you'd have finished by now."

"Forgive me," the false Adena said. "In times of trouble, my prayers sometimes grow long."

"There won't be any trouble," the Imperial said. "Just as long as you do what you're told."

"Of course," James said. "Good night."

He walked away, toward the palace. Montse listened for the sound of the soldier's steps retreating, too, and didn't hear them. She could hear his breathing in the doorway, which made her very conscious to keep her own inhaling and exhaling to a quiet, muted whisper.

What was he looking for?

And might he come in?

Finally, she heard the sound of spitting. "What a sack of shit," the soldier cursed. "Pagans. Snake worshippers, the lot of them."

Finally, the sound of receding footsteps.

"Is he gone?" Luman murmured.

She peered around the wall to see. "He's far enough he can't hear us."

Luman nodded. "To be safe, let's leave under the same bit of gramarye we used on arrival. Your Majesty, we're going to link hands."

"If I'm to travel incognito all the way to Cahokia, you can't call me your majesty the entire time. My name is Shelem. Shelem Adena, since the kings of Adena take their land's name."

"I knew a Sherem once," Luman said.

"It is the same name originally," Shelem Adena said.

Luman nodded. "We will join hands and walk to the Giant. Once there, I'll give you a mask for your face, and you'll walk out with another man's passport and trustworthiness certificate."

"Another man's *forged* passport and certificate,"

Montse said, but she took the king's hand. "Your name is James Goram, if anyone looks at your documents."

Luman cast his *abscondo* spell and they disappeared again. Carefully, they picked their way across the plaza, down the lane between two houses, and in through the back door of the *Giant of Adena*, to where the man called Ritter stood waiting. Once again beneath the skeletal stare of the seated giant, Luman ended his spell.

His face was flushed.

"Are you well, Luman?" she asked.

"The spell to disguise the false king," he murmured. "It cost me. I think it will continue to cost me. I am learning that gramarye has its limitations."

"There is only a very general description in the passports," Shelem said. "And the soldiers don't really look at them when a person is leaving. The real control is upon entry. From here, I'll simply walk out."

"Not a good idea," Luman said, but then he nearly fainted.

"It is a good idea," the king said. "Shall I get you a little port to fortify the blood?"

"Coffee," Luman said. "I can't drink wine."

"More's the pity," the king told him. "With my wife gone, other than my sons, wine is the great joy of my life."

Ritter fetched hot coffee. Luman gulped it, wincing at the heat.

"We must go," the king said. "Queen Sarah lies dying, and the later we leave, the later we get back."

They walked in a deliberate order: Ritter, followed by Luman, followed by the king, who promised to stick so close to Luman that Luman's shadow would cover the king's face. Montse should come last, the king explained, because any guard at the gate who had the slightest inkling that he might wish to look at the king's face would instead be distracted by Montse's beauty.

"And if he is not distracted by my beauty," Montse said, "I will cut his throat."

They approached the gates as Imperial soldiers were preparing to drag it shut by the light of torches. "Wait!" Ritter called.

"Short visit with your family." Pimple Mouth was still on duty, and stepped into the torchlight.

"You know what they say," Ritter answered. "Short visit, sweet visit."

Pimple Mouth nodded. "I've seen all your papers today. Carry on, but watch out—the New Models are on the move."

The New Models?

The four of them passed through a gate just barely open enough for them to fit through. Shelem Adena duly hugged the back of Luman's tunic as he walked, face down, and Montse in turn stuck as close as she could to the king's heels. Nevertheless, as she pushed toward the gap, Montse had the sensation that one of the soldiers standing there was staring at her.

But then she realized that the case was even worse; the man was staring at the king.

"Hurry," she whispered, when they had taken a few more steps together. "Shelem, I think that last soldier might have recognized you."

"Don't look back now," Luman cautioned. "If that soldier thinks he saw the king, then he'll run back to the palace and check. I can tell you with great confidence that the spell I cast is still in effect, because

I can feel it. So the soldier will see the king, and conclude he must have been mistaken."

"And if you're wrong?" Montse asked.

They were leaving the town behind, but were still walking through the town's farm plots, and the band of Imperial soldiers that surrounded the town. To her right and left, men cooked and played cards and sang around campfires, under an Imperial banner. Ahead, tantalizingly within reach, Montse saw the ragged edge of the forest.

"I will stay behind," Ritter said. "To be certain."

"You are needed as a guide, and for your contacts," Montse said. "Luman is needed because he is the wizard. I will stay back, and if we are followed, I will deal with it. And if we are not followed, then I will catch up."

Ritter nodded. "I'll tell the Swords to watch for you."

Less than a minute later, Ritter turned, taking a track through the forest that led westward. Montse followed him, but then as soon as the trees blocked the light of Adena, she drew her knife and stepped off the trail, into the woods.

It took two minutes, by her count, for her companions to march out of her sight. In those two minutes, Montse found a fallen trunk where she could perch, five feet off the ground and in the shadow of another thick tree, only a few feet to the side of the trail. She gripped her knife in her hand.

One minute later, men came from Adena, following.

There were only two men in the tailing party, and Montse couldn't see their faces. As she had feared they might do, they rode horses.

"They turned down this track, sergeant," the foremost rider said. "We'll be on them in a minute."

Montse knew the voice; it was the same man who had stood in the door of the shrine and cursed the goddess for a pagan cult. She let him ride past.

When the second man passed Montse, she attacked. She leaped, striking his head with her shoulder to stun him and wrapping her left arm around his head and neck at the same time. He made a muffled protest and grabbed for the reins of his horse, but Montse's full weight was in motion and he was already flying from the saddle, with her, toward the forest floor.

Montse landed badly on her left ankle, but she still had her hold on her man. By attacking the man second in line, she hoped she had chosen the senior, more experienced soldier as her target. She didn't want to frighten the other man into running away, but she preferred to take down the bigger threat first.

She stabbed the soldier twice in the neck, and then a third time in the eye. He spat blood and launched immediately into violent death throes. His horse panicked, and bolted ahead down the path. Riderless, it shied around the other horse, sending it into nervous leaps that nearly threw its rider.

Montse looked for a sword on the dead soldier's body and didn't see one immediately.

Then the other Imperial got control of his horse and swung back around. In the evening gloom, Montse couldn't see his face, but she did see the glint of some distant light on metal as he raised his sword over his head and charged toward her.

If the man on the ground had a sword, he was lying on it, but he did have two pistols belted across his belly. Montse grabbed both weapons and pulled them free—

and then fell. The earth was slick with blood, and she landed on her back. The horse thundered toward her, the razor gleam of a saber still high above it. She aimed, then considered the volume of the report—she didn't want to bring the entire army camp down on her. Dropping to her hands and knees, she yanked up the dead man's cloak to cover her pistol, and muffle the sound.

Bang!

Montse shot the horse. She was a good shot, and she hit it, though she couldn't be sure where. The report was loud, though maybe a touch softer than it would have been. The beast began to skew sideways and fall, a great neighing bellow rising from its throat. Montse rolled aside, dipping her knee into a pool of hot blood, wrapped the second pistol, and shot the horse again, this time in the neck.

The animal slammed into a tree, sending its rider rolling across the forest floor. Montse's knife was in the dead sergeant's eye, but she still held two heavy pistols. She lurched forward, ankle screaming, and fell upon the second soldier, using the pistols as clubs. She aimed for his head. He swung his sword at her but it was an awkward blow, and did no damage, slapping her instead with the flat of the blade, and then she heard a loud *crack* as the man's skull caved in.

Montse wished she had the time and resources to hide the dead horse, but she didn't. She dragged the men out into the woods, lifted a rotting log, and lay them in the depression beneath. With a little luck, that might slow down the inevitable pursuit.

She threw several large branches, thick with leaves, over the horse.

She kept the saber and the pistols, and grabbed a possibles bag from the dead sergeant's shoulder, hoping it included powder and shot—it made her feel more comfortable to be armed, in any context, but certainly when she was being pursued.

Then she raced after the panicked riderless horse. It had run nearly half a mile by the time she caught it up. The horse pulled away from her and whinnied in protest, but with enough soothing words, it eventually calmed down and let her climb atop it.

She caught up with her companions. She rode calling out her own false name, "Nemia Polog!", afraid that in the darkness, they'd take her for a mounted soldier and hide at her approach.

Luman stepped from a thicket beside the track to wave her down. He was trembling; exhaustion? "Were we followed?"

"Two," she said. "Now dead."

"Their friends will find them by morning." Luman sounded tired, too.

"I hid them well. We might have until noon." Montse slid off the horse, wincing from the tenderness of her ankle, and handed the reins to Luman. "You ride, wizard. You are exerting yourself elsewhere."

"Your Majesty," Luman said, as Shelem Adena and Ritter stepped from the trees. "You should ride."

"Bullshit," the king said. "Listen to the woman. Call me Shelem, and get on the horse."

"Yes, Shelem." Luman struggled, so Montse hoisted him into the saddle.

"I'll check tomorrow through the peep-stone, to see whether James has been discovered," Luman said.

"If you can stand it," Montse countered.

"We need to make as many miles as we can, right now," Montse said. "We walk through the night. We go west. We take every opportunity we can find to confuse the trail."

"We have people in Philadelphia, Shelem." Luman's voice was woozy. "We can reach out to them about your sons, too."

Montse seized control of the pace. She kept the naked sword in her hand, but she gave Ritter the pistols and began to march at a brisk pace, ignoring the pain from her ankle until it simply disappeared. To her surprise, Shelem Adena kept at her side with ease, and it was Ritter who flagged in the depths of the night, falling behind or needing encouragement. They stuck to footpaths, mostly, but in a small town in the early hours, Montse stole a canoe. They freed the horse, having lightened it of powder and shot and a little dried beef and a waterskin, and they rode the stream down several miles to the next bridge. There, Montse sank the canoe with two large rocks and a slash of her saber, hiding it beneath the stone arch of the bridge, and they continued. Sore and tired, their walk had become a shuffle, but perhaps now they had come far enough that the Imperials surrounding Adena wouldn't be able to catch them.

The sky had turned from black to stormy slate-gray when Montse saw a tree ahead of them move.

"Stop." She held up a hand. "Something is happening up there."

Luman snapped his chin up from his chest. "James is still hidden."

"What did you see?" Shelem Adena asked.

Montse pointed. "Over there. Perhaps a mile. A tree moved, I would have sworn."

"I can go ahead and scout the trail." Ritter looked peaked, if not as spent as Luman.

"No, wait. There may be a better way." Montse looked about her, eyes finally lighting on a tall pine tree on a low rise. From where she stood, she could see that the top of the pine poked out above most of the forest. "What we need now is a crow's nest."

She handed the king her stolen sword. Then she jogged up the rise, making light of her own fatigue, and hoisted herself hand over hand up the evergreen tree. Near the top, the branches got lighter and she had to move with more care, but within five minutes, she was raising her head above the forest canopy to look west.

At first, she thought was seeing church steeples, of some strange, rounded, Ohioan design. A row of wooden knobs the size of church bells protruded above the trees. Some of them, she saw, were painted. One even had a face painted on it, a greenish goblin face, with one eye five times the size of the other, two slits for noses, and an open mouth full of teeth.

What were they?

Then the goblin face moved.

It rose slightly, and Montse nearly fell out of the tree in surprise. Clinging to the branches, she watched as the face turned out of view, exposing an unpainted wooden surface and then moving away in lurching, shuddering leaps.

The others began to move, and she tried to count them. Twenty? Thirty?

And then the goblin-headed post moved into a gap between trees, and she could see the entire object for what it was: a humanoid form, with two arms and legs, carved entirely out of wood and hung together with steel cable like a doll. But these gigantic wooden dolls were marching, apparently of their own volition, westward.

And they must be at least fifty feet tall, and maybe as tall as seventy feet.

She scrambled to the ground, falling to earth among her companions with her heart racing and her mind full of fear.

"What is it?" the king asked.

"Doom," she said.

*"Our arm is extended still, to grant mercy to those
who wish to return to our embrace."*

<hr>

CHAPTER SIXTEEN

Calvin crossed the Ohio at a blind run. He carried
money, so he wasn't stealing horses as he traveled,
but he was buying them, trading them, and wearing
them out in quick succession.

He rode through the fringes of a great storm that
filled the Ohio. From Youngstown, which was overcast
and raining, he plunged into a bowl of lightning and
wind and sheets of water so large that they nearly
hurled him from the saddle. Despite the wind, that
tore at Calvin's clothing and whipped his long red hair
into a sopping wet scarf around his neck and chin, the
clouds never cleared. They moved in circles, or they
moved and were replaced by more clouds. Sometimes,
Cal would have sworn, the clouds moved away and
then moved back.

The weather eased as he crossed the river into
the Kentuck. Cal couldn't be certain that he saw
any ghosts, but he did hear a birdsong that sounded
backward to him one morning, and in the middle of
one night he awoke to see a procession of very tall,

red-headed men walking past the thicket where he'd bedded down. They carried copper axes and copper-headed spears, their eyes were fixed on the horizon, and they said nothing to Cal.

He went back to sleep. Lord hates a man as is scared of strangers.

He lost track of time, but it was something like a week after leaving Youngstown that he staggered up the draw and onto Calhoun Mountain. Black Charlie and Abraham Calhoun were on watch, and ushered him up the slope with whoops of victory. Cal's heart was far too heavy to join the shouting, but he grinned and clasped forearms with his cousins.

"We need to git everyone together," Cal told them. "Bring 'em to the Thinkin' Shed."

"Who's everyone?" Abe spat a squirt of tobacco juice into a bush. "Young'uns, too?"

Cal shook his head. "Grown-ups is all. I got heavy news, folks'll want to tell their children in their own fashion."

"I's hopin' you's bringin' word that Tommy Penn had gone and got hisself booted back to the Slate Roof House," Black Charlie said, squinting and looking into Cal's face.

"I'll tell you two now, what I aim to tell everyone at the shed." Cal felt tired. "Grandpa's dead. Caleb, too. Murdered in Youngstown."

"Some folks are gonna blame *you*," Abe said. "I ain't sayin' that's right, I'm jest sayin' don't be surprised."

Cal snapped to alert despite his fatigue. "Me? What in Jerusalem for? For not bein' able to protect 'em?"

"It was you as summoned 'em to Youngstown," Abe explained. "Or anyway, summoned *Grandpa*, and then

Caleb went with. A body might say it was your fault, you're incompetent."

"I ne'er summoned Grandpa," Cal said. "Hell, I'd ne'er do that. What kind of puffed-up fool do you take me for, to treat Iron Andy Calhoun like he's my servant? Jerusalem, *he* called *me*."

Abe shrugged. "That's how I heard it, Cal."

"So did I," Black Charlie said.

Cal's heart fell. He'd raced home because he knew he needed to deliver the news. He'd also raced home because someone was going to take over for his grandpa and become the Calhoun Elector, and Cal wanted to be certain that that person supported the impeachment. He hadn't imagined that anyone would hold him responsible for his grandpa's murder.

"Git folks to the Thinkin' Shed," he told his cousins. "Tell 'em it's me come back, and I got somethin' important to tell, but don't tell 'em Grandpa's dead. Let *me* do that."

They nodded and clasped his arm again, this time with shared sorrow. Abe quickly found someone else to watch the draw, while Black Charlie began rushing from door to door with the summons.

Cal entered his grandpa's cabin. He needed a moment to think, and didn't want to be interrupted by running into any kin. Standing alone in the small house his grandpa had built with his own one hand, Cal felt something break inside him, and he began to cry.

After a few minutes of weeping, thrashing mindlessly about in thought-free grief, Cal collected himself. People would be gathering, some were likely already standing outside, and Cal was a mess. His clothes were filthy and holed from the long ride.

He set his things on the floor and looked in the wooden chest of drawers for clothing he could borrow. He found a black shirt and breeches and began to put them on. His grandfather was near enough to Calvin's size that Cal could wear his clothing, and black—Iron Andy's favorite color, as long as Cal had known him—was suitable for the occasion.

Cal noticed multiple pin pricks in the cuff of one sleeve and he blinked, trying to figure out why his grandpa's shirt would be scarred in this fashion. Then he realized: having one arm, Andy Calhoun pinned his sleeve to the side of his shirt so it wouldn't flap loose.

Cal wept again. Then he dried his tears, tucked the letter that had summoned him to Youngstown into his pocket, and walked out onto the porch.

His kin had gathered. Cal stood on the planks, looking out over the heads of aunts and uncles, cousins of various specifications, and more remote kin whose precise relationship with Calvin had no specific name. They looked at him, some with expectation in their faces and others showing fear.

"I'm the wrong feller to do this," Cal said slowly. "But I been the wrong feller to do lots of things in my life that I jest went ahead and did anyhow, on account of I's the one standin' there. I wasn't the right feller to take Sarah off to the Ohio, she needed a warrior or a wizard, and I wasn't the right feller to go to Philadelphia, either. That turns out to be a bunch of lawyerin', and I can't abide lawyers. And mebbe there's no right feller for this task, anyway."

"Git on with it!" Polly called.

Cal nodded. "No easy way to say this," he started, but then he cut himself short. He was saying everything but what he needed to say. Was it because he was afraid people would be angry with him? Was it because he had no idea what the consequences were, and the world that lay beyond his next utterance was an unimaginable void? Was it because he felt that it was only when he actually pronounced the words that his grandpa would truly be gone? "The Elector Andrew Calhoun is dead."

He shuddered with the weight of his words, and gripped the timber of the house to support himself.

"Jesus!" someone in the crowd cried. It was a plea, not a curse.

"What happened?" David Calhoun, who had named his own son Andy after the Elector, was Cal's uncle and Iron Andy's son. He was twenty years older than Calvin, and his black hair and beard were just beginning to go gray. People often said, with admiration, that David was the spitting image of a young Andrew Calhoun. "Were you there?"

"He was murdered," Cal said. "I got this letter as said it was from him, and called me to Youngstown for a meetin'. I went, thinkin' we's gonna discuss the impeachment." He took the letter from his pocket and held it up.

"Who killed him?" Red Charlie bellowed. "And what about Caleb?"

"Abe and Black Charlie told me that Grandpa got a similar letter, only the letter said it was from me," Cal said. "Which means someone wanted me and him both in Youngstown. I reckon that somebody is the one as killed him. I'll give you three guesses who *I* think done it."

"Shit!" Black Charlie yelled. "We already knew

Thomas Penn was a murderer. This jest makes it real personal."

Uncle David's eyes narrowed and he folded his arms across his chest.

"I got to Youngstown," Cal continued, "and somethin' didn't feel quite right. So I did a little creepin' around, like Grandpa taught me when I's little and we'd play at Indian Wars."

"Like you done all those years of rustlin' beef," Abe said.

Cal grinned, tears in his eyes. "Lord hates a man as won't feed his family."

That drew a melancholy chuckle from the crowd. Uncle David continue to stare at Cal.

"I found Grandpa and Caleb dead. Shot. And I found the fellers as must a done it. They was waitin' in my hotel room, three men, with knives."

The crowd fell quiet.

"Go on," Polly said.

"You kill an old man by a trick," Cal said slowly, "I reckon you give up your right to fair warnin'. I shot one of 'em in the back. When the other two objected, I cut their heads off with my ax."

Murmurs ran through the assembled Calhouns. "Damn right." "Had it comin'." "Hell of a feller, Iron Andy." "Hell of a feller, Calvin."

Cal had nothing else to say, so he just stood, arms at his side.

"So you came running back to tell us," Uncle David said.

"It was the right thing to do," Cal said. "Iffen you and I had switched places, I'd a wanted you to tell me, quick as you could."

"You didn't want to come lay a claim to being the new Elector?" David asked slowly.

"Hell, no!" Cal tried to say the words emphatically, and they came out in a near shout. "No, I ain't the feller to do that. But someone's got to be the Elector."

"Might not be someone from the mountain," Black Charlie said. "They's Calhouns up in Pennsland, and the mountains of Virginia, and down in Nashville itself."

"And down in the hills in Igbo country," Polly added. "Some of those folks might fancy themselves as a new Elector."

"Or someone else right here on the mountain," David said.

"Of course," Cal said. "And since I's only in Philadelphia on account of I held Grandpa's proxy, I figured I needed to git back here and find out who the new Elector was, so I could git *his* proxy instead. You know how lawyers are, complainin' about the little technicalities like metes and bounds, and who only has a life interest or a term of years. They're the same in the Assembly, only much worse. Iffen I don't have a valid proxy, I'll git thrown out and the impeachment might collapse."

"*Iffen* the new Elector wants to continue the impeachment," David said.

There was a thoughtful murmur in the crowd.

"*Iffen*? The *hell* you say!" Cal snapped, feeling rage rise in his chest. "I jest told you that your father was murdered by Thomas Penn, and now what you want to do is let Thomas git off without his just desserts? What the hell is wrong with you?"

Cal felt a little strange, addressing his uncle as he would a peer, but he was angry, and his words felt right.

"You jest told me my father was murdered," David said. "Might a been at Thomas's doin'. Might a been the work of someone else. Mebbe it's time we cut and run from the impeachment, and worried about things as matter."

"Things as matter?" Cal's heart raced. "Like what?"

"Like the beastkind in Missouri, ragin'," David suggested. "I read as Shreveport's about to collapse. Machogu's got his own soldiers and Imperial troops and they's even some feller callin' hisself Judge McCain, runs a militia, and it ain't enough. Like keepin' folks here fed and in good homes. Like the war in the Ohio." There were nods of agreement throughout the crowd.

"This is all about the war in the Ohio!" Cal nearly screamed. "Who do you reckon is doin' the fightin'? And iffen you think it wasn't Thomas Penn as killed my grandpa, who do you think did it?"

David shrugged, and was slow to speak. "Could a been lots of people. Mebbe an old enemy, from one of his wars. Mebbe he jest got in a fight with someone because he was a cantankerous old men, and the fight went bad. Or mebbe he was killed by someone as wanted to replace him as Elector."

"Who would that be?" Cal asked.

David shrugged. "Mebbe someone who summoned him away from all his kin under false pretenses with a letter."

Calvin's blood ran cold. "What the hell are you sayin'?"

"Mebbe someone as raced back here to stage a bit of theater, claimin' he'd avenged Iron Andy Calhoun, standin' on Iron Andy Calhoun's own porch to say it."

Cal's head swam. He could scarcely hear the words

coming out of his uncle's mouth, his own heartbeat and the breath in his lungs sounded so thunderingly loud.

"Mebbe someone as put on Iron Andy's own clothes," David said. "As iffen to say, look at me, I'm the new Iron Andy."

Cal wanted to hit David. He wanted to go back into his grandpa's cabin, take up his tomahawk, and chop his uncle's head off.

But his grandpa wouldn't want him to do that. David was kin, even if he was insulting Cal, and making false accusations. David was a Calhoun, and he was not the enemy.

"You're wrong, David," he said. "You're wrong and you're sayin' hurtful things. But I love you jest the same, and I ain't gonna fight you." Cal stepped down off the porch. "Youins tell me when it's decided who the new Elector is. Then I'll ask that feller for my proxy."

Cal walked away, making the shortest line that would get him out of the cabins and into the woods on top of Calhoun Mountain. He wept freely now, for the grief of his grandpa's death, and Caleb's death, and also for Uncle David's hard suspicions and fierce accusations. He found he was weeping for Sarah, too, because he missed her and because she was at war, and he wished he could be a young'un again, taking tobacco to the fair to sell for his grandpa.

"Cal," Abe said.

Cal looked up. He found himself sitting on a stump at the edge of a small meadow, warm sunlight soaking through the black fabric directly in his bones. He felt empty, deflated, and no more at peace than he had been before.

Abe and Black Charlie stood before him.

"Uncle David's called a meetin'," Black Charlie said.

Cal stood. "Back at the Thinkin' Shed."

Abe shook his head. "At the Temple."

"He's called the Lodge together?" Cal took a deep breath. "So you two were sent to invite me?"

Black Charlie laughed. "No, we's told *not* to let you know about it. But that's horseshit, and jest about everyone knows it. You need to go."

Oranbega lay at the southwest end of Lake Erie, on the west bank of the Maumee River. Cathy had grown accustomed to the architecture of mounds from her time in Cahokia, including the low residential mounds and the great monumental mounds with public or sacred significance, such as the Sunrise Mound, the Serpent Mound, the Great Mound, and others.

Oranbega had mounds, but they were towers.

The sight of the mounds made Cathy think of Bill, and the home he had not yet built for Cathy and himself. When he built it, it would certainly be a mound in the Cahokian residential style, low and built around a house.

But would he ever build a house now?

Would he want to?

Oranbega had no walls, which in itself was striking. And twinned mounds, steep-sided like the mound at Irra-Zostim, but much taller, rose on the lake shore, and also irregularly around the oldest, densest part of the city. Lacking a wall, Oranbega sprawled beyond its original boundaries, as Philadelphia did, with avenues running along the lake shore in both directions as well as up the river. Atop each twinned mound was a fortress consisting of two stone towers, rising another hundred feet up above the top of its mound. Each pair of twinned towers was then bound together by a slender arching bridge of stone.

The buildings of the city were of various styles, and tended to run in patches. Cathy passed a section built in half-timber style with thatched roofs; an avenue that ended the area marked the beginning of a new style, in this case, horizontal boards, mostly painted white, and tar-paper roofs. Cathy saw low mounds, rectangular stone buildings, log cabins, brick, and even something that looked like adobe.

"This city is much larger than Cahokia." Cathy tore her thoughts away from her lost husband.

"Yes," Zadok Tarami said. "I fear that will be our challenge. The rulers of large cities are rarely humble, or easily persuaded."

They rode side by side with the Podebradan Yedera. As they had drawn nearer to Oranbega, the weather had improved, but they had not seen the sun yet on their journey. Here in Oranbega, the sky was scored gray and black, and light showers dappled their road from time to time. A strong wind blowing in off Lake Erie hurled high waves against Oranbega's docks and seawall; the waters of the Maumee were so flooded that they nearly overflowed their banks, even along the last mile, where the riverbanks had been built up with dressed stone.

"The towers near the lake are the oldest," Yedera said. "They were built to signal to those who followed, and they have been maintained by Oranbega since."

"This is another source of pride," Zadok noted.

"And then the city preferred to keep building towers," Yedera continued, "rather than walls. The first king of Oranbega was a man named Amun. He had been a war leader, and he had buried his weapons of war and forsaken all his warrior arts. He said he would build towers rather than walls, so he could see friends coming, and run out to embrace them."

"Has Oranbega always had peace, then?" Cathy asked.

"No," Yedera said.

"And yet it does not seem to have suffered."

"Many of those who came with Wallenstein arrived at this city and simply stopped," Zadok said. "They had come far enough. So you will find Germans here. But it is also well situated for trade. Acadia, and Haude-nosaunee territory, and the Republic, and Pennsland are all quickly and easily reachable by water, and so those tongues, too, have a place here. And trade along the Maumee reaches deep into the heart of Talega. The enclave of Lenni Lenape towns where their king lives is located at its headwaters."

"Perhaps this should be the capital of the empire," Cathy mused. "This city is closer to its center."

"The Kentuck would be closer still," Yedera said. "Maybe the emperor should build a city there. It was a sign of the great empire builders, once, that they made cities to be their capitals."

"The empire has no capital city," Zadok said, "though the Assembly meets at Philadelphia. But if the empire is to acquire a capital, it will not be Oranbega. Not while Thomas Penn has any say in the matter."

"Does the King of Orenbega hold court in one of the towers?" Yedera asked. The question made Cathy stare; she thought of Yedera as a person who was strange and powerful, in her way, and the question was a reminder that Yedera was in some senses a provincial woman. Perhaps she was seeing a large city for the first time in her life.

"We are almost to his hall," Zadok said. "I am known to his father confessor, who was one of the twelve men who undertook the pilgrimage of the Onandagos Road last year. I've written again, and we will be welcomed. By the chaplain, at least."

The king's hall was a long stone building with an arched roof of stone and stocky buttresses on all sides. It looked rather like a cathedral, if an ugly one, with its wings shorn off. It lay on the stone retaining wall built around the mouth of the Maumee, and the muddy brown floodwaters now swirled only a few paces from his stones. The door was shut, and a young man in a brown robe stood on the stone porch, hands folding together and smiling.

Zadok rode to the bottom of the steps and called to the young man. "I'm looking for the king, or if not him, then for his father confessor."

"Father Vaudres is expecting you," the young man said. He pronounced the name with a French silent S, though Cathy knew it had a Cahokian spelling and pronunciation. "You are the Metropolitan Zadok Tarami, and I have been waiting for you."

"Not for too long, I hope." Zadok dismounted and handed Cathy his reins. She led his animal, while he walked alongside the other priest.

"My vigil began the day before yesterday. I'm Father Jean-Claude."

"You are taking us to meet with the king," Zadok suggested.

"No, just Father Vaudres."

Zadok looked up to meet Cathy's eye and frowned.

Father Jean-Claude led them a few streets away, to a chapel of reddish brick. Around the side of the building stood the rectory, and Father Vaudres rushed from its door into the rain to embrace Zadok Tarami. He was taller than Zadok, and younger, but similarly thin, and with a similarly long beard.

"I worried," Zadok said, "leaving you in the hands of the Imperials, as I did."

Vaudres laughed. "You worried for me? But you were the one who crawled into a city under siege, on his knees."

Cathy and Yedera dismounted.

"I had hoped God would take my sacrifice and give us peace."

Vaudres's face fell. "And instead, we have more war. Perhaps we failed God, and He withholds His blessing."

"Perhaps we have failed God," Zadok agreed. "We, as God's children, are certainly failing each other."

Vaudres nodded slowly. "Jean-Claude, will you please see to the horses?"

The French priest took the beasts and led them into a stable behind the rectory. Vaudres ushered the travelers through the rectory door and into a cloakroom. Cathy peeled away her cloak and hat, hanging them on pegs. The sudden lightness of her shoulders, after many days of wearing wet, heavy wool, contrasted with a foreboding in her heart.

They sat at a dark wooden table in a cozy kitchen. Rain beat against the glass of the windows and the smell of baking bread set Cathy's mouth to watering. Finally, Vaudres spoke again.

"I know I am disappointing you," he said. "I cannot get you an audience with the king."

"Does the king wish Cahokia ill?" Zadok asked gently.

"He wishes peace and health for Cahokia. And he will not himself participate in the Serpent Daughter Anointing."

"Did you advise him thus?" Zadok asked. "I know that, in your stead, six months ago, I would have told him that this was an old pagan rite, and probably harmless, but possibly connected with the worship of a demon."

"You would have said exactly that," Vaudres agreed.

"But I was wrong."

The two men talking to each other across the table looked so much like one man talking to himself in a mirror that Cathy struggled not to laugh out loud.

"I advised him differently," Vaudres said. "I advised him that the rites of kingship were beyond my ken. I advised him that he should make the decision dictated by his own conscience. I also advised him that if he were to save the life of the Queen of Cahokia, then she would be likely to think well of him. I advised him that Cahokia could be a very important ally, not to mention trade partner."

"But he will not meet us," Zadok said.

"He has informed me that he finds Thomas Penn to be a more important ally and trade partner. 'The Erie trade dwarfs the Maumee trade,' he told me. 'It always has.' I told him you were coming, and he became angry. He said that he regards your queen as an upstart, illegitimate, and a criminal. He said that the only appropriate response to emissaries from a bandit queen is to treat them as bandits."

"He said he'd imprison me?" Zadok's eyebrows raised.

"He said he'd hang you." Father Vaudres collapsed

forward, resting his forehead on his folded arms and hiding his face.

Zadok Tarami began to laugh. Vaudres raised his head to stare at him.

"At least," Zadok said, "it won't be a *lukewarm* reception!"

Vaudres smiled, but shook his head. "Really, this time, it falls to me to save you from yourself."

"Did the king order you to arrest me?" Zadok asked. "Is there a warrant?"

"There's no warrant, as far as I know," Vaudres said. "And I was given no instructions regarding you, except that I was not to arrange a meeting. I asked Father Jean-Claude to wait at the king's audience hall, fearing you might go there directly rather than come here first."

"You know me well." Zadok smiled. "So you will not be surprised when I tell you that I plan to stay a few days. It will allow me to reminisce on our pilgrimage together, and enjoy the waters of the Maumee."

"The Maumee is flooding," Vaudres said. "Its waters are barred to trade and travel now, because they are dangerous. If you wish to enjoy the waters of the Maumee, consider doing so in Talega, where they are smaller."

"Dangerous waters are the ones in which I am wont to swim," Zadok said, smiling.

"Dangerous waters will one day bring you death by drowning." Vaudres didn't smile back.

"Is he married?" Cathy asked.

"What?" Vaudres seemed startled, as if he had entirely forgotten that she was there.

"The king threatens us with hanging." Cathy's

thoughts jumped easily from the King of Oranbega to her husband, so she struggled to speak clearly, and without blushing. "In my experience, when a man threatens violence, it usually means he has reached the point of the conversation in which he has foregone negotiation. He will no longer hear ordinary offers."

"Yes," Father Vaudres said. "This is exactly what I am trying to tell you."

Zadok frowned and raised an eyebrow.

"Sometimes, a married man," she continued, "that is to say, a happily married man, may still be brought to the negotiating table from that point, if he is approached by his wife."

Zadok folded his arms. "This is beyond my personal experience, but I can think of cases I have seen secondhand."

"This is because he trusts her. Many years of repeated acts of generosity, many years of mutual cooperation, and many years of mutual forgiveness, create a bond between longtime lovers that is unlike any other." The priests both looked pale, so Cathy tried to smile with compassion. She wanted to weep. "So I ask again: Is the king married?"

Thomas waited in a nearby sitting room for the Shackamaxon Hall to fill. Julia sat beside him, sharing a deeply cushioned sofa made of dark walnut and embroidered with narwhals and foxes. Julia was smiling; since their meeting at the *Huig de Groot* hotel, at which Thomas had had to reprimand her for her isolation, she had been pleasant and available. There had been no more talk of hoping the wedding might be called off, and Julia had been available to be seen at the theater, at dinner parties, at balls, and even simply riding the streets of Philadelphia.

Now they were married. They had been married that day, the ceremony performed by a suitably fashionable, distinguished, and compliant member of the great Winthrop family, and in the Lightning Cathedral. Thomas had been mildly disappointed that the cathedral had performed no great feats of electricity in his honor, but Bishop Winthrop assured him that the cathedral had done its part admirably. The city had attended, packing the streets as well as the pews, with a large number of Electors filling the front quarter of the church's seats.

Some had stayed away. Calhoun was dead and his proxy had disappeared, facts in which Thomas took discreet joy. The scheme to kill both Iron Andy and his grandson had been Temple's last act before departing for Missouri, bearing the emperor's gift to the Heron King. Other Electors, notably those seeking Thomas's removal, had been absent from the wedding as well. He planned to make them regret their absences.

Gottlieb came to tell him that Shackamaxon Hall was full.

No, not Gottlieb. This was Gottlieb's replacement, a thin fellow somewhat ironically named Hercules. Gottlieb had betrayed Thomas, and when Thomas had sent him to the Ohio to be disposed of, he had given Thomas the slip.

Out of Thomas's sight and mind, Gottlieb had become harmless. The real purpose of sending Gottlieb along with Franklin was to test *Franklin*. When there was betrayal within his house, Thomas wanted to be certain that his private counselor was a person he could trust. Gottlieb was a traitor, and spent many hours in the presence of Temple Franklin, under careful observation, through the Parlett traveling with them, by Oliver Cromwell.

If Franklin and Gottlieb had shared any treasonous communication, they had done it without Cromwell noticing. That put Thomas's mind at ease, also. And it further meant that he didn't have to offer up Franklin as one more appetizer on the plate to the Heron King.

He would like to have had his new alliance in place before today, but the weather in the Ohio meant that Franklin traveled slowly. He neared the junction of the rivers now, but was not in Missouri yet.

"The hall is full," the servant said again. "Thirty-five of the people on your list are present, Your Imperial Highness."

Thirty-five Electors. It was a start, at least.

"Thank you, Samson. That will do."

The servant bowed and retreated, and only then did Thomas realize that he had bungled the fellow's name. "Blast," he murmured. Julia rested a feather-light hand on his arm.

They descended to the hall together. Julia wore white and pearls, a simpler dress that nevertheless echoed her splendid wedding gown. Thomas wore Imperial blue, with as many gold accents as his tailor would permit him. The seal of Jupiter was stitched into the suit in gold thread; the first time the tailor had shown the result to Thomas, Thomas had ordered him to go back and quadruple the amount of thread. He would not have his victory missed, and, as a result, he dazzled. The light reflecting from his own clothing nearly blinded Thomas whenever he passed a mirror.

He wore his thick hair up and powdered white, and he carried his saber at his side.

He wore kid gloves dyed the same blue as his coat.

The doors to the Shackamaxon Hall opened. A herald cried out, "His Imperial Majesty, Lord Thomas Penn. Her Imperial Majesty, the Lady Julia Stuyvesant Penn."

He had invited Julia to continue to use her name, both as a concession to her tender sentiments and as a sign of good faith to her father. Her acceptance had been gracious.

Thomas walked to his throne, head held high. The Shackamaxon Throne still sat in the center of the low dais at the far end of the hall, but he had caused a second chair to be placed beside it. The second chair was smaller, off center, and set very slightly back. It featured similar stitching and embroidery, though of course it was carved from a lesser wood.

Electors, their husbands and wives, the great and good of Philadelphia, and assorted other notables of the empire stood and faced Thomas as he strode to his throne. At the edges of the hall were scattered servants and bodyguards, as well; the room was packed, so that there was scarcely room for guests to maneuver to gain access to the wine and the punch bowls standing on tables along two walls. Thomas prowled like a lion, chin up and hair back, each step a deliberate paw placed forward on the savannah.

He seated Julia, and then he sat, and then the crowd applauded. It was their first appearance together as a married couple. As *the* married couple. As the first couple of the empire.

"You are my Eve," he whispered to her as the applause died down. "Allow me to be your Adam."

She nodded, with charm and composure.

She had required correction, but he was finding her delightful.

"I welcome you all to this reception," Thomas said. "Many of you have not seen this throne before, so I wish to take a moment to present it to you." He clapped his palm on the arm of the chair. He was understating the novelty; none of those present but Thomas had ever seen the chair before. "I had this made of the wood of the Shackamaxon Elm. For those who come from remote powers of the empire, or from beyond its borders, I will tell you this much of my family history. The Shackamaxon Elm was the tree beneath which William Penn signed his first treaty with the Lenni Lenape and the people of the Ohio. They were beset with enemies, and they begged for Penn's help. Penn's valor in battle won him the land which is mine today. The wood of the throne is stained red, to remember the Three Wounds of William Penn, three injuries that he suffered in battle in the Ohio, keeping his alliance."

The crowd murmured and nodded.

"We shall be grateful to see you individually," Thomas said, "only first I wish to make two announcements of general interest. I say of general interest, but perhaps they are of *particular* interest to those of you here who sit in the Assembly."

An excited murmur ran across the room.

Charlie Donelsen of Appalachee caught Thomas's eye. Donelsen flared his nostrils and sneered. No doubt the cattle-thieving rascal Donelsen hoped that Thomas would announce his resignation.

"Three things, rather," Thomas said, deciding on

the spur of the moment. "You will forgive me the little slip; my mind is rather elsewhere this afternoon."

He beamed at Julia. She beamed back.

"The first announcement is this." Thomas met Donelsen's gaze and smiled. "We regret to announce the death of the Elector Andrew Calhoun. Our messenger had only imperfect information, but it seems that Calhoun met his untimely end at the hands of ruffians in the Ohio, some days ago."

The crowd gasped. Donelsen's sneer became envenomed.

Ruffians in the Ohio was excellent, Temple Franklin himself couldn't have done better. It implied that Calhoun had been killed by Firstborn, when in fact the assassins had been men employed by Thomas himself, through Franklin.

And men who, Franklin had assured him, would in turn be killed by others, so as to leave no trail of witnesses.

"Our second announcement is a much more joyful one." Thomas cleared his throat. "We have won a major battle in Koweta. The New Models constructed by the Philadelphia College of Magic continue to prove their worth, and this very week have routed a rabble of outlaws calling themselves the Swords of Wisdom. We have sealed the rebel prince Koweta in his own burrow. Our forces shall soon be converging upon Cahokia and its urchin pretender."

The Philadelphia College of Magic had had nothing to do with the New Models. They had been assembled in Pittsburgh and elsewhere in western Pennsland, and given life by Oliver Cromwell. But the College was so big and so locked into separate faculties and campuses that even the College couldn't be sure that the College wasn't responsible, and in any case, they weren't about to turn down credit for a victory.

One of the Memphite Electors raised his glass to make a toast. Two of them, princes whose shocking height betrayed Anak ancestry, had come to Philadelphia for the wedding. The celebration was a little premature, as Thomas hadn't finished his announcements, but this was a day on which he would indulge people. He waved permissively.

"To Lord Thomas, and to his victories!" the Elector proposed.

"To Lord Thomas, and to his victories!" others in the room echoed. They variously sipped their wine or their spirits.

Charlie Donelsen drank nothing, and looked as if he had a sour stomach.

"It grieves us that the Ohio," Thomas continued, "which was home to the first allies of my greatgrandfather, William Penn, and which was even home to my sainted sister's husband, has so turned on us. Our arm is extended still, to grant mercy to those who wish to return to our embrace. But that same arm shall not hesitate to deal justice to those who wound and betray."

General noises of assent.

"I said I had a third announcement. To the end of defending against the reavers and marauders who nibble at the flanks of our empire, I make public today a project that I have been assembling in quiet for months. I do it as a gift to my bride, and to her father, the Elector Adriaan Stuyvesant."

He found Stuyvesant standing near the back of the

crowd, holding the cylindrical case, as he was tasked to do. Was that Dutch modesty, or was Adriaan trying to look inconspicuous? It didn't matter.

He nodded toward Stuyvesant.

"Today I announce the formation of the Shackamaxon League. The League shall be an alliance for mutual defense and reinforcement, and it shall not be coextensive with the empire. I therefore form this league and make the announcement not as His Imperial Majesty, Thomas Penn, but as Thomas Penn, the Penn landholder. We invite all powers of this continent who wish to, to sign the League Charter. Indeed, I may tell you that I am currently negotiating with powers beyond the borders of the empire to join the League, and hope to be able to formally welcome some of those powers shortly.

"Today, I present to you the League Charter, which shall be signed on behalf of its founding members: Pennsland, the Hudson River Republic, the Kingdom of Memphis, and the Principality of Shreveport."

Thomas raised a hand and signaled to Hercules. He led two footmen forward through the crowd. The footmen carried a table, so going was slow as the assembled guests had to shift aside to make room. They set the table on the floor a few paces in front of Thomas, and then Hercules produced a single chair.

Adrian came forward, carrying the case. He opened it, to the hushed fascination of the crowd, and removed the parchment containing the Articles of the Shackamaxon League. He unrolled the parchment on the table, weighting it on one end with its case and on the other with an ink pot produced by Hercules.

"I am happy to sign this," Stuyvesant said. "I join

with the Penn landholder Thomas Penn... my son-in-law... in an oath of mutual defense against threats within and without the empire."

He sat, signed, and then stood to a round of applause. Then he pushed through the crowd, toward the nearest punch bowl.

Kimoni Machogu sat next. "I am grateful to all who will sign this charter," the prince said. "Today it is my lands that are ravaged, but tomorrow it will be yours. And as you send men to my aid," he nodded to Thomas, "I will aid you when the time comes."

He signed, and then stepped away.

The Memphite Elector wanted more attention, and spoke from his feet. "I will not say that the empire has failed," the prince said. "But the empire has elements within it that are *not cooperating*. Until they can be brought into a more amenable frame of mind, I urge all those powers who are serious about peace to join the Kingdom of Memphis in entering into this alliance. Kimoni, my friend, our troops are at your disposal, as are our hearts."

He finally withdrew, and Thomas took his place at the table. "That this is a great day in history is already clear," he said. "How great a day it shall eventually prove to be, only the unraveling of history will tell."

He signed, to applause.

"There is always a risk I might eat the boy."

———◆———

CHAPTER SEVENTEEN

As a boy, Calvin had never realized that Broken Finger Clearing was the Temple of the Calhoun Mountain Lodge; he had known it as a clearing with great rocks for sitting on and a spectacular view of the valley below. He had also known it as a clearing that was haunted—Granny Clay had warned him repeatedly, cackling her most witchlike laugh, about the many haints that were to be encountered around Broken Finger after dark.

At the turn of his manhood, on a dare, he'd crept up late one night. He would prove his courage by recovering a notched stick Red Charlie had left in the clearing for the purpose; approaching, he'd heard songs he didn't recognize, and through the trees he'd seen what looked like people wearing white sheets, but he'd figured, Lord hates a man who can't stand up to some old ghost, so he'd been about to run into the clearing to grab the stick, anyway.

Instead, his uncle David had stepped from behind a tree and grabbed him by the arm.

David had chased him back down the mountain with a stern warning to listen to Granny Clay. Only later had Cal put Broken Finger Clearing and Free-masonry together.

He walked up the mountain now by little-used paths. They were little used because they were steep and had bad footing, mere deer paths, so his going was slow.

He chose the bad path on purpose, because he was going to sneak into the Temple. If David had directed men not to invite him, likely he had also directed the Tyler and his lookouts to keep Calvin out. He carried a big handful of pebbles in his pocket; to keep them from rattling, he pressed them against his hip with one hand.

He carried no other weapon.

Cal's path turned up steeply, and he had to scramble on all fours to make it to the top of the rise. There he remained in a crouch, scanning the trees. He was close enough to see the light in Broken Finger now, so he was in the area watched by the Tyler, who was Jeffrey Simmons Calhoun, a distant cousin from down in Nashville.

After a couple of minutes of patient watching, he spotted the lookout on this side of the hill. The man was good; he stood in the shadow of a pitted boulder to avoid being struck by moonlight or making a sil-houette, but when he shifted his posture to keep his legs from falling asleep, Cal heard him. From that sound, he had an approximate direction, and then it was a matter of peering deeply into all the shadows until he found the one that wasn't empty.

The mosquitoes were swarming, which meant that the bats were out as well. This was to Cal's advantage; a man who had been seeing tiny bats swoop through his field of vision all evening would take a thrown pebble for just one more bat. Cal gauged his throw to get the pebble onto the other side of the boulder. He kept his arm low to the earth as he threw, so as not to emerge from shadow himself.

He couldn't hear the pebble hit the ground, but he saw a shift in the boulder's shadow.

He threw a second pebble. He wanted this one to sound closer, but if he hit the boulder, he might give the game away. He judged the weight of the rock in his hand, took careful aim, and threw.

This time the lookout peered around the boulder— Cal could see his silhouette against the moon-silvered hill beyond—and Cal moved.

He didn't move far, just into the next big pool of shadow, this one in a cluster of trees beside a fallen log. He waited until the lookout had satisfied himself that no one was sneaking up on him on the other side of the boulder and settled back into his watch.

Then Cal threw another pebble.

After he lured the lookout out of position a third time, Cal guessed that he was beyond the man's vision. He slipped past a second lookout with the same tricks, and then reached the edge of the Temple of the Calhoun Mountain Lodge. He didn't want to spy because he didn't want to be *caught* spying, but he did want a sense of what he was stepping into.

The men of the Lodge stood arrayed in a semicircle, facing Cal. They wore their aprons, so this was a solemn occasion and they'd already completed the liturgy. Slightly to Cal's left and facing the men were Cal's uncle David and a man Calvin didn't know by name, but recognized as a Calhoun from down on the Cumberland.

He was tall and clean-shaven, which made him look a little citified, but he ran cattle. Cal had never stolen from his herd, of course; he was kin.

"We sent word by brothers to other family centers," David was saying. He seemed to be answering a question, since one of the younger men, standing in the front of the assembled masons, was meeting his gaze expectantly. "Iffen any man wants to throw his hat into the ring, they'll let us know. But this here is Calhoun Mountain, it's where Iron Andy made his home for twenty years, and I reckon the family looks to us. We select a man here tonight, that man is the Elector until some other Calhoun comes along and makes us take it back. The Lodge will send a letter to the Assembly to say so."

The man he was talking to nodded.

"I'm Jet Calhoun," the citified kinsman said. "Jedediah's the name my pa wrote in the family Bible, but on account of I had thick black hair, even as a baby, my sisters took to calling me Jet, and hell if it didn't stick. I run cattle about forty miles down the Cumberland, near five hundred head."

"Forty miles . . . ain't that the Kentuck?" Red Charlie asked.

"Or near enough," Jet said, "but I ain't afraid of ghosts."

"You're afraid of Thomas Penn, though."

"I ain't afraid, but I ain't a fool, either. Iron Andy was a good man, and sometimes a good man gits led by his good heart into doin' somethin' foolhardy. I understand the Queen of Cahokia was fostered here, youins all unawares, and I reckon Andy decided to make war on the emperor for the girl he raised as his daughter. That's love, and that's admirable."

Cal found himself liking Jet's manner, if not the direction of his words.

"Andy's dead, now. Change of leadership means a change of compass, and this is a good opportunity for the Calhouns to git ahead. It's time to embrace the empire. It's happened, folks, it ain't goin' away, so what we ought to be doin' is makin' it work for us. We ought to git our boys on the town council down in Nashville, and git ourselves exempted from the Toll Fare."

A year earlier, Cal might have been convinced.

Jet continued, "We ought to git our boys into the Foresters, so we can be certain the Imperials'll look the other way when a few cattle trade hands now and then. And as for the impeachment, I think we ought to consider it a bargainin' tool."

"How do you mean?" Black Charlie asked.

"The emperor wants it to go away," Jet said. "How *bad* does he want it to go away?"

This was the moment. Cal stepped from the trees and into view.

"Bad enough that he murdered Iron Andy Calhoun," he said.

The assembled men started, though Cal saw more than a few grins.

"I'd crack a joke about not havin' my apron and bein' late," he said, "only I's specifically not invited."

"I'll have the Tyler expelled," Uncle David growled.

"The Tyler's a good man," Cal said. "So are the lookouts. I'm jest a *better* man."

Someone in the back hooted.

"Did you come to throw your hat into the ring?" David asked.

Cal shook his head. "I ain't the feller to fill my

grandpa's moccasins. He was a hero, in every sense of the word, and I'm jest a poor, dumb cow thief. But I *am* the man who stood up in the Electoral Assembly and called for the impeachment of Thomas Penn. It was what my grandpa wanted, and it was the right thing to do, and I'm here to see that we carry through with our commitment."

"How many Calhoun lives are you willin' to lose for that impeachment?" Jet asked.

Cal shrugged. "Many as it takes, I guess. I risked mine, and hell, Tommy Penn hisself tried to take it from me." He turned to David. "Jet might a been a good Elector in more normal times. I like his concern for takin' care of the Calhouns, for instance, and makin' the empire work for us. Only we live in times when the empire is flat out tryin' to kill us. It already killed our hero, and it's prepared to kill any other man as sticks his head up to object. Hell, that's what Jet's sayin'. Thomas Penn murdered my grandfather, the hero to every man here, and Jet thinks what we ought to do is jest shut up and take it."

David looked at his feet.

"How about it, David?" Cal asked. "We're politickin' here, and I got a question for the speaker at the stump. What are you gonna do about Thomas Penn?"

David fixed a glare on Cal that would have peeled the paint off a barn. Then he turned slowly, to face his brother masons.

"Jet's right about one really important thing," he said. "We're Calhouns. We ought to be seein' to Calhouns. Yeah, the emperor killed my father, and iffen my *nephew* don't reckon I'm grieved by that fact, he might oughta think a little more on the meanin' of family. My father was murdered. I don't want the next death to be my brother's, or my wife's, or my nephew Calvin's. No more Calhoun deaths, that's the first thing."

"That's what Jet said," Black Charlie called out. "I wanna know what you think that's *different* from him!"

"Jet wants to involve us more in the empire." David shook his head slowly. "That's a mistake. The empire is goin' away. It weren't e'er but an artificial creation anyhow, a dream that was dreamed once by Ben Franklin and John Penn. We held together through the Spanish War, all right, because we had common interests. Now that our interests ain't aligned, what do you see? Impeachment. Lawsuits. War in the Ohio. War in Louisiana. It's comin' apart."

Cal heard murmurs of agreement among the assembled.

"Gettin' us more involved in the empire is a big mistake," David said. "Any ties we have with the empire will be the ties that drag us into one of these wars. What we need to do is git out. That's what I'll do as Calhoun Elector, is keep us from gittin' involved, and when war comes this way, I'll keep us safe up on this here mountain."

Cal ripped the sleeve off his shirt. It was his grandpa's shirt, and his grandpa's sleeve, and he raised the black cloth over his head. This was not a gesture he had planned, but in the moment, with his own heartbeat loud in his ears, it felt like the right thing to do. "Are you hearin' what I hear, boys? Jet thinks we ought to go beggin' to Tommy Penn for Imperial jobs, and David wants to pretend there ain't no empire at all. Neither one of 'em's got any kind of response for the murder of Andy Calhoun, other than we should ignore it."

"I heard tell you already killed the men that done it," Jet said. "I thank you for that. Perhaps we can consider three deaths for one vengeance enough, and let the murder lie."

"For two!" Cal snapped the sleeve in the air. "Caleb Calhoun was assassinated, as well. That's my uncle, and iffen you's keepin' score, it's Andy's son, so it's too late to worry that the next death might be David's brother, on account of that death already happened."

"Damn straight!" someone shouted.

"I have more brothers," David said.

"You offerin' 'em up?" Cal asked. "I expect the Imperials'd be grateful for some target practice."

"*You're* offerin' 'em up!" David shouted. "Antagonizing Thomas Penn got two Calhouns murdered, and you want to go on pokin' him with a stick!"

Cal shook his head. "I don't want to rile him up. I want him gone. Iffen a copperhead bites one of my dogs, or my child, or my neighbor, the answer ain't to make friends with the snake, and it ain't to pretend the copperhead's gonna go away on its own, either. The answer is to kill the serpent."

"Prosperity!" Jet called. "That's what we need!"

"Peace!" Uncle David countered.

Cal turned to face the crowd. "I expect we'll have to wait for someone else to show up. These fellers are both fools."

"Calvin!" someone shouted. "Calvin Calhoun for Elector!"

"Jerusalem, but that's a bad idea." Cal chuckled. "Mebbe we can send down to Nashville for someone? They's Calhouns down in the Igbo lands."

"Calvin!" came another shout.

"He's a boy," David sneered. "He wants to take us to war."

"I don't want war," Cal said. "War's here, and that's a fact. And I don't love the empire, but it ain't goin' away, either. The only way to make peace with both those things is to be on the right side of the war, and fight to git the right people in charge of the empire. So my vote is goin' to who says those things, and it ain't either one of you."

"Then don't vote," Uncle David said.

Calvin's heart sank.

"All in favor of Jet Calhoun, show it by the uplifted hand," David said.

Three hands went up.

Dammit. David was going to win, and all Cal's work on the impeachment would be wasted. Iron Andy Calhoun, the greatest hero the family had ever produced, had died in vain.

"All in favor of David Calhoun, show it by the uplifted hand," David said.

Five hands went up.

"All in favor of waitin'!" Cal cried, raising his grandfather's empty sleeve again. "David's a good man, but he's wrong!"

No one raised a hand.

"All in favor of Calvin Calhoun, show it by the uplifted hand," Black Charlie said. "And while you're at it, hoot like a banshee."

Hands shot up. The cry that rang across Broken Finger Clearing nearly left Calvin deaf.

The first destination of the emperor's honeymoon tour was New Amsterdam. As the Lady Julia's Dutch servants, Jacob and Margarida, Nathaniel and Margaret wore a simple blue livery and rode in a wagon near the back of the train.

Thomas and Julia rode horses, and ranged sometimes in front and sometimes behind their wedding procession. Sometimes they rode parallel to it, out in the woods. Julia was patient and cheerful, though she did remark in the middle of the first afternoon's riding, in Nathaniel's hearing, how much her legs hurt. He took then to singing healing songs, and her smile seemed less forced.

Thomas talked much to Julia. He told stories of his battles in the Spanish War, and his actions with the Imperial Foresters suppressing bandits and tax evasion. He was polite to Julia, and he never mentioned any other women, except in the most respectful and objective tones.

He also listened, to Nathaniel's surprise, to stories of Julia's youth on the Hudson.

The Philadelphia Blues, mounted dragoons in simple blue uniforms, rode as Thomas's bodyguard. Two of them rode at the head of the procession, carrying the Imperial banner of horses, ship, and shield. The others moved flexibly about, maintaining a loose net about the Imperial couple at all times. They were fierce-eyed soldiers, and they were armed to the teeth, each with a carbine rifle and a pair of pistols as well as knives, a bayonet, and a sword. The two who rode most consistently near Nathaniel and Margaret were named Stambo and Pottles. They muttered jokes under their breaths to each other, and when they looked at Nathaniel, it was to sneer.

Stambo was the taller of the two, and had mottled gray skin; Pottles had a dark brown complexion. The men took turns offering fruit and biscuits to Margaret for the first several days, undeterred by her glares.

"And I had heard that Dutch girls were sweet," Pottles said, when they finally surrendered and left her in peace.

Nathaniel was careful not to bother any of the Blues. While riding, the emperor wore a coat that seemed to block Nathaniel's ability to hear him, and his ability to see him while riding the starlit plain. In the evenings and mornings, and occasionally at other times, he would take the coat off. Nathaniel watched carefully, blacked shoes and fetched water and set out food, and waited for his opportunity.

The train included a wagon for the Imperial baker (containing a portable brick oven) and another for the butcher and a third for the cook. There was a wagon carrying wine, water, and beer. In addition, there was a wagon inside which Thomas and Julia could sleep, if the weather grew too fierce for their pavilion alone; everyone else slept in tents at all times. There was a phaeton that carried only two people, one the emperor's body servant, a man named Hercules, and the other a bald-headed youth in blue who said nothing and stared at the woods. Nathaniel found the boy's gaze unsettling, and tried to avoid his presence, when at all possible. There was an empty coach, in which Julia rested when she tired of riding. There was an armorer's wagon, carrying weapons and ammunition. This was not for the Blues alone; more than once, Thomas called a halt to the procession so that he and Julia could shoot, either because a herd of deer had crossed their path or because they had found a long clearing with clean lines of sight.

They also stopped to picnic, at least once a day. Other meals were provided, either by taverns along the road—swept and scrubbed into an unnaturally white state of affairs, and serving surprisingly good wine—or in good houses, usually set back from the Imperial pike.

At the end of the train came two wagons that carried the servants and their gear: tents, bedrolls, and the implements of their various roles. Nathaniel and Margaret rode with Lieke, who mostly paid attention to her needlework. Their position at the back of the caravan kept them generally out of sight of Thomas and also the boy in blue, and Nathaniel was grateful for it.

Messengers came and went, always in Imperial blue. Occasionally, Thomas dashed off a reply and sent it back with the delivering messenger. Generally, he sat at night after dinner, writing out replies for a messenger to carry through the night to Philadelphia. While he wrote, Julia sat beside him and read a novel.

During the day, Thomas and Julia picked mushrooms, gathered birds' eggs, plucked berries from wild brambles, examined birds through a spyglass, and discussed the arrangement and meaning of collections of standing stones they encountered. They also pored over maps, and Julia herself chose their route at crossroads. At her decision, Hercules would mount a horse and ride ahead, in the company of two dragoons, to secure places to eat and rest for the coming day.

Thomas never took off his blue kid gloves.

Choirs met them along the roadside, to sing as they passed; these must also be arranged by Hercules. Puppet shows were presented beside the pike, and Thomas and Julia would laugh at the misbehavior of

Punch or the Heron King. Poets approached to bestow compositions upon the emperor and his wife, florists brought bouquets for their picnicking, farmers presented cured hams and fresh eggs. At one crossroads, Algonk actors from a pair of nearby Praying Towns competed in reciting monologues from Shakespeare.

Thomas in every case spoke words of gratitude and praise.

Each day, Julia rode closer to him. By the third day, she was spontaneously reaching out to touch his arm.

To stay dressed in blue livery, rather than putting on his inside-out purple coat, Nathaniel had to constantly carry Isaiah Wilkes; this also allowed him to endure the inches of separation from his drum, which rode beneath their seat. To speak Dutch, as the emperor expected, he had to constantly carry Jacob Hop. His limbs dragged from fatigue, and he lay himself down at night tired and awoke exhausted.

He resolved to do what he could for Thomas, and then leave the honeymoon train.

"I hate him," Margaret whispered, as she and Nathaniel together carried a folding wooden table out into a grassy meadow to set up a picnic lunch. "I know he tried to kill us, and if he knew who we were, he'd kill us now. Probably right in front of his bride. But he's not the worst man I ever knew. Maybe in another life . . . he could have been an uncle I loved."

"Maybe still in this one." Nathaniel folded down two of the table's legs.

"He killed both our parents," Margaret said, folding down the others.

Nathaniel nodded. He hadn't forgotten, but somehow the importance of those murders had begun to fade.

"You're right. But...maybe there is yet a possibility of healing."

Together, they stretched a tablecloth over the table and then headed back to the wagon for chairs. "I know that's what you want," Margaret said. Her hand shook slightly. "But what I want is to kill him."

In his spirit-ear, Nathaniel heard the words slightly differently.

~But what I want is to kill you.~

"Margaret," he said, "are you angry?"

"Why should I be angry?" She sniffed.

"Sometimes people are just angry."

"So if I'm angry, you would expect it to be for no reason?" she pressed. "You would expect me to be irrational?"

Nathaniel shrugged. "I'm here to listen."

"Go ahead and listen." She set her chair in place. "Listen to me, who was raised by a pirate queen, as I go fetch silverware and lay it on the table."

By agreement, Margaret handled the silverware, because Nathaniel couldn't make himself touch the knives. Margaret handled it only briefly, because extended handling would irritate her skin.

Nathaniel dropped his questions, but he tried to pay more attention to Margaret. She often seemed angry, and Nathaniel could never quite understand why. She went from smiling to breathing out fire at the drop of a hat, and when she was angry, Nathaniel heard her voice, the voice that no one else could hear, breathing out threats against him:

~I should break your legs.~

~How would you feel, if I threw you beneath the wagon wheels?~

~If I killed you and hid you in these woods, no one would ever find your body.~

He tried to sing songs of healing for her, too, but she didn't seem to hear them.

They reached New Amsterdam by ferry and took rooms in a hotel called the *Willem Barentsz*. Hercules informed them that Jacob and Margarida would share a room with Lieke, one floor beneath the Imperial couple, and handed Margaret and Lieke each a key.

Finally, he could play his drum and summon Makwa to his dormant body with enough privacy. Nathaniel felt prepared to make an attempt.

After the last boot had been blacked and the last dishes all put away, Nathaniel and Margaret retired to the hotel room. Lieke was there already, sitting in a wooden chair in the corner. "Tonight you will do it?" she asked, in Dutch.

"*Ja.*" Nathaniel's head felt like a pile of bricks on his shoulders, but he would feel no relief until he set down the spirits he was carrying, and that required him to heal Thomas. He lay down on a carpet in the center of the small room. "Margaret, would you like to come with me?"

She hesitated, but nodded yes and then lay beside him.

Then he drummed. He had grown accustomed to rattling out a quick series of beats that raised him to the starlit plain in moments, but this time it took longer. Nearly a minute. Was it fatigue? Or the weight of Margaret?

He ascended the seven steps and found Jake, Wilkes, and his sister Margaret all with him.

~What is this place?~ she asked.

~*Hello, Margaret.*~ Jake smiled at her. ~*It's a place of spirits.*~

~*The dead?*~ she asked.

~*Some of them are dead.*~ Jake nodded. ~*I'm dead, and so is Wilkes. But many of the dead move on. And also, the living can be here. Like you.*~

~*But the unborn are elsewhere,*~ she said.

Nathaniel nodded.

Margaret looked around. ~*This is beautiful. Why are you not here more often?*~ As she spoke, a spider crawled from her mouth. It sat upon her chin and looked up at Nathaniel. Though the creature was tiny, Nathaniel could see hundreds of iridescent facets in its eyes. Margaret frowned.

~*Because I like spending time with you,*~ Nathaniel said. That seemed to satisfy the spider, which lowered itself onto Margaret's chin and pulled its legs in, so that it looked like a mole.

While Margaret continued to look around in wonder, Nathaniel listened for the sound of Thomas Penn's voice. He heard the man, and it sounded as if the voice were coming from the top of a small peak. With his companions following, Nathaniel trudged up the hill.

He still felt weary.

He found Thomas and Julia, sitting on a sofa and singing a song without words.

~*Is this what they're really doing?*~ Margaret asked.

~*It's hard to say,*~ Nathaniel told her. ~*In this place, things seem to be boiled down to their bones. Only that's not a very helpful description. Here, we see the essentials of a thing. And sometimes, seeing the essentials of a thing means being able to see what's wrong with it.*~

~*Not always?*~

~Not always.~ Nathaniel thought of the Lazar Robert Hooke, and the wiindigoo Ezekiel Angleton. He had seen both men on the starlit plain, and neither one had seemed susceptible of healing.

~So maybe Thomas and Julia aren't really singing,~ Margaret continued.

~I don't think the word 'really' is the right word. I would say, in their physical bodies, sitting in their hotel room above us, they are probably not singing a song together. Whatever they are doing, it's like they're singing. And listen, they're not just singing, they're harmonizing.~

~It's like singing, is it?~ she teased him.

Nathaniel decided not to take that bait. Instead, he examined Thomas.

From the waist up, the emperor wore a white night-shirt, and no gloves. He was muscular and his motions free and nimble and he sang, and then began to dance with Julia, who wore a matching nightshirt; both were embroidered with the ship, eagle, and horses of the empire, though to Nathaniel's eye the horses seemed to have stepped back and let go of the ship in the middle. Below the waist, Thomas was covered in vines. They were dark green, like holly, and they seemed to sprout from the ground in two thick trunks. The vines were leafless, shooting out only tendrils that wrapped themselves around Thomas's legs, inserting themselves underneath his skin and into veins that bulged green.

And then Nathaniel realized that the emperor only *appeared* to be moving his legs as he danced. Instead, the vines were dancing, and moving Thomas about. Thomas himself seemed to have no notion that, while his arms looked young and strong, his legs appeared as withered spindles, atrophied, capable of no motion

other than as they were moved by the tendrils of
their plant puppeteer.

~*I have no knife,*~ Nathaniel said.

Then he saw that the tendrils digging into Thomas's
legs poked out the other side. They waved and trembled, and as the couple danced, the tendrils groped
toward Julia.

He knelt and grabbed at the tendrils, but for each
one he shattered with his hands, another grew to
replace it. Blood flowed down the emperor's leg, only
the blood was dark green. Nathaniel sang at the vines,
while Margaret and his two familiar spirits knelt and
worked with him to tear away the vines. They couldn't
tear faster than the vines could grow.

~*What is this?*~ Wilkes tugged without effect on
one of the large vines.

~*I don't know!*~ Nathaniel screamed, but every time
he touched the vines, he heard a voice in his mind:

~*Death! Death to Elytharias! Death to the Firstborn
and their goddess! Death!*~

Nathaniel screamed and fell. He bounced down
the seven steps, each one more painful than the one
before, and lost his grip on his familiar spirits. When
he hit the ground, he found himself lying on the hotel
room again, and weeping.

Of the nearly five hundred prisoners he'd brought
from the Walnut Street Prison, Temple Franklin thought
that three hundred fifty remained, give or take a few.
After they were ferried across the flooding Mississippi
and had entered the Heron King's lands, he'd had the
dead pulled out of the wagons. To be certain that none
of the prisoners was feigning death in order to escape,

those removed had been weighted down with stones and thrown into the river.

The Mississippi in a calm season was a mighty river. In a season of storm and flood such as this spring, it was an unholy terror. The ferry, aided by filthy, soaked men who swore they were professional rivermages in the employ of the Imperial and Dutch Ohio Company, shepherded the thirteen wagons across five miles of water. Franklin watched the tops of elm and oak forests drift past as if they were shrubs. He saw church steeples poking from the brown sheet, with the churches entirely submerged.

And the rain was not abating. It had grown worse as he had come west, growing from drizzles and sprinkles over Youngstown to steady rain on Koweta lands to a howling fury of thunder and lightning on the river.

Once the river was behind him, the storm fell off. Turning back, half a mile from the Mississippi and heading into thick forest, Temple Franklin had the impression that the river was flooding and flowing up into the sky, rather than the other way around.

Should he have kept the bodies of the dead? Perhaps Simon Sword would eat carrion, or some of his followers would.

But no, this was not a meal being offered to a beast in a zoo—it was a sacrifice being laid on the altar of a god. The old high priests of Jerusalem slew rams and bullocks and sheep and goats and turtledoves, but they laid no rotting flesh on the altar of the Lord.

The soldiers guarding the wagons were veterans, soldiers rather than Company men, though there were several scouts whose experience was in running the great rivers in canoes for the Imperial Ohio. The first night that Franklin and his wagons camped in the Great Green Wood—or was this Missouri? he was unsure quite where the border lay—those same scouts went into the forest. When they returned there was one fewer of them, and they had frightened looks on their faces, but they also brought back beastmen guides.

A man with a badger's head entered the circle of the campfire. Franklin sat reading by the light of a small lamp; it was Ibn Battuta's *Travels*, and he was enjoying it immensely. Its proper title was *A Gift to Those Who Contemplate the Wonders of Cities and the Marvels of Traveling*, and those were things Franklin received as gifts, indeed. Someday, he should like to travel the New World as Ibn Battuta had traveled the old, or as Sir John Mandeville or Benjamin of Tudela had done, recording its mountains and rivers as well as its monsters and marvels. Beside him, the Parlett he had brought dozed on a camp cot. The cot, chair, lamp, and fire were all sheltered from the rain by an oilcloth tarpaulin. Similar tarpaulins were strapped all around the outside of the prison wagons—from behind those sheltering sheets, Franklin heard a low symphony of groans.

"I am Fftwarik," the badger-headed man said. "You wish to see the Heron King?"

"I have brought him gifts." Franklin set Ibn Battuta aside, on a small table, and stood. "And my master wishes to speak to him."

Fftwarik looked at the sleeping Parlett. "Is this creature your master?"

"This boy is a kind of idiot seer," Franklin said. "My master will speak through him."

"Ah," Fftwarik said. "I, too, am an idiot seer, and my master will speak through me."

"I had rather hoped to see your master in person," Franklin said.

"But your master is not here," Fftwarik said. "Does Thomas Penn exceed the stature of the God of the Mississippi and the Ohio Rivers?"

Franklin was not about to be drawn into a conversation about precedence baited with such traps. "Of course, you are correct. When shall we proceed?"

Fftwarik was silent for a moment.

Then he said, "I am Simon Sword. You stand in my kingdom now, and I am in my power. I have been held back for many lifetimes, but no longer. The sword has returned home. The rod is mine. This time, I shall break the cycle, and I shall reign with blood and horror upon this valley for all eternity."

The Dutchman Jacob Hop had said something similar to Franklin during his final hours. A member of Franklin's Conventicle, he thought, had told him that the sword had gone back. Hop thought that meant an empowering of Simon Sword. Apparently, Simon Sword thought the same thing.

For the first time on this journey, and possibly the first time in his life, Temple Franklin wondered whether he had overreached. He dragged the Parlett boy into a sitting position and prodded him awake.

"I am Temple Franklin," he said. "Confidential advisor to His Imperial Majesty, Thomas Penn. His Imperial Majesty will be available in a moment, and will speak via this young man."

"Temple Franklin," Simon Sword purred. The thunder over the Mississippi rolled with his words. "Son of Benjamin Franklin. The Lightning Bishop."

"Grandson," Franklin said.

"I hate your grandfather," Simon Sword said.

Franklin's heart raced. "We are not in strong disagreement there, Your Majesty. He was a quixotic man, a builder of purposeless devices and Weishauptian conspiracies, and I have spent my adult life trying to rid myself of the chains he laid upon me and upon the empire."

Simon Sword laughed. "You hate your grandfather because he gets in your way. I hate my own father for the same reason. Perhaps you, Temple Franklin, are a person I can like."

Franklin smiled uneasily.

"I AM HERE," the Parlett said, in that voice of breaking glass that mean that Cromwell was inhabiting the Parlett on the other side.

"There are two of you," Simon Sword said.

"I AM THE EMPEROR THOMAS PENN. AND I AM HERE WITH ONE OF THE PARLETT BOYS. YOU MUST BE WITH THE OTHER. WITH WHOM AM I SPEAKING?"

"You are also with another person," Simon Sword said. "A dead man is with you. I felt his presence before, when I was trading with the Queen of Cahokia, wooing her." He nodded at the storm and the flooded river. "She turned down all this grandeur and glory, can you imagine it? But you, dead man, you were nearby. Your servants came to the Serpent's hill on your behalf, but you lurked in the forest to watch."

"I AM OLIVER CROMWELL. THEY CALL ME THE NECROMANCER. I AM COMING INTO MY POWER."

Could Director Schmidt in the Ohio listen in on this conversation, if she wished?

"Ah." Fftwarik, with Simon Sword inside, nodded. "And what is your power?"

"I SEEK TO END DEATH FOR MANKIND. MY SERVANT THOMAS PENN WILL RULE OVER AN ETERNAL KINGDOM OF THE UNDYING."

"I do not agree with this goal," Simon Sword said. "I live to bring change, and change comes by means of death."

"THE ETERNAL COMMONWEALTH OF PENN-SYLVANIA WILL BE A CHANGE. IT WILL COME ABOUT BY THE DEATHS OF EVERY OPHIDIAN LIVING IN THE OHIO. THE DEATHS OF EVERY OPHIDIAN AND THE DEATH OF THEIR GOD-DESS."

"Ah." Simon Sword leaned forward, and suddenly, the badger-headed man was gone. In Fftwarik's place, and towering over Franklin's pavilion, sat a giant. He was covered with iridescent feathers, his head was the gigantic head of a heron, and he held a golden sword across his lap, a blade so huge, Franklin thought it might slice through the mast of a sailing ship in a single blow. Wind and rain blasted from the giant's body. "Now we are in agreement. This is the last thing I need for *my* kingdom to become eternal, that the serpent goddess and her serpent daughter be scoured from the earth. And yet, I find that I cannot act against her directly, as I would."

Franklin's hands trembled. He clasped them together and smiled.

"AS A TOKEN OF OUR GOOD WILL, WE HAVE SENT YOU A SACRIFICE."

"I smell the men," the giant said. "Are they all for me?"

"WE ASK THAT YOU SPARE FRANKLIN AND

THE PARLETT," the voice that sounded like shattering glass said. "CONSIDER IT A TOKEN OF YOUR GOOD WILL. BUT THEIR LIVES, TOO, ARE IN YOUR HANDS."

Simon Sword laughed, a sound like the howling wind. He stepped past Franklin and seemed to grow. Was he fifty feet tall? One hundred? Simon Sword raised his golden blade and swung it in one long blow, parallel to the earth—

that sliced off the top of a wagon. With a loud *clang*, the roof flew away, like a lid knocked off a kitchen pot. Oilcloths, snatched up by the wind, immediately disappeared into the gray storm, and the men in the wagon screamed in discordant terror.

Simon Sword reached into the wagon and seized a man. He raised the hapless fellow, shrieking, over his head, his white feathered fingers wrapped around the victim's legs. The doomed man squealed, waved his arms, and tried to dodge, but failed.

Simon Sword bit his head off.

Blood poured onto the iridescent feathers. Simon Sword smiled. "Guilt," he rumbled. "All mankind tastes of the same thing to me. Sin and guilt. You all deserve judgment, and I am the great judge."

The screams coming from the wagon grew louder. In three bites, Simon Sword ate the rest of the fellow: one leg, then arms and torso, and then finally the remaining leg. He ate the rags the man wore, and swallowed his bones.

Franklin managed not to vomit, though only barely.

Simon Sword returned to crouch beside the pavilion. The rain hurled from his body seemed warmer now; and had it darkened in color?

"You mistake me," the god of the Mississippi and Ohio rivers rumbled. "I have no good will."

Franklin stumbled back a pace, sucking in air and tightening the muscles of his stomach as he braced for sudden death. He stepped out of the pavilion and rain drenched him instantly.

The Heron King laughed. "I will not kill you, Franklin. Penn, I accept your offer of alliance. Your name is one I have heard before, and it was not as the name of an ally. I am amused that the descendants of William Penn and Benjamin Franklin should aid me in founding my unending reign."

Franklin bowed, ushering himself back underneath the shelter of the pavilion.

"WE ARE PLEASED," the Parlett said.

It was not Thomas's habit to speak of himself in the plural. Who were the "we" to whom he referred? He and his new bride? He and Cromwell? He and Franklin?

"We are pleased," Franklin decided to say, and bowed again.

"Tell me, Penn," Simon Sword said. "Do you intend to leave Franklin in my kingdom, so that we may speak?"

"WE MUST HAVE SOME MEANS OF COMMUNICATION," the Parlett said. "ON THE WHOLE, I THINK I WOULD LIKE TO HAVE FRANKLIN BACK. THE IDIOT SEER IS NAMED PARLETT. IF I LEAVE HIM WITH YOU, WILL HE SURVIVE?"

"There is always a risk I might eat the boy." Simon Sword stood again, scooped his hand into the roofless wagon, and plucked out another man. This time, he tore off both the man's legs with his beak, so the man thrashed in his grip and continued to scream.

"I will stay." Franklin took a deep breath. "If it is necessary to the alliance."

Simon Sword laughed and swung the legless, screaming torso in a circle, spraying blood on Franklin and on the Parlett and on the wagons. "Excellent, Franklin. But no, Parlett will be safe in my kingdom. And I shall send my herald Fftwarik with you, Franklin. I may not appear thus in the Land of Penn, but Fftwarik shall bear my presence into the Ohio, and be my voice there."

"Thank you," Franklin said.

Simon Sword bit off the head of the man in his grip, and the screaming stopped. Raising the body above his head, he tilted up his beak and then squeezed, forcing the man's blood to rush out and gush into the god's open maw. He tossed the exsanguinated torso into the forest.

The men in the open wagon begged for mercy.

Franklin forced himself to keep breathing.

"When I am done glutting myself," Simon Sword said, "I shall give this body again to my servant Fftwarik, and you shall return with him into the Ohio."

Franklin nodded.

Simon Sword reached once more into the open wagon.

"And bring me a young man for company."

CHAPTER EIGHTEEN

Chigozie and the Merciful cornered Absalom in a ravine near the Mississippi River.

Were the river not flooding, the ravine might have been two miles or more from the water. At the mouth of the ravine, the roof of a barn protruded above the flood, making a low-peaked platform from which Chigozie and his flock could survey the ravine. Where there was a barn, there was likely also a farmhouse, not to mention possible chicken coops, sheds, or stables. None of those buildings was visible.

"God," Chigozie murmured, wiping cold rain from his face, "bless the people who have been driven from this land."

"Amen," Ferpa lowed.

The mouth of the ravine was submerged in a slow eddy created by a pillar of rock. Words had been painted on the rock with whitewash, but the rain had all but obliterated whatever message there had once been, leaving only the letters *RM*. But the ravine rose steeply into the cliff from which it was carved, the rocky floor of the canyon resisting destruction by the storm. A few twisted trees, blasted naked by the wind, clung to crevices in the ravine wall.

"Kort and the others should be at the top by now," Chigozie said.

"I will go first." Ferpa had a long coil of stout rope over one shoulder, taken from an abandoned tack and saddle shop. Kort carried a matching length.

"No," Chigozie insisted. "I go first. It is the shepherd who confronts the wolf, not the sheep. Especially when it was the shepherd who brought the wolf into the fold."

"I am reluctant to say that my Shepherd is being silly," Ferpa growled.

"Good." Chigozie plunged into the icy water.

The eddy would have pulled him under and made an end of his career as Shepherd, his bravado notwithstanding, but for Ferpa. She was tall enough to stand where he struggled to touch the bottom with his foot; grabbing him by the back of his fur cloak, she hoisted him up onto the rock. Water dripping from his furs, Chigozie clambered the ravine.

He did not want to be seen as sneaking up on Absalom. He still believed that he could touch the heart of the Heron King's son, somehow, and kindle compassion in him. To avoid surprising his quarry, he sang. The Merciful joined him, and because it was not a song they had sung much together, they sang it in call and response fashion.

> Come, we that love the Lord,
> And let our joys be known;
> Join in a song with sweet accord,
> And thus surround the throne.

We're marching to Zion, beautiful Zion
We're marching to Zion, the beautiful city
  of God

Chigozie was pleased to find that he could sing while marching uphill. Life in Missouri had strengthened him, at least physically.

Had it strengthened him morally?

But he must not let it harden his heart.

"Great God of Heaven," he prayed out loud. "Give that we may find our brother Absalom, and soften his heart, that he may be willing to return with us, and be one of Thy flock, and know mercy."

A massive weight struck him from above, accompanied by a terrible shriek. Claws dug into his back; but for the heavy furs, Absalom's talons would have pierced his ribcage and torn out his heart.

A bellowing and snorting racket enveloped Chigozie, and the talons were yanked away. Cold rain sluiced in through new rents in his cloak, stinging his torn flesh.

One of the Merciful dragged Chigozie to his feet and snuffled at his ear and neck with a canine nose. "Do you live, Shepherd?"

"I live!"

The exploding chaos of noise continued. The Merciful propped Chigozie against a wall of the ravine. Leaning against a limestone bulwark, he was sheltered from the wind and rain. He wiped water from his eyes again, and witnessed battle.

Absalom had killed one of the Merciful. Sthoat, his name was, and he looked like a man-sized ferret who walked on its hind legs, those hind legs and the tail behind them being the hindquarters of a lizard.

Sthoat had always sung with a beautiful tenor; now he lay over a boulder, back twisted at a fatal angle, not breathing.

Kort, Ferpa, and two others of the Merciful tackled Absalom. He tossed Ferpa against the stone wall and dove at her headfirst, slashing with his beak at her throat—

and Kort punched him in the side of the head.

Absalom staggered sideways, and a Merciful named Roppet, who looked like a large man with a pig's ears and snout, and who had never in Chigozie's presence spoken any intelligible word other than "amen," wrapped his arms around Absalom's knees. Absalom fell and Kort lunged forward, a loop tied in the rope.

Absalom yanked one knee up to his chest and then kicked downward. His talons raked through Roppet's chest, shattering ribs and spilling entrails and blood. "Amen!" Roppet shrieked, wrapping his arms around Absalom again in one last, fatal effort.

Kort got his noose around Absalom's neck. He hauled the Heron King's son back to his feet and then pulled the rope down, curving it beneath a large fang of rock. He pulled, and Absalom's head was yanked down to ground level.

Absalom kicked and slashed, wounding two more, and then Ferpa looped her line around one of Absalom's birdlike feet. She pulled, and she and Kort had Absalom stretched out between them.

"Mercy!" Chigozie cried.

"I scorn mercy," Absalom shrieked.

"Mercy may be to kill this child," Ferpa said. Her voice held sorrow.

"No." Chigozie ground his eyes with his palms. He

hadn't slept much, crossing Missouri on the trail of this monstrous child. He had a hard time thinking through the exhaustion, and now through the lancing pain in his back, but he wasn't yet ready to surrender. "There must be hope yet."

"We are near Cahokia," Kort said.

Chigozie had never seen Cahokia, or any of the capitals of the Ohio. "Are you thinking of their sorcerer queen? But she will bear no love for us if we bring a murderer within her gates."

"The Queen of Cahokia is a giver of mercy," Ferpa said. "She would not despise you for your compassion."

"I know little of the queen," Kort said. "It was in Cahokia that I first learned mercy myself. There is . . . something there."

Absalom shrieked and writhed, but could not escape his bonds.

Chigozie stepped away from the limestone to stare up into the clouds. Rain spattered his cheeks and fell down the open neck of his shirt; though he was shivering nearly to the point of illness, the cool rain felt good on his skin.

God in heaven, what is your will?

Lightning flashed across the top of the ravine. A split second later, thunder rolled through the canyon, making Chigozie's spine tingle.

It was not an omen. God did not communicate through omens, omens were the tool of the mystères. God answered prayers.

But if God had answered Chigozie's prayers, Chigozie didn't recognize the answers. He needed to do something, and he was loath to cause the death of even so strange and violent a creature as the Heron

King's son, and Kort's idea was the only other option he seemed to have.

So perhaps that was an answer.

"We take him to Cahokia," he said. "We ask for their help."

Lightning flashed again, but if there was thunder, Chigozie missed it.

The Merciful tied Absalom hand and foot, lashing him so thoroughly he could not move. Then Kort and Ferpa dove under the waters around the barn roof, emerging with axes and saws, with which the Merciful chopped the rooftop of the barn, severing it from the rest of the building. When it was free, the rooftop floated. They held it in place with poles recovered from inside the barn.

In the meantime, Chigozie had gathered the remains of Sthoat and Roppet. Ferpa brought up sheets of burlap from beneath the waters; Chigozie wrapped Sthoat and Roppet in the rough material, weighting the funereal bundles down with stones from the ravine.

Standing on the rooftop raft, surrounded by the Merciful and gazing upon the dead bodies of two beastmen—two *people* who had *died* following Chigozie's vision of mercy—Chigozie was overcome with grief. "I am not fit to be a shepherd."

"No one is," Ferpa said. "And yet, someone must guide us."

"I am the resurrection, and the life," Chigozie recited. "He that believeth in me, though he were dead, yet shall he live: And whosoever liveth and believeth in me shall never die."

"Amen," the Merciful said.

Absalom twisted, but could not escape.

"As our friends Sthoat and Roppet were baptized to a new life in mercy," Chigozie said, "may they now descend into these waters, to be born again in a new and eternal life with Thee."

"Amen," the Merciful said again.

Chigozie rolled both bodies into the water, watching them as they sank.

Then he stood. "Is there a pole for me? A shepherd works for his keep."

"There is tending for your wounds," Kort said. "And you must rest. We shall pole. But if you wish to lead us, I ask that you continue to lead us in song."

Chigozie raised his voice again.

> Let those refuse to sing
> Who never knew our God;
> But children of the heav'nly King
> May speak their joys abroad.
>
> We're marching to Zion, beautiful Zion
> We're marching to Zion, the beautiful city
>   of God

In the crossing of the flooded Mississippi, they passed swimming beastkind. The Merciful invited none aboard their vessel, and also had to repel none. Perhaps the beastkind in their rampaging looked for children of Adam to attack, or perhaps the raft left them perplexed, so they ignored it.

The river carried them downstream, despite all that they could do on the poles. Several hours later, they reached, if not quite the other side of the flood, then a no man's land between the river and the earth, a wooded plain soaked to the depths of Chigozie's knees. Stepping into the water, Chigozie straightened his back and looked around.

"I am lost," he complained. "In this storm, time and direction don't matter at all. I see wind and rain. Was this what it was like on the day of creation?"

"Upstream," Kort bellowed. "Cahokia lies on the river. If the water becomes too deep, bear right. If we leave the water entirely, bear left."

It took them twelve hours of walking to reach the walls of Cahokia. They smashed the barn rooftop down into a smaller raft and laid Absalom on it, pulling the craft with rope. At his insistence, Chigozie took occasional turns pulling. At the insistence of the Merciful, he mostly led the way and sang.

The fabled Treewall was standing, despite the storm. Cahokia was built on a very slight rise above the surrounding flat land, so that its gates were not submerged. On the western side of the city, where there ought to have been wharves and docks, the water lapped directly against the wood of the wall. There were ships anchored there, or struggling with pole and sail against wind and wave, making a ragged patrol of the river.

Chigozie led the Merciful to the city's southern gate. The gate was open, and soldiers in gray sheltered from the storm within the gatehouse. They wore small steel helmets and were armed with spears and carbines. When the Merciful approached—Kort and Ferpa slinging Absalom along between them—the Ophidian soldiers stared.

Chigozie found that he hadn't planned what to say. "We are here to see your queen," he said. "To ask for her help."

The captain of the guard hooked his thumbs into

his belt. He and all his men had an image of a bird on their chests; it had the outline of a raven, but was white. "You're beastkind."

"We know," Kort said.

Chigozie could not bring danger to the city with a lie. "This prisoner we carry with us is the child of the Heron King. We have striven to teach him mercy and love and restraint, and we have failed. He kills, and he will kill again. We hope that there may be healing for him in Cahokia."

"I'll send a messenger." The captain's expression was openly doubtful. He gestured to one of his men, who grumbled, drew a wool cloak about him, and then ran north into the city. "The Vizier is laying sandbags against the flood in Riverside, so he may not have time to meet you."

"I understand." The gashes in Chigozie's back had ceased to trouble him, no doubt because he could no longer feel his back. He could no longer feel his legs below the middle of his thigh, either.

He stood with the Merciful. Absalom glared at him with a glittering black eye and opened his beak. "You will not make me a child of Adam."

"I do not wish to," Chigozie said. "I wish to give you a new heart."

A few minutes later, the dispatched guard came running back, sloshing through the puddles of the field beyond the gate. With him was a second person, a young man in simple gray, huddling under a wool cloak. "I only got halfway there," the soldier panted to his captain, "and I was met by this runner from the Temple. The queen says to let them in."

❖   ❖   ❖

"They are at the door," Sarah said. "Open the veil."

The Lady of Tendance was one of those who flocked around the Lady Alena; like Alena, she had taken a vow of silence. She bowed and stepped toward the corner of the sanctum, to take the veil in hand.

"Are you sure that's sensible, Sarah?" Kodam Dolindas asked. The King of Tawa had returned from his palace with the promised oils and incenses, and clothing in a package he wouldn't let Sarah see. The kings of Tawa, Talega, and Talamatan took turns sitting with Sarah as she handled Maltres Korinn's administrative reforms and waited for her friends to return.

She was afraid to look too often at her friends, traveling in the Ohio and elsewhere, because the looking took a terrible toll on her, in fatigue and sometimes in bleeding. The knowledge that she could see them and was choosing not to ate at her, and left her feeling antsy.

"I ain't sure I e'er done a sensible thing in my life, Kodam," Sarah snapped. "It's a queer irony of this world that a goddess called Wisdom would take an interest in me."

Kodam laughed. "I reserve the right to shut the veil again, if your health requires it." He nodded at the Lady of Tendance, who pulled the curtain open with measured, decorous paces.

Sarah nodded. "Iffen I'm unconscious, I can't stop you."

"I begin to see how you got into this predicament with your health," the king said. "And also why people follow you."

"They follow me 'cause they ain't got better options. Ain't that usually how it goes?"

And they follow you into an abyss.

The presence of the kings distracted Sarah enough that sometimes she almost forgot that the voice of Simon Sword spoke to her through an open door in the sanctum. Almost.

"Perhaps," Dolindas said.

Sarah watched a dozen beastkind troop through the Temple of the Sun. Before them came a child of Eve, a dark-skinned man who looked familiar . . .

"Chigozie!" she shouted out. "Chigozie Ukwu!"

She nearly bounced to her feet out of pure reflex. The King of Tawa restrained her with a hand on her shoulder.

"Sarah?" The New Orleans priest wore furs like one of the Rangers, and his face was gaunt. "Sarah Carpenter?"

"Mostly they call me Sarah Elytharias now. Except in the lawsuit Maltres is getting together for me. In that, I'm either Sarah Penn or the Claimant."

"You look . . . like a queen."

"You mean dead, and white as marble? You look twenty years older."

"Forgive me, I had not . . . I didn't know." Chigozie shrugged. "What a delight to see you. I feel *fifty* years older. But no, you look . . . mighty."

Sarah laughed. "You're traveling with beastkind. Only there's something . . . different about them." She wasn't sure what she was seeing, exactly, but the green aura she usually saw when she looked at beastkind with her Eye of Eden was slightly different with Chigozie's companions. It was paler. It was closer to the white that she expected when looking at one of the Children of Eve.

Then she recognized one of the beastwives. "Ferpa!"

"Your Majesty." Ferpa bowed her head. She and a large bison-headed beastman held a roped bundle between them. The bundle wiggled, and Sarah saw that from one end of the rope cocoon emerged a pair of talons, while from the other protruded a beak.

The beastman sharing Ferpa's burden looked more cowed than the rest of the beastkind. He cringed, as if expecting to be struck down.

"Father Ukwu," Sarah said, "if that's the Heron King you got roped up there, then you've done me an astonishing service."

Fool hope.

"I regret that it is not," Chigozie said. "But it may be fair to call this child the Heron Prince."

The King of Tawa again restrained Sarah from bounding to her feet.

"Peter Plowshare?" she asked.

"I do not know," the priest said. "I do not think so."

"It is not Peter Plowshare," Ferpa said. "The Shepherd of the Merciful gave this child the name Absalom."

"Who's the Shepherd of the Merciful?" Sarah imagined some new demigod, sweeping down off the plains to attack her kingdom.

"Humbly," Chigozie said, "I am. It was the least outrageous thing that my flock wanted to call me."

"Flock. Jumpin' Jerusalem, as Calvin Calhoun might say, you've gone Wobomagonda one better and you're preachin' to the beastkind."

Chigozie nodded.

Kodam Dolindas leaned in close to Sarah's ear. "Forgive me for appearing to give secret counsel in front of your friends, Sarah, it is impolite. That creature, whatever it is, cannot be Peter Plowshare. If you did not know this piece of royal Ophidian lore before, then know it now: if Peter Plowshare comes into the world at this time, it will only be because you are his mother."

Sarah's breath caught in her throat. The king gripped her shoulder, as if to impart strength to her by physical contact.

Sarah felt ambushed on two sides. Her mind raced. Her heart seemed to have stopped beating entirely.

"You have Absalom tied up," she said finally. "Is he dangerous, or does he try to escape?"

"Both," Chigozie said. "He has developed a taste for the flesh of men."

"How old is he?"

"His mother, a Vodun mambo from New Orleans, gave birth to him this spring." Chigozie paused. "He tore apart her body to come into this world. And immediately upon seeing the light, he attacked his mother's flesh."

Sarah stared. Even tied up, Absalom looked like the Heron King.

You see that I do not need you. You see that you are doomed.

And the King of Tawa had just suggested to her that she might give birth to another son of the Heron King. Or rather, that only she *could* do it.

Or *only* she could do it, if the child were to be Peter Plowshare. *This* was some other son of Simon Sword. A bastard son. A castoff?

If this creature were not to become Peter Plowshare, then what would it be? A general in its father's horde? A rival to its father? A murderous beast, loose in the countryside?

And if Sarah gave birth to a son, was the King of Tawa saying that it would look like this monster?

She sighed heavily.

"We have prisons," she said. "Not many. My people prefer to impose fines, or put offenders in the stocks, or occasionally hang them. We have places designed to hold prisoners for short periods of time. They may be sufficient to contain him. My own powers are drained, and I am weak, but we have a few magicians still in Cahokia, and perhaps they would be willing to ward him."

Chigozie looked crestfallen. "I had hoped that Absalom might overcome his evil inclinations."

"You have any idea how to help him do that?"

Chigozie shook his head.

"Neither do I." Sarah sighed and squeezed her cheeks and jaws between the palms of her hands. "I could try, but I'm none too vital, just now. And I'm none too certain that our cells will hold him. How strong is he?"

"Strong," Bison Head said.

"Perhaps the safest thing is to treat this creature like a monster," Sarah said. "If a wolf is eating your cattle, you don't try to get it to repent. You kill the wolf."

"Or your sheep." Chigozie looked stricken.

"We had considered this possibility," Kort said. "Perhaps, after all, it is the only thing we can do."

"There is another way," Kodam Dolindas said. "We could imprison it within the Well of Souls."

The Ghostmaster Auntie Bisha awoke in Gazelem's house, on a reclining chair, beside a pitcher of shikaram and a bowl of berries and cream. Looking up at Gazelem and Naares Stoach, she then noticed the berries.

Without a word, and without using the spoon provided, she ate the berries, swallowing entire handfuls whole and licking the bowl to get all the cream. When the fruit was gone, she took a long drink from the pumpkin liquor.

"I have never understood," Gazelem said, "why you Ghostmasters are tattooed about the mouth."

"Never had occasion to consult the dead?" she asked, her voice cracking like an adolescent boy's.

"I have generally been more concerned with steering the future than with examining the past," Gazelem said.

"Only now it seems one key to the future might lie in the past," Stoach added.

Auntie Bisha laughed. "That's always true. The future is only consequences, and everything that has ever been done that matters was done in the past. By the dead."

"Hmm," Gazelem said.

"You are the poisoner prince," the witch said.

"I had to master narcotics, philtres, toxins, and antidotes as a very young man," Gazelem said. "My brothers and cousins kept paying people to use them against me."

"Yes, but *you* didn't pay an apothecary. You did it yourself."

"I trust myself more than I trust any old fool with a mortar and pestle and a red cap. What do your tattoos say?"

"In the process of becoming a Ghostmaster, one tattoos one's dying words around one's mouth. These tattoos are the sign that makes me visible to the dead, and the net that allows me to capture their words."

"In what script are the words written?" Gazelem didn't recognize the characters.

"An old one, long forgotten."

"Did someone look into your future to see your dying words?" Stoach asked. "Or did you choose them?"

"I chose them. Before ever I could get the tattoos, I spent many months meditating upon my own death."

"We need your help, Auntie Bisha," Gazelem said. "This is my home; you may stay here. If you have family, and they are a reasonable number, they may stay here also. Tell me what else you require, in order to help me."

"It depends what you want from me." Auntie Bisha turned her head sideways and squinted. "Maybe that's enough, if you want something simple and obvious. If you want something difficult—say, the voice of someone who is long dead, or the voice of someone who died far from here, or the voice of someone who is warded—then I might require a very large payment."

"I wish to speak with Turim Zomas," Gazelem said. "Lord of the White Towers."

"The baby?" The Ghostmaster frowned.

"Turim Zomas the *first*," Gazelem said. "Not the *third*."

"Kings are difficult," she said. "Kings are bound by oaths. Often, they lie in dark hells, and are hard to find, because they are commonly committers of foul deeds. Or they refuse to divulge secrets."

"The ghost will see me, will it not?"

"Yes, the king will see you, and he will have memories, so he will know you for his kinsman. Did he bear you great love in life?"

Gazelem considered. "He exiled me, but I believe it was to save my life."

"Because the other princes wanted you dead?" the Ghostmaster asked.

"I was good at many things," Gazelem said. "I was not always good at making allies. I cultivated an air of mystery that helped protect me, but that same air of mystery kept friends away. When my grandfather heard that other princes were conspiring to move against me, and in a direct fashion for which I had no counter... he had the funeral rites conducted for me. I had to leave Zomas with my shoes tied together, like a corpse."

"Ah." Auntie Bisha nodded. "And this man came with you into exile? This man is also ritually dead?"

"I fought for Zomas until she fell," Naares Stoach said. "But I knew there was one prince remaining. I came to him with... tidings."

"Does it help your work that I have been excommunicated from among the living?" Gazelem asked.

"It may," the Ghostmaster said. "I will certainly incorporate it into my song. Can you tell me what you wish to know from the mighty warlord Turim Zomas?"

"On certain occasions, the King of Zomas bore a wooden staff," Gazelem said. "It was tipped with an iron horse's head. Do you have it in mind?"

"Only on certain occasions."

"Correct. At other times, it was kept in a vault beneath the city. I believe that it was also used in that vault, beneath the city. Since it appears, for various reasons, to be in use now, that suggests to me that the staff is still in that subterranean vault."

"Your reasoning seems sound to me, Prince."

"The staff is called the Earthshaker's Rod, but sometimes also called the Staff of Zomas or the Staff of the Gods. I would know how to find it, and I would know the secrets of its use. I am the only living heir to Turim Zomas, so the knowledge is rightfully mine. Tell me what it will cost me for me to speak to my grandfather."

"I shall make the attempt," Auntie Bisha said. "I shall require gold. One hundred pieces. Louis d'Or, or something of equal value."

"Done," Gazelem said. "That is little. What else?"

"I will live here," she said. "I have no family, but I will live here, as a Prince of Zomas lives, for a year."

"You will eat what I eat, or better," Gazelem said. "You will drink what I drink, or better. If I must travel, though, you will travel with me. And you will have your choice of beds in the place we shall share."

"Good." Auntie Bisha nodded. "And bring me a young man for company. Not more than thirty winters old, but not fewer than twenty. Let him be a player of games, witty, and able to read. I desire entertainment."

"That can be arranged," Gazelem said.

"I shall tire of him within a week," Auntie Bisha warned him. "Be prepared with his replacement."

Gazelem nodded.

"It is enough," she told him. "Leave me. I must prepare my song."

Maltres Korinn walked through the darkness at the head of a file of the wardens. These men did double duty now; having been re-formed as members of the Cahokian Military (now commanded by Jaleta Zorales, with William Lee, at Sarah's insistence, officially designated on leave), they nevertheless continued to operate as the day-to-day law enforcement personnel of the city. They wore a slightly different uniform as wardens, and it didn't bear the white Cahokian crow. The wardens carried cudgels, though they were also armed with swords and knives under their cloaks should the occasion arise. A few had pistols, kept carefully under their heavy gray cloaks so as not to wet the powder.

Maltres was armed, too, though he left his sword in its sheath. He had his face wrapped in a scarf, and he tried to pull his head, turtle-like, as deep into his hood as he was able. The rain and the puddles on every street made going slow and footing uncertain, but the noise of the perpetual storm that had engulfed Cahokia hid the sound of a few passing pairs of feet very well.

He reached the end of the alley and stopped, holding up a hand. From here, he could see the Sunrise Mound. He could also see the people who were gathering at the edges of the mound, around the seven toothlike Eve Stones that bounded the sacred space.

He saw no faces; whether it was because of the rain, or due to ritual considerations, or for the sake of discretion, the people gathering at the mound had all hidden their faces. They wore cloaks and scarves, like Maltres, or robes with veils; a few had hats with the brims turned down, and flaps that concealed their faces.

Maltres had received a tip that blood sacrifices were being performed here.

It was too early to arrest anyone; there was no law against gathering in public, even with hidden faces, even at night and in a storm.

Nor was there any obvious, ordinary reason to gather in this manner.

He couldn't hear their words. If Luman Walters were in the city, Maltres might have asked for his help, and the mage would have given him a charm for better hearing or seeing. Sarah might provide the same assistance, but her body was already wracked from overuse of her arcane powers.

Four women in robes and veils ascended the low mound. One held something black in her hand, that might be a stone. Two others led a goat each, large-horned beasts of equal height, and brought them shoulder to shoulder at the top of the mount.

The fourth woman began to sing.

Maltres couldn't hear the words, but he could almost hear the melody. Even as that registered at the edges of his hearing, he felt he was only hearing the echo of the song, or a mirror image of it, as if the true song were hidden inside what he was hearing, and the true song was backward.

He tried humming a few notes under his breath, and couldn't quite pin it down.

"Sir," the captain of the wardens said. His name was Fridrich, a German name that maybe was influenced by the proximity of Talamatan, or maybe meant that his family had come to this land with Wallenstein. He was a sober-eyed veteran of many combats, with a crooked nose from having been struck in the face by an Imperial club during the Siege of Cahokia. "Should we intervene?"

"Not yet, Captain," Maltres said.

More than an arrest, what he wanted was information. He didn't much care what gods the people of his city worshipped, as long as they supported the city, and as long as the city's native goddess, the Virgin

Wisdom, was not offended. But people who met at night and worshipped in secret might also support secret leaders and secret aims.

The song rose in pitch, at least an octave. Men joined in the song, laying down an undergirding bass line beneath the melody. A rhythmic sound began, that wasn't drums; maybe sistra, or rattles, or bones being played together in rolling triplets. He could see some of the congregants shaking, and in flashes of lightning, their instruments.

A man cast his robe aside; he was naked underneath, and his body was covered in blue tattoos. He began a slow walk around the outside of the ring of Eve Stones, with the stones on his right hand and the surrounding crowd on his left. The crowd sang, and in time with the music, struck the naked man as he passed, with sticks and with whips and sometimes even with knives. It was only when he saw blood rise on the man's back that Maltres realized the blows weren't simulated.

The man's step was steady, and though blood began to flow over his tattoos in more and more streams, turning him from a mottled blue into a vivid crimson, where the rain didn't quickly wash him clean, he continued his measured circular journey. As he passed each stone he stopped to kneel at it, touching his forehead to the time-gnawed old rocks. When he knelt, the crowd at his back continued to sing, and continued to strike him.

"I don't like this," Captain Fridrich said.

"I don't either," Maltres murmured. "But do you know what it is?"

"It's strange."

Maltres nodded. "It also feels...*old*. And why are they doing it here, of all the places they could have chosen? And who are they? And are they trying to accomplish anything?"

"We could ask those questions," Fridrich grunted. "Or we could just run them off for disturbing the peace, and put a guard here from now on."

"And would they then merely go elsewhere?" Maltres wondered. "I want to understand more, before I order this stopped. And besides, they're not disturbing the peace."

"They're disturbing *my* peace," Fridrich said.

"That's not a crime."

"What if they sacrifice the goats?" Fridrich asked.

"Then I definitely want to talk to them."

The naked man had finished his circuit, and stood where he had started, standing beside one of the Eve Stones and facing up the low mound toward the four women. Priestesses, but of what god? He pumped his hands in the air above his head, and seemed to be singing still.

The two priestesses holding the goats moved to the beasts' heads and knelt, each holding one of the animals by its ears, or its horns. The naked man ascended the hill, stopping beside the goats. The animals made no move or sound of protest. Were they drugged? Was the man drugged? If the priestesses sacrificed the goats, Maltres wasn't sure it was any of his business, other than maybe misusing public land. He'd want to discuss it with Sarah.

But was it possible they were going to sacrifice the man?

Could this be some way of worshipping Simon

Sword? Simon Sword's display of might, in driving the rampaging of the beastkind, in hurling a perpetual storm across the Ohio, and in commanding the quakes that slammed recurringly into Cahokia, could certainly inspire devotion. Some liked their gods distant, and to be given responses in need of interpretation, but many favored an immediate and intelligible deity.

He drew his sword.

"Now?" Captain Fridrich asked.

"Hold," Maltres said.

The third priestess, holding up the black object in her hand, moved to stand behind the naked man, while the fourth, the singer stood to one side.

The man raised a leg, twisted to one side, and stepped onto the back of the nearer goat. Then, while holding the hand of the singing priestess, he pushed himself up and placed his second foot on the back of the other goat. The beasts didn't object. The music rose in pitch and now in tempo, too. The priestess let go and the man raised his arms over his head, balancing and singing.

"Vizier," the captain muttered. His men, behind him, stamped and fidgeted.

But Maltres still saw no violence, and no reason to rush in. What *was* this?

The kneeling priestesses were doing something. Each kept one hand holding her goat, and with the other hand, reached up to grasp the naked man by an ankle. The music rose in pitch again, the sistra reached a fevered tempo—

and then the music stopped.

The kneeling priestesses yanked sideways, and the man's legs jerked out from under him, left and right.

With a squeal of ecstasy, he fell on the backs of the goats. Finally, the animals responded, bleating in panic and surprise. The naked man's cry warped from delight into an acheful keening, and then the priestess standing behind him reached between the two goats.

The man screamed. He struggled and rose into sitting position, again raising his hands over his head, and there was blood on his arms and on his belly.

The priestess behind him stood and held up two objects. One was the black thing, now red with blood despite the rain. The other was a lump of flesh, also bleeding.

"Dammit," Captain Fridrich bellowed, nearly shouting. "They've castrated that man!"

"Arrest them," Maltres Korinn said. "All of them if you can, but especially the four women in the center."

The wardens rushed past him, shouting. Maltres took a deep breath, and then he followed.

As the wardens charged, the woman holding the two objects ran left, toward a nearby huddle of houses. She might not have seen Maltres yet; he ran too, aiming to head her off. To his left, the Cahokia wardens grabbed two more of the priestesses, and several of the people holding musical instruments.

The naked man fell slowly off the two goats and landed on the grass. He lay there on his side, his bleating indistinguishable from the sound made by the animals.

The woman Maltres was chasing was faster than he'd expected. She was going to beat him to the opening of a small side street, and from there she'd soon have many doorways and alleys in which to hide. In the darkness and the rain, he might lose her.

He threw his sword.

There was no way he'd wound her seriously with such a throw, and he had no desire to do so. He wanted to slow her down. His throw was clumsy, backward, and spinning, the straight blade flashing in and out of his view—

and he hit her in the side.

The woman slipped and fell. Maltres overtook her as she struggled to stand. Ignoring his sword on the ground, he jerked her to her feet. She still held severed and bloody testicles in one hand, and the black object in the other, he could see now, was a large, sharp flake of obsidian.

He still wasn't entirely sure that what he'd seen was criminal, but he knew that he wanted it stopped. Holding the woman's shoulder with his left hand, he ripped away her veil with his right.

And saw the face of the Lady Alena.

"Tell him quickly, or the spirit of wisdom
is liable to catch a few musketballs."

———◆———

CHAPTER NINETEEN

Bill frowned down at the headstones. The humidity
had been choking him, so he'd removed his coat and
left it hanging over the fence to which he'd hitched
the horse. Out of respect for the sacred ground of
the churchyard, he'd left his horse pistols with the
animal, too. Now he couldn't find the stone he wanted.

"Well, saints pickle me!" cried a cracking voice to
Bill's right. He recognized the voice, because it was
one he had thought of, on his journey here, and one
he'd believed he couldn't possibly hear. "If it isn't Sir
William Johnston Lee!"

"Parson Brown." Bill removed his hat and bowed.
"You will not take this amiss, but I am pleasantly
surprised that you are alive. I can feel the fingers of
old age gripping my own spine and its teeth gnawing
at my entrails, and you must be my senior by twenty
years."

The parson laughed, showing toothless gums. He
was dressed in clerical black, and his completely bald
head was deeply tanned by the sun. "You will not take

this amiss, but go to hell. I baptized you at eight days old, and I plan to bury you at eighty years."

Bill grunted. "You do not express astonishment at my appearance."

"I knew you were writing Sally, for many years. If you'd died, it would only have been recently."

"She remained in the house, then?" Bill asked. "You were her confessor?"

The parson nodded. "She confessed to hating you quite a bit, especially at first. She calmed, with the passing of time, though I think it's fair to say she didn't *heal*, exactly."

Bill sucked his teeth. "I always did admire her ability to hold paper on a man."

"She held paper on the earl, too," Brown said. "Never stepped foot in his hall again."

"Not even when Charles was given his commission?" Bill felt shock.

"She had died by then. The doctor said it was a tumor. By the time she told anyone she was bleeding, there was nothing he could do."

"She never wrote me back," Bill said.

"Of course not. Instead, she told me all the things she would have told you."

"To go to hell, I expect."

"That was one of her more polite expressions."

"You never wrote to inform me of her death."

"She forbade me."

Bill sighed. "She remained your parishioner, and yet I do not find her stone here." Hs breath came shallow at the dagger of doubt that stabbed him. "Please tell me she was not excluded on my account."

Parson Brown shook his head. "The graveyard here

is full. If we are to bury anyone else within these fences, we shall have to dig up some of our older dead to make room."

"I have been told that in Boston and New Amsterdam they stack them," Bill said.

"Instead of doing anything so drastic, we built a new church. It serves some of the newer settlements, down along the river, and we built it with a very large plot of land for burials. You'd like the young priest we found for the chapel. He's a shooter, takes prizes for marksmanship at the fairs."

"I do not hold with new churches," Bill said. "A church should be old, so that it may be respected. And I dislike young priests, for the same reason."

"As I recall, you dislike priests, generally."

"Yes, but with age, you are endearing yourself to me."

Parson Brown turned to point an arm down the long hillside on which the church stood, toward the thick green forest at its base. "You may remember the bridle path at the foot of the churchyard. If you ride it two miles straight on, and then turn left at the river, another five miles will take you to the new church."

Bill grumbled to himself for the entire seven-mile ride. He grumbled because the minute he stopped grumbling, or talking to himself, or maintaining his pistols, he thought about Cathy instead, or reached for his cherry brandy. He didn't want to think about Cathy; such thoughts hurt.

The new church was the abomination he expected, a tidy stone building without a single vine creeping up its wall, and no sign at all of repainting or renovation. Sparing himself an unpleasant encounter with a young man passing for clergy, he hitched the horse again to a fence post, in easy reach of a thick patch of tall grass, and climbed the fence into the churchyard.

Only a small portion of this yard was yet filled with graves, so Sally was easy to find. The words carved into the stone appeared chosen to be a barb aimed at Bill. *Sally Tazewell, QUOADUSQUE FINEM FIDELIS*. Latin, he thought. His wife had died so angry at him, she had not only omitted their shared name from her tombstone, she had also had the stone carved in a language Bill couldn't read.

His *first* wife, Bill thought.

He tore his mind away from the bloody whorl of pain that that idea raised in him.

Finem looked like *fine*. Sally had been a fine woman. Handsome, dowered with land, good with horses, vivacious, brave, and intelligent. God's bones, the woman could read Latin. She had deserved better than Bill from this life.

So did Cathy.

"Dammit!" he growled.

He felt dry and prickly and irritable. He would not drink.

Beside Sally lay a second grave. *Lieutenant Charles Tazewell Lee, Alive forever in his fame.*

Bill sat on the churchyard grass and wept.

Later, when he had collected himself, he rode to the earl's hall.

The earl's lands showed nothing of madness. The tobacco and other crops grew thick and lively, the walls were mended, the roads in good repair. No sign of madness, and also no sign of the war that ravaged the Ohio.

Except that there seemed to be too few men. Where Bill expected to see men on horseback, directing the

Irishmen working their fields, he saw women. Before the public houses, there were too few horses tied to the posts. And when Bill approached the earl's hall, he was challenged only by one man, and only at the very lane leading to the hall itself.

Johnsland *was* at war, only its men were fighting somewhere far from home. Some of them were in the Ohio, fighting for Cahokia, and the thought shamed Bill. He had abandoned his men.

Only one of those men was Landon Chapel, who by rights should have been called Landon Isham or perhaps Landon Filmer, the man who had confessed to murdering Charles.

But where were the others?

"Good afternoon, stranger." The man challenging Bill sat astride a big black horse, a carbine resting easily across his saddle. "Do you have business at the earl's hall?"

"John Parshall," Bill drawled. "I knew you when you were still wearing dresses, though your father called you *Jack*, then. How are you called now?"

Parshall squinted. "My God, William Lee. I didn't know you were alive."

"Sally hoarded her knowledge of me. You ride in the earl's service. Did you ride with Charles?"

Parshall nodded. "He was a hero. He stood up for others."

Honor in defense of innocence.

"Yes," Bill said. "Those are always the ones who get killed."

He urged his horse on, and Parshall offered no more challenge.

No servant offered to take his horse, so Bill rode

directly to the stable. He removed the saddle, brushed the beast down, and let it out into the pasture. These simple actions gave him time to gather his thoughts, but that effort continued to be a battle between different sources of torment. Sally had turned her back on him. Cathy's son had killed Charles.

Dammit, they'd buried his son in a new church!

Bill walked to the hall. At the door, he stepped back in amazement before a vision of Earl Isham, forty years younger than he had any right to be. "My Lord Earl!"

The man in question was reviewing a sheaf of papers with someone who looked like a builder or an architect, given his spectacles and his fistful of pencils. "No," the young man said, "but I'm his son. George Randolph Isham." Then he stopped, and his eyes widened in surprise. "General Lee!"

"I fear I am Cahokia's general no longer." Bill felt the truth of it heavy across his shoulders and in his belly. "Nor do I possess Imperial rank."

"Sir William, then."

"Ah." Bill took a steadying breath. "Well, if *you* say it, then *that* may well still be true. But to be honest, suh, I'd rather have military rank. I notice that Johnsland seems to have ridden to war."

Isham nodded. "Our men ride our own northern bounds, and also fight in the Ohio. And again, a number have accompanied the earl to Philadelphia. He has learned that he cannot trust his proxy, and is determined to be in the Assembly for the impeachment vote."

The architect wandered away, poring over the papers.

"I would be honored to join your men in any of those places," Bill said. "I can take orders as well as give them."

Isham nodded, his face sober. "Sir William, I regret my part in Charles's death."

Hell's bells, the whorl of pain was a storm, and it would engulf Bill and swallow him whole.

"What can you mean, suh?" Bill's breath came tight. "I understood from Landon Chapel that Landon himself killed my son. Challenged to a duel, and rather than face that prospect, he shot Charles immediately."

"That's all true," George said. "It happened here, just on the other side of the house. Landon is my half brother."

"I know his parentage," Bill said grimly.

"I did not treat him well. I did not treat Charles as well as I should have, either, but I respected Charles, for his rank, for his discipline, for his accomplishments. I had no respect for Landon, and Landon knew it."

"A man *earns* respect."

"But Landon deserved better than he got from me. He has a good heart, he wants to do his duty, but I rode him hard. I made him the smaller man at every opportunity, the brunt of every joke. He afflicted his own pain on those beneath him."

Bill drew himself upright. "Charles was beneath a bastard?"

"Never. Landon tormented a young man you know. Another of the earl's foster sons, but in this case, not one of his bastards. The child you brought here. And Charles defended him."

Bill felt old. "You tormented Landon. Landon tormented Nathaniel. Charles stood up for Nathaniel."

"And Charles died." George Isham sighed. "The best of us."

"My god," Bill said. "What hell it is to be a child of Adam."

The earl's son put a hand on Bill's shoulder. "We would be honored to have you in our service. If you are truly determined to do this, the earl will not waste you as a mere dragoon. You can have a commission and fight where you want. But I think that you should go see your daughter."

Bill nodded. His eyes stung. "Only one? Have I lost a daughter as well as my son?"

"Caroline moved away," Isham said. "She married a planter from Henricia. Mary still lives on your land."

"Is she a married woman?" Bill asked.

"I believe there are still several men competing for her hand."

Bill hesitated. He felt there was one more thing he had to say. "I killed your brother Richard."

"I know." George Isham nodded, and his face took on a somber cast that made him look even more like his father. "That is old history, and something that happened in another country."

"Thank you, suh." Bill bowed deeply and headed back to the stables.

Koweta was encircled by enemies.

The Ohioan capital itself was contained within a circular stockade wall. Green leaves and flowering branches sprouted from the timbers, suggesting that this was something like Cahokia's Treewall, only on a much smaller scale. Water flowed out underneath the wall but not, as far as Montse could tell, into it. That suggested the town had a spring.

She sat again in tree, looking down at Koweta

through sheets of rain; the land around it was too flat to afford any good vantage point otherwise. Luman, Ritter, and the King of Adena stood at the base of the tree.

The stockade was surrounded. Montse estimated that five hundred soldiers were camped around it, their pickets and lines a few hundred feet back from the wall. Beyond them walked two of the gigantic wooden men, pacing in an unending circle. Seeing their entire frames clearly now, she saw that they had no fingers, but mere balls of wood for hands and feet both. Between the wall and the soldiers, cattle roamed.

"Why are the cattle licking the ground?" Montse asked. "Is this some Ohioan breed of cow, that eats dirt?"

Shelem Adena laughed.

"There must be a salt lick here," Luman said. "There are places where the ground is salty, often near water. Animals come and eat the dirt because they need the salt."

"Koweta was founded precisely because of the lick," Ritter said.

"On Onandagos's journey west," Shelem added, "the people's flocks were dying, and no one could say of what."

"They brought flocks from the old world?" Luman asked. "How Mosaic of them."

"And yet before Moses," Shelem said. "These things happen again and again. And Onandagos consulted the goddess, and she told him to trust in the wisdom of the beasts. So he released the flocks, and found, to his surprise, that the sheep and cattle and other beasts that came down here recovered. So Onandagos himself planted that wall, as he planted the Treewall at Cahokia later, to hold the people's animals."

"This is why Koweta is sometimes called the Onan-dagos Lick," Ritter added.

"Like limes and oranges for sailors," Montse said.

"I suppose," the king agreed.

"I would dearly like to commandeer one of those vessels," Montse said.

"What vessels?" Ritter asked. "If you see any canoes, and we could steal one, we're not far from the river."

"The man-shaped machines," Montse said.

"Those aren't vessels," Luman said. "Those are fighting monsters. Do you see anyone aboard them?"

"No," Montse said. "But someone must guide them. Perhaps sitting inside the chest."

"The spirits of the dead guide them," Luman said, "is what I was taught in school. Is Oliver Cromwell not part of a child's education on the Gulf coast?"

Montse shrugged. "We learn the kings and queens of Valencia, the Bourbon kings, the Caliphate, the expulsion of the Jews. Cromwell . . . was a sorcerer who ruled the English for a time. I know he fights against Sarah, but I know nothing of giant walking wooden men."

"In England, he had walking wooden men, which he called the New Model Army. They are not said to have been giants. This is an innovation."

"If we cannot commandeer a giant, then we shall need to go into the fortress on foot. Night will be best. It will also be helpful if we can steal some uniforms. Unless you have the strength to disguise us, Luman?"

"I am tired," he said. "In part because I am still maintaining the illusion of James Goram. He has not been found out yet."

"Good," she said. "You maintain that illusion. After

dark, I shall steal us some uniforms, and then we shall go get the Salt Lick King."

She scrambled down the tree and they sheltered from the wet weather in a thicket. Their hiding place was away from the roads leading into Koweta, and beyond the sentry lines of the Imperial camp, so they passed a few uneventful hours listening for the sound of footsteps and seeing the occasional small herd of deer. Even this far from the stockade, the animals would stop and lick the earth.

When night fell, they waited two more hours, measured by Montse's internal clock. Montse stole four blue coats and four blue tricorn hats from the tents at the fringes of the camp. Buttoning up as if against the night's chill and damp, she then led the four men on a march straight toward the wall.

They passed the first campfire, surrounded by tents that were still being erected. Five men struggled to raise the central pole of a tent larger than the others, and a young officer shouted at Montse. "Give us a hand with this tent!"

"Sorry!" Luman shouted. "Orders!"

That was Luman's role, agreed in advance. He was a child of Eve, and he sounded like any English-speaking Pennslander, so he would raise the least suspicion.

A second officer demanded that they lead away a string of horses.

"Sorry!" Luman shouted again. "Orders!"

A sergeant barked out them for being away from their unit.

"Sorry! Orders!"

A captain asked which way he had to go to find a latrine.

"Orders!"

They reached the open ground around the stockade and kept walking. Montse kept her eye on the wooden giants, fearing they would turn and attack her. They had painted eyes only, but they must be able to see, since they avoided stepping on the men around them.

"I am remembering now," Luman said, "that you entered Cahokia in much the same way."

"I had a rope," she said, "and I climbed."

"We should have stolen a rope while we were at it," he said.

"We have something much better," she told him.

They marched to the front gate in the mud. Montse wanted this part to happen very quickly. She had enough experience with large groups of men to know that no one in the army would think twice about a few stray soldiers picking their way across the field of the siege. They could be drunk, or looking for mushrooms, or trying to find a lost powder horn, or collecting souvenirs, or doing any one of a thousand other things.

But if they stood very long at the gate, someone would grow curious.

Shelem Adena took off his hat as they neared the gate.

"Awaken, gatekeepers!" he shouted.

Two men in sallet helmets looked down from behind sharpened timbers. "Ah, look," one said. "It's the Imperial army, come to offer its surrender."

"I don't want their surrender," his comrade replied. "Then I'd have to keep an eye on them. Tell them they can just lay down their food and leave."

"Good," Shelem said. "Bravado. But I'm no Imperial. I'm Shelem Adena, King of Adena, and I have come to see my Sister King of Koweta. If you don't let us in promptly, the Imperials will realize that we're not part of their army, and your names will be recorded in one of the saddest footnotes in the entire history of the Ohio."

"How do we know you're Shelem Adena?" one of the guards asked. "For all I know, you might be Tommy Penn."

"Tell your master that the spirit of wisdom has come calling on the spirit of might," the King of Adena said. "But tell him quickly, or the spirit of wisdom is liable to catch a few musketballs."

Auntie Bisha chanted. She would repeat the same few syllables again and again for what seemed like five minutes at a time, and then explode into a glossolalia of apparent nonsense for fifteen. As she chanted, eyes closed, her voice slowly dropped in pitch and fell in volume. If he closed his eyes as well, Gazelem could imagine the sounds the Ghostmaster was emitting to come from a man.

They sat in a parlor in Gazelem's house. Woodcuts on the walls depicted Zomas, before it fell, and the Great Green Wood, full of giant beasts. They were inside because, as Auntie Bisha had informed them, "In wintertime, the trail of the dead is visible in the sky, and one must sing the songs of the dead where they can hear them. In the summer, the trail of the dead is beneath our feet, so it is best to be low to the ground, so as to be as close as possible."

Auntie Bisha sat cross-legged on a low table. A stick of reeking incense burned in a wooden bowl beside her. Gazelem Zomas and Naares Stoach sat on cushioned chairs.

"I have heard that the son of the Heron King has been brought to Cahokia," Gazelem murmured.

Stoach was startled out of a reverie. "What?"

"They named him Absalom," Gazelem said. "He has been brought here, to be cured of being a beast."

"One can't be cured of being a beast," Stoach growled.

"No? That's what I thought it was to raise children. I shall have to reconsider."

"You haven't seen this child."

"But I will. That's what I am telling you, that the opportunity you suggested to me has not gone away. Indeed, it has only come closer."

"Will they keep it in the Hall of Onandagos?" Stoach asked.

"The priestess who informed me also said that they planned to contain Absalom within the Temple of the Sun. This information is so extraordinary that it seems it must be a mistake, but I will investigate."

"The Heron King's son replaces him," Naares Stoach said. "If you were to control the Heron King's son, then one day you control the Heron King."

"He certainly sounds fearsome in war," Gazelem murmured. "But shh."

As if she had heard Gazelem, Auntie Bisha stopped chanting. Gazelem leaned forward, hands on the arms of his chair.

"Gazelem," Auntie Bisha croaked. Her voice was now not merely low, but definitely a man's voice. And not just a man's voice, but the voice of Turim Zomas the first, Lord of the White Towers.

"I am here, Grandfather."

Auntie Bisha's instructions had been simple. Gazelem

was to speak to the dead person as he would have spoken in life, he was to make no promises and offer no deals, and, no matter what, he was not to touch her until the spirit of the dead person was gone.

In a box beside his seat, a chicken scratched and pecked at a handful of grains. Auntie Bisha had told him he would know when the time came to involve the bird.

"What is this place?" Turim Zomas sounded offended. "I am not on my father's soil, nor am I buried in it."

"This is Cahokia," Gazelem said. "I am in exile."

"I remember that day, child." Auntie Bisha reached forward with one hand, and Gazelem did not take it. "I did it so that you could live."

"I understand, Grandfather." Gazelem hesitated. "I have brought you here to ask your help."

"I am dead."

"You are dead," Gazelem agreed. "I need your help in returning to Zomas."

"I cannot make you king. I could not do it in life, how could I do it now?"

"He *is* king," Naares Stoach said.

"Who is that?" Auntie Bisha hissed, clawing in the direction of the outrider. "Who is there, watching in the darkness?"

The chicken squawked, a panicked sound.

"I am Naares Stoach. I served you as outrider."

"Sergeant Stoach, I remember you."

"Captain, now."

"General." Gazelem laughed. "If we are all that is left of Zomas."

"Let me feel your face, Captain." Auntie Bisha reached toward Stoach. "It is so dark in here."

Stoach started forward, and Gazelem held him back. The Ghostmaster groped at the air without touching anything, finally hissed in frustration, and gave up.

"You speak as if you are all that is left," the dead king hissed.

"Zomas has been destroyed," Gazelem said. "By the Heron King."

The Ghostmaster nodded. "Ah. I have seen so many new-made dead, and I have wondered. Our stargazers warned us that the time of Simon Sword was nigh. Are you the one, then, who has been tasked with removing Simon Sword's child from his grasp?"

Gazelem was startled at the question. "Not I. But I understand that it has been done."

"He must be made to keep the old covenant," Turim Zomas said. "It is the only way to shorten his reign."

"Grandfather, Simon Sword has destroyed Zomas, and now he sends earthquakes upon the Ohio."

"Ah. The Staff of the Gods."

The chicken flapped its wings furiously, but its feathers had been clipped long before, and it only succeeded in making a little noise.

"I would recover it. If possible, I would use it against the Heron King, but I would also use it to protect Cahokia."

"Usurpers." Turim Zomas sighed. "And yet, the covenant is with their queen."

"I do this because it is right," Gazelem said. "I also hope that, in doing it, I will gain the Cahokian queen as an ally, and she may help restore Zomas. She is young, but powerful. She has a remarkable gift for striking at the heart of any matter."

"Do it for one more reason, then," the Ghostmaster

said. "Do it because I too am sworn to uphold the old covenant. If you are king of Zomas, crowned or not, then the covenant is binding on you."

Gazelem pressed his fingertips together. "I don't know the covenant."

"The throne knows it," Turim Zomas said. "The throne does not forget."

"I wish to recover the Earthshaker's Rod."

"Let me put my hands on your head," the Ghostmaster wheedled. "I wish to give you my blessing."

Naares Stoach looked at Gazelem and raised an eyebrow.

"No," Gazelem said. "Tell me how to find the Staff of the Gods, and what to do with it."

"You would be king, but will not allow the old king to lay his hands upon your head?"

"You are dead, Grandfather. Tell me where the rod is kept."

"Only it has been so long since I have felt warm flesh," Turim Zomas whined. "I am so cold, and you are so warm. If I tell you what you want to know, may I rest my hands on your head to bless you?"

"No," Gazelem said.

The dead king whimpered.

"Do not make me put my clothing on backward," Gazelem said.

"You would not do that! I am your grandfather!"

"You are my grandfather, and you will not aid me?"

"I will, only..."

"Only what?"

Breath rattled in and out of the Ghostmaster's lungs. "Only let me drink your blood."

"Get down!" Gazelem sprang to his feet. "You

cringing, whining beast, you are but the shadow of the great man my grandfather was! Back!"

Stoach leaped to his feet, too, hand on the hilt of his sword. The Ghostmaster whined and retreated into herself, lips trembling.

"You will tell me what I want to know!" Gazelem stared the Ghostmaster in the eye. "If I demand it, you will lead me there in person! You will tell me what key words or secrets I require, and you will cease your attempt to touch me! Understood?"

Auntie Bisha trembled. "You are the king."

"I am the king." Gazelem bent to pick up the chicken, holding it against his body with his left arm. "And as your king, I have a gift to give you, Grandfather." With a small belt knife, he sliced off the chicken's head. Blood spurted from the open neck, jetting onto Gazelem's floor. He handed the fowl to the Ghostmaster, careful not to put his fingers within her reach.

She seized the bird and fell on it, sucking blood from the severed neck. The bird flapped its wings vigorously and worked its claws in midair in a futile attempt to run. The Ghostmaster sucked harder, the bird shuddered and fell still, and Auntie Bisha finally cast aside the lifeless body.

She hissed, mouth open wide, blood smeared around her tattooed lips.

"Tell me where the Earthshaker's Rod is kept," Gazelem said.

"It is kept in an ark of white stone," the dead king said. "The ark is the altar in the Chapel of the Rod."

"This is not the royal chapel." Gazelem had been

in the royal chapel many times as a child, and did not remember an altar of white stone. "Is it beneath Zomas?"

"It is not. In the floor of the Chapel of the Rod is one of the crosses of the earth. At the hinges of the year, the Brotherhood of the Rod removes the rod from the ark, places it into the cross, and sings the peaceful hymns of the Earthshaker. This holds the earth beneath Zomas firm."

"But does the brotherhood also know songs to make the earth shake?" Gazelem asked.

"The war hymns of the Earthshaker." The Ghostmaster nodded. "These are only sung upon the order of the king. They were never sung in my time."

"Where is the chapel?"

"Many of the Brotherhood of the Rod are dead," the king said.

"Do you mean dead priests from ancient times? Or newly dead?"

"Both," the king said. "Maybe Simon Sword is killing them."

"Some must live," Gazelem suggested. "Or how does the Heron King work the rod now, and send earthquake upon earthquake against Cahokia?"

"But Cahokia has a rod, too," the king wheedled.

"But its magician-queen is ill. And the crosses of the Ohio are in enemy hands."

"Perhaps the Heron King's own sorcerers have learned to work the rod," Turim Zomas suggested. "A song one man may sing, may always be learned by another."

"Can you teach me the songs?"

"I don't know them."

"Where is the Chapel of the Rod, Grandfather?"

"It lies within the great necropolis of Zomas."

"Zomas has no necropolis," Gazelem said. "Its dead are cast out."

The dead king said nothing.

"You mean the Great Green Wood," Gazelem said. "The dead are cast out into the forest, that is our necropolis. The chapel is in the Great Green Wood... on the borders of the Heron King's own land? What madness is that?"

"If it is madness," Turim Zomas said, "it is madness I inherited, and did not make."

"How do I find it?" Gazelem asked. "I recall no chapels in the wood, and no roads leading to chapels."

"From the top of the Northeast Tower, the Chapel of the Rod is visible."

"The Northeast Tower is shattered," Gazelem said. "Standing on the rubble, I will see only the woods."

"It lies four hours from north," the king said. "Twenty miles, in a line a cuckoo would fly."

"I understand," Gazelem said. "Is the chapel defended?"

"It doesn't have to be defended," the king said. "It is hidden."

"Simon Sword has found it," Gazelem pointed out.

"Zomas has fallen, as you told me." Turim Zomas fawned and cringed. "She is plundered."

"What one man may plunder," Gazelem said. "Another may learn to raid."

The Ghostmaster chuckled. "Yes, My Lord." She reached toward Gazelem.

"Down, Grandfather!" Gazelem snapped.

❖   ❖   ❖

The chevalier and his men beat Achebe. In the days following his failure to kill the chevalier, the chevalier proved that he could make Achebe bleed, and pass out, and scream in pain. He could do it with sticks, with hot irons, with knotted ropes, with blades, with salt water, and even with splinters.

But they could not make him betray the Eze-Nri.

They did not have to compel him to name his master. He was proud of it.

This, too, was a demonstration of the Eze-Nri's power.

"Who sent you?" the chevalier asked at the first interrogation, after Spanish soldiers had stretched his arms and legs out until the joints made popping sounds and sprang from their sockets.

"No one sent me," Achebe said proudly. "I chose to come myself, and my chi agreed to our fate. But my lord is Etienne Ukwu, the Bishop of New Orleans."

In response, the same soldiers beat Achebe senseless. It did not matter. He still served the Eze-Nri.

On another occasion, after Achebe's fingernails had been pulled and he had spit out three teeth and the chevalier had asked him repeatedly how he had crossed the Mississippi River, where were the tunnels the chevalier had heard so much of, Achebe said, "There are no tunnels. I know of no tunnels. I swam across the river."

"The snakes did not hurt you," the chevalier said. A Spaniard stood with the chevalier, and also a Pennslander lawyer named Burr. "The snakes have killed hundreds of our men."

"Thousands," the Spaniard said.

Achebe laughed. The god within him was powerful, and could laugh even as he was being tortured.

"How did they not kill you?" the chevalier asked.

"By the power of my own chi," Achebe said. "My god protected me, with the blessing of the Eze-Nri."

This could not help the Spanish, who did not have the Eze-Nri to help them. It might even discourage them.

Later still, when the Spanish had placed a knotted rope over Achebe's face, with a large knot pressing down against each eyeball, and told him they would blind him if he did not agree to betray Etienne Ukwu, Achebe said, "Blind me, then. I will still contemplate the glory of the Eze-Nri with the eyes of my spirit. You cannot take that from me. My chi and I are content."

"What the hell is this chi you keep talking about?"

"It is a Celestial term," Burr said. "Ask your *nanwu* and your *wuyu* for more detail, but I understand that it means breath. Life, if you will. Or orenda, as the Haudenosaunee have it."

Achebe laughed. "There is no fool like a learned fool."

"Why do you call Etienne Ukwu the Eze-Nri?" the chevalier asked. "Doesn't that mean a king? Or god-king, my interpreter tells me. You think Etienne Ukwu is some kind of divinity? The man is a gangster, a cutthroat. What has he done to convince you that he is a god?"

Achebe laughed. "I have a chi inside me. As do you, if you have not chased yours away with wickedness."

"A breath?" the Spaniard asked. "What are you talking about?"

"A chi is not a breath. A chi is man's god. All men are born with gods inside them, and it is our chi that chooses our fate, along with us."

The chevalier snorted. "You think *you're* a god."

"We each have a god," Achebe said. "Only a very special man can be king to the gods."

"Blind him," the chevalier said.

After he lost his eyes, Achebe held no interest for the chevalier. He was not again chained to the iron cot, but thrown into a thicket.

He passed in and out of consciousness. Eventually, the sound of gulls woke him, and he stood.

He was not at the seashore. He must be a hundred miles from the seashore.

And yet he heard gulls. Ahead of him. They must be calling from the Gulf.

Achebe breathed in clean air. The air and his chi gave him strength. This was his destiny, to be free of the Spanish, and not to languish in captivity.

He was blind, and he could not straighten his back, but his limbs were still strong. If he turned left, he could walk until he came to the river. There, he knew the gift of the Eze-Nri could protect him from the serpents, but he did not know how to avoid the Spanish.

If he turned right, he could eventually get to New Spain. He could also turn and go back into the Spanish camp, though how that could possibly end well for him, he did not see.

The sound of the gulls lured him forward. He took several steps, crashing through thick brush.

He should turn left. His chi and the Eze-Nri's blessing brought him across the Mississippi once, and could do so again. He could ignore the Spanish.

But if he turned his head forward, he heard the cry of gulls, and he could see. A field of warm yellow, it seemed to him, filled his vision.

Even though he knew that he no longer had eyes.

He took several more steps. The ships of Jean and Pierre Lafitte, and New Orleans's other naval defenders, were in the waves somewhere before him.

He should turn left.

He had defied the chevalier and his Spanish allies. He had made a mockery of their torture, and struck fear and confusion into their hearts. This was enough destiny for any man. And ahead of him, somewhere, lay the Gulf, and friendly ships.

He should turn left.

But he walked straight, instead. His chi walked with him, and accepted their destiny.

"What loyalty does the forest fire owe the earthquake?"

━━━◆━━━

CHAPTER TWENTY

Maltres Korinn stood beside the Lady Alena at the foot of the steps leading up to the Serpent Throne. Sarah sat upon the throne, and surrounding her stood the three visiting kings. She was mere skin stretched over bone, but her eyes were brilliant.

As she gazed on him with her Eye of Eden, he hoped she would see his devotion to her city, his fear, and maybe his puzzlement. What would she see, looking on the Lady Alena?

The three other Ladies of Tendance who had taken vows of silence were also present. Maltres's wardens had collected them all at the Sunrise Mound, along with several other participants in their rite. The four Ladies of Tendance, Maltres believed, were the four women who had performed the ceremony. He couldn't be entirely certain, because the scene of the arrest had been chaotic, and because the women, despite their earlier willingness to sing their modal castration song, had stuck to their sworn silence. He had left the other arrestees, including the new eunuch, in the cells beneath the Hall of Onandagos.

Maltres had just finished a spare account of the rite and the arrests. To try to keep himself objective, he omitted adjectives, and avoided using emotionally charged verbs. In his account, the Lady Alena had not *trespassed* upon the mound, nor had she *fled* the scene; she had *gone* to the site and then she had *exited*. He also spared the description of the large amounts of blood he had seen, and he was careful to stipulate his own delay to act, so as not to sound self-exculpatory.

If the Lady Alena recognized his care in presentation, she didn't show it. She had showered him with a scornful stare during his entire account.

When Maltres had reached his account of the rite's climax—"one of the ladies caused the naked man to fall astraddle the goats, and then the Lady Alena severed his testicles with a flake of obsidian"—the other three Ladies had crouched. Knees pointed upward, the Ladies had hung their chins between their knees, faces pointed downward. They swung their heads back and forth and breathed in and out in great rushing gasps. Though their behavior unnerved him, Maltres tried to ignore them, and focus on the space between himself, Alena, and Sarah.

Sarah looked at Maltres long and hard. Then she turned her eyes on Alena.

"Have I been unkind to you, Alena?" she asked. "Did I punish you for opposing me? Did I impose a penance on you when you violated your own vow, before allowing you to reinstate it? Did I replace you in your office with my favorites, or take the revenues supporting your order and give them to my allies? Did I wrong you in some way?"

The Lady Alena stood straight-backed and held her silence.

"Let me be clear," Sarah said. "You will explain yourself, in words we all understand. I suspend, for this conversation, your vow of silence and the vows of the other Ladies of Tendance present. If I am not satisfied with the answers you give me, you will leave here with no priesthood at all. If you anger me, there is a good chance that you will walk out of here and directly into exile. I will do these things, Alena, not as the queen, but as the Beloved of my goddess, and as the holder of the Serpent Throne."

"What you do," Alena said, "what you *have done*, is not enough."

The three Ladies began to weep, a high-pitched, keening sound.

"Explain yourself," Sarah said. "Do you mean you are still ambitious to hold the throne?"

"I mean that the goddess condemns you," Alena said.

The three squatting Ladies of Tendance threw their heads back, staring upward at the ceiling. "Blood!" one cried. "Blood is life!"

"Horses!" cried the second. "I long for the blood of horses!"

"And sons!" cried the third.

Maltres's breath froze in his lungs.

"You are the Beloved of the goddess," the Lady Alena said. "She is pleased with you. But what you have done is only a beginning. It is not enough to return to the lukewarm practices of your great-grandfather. Why do these storms and tremors assail us? Why is Simon Sword on the warpath? Why does the empire yet threaten? Because the goddess holds Her full blessings in reserve, until we are willing to fully commit to Her worship."

"Eunuchs," Sarah said. "Is that what you think is missing, more eunuchs?"

"Blood!" cried one of the Ladies.

"Shut up," Sarah said, "or I'll shut you up."

"If you would not presume to shut the mouth of the goddess," Alena said, her words slow and deliberate, "then you should not speak so to Her sibyls."

"Don't threaten me, Alena."

Alena said nothing.

Sarah shook her head. "I fought through Zadok Tarami's reformation on the side of the priestesses," she said. "I thought we had reached an accommodation between all the parties."

"An accommodation between truth and error is nothing but a different error," Alena said. "The goddess's hand is extended to you, Beloved. It can be a hand that grasps in kinship and gives reward, or it can be a punishing fist."

"You don't want the throne for yourself."

"I want *you* to take the throne in full."

"Where is this coming from, Alena?" Sarah asked. "I figure you're going to tell me one of two possible stories. Either the goddess has revealed to you these ideas, or else you were the bearer of them all along, probably because they were taught to you as a young priestess. Back when my grandfather was tearing down the veil, I expect. I bet it's the latter, because I know you've had eunuchs all along . . . I guess I just thought they were made in a more . . . respectable fashion. But your mentor, your superior when you were young, she must have told you that the goddess is really a drinker of blood, and that the day would come when you would restore this great truth to the land. That's it, isn't it?"

The Lady Alena was silent.

"Only I've seen Her," Sarah said. "Do you understand me? I have stood in Her land, Unfallen Eden, and I have passed through the gates of Her city, and I saw no sacrificial knives, no blooded altar stones, no fire of burned sacrifices. The tradition that was handed down to you is a mistake."

Alena said nothing.

Sarah turned to the kings. "Do you have priestesses performing blood sacrifices in your lands? Am I missing something here?"

"No," the King of Tawa said.

"We do not," the King of Talega agreed.

"In my lands," the King of Talamatan said slowly, "there are such women. I had taken what they do to be a borrowing from our German neighbors. In Chicago and Waukegan, blood sacrifice and even self-sacrifice are common."

"There you go," Sarah said. "We ain't so far from Chicago, ourselves, that's the answer. Your old priestess didn't know it, but she was copying the Germans. Hell, maybe this is something that came in with Wallenstein. Maybe the immigrants that came with him and made it all this far across the Ohio got a little of that German blood-fascination mixed into their religion, only the books didn't support what they did, so they had to pass on their practices as a secret tradition, lore from the mothers who went before."

"It is not merely word of mouth," the Lady Alena said. "Sherem, and others, those who sacrificed themselves during the siege. They were acting on memories contained deep within their bones. The goddess was speaking to them, and they saved us."

"No," Maltres murmured.

Sarah stood. She wobbled, but managed to stay on her feet, even when she bent to pick up the Earthshaker's Rod.

"And if the goddess Herself tells you to stop this nonsense," Sarah said, "will you back down?"

"Of course," Alena said.

Sarah nodded. She took a deep breath, and then she slammed the staff's tip on the floor. "*Signum quaeso!*" she cried.

Nothing happened.

Maltres's heart fell.

"Blood!" one of the prophetesses cried.

Sarah suddenly leaned all her weight on the Earthshaker's Rod, as if she might fall. The King of Tawa rushed to her side, and she waved him away.

"Sign or no sign," Sarah grunted. "Iffen I learn you're attempting human sacrifice, I will crush you. No self-sacrifice, no slaves, no prisoners, no one. Vizier, this is my instruction to you, too. If I hear you take one action—you buy a new slave, you teach this doctrine to another person—you will feel *my* punishing fist."

Alena said nothing.

"Make your eunuchs," Sarah said. "But do it somewhere else."

"The rite may only be performed on sacred ground," the Lady Alena said.

"Pick another sacred ground," Sarah said. "And not *this* one."

Alena hesitated, but nodded.

"Are you offering some other kind of blood sacrifice?" Sarah asked.

"Chickens and goats."

"That's fine," Sarah said. "Chickens and goats. No horses, understood?"

"You cannot stand in the way of the goddess," the Lady Alena said.

"Nor can you. And from now on, every circumcision, every sacrifice, you have two of Maltres's wardens present. This is the condition of the license I am granting you, and it is not negotiable. Can you accept?"

Alena looked at Maltres, contempt in her eyes. "We will notify the wardens."

"We will be present," Maltres said. "At least two of us, each time."

Sarah looked at Alena again, squinting. "When Catherine Filmer gets back, she will resume her place behind the veil. You will not object, privately or in public. If at any time after that you attempt to put your accomplices into a majority of the days of tendance, I will break you."

The Lady Alena nodded.

"Your vows are reinstated," Sarah said. "Now go. Leave the mound. Maltres—stay."

The four priestesses retreated.

"I rather wish you hadn't allowed them to speak," Maltres said. "At least, the three sibyls. I found their cry of 'blood' unsettling."

"I've heard worse cries," Sarah murmured.

Maltres could only nod.

"I do not understand why this has to be so hard." Sarah handed the rod to the King of Talamatan and climbed gingerly onto the Serpent Throne.

"You have given the Lady Alena respect, and the

room to serve the goddess as she wishes," the King of Talamatan said.

"Did I not see her activities because she was castrating men on sacred ground?" Sarah murmured. "And does that mean the goddess abets her?"

"One thing she said is, after all, true," the King of Talega said. "The compromise between truth and error is still error."

"I have heard these old stories of sacrifice," the King of Tawa said. "I would like to believe that they came with Albrecht von Wallenstein and his Germans, because the stories tell of the sacrifice of horses instead of sons, but before that, of the sacrifice of sons instead of kings, and before that, of the sacrifice of kings when they had lost the favor of the goddess."

"Stories." Maltres waved a dismissive hand.

"What was the sign you sought?" the King of Tawa asked.

Sarah buried her face in her hands.

"When she was first arrived here," Maltres said, "the Beloved was in a privy council meeting, not unlike this one. She struck her staff upon the ground in that meeting, and the goddess favored her with a sign in the staff itself, which flowered."

"I used my gramarye," Sarah said. "The goddess . . . perhaps aided me. Perhaps inspired me to choose the staff and the flowering tree."

The four men all nodded, none of them saying what Maltres thought: that on *this* occasion, the goddess had done nothing.

"My gramarye is weak," Sarah said. "I am too weak, in this state. It was a stupid idea, I shouldn't have done it. Or I should have used the Orb of Etyles."

"Channeling more power than your body is able to handle is precisely why you are unwell," the King of Tawa said. "I do not believe that encounter could have gone any better."

Sarah laughed. Her voiced sounded thin and hollow. "Thanks for your optimism, at least."

"Your Majesty," a voice piped from the temple door. "My Lords. Someone asks admittance."

Maltres turned, to see one of the gray-clad messenger boys leaning into the room, standing on the balls of his feet.

"Who is it?" the King of Talamatan asked.

"My Lord," the boy said, his voice trembling with enthusiasm, "it is *giants*."

"Let them in," Sarah told him.

Before any giants, three children of Adam walked into the Temple of the Sun. First came a woman, dark-complected like an Indian, dressed in a red blouse and boots and a black skirt. Following her were two men, one an Algonk in breechclout and leggings and the other a frontiersman in fringed leather jacket and a badger-pelt hat. All three stopped in the entrance to set down knives, firearms, axes, and in the case of the Algonk, a bow, before accepting a quick anointing and then proceeding up the nave.

Behind them came giants. Maltres counted, eventually reaching twenty-two. Their sheer mass, combined with their number, took his breath away. He had seen the occasional Anak, down from the Great Lakes to trade or hunt, but he had never seen two together, and here was an entire platoon. They set down weapons too, spears and swords and axes and bows; they were covered with fur and leather and copper armor, and their clothing had a piebald appearance, as if they were unable to come by an entire outfit, and instead made do by strapping mismatching pieces to their bodies. They were red-haired or blond, and as they entered the Temple, they lowered their chins and began walking on tiptoe.

The entire procession stopped beside Maltres and faced Sarah.

"I am Ma'iingan," the Algonk said. "You are Queen Sarah. I have never seen you before, but you look very much like my friend, the healer God-Has-Given. He is called Nathaniel, in Zhaaganaashii. So much like him, he could be your brother."

Sarah nodded. "You rescued my brother."

"Henh. I did what my manidoo said I should do."

"And I see a face I know," Sarah said. "Kinta Jane Embry."

"You remember," the woman said.

Sarah gasped. "You speak!"

Kinta Jane laughed. "It is a long story, but the short of it is this: I have regained a tongue."

"I regret that we were rough," Sarah said. "And I am sorry about your brother's death."

Kinta Jane stiffened. "I assumed he was dead, but I did not know for certain."

Sarah looked at her closely. "He died faithful to his oaths, if that matters to you."

Kinta Jane's eyes filled with water. She nodded.

"And the buckskinner?" Sarah asked.

"Name's Dockery," the man said. "I'm with Kinta Jane."

"I am Chu-Roto-Sha-Meshu, son of Shoru-Me-Rasha." One of the giants stepped forward and bowed. "I am a worm and unworthy of being introduced to Your Majesty at all, much less being introduced before the mighty warriors who stand with me. That I step forward at all is at their insistence."

Maltres was tired. "Fewer words, Talligewi."

The giant spun quickly upon him. All trace of fawning and self-deprecation fell from him, and he rose like a snarling beast. "I was not speaking to you!"

Maltres stumbled back, fighting to breathe with the sudden fear that seized his chest.

"Anak!" Sarah shouted. Her voice boomed like thunder, echoing in the nave.

The giant caught himself. He blinked, his face growing calm as he gazed coolly at Maltres, and finally he smiled. "Forgive me, Your Majesty." He turned to face Sarah again.

"When you talk so much," Sarah said, "it doesn't make you sound humble. It makes you sound insane."

The giant bowed again. "I fail even at being meek."

"If all your Anak warriors have names as long as yours, let's save the rest of the introductions for later," Sarah said.

"You may call me Mesh."

"Mesh it is." Sarah looked back to Kinta Jane. "Through my brother, I am aware of the activity of Isaiah Wilkes, whom I believe you know."

Kinta Jane gasped. "Your reputation for perception is deserved."

"Like hell it is," Sarah said. "I got friends is all. Are you here on Wilkes's errand?"

Maltres had no idea what *Wilkes's errand* might be.

"Wilkes's errand has failed," she said. "At least on Wilkes's terms. But I have seen Franklin's vision, and

I continue to fight against Simon Sword. Mesh, though he cannot bring himself to say so directly, is a prince of the Talligewi."

"Is this his entire army," Sarah asked, "or just his bodyguard?"

"Not all his people follow him."

"Another prince in exile." Sarah nodded. "Will you fight with me against Simon Sword, Mesh?"

The question made Maltres uneasy, but the choice was not his.

"We will." The giant nodded. "We will also fight against your empire, if that if what is needed. In return, we hope that we may ask a boon of you."

"A boon." Sarah smiled, and for a moment, she looked again like the girl she really was. "Hell, I don't think anyone's ever asked a *boon* of me in my entire life."

"I seek a place called Kanawha," the giant said. "It is an ancient land, a watered hill. The dead of my people are buried there, and monsters bar the path. It is in the Kentuck, and I have seen it in spirit, but in years of walking over all that land's hills, I have never found the one I was looking for."

"I've never been to the Kentuck, Mesh," Sarah said.

"But you have a gift of sight." The giant smiled. "As far away as the far shores of the Michi-Gami, we have heard of your gift of vision, and you have demonstrated it to us today."

"I told you, I have friends."

"That does not make you sound humble, Sarah."

Sarah laughed out loud. "You wish me to use my vision to help you look. Tell me why this land is so important."

"My ancestors died there," Mesh said. "Fighting

against your ancestors. And there we lost our memory, our power, and our gods. I believe those things can be recovered, if I can find Kanawha."

Sarah looked at the giant intently. "Does the tale of my mighty vision that has reached all the way to the remote shores of the Michi-Gami tell that I can look upon the hearts of men directly?"

"Yes," Mesh said.

"I believe you're telling me the truth."

Mesh bowed.

"I believe you wish me and my people no harm," Sarah said.

Mesh nodded.

"If Kanawha is a watered hill, that's good," Sarah said. "I see best along the rivers and their tributaries. Is your quest urgent?"

"It is vital," Mesh said. "But I do not believe that it needs to be accomplished today, or this week, or this year."

"Good." Sarah nodded. "I grant your boon, Prince-in-exile Mesh. Only I am not at present well enough to search with you. If you can wait, for what I hope is only a short period of time, these men here will help me regain my strength, and then I will help you find Kanawha."

"Thank you." Mesh knelt, placing both hands over the center of his chest. The score of giants behind him assumed the same posture. "Until then, I am your servant, and at your disposal."

"I am your servant," the other Anakim echoed.

"Tell me what this Well of Souls is," Sarah said. She sat upon the Serpent Throne, facing her three counselor kings.

It cannot hold my son. No power can hold him.

"Some say that it is a shaft that leads to the waters of the great flood," the King of Talega said. "That when God commanded the angels of rain to cease, it was not enough, because there was nowhere for the waters to go. Therefore, God also taught Noah sacred names by which he could open a hole in the earth. When Noah chanted the names, the pit opened, and the flood waters subsided, draining down through the hole. Then, to hold them there, he placed a great stone over the opening."

"Noah landed his ark in the Old World," Sarah said. "Mount Ararat."

"Did he?" the King of Talega asked. "But the stories I heard said it was here. That also here, in the so-called New World, is the great stone that Enoch erected, the only thing that was not buried in the waters of the flood."

"Where's that, then?"

The King of Talega shrugged. "And when Onandagos arrived, his own lands having been destroyed by flood, he raised this mound atop the pit, and set the Serpent Throne upon the mound as a final seal to stop the waters of the cosmic flood from ever rising again."

"It ain't working." Sarah laughed grimly. "You looked outside recently?"

"I have heard different stories," the King of Tawa said. "That in order to raise this mound, Onandagos battled a cosmic monster. He defeated the beast by tearing open the earth at its feet with his Earthshaker Rods, finding beneath an endless void. Having hurled the monster into the void, Onandagos found that he could not again shut the rent with his staffs. Instead, he placed the Serpent Throne over the pit, both as monument of his goddess's victory and as impassable gate to the beast's prison."

"We are Dutchmen here." Sarah turned to the King of Talamatan. "You will have heard a third account still."

He laughed. "I have heard that beneath the Cahokian throne is a bottomless pit full of stars."

"Why 'souls,' then?" Sarah asked. "None of you said that there is a pit full of souls."

Your advisors are fools, with heads void of useful lore.

Sarah took a deep breath. That Simon Sword seemed to voice doubts that occurred to her own mind did not make her feel at ease.

The kings frowned, and shrugged, and shook their heads.

"Well," Sarah said, "I expect I'd better at least try to take a look before we go popping the Serpent Throne out of place."

"Are you certain you have the strength, Sarah?" the King of Tawa asked.

"No." Sarah laughed, her laugh choking into a cackle before it ended. "But if I die, it's not my problem. Here, help me down."

All three men assisted her off the throne. The gauntness of her own calves and feet shocked her. Her joints seemed to slide around in their sockets, they felt so loose. She walked to the corner of the sanctum—the far corner from the menacing door, that only she and the kings were able to see, and squatted to look at the floor.

She saw only floor.

She closed her mundane eye, looked only through her Eye of Eden...and still saw only floor.

"Should I be looking for something in particular?" she asked.

"A hole." The King of Talamatan laughed hard at his own joke. The other kings chuckled too, but softly.

"Smart ass," Sarah said. She would risk a little magic. "*Visionem quaeso.*" Fatigue poured through her veins instantly, nearly knocking her prone. She saw something, briefly, like a shadow beneath the Serpent Throne, but then it was gone.

She took deep breaths and wiped sweat from her forehead.

Then she stood, and the men reached out to help her again. She waved them away. "I can do this."

You have no vision because your goddess has no power.

Sarah walked back to the throne and took the Orb of Etyles into her left hand. Touching the first two fingers of her right hand into the oil of one of the throne's lamps, she closed her eyes and anointed her own eyelids. Then she hobbled back into her gazing spot and crouched again.

"*Visionem quaeso.*" This time, as she cast the spell, she reached deep into and through the iron Orb of Etyles. The Mississippi River's ley line lay immediately beneath it and within her grasp, and she gripped as much power as she dared, forcing it all into her vision.

She saw a man, like a shimmering golden shadow, sitting on the throne and watching her. She saw salamanders dancing in all seven lamps of the Serpent Throne.

Lowering her chin, she looked down. As her head

moved, the salamanders leaped from their bowls and climbed down the Serpent Throne and onto the floor. The kings gasped, and with her ordinary eye, Sarah saw that fire spilled from the lamps and pooled in a flaming circle around the throne.

There was a shadow beneath the throne, but Sarah could still not quite see what it was. The salamanders ran in a circle, and the light that sprang from the faint trails they left behind seemed to show letters. Strange characters she didn't know, though she could now read most Eldritch writing. The letters were arranged as if carved into a circular plate, and then the salamanders passed, the letters filled with gold, slowly fading afterward.

"*Animarum fontem invenite!*" she hissed at the salamanders, drawing more fire from the orb. The effort knocked her to her knees, but the salamanders heard her command—

and dove.

They plunged down into the stone, and whatever Sarah's mortal eye was now seeing, she did not have the strength to notice it. The diving salamanders left long trails of light, and where those trails were anchored to the floor, the light spread in puddles, until Sarah saw a circular stone, carved with characters that were laid out like spokes on a wheel, set into the floor and entirely covered by the base of the Serpent Throne, and beneath it, a pit that descended without bottom.

She tried to stretch her vision, and look deeper into the pit, without seeing an end. She stood, wobbled closer to the pit to crane her head and look downward—

and then collapsed.

Her vision swam. She heard the laughter of Simon Sword, and distant screaming.

The kings rushed to lift her from the floor. "Your Majesty!" a young voice called from the pit. "A petitioner seeks audience!"

No, not from the pit. From the other side of the veil.

"The petitioner must wait!" Roland Gyanthes cried.

"Stop!" Sarah yelped.

"What petition cannot wait?" Kodam Dolindas whispered. "You are spent."

"It's Gazelem Zomas," Sarah said.

"A Zoman?" Ordres Zondering was skeptical.

"He's never come to me here," Sarah said. She felt drained, but lucid. "He must really want my attention. Put me on the throne, open the veil, and let him in."

She resented how little effort it took the kings to hoist her into the seat. With grim determination, she took the Sevenfold Crown and lifted it onto her own head. She also reached for the Earthshaker's Rod, and when Zondering handed it to her, she laid it across her lap.

"I may be a skeleton," she said, "but I'm a skeleton all dressed up for the ball."

When the veil opened, Gazelem stood at the foot of the steps, head inclined in a small bow.

"Your Majesties," he said. "I am Gazelem Zomas, presumptive King of Zomas."

"Gazelem," she answered. "I know you're a serious fellow, so I know if you're using that title, you think you have something really important to discuss. If you're looking for help to claim your throne, I don't know what help I could give. Do you want recognition of your claim?"

"Not yet." He looked up at her. "Though that time will come. I came to discuss things with you that pertain, I believe, to the safety and stability of your throne . . . and mine."

Sarah was suddenly mindful that she was sitting on top of an apparently bottomless pit. She felt old. But looking at Gazelem's aura, she saw no deceit or hostility.

"I'm curious," she said. "Go on."

"I have searched among the refugees from Zomas," he said, "and found a Ghostmaster."

Sarah closed her eyes and discovered that, in her memory, she could see Gazelem finding a woman with tattoos around her mouth, and that woman summoning the spirit of a dead man in Gazelem's palace. "You have learned where Zomas keeps its Earthshaker's Rod."

"Yes." He looked startled. "I intend to seize it from the Heron King."

"I have no men to spare to send with you," she said. "Perhaps Chigozie Ukwu and his flock might help. They are the Merciful. Ah, I see that Naares Stoach has already told you of them."

Gazelem looked more startled still. "In fact, it was my intention to ask Your Majesty if I might beg the assistance of the Shepherd of the Merciful."

"Only be careful," Sarah said. "I think he takes his Christianity seriously."

"Is Your Majesty also aware," Gazelem asked slowly, "of what I witnessed on the Sunrise Mound, the same evening that I met the Ghostmaster?"

Sarah tried to slip into her memory and see what she had witnessed, without being aware of it. "I'm not," she said, "but let me guess. Was it wild singing, two goats, and a ritual castration?"

Gazelem laughed; judging by his aura, he was

uncomfortable. "No, but I believe I saw animals being sacrificed."

"Same damn people," Sarah muttered. "Alena."

Gazelem shook his head. "This city was staggeringly lucky that you came along. Imagine what a disaster Eërthes would have been in your place. Not to mention me."

"Stop it," Sarah said. "You sound like a giant."

"Do you already know the third thing I wished to discuss?" Gazelem asked.

"I don't really want to get into the habit of playing a guessing game with you." Sarah considered. "But I expect you came to talk to me about the Heron King's son. Absalom."

"I have no secrets."

"Don't forget it. I'm planning on throwing Absalom into a pit. He's dangerous."

"Could he not be used against his father?" Gazelem asked. "If he could be made into Peter Plowshare—"

He can't! The Heron King's cry was triumphant.

"He can't." The words were heavy on Sarah's tongue.

"Or he could be turned upon his father's troops, as an engine of war."

"We can't control him," Sarah said.

"Have you really tried?"

Sarah thought about it. "There is *one* more thing I could try."

Maltres Korinn and Captain Fridrich trailed the giants through the dark streets of Cahokia. The giant prince, Mesh, had asked for permission to sleep within the city's walls and Sarah had granted it. Now the twenty-one Talligewi trooped through the rain toward the eastern wall and the Ohio Gate, where the land was least submerged.

What did Maltres fear?

It wasn't that his queen had a fault of vision, and misjudged the Anak. He had seen too much of Sarah's power to doubt her.

It was rather his own people. He had had to contend with his own people many times in recent months, over burial rites, over animal sacrifice and circumcision, and over actual treason. Now he couldn't quite trust his own people to have a calm reaction to the presence of the giants among them.

And he had niggling doubts that there was something else.

Six wardens trailed behind him and the captain. They carried spears—Maltres expected no violence, but if he had to fight, he wanted his men to have the advantage of reach. *Especially* if they had to fight Talligewi.

The giants passed through one thick clump of Ashtares, the trees that had sprung up after the Siege of Cahokia, heading through the rain for a thicker clump beyond, just within the Treewall. Maltres felt some relief; other than a few Missourians or Zomans camped in the same trees, the giants shouldn't trouble anyone there.

He watched the blurred line of shadows troop from one grove to the next, and then he beckoned Captain Fridrich to come with him. With the wardens a few steps behind, the two men crossed from the shadows of a long storage barn to the nearer grove.

Maltres stepped ahead of Fridrich, pressing to the edge of the trees to watch the giants. The captain followed close at his shoulder. Dockery and Embry and Ma'iingan were with them, and they seemed to be conversing with people camped around a small fire, sheltered from the rain by the grove of Ashtares and the Treewall.

Thud!

Maltres flew forward, struck from behind by a heavy force. He splashed into the mud beyond the edge of the trees, and when he stumbled to his feet and turned around, he saw the giant Mesh. In his right hand, the Anak held a spear with a reddish head, pointed at Maltres's chest. With his left, he held Captain Fridrich off the ground by his throat. In the darkness, all Maltres saw of the giant's face was a row of teeth that seemed as wide as his head, and the glinting whites of his eyes. Beside him were two enormous dogs, wolflike in appearance and snarling with the volume of an entire pack.

The other wardens hesitated, spears trembling.

"Hold!" Maltres barked at his men.

"Maltres Korinn," Mesh rumbled. "Your queen invited me to stay. Do you have an objection to me and my men making camp here?"

Fridrich's boots dangled three feet above the earth. Where had the giant come from? Had he been up a tree, or lying flat in the mud?

"Unhand my warden," Maltres growled.

"Do you have a personal grudge against me?"

"He'll die," Maltres said, "and it will be murder."

One of the dogs barked, and Maltres shuddered.

"He's in no danger," Mesh said, "unless I wish it. He'll pass out long before he dies. And you and I should only require a few seconds to clarify our situation. Wouldn't you agree? Or is there some complexity of which I am unaware?"

"I have no objection to you making camp," Maltres said slowly.

"I am very glad to hear it. And do you intend to have me and my men followed, wherever we go in this city?"

Maltres ground his teeth. "No."

"Excellent. Remember," Mesh said, setting Fridrich gently on the ground, "I could just as easily have grabbed *you*."

Turning his back on the Vizier and the wardens, the giant walked slowly to the second grove to join his men. The dogs fell silent and padded in his wake.

Gazelem waited at the base of the steps leading up to the Serpent Throne, facing away from the sanctum. To his left, on the other side of the stairs, stood a red-headed Talligewi. At Sarah's insistence, Gazelem wore a red silk tunic emblazoned with the crown and cuckoo of Zomas; the giant was wrapped in oiled bear furs, without any insignia. He smiled at the enormous man and received a smile in return.

So, he was to be a spectator to the imprisonment of Absalom.

The veil to the inner sanctum was open. Sarah sat on the throne, the three Ohioan kings around her. She wore her iron crown and she held in her hand something that glittered like gold, but had other colors mingled into it, white and green and purple, flashing a miniature iridescent rainbow.

Seven senior priestesses, the Ladies of Tendance, sang wordlessly in the temple's front door. They had anointed Gazelem and the other participants in what was about to unfold.

"Bring him in!" Sarah's voice boomed down the temple's nave. Enhanced by her gramarye?

Eight more giants entered. Gazelem had never seen so many Talligewi all together, and watching them now gave him the impression that he was in some unearthly zoo. Each giant held an iron chain; four of the chains linked to an iron belt, and four linked to an iron collar. Belt and collar were both worn by the creature called Absalom.

Naares Stoach had described this godling; man-shaped, but much taller, covered with iridescent feathers, and possessing the talons and head of a heron. Seeing the thing in person was a completely different experience from hearing about it. Gazelem took a step back.

The giants pinned Absalom in place by all keeping their chains taut. In any direction in which he could try to move, at least four giants could hold him back, and maybe as many as six. They chanted as they walked, like sailors heaving on a capstan, their steps in time with the first beat of each line of their thudding, rhythmic song.

Gazelem cleared his throat and stepped back into his place. The giants held the creature in place while twelve other giants emerged from a side door at the bottom of the nave. All eight giants leading Absalom and the twelve arriving now wore linen tunics, and their faces gleamed from their anointings.

The twelve newly arrived giants walked around Absalom and his captors in two files, then ascended the steps, two by two, like animals trooping up into the ark.

"Bring Absalom to me," Sarah ordered.

The giant gaolers marched Absalom forward. One of

the giants stood within arm's reach of Gazelem, and Gazelem could look the Heron King's spawn in the eye. Only the giants holding him back on the other side kept him from leaping upon Gazelem.

Absalom fixed his black eye on Gazelem and said nothing.

"Chigozie Ukwu baptized you *Absalom*," Sarah said. "Is this name acceptable for me to use in addressing you?"

"I care nothing for your Adam-names," Absalom said. "Does the eagle care how the hare addresses it?"

"You are the son of the Heron King," Sarah said. "Not Peter Plowshare, but a son of the king nonetheless. A Heron Prince. Mine is a land in which other princes are welcome, indeed, in which other princes make their homes."

This was why he was here.

Then Gazelem realized that Sarah had stopped talking; he had almost missed his prompt. "My name is Gazelem Zomas. I am the grandson of Turim Zomas the first and the last surviving member of his line. The throne of Zomas is rightfully mine, though it is occupied by an invader at this time."

"And I am Chu-Roto-Sha-Meshu, son of Shoru-Me-Rasha," the giant in bear furs said. "In the fashion of my people, I am what you would call a prince. I have been cast out for my vision, but Queen Sarah Elytharias has taken me into her service."

"A king of rubble," Absalom sneered, "and a king of lake-fish."

"Nevertheless," Sarah said, "you would be welcome here. You would be the Heron Prince, and you could be a member of my court. You could be a prized ally."

"In your war against my father?" Absalom's voice was a harsh shriek.

"Yes," Sarah said. "What loyalty do you owe him?"

"What loyalty does the forest fire owe the earthquake?"

"There would be a single condition to your remaining at my court," Sarah said. "It would not be subject to negotiation."

Absalom hesitated. "Tell me your condition."

"You would swear an oath," Sarah said. "You think as I say this that you would break your oath. What oath does the thunderbolt respect? But this oath would bind you, Heron Prince. You would not eat the flesh of men. You would obey me, and you would treat my servants and my allies with dignity and respect. You would not flee. You would not attempt to break the oath. And if you did break the oath, it would kill you. Did I say *obey*? You would *worship* me. But in your worship, you would be free."

"You think you are a god," Absalom said. "But Chigozie Ukwu has told me what your people do with their gods. You eat their flesh and you drink their blood. In this fashion I will worship you, Serpentborn witch, and in none other."

"Let all here witness," Sarah cried, "that I tried to save this creature. There is only one other fate that I can permit you, Absalom, and it is by your choice. Gazelem, Mesh—step back."

Gazelem and the fur-wrapped giant retreated. Gazelem turned to watch, and saw Sarah raise the flashing object in her hand. "*Scalam creo!*" she cried, then sank back unsteadily on her throne.

Absalom snarled and yanked at his chains, but

accomplished nothing. One to one, he looked more than a match for any of the giants. Eight to one, they had him pinned.

In the sanctum above, eight of the giants surrounded the Serpent Throne. Kneeling, they gripped it around its base, and then stood—

Lifting the throne entirely off the ground.

Sarah was chanting, and the three kings chanted with her. The eight bearers stepped back, carrying the Serpent Throne into a far corner of the sanctum. The four remaining giants in the sanctum knelt and gripped something out of Gazelem's sight. When they stood again, they held a large, round stone. They strained at the weight, knees buckling, but held. Then they, too, backed away, easing themselves into the other back corner of the holy of holies.

The giants holding Absalom's chains advanced. Their prince with the long name burst into song and they sang with him, a new and darker melody. One coordinated step at a time, they hauled Absalom into the sanctum. The giants scarcely all fit, though those pulling Absalom along by his chains adjusted their grip at each step to shorten the bonds.

Sarah sang also, a different song. The three kings sang with her. And then she paused.

"This is your last chance, Heron Prince." She sounded tired.

Absalom shrieked and wrapped his arms in the chains, trying to yank giants toward him, trying to drag them to the floor, slashing at them with his beak.

The giants held fast.

Then they threw Absalom to the floor. Absalom disappeared, and Gazelem heard a long shriek that slowly faded out of audibility. Absalom had been hurled into a pit out of Gazelem's view, and then the four giants replaced the stone they had lifted, and then the eight giants set the Serpent Throne again on the floor.

"*Sigillum repono*," Sarah said, so softly that Gazelem could scarcely hear.

Was there blood on her face?

Two priestesses closed the veil before Gazelem could see any more. The twenty giants trooped out one by one. Their faces were full of wonder, and they said nothing.

The rain didn't bother Ezekiel. The snow didn't bother him, either, since the Lord Protector had raised him in the first resurrection. Ezekiel felt the cold, but he wasn't harmed by it. His own flesh felt like ice to the touch.

But the flooding was an obstacle.

The draug followed Ezekiel. They heard his commands and obeyed, but each obeyed in his own time, and none of them was quick to respond.

They didn't stop to eat, or to sleep, but the flooding rivers of the Ohio swept them away from time to time. They could neither swim nor drown, so individual draug were deposited miles away from the main body, to resume their shuffling march on their own.

The result was a ragged fan-shaped tail of shuffling dead men, former inmates of the Walnut Street Prison, that stretched over several miles. Ezekiel Angleton walked at their head, ignoring towns and farms and fields, bent on their destination at the far end of the Ohio.

They were bound for Cahokia.

"The question is whether you will defend yourself."

CHAPTER TWENTY-ONE

The Vieux Carré of New Orleans had many decadent pleasures, but sweat lodges were not among them. Raised as a proper horse-riding young woman of Virginia, Cathy had never before had a sweat.

But she was desperate.

She left her clothing with an attendant in the dressing room. She had brought no valuables that could be stolen, by the attendants or by other criminals, and had only brought enough money to pay for the sweat itself.

If she needed more cash, Yedera stood across the street from the long wooden sweat lodge, fully armed and armored and holding a purse. For her planned encounter with the Queen of Oranbega, Cathy had left the hard-hitting Firstborn paladin behind.

It was Father Vaudres who had suggested the sweat lodge. He knew, as the king's confessor, that the queen had a weekly sweat, this being a habit she had learned young from her Algonk grandmother. She went anonymously, without ladies in waiting, and at a time when the lodge had little business. He had been distraught at sharing the information, pacing up and down and pulling out his own hair in grief at his betrayal. Zadok Tarami had looked similarly troubled, but had helped persuade the Oranbegan priest with clerical nostrums and Latin saws. Afterward, Vaudres had had to drink a large glass of port wine and lie down.

Cathy saw no sign of the queen in the dressing room. Wrapping herself in a linen towel and stepping into thin leather sandals, she moved into the sweat room proper. Three women sat in the room, two side by side, next to a disheveled pile of towels, and the third alone. They leaned over the heated bricks to ladle water onto them, generating clouds of steam, and then leaned back to feel the steam on their bodies and sweat. Attendants brought in more heated bricks from time to time, holding them in thick pads. None of the three women was the Queen of Oranbega.

Two stacks of bricks sat without customers. Cathy sat at the one nearest the door and ladled water onto it. She wasn't sure yet whether she was enjoying the experience, but the thick sheen of sweat springing out on her skin definitely reminded her of New Orleans.

Ten minutes passed, and then the queen arrived. Cathy knew her from Father Vaudres's description; she was tall, thin, and dusky with a long nose and a small chin. Surely, the attendees of the sweat lodge must know who the queen was. How did she manage to gain so much privacy, without being flocked by petitioners?

Petitioners like Cathy.

The queen ladled water, sat, and leaned back against the wooden wall. Cathy waited another ten minutes; she wanted the queen to feel relaxed. The other three women didn't leave, but continued ladling water onto heated clay. An attendant came and changed out two of Cathy's bricks.

Finally, Cathy crossed to the queen, kneeling on the floor before her. The floor was hot, but the sandals protected her feet and she protected her knees with the towel.

"Your Majesty," she said, "forgive my intrusion."

The queen opened her eyes and sat upright. She raised a hand, palm out—was this an Oranbegan gesture of greeting?

Cathy leaned forward and touched her head to the floor. It was a highly unnatural gesture for her, a gesture of deep respect, one she had learned from the priestesses of the goddess and which she had only performed before this moment in entering the goddess's sanctum.

"I have no merit to deserve even your time," Cathy said. "I have no status to deserve your notice. I can only bring myself to approach you at all because I do so on behalf of others, and they are truly needy."

The queen's expression was dignified. "Does being one of the Ladies of Tendance of the Temple of the Sun in Cahokia not give you status worthy of my notice?"

Cathy was still wrapped in her linen towel, but she suddenly felt naked.

"I cannot use my priesthood to ask the favor I must ask, Your Majesty."

"You came with a Podebradan and with the Metropolitan of Cahokia," the queen said. "You are on the errand that Father Vaudres raised with my husband. You wish my husband to come with you to Cahokia and anoint your queen."

"She is dying," Cathy said. "We believe this may save her."

"Cahokia has been without a queen before."

"And suffered for it. And it needs her now more than ever. The empire's troops ravage the Ohio."

"You do not need to tell me what the empire does in the Ohio."

"Forgive me." Cathy looked at the floor. "We groan with the weight of our refugees, and earthquakes and storms come from the west to shatter our roofs and walls. Before, we starved. Now we are being crushed."

"My husband has heard this appeal from Father Vaudres," the queen said. "He has said no. He will not relent, not on this."

"Perhaps if *I* spoke to him. If I *begged* him."

"Do you believe that you are more eloquent than Father Vaudres?"

"Perhaps the king merely needs to hear it again, from someone else. Perhaps if he heard it from *you*, Your Majesty."

The queen's eyes looked deeply sad. "On *this*, he will not relent. I have already asked, on behalf of your queen, and my husband has already told me no."

"Your Majesty, *please*!" Cathy lost her composure and started to rise—

and felt a sharp, burning hot prick in her shoulder blade.

"Remain kneeling," a voice growled in her ear.

Cathy eased herself back down to the floor and looked behind her. The woman alone had disappeared. The two women sweating together now stood behind Cathy, both stark naked and each holding a long-shafted wooden spear with a steel head.

"Forgive me," Cathy said. "I have great love for my queen. She brought me and my husband together, and raised me—" Cathy sobbed, and stopped talking.

"I too have great emotion," the queen said. "I would not abandon Sarah Elytharias, even if she were not the daughter of the Lion. And I have no love for Thomas Penn, whose troops and machines pillage my land. I had two sons, Cathy Filmer. The older is safe; he is here, learning the craft of rule from his father. The younger rode with the Swords of Wisdom. He left home five years ago, and at first, we believed that he was studying at a university in Philadelphia ... only that was a lie. He rode the Ohio, as Kyres Elytharias once did, defending our people against outlaws and Imperials. And three years ago, in a small square in front of the public gaol in Cleveland, he was hanged."

Cathy wept. She was not prepared for the strength of the feelings that washed over her. Her heart broke for Bill, for herself, for Landon, and even for Charles, whom she had never met. Her heart broke for Sarah and her father, a man who had also died for justice, and who himself still waited for justice to be done on his behalf. She steadied herself with a hand on the floor, ignoring the heat that threatened to burn her knuckles.

The queen wept, too, but with more dignity, and without making a sound.

"I have not lost a son," Cathy said. "But I have lost my husband. After many years of being kept apart, we were finally able to marry. And on the day of our marriage, my husband learned that my son had murdered his son. My husband fled our wedding, and I have not seen him since. I do not know whether he is alive or dead."

The queen reached out a hand to Cathy. "Come sit beside me, Cathy Filmer. Or you will burn your hands and knees."

"I would burn my entire body if it would bring your husband to Cahokia." Cathy sat with the queen.

The two women with spears stepped back and stood at ease, but they didn't go back to their earlier seat or put away their spears.

The queen sighed. "I know you would."

"I grieve for your loss."

"I grieve for yours."

They sat in silence for a time.

"Perhaps," the queen said. "There is something that can be done."

"Tell me," Cathy said.

"I'm afraid to say it out loud," the queen told her. "I think it will sound like a very bad idea."

Luman Walters was cold and wet, but above all, he was tired. The physical fatigue of his journey was a factor, as was his lack of sleep in the days of their zigzagging across the Ohio. But also, it was very draining to maintain an act of gramarye.

His Memphite spells were different, as was his braucherei. Creating a himmelsbrief cost him coin and time and concentration, but then it existed, and would do its work, with no further effort from Luman. The same was true, for instance, of the spell he had cast for Notwithstanding Schmidt, to monitor the activities of Reuben Clay and the Hansa of Parkersburg. Luman had to know the spell, and have the ingredients, and do the work, but then the spell had disappeared from his consciousness until it had gone off, a tripped alarm.

His spell to monitor James Goram, to be sure that that false King of Adena was not discovered, was different. It seemed to follow him around like a weight on his shoulder.

Why should that be?

In the meantime, his steps across the muddy stockade yard of Koweta felt weighted down by lead, as well as by the rain that pounded down on his stolen army coat. Koweta was a small town, only modestly larger than Adena, but its buildings were more uniformly in the Eldritch style, low mounds and houses made of timber and thatch. Koweta had no tall mounds.

They left the soldiers at the gate behind and headed toward a long hall with a thatched roof built atop a low mound. The beams protruding from the face of the building were carved like serpents, and a motif of interlaced leaves and branches ran up the building's planks, lacquered green and gold.

A man stood outside beside a pile of split wood and a stump, bare to the waist and holding an ax in his hands. Water poured over him as if he were a statue; he seemed impervious to the cold and wet. His long black hair lay in a plastered braid between his shoulders. As Montse breezed past on her way toward the front door, the man called out, "There's no one there."

Montse kept going, but Luman stopped. Ritter and Shelem Adena stopped with him.

"Has the king already fled?" Luman asked.

"The king will not flee," the woodchopper said. "The king's people are here."

"The king could probably let someone else chop firewood, though," the King of Adena said.

The woodchopper smiled. "Most of the time, some-one other than the king should chop firewood, sweep floors, plant corn, bake squash, and do many other things. But the king is not above such things, he simply has a different role. I find it a helpful reminder to undertake simple tasks, from time to time."

Montse, hearing conversation, returned.

"Thou art the King of Koweta," Luman said.

"Aha," the king said. "Understand that I am not saying *ah ha*. That is my name, Aha. It's an old name, and like my friend Shelem here, I carry on the fashion of being called after my kingdom, so I am Aha Koweta."

"Your Majesty," Luman said.

"Pfff," the king said back.

"Did you receive messages from the Queen of Cahokia?" Montse asked.

"No." The king waved beyond the wall, to where one of the giant wooden men was visible, pacing. "Likely they were intercepted."

"She is dying," Shelem Adena said. "She requires the Serpent Daughter Anointing."

Aha Koweta's eyes widened. "To skip death and become an angel? Bold."

"It was Kodam's idea."

"Ah, of course."

"How is it that you are not destroyed already?" Luman asked. "I see your defenders on the wall, but you have no large guns, and those monsters are enormous. Why do the wooden men not simply step over the palisade?"

The King of Koweta swung his ax, sinking its head into the chopping block and leaving it there. "I am no scholar of magic and cult practice like the King of Tawa is, but I have some little art. It requires all my will and strength, but so far I have been able to keep the wooden giants from the wall. Mind you, some of the magic is in the wall itself; without it, I think the giants would have crushed us already. But without their machine-warriors to help them, the Imperials are only ordinary men. They outnumber us, but not by much, and we have a wall and the water. We will eventually starve, but not until winter."

"Sarah would relieve your siege," Montse said.

"The dying queen?" Aha asked. "It speaks well of her that you think so. But I do not see how *I* can relieve *her*. If I leave my people, the wall will be lost, and they will at best become Imperial prisoners. And do you know what Thomas is doing with his prisoners, these days?"

"Recruiting them into the army," Luman said. "We fought some of his recruits in the siege this spring, and interrogated a few in the aftermath."

"Yes," the king nodded, "if you are willing and able to fight for the empire. But if not, there remain at least two ways in which a prisoner can serve the interests of Thomas Penn. Some of them he kills, and then raises as his undead militia. Draug warriors."

"We saw those at the siege too," Luman said grimly. "I didn't know they had been . . . created . . . on purpose."

"Yes. It takes dark magic to do such a thing, and a darker will."

"And the third fate of Thomas's prisoners?" Ritter asked.

"A caravan of prison wagons recently crossed our land," the king said. "Heading northeast to southwest, like some perverted pilgrimage on the Onandagos

Road, only the wagons were too large for the good old track, so they used Imperial pikes instead."

"But not to fight," Luman said.

Aha Koweta shook his head. "I had a small company of scouts follow them. The prisoners were ferried across the Mississippi River, and fed to the Heron King."

Luman felt ill. Ritter turned his head, and Montse cursed in Catalan.

"Thirteen large wagons," Aha Koweta said. "Perhaps five hundred men."

"Who would cooperate with such a monster?" the King of Adena asked.

"A man who is already cooperating with monsters," the King of Koweta answered. "A man to whom monsters have come to seem normal, and perhaps even effective allies. A man who has become a monster himself."

"Thomas Penn hates Sarah more than any other enemy he has," Luman said.

"Because she escaped him as a child," the king answered.

"Because his wealth is rightfully hers," Montse said.

"Because she stands up to him!" Luman snapped. "And she inspires others to stand up to him! And she calls you now to help her stand. Do you loathe and fear the beast that Thomas has become, and the beasts with which he yokes himself? Then keep Sarah alive!"

"And who will stay here and keep the wall up to shield my people?" the king asked. "It is possible that the only life they have remaining is through this summer, but even if that is true, then they deserve to have that life. Will you stay, Pennslander? Have you the might to hold the wall?"

"I have . . . some craft," Luman said. "I doubt I can hold the wall."

"What about you, Catalan?" Aha asked Montse. "Are you a sorceress with the strength to stand against the Imperials outside my capital?"

"I am no wizard at all," she said. "I am Montserrat Ferrer i Quintana, and if you have not heard of me, it is only because you live so far from the sea. I follow my mother's trade and I sail her ship, and I am second in fame on the Gulf coast only to the Lafitte brothers."

"Ah." The King of Koweta smiled. "So if you cannot defend my wall, perhaps you can lay alongside the Imperial camp, board their ship, and make them all walk the plank."

"I am a pirate when I must be," she said. "But at all times, I am a smuggler. I can cast no spell, and I have no men with which to defend your wall. But if what you wish is to preserve your people, then I can help. I can *smuggle them out.*"

The King of Koweta smiled politely. "Will you dig a tunnel? The earth here is wet, due to the springs."

"How many people live here?" the smuggler captain asked.

"Five hundred."

"How much blue fabric can you collect?" Montse shrugged out of her stolen Imperial coat and held it up.

The king shook his head. "I don't know how much cloth the seamstresses of Koweta keep on hand, but it won't be enough to make coats for five hundred."

"I do not mean merely virgin cloth," Montse said. "Tear up sheets and curtains, take down wall hangings. Dye your white cloth blue, and when the dye runs out, then empty your inkpots. The cloth does not have to stay blue for long, or stand close scrutiny."

"Indeed," Luman said, "you and I may perhaps aid the coats in appearing as blue as possible, Your Majesty. With a little craft."

"We must collect the fabric tonight," Montse said. "And disguise our movements as much as we can—who knows how much those giants are seeing, when they peer over our walls?"

"We sew tomorrow during the day," the King of Adena said.

"We?" the King of Koweta asked.

"As you said," Shelem reminded him. "The king is not above menial tasks, and it is good on occasion to perform them. To remind ourselves of all we share with our subjects."

"Including our shared peril in attempting to escape." The King of Koweta snorted. "But still, I am not fully understanding this plan of yours, smuggler."

She told him her plan.

"That is completely insane," he told her.

"Do you prefer some other plan?" she asked.

"I will begin gathering blue fabric," he said, "and organizing those who know how to sew."

Yedera looked entirely too eager.

"We're not going to kill him," Cathy said.

"I understand," the Podebradan said.

"We can't even hurt him. We need him."

"I understand why we came to Oranbega."

"I mention this because you heft that scimitar in such a convincing manner, I worry you might get carried away in the moment, and slice the king."

"Isn't it important that he think I will harm him?"

Cathy nodded slowly.

"Then I am doing my job well."

Cathy nodded.

"You understand that, even if you and I do not plan to fight, the king may still wish to execute us. And Father Vaudres. And the queen."

"Shh," Zadok Tarami said.

The three of them stood in the corner of a tiny royal chapel, which was not a separate building, but a room in the palace of Oranbega. They all wore clerical robes provided by Father Vaudres, who had brought them into the palace early in the morning, and their corner, which was lined with shelves and served as a closet, containing a selection of books and a few vessels, was concealed from sight by a hanging tapestry. Yedera wore her scale mail beneath her robe, and held her scimitar in her hands; Cathy was armed with a pair of pistols.

And beneath the clerical robe, she wore the brocaded presentation dress. It had two white crows embroidered across the breast. She felt she must be dressed to meet the king, even if it was beneath a disguise.

Father Vaudres stood on the other side of the tapestry, waiting.

The door opened abruptly and feet stomped into the room. More than one pair.

"Your Majesty," Father Vaudres said.

"Shut up, Vaudres," a man's voice snarled, "or I'll have you hanged."

Cathy heard the ragged click of multiple hammers being cocked.

"You, standing behind the tapestry," the man's voice

said. "Set your weapons down now and come out, or we'll shoot. I'm counting down from three. Three—"

"Don't shoot!" Zadok Tarami raised his hands and exited from behind the hanging. Shaking her head, Cathy set down her guns. With a grimace, Yedera laid her sword on the floor, and then the two women followed the Metropolitan.

Had Vaudres given them up?

Shrugging out of the priestly robe and emerging from hiding, Cathy saw the Queen of Oranbega. Her facial expression was rigid, as if controlling great pain. She stood beside a short, broad-shouldered man with black hair but a white beard, who wore a leather jerkin, and four men with muskets, pointed at the tapestry. They wore steel bonnets and metal breastplates, with green kilts and puffed green sleeves, and one of them aimed his weapon at Cathy's chest.

"Your Majesty." Zadok Tarami bowed.

"Ha!" the King of Oranbega snapped. "Is that what you would have called me when you kidnapped me? Your Majesty, we're tying your hands now? Your Majesty, get on the horse? Your Majesty, stay silent or we'll have to kill you?"

"Actually," Yedera said, "we were going to stuff you into a barrel, and then we wouldn't have had to say any of those things."

"Only until we got you out of the city, Your Majesty," Zadok said.

"And it is a very large barrel," Cathy added.

"Thank you for your confessions," the king said. "And your dress is lovely, Mrs. . . . Filmer, is it? Having agreed together to commit kidnapping, and having taken the overt act of gathering here in my private confessional, you are all conspirators and meritorious of hanging. What do you have to say for yourselves?"

"That the empire depends upon resisting tyranny," Zadok said.

"That we have no time," Yedera added. "My queen is dying."

"That your son understands," Cathy said.

The King of Oranbega stared.

"Damn you, woman," he said. "Why do you say that? Why not, 'if your son were here, he would go along with us'?"

Cathy shrugged; her shoulders felt very heavy. "I don't know that he would. Perhaps he would urge you to hang us. But I know that you think of him, and I know that, like him, you want to protect your people, as well as your wife and your other son. So I think that your son understands what you're doing."

The king watched Cathy's face closely. "And do you believe that my son understands what *you* are doing?"

"I didn't say that."

"You didn't. I'm asking."

Cathy sighed. "I hope so. I haven't ridden at night across the Ohio to report Imperial troop movements, or to bring food to the starving, or to rescue Imperial prisoners, but I have done other things. I have stood beside an altar to defend Kyres Elytharias's daughter from the pale-faced dead of Oliver Cromwell. I have held the Serpent Mound and Wisdom's Bluff against the Philadelphia Blues, to protect that same daughter. And now I came here, risking my life again, to save the same young woman a third time. And I see that I was wise to trust your queen's love for you, but foolish to expect her to betray you, even in your own interests."

"Is it in my interests to fight Thomas Penn?" the king pressed.

"*He's* fighting *you*," Cathy said. "The question is whether you will defend yourself."

"Dammit," the king growled. "My wife *said* you knew all the right words to say."

Cathy hung her head. "If you were persuaded by mere words, then I would worry you were accompanying me for the wrong reasons."

"I haven't said I'll accompany you."

"You must do as your conscience requires," Cathy said. "Your Majesty."

The King of Oranbega looked long into Cathy's face, and then shook his head.

"Ha!" he laughed.

Montse dropped over the wall, Ritter only moments behind her. They lay still on the marshy soil, gazing through the tall grass and the sheets of rain toward the enemy camp. The defenders would give them fifteen minutes, but Montse didn't think she needed that much time. The Imperials kept a watch facing outward, into the surrounding forests of the Ohio, but no watchmen within the siege ring to challenge and to demand passwords.

The Imperials remained quiet, a few fires burning and a few men moving about the camp on nighttime duties. Behind the section of tent and campfire in Montse's vision, one of the wooden giants ambled slowly past. Montse's plan had no special provision for the giants—she hoped that they, too, could be fooled, and could be caught by surprise.

She and Ritter both wore blue coats and hats.

She rose to a crouch and began to creep forward. Here, she moved through shadow and tried to avoid noise. When she had crossed two thirds of the interposing space, she turned to Ritter and they both stood.

Whistling under her breath, she walked toward the camp.

A corporal stood beside a campfire, pulling a pot from off a metal rod passing through the flames in order to pour himself a cup of hot coffee. He looked up, and offered a cup.

"Thanks." Ritter took the drink.

"Any movement from the Wigglies?" the corporal asked.

Ritter didn't flinch. "Not a damn thing. They'll get hungry come September."

Montse took a cup as well. These men wouldn't know her, but they would recognize her for a foreigner if she spoke, and would remember an accent. With her hair still blacked, and tucked up into an Imperial tricorn, he might not be able to say anything at all about her, if he were ever asked.

Her job was to wave, and join Ritter in the danger.

Luman Walters had volunteered to climb down with the Sword of Wisdom, but he was clearly the wrong man for the job.

She and Ritter drifted away from the fire before any revealing small talk. They found a supply wagon, with an abundance of pots, pans, and mess kits hanging from nails pounded into one of its sides. The rain hammering on the wagon's roof sounded like the pounding of drums. Leaning against the wagon, she watched the walls of Koweta.

What were the wooden giants seeing?

BOOM!

A column of fire abruptly jetted up into the sky from the center of the village. That would be the shrine. The King of Koweta had insisted that they not leave the shrine behind to be defiled, but instead destroy it in the one approved way—by fire. It was his great offering, the reduction of his house of worship, and he had shed tears as he had explained what he would do.

Cursing erupted from the tents. She grabbed two pots and began banging them together. "Attack!" Ritter cried. "Koweta is falling!"

With a second explosion, a stretch of the wall fell apart. Most of it toppled over, some burst into flames, a few stray timbers were launched straight upward, falling to earth a few seconds later.

Someone blew a horn.

"Charge!" Ritter yelled. "The wall is down! Those bastards are getting all the loot!"

In the wake of the two explosions, smoke billowed from the town. This, too, was part of the plan. Montse and Ritter didn't lead the charge, but once the first squads of Imperials were charging across the open ground toward the fallen wall, they joined in the attack. Montse waved her saber and roared wordlessly.

They found themselves slogging forward across damp ground at the side of the corporal who had given them coffee. He ran with his musket pointed forward, bouncing in his cupped hands.

"Gold!" someone shouted.

Clambering over the fallen timbers of the wall, Montse saw a small chest flung laterally before her eyes. Blue-backed coats charged toward the chest and the ground around it. Others rushed into buildings, where men and women in blue were already tearing hangings from the wall, shattering windows, and even picking up furniture.

"Hey, is that the third?" another soldier shouted. "Why didn't you wait for us?"

Montse scanned the horizon, searching for the wooden giants. They were both ahead of her, on the other side of the town, and separated by an arc of ninety degrees. Turning toward Koweta, they began closing in, with long steps.

More buildings burst into flame.

Some of the people in blue coats marched back out, over the top of the fallen wall. They carried rifles on their shoulder...or broomsticks, or timbers roughly cut and blacked to look like rifles. They were only lightly burdened, carrying bedrolls and water bottles, and a little food.

And there were children among them.

Ritter, and a few others, continued to sow confusion by shouting out false directions. "Marksmen on the roof! They've got spears! Infantry to the town square!" He ran into the open mouth of a narrow street.

Bugle calls competed with different signals, and two different drums began to beat. The last of the Kowetan people, disguised in blue coats, slipped out the crushed wall and into the forest. Montse hadn't noticed Luman Walters, but he must be among them.

"Ritter!" Montse called.

She charged down the street he'd entered. She found him fighting, his back to the low stone wall of a well and turned to face Montse, keeping two blue-coats at bay with a long spear. They had the advantage of numbers, and were coming at him from two directions at once. He swung with the butt of his spear as well as his point, and for the moment he held them at bay...but it wouldn't last.

Montse ran.

The soldier to Ritter's right sacrificed himself, taking a hit to the chest with the spear shaft and then falling on it, dragging the weapon from Ritter's hands. Montse stepped on the stone wall of the well and leaped—

the soldier to Ritter's left rushed in low, bayonet fixed and pointed at Ritter's belly—

and Montse slammed into the soldier, striking him in the sternum with her own shoulder and knocking him to the ground. At close quarters, he couldn't bring his bayonet to bear. While he tried, she drew her smallest knife from her belt and cut the man's throat.

Ritter kicked the other soldier twice, then picked up the man's own musket and shot him with it.

"They are out!" Montse cried.

They fled toward the shattered wall.

Timbers exploded in front of them, blocking Montse's view. Something heavy struck her and knocked her down, leaving her lying in a cloud of dust and coughing.

She heard collapsing and crushing sounds, and screaming. The Kowetans? But the screams were too close.

"Capità!" she heard Ritter shout.

"Here." She pushed away a mass of thatch that had fallen across her legs, and managed to stagger to her feet. Her eyes watered from smoke—the Kowetans had created the smoke themselves, heaping green leaves onto every fire in town simultaneously.

Ritter stood up beside her, spitting onto the rubble.

"Which way?" Montse asked. In the confusion, she had lost her sense of direction, and the Imperial assault, combined with the Kowetans' own actions, had obliterated her landmarks. Blazing buildings lit the town, and in the orange light, she saw at least three gaps in the wall.

And then she saw a giant foot, thudding to the ground right in front of her.

The foot was flat on its underside and curved on top, rising to a bronze ball joint where a child of Adam would have an ankle. The foot was nearly ten feet long, toe to heel, and four feet tall from sole to joint. A life aboard ship gave Montse an instant appreciation for the monster's carpentry—it was planed smooth, contoured to resemble a foot, and lacquered blue.

"Move!" Ritter tackled Montse, shoving her aside and up against a few timbers that had once been a wall.

The ground where Montse had been standing disappeared, flattened by the sudden crashing to earth of one of the giant's enormous wooden fists.

"Run!" Ritter shouted.

They sprinted toward the nearest gap in the wall. Looking over her shoulder, Montse saw the giant stand again, shattered wood and shredded earth falling from its fist. Then it raised its foot and took a long step, following Montse.

In a second step, it would catch her.

Ritter ducked into the door of a mound and Montse followed. Overhead, the roof burned, and within, the building had already been looted. Either the Kowetans or the Imperials or both had shattered and overturned furniture and broken windows.

The sudden respite of the rain was a relief, but Montse feared the giant more when she couldn't see it. "Out the window!" She set the example by leaping through a window that had once held oiled paper, rolling down the slope of the mound on the other side. Ritter had barely squeezed through when the giant swung its foot and flattened the house. Flaming thatch and timbers flew in three directions, and Montse ran away, at a right angle from her previous path of flight.

Would the turn throw the giant off? She looked over her shoulder and saw the giant pivot to follow.

And where was the second giant?

She turned again just beyond a hedge, pulling Ritter with her. The man was slowing down. "Are you feeling your age, Sword?"

The giant ran two steps beyond the hedge and stopped. A platoon of Imperial soldiers scattered in front of it. "The giant is amok!" someone screamed.

Then it turned and looked in Montse's direction. It had a single painted eye, flame-red.

"I'll keep up," Ritter said.

Blood soaked his trousers and his shirt. Montse lifted his coat away from his body and saw a splinter, a foot long, stuck in the man's side.

Montse grabbed his hand and pulled him. They ran down a short lane—ahead she could see an intact section of wall. Looking back and seeing the giant running her way, she turned again, running between a chicken shed and a cattle byre, and then between two mound homes.

The chickens squawked at her passage, and then were silenced in a single enormous *whumph!* as the giant flattened them under its foot.

Emerging into the street on the other side of the

two houses, Montse saw the other giant. It faced toward her right, as if looking at one of the town's plazas, a grassy space with a well in the center of it.

She dragged Ritter toward the plaza. Behind them, the pursuing giant exploded into the street. It turned slowly, smashing through the corner of another building as it did so. Montse drew a pistol from the pocket of her coat and took aim.

"What are you doing?" Ritter asked.

Her aim was rendered unsteady by the fact that she was running, but her target was enormous. Montse fired at the center of mass of the second giant.

She must have hit it, because the second giant turned to look at her.

And then began to run in her direction.

Ritter stumbled, but Montse wouldn't let him fall. She dragged him with all her strength, developed in years of climbing rigging, pulling lines, heaving cargo, and fighting hand to hand. Gauging her distances, she didn't quite like them, so she ducked behind a flattened house to change her angle. Breaking into the plaza, she risked a last look at the giant following her, and saw it leap over the ruined building in one long step.

Hitting the center of the plaza, Montse pushed Ritter down the well, and then threw herself to the cold mud alongside.

The two giants both dove to strike at her, and collided. One giant's ball-fist struck the other in the joint of its elbow. Splinters flew, wooden and bronze both. The elbow shattered and the disconnected ball of wood crashed to earth, flipping over several times and plowing a furrow in the plaza with the wooden forearm it dragged behind it.

Then the giants' heads struck each other. One cracked open and swung loose, its ball joint barely holding it to the giant's body. The other came completely off, and disappeared from Montse's view.

The bodies tumbled to earth. One torso thudded to the ground directly in front of Montse, and the other landed on the far side of the well. After one terrifying bounce, the torso before her came to rest. The head attached to it banged once against the giant's shoulder and then fell limply to the ground.

Montse rose, unsteady on her feet.

From the cracked visage of the wooden monster, something was trying to emerge. It had tentacles, and it was a pale, fleshy pink, and as it groped to pull itself from the crack, Montse drew her saber and stabbed the creature. White gel spurted from the cracked wood; where it struck the soaked earth, it made a hissing sound and threw off vapor.

Montse lowered the bucket and helped Ritter up. They walked away from the fallen giants before a crowd gathered, and marched over the breached wall as if headed for the Imperial camps.

They stopped in the camp. The Imperial soldiers were still fighting imaginary enemies from house to house in town, and arguing over who had destroyed their wooden giants. Ritter lay across a camp table long enough for Montse to pluck out the splinter, clean the wound with whisky, and then bandage it with a roll of clean lint she found in a supply box.

"I can't walk," the Sword said. "We must let Thomas Penn take at least one prisoner."

"Go to hell," Montse said. "He gets nothing." She pushed her shoulder up under his arm and levered him to his feet, carrying him out of camp before the soldiers could return.

They limped together to the rendezvous point in the forest, but the Kowetans had moved on.

"Here is where I must stop." Ritter pulled himself from Montse's shoulder and collapsed against the trunk of a tree. "You should leave me."

"I don't know where they went." Montse crouched and began reloading her fired pistol. "Except that they were going to Cahokia. We can catch up to them there."

By the time her words finished, he had passed out. Montse dragged the Sword of Wisdom beneath a wet tangle of bushes to hide him, and then stood beside him, leaning against a tree, watching as Koweta burned.

"We ride into the storm."

———◆———

CHAPTER TWENTY-TWO

Olanthes Kuta had no standing in the Electoral Assembly; he was neither an Elector nor a proxyholder, nor yet was he one of the Electoral Clerks. He had inquired about working as one of the Assembly Bailiffs, the armed men who guarded the Assembly's doors and stood at the corners of the room to keep the peace, when occasion required. In its thirty-year life, the Assembly had so far only seen two duels fought in the actual Hall, and those had both been before Thomas's time. Olanthes had been told that the Bailiffs were few, and the jobs so well paid that no man ever quit, so the posts were occupied by retired Imperial officers.

Therefore, Olanthes had no right to enter the Assembly Hall. But the Bailiffs didn't actually check the credentials of those who entered; that was left to the Clerks, at the time of taking roll. The Bailiffs merely counted. That meant that Memphis, for instance, which generally sent a single proxyholder for its entire royal family, could also send a few bodyguards, who would sit around the diplomat and scowl stoically at their neighbors.

The disappearance of Calvin Calhoun left an empty seat, and, at Charlie Donelsen's insistence, Olanthes had walked in at Donelsen's side to take it. "Iffen the clerks call for the Calhoun vote," the toothless Appalachee muttered as they entered the Assembly Hall side by side, "vote how I do."

"Isn't that a violation of the Compact?" Olanthes asked. "And therefore a crime?"

"What's a crime is that Thomas Penn murdered my friend Andy Calhoun," Donelsen said. "The bastard can barely even be bothered to pretend it wasn't him as done it. And Cal's gone. You e'er know Calvin Calhoun to jest up sticks and light out for the Kentuck?"

"He doesn't seem the type." Although Calvin had done just that, the night that Sarah Elytharias Penn has been selected as the goddess's Beloved. But Olanthes gathered from Cal's refusal to discuss the subject, the two times it had come up, that his flight had had a romantic cause at its root. Calvin didn't seem like a coward.

"So I make *him* murdered, too," Donelsen said. "And I can't git Stuyvesant to even accept my callin' card, much less talk to me, so I expect he's gone over to Thomas. I keep tryin' to count the votes, but dammit, it's close, at best, and I reckon it's more'n possible we might lose. So iffen the clerk calls 'Calhoun,' that's his mistake, not ours, and you jest go ahead and shout yea or nay, whate'er I'm shoutin'."

They stopped talking while they stood at the top of the Assembly Hall steps to let a Bailiff check them for weapons, then descended to their seats.

Thomas was not in his seat in the Well of the Assembly. He was still on his honeymoon, wandering the lands of his Electoral allies. Did the Swords of

Wisdom send assassins against him in the woods of the northeast? Olanthes hoped they did, though the only instruction he ever received was to continue to monitor the impeachment proceedings. In his absence, Thomas sent his proxy with one of the other Philadelphia Electors, a thin, stiff-faced Magister Superior from the College of Magic named Byrne. Byrne voted on his own behalf as Elector and on Thomas's behalf, and also chaired the Assembly.

But this morning, Byrne sat in his usual seat between the Electors from Newark and the Delaware. In the Well of the Assembly stood only the Clerk of Proxies, his bulk nearly bursting the seams of his bottle-green coat and breeches. He looked proud of himself, his mouth twitching as if about to slip from its solemn, duty-driven line into a broad grin.

"Somethin's happenin'." Donelsen had noticed the change, too.

"Point of order!" the Ambassador of Adena shouted. "We are late. Byrne, what are you doing?"

"We are late," the Clerk replied, his voice adopting a stentorian boom. "As Clerk of Proxies, I am waiting for the arrival of the new holder of Lord Thomas's proxy. The proxyholder shall then preside over the Assembly."

A buzz of surprise, mixed with equal parts irritation and wonder, swept the room. Had Magister Superior Byrne offended His Imperial Majesty?

"Why the delay?" the Ambassador shouted. "Do your job and get on with it."

The Clerk of Proxies bowed. "First, Madam Ambassador, the Clerk of the Rolls must do his. Lord Thomas's new proxyholder is himself an Elector."

"Dammit," Donelsen muttered. "Dammit, dammit. That's us down one vote, almost certainly. Whoever jest showed up has to be a friend of Thomas's."

"Who is it?" Olanthes asked.

Donelsen shrugged.

The buzz hushed, and Olanthes heard footfalls on the steps. He turned slightly, to see a thin man with dark hair, cropped short and beginning to go gray, descending the stairs. He wore a blue military uniform; not the rich Imperial blue, but a lighter color, closer to the shades of a summer sky, with gold trim and loops of gold over one shoulder. A golden fleur-de-lis figured prominently in the uniform, as buttons, and buckles, and stitched border designs, and he had new scars across one cheek.

Behind him came a tonsured man in a friar's brown robe.

"The Chevalier of New Orleans has finally sent a proxyholder," Olanthes murmured.

"That's no proxyholder," Donelsen grunted. "That's Le Moyne himself. But who's that with him?"

"I move that the Bailiffs be ordered to arrest Gaspard Le Moyne!" The shout came from the Creole accountant from New Orleans, Monsieur Bondí. "On charges of blackmail and extortion!"

Gaspard Le Moyne smiled and continued his measures steps.

"Point of order, Bondí!" cried one of the Igbo Electors. "The Bailiffs have no authority to arrest, other than in the event of a physical disturbance in the Assembly Hall itself."

"Point of order!" the Memphite proxyholder added. "The Chevalier of New Orleans has been admitted by the Clerk of the Rolls. He has immunity."

"Mebbe it's a good thing Cal ain't here," Donelsen muttered. "I gather the chevalier might have somethin' personal against the man. And Thomas was bein' blackmailed by the chevalier, so how much can they really be allies?"

"They are both subject to this impeachment proceeding." Olanthes said. "And Thomas seems to have given Le Moyne his proxy, and the chair."

"Dammit," Charlie Donelsen agreed.

Le Moyne handed a document to the Clerk of Proxies. Then he stood in the Well of the Assembly, behind the podium, and smiled at the assembled Electors.

The friar moved into an empty seat, beside the proxyholders of La Fayette and Champlain.

The clerk reviewed the document, then cleared his throat. "The Assembly recognizes Père Augustin Gagnon of Acadia, Elector."

"The Acadians vote against us." Donelsen groaned.

The clerk continued. "The Assembly recognizes Gaspard Le Moyne as the Chevalier of New Orleans, Elector. The Assembly recognizes that Gaspard Le Moyne is rightfully appointed President of the Assembly *per procuriam*, and will now preside over this session."

At least a hundred hands shot for the ceiling, and a hundred throats opened to howl surprise or protest.

Gaspard Le Moyne lifted the gavel from the podium, then slammed it down on the wood three times, loudly. The shouting died to a low rumble.

"The chair recognizes the Electoral deputation of the Kingdom of Memphis," he said.

The Memphite proxyholder stood. "We've had a spirited debate," he said slowly. "We've heard allegations of murder and blackmail. We've listened to much detail from an accountant, much more than I think most of us would ever have wanted to tolerate, frankly."

Several Electors chuckled.

"But have we listened to *enough*?" Donelsen roared.

"No law defines how much evidence we must hear," the Memphite said. "Only our own sense of what is appropriate. And I, for one, believe that I have heard sufficient."

"You decided they're guilty already?" the Ambassador of Adena called.

"We have to decide not only innocence or guilt," the Memphite said, "and those according to whatever standards we ourselves choose, but also whether the behavior, if proved, merits removal."

"Yeah, we know which way you're a-votin'!" Donelsen snapped.

"On the merits of the motion to remove Thomas Penn as emperor, et cetera," the Memphite said, "and as a wedding gift to the emperor...I call the question."

"Seconded!" the proxyholder sitting in the Assembly for Kimoni Machogu leaped to his feet to shout his enthusiasm.

The chevalier banged his gavel again. "The question has been called and the motion seconded. We will now proceed to a roll call vote. The emperor would very much like everyone's vote on this particular issue to be a matter of record." He scanned the Electors, still smiling neutrally. "As would I. Memphis, on the motion to remove Thomas Penn as emperor, et cetera, how do you vote?"

"Nay!" Memphis said.

"Shreveport?" Le Moyne asked.

Olanthes's heart sank.

"Nay," the proxyholder of Shreveport said. "And the Prince asks me to record his gratitude to both the Emperor Thomas and the Chevalier of New Orleans for sending troops to Shreveport in its time of trouble. He, too, felicitates with Lord Thomas upon the event of his nuptials."

"Noted," the chevalier said. "And, speaking for myself, you are very welcome."

The chevalier then proceeded to call for the remainder of the votes in their Compact order. When he called for the votes of the Hudson River Republic and they were all in favor of dismissal, Olanthes shed a tear. With that revelation, and with the chevalier himself voting, the motion of impeachment was doomed.

The chevalier never called for the Calhoun vote.

After a week of being kept in a dark tent—fed well, given plenty of water and even halfway decent beer, but not allowed to speak to anyone other than the close-lipped Schäfer—Gottlieb was dragged forth.

He half expected to be blindfolded and paraded before a firing squad, and so was pleasantly surprised when he was placed on a horse. Schäfer mounted another horse and led Gottlieb's beast through the rain, but Gottlieb's hands weren't tied and his face was bare.

Schäfer led him from the camp and into a clearing in the woods. The sun hit the western horizon during the short ride, and the shadows through which Gottlieb's mount picked its way were tangled thick and deep along the path. In the center of the clearing stood a tent, tall enough to stand in and wide enough to sleep twelve men. It was made of blue canvas, but unmarked with any insignia.

His initial relief was beginning to fade to jangling nerves once more. "If you're going to shoot me, I suppose you may as well do it here. That tent isn't going to mask any more sound than the distance already will."

"You might give me ideas, if you aren't careful." Schäfer pointed at the tent door. "Inside."

Gottlieb entered the tent. Within, a single lantern gave dim light, revealing a folding wooden table and two camp chairs. The floor, muddy from rain, was covered with scattered straw to create a simple carpet. Atop the table stood a green glass bottle and two cups; Gottlieb poured himself a drink and was disappointed to find that it was water.

He sat and waited.

Surely, Director Schmidt was not going to kill him. She had gone to too much work.

The burst of confidence and hope was just beginning to crumble beneath the mass of his gnawing doubts when the tent flap opened and Notwithstanding Schmidt entered.

Gottlieb gestured at the empty chair.

"No apparatus," she said. "You said it was unnecessary."

"Yes," he agreed. "I should warn you, though, that some who undergo the experience emerge mad."

"Weak-minded fools."

"That's what we say about them in hindsight, of course. But if the only evidence of their weak minds is that they were crushed by the vision, then perhaps the cause lies rather in the experience than in their weakness."

"I have stood all manner of weights that were supposed to have broken me," Schmidt said.

"Also, I can give you the names in any case," Gottlieb said.

"I will have the vision." In the light cast by the lantern, Schmidt's eyes looked cavernous, her yellow slab of a face resolute. "I will have it all."

"And Schäfer?" Gottlieb asked.

"He will stand outside," Schmidt said.

"Is he loyal?" Gottlieb asked.

"That is *my* concern," the Director said.

Gottlieb nodded. "You will want to lie down. And candidates usually wear looser clothing—white shifts, things of that nature. If you do not think it presumptuous, perhaps you would at least remove your coat."

Notwithstanding Schmidt stepped out of her coat, laying it on the ground like a pallet and setting her hat on the table. She stepped out of her boots and breeches as well, leaving herself dressed in a long white nightshirt and short pants.

Gottlieb nodded. "You'll breathe better, unrestricted. Take this, and drink it down with a full glass of water. Otherwise, it will burn a hole in your stomach."

He handed her a pea-sized bead of the green paste.

Schmidt hesitated, for just a second, looking at the yellow-green lump held in her fingers. Then she placed it squarely on the center of her tongue, raised the bottle to her lips, and drank off half the water. She fixed a stern eye on Gottlieb. "When do I begin to see seraphim?"

"Would you lie down?"

She stretched herself out on the coat, her stockinged heels resting on the dirty straw.

"Breathe deeply," Gottlieb said, "and say the following: 'The father of the son is the son of the father, the son of the father is the father of the son.'"

Notwithstanding Schmidt closed her eyes. "The father of the son is the son of the father," she said, "the son of the father is the father of the son."

"Good," he told her. "Now keep saying it."

She continued the mantra, not slipping or hesitating.

He sat at the table and began to drum with his palms and fingers. The pattern was not complex, but it was important that it be repeated consistently. He found the rhythm and kept it, and Schmidt's words immediately fell into time with the percussion.

Gottlieb sang:

> *Peter Plowshare's the final man*
> *The keeper of the old accord*
> *Who breaks all oaths and burns the land?*
> *The lightning, Simon Sword*

Notwithstanding Schmidt's breathing had become deep and steady. Her lips moved, but no sound escaped them. "Tell me what you see!" Gottlieb cried. He himself had no conscious memory of his own dialog with the singers and drummers of his own initiation, but such a dialog must have taken place.

"A green land," Schmidt murmured. "The greenest land there could be. Flat and fertile. Broad as the world, beneath a sun that never sets. The land groans with the weight of its own fertility, but rejoices in the burden."

Gottlieb did remember a similar image, though he remembered it as something fleeting, that escaped from just before his fingertips when he reached out.

> *Peter Plowshare's the lord of peace*
> *The book of life, the law restored*
> *Who brings murder without cease?*
> *The waster, Simon Sword*

"Tell me what you hear!" Gottlieb commanded.

What was he doing, really? Did he think he could turn the director's ambition into a desire to help him not only survive, but in fact to continue to serve the ends of the Conventicle? And if not that, then why else share Franklin's Vision with this iron-hard woman?

"The shrieking of innocents," she murmured. "The burbling sounds of a running river of blood."

Was he mad to think thus?

> *Peter Plowshare's the angel king*
> *Of star the priest, of sky the lord*
> *Who calls the fault in everything?*
> *The devil, Simon Sword*

"Tell me what you feel!"

"My womb rips apart." Schmidt's voice was shaky, riven through with a flood of tears. Gottlieb had heard men say similar things in a similar tone. "A new world is born, and it is born of my flesh."

> *Peter Plowshare is stasis-bound*
> *The wheel won't move, the ox is gored*
> *Who gives birth to a virgin ground?*
> *The midwife, Simon Sword*

"No new world is born before the old one dies," Gottlieb said.

"No new world is born," she repeated.

"No old world can be buried before the new one arrives to cover it."

"No old world can be buried."

"Your heart belongs to the vision. Your body belongs to the vision. Your strength belongs to the vision."

"My heart," the director said. "My body. My strength."

"The father of the son is the son of the father. The son of the father is the father of the son."

"The son of the father," Schmidt repeated. "The father of the son."

"We found David," Black Charlie said.

Cal struggled to tear himself away from the written letter in his hand. It was a missive from the Firstborn warrior Olanthes Kuta, and it was both horrifying and intriguing. The letter horrified because it was the first news that had come to Calhoun Mountain about the failure of the impeachment.

It was also horrifying, because Olanthes passed on news from Charlie Donelsen—Thomas Penn had started something called the Shackamaxon League, which was a union for mutual defense. Many powers had flocked to this new banner, within the empire, and apparently also without. Thomas had made the League attractive by sending troops in defense of Shreveport, including troops from the Spanish army that besieged New Orleans.

Was this an impeachable offense? Cal rubbed his temples. Thomas Penn as the Penn landholder had made common cause with New Spain, but he hadn't done so to make war on the empire . . . at least, not yet. Indeed, he had done so to defend one of the powers of the empire, and Kimoni Machogu was publicly and effusively grateful. Cal hadn't committed the entire Compact to memory, but he didn't think Thomas was doing anything that violated any specific provision of the document.

But wasn't Thomas *thoroughly* violating the *spirit* of the agreement? He was, in effect, setting up a second empire, within and alongside the first. And what might he do with that shadow empire, beyond defending Shreveport from beastkind? And if the Spanish were on his side, could any alliance of other powers on the continent stand against them?

Was the Philadelphia Compact to last only thirty years, to be torn up and replaced by the grandsons of its architects?

And if Thomas had the military force at his command to cow and subdue the other Electors, how could Sarah possibly stand up to him?

Cal sighed and ground knuckles into both his eye sockets. He hadn't slept a wink, it seemed, since the night he'd intruded on the craft meeting in Broken Finger Clearing. Both men he'd defeated in that midnight election had disappeared, but Black Charlie swore up and down that neither had been harmed.

Cal worried his Uncle David might be off rallying support. For the moment, Calvin seemed to have become the Elector Calhoun, but his leadership was only as strong as his kin allowed it to be, and he wasn't sure it was strong enough to survive a challenge.

The other fellow, Jet Calhoun, had been given a ride down the mountain on a rail. Black Charlie assured Cal that the man had walked away from the experience alive—and therefore, by Black Charlie's reckoning, unharmed. A bit bow-legged, perhaps, but moving under his own power.

The intriguing thing about Olanthes's letter was a short paragraph that hinted at long conversations, and possibly action, to come. It read:

> *I know how you and your grandfather were betrayed. The betrayer believes himself unde-tected.*

The letter was postmarked from Cambry, which meant that Olanthes had ridden out of Philadelphia to send the letter. Was it to escape detection by the betrayer he wrote of? And yet, he had still been circumspect about naming the man.

"We found David," Black Charlie said again.

Cal set the letter and his thoughts aside. "He's uninjured?" Cal sat in the Elector's Thinkin' Shed, which he'd taken to using as an office, as he'd started sleeping in his grandpa's feather bed. No one had objected.

Black Charlie and a couple of the other younger Calhoun men had taken it upon themselves to find David, when he turned up missing. No one said openly why they wanted him found, but Cal knew it was out of loyalty to Calvin, and the desire to have a stable leadership for the clan.

"He stinks." Black Charlie leaned against the door-frame. "We can't git sense outta him, and we figure he's been sleepin' rough. I guess he wanted to be Elector more'n I e'er knew, iffen losin' the vote hurt him this bad."

Cal stood, putting his war ax and his looped lariat

both into place on his belt. Home as he was on the mountain, he could walk around without them, but he liked the symbolism of always being armed. It suggested he thought, as Calhoun Elector, that he was at war.

Which he did.

Cal followed Black Charlie. "We got him over in the woods," Charlie said softly. "Don't want to distress his wife or kids none."

Cousins and young'uns nodded at Cal. That was normal enough, but they had a new respect in their faces they'd never shown him before. Stranger than that, his aunts and uncles nodded, too, and showed a similar look of deference. Cal nodded back, and tried to look like his grandpa had always looked: carved out of granite, built to scowl, but face erupting into laughter and tenderness at the drop of a hat.

Black Charlie led Cal into the trees.

"You don't smell too good, yourself," Cal said.

Charlie laughed. "You think I been lookin' for Uncle David in a fancy Nashville hotel? We had to follow him halfway down the Cumberland, sleepin' in the saddle or in hayricks or even in wet ditches."

Something tickled at the back of Calvin's consciousness.

"You reckon he's calmed down since the vote?" Cal asked.

Black Charlie shrugged. "Like I said, he ain't makin' a lot of sense. But you're a better talker'n I am, I figured he might listen to you."

Cal snorted. "My momma'd sit up in her grave with pride at the thought that someone accounted her only son a decent speaker. And I expect it'd make my dad jest spit."

Black Charlie chuckled. "Hell of a feller, your dad."

"Yessir," Cal agreed. He let Black Charlie drift a step or two ahead of him.

Only it wasn't Black Charlie. Indeed, it likely wasn't a man at all, but one of the mud creatures Cal had fought before. Mockers, Thalanes had called them. Cal had destroyed them with silver, because they were creatures of magic, and Sarah had used a magic spell, together with her staff.

Her staff, carved by Cal's grandpa out of white ash.

Cal had no silver in his pocket; his purse was on the table in the Thinkin' Shed. And while there was plenty of white ash growing on Calhoun Mountain, he didn't think he had time to carve a spear of the stuff, much less learn the gramarye Sarah had mastered to be able to burn the clay monsters.

But Lord hates a man as gives up afore he even tries.

Cal lifted the tomahawk from his belt. He stepped forward and swung.

He felt a terrible doubt at the very last second, as his sharpened ax-head hurtled toward its target, but he forced himself to follow through—

and chopped off Black Charlie's leg.

The mudmen had no bones, so cutting through the limb in one blow was easy. The severed leg, wet gray clay showing inside its pale shell of skin, toppled sideways. Not-Charlie turned to glare over his shoulder and then hopped, trying to turn himself around.

Cal swung his ax again, reversing it to hit with the blunted back of the ax-head this time. The Mocker raised its arms, but not quick enough, and Cal struck the simulacrum of Charlie in the shoulder, knocking him off balance and into the trees.

Cal turned and ran.

There could be others. Mockers weren't natural creatures, he didn't have to worry that they always hunted in packs, like wolves. But someone had created this Mocker and sent it up Calhoun Mountain to come after Calvin. If that someone was determined and had resources—and it seemed most likely that the someone was Thomas Penn, or Penn's dark ally, the Necromancer—then he had probably sent more than just the one.

And the Mocker could have anyone's face.

Behind him, Cal heard a long howl. The call was not a wail of despair. It was not an animal cry, but a keen-edged hunting call nonetheless. The hairs on the back of his neck stood up and his heart raced.

Elsewhere on the mountain, to his left, rose an answering cry.

And then again, a call to his right.

Cal wished he had William Lee's horn—he could blow an alarm. But wouldn't his people hear the cry of the Mockers?

He lengthened his stride, pushing himself at breakneck speeds down paths too steep for a mule, leaping over gullies, splashing through streams to take the shortest possible road back to the settlement.

How did Mockers hunt? Cal tried to think through what he'd heard Thalanes say. It didn't seem that they hunted by smell. Instead, maybe they worked like gramarye. What was it Thalanes had said about Isaac Newton? The Laws of Similarity and Contagion, wasn't that it? So the Mockers had found Sarah on the Natchez Trace because they had somehow had a little bit of her, some hair or something. And that was how they had looked like her, too, nearly killing Calvin in an ambush.

But this Mocker didn't look like Calvin, it looked like Black Charlie. And had it been leading him to a Mocker that looked like his Uncle David? Which would mean that the Mockers had made a connection with those two Calhoun men, taking skin or spittle or hair from them.

Were David and Charlie both prisoners?

Was David cooperating with Thomas, and had they captured Black Charlie?

Cal tore through a berry bramble, ignoring the scratches that lacerated both his arms, and onto a path at the edge of the settlement. He began to yell at the top of his lungs, "Foreigners! Invasion! Git to the Thinkin' Shed!"

The sun was hitting the western horizon, smearing long shadows across the settlement. Heads poked out of cabins, and men and women appeared with torches in their hands.

Half expecting to be seized from behind at every step, Cal burst into the Thinkin' Shed and seized his purse. When he emerged, he found a dozen people waiting, with fire and weapons and ferocious snarls on their faces.

"Enemies on the mountain," Cal panted. "They's sorcerous creatures, so we gotta do this right."

More people gathered. Cal knew all their faces, but that meant nothing.

He shook silver coins into all their hands. "They're called Mockers, and they can take the shape of any person. Any person, you hear me? One jest took Black Charlie's shape and led me on up the hill, almost caught me afore I figured out what it was."

"Iffen they can look like anyone, how do we find 'em?" one cousin asked.

"How do we kill 'em?" added another.

Cal held up a shilling. It was slightly tarnished, and bore the likeness of Hannah Penn. "Touch silver to 'em, and they'll react. They'll start wailin'."

"Like a Wiggly?" It was Young Andy who asked. In the circumstances, Calvin decided to let the slur pass without comment.

Cal shook his head. "Firstborn get a rash. These things start throwin' off yellow smoke. So go in groups of three, but first, touch a silver coin to every person you're with." He started passing coins out. "You three, round up all the young'uns. Every single one, touch silver to 'em first, and then git 'em here to keep an eye on 'em."

"This is crazy," someone called from the back. "David made a mistake goin' up against you, and a bigger one, leavin' you out of the meetin', but he was right about one thing. Calhouns gotta be for Calhouns. That's fundamental. Kin first, or you can't rightly call yourself a Calhoun."

The crowd, still growing, parted to open a corridor in front of Calvin. He recognized the face and voice of his cousin Liam.

Cal stepped to the ground, holding his last silver coin in his palm. He walked slowly toward the other man. "Kin first, Liam," he agreed. "David's still my uncle, and I don't hold it against him that he thought he'd be a better Elector than me. Could be he's right. But I'm talkin' about creatures as can take the face of kin. So I'm gonna need you to do what I tell you and help hunt these Mockers down. But first, you need to take this coin in your hand."

He stopped, standing immediately in front of Liam, and knew already that Liam, too, had been replaced by a Mocker. Calvin could smell the wet clay.

Liam lashed out, moving to strike the coin from Cal's hand and to the ground—

but Cal was already moving, grabbing the back of Liam's neck—

and slapping the silver coin against his forehead.

Liam roared in pain, and smoke exploded from his face. He thrashed and punched, but four Calhouns pounced on him. They dragged him flailing to the ground, and hands pressed more silver to his flesh while Cal knelt on his chest. In seconds, the Mocker was reduced to a pile of clay.

When Cal stood up, Polly sloshed lantern oil onto the pile of clay and then lit it on fire.

"They's at least three on the mountain," Cal said to the crowd. "Don't assume they's only three, though. Don't be alone, test everyone you meet with silver. You might be able to smell 'em, too—they're made of river mud, and they smell like it. Don't count on that, though—we Calhouns ain't generally famous for going perfumed."

"How can we be sure we got 'em all?" cousin Elizabeth asked.

"We can't," Cal said grimly. "From now on, no one is e'er alone. You go to the outhouse, you take a friend and a silver shillin'. We don't have enough shillin's to go around, we cut 'em in half, and half again, until everyone's got a bit. But they's at least two more of these things on the mountain, and once we destroy those, we got a task ahead of us of findin' Uncle David and Black Charlie." He looked down at the heap of baked clay that had recently resembled his cousin Liam. "And anyone else as is missin'."

The Vizier Maltres Korinn rode to the Chicago Gate with Gazelem. Beside them rode Chigozie Ukwu, looking thoroughly uncomfortable riding a horse, and Naares Stoach, who looked so utterly at his ease on his mount that he might have been half-horse himself. Behind them came the Merciful.

When Gazelem had asked Sarah for soldiers to support him in his effort to recover Zomas's Earthshaker's Rod, she had demurred. Chigozie, when asked, had promptly volunteered. What was the Igbo priest looking for? Cahokia was not his land, and neither was Zomas.

Sarah knew him and trusted him immediately. Given her gifts of vision, that seemed a strong mark in the priest's favor. On the other hand, Gazelem's land was overrun by beastman warriors, so he felt discomfort at riding homeward with more beastkind at his shoulders.

But they were a troop of ferocious warriors—meek though he might be, Gazelem had difficulty imagining any five men defeating the bison-headed Kort in a contest of arms. And moreover, his warriors would not stick out in Missouri, and he was willing.

And Stoach trusted them. By way of warning, he had simply said to Gazelem, "If the priest and his worshippers fail to keep faith with you, it will be because they are trying to do something…righteous."

Behind the four of them came the beastkind themselves, Ferpa and Kort at their head.

They rode out the Chicago Gate because the Mississippi Gate was underwater. The Memphis Gate was also obscured by flood, but could be used, if one was willing to wade, and pointed more directly toward Zomas—indeed, it had once been known as the Zomas Gate. The south-facing Memphis Gate, though, saw much more activity of feral beastkind, whereas the Chicago Gate faced allies.

Emerging through the gate, Maltres reined in his horse. Rain crashed against his cheeks as he lowered the hood of his cloak to address the leaving party. "We can ferry you across on a raft," he said, reaffirming his commitment to their agreed plan, "and gunboats will protect you until you get to the western bank. From then on... I wish you luck."

Each man had dried meats, portable soups, and parched corn in his saddlebags. Chigozie had politely communicated Korinn's offer of supplies to the beast-kind, which had elicited a blast of laughter from Ferpa and Kort. They hadn't explained their amusement, but had bellowed to their fellows, who had promptly erupted into a racket of humor.

"The Merciful are blessed," Chigozie Ukwu had said by way of explanation. "God gives them each day their daily bread."

"As long as no one thinks I am that bread," Gazelem had said.

Now, saying his farewells to the Duke of Na'avu, he felt considerably more solemn. Would they meet again? "Thank you, Maltres," he said.

Korinn raised a hand in a gesture of parting. "The goddess go with you," he said. "You are a true son of Onandagos."

"Do you think your queen sees that?" Gazelem asked.

"I think she would be happy to see you on your

grandfather's throne," Korinn said thoughtfully. "Since she looks on a man's heart as easily as I look on his face, this speaks very well of you." There was a hint of embarrassment in his words.

Gazelem nodded, happy to take those words as his final message from Cahokia and its queen. Turning his horse's nose westward, he rode toward the ferry.

The final members of their company were the Ghostmaster, Auntie Bisha, and a young Zoman refugee named Belladin. Belladin's skin was dusky and his hair was a shock of white; he was thin, nearly as thin as the Ghostmaster, but she reveled in his body, announcing regularly how much heat he gave off, embracing her through the night to keep her bones warm.

What else happened during those nocturnal embraces, Gazelem chose not to consider. But Belladin seemed content, and ate ravenously whenever food was offered to him, and sang to the Ghostmaster whenever she asked. They both rode ponies, small, sturdy creatures such as the farmers of Chicago loved, and they rode among the beastkind.

Gazelem led them all to the ferry. Even on this mile-long journey, the beastkind showed that they knew how to be useful; two each moved out to the right and the left of the caravan, in a forward flank-protecting position, and two more fell back as a rearguard. Chigozie hadn't given any order, and didn't seem the type to know to give such an order; the beastkind simply performed.

The ferry was a wide, flat barge, poled by six men. Four gunboats anchored out in the Mississippi flood stood watch, their weapons aimed downstream. The horses and the children of Adam would all fit onto the barge, but the beastkind would require a second trip, or perhaps a third.

"We shall swim," Kort said. He and Ferpa and two others struck out promptly into the waters, while the horses were still being hitched to a pole in the center of the raft and hooded. The ferrymen, heavily muscled Germans in leather shirts and breeches and thick fur cloaks, chanted as they pushed the boat out into the water.

These were not Cahokians, but men of Chicago or Waukegan. The upright posts of their ferry were carved with the angular runes of a Chicagoan vitki, the deep angles and slashes stained a dark reddish brown. Gazelem stood near the center of the raft, huddled against the wall of a tiny shack nailed to the raft's timbers, in which the ferrymen kept a small fire burning. Stoach stood beside their horses, murmuring comforting words to the beasts. The Ghostmaster and her boy huddled beside the fire, Belladin cooing an ancient love song about the original Zomas himself, and Gazelem found himself standing beside the New Orleans priest.

"You are an outcast prince," Chigozie Ukwu said.

"As the last prince of Zomas, to my knowledge, I can hardly be said to be outcast any longer. But my grandfather cast me out to save my life, as my aunt taught me skill with herbs and drugs so that I could protect myself." Gazelem smiled, trying to keep his expression inviting. "And you are an outcast prince, too, are you not? The son of the bishop of New Orleans?"

Ukwu nodded slowly. "Sometimes I think that one of the great secrets to understanding this life is that we are *all* of us outcast princes."

Gazelem examined the sky. To the north and west, beyond Missouri and Chicago, the clouds were light, steely blue. But to the south, over the tangled green lands of the Heron King, and over the hills of Zomas, the sheet of rain clouds was so dark it was black. "And you? Why did the bishop cast you out?"

"I . . . he did not," Chigozie Ukwu said slowly.

"Was it your brother, then?" Gazelem tried to remember what he had heard. "Your brother became bishop and exiled you?"

"My brother became bishop and begged me to stay." Ukwu sighed. "Sometimes, I think it was my own pride that cast me out."

"Sometimes, I think that the great secret to understanding this life is that we are all cast out by our own pride." Gazelem's smile really was warm, this time.

The ferrymen whistled, stopping their song as they approached the western bank. Kort and Ferpa stood waiting in waters that were only ankle-deep on them. Gazelem scanned the horizon; gray fog and rain shrouded his vision, but he saw no sign of hostile forces.

Chigozie pointed south. "We ride into the storm."

Gazelem nodded. He took his horses' reins, unhitching the beast from the ferry's post. As he stepped off the raft and into the water, the earth trembled.

"I can be a clod of a man."

CHAPTER TWENTY-THREE

The northern walls of New Orleans had been quiet. After an initial wave of ravening beastmen, the assault had slowed to a trickle, scarcely more severe than what New Orleans experienced in ordinary conditions. Feral beastkind occasionally charged the city's walls, or got loose in its streets; dealing with them was one of the basic responsibilities of the gendarmes.

Some of the reduction in the strength and savagery of the attack might be due to the rains in the Ohio. New Orleans's own spring had been, if anything, slightly dry. Eggbert Bailey only wished the spring had been much drier, to compensate for the flood of brown water that surged down from the north. The flood buried oxbow lakes, forests, and roads. The flood submerged streets in New Orleans and kept pumps busy night and day, uncovering them.

Trade was also strangled. The junction of the rivers was cut off first by Imperial blockade, and then by storms of such unimaginable violence that hardened keelboatmen were frightened. On top of that, there were the basilisks. Occasional smugglers and other bold captains continued to rush up and down the river as far as Memphis, but no farther. On the west bank of the river, the Cotton Princedoms had been fighting their own war against the beastkind, facing a wave that did not diminish with the rising of the river, so trade with Shreveport and the rest of the Cotton League had also died.

The gulf was full of Spanish ships. They were afraid to come in too close, for fear of New Orleans's river fortresses and its pirate defenders. Still, they sailed back and forth and cut off trade, with ports in New Spain and the Caribbean and also with the more distant capitals of the Old World in Europe and Africa.

But for overland trade, New Orleans would have starved. But the trade with the Igbo Free Cities—and through them, much of the rest of the world—had flourished. In other circumstances, the Igbo middlemen might have taken advantage of the Spanish and the Hansa disappearing from trade to raise their prices to the vaults of heaven, but Etienne's partner Onyinye Diokpo had wide respect, and although prices rose, they didn't rise very much. In addition to Onyinye's influence, there was among the Igbo a reverential feeling toward the Bishop of New Orleans. Those who were Christian regarded him as the greatest bishop in the land, and even those who were not, surprisingly, looked to him as a leader.

Etienne, meanwhile, seemed to have lost direction. Having removed the Chevalier of New Orleans from his Palais, Etienne seemed to have been stricken by paralyzing doubt.

Trade also continued with Appalachee, along the

Natchez Trace and other ancient roads. As much as Etienne's and Onyinye's popularity among the Igbo, rivalry with long-shanked Appalachee and the Ferdinandians and Cavaliers who followed with them along the same roads probably contributed to keeping New Orleans in boots and bread.

For weeks, the Spanish had been slowly trying to cross the Mississippi, upriver of the city. They mounted their assault at a spot where the Memphis Pike ran along a low ridge close to the river. The pike was the fastest, most direct road connecting New Orleans to Memphis, and it ran on a bank of artificially raised earth—heaped up, depending on which tale you believed, by John Penn's engineers or by the Bishop de Bienville's thaumaturges—that kept it on mostly dry ground, above the swamp and the bayou. Once they had gained the Memphis Pike, the Spanish would be able to march straight to New Orleans.

Two things slowed the Spanish down. First, the plague of serpents that, according to Etienne Ukwu, had been raised by Queen Sarah of Cahokia, continued to infest the river. In his years in New Orleans prior to this spring, Eggbert had seen half a dozen of the winged basilisks alive, two in a zoo, one in a private collection, and three more on separate occasions when on the river. This spring, he had seen thousands. They killed cattle, wild animals, and children of Adam who strayed too close to the river, and they killed Spanish soldiers by the thousands. The Spanish at the beginning had sent engineers, men who tried to sink pylons into the mud and set planks across the top, but such men were valuable, and not even New Spain had so many that it could afford to throw them away at the rate necessary to sate the basilisks' appetite.

So the Spanish had taken to simply filling the arms of its men with rocks and marching them into the river to be bitten and die.

It was a slow process, and one that required direction. It was impossible to dam off the river in this fashion—merely building a stone weir all the way across the river would not provide a bridge, since the water would flow over the stone. Instead, the men directing those who carried stone to their deaths aimed to build a series of stone islands, tall enough that the water would flow around them and between them, leaving the tops of the islands exposed.

Among Eggbert's men, and then spreading to the people of New Orleans in general, had arisen a new cult, that of Saint Serpent. To Christians, he seemed to be a man with a serpent's head, rising from the river, and his martyrdom was said to have occurred on the day of the Spring Equinox, when a Spanish alcalde had had him drowned in a small town on the Mississippi, only to see Saint Serpent return to bless the poor of the same village with protection and fertility. Among the Vodun, he had the same image, but was said to be one of the mystères of the city, always present but long forgotten, returned now in the city's hour of need.

As Eggbert had watched the men chosen to march, he had seen which troops were more valued by the Spanish, and which less. Unarmored men with shaved heads, Africans and men from the far east, were sent early. So were Indians, in large numbers. Spanish lancers were never made to dismount and carry in stone to die; neither were the more elite troops of other nations, whether Celestial swordsmen or Aztec berserkers.

A second difficulty was the flooding of the river. As the Mississippi rose through the spring, it buried stone islands that then required more men to be sent to hurl their stone upon the heap and die. It also pushed the eastern and western banks farther apart day by day, so that on some mornings the Spanish engineers arrived to find that they had to start one hundred feet west of where they had worked the day before, and that the first task facing them was to heap up a new island in the water where yesterday they had stood on dry land.

Across the tops of the stone mounds, the Spanish stretched wooden planks, with woven wicker walls and ceilings. Initially, they tried building their bridge with stone, but after two lengths of bridge were swallowed by the rising waters, they gave up and opted for lighter material.

Wooden bridges could be more easily raised, but they could also be more easily burned. Eggbert had scouts watching the Spanish at all times, and early on he had had his men throw up banks of earth, and lay long guns that aimed at the bridgeworks. Hitting the far side of the river was out of the question with the cannons he had, but once the bridgeworks reached the middle of the river, his gunners began blasting at it.

For their part, the Spanish responded with muskets from the western bank. To which Eggbert had answered with his own sharpshooters.

Flaming arrows had also taken on a significance that Eggbert had not seen in warfare in his lifetime.

As if they were some medieval unit, he had stationed Choctaw archers—they were the only fighters he could find in New Orleans who still used bows—around barrels of flaming pitch, to set fire to the Spanish woodworks, day and night.

Celestial magicians who had power over water had drawn the Mississippi mud up in waves to put out those flames. Few Polites remained in New Orleans; apparently, defending the city was not part of their sacred mission, and they had quickly taken roads east. Needing magicians, Eggbert had gained time by employing two Vodun houngans, one in the service of Ayida-Weddo and the other a worshipper of Agwé. These were water gods, and when the Celestials had tried to force the waters up to douse the flames, the houngans had chanted and poured out libations that forced the waters back down, allowing the bridges to burn.

Until one night, when the Celestials had done something new on their side of the river, something that stank of incense and burning flesh, and had been accompanied by the screaming of many men. Then a river-hurricano of churned water had ensued, the houngans' chant had grown faster and faster and more and more desperate, and finally, just before dawn, both Eggbert's magicians had exploded into red mist.

Thereafter, the Spanish advance had become faster.

It had taken the Spanish weeks, but eventually they had built a stone island in the middle of the river that was too large to wash away or submerge in the flood. Then, one blood-soaked rock at a time, they had put up stone walls, and brought in their own long guns.

The battle had become one of two artillery forces,

smashing away at each other from fixed positions. The bridge had slowly continued to extend.

Bodies had floated downriver all the time, sometimes in such astounding numbers that Eggbert couldn't see the water beneath them.

The Spanish had expanded their midriver fortress, and advanced sharpshooters to the front position. Eggbert's gunners, exposed to withering sniper fire, had begun to fall in much greater numbers.

Now it seemed, finally, that the crossing of the river was imminent. Eggbert had prepared for the moment with supplies purchased from the Igbo networks of the east, and with prodigious amounts of digging. A trench cut into the earth in a zigzagging pattern raced along the road all the long distance to the city's northern gate, and he had filled it with all the musketeers he could organize. As in 1810, the city had turned out civilian defenders to fight off an invading foe, so gamblers and pimps and dry-goods salesmen stood shoulder to shoulder with gendarmes and hired soldiers, looking over the tops of their ditches toward the direction from which the Spanish would come, waiting.

"Retire the cannons," Eggbert directed the subalterns who passed his orders on to the artillery captains. The men immediately set to hoisting the guns off the embankments where they lay, loading them onto sturdy wheeled carts, and trundling them south along the road toward New Orleans.

As the guns moved south, sharpshooters moved forward to fill in the gaps they left. The men lay on their bellies in the dirt, bullets whistling above them, and fired at the head of the bridge.

Eggbert himself stood, behind a thick timber screen he'd had built for himself, in which he'd had cut a horizontal arrow slit, for looking through. A cask of oil and a lit lantern stood at hand behind the screen, and Eggbert stomped from side to side, watching through the slit. Bullets struck the timbers from the other side and stopped; occasionally, a bullet would whistle through the slit, but so far, none had struck Eggbert.

Men holding wicker shields in one hand, covered with thick leather armor, and holding long planks under their other arm, charged to the front of the nearly completed bridge. The armor was no defense, inasmuch as it left gaps around the men's necks and wrists and eyes. Basilisks darted down from the cloud of snakes hanging above the river, and the screams of men bitten on the throat or on the hand filled the air. Eggbert watched one unlucky man, a short-haired, mustachioed Indian of some sort Eggbert couldn't identify, lose an eye to one of the snakes, and then fall shrieking into the Mississippi.

"Saint Serpent!" Eggbert's men roared.

But the Spanish soldiers who dropped screaming were immediately replaced by men behind them. Some of these fell, too, but others seized the fallen planks and rushed forward.

"Fire arrows!" Eggbert cried. This was the last stand at the river, he knew, and he would now retreat. But every Spanish warrior who fell here was one less warrior who would try to climb the walls of the city, and one more blow to the morale of the survivors.

The Choctaw loosed their arrows. They fired at the wicker walls and planks as far back as they could, even striking the bridge on the far side of the Spaniards' island fortress. The bridge shook with the tramping feet of more men all along its length.

The Choctaw had shot all their arrows and retreated. Only minutes later, the Celestial wizards of New Spain had extinguished the flames, sloshing great waves of river water up and over the wicker walls and ceilings of the bridge.

The men charging out of the mouth of the bridge and up the slope of the river now were Nihonese knights, with their hair back in tight buns, and long, single-bladed swords bare in their hands.

"Retreat!" Eggbert called to the sharpshooters. They fired a single volley and then fell back to the next angled stretch of the trench.

Eggbert shattered the cask of oil against his own wooden shield and the subaltern tossed the lantern into the oil. Flames quickly engulfed the wooden wall; no sense leaving it to the Spanish to use.

Eggbert fell back. Moving away from the river, he lost the ability to look down the slope and see how far away the Spanish troops were, so he could judge his timing. He would have to estimate, and he would err on the side of allowing them closer. The adjutant scampered down the ladder into the trench ahead of him, and Eggbert dropped down in a single jump, sinking into the earth when he struck the bottom.

Turning, because he was a tall man, he could see over the top of his trench. "Fuse!" he called out. His own adjutant took in hand a gunpowder-infused cord that was protected from the soil and rain by running it through a length of pipe; another junior officer in the trench on the other side of the road should be taking into his hand a similar fuse.

"Musketeers, ready!" Eggbert cried.

In the trench that stretched away to his right, angling away from the road, musketeers stood tall and lay their weapons, pointing them at the road where the Spanish should appear.

Seconds later, the Nihonese warriors advanced. They were stately looking men, as dignified a bunch of warriors as Eggbert had ever seen. They advanced with swords drawn, and they were supported by musketeers coming up behind them and on both sides, smoldering lengths of match tied into their long, black hair.

"Musketeers, fire at will!"

Eggbert's men began to fire. The Nihonese riflemen fired back; the earthen banks of the trenches gave protection to Eggbert's men that was significant, but not perfect. Two died in the first volley, shot in the head.

"Light fuse!"

The subaltern struck fire by pulling the trigger on his pistol, sending a shower of sparks into the fuse pipe.

A few of the Nihonese knights fell, but many did not. Eggbert's men had decent aim; the easterners must be protected by wizardry.

"Fall back!" Eggbert shouted.

Half his musketeers took one last shot and then retreated beyond the next bend in the trench; the same would be happening on the other side of the road. Eggbert followed after them, making sure that men with fixed bayonets were prepared to defend the actual bend in the trench.

"Aim at the musketeers!" Eggbert shouted.

While the first half of his men fell back, the second half fired another volley, now aiming beyond the swordsmen, at the men with guns. These men must not be so well protected, as they fell in greater numbers under fire.

"Fall back!" Eggbert shouted again. The men at the front now retreated into the next bend of the trench, under covering fire provided by their fellows at arms who had already retreated.

The road to New Orleans was narrow; to leave it was to plunge into swamp and jungle that was interminably slow to cross, even without the basilisks that now infested it. Eggbert Bailey was prepared to defend the road in this fashion all the way to the gates of the city.

KABOO-OOM!

The first of the explosive charges went off, followed almost instantly by the second. On each side of the road, a buried barrel of gunpowder now exploded. Before sinking the charges in the earth, Eggbert had emptied the top twelve inches of the barrel and packed it tight with nails and small bits of scrap iron, all lying only a few inches beneath the earth, just to either side of the road.

The Nihonese fell en masse, some pierced with multiple wounds and some cut completely in half. A few men, standing close to the blasts, disappeared entirely. The walls of the nearby trenches buckled and sagged, sinking inward and losing their value as defensive cover for the Spanish.

"Bayonets!" Eggbert shouted. This was a command not to the men defending the bends in the trenches, but to the musketeers who now sprang up to attack the stunned Nihonese survivors in hand to hand combat.

"Kaboom!" he heard his own men shouting, farther south along the road. "Kaboom!"

Through the acrid, stinging smoke of the muskets and the explosives, Eggbert saw another unit advancing to take the place to the crushed Nihonese. These men looked like proper Hidalgos, with metal breastplates and steel bonnets, bayonets fixed to their muskets.

"Musketeers, fire at will!" Eggbert shouted, preparing to fall back a second time.

"Oui, Général Kaboom!" several of them cried.

Eggbert was tired already, and had a long way to fall back before he reached New Orleans.

At the ridge above his home, Bill stopped his horse to look.

Tears flooded his eyes. He had forgotten, he would have sworn it wasn't true, that he loved this land. He loved the valley with its natural horse paddock, easily fenced in with a few timbers. He loved the bubbling brook, and the small mill and pond his father had built, and the trees that grew in close to the barn, the stable, and the house, giving one the sensation, sitting in the kitchen and looking out the window, that there were no other houses in the world, but only forest stretching forever in all directions.

Bill emerged from the endless forest with his eyes still moist with memory. He fancied he could see Charles in short pants, climbing over the split-rail fence; Caroline and Mary singing beside the stream; Sally smiling at him from the door of the house. He fixed his blurry vision on Sally as he rode down into the valley and hitched his horse to a post, all under her welcoming smile.

Then he approached the door, and blinked, and she was gone.

He stopped a moment to admire the building his father and uncles had built. The roof still held. The witches' marks on the lintel above the door were more visible than ever; the lichen that had grown up the wall tended to highlight the interlocked Vs and the daisy-like pattern Bill himself had made when he was a boy almost old enough to be a man, tracing a circle in the wood with a charcoal pencil and compass, and then centering six additional circles on six points equidistant from each other along the first. Where they overlapped, the circles created a petallike image, and the image, like the inter-locking Vs that were also an upside-down M and therefore recalled the Virgin Mary, repelled evil intentions.

But wind and water would erase pencil, so while his uncles had hauled timbers up onto the roof, young Will had painstakingly worked over both patterns with a chisel, laying the tool one way and then the other, being careful to take small amounts of wood and work longer rather than risk big mistakes.

"Good work, Will," his uncle John had said, tousling his hair. "The perfection of the lines you are cutting will determine the strength of the witches' marks. What you are doing right there is building a strong protection for your family."

Short strokes. Taking time. Doing the work right.

Building protection for the family.

Bill sighed.

He reached up to rap on the doorpost, and the door opened before he could knock.

Hell's Bells, Mary looked just like Sally.

She had her mother's firm jaw and determined eye, one eyebrow perpetually slung at the top of her forehead. She had her mother's black eyebrows, too, despite the flaxen yellow of her hair. She lacked Sally's mole alongside her left ear, and her lips weren't painted; Sally never opened the door before she had applied at least a little lacquer.

Mary held a blunderbuss in her hands.

"I don't believe I know you, suh," Bill's daughter said slowly. "If you have come calling in the expectation that you would find me alone, I regret to have to disabuse you of the notion. You will see that I am here in the company of my close friend, Old Mortality."

Bill laughed. He couldn't help himself; his daughter looked like Sally, but sounded like Bill. And the gun—he'd forgotten that he'd told his children stories of the Siege of Mobile, and Harmonszoon and his blunderbuss, Old Mortality.

Had Bill named the family weapon after his experience? Or had his family done so? He couldn't remember.

"If you have come calling, suh," Mary said, "it is customary to write first."

"It is *customary*," Bill said, "to first approach the *parents* of the young lady. A marriage is a family alliance. There are genealogies to be consulted, holdings to be reviewed, positions enumerated, titles considered. If one is of that persuasion, there are stars and the Tarocks to be analyzed. And it is always worth a trip to the parson, or the godar, to learn an impartial account of the lady's family's fame."

"Alas." Mary lowered the gun, but only slightly. "My mother is dead, I care nothing for stars and cards, and I would as soon pull a tooth out sober as step inside a church, so the parson is likely to say nothing more of me than that I am a heathen. Do you find your suit thwarted?"

"Mary," Bill said gently. "Has it been so long that you do not recognize me at all?"

Mary frowned. Her lower lip trembled. Then she began to cry.

Carefully brushing aside the blunderbuss, Bill took his daughter into his arms for the first time in fifteen years. His heart melted, and for a long time he could think no clear thought, only reveling in the sensation that he had lost his identity entirely, dissolving again at last into a unity that he had long desired and lacked.

When he could think again, his first thought was of Cathy, that Cathy would love his daughter as Bill loved her. The pang of heartache that followed on the heels of that thought nearly knocked him down.

"Besides," he told her, "I am far too old to be a suitor for you."

"I did not want to be impolite to a stranger," she said into his shoulder. "And you might be a man of property."

"Sadly, I am not."

Mary pulled Bill into the house with a strong hand upon his forearm, clutching him as if she was afraid he would disappear, pulling him onto a chair in the kitchen. At the sight of the heavy trestle table at which he had eaten so many meals, man and boy, and the sturdy, elegant, dark-stained hutch that had come to the home as part of Sally's dot, Bill's eyes teared up again.

"I knew you were alive." Mary pulled a bottle of Kentucky bourbon from the hutch, along with two glasses. She pushed open the curtains, flooding the kitchen with light. Bill set his hat on the table. "I knew that Mother received letters from you, but she would say nothing. Even when I asked."

Bill nodded. "I understand her anger."

"I understand it, and I care not a fig for it." Mary poured whisky and sat. "We were your children, and our right to know that you lived and loved us was not dependent on her right to be angry."

"You sound like a lawyer." Bill nodded at the glasses. "Do you greet every visitor with whisky?"

"If your tastes have changed so much, I have a brick of tea and can boil water."

Bill smiled and took a sip.

"She burned the letters," Mary continued. "Or I would have opened her chest and read them. But twice I intercepted them and managed to read them before she could destroy them. I read both those letters to Caroline, as well. I would have read them to Charles, only he was riding for the earl by then."

"I wish I had thought to write to you separately," Bill said. "I do not intend so, but I can be a clod of a man."

"I know enough of men now to know that they can all be clods," Mary said. "And I think I know enough to know that my father is a man who can stand tall in any company."

Bill tried to respond graciously, but could only bite his lip and nod.

"You were in New Orleans," Mary said. "At least for a time, when you wrote those letters. When I was twelve years old and ran away from home, I wanted to go to New Orleans and find you. I got as far as Asheville, and then Charles found me. He promised me that we'd go together, one day, and that promise was enough to bring me back home."

Mary sobbed, once.

"I heard of Charles's death," Bill said.

"In part, it was because Charles was so good that I knew you must be good, too." Mary smiled sadly. "His death was a terrible accident. The poor young man who shot him...he did not intend the death, it happened in a moment of panic."

"Do you believe so?" Bill asked gravely. "You do not harbor feelings of anger toward the killer?"

"His name is Landon," she said. "I do not hate him."

"But he is not one of your suitors."

"You speak as if I have had a throng at my door, Father."

"It was Parson Brown who gave me the plural."

"Landon has never called at this door to declare amorous intentions," Mary said. "I believe my family fame might have been too...colorful...for him. As a foundling, he might be hoping for a lady with less elevated titles in her family tree, but more conventional respectability."

Bill laughed. What should he say about Cathy?

"My own father killed the earl's son in a duel that had scarcely more reason than the scuffle that took my brother," Mary said. "I do not hate my father, and I cannot hate the man whose shot took my brother from me. This is the way we live, and these are the blows we must take."

Bill nodded. "And Caroline?"

"She lives in Henricia. She married a planter named Bolger. I believe he is kin to the Byrds."

Bill nodded. "Is he a kind man?"

"Her letters to me are full of love and happiness," Mary said. "I will not say I envy her, but she has done well for herself."

"Children?" Bill dreaded the answer as much as he

wanted it. The thought that he might be a grandfather made his breath come short.

"I do not know." Mary toyed with her glass, looking at the alcohol but not drinking it. "Father, have you returned because the earl has regained his mind? Are you again in the service of Johnsland?"

Bill realized that he had been drinking in all the detail he could of Mary's life, and telling nothing of his own. But what to say?

"I am in the service of the Queen of Cahokia," he said. "If she will still have me. But I had news of Charles's death, and of the earl's recovery, and I came to find my daughters."

"Does the Queen of Cahokia grant you land?" Mary smiled. "My throng of suitors might become a nation if the men of Johnsland knew I could expect to inherit large tracts of the fertile Ohio."

"Thus far, the Queen has given me a very small tract, with a house upon it."

"A *mound*?" Mary could barely suppress a smile.

"In fact, yes, a mound. I am not yet become a mound *builder*, but in recent months I find that I am a mound *dweller*." He had to say something about Cathy, if he waited any longer than this moment it would be a grievous admission. "And I dwell there with a woman. With my wife."

"Ah." Mary's facial expression was controlled, hard to read. "How long have you been married?"

"Only a few weeks," Bill said. "I came here directly after the wedding. Her name is Catherine Filmer, and she is a lady of Virginia."

"Shall I call her 'Mother,' do you think?"

"I think she will wish you to call her 'Cathy.' But

I also think that, clod though I be, I am wise enough to remove myself from the decision. You and she are both excellently able to come to terms without me." He hesitated. "The story is long, and I do not understand all of it myself, but she has a son."

"A young man of Virginia," Mary said. "Has he land?"

"He has no land, and he is not from Virginia." Bill swallowed the last of his whisky, a large gulp. "Cathy is Landon Chapel's mother."

Mary sat still, her smile frozen.

"Heaven's curtain," Bill murmured. "Life is a road that takes unexpected turns."

"And does not go to the destination indicated on the map," Mary added. "Do you love Cathy Filmer?"

Bill nodded. "I do."

"Then I shall love her, too. And I have all the more reason to think kindly of my brother Landon."

Bill inhaled deeply, and then shuddered. "Thank you, Mary," he said. "Thank you."

Bill stayed the night in his childhood home. Mary tried to give him back his married bed, but at his insistence he slept in the loft, in the corner that had been his when the house had first been built.

And he required only the tiniest sip of his cherry brandy to get to sleep.

Awake, son.

Etienne sat up. The Palais was dark, and outside his room, the facing sets of stars—those of the sky above, and the lights of New Orleans beneath—told him that dawn was still far away.

The voice he heard was his mother's. Etienne touched the silver locket that he carried at all times.

Mother?

Someone comes, she said to him. *For you. By ship.*

Etienne stood, stretching vigorously to cast off the chains of sleep. He climbed into breeches and waistcoat, but left his sash hanging on the peg in the wall. Standing briefly on the balcony outside the room where he slept—he was hesitant to think of it as *his* room, preferring to style himself a visitor, a guest of the city—he looked westward.

The Spanish army was on the move. He saw their lights shifting northward as units marched upriver. This was no expedition to help Shreveport, no scouting foray, no building crew marching to its doom on false stories that the bridge was nearly complete, and that this time the Spanish army would cross the river. Etienne could tell by the lights from the farthest sections of the Spanish encampment that the entire army was on the move.

This was not a surprise. His sleep had been fitful, because earlier that day, the Spanish had finally crossed the river. Eggbert Bailey was still retreating one exploding barrel at a time toward the north gates of the city, but soon the Spanish would reach the walls, and the siege would well and truly be joined.

Etienne had been preparing, stocking away food in every public building he could. His allies on the City Council had helped, spending their fortunes to make similar preparations, and to stockpile arms and ammunition as well. By midday, the ordinary lines of trade would all be severed. Fortunately, the smugglers were on the side of New Orleans, but Etienne planned as if he would be entirely cut off from the outside world.

He needs you, his mother said. *The Mississippi Docks.*

Etienne took two loaded pistols, conscious that the mameluke assassin was still hunting him. Should he take gendarmes? There were men guarding the Palais, and he could ask them to accompany him.

Instead, he sprinkled a few grains of gunpowder over his own head. "Papa Legba," he murmured, "take me through this crossroads safely and hide my passage from prying eyes."

As an extra precaution, he exited by climbing a tree. Outside the garden walls, nothing grew close enough to aid anyone attempting to climb, but within the walls, some of the chevalier's trees grew quite close to the enclosure. Etienne hoisted himself easily up and over, and set out for the docks on foot.

He passed through the fringes of the Quarter, not far from the Place d'Armes. Despite the besieging army, an atmosphere of festivity prevailed here. The saloons were less full and the rioters less drunk, since prices, including the price of alcohol, had risen in the city, and since many of the people who might be in New Orleans for casual reasons—merchants, travelers, and others—had cleared out in anticipation of the arrival of the Spanish. Still, the Vieux Carré doggedly held on to its will to recreate.

The traffic was busier at Decatur Street and the Mississippi Gate. Soldiers demanded identification of Etienne, but their sergeant recognized him, snapped to a quick salute, and pulled his men away.

Etienne wandered out onto the docks. *Where do I find this man, Mother?* He rubbed the locket between his thumb and forefinger.

Go to the river.

Etienne felt the teasing sensations in his belly,

and the quickening of his breath, that told him that the Brides were active. He hadn't brought cigarettes to appease them, so he controlled his breathing and tried not to focus on their allure.

Ships loaded and unloaded. To the last minute, trade would continue; there was always some Hansard or Igbo daredevil willing to run the Spanish blockade for a good profit, or some calculating Dutchman or Catalan willing to bet that the siege was not about to be joined, after all, and that his competitors would pull back prematurely, leaving the market to him. Etienne walked straight out the dock in front of him, the wood sagging and creaking slightly under his boots. Stevedores passed, carrying bales and barrels, and a ship's captain haggled with one of the dock authorities over the contents of a bill of lading.

Near the end of the dock, a small vessel ladled a dollop of sailors over the side. The men jumped to, securing the vessel and lowering its gangplank. As he drew nearer the ship, Etienne's mother's locket seemed to tremble in his hand.

The captain was a tall, thin-nosed Frenchman. Pushing a sailor down toward the dock, he shouted at the man, *"Amenez l'évêque!"*

The sailor, a squat man with thin legs and arms half again as long as they needed to be, rushed along the dock. The running sailor bellowed at stevedores to move aside, the captain stood with a foot on the gunwale and shouted at the sailor, and the stevedores bellowed a general objection to it all.

Etienne stopped the runner with a hand on the man's arm.

"L'évêque est ici," he said.

The shouting stopped.

The sailor stared up at Etienne with large eyes. Turning back to his captain, he called, *"Je l'ai amené!"*

The captain removed his hat and bowed, and jumped down to the dock. "Your Grace," he said, "God has moved you to be here at this moment."

God, or Etienne's gede loa, his mother. But how fine the line was that separated those two powers, Etienne was not sure. He contented himself with smiling.

"We found a man in the gulf," the captain continued. "He has been broken. I believe he is dying. But he says he is your servant."

"Lead me to him."

"My men are bringing him now." The captain pointed, and sailors on the deck of the ship, exactly where the captain had been standing moments earlier, now began to lower a board over the side of the ship. The board, Etienne saw, was a table, and they lowered it steadily, four men working four ropes and singing under their breath.

Strapped to the top of the table lay a man.

Etienne's breath came deep and fast.

He stepped close as the table was lowered, gently as a mother would lower her sleeping baby, to the planks of the dock. The man strapped to the wood was Achebe Chibundu. He wore only a loincloth. He lay on his back, arms and legs splayed wide and face turned up to the dark heavens above. His body was marked with many scars, and many wounds not yet healed.

His eye sockets were empty.

Etienne touched his bodyguard's shoulder. "Achebe," he said.

"Eze-Nri," Achebe groaned. "I did not kill the chevalier."

Etienne looked into the man's ruined eye sockets. "You must have come very close."

"I came very close."

"I bless you, Achebe."

"Am I dead, Eze-Nri?"

The sailors and stevedores had stopped their work and gathered round. They murmured to each other as they watched, and Etienne heard his name, along with the words *bishop* and *houngan* and *sorcerer*.

What to say to this faithful servant?

He has already died.

"You have already died," Etienne said. "Death is behind you." The power of the Brides swelled within him.

"Death is behind me," Achebe said.

"Once, you were the man Achebe Chibundu," Etienne said. "And from time to time, the mighty warrior spirit Lusipher Charpile rode you as his horse."

"Lusipher." Chibundu grinned.

Etienne took a small knife from his pocket and began cutting the wrestler's ropes. "Now Achebe Chibundu is dead. What remains is Lusipher Charpile, the warrior spirit, who is always mounted, always ready for battle."

"Always in battle," Charpile said. "Indomitable. But how will I fight, when I have no eyes?"

Etienne put away his knife and took his powder horn in hand. He shook a few grains into one open palm, then pinched them between thumb and forefinger. "Maitre Carrefour," he said. "Ezili Freda, Ezili Danto. Give this warrior sight."

He touched his thumb and finger to his own eyelid, eyes closed. Then he sprinkled the grains of gunpowder in both the wrestler's eye sockets. The force of the Brides shook his frame, and his skin burned.

Lusipher Charpile began to laugh. He didn't laugh with the voice of Achebe Chibundu, but with a deeper voice, a voice that had a ferocious edge to it. "I see!" Charpile bellowed. "I see!"

"Arise, Lusipher," Etienne said. "Arise and ride into your eternal battle."

Lusipher Charpile stood. He sprang to his feet in one fluid motion, rolling from the table and landing in feral crouch. Again, he laughed.

"I see through your eyes, Eze-Nri," he murmured, his voice low enough that the sailors and stevedores could not hear him over their own excited babble.

"Then you see how magnificent you are," Etienne said.

Charpile stood. Some of his wounds had opened and were bleeding afresh, but his face was split in half by an enthusiastic grin.

"It is enough," he said. "We ride into our eternal battle."

Ahmed Abd al-Wahid rapped on the door, and it opened. The person standing in the doorway, lit orange and yellow from behind, had a wizened head so small it was scarcely larger than a fist, and a flower-spangled shawl wrapped around its narrow shoulders.

"*Je cherche le bokor,*" Abd al-Wahid said.

"*Je suis le bokor.*" The sorcerer's eyes blinked rapidly. "Have you been told my price?"

Abd al-Wahid produced three gold coins. "I require a doll. And this doll may require particular skill to prepare."

"Well, I don't know, Nathaniel.
What's happening with my hair?"

CHAPTER TWENTY-FOUR

For several days after his experience with the vines growing over his uncle Thomas's soul, Nathaniel could barely speak. The fact that he had to carry both his familiar spirits at all times was nearly too much for him to bear, so on the morning of the fourth day, he begged Margaret to say he was sick, and do all the work.

"Of course," she said.

~*Of course you think I am your slave,*~ he heard her say.

Sitting in the wagon for a day, clutching his drum and dozing, he was able to let Hop and Wilkes go. Beneath the blanket, he wore his coat backward, and drifted in and out of sleep for a night and a day and a night. Dreams of vines and tentacles haunted him; his sister Sarah stalked him in tree form across several landscapes; and when one of the vines finally seized him and tore him in two, green seeds spilled from Nathaniel's own body.

Once, drifting slowly back into consciousness, he

realized that Thomas was riding beside him. The emperor was speaking to Margaret in Dutch, with an expression of concern on his face; the color and direction of the sunlight, piercing the thick forest about them, suggested that it was afternoon.

Margaret chattered glibly but respectfully, bowing her head with every sentence. Whatever she said, Thomas seemed to believe it, because he nodded and made comforting noises.

~This boy only wants me to kill people,~ Margaret seemed to say. *~I am glad he is asleep.~*

~Worship me and I shall take care of you,~ Nathaniel thought he heard Thomas reply. Behind his words sounded a howl like that of a hunting bird.

On the following morning, Nathaniel felt sufficiently recovered to call Isaiah Wilkes and Jacob Hop to him. He was learning to do it without having first to ascend to the starlit plain; he had to call their names in his mind, listen as they came, and then catch them as they fell into him. They were a burden, but as Nathaniel shrugged into his blue Imperial livery, it seemed to him that he could carry a third spirit. Maybe even a fourth.

He was getting stronger.

But the powers he was acquiring . . . did they come from experience, as a man who practices shooting becomes a better shot? Or was he being given additional power because he used the power he was given appropriately?

He thought that if he undertook to heal his uncle Thomas for the wrong reason—in order to gain power—he might fail, and his power diminish.

Nathaniel sighed. His gift was complicated. Why

could he not have Margaret's gifts, which seemed so simple? When in danger, she became mighty. That would be useful without being tricky.

But then, Nathaniel *liked* healing. He *wanted* to heal his uncle.

The more time he spent with Thomas, the more good he saw in him.

"Tonight, we stay in Boston," Margaret told him in Dutch as they ate fire-baked oatcake for breakfast.

Nathaniel nodded. "I've been thinking about a tool. I need something to help me uproot those . . . well, you saw them."

"Plants." Margaret's voice dropped to a whisper. "In that strange place."

"I think I will need your help," Nathaniel said. "To make the tool. Tools. And use them."

Margaret smiled. It was the sweetest, most uncomplicated smile he'd ever seen on her face. "How do I help?"

"Let me listen as we ride," he said. "At midday, or maybe when we stop to rest the horses, I will tell you if I have found what I'm looking for."

They rode in the wagon, Nathaniel listening all morning. He knew what he wanted to find, but he wasn't sure what it sounded like, so he closed his eyes and tried to sort through the sounds that came to his ear.

He heard things from other people in the procession. They weren't thoughts, exactly, or feelings. It was more that he could hear states of being, which sounded to him like thoughts, when he could interpret them. But he heard the spirits of people in the voices of people, so he focused, listening for the sounds beneath those voices, and the voices soon faded away.

Animal spirits struck his ear, too. They sounded like people, only simpler. Their spirits lacked the complication of society, and their needs usually resolved into hunger, or fear, or a desire to rut. Their voices sounded blockier than those of the children of Adam, like the sound of a drum is blockier, simpler and chunkier, than the sound of a fiddle. Nathaniel breathed deeply, and let the animal sounds fade.

He heard trees and berries and brambles. Their needs were simpler still, and Nathaniel heard them as shivering, or as thirst, or as a gentle humming sound such as a parent might make, having forgotten the words to a lullaby.

Nathaniel listened beneath the plants, trying to let their song go.

At first, he heard nothing. After long minutes, maybe hours of contemplating the silence, he found texture to it. The silence had grain, like a piece of wood, and the grain wasn't sound, exactly, but it was *like* sound. It was like the impression sound would leave behind if pressed into wet clay, and Nathaniel could hear it.

In the grain of the silence of the earth, he found stone.

He heard limestone, dripping with the steady passage of water.

He heard slate, anxious to crack.

And finally, he heard what he was seeking: flint.

Flint sounded like the cry of an eagle, sharp and abrupt, a sound to warn the hare that it is about to bleed. Flint sounded strong, but riven through with cracks of weakness, like a young singer who has found his baritone, but whose voice, attacked at the right angle, can crack back into a tenor or even a falsetto.

"There is a bed of flint ahead," Nathaniel said. "Only a few hundred yards. How close are we to the midday meal?"

"Hours to go," Margaret whispered.

"I am going to stop the caravan," Nathaniel said. He listened to the song of the flint, hearing it come closer. "I need you to convince Julia to leave us behind. Tell her that we'll catch up."

"You can't tell her yourself?"

Nathaniel shook his head. "If this works, I'll be unconscious."

"You need me to protect your body." Margaret's voice fell flat. She squinted.

"And harvest flint with me. And find our way to the procession. And come with me onto the starlit plain to uproot that plant."

The suspicion eased from Margaret's face, slightly. "I will do it."

Nathaniel took a deep breath. Before his first ascent into the sky, when ogres had torn him to pieces and rebuilt him with iron bones, he had been subject to falling spells. They had been triggered by his hearing voices, voices which he had come to learn were the sounds of the world and its spirits, channeled to Nathaniel through his ear. His ascent and re-creation had given Nathaniel the ability to harmonize the screech and cacophony of the universe into music, and to choose which sounds to hear and which to ignore.

Now he intended to release that power, and trigger a fainting spell.

He gathered the song of the flint into his ear, and the songs of the other stones. He took a deep breath and readmitted the wordless mewling of the trees. He listened for the deer and the beaver and the badger, and piled their complaints into the noise that rocketed about inside his skull. His breathing was shallow, and coming fast.

~Flee—the children of Adam approach!~

~Saint Christopher, but the captain had better give me a little furlough in Boston. It's been weeks since I even smelled a woman!~

~Earth and leaf, stone and brook, earth and leaf!~

"Flee," Nathaniel heard himself murmur. His own voice sounded as if he were far away. "Earth and leaf!"

"Are you ill?" Margaret whispered.

Nathaniel's eyes hurt. He tried to open them, but the light was blinding and his vision quickly contracted into tiny pinpricks.

"Flee," he gasped. Then he shuddered and fell from the wagon.

Nathaniel awoke with his mouth dry and his head pounding. He lay on the cool earth, his purple coat thrown over him and his hat beneath his head as a cushion. Brilliant dappled green light flooded into his eyes, so he shut them.

"Margarida?" he croaked.

"I'm here," she said in English. "We're alone."

Nathaniel rolled over onto all fours and stood. It took him a minute, during which he felt dizzy, dry mouthed, and unsteady on his legs. Then he climbed into his inside-out, inherited coat, and placed his hat on his head, backward.

"They left us this small beer." Margaret held up a drinking skin.

Nathaniel took the skin and had a sip. He breathed

deeply, trying to clear from his head the cacophony of sound that had knocked him unconscious.

"Did that hurt?" Margaret asked.

"Yes," he said. "But . . . in the way that a bad headache hurts. And I feel . . . dried out now, and light looks queer. But it used to happen and I couldn't control it, and I didn't know what it was, so it was terrifying. I heard voices all the time, and sometimes the voices seemed to attack me. I thought I was mad."

"You *are* mad," Margaret said. "You have sneaked into the honeymoon procession of the man in the world who most wants you dead, and you're doing it not so that you can kill that man, but so that you can help him."

"And you're going to help me," Nathaniel added.

"I am."

"It's this way." Nathaniel started walking.

In a few minutes of picking their way through tangled forest, they arrived at the rock that Nathaniel heard. It was a gnarled stone fist poking up through the leaves and moss of the forest floor.

"What do you want from this rock?" Margaret asked.

"I need a knife."

"There are all manner of knives in the wedding wagons."

Nathaniel shrugged.

"You do not eat with a knife," Margaret said, "as you do not ride a horse and you cannot dress normally. But you can use a sharp edge, if we make one out of this stone."

"I think so. And I think I can take it with us, into the starlit plain."

Margaret nodded. "To use against the strange plants. So we shall make stone knives, as the Indians once did."

"As everyone once did, I think." Nathaniel stooped to pick up a chunk of rock and examined it. "Only I have no idea how."

"I saw a Choctaw do it once." Margaret sat on the stone and took two rocks into her hand. "He made arrowheads, not a knife. They were sharp as razors, sharper than my Tia's sword, and he made them by striking two flints together. He seemed to do it at a certain angle, that knocked off chunks he could use."

"Chunks?"

"Flakes. I think you might need to get a big, sharp flake of flint, and then bind it into a piece of wood as a handle." Margaret struck her two stones together experimentally, and nothing happened.

Nathaniel tried the same, but banging the rocks against each other over and over only resulted in his smashing his own thumb and dropping both stones.

"Maybe . . . your spirits?" Margaret asked. "Maybe Jake or Wilkes knows how to do this?"

Nathaniel shut his eyes and listened.

~Isaiah,~ he called. *~Jake.~*

He felt their presence, though he thought that Isaiah Wilkes was far away in the west, watching events in a throne room, and Jake was in the north, learning the tongue of the giants.

~Does either of you know how to make a flint arrowhead?~ he asked. *~Or a flint knife?~*

They did not.

Nathaniel dismissed them and looked again at the flint. He relaxed, letting the sounds of his sister and the forest and even the distant procession, which still rang in his ear, fade, until he could find again and focus on the deep rhythms of the stone before him.

He held the rocks up to his ear one at a time, rotating the stones slowly and listening to the way they were held together. He heard infinite and infinitesimal cracks through the rocks, as if each stone were a sheaf of sharp blades, pressed so tightly together that they had stuck that way, and then wind and water had worn their collective exterior into a mere knob. He found a large blade within the rock in his right hand and he turned the stone, laying it at just the angle he needed so that he could strike off the excess.

Then he knocked it against the other stone, once.

A third of the rock fell away, exposing a leaflike surface.

Margaret whistled.

Nathaniel listened again, tilting the rock this way and that, until he had found the other side of the blade he wanted. Again, one quick blow, and the excess stone fell away.

He handed the stone leaf to his sister. "Be careful, it's very sharp."

Then he searched among the rocks until he found another suitable stone. The process was quicker now, and he easily fashioned a second leaf-shaped stone blade.

"This will sound silly," Margaret said, "but you have a very powerful ear."

"You are much more impressive than I am," he said. "You actually know how to do things. Such as speak Dutch and French. And sail a ship, and fight, and play card games. I have to use my . . . ear . . . to figure everything out."

Margaret shrugged. "I would trade you."

Nathaniel stood again and listened. "This way."

He quickly found what he was looking for, which this time was an antlered deer's skull. It lay beneath a thick drift of leaves, with damp, dark earth clinging to bone and antler that had long ago lost the last scraps of its skin and flesh. Listening carefully to the skull to hear how it was assembled, Nathaniel thanked the dead deer's spirit and then snapped off both antlers. Knocking off the points and the long thin branchings, he was left with two knife-handle-sized lengths of antler.

"Do you have any leather?" he asked.

Margaret produced the purse that hung at her belt. "The flap on top is much larger than it needs to be."

With one of the stone knives, Nathaniel cut two long strips of leather. Wedging each blade into the largest crack in the point-end of an antler length, he then bound them in place with leather. This last part proved beyond him, until he asked his familiar spirits and discovered that Jacob Hop was adept at a wide range of knots and lashings, having learned them aboard ship as a young man. Nathaniel surrendered his fingers to Jake, and Jake finished the knives.

Nathaniel hid one in his own pocket, wrapping it in a blue handkerchief that matched the livery, and Margaret did the same with the second. Then they ran to catch up to the procession, overtaking the rearguard member of the Philadelphia Blues just as the caravan was coming to a halt for the midday meal.

The Lady Mayor of Boston and the city's bishop met the wedding procession at its gate, which was a full mile after the farms and pastures gave way to cobbled streets and shops. The bishop's jaw looked as large as all the other parts of his head combined, and the Lady Mayor was a pale-faced woman with thin blonde hair.

From the wagon, stone knife hidden in her clothing, Margaret heard the entire encounter.

Thomas dismounted to receive their welcome to the city, which included both a speech by the bishop, about being subject to principalities and powers, and the presentation by the Lady Mayor of a large certificate, its writing in stern black ink, but its corner embellished by the presence of a blue and gold ribbon.

"This is a certificate of exemption from the city's sumptuary laws," the Lady Mayor explained. "Not that we believe the city's tithingmen or constables might undertake to attempt to enforce them upon Your Imperial Majesty, but we wish to share in the abundant joy of the Imperial Wedding. We ourselves shall continue to wear our customary sadd colors, but by this official recognition, we approve all clothing worn, and all food and drink consumed, by this party during your sojourn in our city."

"The exemption extends to anyone celebrating the Imperial Wedding within the walls of Boston," the bishop added. "It has been published in both the *News-Letter* and the *Gazette*, to encourage the people of the town to come out in their gayest apparel."

The buildings within the walls were sober, practical affairs, built of long horizontal planks and long wooden shingles. Margaret had seen these buildings before: the simple Cape Cod, the two-story Colonial, and the lopsided Saltbox were all variations on a simple theme. The structures were stacked side by side as if architecture itself were a sermon on the order of

God's universe, to be preached to all within view. Few acceptable choices, and all in neat rows.

The people inside the actual city also wore noticeably different colors than those without the walls, tending toward dull oranges, forest greens, and browns as well as black, but as the horses and wagons rolled toward the bay, celebrants in sky-blue and vermilion and white lined the streets and waved. They were women more than men, and as many children as adults, but still, their sheer number was striking.

Thomas was loved.

The procession stopped at a hotel called *Imperial House*, and Thomas and Julia promptly changed their clothing to go to a ball. While they were out, Nathaniel and Margaret helped Lieke prepare their chambers, filling pitchers with water and placing flowers on the tables. Then Nathaniel retreated into the servants' room to prepare for his own evening's undertaking.

He napped briefly, and Margaret took the opportunity to collect sustenance for them both. Then she watched the front of the hotel out the window of their room. When Nathaniel awoke, it was late, but not late enough for Thomas and Julia to have returned. The siblings sat on a wooden bench beside the window overlooking the street and ate dried apricots and buttery soft French bread that the hotel baked, washing it down with cold water. They turned the lights down in their room so they could sit in darkness, Nathaniel's face only lit a soft golden color by the light leaking from a window across the street.

"Do you have a plan?" Margaret asked.

"I hope that if I can cut the plants away from Thomas, I'll be able to talk to him." Nathaniel shrugged. "I find that most people, somehow, can be reached. I have to . . . help them with their pain first, or heal their wound, or get their attention. But I believe that, down deep inside, all people want to be good and do good."

Margaret snorted. "Maybe. But for most of us, that kind, good-doing soul is buried beneath many, many layers of selfish, backstabbing bastard."

Nathaniel laughed. "Not you," he said. "You're good all the way to the top."

Margaret felt her stomach muscles tighten. "If I'm so good, why do I kill so many people?"

Nathaniel looked surprised. Before he could say anything, Thomas's coach rattled briskly down the street and pulled to a stop in front of the hotel. Two of the Blues rode ahead of it and two behind, and the four men positioned their mounts in an arc around the carriage standing guard as Thomas stepped out first, and then helped Julia down with a gloved hand.

Thomas kissed Julia gently. Was Nathaniel right? Was there a core of good inside Thomas, that just needed to be helped out?

Julia entered the hotel, passing out of sight. Thomas stretched and looked up at the hotel.

He seemed to look straight at Margaret, and she shuddered.

Thomas whistled and snapped his fingers. The nearest of the Blues dismounted and stepped close, allowing Thomas to whisper into his ear.

"Can you hear what they're saying?" Margaret asked her brother. "With your . . . ear?"

"That's not really the kind of thing I hear," Nathaniel said. "I can hear that Thomas feels content. Even gleeful. And I can hear that Julia feels happy."

"Lucky Julia."

"Doesn't that make you want to help her?" Nathaniel asked. "By healing her husband?"

"I am committed to your plan," Margaret said.

Nathaniel nodded. They watched the street below for a while longer, seeing the coach pull away and into the coach house adjoining the hotel. The four Blues remained standing in front of the hotel as a guard, interrogating an errand boy who arrived carrying sacks of groceries and also a fat gentleman in coattails who stepped out of his coach and wanted to check into the hotel as a guest.

Margaret snorted, feeling slightly more at ease.

The door to the room opened just as they finally stepped away from the window, and Lieke came in. "The Lady Julia is going to bed," Julia's servant announced in Dutch. Then she changed into a night dress and bundled herself into one of the two large beds in the room.

Margaret lay down before Nathaniel told her to, taking deep breaths and preparing for the strange experience of leaping upward into the plain of spirits. She held her stone knife clutched by its antler handle in one hand.

Nathaniel stretched himself out beside her, also breathing deeply. "Are you ready, Margaret?"

"*Estic preparada*," she said. "Yes."

Nathaniel drummed a pattern of beats, and then he took her hand and climbed into the ceiling. In seven quick steps, they were standing in the tall grass, warm breeze in their hair, beside a snorting horse. Margaret looked down quickly, and for a split second, seemed to see the shadowy black bear Makwa looking up at her. Then the grass closed over the vision and it was gone.

Jacob Hop and Isaiah Wilkes stood a few yards away.

~*You have knives*,~ Hop said.

~*But you didn't bring any for us.*~

Nathaniel laughed. ~*I didn't think of it. I'll bring knives for you next time.*~

~*Better if it doesn't come to that,*~ Margaret said. ~*Better if we do this right the first time.*~

Nathaniel nodded. ~*Let me find Uncle Thomas. He shouldn't be far.*~

Margaret's brother cocked his head to one side. He closed his eyes briefly, and when he opened them again, he pointed. "There."

Margaret followed his pointing finger and saw Thomas. He and Julia stood a short distance away, arm in arm and dancing slowly. They both smiled; Julia's smile was dreamy, her eyes closed.

~*Look at the plants,*~ Margaret said.

Nathaniel gasped. The plants that they had earlier seen entwining the legs and lower body of Thomas Penn now wound their way up his waist and chest, reaching nearly to his shoulders. His skin, from the waist down, was a dark greenish gray, and leaves and buds sprouted directly from his flesh, here and there.

The vines also crept up Julia, covering her legs.

~*Better if there is no next time,*~ Nathaniel said. ~*Are you ready to cut?*~

~*Do you mean, am I out of control with rage?*~ Margaret asked. ~*Is my strength upon me? Is my father's gift of might turning me into a monster? Well, I don't know, Nathaniel. What's happening with my hair?*~

Nathaniel staggered sideways. *~No, I...I just mean, are you ready to cut? I...would you prefer Jake to do the cutting?~*

~I can do it,~ Hop added.

Margaret felt foolish. *~I will cut.~*

Nathaniel nodded. Getting a good grip on his own knife, he crept toward the dancing couple. Margaret approached at his side. She held the knife point down before her, pointing at the ground.

The dancers showed no sign that they heard their approach.

Nathaniel sang.

> *I ride upon four horses, to heaven I ride*
> *To seek to free my uncle, and free his bride*
> *I'm armed with bones of earth, and with*
>   *love inside*
> *I seek to free my family, to heaven I ride*

Margaret wished she knew the words to sing along, but Nathaniel seemed to be making them up. The melody was dirgelike, so she hummed along, and Nathaniel sang a second verse.

> *I ride upon four horses, in heaven's land*
> *My sister is a warrior, with mighty hand*
> *I call my father's gifts upon this tiny band*
> *We seek to free our uncle from clutching*
>   *hands*

Margaret felt the electric prickle on the back of her neck that told her that her hair was standing up. She felt energy flowing into her limbs and seeking

to push her forward, accelerate her step. And she
didn't feel rage.

She stopped and stared at Nathaniel. He smiled.

She was afraid to ask him what he had done. She
feared any word from her would end his spell, so she
simply continued to hum, and prepared to cut with
the stone knife.

Something touched her leg.

Margaret slashed with the stone flake. She struck
a length of fibrous plant, dark green, that rose from
the ground and swayed back and forth, probing at the
flesh of her calf. She had missed it, hidden among the
tall stalks of grass of the starlit plain, and her blow
with the knife touched it at an awkward angle and
caused it to dance away.

With her second slash, she severed most of the
plant from its root. The stalk fell to the earth and
lay twitching.

~*Around you!*~ she called to Nathaniel.

He looked down; his legs were surrounded by the
groping plants.

Margaret looked quickly to the Imperial couple;
they continued to dance, but a carpet of writhing,
dark-green stalks spread from where they stood to
Nathaniel and Margaret.

More plants touched Margaret's calf, and she
attacked, mowing them down in numbers.

More rose from the earth to replace those that she
cut. They wrapped around her legs.

Nathaniel slashed too, but his arm was not as strong
and his blows were uncertain, hesitating. The plants
wrapped themselves around him in greater number,
and then he dropped to his knees.

The horse neighed, disturbed. Jacob Hop and Isaiah Wilkes rushed forward, but were forced to step back by a surging wall of vegetable matter.

A stalk reached up toward Nathaniel's face.

Margaret ripped her legs free by brute strength, hauling one limb and then the other from the living thicket that sought to entangle her. She sprang to Nathaniel's side and slashed, slashed, and slashed again. She laid low first the tendril that reached for his face, and then two great swathes of plant to his left and his right. Then she grabbed his forearm and pulled him to his feet.

~Thomas!~ Was Nathaniel gasping in pain and surprise? Was he reminding Margaret of their objective? Was he trying to get Thomas's attention?

Thomas paid no heed. Margaret dragged her brother toward the emperor.

More plants clung to him, which slowed their progress. *~Cut them!~* Margaret screamed. *~They're trying to kill you!~*

Nathaniel nodded and cut, but he still faltered in his attacks.

~Sing, then!~ Margaret threw herself at the plants, hacking and chopping with the stone knife. In her hands, the weapon seemed to elongate into a scythe, and the stalks laid themselves down before it rather than be cut.

> *I ride upon four horses, with healing aim*
> *I am a son of Adam, and of his dame*
> *From them I have dominion, of them I have*
> * no shame*
> *I call the grass to answer my lawful claim*

The grass of the starlit plain responded. The stalks that drifted gently back and forth, ruffled by the warm breezes blowing across this cosmic landscape, leaped into motion. The grasses, pale green and yellow, entwined themselves with the darker stalks. The ground surrounding Margaret and her brother went from a meadow covered knee-deep in tall grasses to a flat, snarled carpet of plant, plant balled up with plant and each indistinguishable from the other, in a matter of seconds.

~*Now to Thomas!*~ Margaret cried.

She charged. She heard pounding hooves behind her, and then Nathaniel passed by her side. He rode his horse, and he leaned forward, left hand curled tightly in a fistful of the horse's mane, right hand swinging low toward the ground, long stone knife poised to cut.

Thomas continued to dance slowly. Julia murmured wordlessly, her eyes still shut.

Nathaniel reached his uncle, passing by on the left-hand side, and swung his stone to cut at the plants that still curled around Thomas's leg—

a huge stalk of dark green plant exploded from the earth.

Dirt flew in all directions. Dirt struck Margaret in the face, stinging her forehead and her eyes. She blinked and her forward momentum faltered. Tears streamed down her cheeks.

The giant stalk slammed into the side of Nathaniel's horse and knocked the beast to the ground. Nathaniel hit the earth and lost his grip on his stone knife, rolling over several times and landing on his back.

Dark green stalks whipped around his limbs and over his neck, pinning him.

Margaret ran toward Nathaniel. ~*Help!*~

~*No!*~ Thomas bellowed. Reacting for the first time to the scene unfolding about him, Thomas Penn turned and bared his teeth toward the two familiar spirits. They charged anyway, rushing across tangled, balled-up plants—

until another thick plant burst from the ground. It struck them both across the legs at the height of their knees, and they fell screaming.

Julia continued to dance and hum.

Margaret hurled herself upon her brother. She swung her blade along one side, cutting so close that she slashed the sleeve of his coat, and then tried to yank him from the grip of the clinging plants.

But there were too many, and she couldn't free him.

She felt other plants wrapping themselves around her ankles and calves.

~*Sing!*~ she yelled.

Nathaniel groaned, but emitted no word. She looked at his face closely and saw that fine green wisps of plant stalk had wrapped themselves around his cheeks and jaws, some of them even piercing his lips and weaving back and forth from one lip to the other, sewing Nathaniel's mouth shut.

She cut twice, once on each side of his head, severing plants. Stalks crawled up her back. The electric tingle on her neck spread to her scalp and spine, and Margaret could feel her hair standing on end.

She gripped the stone knife near the tip to get precise control, and then drew the blade between Nathaniel's lips, slicing away the plant-matter sutures.

Nathaniel sang:

I ride upon four horses, to heaven aspire
I ride above the sky dome, and even higher
I come on mercy's errand, mercy shall not tire
I call the stars to answer and give me fire

As Nathaniel sang, Margaret lurched to her feet. She roared as she jumped, and blood poured from her legs where the dark green plants, which had been burrowing into her flesh, were torn completely away. She staggered, swinging her stone blade at plants that tried to wrap themselves around her and around Nathaniel.

Then Nathaniel finished his song, and fire fell from heaven.

It was not red, or orange, or any color one might name to describe how fire appears. The fire that plummeted from the stars overhead was simultaneously all the colors of the rainbow, and black, and white. Light and heat poured from it, warming Margaret's flesh.

The fire crashed to earth in bucketfuls. Where it struck, it scoured the plant life away, gouging chunks from the earth. A near miss left Margaret scorched and tender on one side of her face.

~Thomas!~ Nathaniel croaked, rising to his knees and pushing to stand. *~Please! Uncle Thomas!~*

Thomas sneered.

Margaret charged Thomas. The emperor turned, keeping one arm wrapped around his bride, and faced his attacker. He smiled and raised his arms as if to catch her in her assault—long green strands of plant fiber hung from his limbs, dancing as he moved.

The fire was falling less and less.

Julia turned to face Margaret, too. She smiled, but

the smile was no longer the dreamy, half-asleep smile
that had marked her face during her dance, but a
knowing smile, the smile of someone who could see
what was coming.

Julia Stuyvesant opened her eyes, and they were
green. White, iris, and pupil, all dark green, all the
color of the writhing plants.

Margaret sprang to the attack low, aiming to cut at
the plants that entangled both their knees. She saw
Hop and Wilkes to the side, pulling Nathaniel to his
feet, and then rushing at his side into the fray. Plants
entangled all three men.

The fire from heaven had stopped.

The stalks wrapped around Thomas's ankles and
calves were thick, mature vines, much more powerful
than the strands that had entangled Margaret. She
grabbed the thickest, near where it emerged from the
ground, and she hacked at it. She cut a second and
a third time, and just as it seemed she was close to
cutting her way through, Thomas kicked her.

She fell back. She lost her grip on her knife for a
moment, but then she recovered it and struggled to
her feet, pulling her arms and legs from the grip of
more vines.

~*Come,*~ Julia Stuyvesant said to her. ~*Relax.*~

The Imperial Consort reached toward Margaret
with a hand, and green tendrils shot from her fingers.
They reached toward Margaret like extensions of the
fingers themselves, and Margaret sliced them all off
in one short swoop.

The emperor grabbed Margaret with his hands.

She punched him with her left fist. It was an awkward blow, and poorly aimed, but Margaret's strength

was upon her. She caught Thomas Penn in the jaw and sent him reeling back. The force of his motion tore him free from the vines wrapped around his ankles and he looked at Margaret with surprise and fear in his eyes.

Nathaniel and his familiar spirits rushed from the other side, trying to grab Thomas Penn from behind.

Dirt clods again stung Margaret in the face as more plants burst from the earth. One rose up directly before her, obscuring her vision. She cut at it, and cut again, but it was too thick for her to sever, and then the enormous stalk slammed into her chest—

throwing her to the ground—

throwing her *through* the ground.

She fell.

The stars disappeared, and then Margaret saw the starlit plain recede from her view above her. She saw large plant tendrils seize Nathaniel, Hop, and Wilkes, and drag them to the ground. She saw Thomas look about him stupidly, wander in a small ragged circle, and then stand still again as plants rooted him to the earth.

Margaret crashed to the floor. She lost her grip on her stone knife, which clattered to the boards. Lieke snored. Nathaniel whimpered, his breathing erratic. The black shadow bear Makwa growled.

Margaret heard an urgent knock.

"Open, or we kick the door down!"

"And yet you have not yet taken the city."

CHAPTER TWENTY-FIVE

Margaret groped and found the knife in the dim light. Makwa growled again.

"Wat is dat geluid?" Lieke called from her bed.

BAM!

"Nathaniel!" Margaret hissed.

He didn't answer. No time to wait for him to wake up, so Margaret grabbed her brother to hoist him onto her shoulder—

and Makwa attacked her.

The bear looked like shadow, but it had a thoroughly corporeal presence. Smelling of ancient, undisturbed air, a full bear's weight slammed into Margaret and sent her skidding across the hotel room floor. She hit the wall hard—an ordinary fighter might have been knocked unconscious, or had her neck broken.

Lieke screamed.

Margaret stood, the stone knife gripped in her hand. "Makwa, you're coming with me!"

The bear snapped its jaws at her.

She punched it in the snout, sending it reeling.

The door shook again and burst open. Yellow light from the hallway lanterns flooded into the room, but the men pouring through in blue tricorn hats would be unable to see very well, for a moment.

"He's on de floor!" she shouted, in her best imitation of a Dutch accent.

The men entering the room—Philadelphia Blues—jumped toward Nathaniel.

Makwa roared and hurled himself into their midst.

Margaret hoisted Nathaniel into her arms. He felt light, because her strength was up. He'd feel even lighter on her shoulder, but she was afraid to expose him to too much fire. Instead, she spun around, pointing her back toward the attacking dragoons.

Bang! Bang!

She felt a bullet strike her, but it didn't pierce her skin. Makwa howled—

Margaret rushed away from the fighting, hoping to escape Makwa's attack if he came after her—

but instead, she heard dragoons screaming.

Lieke screamed again.

Margaret jumped out the window.

She landed on her feet on the cobblestones. She swayed briefly, caught her balance, and then ran.

"Is that one of them?" she heard a man shout.

"It's both! Fire at will!"

Bang! Bang!

Shots whined off the cobblestones around Margaret, and again struck her in the back. A bullet knocked her hat off and rapped on her skull, hard enough to give her a headache, but she knew it wouldn't draw blood.

Where was Makwa?

She heard roaring again, and then a heavy *THUD*.

Whatever Makwa was made of, it was heavy.

"Forget the children!" she heard a shout. "Kill the beast!"

More gunfire, and then she turned a corner and was out of sight of the hotel. She slung her brother over a shoulder.

Time snapped at her heels. How long would she stay in this state, and how far could she get? She had carried Nathaniel unconscious once before, though he hadn't had the bear guardian to attack her at the time, and she had had enough energy to run a few miles before her rage had run its course.

But this time . . . what had Nathaniel done? He had sung a song on the starlit plain, and the song itself had activated her strength. What did that mean? Did it mean that her strength and her impervious skin were now permanent, active at all times?

She didn't think so.

But then how long would they last? And then what?

The screamings and gunshots had stopped. Were the dragoons all dead?

It was much more likely that Makwa had abandoned them and was chasing after Margaret. Makwa didn't seem to recognize her as a friend, or perhaps Makwa was a simpler creature than that. Perhaps anyone touching Nathaniel in this state was by definition an enemy.

Margaret needed a place to put Nathaniel down.

A safe place. A place, ideally, where they could still move, so that if the emperor sent men after them, including wizards with finding charms, they wouldn't be easy to find.

She turned downhill at a crossroads. Boston was

a port town, on the Charles River. Somewhere, she had to be able to get onto a boat.

She heard the heavy padding of Makwa's feet behind her. She spun about, holding the stone knife up. If that blade could continue to exist, could come with her onto the starlit plain of spirits, then maybe it was also a weapon that could damage a spirit-bear.

Makwa bore down upon her and she slashed at it. She connected with the creature's forearm, and Makwa roared. It pulled back, leaving a black smudge on the air like a cloud.

"Ma'iingan," Nathaniel murmured. "Ma'iingan."

Blood dripped from Nathaniel's arm and spattered on the cobblestones. When had he been wounded? Had one of the dragoons managed to shoot him? Had Margaret accidentally squeezed him too hard in the fall, breaking his skin?

But Nathaniel was wounded in the same spot where she had cut Makwa.

Margaret had cut the bear, and wounded her brother.

"Stay back!" she shouted at the bear.

A light came on above her, in the second story of a plank-built house. Margaret turned and ran.

She smelled water. Then she saw the streaks of light, where yellow lanterns sent smears of color across the surface of a river. Ahead of her, the street dissolved into a wharf. Men carried supplies and cargo up and down the creaking wooden platforms, loading and unloading boats. Beyond the long docks, moving lights revealed barges and ships moving upriver and down.

But Margaret was feeling weaker.

Makwa struck Margaret from behind and knocked her down. She rattled across the stones and lost her grip on her brother. The bear Makwa pounced on her, clamping its jaws on the forearm she raised to protect herself—

and drawing blood.

She grunted, managing not to scream. She didn't want the town watch coming, any more than she wanted some burgher to come rushing to her aid. Eventually either of those things would lead to the Imperials finding her.

She stabbed the bear.

She didn't really mean to do it, but she was a fighter, and she defended herself. She struck the bear in its chest with her knife, and she felt the cold liquid of its blood flow over her hand.

The bear released its grip and whined.

Margaret wanted to grab Nathaniel and run, but the spirit-bear still stood over her brother. She ducked and slammed her shoulder into the bear's chest.

"Damn you," she grunted. "Don't make me hurt you!"

The bear swiped with a paw, knocking her to the stones and tossing her sideways.

Margaret struck the stone foundation of a house. The blow was hard enough to rock her vision akimbo, and she sucked in cold air, trying to get control over the images that spun before her eyes.

The blow didn't hurt.

It *did* make her *angry*.

She stood and pocketed the stone knife. Then she marched on the bear, swinging her arms. The beast leaped at her—

and she jammed her left forearm into its mouth.

Makwa snarled and tried to chew, but he could not break Margaret's skin. He growled and pushed, trying to knock her away. She strained and pushed back, but couldn't move the bear.

"Let me save him," she grunted.

The bear growled. In its dark eyes, she saw the twinkle of stars.

From the hill above, Margaret heard shouting, and the thunder of hooves.

She bent a knee, let the weight of the bear surge toward her, and then stood, hoisting Makwa into the air with both hands. The bear yelped in surprise.

She turned and threw him aside, down the open mouth of a nearby alley.

Then she grabbed Nathaniel, swung him onto her shoulder again, and ran toward the wharf.

She didn't look back to see whether the dragoons had spotted her. The light on the street was spotty, coming from scattered windows; perhaps the pools of shadow through which she ran were enough to keep her from searching eyes.

She was more worried about the dowsers and charmers who might try to follow. She reached the docks, the cobblestones giving way to wet dirt, and then to planks nailed together, parallel to the shore, stretching out over the water in several docks.

She picked the one that was the least lit. Beyond its end, in the river, she saw a light drifting past. She accelerated her step, racing past bent men shouldering casks and bundled lumber. Her footsteps pounded loud in her own ears.

She heard Makwa's roar behind her, but it wasn't immediately at her heels. Was the bear challenging pursuing dragoons? Was it angry at some sailor or stevedore?

She kept running.

The boat at the end of the dock was a barge, and its cabin, containing the lantern, was now past. The vast, flat portion of the barge was heaped high with what looked like rocks. Margaret raced to the end of the dock, angling her line because the rear of the barge was fast approaching, and then jumped. She sailed over the dark waters of the Charles River, crashing with a heavy rattle onto a bed of coal.

Nathaniel cried out as he struck. "Ma'iingan!"

Margaret thought she had heard that word before, but she didn't remember what it meant. She watched to make sure that the dock was well behind them, and she saw, in the street beyond the wharfs, three mounted dragoons tangling with the shadowy spirit-bear. They fired, but their shots did it no harm. It brought down one of their horses by tearing open the flesh of its neck with its jaws, and then the other two men scampered back, shouting for help.

The barge was long and wide. Men walked along its side, poling the boat steadily upriver and singing.

> *Oh Shenandoah, you chieftain's daughter*
> *Away, you rolling river*
> *I'll bear you 'cross yon rolling water*
> *Away, I'm bound away, across the wide*
>   *Missouri*

Each man pushed with his pole, driving the boat forward, as his companions one by one walked past him. When the motion of the boat brought him to the end of the vessel, he pulled up his pole and marched to the front of the boat, to begin to push again. The song kept the men walking in time together. The men working the poles didn't see Margaret, and she didn't try to attract their attention. Instead, she turned Nathaniel around on his bed of coal, getting his feet elevated. Before she threw her own coat over him, she saw not only his wounded arm, but a gash to his chest.

A gash she herself had cut, into the chest of Makwa the bear.

And his drum was there, though she did not remember having carried it.

"Ma'iingan," Nathaniel murmured.

It sounded like an Indian word. Or name? Could it be the name of the Algonk who had rescued Nathaniel in Johnsland?

But how could Margaret find this Ma'iingan, if Nathaniel *was* calling for him?

She heard the soft splashing of Makwa approaching in the water. The boatmen didn't hear the noise over their own raucous singing; Margaret watched the bear come over the back of the barge, where there were no men poling, and clamber over the coal.

"I'm sorry," she whispered into Nathaniel's ear, hoping the bear would hear, and then she scooted back. She held the knife in front of her defensively, but sat ten feet from Nathaniel and made no threatening moves.

"I'm sorry," she murmured again, as the bear Makwa sat down curled beside Nathaniel, and licked his face.

Neither the bear nor her brother answered.

"What happened to the smuggler?" the King of Koweta asked.

"I still do not know, Your Majesty," Luman said. In his own imagination, he hoped from moment to moment to see Montse and the Sword of Wisdom step from the dripping trees onto the cow path he was following. But it didn't happen.

"And if she is captured?" the king asked. "What will she tell them?"

"At most she will lead them to the rendezvous point," the King of Adena said.

"And then the Imperials will track us from there," the King of Koweta said.

"They can track us from Koweta, just as easily," Luman said. "But I am doing what I can to obscure those tracks."

"You look very tired to me, wizard," the king said. "Are you doing enough?"

"I am doing all I can!" Luman snapped. Then he took a deep breath. The king was right, Luman was indeed very tired, and he was near the limits of what he could do with his newfound gramarye. "I'm sorry. I do not know the answers to all the questions you have. But we do not have the strength to fight the Imperial army." He gestured at the ragtag collection of fugitives that marched behind them, a third of them armed men, but the other two thirds women and children, villagers who had had the bad fortune to be caught up in a siege. "We have a head start. And we may hope that it will take some time for the Imperials to determine our direction. Hopefully, it is not obvious that we would take the road into Cahokia, deeper into the storm and the tremors. Possibly, the Imperials have orders simply to seize the town, and not enough ambition or imagination to pursue the people. But ultimately, our salvation comes from speed."

"If your people dispersed into the woods," Shelem Adena said mildly to his colleague, "perhaps they would be safe from the Imperials. There are other Koweta villages and farmhouses where they might take refuge, are there not? Or some could walk to Tawa, or even south into the Kentuck. And if we were not leading this entire procession, if it were the three of us, and perhaps a handful of soldiers, we might make better time, and it might be easier for the wizard to erase our tracks."

Luman smiled. He was exhausted, stretched thin physically and spiritually, but he still found it gratifying to be referred to as *the wizard*, rather than as *the hedge-wizard* or *the cunning man* or any other dismissive title.

"No," Aha Koweta said.

"You do not wish to abandon your people?" the King of Adena's words contained a wistful note of admiration.

"I have brought my people out from the walls of my capital for one reason," the King of Koweta said, "and that was to save them. Not as individuals, but as a people."

"Because without a people, you cease to be a king?" Luman asked.

"Because if I do not *serve* them *as* a people, then I cease to be a king," Aha Koweta answered. "Because serving the kingdom is the burden I inherited from my father, and it has defined my entire adult life. Because it is what they expect of me. If we run, helter-skelter, in all directions, then Koweta ceases to exist."

"They might be safer if they are not in your presence," Luman said.

"But they would no longer be Koweta. And the farmers, and the scattered villages here and there, would also cease to be Koweta, and I would have failed entirely."

Luman nodded slowly. Would the anointing that Sarah wanted from these men fail in its power, if the King of Koweta were no longer king of any nation? Kingship seemed sometimes to be a magical thing, and to operate on Newton-like principles. "Then we must choose a road that is fast, and direct, and secret, and can be defended."

The King of Adena laughed. "We are in the Ohio, Pennslander. We have no high mountain roads, no narrow passes where ten men may hold off an army, so long as they have food and water. Here, if we are lucky to have a hill, we call it a mountain."

"At least we can stay on the forest paths," Luman said.

"Which are slower than the pikes," the King of Adena pointed out.

"There are the caves," Aha Koweta said.

"Tunnels?" Luman asked. "Surely, Cahokia is too far for any tunnel to take us all the way there."

"I said caves, not tunnels," the king said. "They are half a day's journey from here. There are supplies there, dried food and blankets and weapons, and water flows inside the caves. The Kings of Koweta fled there in times of great peril, even when our lands were young and Onandagos himself was yet the spirit of counsel. We have maintained it always as a refuge."

"Are you suggesting we shelter your people there?" Luman asked. "If they are ensconced within the cave, will you continue on with us to Cahokia?"

The King of Koweta looked at the King of Adena, and hesitated. "We can at least shelter there tomorrow night, since my people cannot walk forever. And there we can discuss more. Perhaps some other path, that now escapes my memory, will occur to me."

"I have heard that your queen flies, for instance," the King of Adena said to Luman.

"That is true," Luman said. "I know this of my own experience. But she is not here, and I do not believe I have the strength to fly, even if I were required to cause only the three of us to soar through the air. And if the call were to cause the entire nation of Koweta to fly like birds, then I think even my queen would balk."

"I am no tracker," Montse said. "I am relying on you."

Ritter shook his head. "I have no idea whether these Imperials are going in the right direction. It's possible the two kings and the magician went south and are in the Kentuck already."

Montse and the Sword of Wisdom had tried to track the Kowetan refugees during the night, and failed. When several platoons of Imperial soldiers, detached from the looting and burning of the city, had arrived at the forest rendezvous point, they had hidden, Montse with pistols loaded and cocked, expecting to be thrust momentarily into a running battle in the woods.

Instead, the Imperials had produced a tracker. He was dark skinned, likely some sort of Indian, though Montse couldn't immediately place his people. He had two long yellow feathers tied to hang down from the back of his black bowler cap, and he wore leather britches and a brown woolen vest. The tracker had scanned the ground, not through his natural eye alone, but placing a dark patch over one eye and staring through that. Montse had been a little far away to be confident in what she saw, but she thought the patch looked rough-woven, something that had been improvised rather than crafted.

A magical lens? A patch woven from the hair of the

King of Koweta, looking through which the tracker was able to see the king's tracks?

The tracker had confidently rushed off along a thin track through the woods, one of several trails that was most likely made by deer, coming to and from the salt lick. The Imperials had marched after him double-time, rifles over their shoulders and more than a few longing glances cast back at the burning town and its imagined loot.

Montse and Ritter had followed. They had trailed at a distance, not wanting to be seen. Ritter kept an eye on the ground, assuring Montse that they were still following the soldiers every few minutes, even though there could be no assurance whatsoever that the soldiers were following the Kowetans.

Ritter moved slowly, and sometimes grunted. He made no mention of the wound he had received, and Montse kept an eye on the lint bandaging: blood had seeped through the bandages, but the bleeding now seemed to have stopped.

They were still following when the sun came up, and even Montse could see the tracks. The soldiers left a trail of snapped branches, stones kicked aside, and overturned leaves, as well as the occasional cigarette butt, squirt of tobacco juice, scrap of torn cloth, or improvised forest latrine.

They marched through the morning, careful at each low rise or at the beginning of each clearing to stop and be sure they weren't too quickly approaching the rear of the enemy, and then accelerating their pace to make up for the small delay. Montse grew weary. Ritter must have phenomenal physical stamina, to still be on his feet despite his wounds and the miles.

"If these men are following fleeing women and children," she said. "They will soon overtake them. Fear will push a person to unusual strength and endurance, but a child is still no match for a soldier, accustomed to marching."

"We could circle ahead of the Imperials." Ritter winced. "Move laterally into the forest and run."

"Or we could attack the Imperials now," Montse said. "From behind. If we slow them down, the Kowetans can get farther. Maybe get to a river, and hide their trail."

"The trail *is* being hidden," Ritter pointed out. "The tracker is using magic to find the trail anyway."

"Too much talking," Montse said, "and the moment is gone. We shoot at them from the trees. We don't have to be accurate, we just have to make them slow down."

They ran into the woods until they were a hundred yards from the trail, then turned and ran forward, parallel to the path. They were far enough away that they had to guess where the track was, and they couldn't be certain their guess was correct until they saw the Imperial rearguard. A dozen men in blue, marching briskly up the trail, stopping every few minutes to look back.

"If we attack the main body, we slow them down immediately," Ritter said. "If we attack these men, we risk the possibility that the main body may not notice."

"We attack these men, and rely on them to signal," Montse said. "To do otherwise is to risk that this rearguard attacks us on our flank. And we do it now, while we have the advantage."

To end the argument, she cocked a pistol, fired at the rearguard, and stepped behind a thick tree trunk.

Ritter dropped to a crouch, hiding himself behind a large stone.

A cry of pain and surprise told Montse that she had hit. She reloaded, then indicated a path for Ritter to take, where they could stay out of sight and get ahead of the rearguard by jogging behind an earthen bank.

Ritter took the lead and she followed. Letting the rearguard out of her sight meant they might sneak up on her, but she didn't think they could possibly know where she was just yet, so switching positions was strategically more valuable.

A stone's throw farther on, the earth bank dipped, and she and Ritter crawled up it on their bellies to look.

"I only count eight now," Ritter said. "Four of them have disappeared into the brush to look for us."

"They don't know yet how many we are," Montse said. "Let's look numerous."

They both checked firing pans, and then Montse unloaded her pistols at the men in blue huddled in a knot of trees. Ritter fired his rifle, reloaded, and fired again.

At least two men fell.

Answering fire came in their direction, but they had already dropped back below the shelter of the bank.

Montse reloaded, then waited to be sure no one was following them behind the bank of earth. While they waited, they heard the *hiss* and then the *bang!* of a rocket being fired. The sun was beginning to sink into evening, which made the cloud of smoke the rocket left behind hard to see, but enhanced the visibility of the explosion itself.

"That's the signal," Ritter said.

Montse nodded, and they ran further up along the bank.

A minute later, as they again crept up the bank of earth to peer through the deepening shadows at the Imperial rearguard, they heard two more explosions, with two more flashes of light, from the west.

"I don't like that there is a return signal," Montse muttered. "I would prefer for the main body of soldiers to simply stop, and send back troops to help."

"You fear they call for reinforcements?"

"I fear nothing," Montse said. "But yes, that is what I think they are doing."

She heard a loud whistle directly to the east of them. It might have come from someone on their trail, standing where they had stood behind the bank of earth.

"They've found us," she said.

"Let's give them cause to regret it. I'll bring them running, if you lie in wait."

Montse nodded.

The Sword of Wisdom shouted, "Run, hetar!" Then he staggered up the trail.

Montse hid to the west side of a thick-boled pine, both pistols ready. There might be as many as four men coming up the bank, but it was more likely there were two, and there might be as few as one.

To the west, she heard the report of Ritter's rifle. That meant that the Imperials on the trail had moved forward, or tried to. A minute later, he fired again, and there were answering shots.

She heard the Imperial soldiers running toward her. They were behind her, and on the other side of the tree, and she could tell by their footsteps and their labored breathing that there were two of them.

They came closer...closer...

Ritter appeared, farther along the earth bank, and

fired a shot that whistled past Montse and caused the soldiers to stop running, briefly. They fired back, two shots—should she take her opportunity now? But Montse couldn't be sure how many weapons each man had.

Ritter disappeared again.

She waited.

There came another sharp whistle, close behind. The two soldiers ran forward again, and a few seconds later, they passed her.

Montse gave the soldiers no warning, and no opportunity to defend themselves. She shot the nearest in the back, squarely between his shoulder blades. Dropping her pistol while the other man turned, she took her second pistol into her hand, and before he could get his carbine up and into position, she shot him in the stomach.

He fell, firing his carbine—a miss. Montse drew her sword, stepped forward, and ran the man through. He died instantly, his face invisible in the twilight. To be certain, Montse stabbed the other man through his neck, then wiped her blade clean and sheathed it.

They had to abandon the attack now. The Imperial rearguard still outnumbered them, maybe by as much as five to one. But hopefully, they would now lose time investigating the attack, so Montse and Ritter could fade into the woods and escape, having bought the Kowetans a few hours of time.

She ran ahead to catch Ritter, and she found him staring eastward, over the tops of the trees. Her heart sank at the sight, and she knew what she would see when she turned back around to look.

Two of the giant wooden men marched in their direction, heads bobbing above the trees.

"The second signal," Ritter murmured. "It called reinforcements. They have already trapped the Kowetans."

His wound was bleeding again.

Notwithstanding Schmidt stood at her table in her tent, contemplating what she read, having worked through the ciphered text with the belt and staff that gave her the key: *The King of Oranbega has left his city. Only a personal bodyguard left with him. The queen remains behind. His location and his destination are unknown.*

It was a missive from an intelligence agent in that great Ophidian city. Greatest of the Serpentborn's cities, larger than Cahokia and more open to the world. In a better world, Oranbega would be the capital of the Ohio, and Cahokia would be a hinterland, a historical curiosity.

Perhaps, after the Ohio was fully pacified, Oranbega could assume its rightful place.

What did it mean that the King of Oranbega had sneaked out of his capital? He was on no official state business, nor yet on a personal holiday, or the spy would have sent that information. Oranbega had evaded the spy network and slipped out, which must mean he was attempting something the emperor wouldn't like.

He wasn't marching to war, because he had left his army behind.

This information alone would have been intriguing, but not more than intriguing. As it was, the news dovetailed with another piece of news that Schmidt had, from an informer within Cahokia. Three of the kings of the Ohio were within the walls of the serpent city: Tawa, Talamatan, and Talega.

Was the King of Oranbega bound for Cahokia?

The Imperial siege had been lifted from the city. Floodwaters penned it in on its western side, but traffic moved more or less freely in and out of the city. Soldiers from various powers friendly to Cahokia—Chicago and Johnsland and some of the Appalachee clans and others—patrolled the lands around it. If there were to be a council to discuss throwing off the yoke of the Pacification, or other plans of war and insurrection against the empire, Cahokia might be a logical place to hold it.

The rain beating against her tent very nearly drowned out Schäfer's shouting voice at the tent door. "Franklin's back, Madam Director!"

The muscles of Schmidt's shoulders tightened. The emperor's confidential advisor had driven a caravan of prisoners to Missouri, to offer them as a gift to the Heron King. What had occasioned his return?

"Come in, Schäfer."

The Youngstown agent sluiced water from his hat and shook it from his oilcloth slicker as he entered. "We've finished relocating the camp."

Schmidt had ordered the tents moved to higher ground, because the constant rain was turning the lowest valleys and roads into swamps. The elevation change was a matter of a few feet, here in the flat Ohio, but that made the difference between standing on muddy earth and swimming. She nodded. "Did Franklin return with all thirteen wagons?"

"No. The muleskinners came back," Schäfer said. "I haven't had a chance to talk to them yet, but they look scared. I've got them drinking coffee and soup in a mess tent, and I'll get them to tell us what they saw.

No prisoners. But Franklin's also got a badger-headed beastman with him. Calling himself Fftwarik, saying he's a messenger from the Heron King. I've got them drinking coffee and soup too, but in a private tent."

Schmidt tore the message she'd been reading into quarters and fed it into the iron camp stove. "Bring them both here, please."

Schäfer went.

She had only a minute or two before Franklin and the beastman arrived. She took a deep breath. Her inner peace was disturbed, shaken by her experience at Gottlieb's hands. Having had Franklin's vision—the end of this world in blood, and the birth of a new world of endless and eternal murder—she had found herself hesitant to kill the emperor's valet.

The vision was indeed horrifying. Simon Sword, a creature she had been raised to think of as mythical, or perhaps as an allegory, like Satan, for mankind's own worst inclinations, turned out to be a very real person, apparently committed to bringing Franklin's vision to pass, with himself as chief bloodletter and king.

What to do?

Notwithstanding Schmidt had reached the top of the ladder she had been climbing. Thomas Penn had appointed her Sole Director of the Imperial Ohio Company, which had shortly thereafter merged with the Dutch Ohio, making Schmidt the single most powerful person in the Ohio trade. There were Hansard traders and Frenchmen and New Muscovites who came down the rivers in their canoes, but, especially given the Pacification, most of the trade happened with Schmidt's consent, tacit or explicit.

Her salary was enormous, and had been impressive

for years. Given her personal abstemiousness, her wealth—socked away in bonds and land and joint-stock certificates, with a small amount kept in the form of gold coins—was more than enough for the rest of her life. And now she had had this vision, and she had seen the list of the top members of this leather apron society that the Lightning Bishop had founded. What did she want?

She could be honest with herself; one thing that had always driven her was a desire to win. Money and titles and men under her command were ways of keeping tally in the game of life.

But also . . . she believed in what she did. Commerce made everyone who participated in it wealthy. If it made Thomas wealthiest of all, and therefore benefited Schmidt, so much the better, but commerce meant new luxuries, and falling prices for staples. One reason why Notwithstanding Schmidt wanted a pacified Ohio was so that normal trade could resume again. She was the inventor of the passports and the trustworthiness certificates that the emperor had imposed on the Ohio as well as on the rest of the empire, but she cordially disliked them as necessary, and necessarily temporary, expedients.

If the Heron King were to succeed . . . that is to say, if Franklin's vision were to come true, then there would be no more commerce in the Ohio, ever.

Which would mean the end of the Imperial and Dutch Ohio Company, as well.

Schmidt felt deeply uneasy.

She did not want to betray her shareholders. She was not unduly troubled by the involvement of Oliver Cromwell and his minions in her affairs. But she did not want to see the end of trade.

She must look more into Gottlieb's leather apron society.

Temple Franklin entered without knocking, stooping to shrug off the rain. The beastman that followed him shook himself, as a wet dog would do.

"Mr. Franklin." Schmidt smiled. "You successfully made a trade."

"Indeed." Franklin smiled, a slight manic energy about his eyes. "A few carts full of worthless prisoners in exchange for an ambassador of a mighty power."

"Those prisoners might have been trained to hold a bayonet and charge, or even to dig ditches." Schmidt smiled back. "So if the ambassador's worth exceeds the worth of that many men, it must be great, indeed."

"I am Fftwarik," the badger-man rumbled. "I serve the Heron King, and I am his emissary to this camp."

"The Parlett remains in Missouri with the king," Franklin added. "So the Heron King may communicate directly with Lord Thomas."

"Has an alliance been agreed?" Schmidt asked.

"We have a common enemy," Franklin said.

Schmidt nodded. She wanted to discuss the terms of this alliance with Thomas, but not in front of the Heron King's ambassador. "I have not yet the strength sufficient to attempt to take Cahokia again."

"More strength is coming," Franklin said. "If it has not yet arrived, it is only that the emperor's forces are taking the time to crush opposition en route."

"We have the strength," Fftwarik said.

"And yet you have not yet taken the city," Schmidt pointed out.

"We have the strength," Fftwarik clarified, "when our ally will assist us in the assault."

"Madam Director!" Schäfer called from the door again. "A message!"

Schmidt turned, expecting to see another emissary. Instead, Schäfer handed her an oilcloth envelope, marked with the Imperial seal. She extracted the sole contents of the packet, which was a slim letter, and stepped to the lantern to read it, thus protecting the letter's contents and also communicating to Franklin and Fftwarik that she was important enough to ignore them, even when they stood in her presence. The gesture also gave her a moment to think.

This message was not encoded, and was from a Captain Twitchell of the 4th Pennsland.

> *Madam Director*
>
> *Last night we successfully took the town of Koweta, and today we have pursued the survivors, including the king. As of this writing, we have pinned the Kowetans into a cavern. Coordinates follow. Absent other instruction, I understand my orders to be to capture the King of Koweta.*

She set the letter on the table for the two men to read it while she examined a map. "The King of Koweta is trapped in a cave on the borders of this land. The Kings of Talamatan, Talega, and Tawa have gathered in Cahokia already. The king of Oranbega has left his throne, none can tell where he has gone."

Franklin narrowed his eyes. "What are you saying?"

If Notwithstanding Schmidt made the Heron King's aid unnecessary, then she could cement a victory for Thomas in which the Ohio could still exist, and prosper, and in which she was still Sole Director of the Company.

"The Kings of the Ohio are gathering. For what purpose, I can only guess." Schmidt looked at the beastman ambassador. "We will take the city of Cahokia together, but first we must set roadblocks, on every road that leads to and from Cahokia. I will have the King of Adena thrown into a dungeon. Oranbega and Koweta must be bound for Cahokia—we will intercept them, and end this insurrection now."

"The trick is picking the idea that is the least bad."

CHAPTER TWENTY-SIX

In the weeks following the dismissal of the motion to impeach, nothing was voted on in the Assembly. The Electors met only a handful of times in the Assembly Hall, but constantly in the coffee shops and taverns and salons of Philadelphia.

A thousand questions were debated, chasing themselves in circles around pints of lager and tall cups of coffee and saucers filled with tea, but all the questions resolved themselves ultimately into this: Was there still an empire?

Item, Thomas had not been removed from office. That implied that he was still the emperor, and he had certainly not said anything to indicate that the empire was diminished. Indeed, he had set out directly on his honeymoon, as if he were a man without a care in the world.

Item, not only had Thomas not lost his office, he had, if anything, grown in power. His alliance by marriage with the Dutch gave him votes in the Assembly, cash in his pockets, and a virtual monopoly over the

Ohio trade, in the form of the now-united Imperial and Dutch Ohio Company.

Item, Thomas had formed a military alliance with the Spanish. This was not an alliance between the empire and New Spain, but among Pennsland, New Spain, and any other power that wished to join. To some, such as Charlie Donelsen, this seemed to be a New Empire, although the Shackamaxon League expressly had no ability to impose taxes or pass laws, and seemed on the face of its charter to be military alliance. Others said that, while the Shackamaxon League was not a replacement empire, its formation was an act of treason. Thomas had allied with a foreign power without the consent of the Assembly, which was not specifically prohibited by the Compact, but an affront to the dignity of the sitting Electors. And his alliance had marched to war not on some foreign shore, but in the Cotton Princedoms. Still other Electors (and news-paper-men, and gadflies, and citizens) wondered what had been the price of Spanish entry into the League? In what currency had Thomas himself paid?

Charlie Donelsen spat on the floor. "I keep askin' myself, how could we a seen this a-comin' in 1784, and what could we a done to prevent it? And I ain't sure they's a good answer. We might could a had rules in the Compact about bargains between foreign powers and powers in the empire, but the Chicagoans would a got angry about their trade with the Sioux, and Boston would a wanted to exempt its agreements with the House of Spencer, and on and on." He took a long drink from his leather mug. "I reckon we jest tried to do an impossible thing."

He and Olanthes Kuta and the Creole accountant sat in the back of a tavern called the *Jolly Whalefish* and drank. Monsieur Bondí sat with his back to the wall and his eyes on the door, a position he had always liked, but had begun to insist upon the day the Chevalier of New Orleans returned to the Assembly.

"If it is a consolation to you," Bondí remarked, "consider that Benjamin Franklin and John Penn failed right along with you."

"I wonder iffen they's anythin' left to do," Donelsen mused. "We might could quit the empire entirely. Or we could go along, give Tommy Penn the soldiers he wants."

"There's a third option." This was a new voice, and it came from a rangy man, tall and cloaked, and wearing a battered slouch hat that hung down over his face and tended to conceal it.

Only it wasn't a new voice at all; it was the voice of Calvin Calhoun.

"Hot damn, iffen that ain't Calvin," Charlie Donelsen murmured, his voice low. "How'd you git past my boys watchin' the door?"

"Slipped them a grip," Cal said. "Showed 'em my face."

"You in hidin' on account of you think Tommy Penn still wants to kill you?"

"That's one of several reasons I got," Cal said. "I'd rather folks not know I'm here."

"The impeachment failed," Olanthes said.

Cal nodded. "My grandad got killed. They wanted me dead, too."

"Thomas announced that, from his shiny new Shackamaxon Throne." Donelsen chuckled. "He seemed pretty pleased with hisself."

"Someone tricked me," Cal said. "Someone as knew enough to write me and Iron Andy both, someone as could get forged letters to both of us."

"Logan Rupp," Olanthes said.

"The lawyer?" Cal asked.

"It does seem like a breach of client trust," Donelsen said.

Cal looked carefully around the tavern. "You haven't killed him, have you?"

"We's waitin' on you, Cal." Donelsen grinned. "Thought you might take it personal iffen we started without you."

Cal nodded. "Good, that'll be useful. Listen, I got a plan, but I needed to talk to the heads of all the families in the Ascendancy, and I reckoned I could git most of 'em together down here."

"*All* of 'em," Donelsen said, "except Calhoun. And jest who is the head of the Calhoun family?"

"I am," Cal said.

"Says who?" Donelsen probed, narrowing his eyes.

"*I* say it," Cal said. "And so far, ain't no one really tried to gainsay me. They was a vote of sorts, in the Calhoun Mountain Lodge. Iffen you like, I can git you the minutes of that meetin'."

Donelsen chuckled. "No, your say-so'll do fine for me. I'm sorry for the death of your grandfather, Calvin, but I'm sure as hell glad the Calhouns got someone to stand up in his place."

"Thank you." Cal nodded. "It was sort of the vote at the lodge that got me thinkin' up this plan, as it happens. My uncle David and a cousin named Jet Calhoun proposed themselves to the lodge as Elector."

"I know Jet," Charlie said. "He's a decent man, but

his feet ain't big enough for Andy Calhoun's boots. So I see why you proposed yourself."

Cal scratched the back of his head. "Well, really, I snuck in. But when I pointed out neither of those fellers was seein' straight, those old apron-wearin' boys went right ahead and elected me instead."

"A hell of a fellow," Monsieur Bondí said. "Is this not how you say it?"

Cal nodded, blushing a bit. "Anyway, then David disappeared. We had a little trouble on the mountain, and it looks like the emperor is sendin' out Mockers as assassins. You know what Mockers are, Mr. Donelsen?"

"Call me Charlie, dammit. Yeah, I know what they are."

"Best tell your people to be on the lookout, and what to do about 'em. Anyway, I figured the assassins most likely came from Thomas, that's Cromwell tactics right there, which meant that Imperials had kidnapped my uncle, or mebbe killed him."

"The uncle who opposed you in the election?" Olanthes asked.

"Still kin. So Black Charlie and some of the others did a little inquirin', and it turns out uncle David is bein' held in a gaol cell by the Nashville Town Watch."

"And you left him there?" Charlie Donelsen asked. "What you got cookin', Calhoun?"

Cal chuckled drily. "Iffen you look at a map, and think about the Imperial towns, where are they?"

"All over," Bondí said.

Cal shook his head. "That's what I'd a told you myself, six months ago, only it ain't true. Course I never looked much at maps, I got around by stars and rivers and mountains, and knowin' a few good old roads, and

sometimes by the straight smell of a place. But no, they's
a definite pattern. Think on it a minute." He sang:

> Youngstown, Chattanooga, Trenton
> Blacksburg, Akron, Scranton
> Knoxville, Johnson City, Asheville
> Cleveland, Providence, Nashville
> Twelve Electors, nary a crown
> One from each Imperial Town

"They're mostly in Appalachee," Olanthes said, "or
in the Ohio."

Cal thumped his fist on the table. "There it is. Set
aside Providence and Trenton, which are different. Or
maybe they ain't. Maybe the reason Providence exists
is to exert control over the folks of the Covenant
Tract, and Trenton keeps a garrison of soldiers as can
march into New Amsterdam, lickety-split. The other
ten, ten of the twelve, are in Ohio and Appalachee."

"The Imperials say their presence is to protect
roads and hold fairs," Bondí said.

"Yeah, but you gotta be gone gump to believe that."
Cal laughed. "What, afore John Penn came along, we
couldn't figure out how to have a road? We weren't
able to hold a Tobacco Fair until the Lightning Bishop
showed us the way?"

"I's jest a young man myself," Charlie said, "and
not the Elector, but the way I heard my uncle tell it,
givin' John Penn those towns and the Imperial Pikes
was a way for him to get some revenue, so's they
could be an empire."

"I believe that," Cal said. "But then why are they all
in Appalachee and the Ohio? Why no Imperial towns

among the Igbo, or in Ferdinandia, or Louisiana? Iffen you really wanted to raise cash for the empire, why not make New Amsterdam and New Orleans Imperial towns, or at least put Imperial markets in 'em?"

"Because the Imperial towns are really about control," Charlie Donelsen said slowly. "Damn iffen I don't think you're right."

"So what's the plan, then?" Olanthes's heart beat a little faster.

"The way I see it," Cal said, "any old town, whether you want to call it an Imperial town or not, but any old town sittin' on Calhoun land belongs to the Calhouns."

Charlie Donelsen slapped his thigh and grinned. "This is insurrection, you know."

Cal shrugged. "Against what? Against a feller who takes our money so that he can send soldiers against our neighbors? Against a man who can't convince Appalachee, so he goes and ties himself hip to hip with New Spain? Against a pawn of Oliver Cromwell?"

"Yessir," Donelsen said. "Against those things."

"You're going to want allies in the Ohio," Olanthes said.

"That's where I hoped you might be able to help," Cal said. "I don't expect I have time to propose the plan to Sarah, git her approval, and then go win over the other six kings of the Ohio, so I's rather hopin' there might be patriotic people willin' to raise a little hell, for freedom, and for the empire that used to be. I's rather hopin' you might be able to git in touch with such people."

"As it happens," Olanthes nodded, "I *am* in touch with such people. And what do we do about Logan Rupp?"

Calvin Calhoun grinned.

✦　　✦　　✦

The caverns ran deep, they ran in a straight line, and they went nowhere.

"I suppose you call these the Onandagos Caves?" Luman had said to Aha Koweta, half in jest, when he'd seen the low bluff with the narrow crack in its face. No trail led to the crack, and the climb up to the cave entrance was a scramble over loose scree that shifted and slid beneath one's feet.

The King of Koweta had laughed. "We call it Irra-Chalonam. It's an old name, and it means something like *the place of many visions*."

They had sheltered for the night in the cave, glad to have its stone walls to keep out the rain, but within hours, the Imperials had arrived: perhaps half the soldiers who had besieged Koweta, and two of the large wooden mannequins.

The Imperials had come following a tracker, a man with yellow feathers tied to his hat and an eyepiece he looked through. The eyepiece had led the tracker to the bluff, and then straight up to the cave opening, before Aha Koweta had finally given the order to fire.

The tracker had survived, but had to be dragged away into the trees by soldiers. Seven of the Imperial infantrymen with him had fallen, and then the Imperials had dug in.

Before the Imperials' arrival, Luman had walked to the back of the caverns. One cave followed after the next in a series that descended nearly a mile, each long, noodle-like chamber connected by a mere crack, or a corkscrew passage, with the next. Water flowed through several of the lower chambers, giving plenty to drink, but entering and leaving through apertures too small or too submerged to see.

In a pinch, could Luman give himself and the two kings the ability to breathe underwater, and try to escape? But there was no guarantee that the streams ever flowed to the surface, or that they did so through openings large enough for a person to exit.

Crates stacked in the caves contained food and blankets, enough, the king suggested, for several weeks. "Enough to march to Cahokia on."

"Where does the air come from?" Luman had asked. He'd looked up and saw no shafts of light that might indicate openings to the surface.

"Various cracks above our heads," the King of Koweta had said. "Bats and snakes pass through, but nothing as large as a bobcat."

Luman had heard the story of Sarah Elytharias Penn transforming her entire entourage into a flock of pigeons, but he'd never seen his queen repeat the act. The mere thought of attempting it exhausted him, but still, the upper passages through which air entered the caves must remain in his consciousness.

These thoughts had been hypothetical when he had had them, on his initial inspection of the caverns. But then the Imperials had shown up, and what Luman had intended to be a rest overnight had instantly become a siege.

He and Shelem Adena deferred to Aha Koweta. The king posted men with rifles in the opening of the cave, and then stood in the cave mouth with Luman and Adena and the watch, while below his people lit fires to dry themselves and prepare a little food.

"They are not so many," the King of Koweta said. "We could attack them in the night, and take them by surprise."

"They would shoot us as we picked our way down the scree," Luman said.

"On the other hand, they cannot do much to us here," the king said. "We can wait them out."

"Only as long as we have food," Luman pointed out.

"I worry about gunpowder," the King of Adena said. "Or cannons. Guns fired into the mouth of this cave might cause a collapse, as could a single lit powder keg, if they could hurl it in here."

What Luman didn't say was that he was worried about the wooden giants. He looked out at the Imperials, setting up tents in the woods around the base of the bluff, and lighting fires, and he saw a siege coming.

When he looked at the two wooden giants, and did so through his own lens—his seer stone, after murmuring over it the quick bit of gramarye, *oculum aperio*—he saw demons. Or if not demons, then he didn't know what. Within each wooden construct, stretched between the head and the chest, rested something he could not see with his natural vision. That something was shaped like a squid, with its long body nestled point-upward in the lower part of the giant's wooden head, and its tentacles falling an unnerving distance within the giant's chest. The giants' motions seemed determined by the motions of the squids' tentacles within them, as if the wooden constructs were enormous marionettes, and the squids worked the strings. Thick black ichor seemed to flow from pores in the tentacles and crawl sluggishly within the giants, flowing like blood to their clubbed hands and feet, and accelerating when they moved.

"Your Majesties," he said. "A word."

He stepped back in from the cave mouth, onto a sandy shelf out of earshot of the men on watch. "I believe I could get us out of here. The three of us, right now. But I worry that, the longer we wait, the more likely the opportunity goes away."

The King of Koweta frowned.

"What do you mean?" the King of Adena asked.

"I can place a cloak of obscurity over me and over you two," Luman said. "We can simply walk out of here, right now, through the Imperial camp and on to Cahokia. We can send help from there."

"By the time help returns," the King of Koweta said, "my people may have starved to death, or have had the cavern collapsed on them."

"Which might happen to you, too, if you stay here," Luman pointed out.

"Why does the opportunity go away?" the King of Adena asked.

"The man who led the Imperials here," Luman said. "Did you notice him?"

"The man with two feathers in his hat." The King of Koweta smiled. "We shot him."

"And he lived. He is wounded now, and we can hope that the Imperials lack whatever arcane vision it was that allowed him to track us here. But if we don't slip out now, I worry that, by morning, he will be recovered, and looking again through his lens, and I will be unable to smuggle us out the front door."

"But if you did smuggle us out the front door," Aha Koweta said, "it would only be a matter of time before the man was healed, and following us again."

Luman nodded, frowning.

"Why must we flee at all?" Shelem Adena asked. "If we run, we only continue to be chased. Why not go on the offensive?"

"If Your Majesty imagines Franklin bolts and an army of summoned Valkyries, I fear I must tell you that such feats are beyond my strength."

"You have said you could conceal the three of us."

"I believe I could." Luman nodded.

"Then conceal three of our men instead, and let us send them into the Imperial camp. If nothing else, they may slay the wizard with yellow feathers, so that if we escape later, we may do so without being followed."

Luman laughed, embarrassed. "Of course, I . . . forgive me, I am not a battle wizard, and that thought had not occurred to me."

The King of Adena looked at his royal colleague. "Is any of your men up to this task? Koweta is very different from Adena indeed if you have experienced assassins in your retinue."

"I do not," Aha said. "Nor, I fear, do I have any magic that can help us, away from my city as we are."

"Don't worry," Luman said. "I have someone in mind."

He took his peep-stone in hand and moved deeper into the cavern, looking for a dark corner in which to sit and work.

Two hours after sunset, Montse squatted beside Ritter beneath a natural lean-to formed where two pine logs had fallen across a third. She thought the Imperials had given up trying to track them, thwarted by the darkness of night and the muddying effect of the rain.

Though neither of those was likely to stop the man with yellow feathers in his hat, if he were set to tracking them. And in any case, once the sun was up again, she expected that the Imperials would send out patrols.

In the meantime, they crouched in their natural shelter and watched the Imperials set up camp in a half circle about the base of a low, rocky knoll.

Ritter's breathing was irregular, and from time to time his eyes fluttered as if he were on the verge of passing out. The linen bandages around his torso were soaked through with blood, and blood stained his leggings.

"There must be a cave in that hill," Montse said.

"We can run for reinforcements," Ritter suggested.

Montse considered the size of the camp. "How long would it take you, and how many could you bring?"

"I do not know how many Swords of Wisdom live near here," Ritter said. "If I am lucky, in a day or two, perhaps I can bring back two dozen armed men."

"Two dozen armed, skilled fighters, could be very effective against the Imperials," Montse said. "You should do it." She feared the Sword of Wisdom was little use to her in a fight, with his wound.

Ritter cleared his throat. "What are you going to do?"

"I will stay here and harass them. I can think of no better use for my time. I will be no help recruiting Ophidian warriors. Perhaps, when the Imperials bring up their reinforcements, I will be able to delay them a few hours."

"It seems inevitable that you will be caught, and then hanged."

"Men have been saying that about me all my life, hetar." Montse grinned. "Go. Bring your men. I will be here, alive and stinging."

Ritter nodded and then staggered into the forest.

Montse crept toward the Imperial camp. She moved

slowly, looking for sentries and picket lines, and suddenly a voice spoke clearly into her mind.

Montserrat, this is Luman Walters.

She laughed out loud. Hope was deceiving her into believing her own wishful thoughts. "Why stop at Luman Walters?" she asked. "Why not say you are Sarah Elytharias Penn? That would truly inspire hope in this old smuggler's breast."

Because I am in fact Luman Walters.

Montse hesitated. "How can I believe you?"

I am watching you now. I can see that Ritter is gone. Was he killed?

Montse snorted. "You cannot convince me you are Walters by telling me things that I already know. I think you are my own mind, deceiving me."

Then how can I possibly convince you?

That was a good question. Montse considered it. "You are a wizard. Cause something unnatural to happen."

That is exactly what I am going to do. I am very tired, Montse, so I think I can do only one thing, and it might not last very long.

"I'm listening."

I'm going to make you invisible. I hope I can make it last as much as an hour.

"Is there a cave in that hill?"

Yes, and I am in it. We need the man with two yellow feathers assassinated.

"The tracker. The magician. You understand that I am a pirate, and not an assassin."

Oh. Is there a . . . code of ethics, or something?

"No. But I am saying that assassins are very precise. As a pirate, you understand that I may be prone to getting carried away."

What might you do, if you were carried away?

"We shall find out." Montse gripped the hilt of her sword. "How shall I know when the invisibility has come upon me? And how shall I know when it has passed?"

I'll start the enchantment in a moment, you'll hear me. And you'll know it has passed when people start seeing you again.

"It seems as if there could be a less dangerous way for me to know the spell was ending."

There probably is. But I'm exhausted, and this is what I can do tonight. After... afterward, you should consider running away. Or at least hiding. Pirates can hide, can't they?

"Pirates can hide."

I am casting this spell now. Oculos obscuro. Good luck.

Montse drew her saber and began walking into the Imperial camp. Just as she spotted the first sentry, face cocked at the outside world, carbine gripped in two hands, it occurred to her that she should have asked Walters more questions, such as: Would she remain invisible if she killed people? Would her clothing be invisible as well? Would she be able to walk unseen in front of the giant wooden men?

But it was too late for that.

She walked up to the sentry, naked blade in her hands. He saw nothing, and in the rain, he couldn't hear her footsteps, either.

She hacked his head off with a single blow.

The soldier collapsed to the wet leaves of the forest floor. He was an innocent man in some theoretical sense, but it was not a sense that interested Montse.

These men—every single one of the Imperials in the camp—stood between Hannah's daughter Sarah and the healing she needed. They might not have chosen that, specifically, but they had chosen to serve the Emperor Thomas, and now they must pay the price of their choice.

But she did want to escape notice.

She looked for the center of camp, and found it easily. Tents housing ordinary soldiers stretched in a smallish semicircle around the base of the knoll, but the command tents were clustered in a single location.

She might only have seconds left of the cloaking spell. If she did have longer, she wanted to use Walters's power to accomplish something else.

She marched up to the first command tent and stepped through the single open flap. Within, two men in officer's uniforms stood poring over a map.

"We are close to the Sole Director's camp," one of them said, touching the map with a fingertip. "She should already have my message, and we should receive reinforcements soon. If not from her, then from the forces behind us at Koweta."

Montse ran the man through. He fell forward onto his map, blood gushing over the yellowed paper, and the other man cursed, looked around in confusion, and grabbed for his sword. Before his steel could clear his scabbard, Montse planted her knife in his neck.

She wiped both weapons free of blood on the officers' coats and kept the knife in her left hand as she walked on. This was good work, these were efforts that would at the very least sow confusion in the Imperial forces, and possibly inculcate real fear. A man who woke up to find his officers all dead might be tempted to simply take his rifle and run home, which would please Montse.

She found the drummer and bugler in the next tent, both asleep. She cut off the drummer's head with one blow, and then slit the bugler's throat.

Finally, she came to the field hospital. A doctor slept on a cot, and she let him live. An honest doctor kept his oath and treated all people who needed it, including pirates. Three wounded men lay on cots.

Montse recognized one of them; she'd seen his face in the Imperial rearguard, as she had shot at him, and before he fell. Looking at him now, she saw a pale, drawn face and heavy bandaging over one shoulder. He would live.

Montse nodded. Let life be his fate, then.

The second man she ignored, a stranger with two bullet wounds treated and bandaged. And the third was the man with the feathered hat. He didn't wear his hat now, but it sat on a small folding table beside his cot. He lay flat on his back, face staring up at the ceiling of the hospital tent. A small iron charm, like a cross with letters engraved around it, sat on his chest. He was bandaged with liniment-stained gauze as if for five or six different wounds, and blood-soaked lint in a basket at his feet testified to mighty efforts by the doctor on his behalf.

Too bad for him.

Montse stepped to the side of the hospital cot and raised the sword over her head. Her knee touched the cot, and she felt a tingle, such as one might feel a little too close to a lightning strike.

The magician's eyes opened and he met Montse's gaze.

"Don't do it," he said.

"*Fotut.*" She chopped his head off. The blow was stronger than it needed to be, perhaps, or a little less well controlled than it could have been, because she struck the frame of the cot as well and the cot collapsed to the floor with a loud crash.

The doctor opened his eyes. "Hey, there."

She ran the doctor through, holding his shoulder with her left hand while he shook violently and vomited blood over her right.

She blew out the lantern in the hospital tent and held still, listening.

A soldier walked past. He whistled a sad tune, maybe a love song.

When he had passed, Montse crept back into the command tent. Coats hung on a standing rack and blue tricorn hats stood on a folding table. She shrugged into the Imperial uniform, ignoring the fact that it was slightly too big for her. She belted her sword belt on, shoved her pistols and shooting gear into the borrowed coat's deep pockets, and exited the tent.

Rain crashed onto the tricorn and into her unprotected face. She took her bearings and headed straight for the gap by which she had entered camp. She passed men huddled around small fires under tarpaulins, stacked wood, and dark tents from which issued gentle storms of snoring.

She passed beyond the firelight, eyes fixed on the path by which she'd entered camp; this stone, that tree, that wide depression. She passed the very tree where she'd killed the sentry and didn't look back to see his body.

"Stop," a voice said behind her. "The password."

Montse ran.

Bang!

The bullet struck her in the buttock and threw her forward to the ground. A second ball hit her in her left thigh.

They would connect her with the deaths in camp. They would hang her, and possibly worse.

She rolled onto her back, drew her knife, and threw it. It was a wild attack, but she hit a man square in the center of his chest and he went down.

Only there were two other soldiers behind the one who fell. They held cudgels in their hands, and Montse leaped to her feet—

but her leg muscles didn't cooperate, and she only succeeded in flopping from one side over onto the other, and losing her grip on her sword. Then the cudgel blows began to fall.

Sarah awoke to the sound of her name. The interior of the Temple of the Sun was dark.

"Who called?" she asked.

Kodam Dolindas stepped to her side and touched her forehead. "You're feverish, Sarah."

"I know that, dammit!" she snapped, then softened. "I'm sorry, I . . . I'm sorry. But I heard a voice call my name."

"You are very weak, my friend. The next world stands very close to you now."

Maybe the voice had been Simon Sword's.

Sarah.

But it wasn't Simon Sword.

"There it is again," she said.

"I heard nothing, Sarah."

"Maybe that's because I'm closer to the other world than you are." Sarah thought about it. "The voice sounded like Luman Walters, though. He's on my errand, I'll use the veil and see him."

"I don't advise it. You're not well."

"Yes, yes!" She was nearly shouting. "We all agree I'm sick!"

"And if the effort of seeing through the veil kills you?"

"If Luman Walters can't bring me the Kings of Adena and Koweta, I ain't a-gittin' better, anyway!"

"If you're indeed hearing his voice." The King of Tawa's voice was level and soothing. Was that his natural tone, or the result of his long work as a healer?

"You're correct, that is the risk." Sarah raised her eyes and hands to the veil. "And it's my risk to take. *Quaeso Walters.*"

She saw the shifting landscape of the Ohio race, turn, and come in and out of focus. Rain battered Sarah's land, its rivers were swollen, its towns floating away. The earth continued to shake, as well; walls were tumbled down, hills split open. She found Luman Walters in a cave. He leaned against a rock wall and firelight played on his face.

"Luman," she said. "What are you doing?"

I am cringing in a hole, he said, *hiding from the Imperial army.*

"That about describes what I do, myself," she said. "Been doing it for months. You sound tired."

So do you.

"People keep saying that to me. Tired and sick. Tired and about to die. Sick and very close to passing through the veil. I'm gonna start demanding a little flattery from my courtiers."

I have the Kings of Adena and Koweta with me, Luman told her. *They're prepared to help you.*

"You're in Koweta," Sarah said, hesitantly, as she tried to gauge the distances by what she saw in the veil. "You're a week's march away. Maybe less, with fresh horses or good walkers, but not much less. I could make it faster . . . much faster . . . with a little gramarye."

"You'll die," the King of Tawa said.

"You don't know that," Sarah said. "And if you knew me at all, you'd know that telling me I can't do something is a surefire way to get me to try it."

Oranbega? Luman asked.

"He isn't here yet." Sarah took a deep breath. She felt hollowed out, burned, fragile. Maybe the King of Tawa was right. Maybe she shouldn't be working the veil like this. "Let me look."

"Your Majesty," the King of Tawa murmured his objection.

"Sarah, dammit," she shot back.

She shifted her vision, looking for Cathy, and was pleased to find her on the Onandagos Road. She was asleep, camped with Zadok and Yedera and a Firstborn man in a large lean-to in a soggy thicket.

"The King of Oranbega," she said. "He's middling to short, but big chested? Black hair, white beard?"

The King of Tawa nodded.

Sarah returned to Luman. "He's not far from you, but I don't think he has any troops that can come to the rescue. Any chance you can sneak out of the trap you're in? Maybe join him and come here together?"

We're here with the entire town of Koweta. If we leave, I fear they'll be massacred. And therefore, their king will not leave.

Sarah's head spun and her breath came shallow.

Dolindas gripped her elbow to support her. "Breathe."

"If you don't leave," she said, "then the kings never arrive here. Eventually, you get starved out and the kings get arrested. Maybe they get stuffed back into their villages, maybe they get imprisoned, maybe they get hanged."

True, Luman said. *There's one more thing you should know, Your Majesty.*

"I'm dying," she said. "Don't waste my time warning me that you're going to tell me something. Just jump to the telling."

The Imperials have captured Montserrat. There's some confusion in their camp, because she killed their ranking officers, but I believe they plan to interrogate her tomorrow, and hang her forthwith.

Sarah ground her teeth, ground her palms into her eyes, ground her hips against the Serpent Throne. "Dammit," she murmured. "Dammit, dammit, dammit. I do not want to pick and choose who has to die."

"Sometimes, that is what a queen must do," the King of Tawa said.

Sarah took a deep breath. "If you're going to insist I choose, then you have to live with my choices."

"Sarah?"

"Luman," she said, "hold out. We're coming to get you. If there's anything you can do to delay the Imperials, an offer of parley, an illusion, anything...do it."

Your Majesty should know that the Imperial forces include giant wooden constructs, Luman said. *Wooden men who move and fight. This is the New Model Army of Cromwell's Eternal Republic, worked in Pittsburgh on a much larger scale.*

"So be it. Hold out."

Sarah pulled away from her vision of Luman Walters and returned to Cathy and her companions.

"Whatever you're thinking, it sounds like a bad idea," the King of Tawa said.

"One thing I learned in my short life," Sarah said, "is that all my ideas are bad. The trick is picking the idea that is the least bad. Cathy. Cathy, it's Sarah. Please wake up."

Cathy Filmer, God bless her, sat right up on her bedroll and looked at the sky. *Sarah?*

"Cathy, there's a change of plans. I'm going to meet you tomorrow night at a cave in Koweta. You're not far, you should make it easily. Get Zadok up so I can explain it to him."

But the sound of Cathy's voice had already awoken the Metropolitan. Sarah explained the location, the low hill with the rocky face, the cave, and the Imperial soldiers surrounding it.

I know the place, Zadok said. *I visited it on my pilgrimage. We can be there by the afternoon.*

"Don't let the Imperials catch you," Sarah said. "Keep Oranbega safe. And be ready—when we come, we'll be coming fast."

She let Cathy and Zadok go. Then she took a deep breath, trying to still the shaking of her limbs, and the breath triggered a spasm of vomiting. She spat thin bile and black blood onto the floor of the sanctum.

"You cannot leave the holy of holies," the King of Tawa said. "You will die."

"I'm choosing who dies," she told him. "And I choose *me*. But I'm willing to bet you're wrong. Only I can't do this alone."

"I will do anything you need me to do."

Sarah laid a hand on the king's forearm. "I know. Only it isn't so much *your* help that I need."

"Instruct me."

"I need the giant Mesh, the prince of the Anakim." She considered. "As much coffee as you can round up. Waterskins. Dried meat and fish, whatever is portable and packs a lot of nutrition. You know what, get Maltres Korinn on it, no one can organize better than that man."

"Done."

"Gather up the clothing and oils and incenses you'll need for the anointing. Pack them for travel. Get the other kings. I hate to interrupt their sleep, but better they be warned than we wake them at dawn and throw them on the road."

"We all sleep poorly with your ill health. No doubt they are both awake already, praying."

Sarah laughed. "Talega, maybe. But I bet Talamatan had half a bottle of that pumpkin liquor before he went to sleep, and is snoring to cut logs."

"What else?"

"I'm going to need the Lady Alena," Sarah said. "Like it or not."

> *"I reckon it's time for you to shut*
> *up and start anointin' giants."*

✦

CHAPTER TWENTY-SEVEN

Etienne dreamed of his father. He slept and woke in fits, and in his dreams his father laid his hands on Etienne's head. He anointed his son, pouring oil from a silver cruse, and repeatedly pressed his fingers to his son's crown and temple.

But no words came from his mouth.

Finally, as the former Bishop of New Orleans gripped his son's head, squeezing as if to drive a blessing through flesh and bone by main force, Etienne wrapped his hands around his father's fingers. Gathering his father's hands in his own, he stood and turned.

His father was a skeleton. He was mitred and robed as if for high mass, but darkness gaped in his eye sockets and his open mouth, and the bone of his skull gleamed white.

Etienne sat up in bed.

He was soaked in sweat and his hands shook. Dragging himself from underneath the covers, he took the ewer of water sitting beside his bed and carried it out onto his balcony. Looking west, he saw the tail end of the Spanish army marching slowly northward along the Mississippi. Looking north, he saw the same Spanish army approaching. Eggbert Bailey had fought them for every inch of ground, as if by refusing to surrender to the Spanish now, he was redeeming his surrender to the French six years ago, with Andrew Jackson. But the road was not infinite, and the Spanish had nearly reached the city walls.

Etienne set the pitcher down and shrugged out of his nightshirt. He poured the water over his body, washing away the sour smell of sweat and the cramped, heated feeling of an uncomfortable sleep.

Taking a deep breath, he didn't feel reborn, but he felt better.

He took his mother's locket into his hand and wrapped his fingers around it. He felt and heard nothing.

The image of his father as a skeleton lingered in his mind. He felt a yearning to receive the blessing his dream had seemed to promise, and he felt a pull that attracted him out of the Palais to get that filial benediction.

Mother?

Silence.

Was this vanity? Etienne's father had always loved him, but of course had never blessed him in life, not as an adult. Etienne had been a gangster and a gambler, and a Vodun houngan, and his father had been a deacon and then a priest and then a bishop. Chinwe Ukwu had never known of the promises his son had made to his wife on her deathbed, and likely would not have approved of them.

But perhaps he would have.

Etienne wanted that approval.

Mother?

He dressed quietly, in his customary black trousers, waistcoat, and hat. He put on the red sash, hesitating and then wrapping it around his waist. He armed himself with a dagger, brass knuckles, and a pair of pistols, along with shooting accouterments in a small belt pouch.

Achebe was sleeping outside Etienne's door, and Etienne didn't want to wake the man. He knotted his bedsheets into a rough rope, tied the rope to the balcony balustrade, and then lowered himself down into the garden. He climbed a tree, threw himself over the wall, and headed across New Orleans.

The Quarter had grown more somber day by day as the Spanish got closer. The work on the new cathedral continued apace; the old foundations had been reinforced and the walls were beginning to rise. Under the supervision of a small group of specialized craftsmen recruited by Monsieur Bondí, the invisible part of the restoration also proceeded; the new cathedral, like the old, would be connected with other buildings by secret tunnels.

The Faubourg Marigny was rowdier. Fires burned in the center of several crossroads, celebrating some snake-like saint or mystère or godlet that Etienne had forgotten, but he took the fires as a good sign. Papa Legba stood at the crossroads of life and death, as well, and if he were really to ask his father's blessing, it was the loa of the crossroads whose help would be needed.

The farther he got from the Palais with no sign of pursuit, the more Etienne relaxed. The Franklin

Gate was open; the commercial traffic with Onyinye's cousins passed through this gate, at least for now, and much of it preferred to come through under cover of darkness. At some point, the Spanish would reach this side of the city, as well. In the meantime, gendarmes quickly examined the Igbo muleskinners and Catalan boatmen, and then let them through.

Etienne had not been out this gate since his father's funeral. He remembered that night, the slow procession, the wailing and the dancing, the rumbling groans of unseen mystères in the alleys as the living and the dead of New Orleans all mourned the loss of their bishop.

The path he walked was quiet, now.

He passed small clusters of houses, farming villages whose names he had forgotten, and approached the St. Vincent de Paul Cemetery, shrouded in moss-draped oak. At the base of the cemetery's low hill, Etienne stopped. The night air was warm, and he was sweating slightly from his walk. He raised his arms.

"Father."

Silence.

Etienne took his mother's locket into his hand and looked at it. It seemed to tremble, which sometimes meant his gede loa had something to say, but he heard no words.

Etienne climbed the hill. He knew precisely where he had buried his father, and he now took long steps to that spot. He turned left and right to avoid recent graves, marked by wooden stakes or simple crosses, but the truth was that the entire hill was a single burial mound, a paupers' grave, where all who were buried, were buried together.

Which would have pleased his father.

He came to the actual burial spot and stood at its edge. In the months since he had interred his father, grass had grown thick and tall over the coffin. This, too, would have pleased his father, and Etienne found himself reciting from the Gospel of Matthew. "Wherefore, if God so clothe the grass of the field, which to day is, and to morrow is cast into the oven, shall he not much more clothe you, O ye of little faith?"

Was that Etienne's own problem, that he lacked faith? He believed in God, and in the gods, though he wasn't always certain he knew where the boundaries between them lay. Was Legba an angel? Was he indeed the same as St. Peter, and did they both answer to God the Father in a great heavenly chain of command? Or were the three all different, and peers, who might consult with each other and make treaties? Or did they all exist and interact, but as different clans, possibly even clans at war with each other?

These questions were theological, though, and Etienne concerned himself little with theology. His concerns were practical.

"Father." He raised his arms again. "Father, in life, we did not speak enough. Or at least, we did not speak enough to each other. You and I were both men of many words."

He found he felt a need to explain himself. "I have not done everything I have done for honorable reasons. As a boy, I studied with Bishop de Bienville, along with Chigozie, but that canny old criminal saw the difference between us from the start. He knew that Chigozie was going to go on to the priesthood, but to me he offered a job breaking legs. 'You will not perform marriages,' the old man joked, 'but you will officiate at funerals.' He showed me that I could be part of the class of men that really ran the city. I could have wealth and respect, whereas if I struggled through with my lessons on the sacraments and giving homilies, I would at best be an admired parish priest.

"I have not spent my years filled with regret, Father. I followed in the bishop's footsteps and got what I wanted to get. It was mother who introduced me to Vodun."

He took out her locket and held it, quiet and warm in his palm.

"She had promised you that she would stop serving the mystères, and mostly, she did. Mostly. But she knew that Papa Legba and Maitre Carrefour were more likely to help me in my professional path than St. Christopher and St. Vincent de Paul, so she brought me to initiation. And perhaps, through me, she continued to enjoy a little contact with the loa.

"On her deathbed, she made me swear to protect you, and, should it come to it, to avenge you. I think she understood very well that you were made bishop to aggravate the chevalier, and that, given your personality, you would make enemies on all sides. And, Father, this is what I have striven to do.

"Lately, I have come to feel... remorse for some of my criminal career. Remorse is a strong word, what I mean is that I wish I might have been able to live a different life, a life in which I could have given offense to none. But that was not the life that was set before me, Father. I gathered wealth and power, and I used it against the villain who took you from this life. I have killed men, it is true. But I have not lived as a glutton. I have been as chaste as Chigozie. Perhaps I shall go to hell, Father, but perhaps not. Perhaps there can be forgiveness for even such a criminal as I."

Far away, he heard the croaking of frogs and the chirp of insects.

"Father, whether God can forgive me or not, I would have your blessing. Perhaps you cannot forgive me, but can you at least tell me that you understand?" Tears flowed down Etienne's cheeks as a wave of emotion struck him. "Can you tell me one more time that you love me?"

Etienne felt a sudden sharp pain in his back and he fell to the ground.

Rolling over, lying on his father's grave, he saw a tall, shadowy form standing over him. The night's dim light glinted on the blade of a long knife in the shadow's hand.

"*Vous m'avez échappé trop de fois.*"

The mameluke.

Etienne chuckled, feigning a nonchalance he didn't feel. "*Je t'ai laissé vivre. C'était une erreur.*"

"*Une erreur que je n'imiterai pas.*" The mameluke dropped a small object onto Etienne's chest. Etienne plucked it from his body and examined it; it was a figurine, wrapped in a red sash.

"You used my own enchantment against me," Etienne said in French. "This is the doll I made to curse the chevalier. You have used it to summon me here. Is that silk from some garment of mine?"

"It is from priestly garb your father wore." The mameluke circled. He was preparing to strike a mortal blow. Etienne steeled himself to roll aside, but he felt his muscles slow and reluctant to respond, and his life seeping out into the earth.

"You wish not merely to defeat me," Etienne said. "You wish me to know you have defeated me. For the glory of your god, and your honor. And on behalf of your fallen comrades."

"You would do the same," the mameluke said.

"Once, perhaps," Etienne agreed. "But now, I think not. Now, I think I would forgive you."

"You arrogant bastard."

"I do not feel arrogant," Etienne said.

The mameluke dropped to one knee, slashing down with his knife, overhanded—

Etienne tried to roll in toward the attack, to knock the Mussulman fighter back, but his legs wouldn't respond—

and a new shadow flashed over his body, slamming into the mameluke and knocking the other man aside.

Etienne gasped in surprise and fumbled for his pistols. He'd lost one in the darkness, but the other was still on his belt, and he managed to draw it. He pushed with his free hand and managed to roll himself over onto his belly.

He could see well enough to make out two men fighting, and which was which. The mameluke wore his black pourpoint, and other man wore only a pair of short breeches—it was the wrestler, Lusipher Charpile.

The shadows between the two men and the darkness of the night obscured some of their motions, but the two fighters circled, grabbing and slapping at each other, until the mameluke overreached, and the wrestler stepped underneath his arm, planted a shoulder into his armpit, and hoisted his enemy into the air.

How was Charpile seeing?

Through Etienne's eyes. Had he awakened with Etienne, then, and followed Etienne silently all the way here? It was a superheroic feat, the act of a fairy-tale guardian rather than the work of a mere bodyguard.

The mameluke tried to stab Lusipher, and the wrestler leaped into the air, arching his back, and falling, shoulder first, on top of his enemy. The mameluke grunted, but didn't lose his knife, and stabbed Charpile in the arm.

Charpile rolled away to avoid a second attack, and Etienne had a clear shot at the mameluke. He pulled the trigger—

click.

The evening was dry, so the powder must have been knocked out of the weapon's firing pan. Etienne reached for his pouch of powder, pick, and brush, but he was lying on top of it, so it was hard to reach, and the movement made his back feel as if he had been stabbed again.

The mameluke rolled away to return to his feet. Charpile lunged and grabbed twice, but missed. Etienne struggled to keep his eyes on the fight—if he looked away, would his defender be blinded? But Charpile didn't move as if he were half-blind. He moved like a demon, slapping aside a knife thrust, dodging back away from a kick, and then catching a punch from the mameluke that would have connected with his jaw.

Etienne got his fine-grain powder horn out. With the hammer pulled back, he blew softly to dislodge any dirt or bad powder from the firing pan, then shook in a pinch of fresh grains. He tried to put the horn back into his pouch, but he fumbled, dropping the powder horn to the ground.

The mameluke slashed with the knife and the wrestler pulled him aside, forcing his attack to miss. As the mameluke fell forward, Charpile headbutted him, smashing his own forehead against the other man's temple.

The Mussulman warrior turned as he fell, landing on his back. In his fall, he produced a small weapon. Small, but deadly—even in the darkness, Etienne recognized it as a pepperbox pistol.

Bang!

Lusipher Charpile staggered back, hit in the body. The mameluke stood, swaying back and forth slightly on his feet, and rotated the barrel of the pepperbox.

"Father, help me now." Etienne raised his own pistol. His hand was shaking, but he raised the weapon at the same moment in which the mameluke raised his, and squeezed the trigger.

Bang! Both pistols went off in the same moment.

The mameluke and the wrestler both dropped to the ground.

Etienne nearly lost his grip on the pistol when it discharged. He didn't see the pepperbox—was it still in the mameluke's hand? He kept his eyes on the would-be assassin, in case Charpile wasn't dead, and dug into his pouch for a paper cartridge.

Charpile groaned, and Etienne tried to move faster. He tamped the cartridge into place. Then he felt around in the darkness, eyes still fixed on the mameluke, for the fine-grain powder horn.

The mameluke rolled onto his side and began climbing to his feet. He was patting the ground, looking for something.

He'd dropped his weapons.

Etienne found the powder horn. He shook a pinch of powder into the firing pan and raised his pistol again.

"Stop!" he croaked. "I'm willing to forgive you, but make no mistake, I'm willing to kill you, too."

Lusipher Charpile crawled to his feet. His movements were slower, and Etienne saw blood streaming down his side. He lurched to the other fighter, hauled back, and punched the man in the side of the head.

The mameluke fell to the ground again. The wrestler staggered back, shaken by the force of his own blow, and toppled over.

Etienne's legs responded slowly, and with great pain, but they responded. Gritting his teeth and cursing, he managed to get one knee on the earth beneath him, and then he levered himself up into a kneeling position.

The mameluke was crawling, but not away. He crawled toward Charpile.

"I will shoot you," Etienne warned the man.

The Mussulman assassin groaned and reached forward, groping for something Etienne couldn't see. The knife? The gun? But his forward motion stopped, and then he collapsed, his own head on his forearm.

Etienne groaned, too, as he pulled one knee up and got the sole of his boot planted on the earth. When he stood, pain lanced into his back and he abruptly lurched sideways, staggering several steps before he managed to regain his balance.

Charpile moaned.

"Get out of here," Etienne said to the mameluke. "Go home to Paris, or Egypt. Go sit in your sunny gardens and forget you ever had anything to do with the bloody-handed Chevalier of New Orleans."

He saw the pepperbox. Stooping, he nearly fell over from pain, but managed to pick up the weapon. He had no free hand to rotate the barrel, but he pointed the weapon at the mameluke, anyway.

"You can let me go." The mameluke stood, unsteady. "But you cannot send me away. You and I are not finished, Ukwu."

"I rejoice to hear it," Etienne lied. "Now get out of here."

The mameluke limped down the hill, disappearing into the darkness. Etienne helped Charpile to his feet—the wrestler had taken more wounds than Etienne had noticed, and Etienne stopped, tore his red sash in half, and used it to bind the two that seemed to be bleeding the most.

He also stopped to pick up the little doll the mameluke had used. He would have to destroy it, though the more urgent task was to get his wound and Charpile's injuries tended to. He should have to go no farther than the gendarmes at the Franklin Gate to get that help.

"Well, Father?" he asked.

The only sound that broke the silence was the groaning of Lusipher Charpile.

Etienne turned, and the two men limped back toward the city.

Right before the northern gates to the city wall, Eggbert had dug the ditch across the road.

Truly, at this point, one was inside New Orleans. Like any prosperous city, New Orleans had long burst the dikes that held her, casting villages out her east gate, and fishermen and merchants into the Gulf, and a long town called Tammany out to the north. Tammany was named after a Lenni Lenape saint, and like Lenni Lenape towns, Tammany was unwalled. It had its own government, with an elected council called a Police Jury, headed by a President. Eggbert had learned this when he had begun to blow up and knock down the buildings of Tammany for defensive purposes.

Once he had thrown the President into gaol ("Yes, without trial, who do I look like, Robespierre?"), the Police Jury had come to heel. They had even helped, giving every resident of Tammany the pointed choice to be evacuated with whatever possessions they could carry through New Orleans and out the Franklin Gate to the Igbo Free Cities, or to be allowed within the city walls to make whatever accommodation they could arrange for themselves. The clearing out of Tammany had happened very quickly, without Eggbert having to arrest anyone else.

Eggbert had then used the buildings of Tammany as he'd used the ditches he'd dug, as defensive barricades. Knocking down the weaker walls in advance, his men had retreated from one stone wall to the next, sheltering behind the walls to shoot at the various forces of the Spanish empire. As they'd abandoned each wall, Eggbert had dynamited it, leaving no defensive works behind for the Spanish to use.

The Spanish army seemed infinite. No matter how many men and of what unrecognized nationality Eggbert killed, more stepped in to fill the gap. If the Spanish were to have the advantage of numbers in perpetuity, then at least Eggbert would insist on squeezing every advantage he could from the terrain.

At the last, he had flattened every building in Tammany within a hundred yards of the walls of New Orleans, and dug his ditch. The ditch was thirty feet wide, and he knew that his men had cursed his name as they'd had to alternate shifts being shot at by Apache braves and Nihonese knights with shifts shoveling earth out of the bottom of a wet-walled trough.

Water seeped continually into the ditch, and Eggbert had requisitioned pumps from several shipowners to suck the water from the bottom of the ditch to keep it, until the moment he needed it, mostly dry. The pumps sat at the end of the ditch that was nearest the flooding Mississippi and there, on the morning when the Spanish were making their final advance, Eggbert buried his last explosive charges. If the Mississippi were at its ordinary depth, or even flooding at customary levels, the river would be out of Eggbert's reach. As it was, he struggled to keep it out of his works.

At its eastern end, the ditch ended just before the soil became too swampy to retain a ditch form. Here again, Eggbert planted explosives. In both cases, gunpowder-impregnated cords ran from the explosives up and over the wall, to men who waited for Eggbert's signal.

The last wall would be the most dangerous to abandon. To this point, the defensive walls were fifty or a hundred feet apart, which a man might run in a few seconds. But the hundred yards from the waist-high brick covert and parallel ditch to the big ditch beside the gate was daunting. Eggbert planned to cover his retreat by introducing the Spanish to the guns of New Orleans, and he planned to be the last to retreat.

His officer on the left side of the road retreated

first. Eggbert and his men on the right gave cover. Eggbert fired a pistol, handed it to his aide to reload as he fired the second, then handed the second over as he fired the third. The advancing forces, Spanish infantrymen in blue and red, had no cover to protect them from his shots and the shots of his men, so they advanced grimly, bayonets fixed and jaws resolved.

The men on the left scrambled down into the ditch and up the other side again, hauling themselves on knotted ropes thrown down to them for the purposes.

Eggbert fired again, nodding grimly as one of the advancing Spanish troopers dropped.

"Retreat!" he bellowed.

The guns on the wall should be going off by now.

The rest of his men headed for the big ditch. His aide had left Eggbert a row of six pistols, loaded and primed, and a canvas sack. He fired at the oncoming Spanish, then fired again.

Where were the big guns?

The Spanish marched forward. They were only a few short seconds away.

Eggbert stood and fired twice more, simultaneously, a pistol in each hand. Then he tossed the four spent weapons into the sack, shoved the two loaded pistols into the pockets of his coat, grabbed the sack, and ran.

Still the cannons didn't fire. Ahead, he saw his subaltern standing on the wall, waving both his arms. It was a gesture that usually meant *no, go back*, or *canceled*.

But there was no going back. With a roar, the Spanish behind Eggbert broke into a charge.

Why weren't the cannons firing? This was the moment when Eggbert needed them.

Still, he had a good head start. He was tired, but he was also highly motivated, and he charged for the gate.

The subaltern atop the wall was alternating his gestures. First, he waved his arms *no*, and then he pointed toward the Mississippi.

What was the man thinking?

The cannons weren't firing. And the explosives weren't igniting, either.

It could be just bad luck, but it was more likely the result of sabotage. Someone inside the wall, or some wizard on the outside, was preventing the igniting sparks.

Ahead, Eggbert saw the last of his men scramble up the muddy ditch, hand over hand up the knotted ropes, and into the gate. "Close the gate!" he yelled, grateful for his big lungs and their capacity.

Then he turned right and ran toward the explosives. He tried to stick behind the few trees that remained at the edge of the ditch, but they wouldn't provide much protection, because Eggbert himself had knocked down everything that might eventually give cover to the Spanish.

The Spanish had to follow more or less exactly in his footsteps, prevented by the boggy ruins of Tammany from angling right to intercept him. That was good. With a bit of luck, maybe they'd even ignore him, and run forward, trying to get to the gate before it closed. Eggbert didn't have time to check; he ran.

He could hear Spanish feet gaining on him: some enterprising sprinter who recognized an officer and hoped for a commendation, maybe. Eggbert hooked a narrow tree trunk with his left elbow and used it to spin himself centripetally around, uncoiling the sack full of spent pistols as he did so.

He whirled into the face of two Spanish troopers, both with surprised looks on their faces. He smote the first across the neck with his sackful of pistols, and the improvised flail knocked the man instantly to the ground. The second crashed into Eggbert, awkward and off-balance. Eggbert seized the man, noticing for a moment his thick eyebrows and square nose before he tossed him down into the ditch.

He looked at the gate—it was closed.

More troopers followed, though farther away. Eggbert ran again.

His own chances of survival were dropping by the moment, but he wanted the moat flooded with water. He wanted to prevent the Spanish from using a battering ram, or even simply heaving explosive charges against the gate. They would eventually fill the moat, as they had crossed the Mississippi, but every additional day Eggbert bought was a day in which Etienne could find new allies, or the Spanish could give up and go home.

He reached the charges. The gunpowder-filled casks were still buried, and the fuse still emerged, pristine, from the pipe that protected it from being rendered useless by the mud. Under his boots, Eggbert felt the ground soften, and his pace slowed as the sodden earth sucked at his heels and toes.

Above the shouting of the Spanish behind him, he heard the zip and hum of the basilisks. They had risen with the floodwaters, and were close.

One more reason this might be Eggbert Bailey's last day.

But if it was his last, then let it be memorable.

Eggbert took the fuse gently in his hand, careful not

to pull it lest he detach the cord from the explosive charges. Pulling one of the two loaded pistols from his pocket, he carefully laid the weapon alongside the cord, close to the ground, angling the gun so that the sparks from its flint and its firing pan should ignite the fuse. He had a second pistol in his pocket, as a backup.

Bang!

The fuse lit, the first time.

Eggbert looked at the sparks and smoke that burst into being, creeping toward the top of the pipe and the gunpowder beneath. He had only a few seconds.

Turning, he took his last loaded pistol in hand. Half a dozen men charged his way in a knot, which meant he couldn't shoot them all. But it also meant that he couldn't miss. He fired into the mass of them, and then ran back toward the gate, on the inside of the ditch, pressing himself against the city wall.

Three of the troopers turned and dropped into the ditch to cut across it and intercept him. The other two raced around the end, tracing his footsteps.

KABOOM!

The shock of the explosion threw Eggbert Bailey to the ground. Mud thrown by the explosion stung his cheek, and something heavy struck him in the head and left him reeling for a moment. When his vision straightened out again, he looked at the ground before him and saw a severed head wearing a steel Spanish bonnet. His ears rang.

Did he hear shouting?

Eggbert lurched to his feet. Water rushed into the ditch, and then men who were in it struggled to climb out, or be swept away. One man scrambled up the slope toward Eggbert, using his musket as a staff. Eggbert placed his boot on the man's shoulder and kicked him back into the muddy, roiling waters.

A basilisk slapped Eggbert's head with its tail as it dove past to bite one of the drowning men. Eggbert had left himself a target—left and right, there wasn't enough ground for him to walk in either direction, with the waters of the Mississippi now sloshing up against the city wall. On the other side, the Spanish scrambled. For the moment, they were ignoring him, trying to drag their own men from the water, or take cover from the flying snakes.

Any moment now, though, they would see and start shooting. And if not, then the basilisks would get him instead.

Eggbert planted his fists on his hips and spread his feet shoulder width apart. "Go to hell!" he shouted at the Spanish, though he himself heard his own voice muffled, far away, and cloaked by a dull ringing sound. "You and your grandees and your alcaldes and your sacerdotes and everyone! From New Orleans to you, sincerely! Go! To! Hell!"

Something scaly struck him in the face. He flinched, expecting death by venom to take him instantly, but the object was a knotted, muddy rope, and it hung down in front of him. Eggbert took the cable in hand and looked up; his subaltern stood at the top of the wall, waving his arms. But this time, he wasn't waving *no*, he was waving get *up here.*

"Midnight Captain!" he heard, and, "*Général Kaboom!*" and now also, "*Le guerrier final!*"

Eggbert grabbed the rope and began to climb.

❖   ❖   ❖

Maltres entered the nave of the Temple of the Sun, standing still to be sanctified by the sleepy priestess on duty. It was the middle of the night, the veil was open, and the only light came from the lamps of the Serpent Throne. He interrupted a conversation with his appearance. The giant Mesh stood to one side with a flat mouth that kept wiggling upward at the corners. Maltres thought he looked at least *pleased*. Perhaps *honored* and *gratified*.

The giant bowed his head. The three Ohioan kings standing in the inner sanctum, on the other hand, looked with wide open eyes at Sarah, who sat up on the Serpent Throne and leaned forward, and Alena and her eunuch mouthpiece, who knelt on the steps below.

Sarah and the eunuch stopped talking at the sound of Maltres's boots.

"What I have heard is madness," Maltres said. "It cannot be true."

"Oh, iffen that's the standard," Sarah quipped, "I ain't heard nothin' true since I left Calhoun Mountain."

Maltres turned to the King of Tawa. "The messenger who awakened me told me that she plans to leave the temple. But you told me earlier, you thought she could not live outside the sanctum. That the goddess Herself kept Sarah alive, and could not do so if Sarah touched unsanctified earth."

"That is what the messenger was sent to tell you." Dolindas nodded. "And that is the queen's intention. And you are correctly summarizing my advice to her. And yes, this all may be madness."

"Youins ain't even listenin'," Sarah growled.

"I'm here," Maltres spread his arms. "My ears are

open. I will do as you wish, Beloved, but please tell me something, anything, that makes what I have heard not insanity."

"Sanctify yourselves," Sarah said. "For tomorrow the Lord will do wonders among you."

For a moment, Maltres wasn't sure she'd heard correctly. "What?"

"Joshua," Sarah explained. "How did he fight the battle of Jericho?"

Maltres tried to rub sleep from his eyes. "The ark of the covenant," he said. "Joshua didn't fight the battle at all, God did it for him. Levites carried the ark—"

"Not Levites," Sarah said. "Priests. 'Out of every tribe a man,' it says, so they weren't Levites."

"Yes, Beloved." Maltres nodded. "And they marched around the city, once a day, and seven times on the seventh day, and priests blew horns, and the walls fell down. But what does this have to do with anything? Are you planning to march around Philadelphia with a cadre of Jewish musician-priests?"

Sarah laughed. "I'd be willin' to try that, jest to see the look on your face. But no, the point is the ark could leave the temple and still be sanctified."

Maltres stared. Was she serious? "But the Serpent Throne is not the ark."

"Isn't it?" She shrugged. "But I heard the same thing about the throne, in any case. It came from the Old World, by ship. And while it was traveling, it still had all its power, because people who touched it without being sanctified died. Alzbieta Torias told me that story. So the Serpent Throne, too, can leave the temple and still be holy."

"You intend to make the temple mobile. You wish

to carry it around with you, travel in a pocket of the goddess's power."

"Yes."

"Will that work?" Maltres asked the kings. "Can holiness be a moving field?" He vaguely remembered the story to which Sarah alluded, but it was a story from the time of Onandagos, at least as old as the story of Joshua and the Ark.

They all shrugged.

"If it works, will it keep her alive?" he pressed.

"Maybe," the King of Tawa said.

"And will the effort of moving itself, the strain of . . . of what, of traveling around in the Serpent Throne . . . kill her?"

Dolindas looked at his feet. "I do not know."

"Oh, I reckon it'll kill me, all right." Sarah's voice was cheerful. "I don't think this'll work without me openin' myself up and running the whole damn ley of the Ohio River right through my itty-bitty soul, and if that don't tear me to shreds, it'll burn me to a cinder. But then, I'm a-dyin' anyway, ain't that what this is all about? I can't git the kings together in time to anoint me, I die. And now, jest to make it even more fun, iffen I can't git to the kings in time, *they* might die, too."

"But how?" Maltres shook his head. "You want to move the Serpent Throne? Do you intend to *fly*?" He tried to connect pieces of the puzzle in his head. He knew the throne could be lifted, because he had seen it. He knew that Sarah could consecrate ground, because he had seen that, too. He remembered her alighting in a rowboat she had made to fly from the junction of the Mississippi and the Ohio Rivers all the way to Cahokia, arriving at the close of a funeral. "Do you think you can do this alone?"

"Well that is precisely what we were negotiating. Mesh has promised that he and his men will do the physical labor, and the Lady Alena is explaining to me why she feels entitled to commit an act of extortion against her own goddess." Sarah turned back to the Lady Alena and smiled coldly.

"It is not extortion," the eunuch said. "The Lady fears that, although many things have been done to restore the full and correct worship of the goddess, many other things remain undone. With the cult in such a partial state, the Lady fears that the goddess will not give Her approval, and the rites that you wish performed will be ineffectual."

"You want eunuchs," Sarah said, "I gave you eunuchs. Only no more sneaking around. You have official witnesses every time you do it. Maltres's people. And no one gets made a eunuch who doesn't really want it."

"But Your Majesty once assured me that you could simply 'make 'em grow back.'" The eunuch's smile was oily, oiliest when he imitated Sarah's Appalachee twang.

"Test me one more time," Sarah growled, "and I will kill you where you stand. That's all you get, you can make eunuchs. I will even let you do it on the Sunrise Mound. You want holy ground, that's some of the holiest in the city, and you can use it. Hell, they can be official government eunuchs'n all, we'll put a stamp on 'em, won't even tax 'em. But you fail to toe the line with my requirements, and I'll take that away, too."

"I will happily cooperate in monitoring the Lady Alena's unorthodox cult activities," Maltres said. "Help me understand why her assistance is required. You are the gramarist, Beloved."

"There's more'n gramarye goin' on here." Sarah's accent slipped in and out of its Appalachee rhythms, her eyes bulged from her head, and her skin was whiter than white. "I need the giants consecrated, all of 'em."

Maltres shook his head sternly at the Lady Alena. "You pretend too much."

"She also requires the Lady Alena to perform rituals which few priestesses know," the eunuch said. "In a circumstance in which the Lady will risk life and limb."

"What are you talking about?" Maltres felt slow.

"You gotta keep up," Sarah said. "I'm a-goin' down to Jericho, and I need someone to blow the horns. Only Alena and her coterie know the tune."

Maltres felt ill. He was tired of seeing his country undercut by greed and internal bickering. He was tired of showing restraint with recalcitrant nobles and priests, and above all, he was just tired. "Say the word, Beloved. I shall begin hanging Alena's coterie, one by one, until they choose to cooperate."

"Why, Maltres," Sarah said, "I always *did* like you. Which reminds me, there's something else I gotta tell you, since you'll stay back to run the city."

Maltres braced himself. "Beloved."

"When we leave, the Well of Souls stays behind. Absalom stays here, or *there*, wherever there is. Under the Temple of the Sun, out there in the stars, whatever. I think he should stay trapped, shouldn't be a problem for you, but just in case . . . be ready."

Maltres nodded.

"Like I say," Sarah said, "I don't think he should

be able to get out, but...I have this feeling I'm going to see him again. So..."

"I require one more thing," the Lady Alena said.

Maltres was startled to hear her voice, but Sarah didn't bat an eye.

"Best tell me what you have in mind," the queen said.

"From now on, the Ladies of Tendance are independent. As a quorum, we will select our own successors and fill our own vacancies, without objection from the throne."

"Like hell." Sarah sat back and folded her arms across her chest. "I'd rather die."

"Then perhaps you will," Alena said.

"There is a thing that must be said between us, Alena," Sarah said.

The Lady Alena raised her eyebrows expectantly.

"I hear tales of human sacrifice," Sarah said. "Firstborn kings who would sacrifice their own sons to the goddess. Zadok Tarami, for instance, might say that circumcision is a reminder of the castration that was a reminder of the sacrificial murder."

"Is that a question?"

"Your words are half an answer, Lady. Know this: While I live, there will be no human sacrifice, and no preaching of it, do you understand? No whispered instruction, no pointing out things that can be read between the lines."

"I understand."

"That will do." Sarah squinted at the priestess. "I'll make you a counteroffer. During my lifetime, I will not again appoint Cathy Filmer to be one of my Ladies of Tendance. That's what you really want, isn't it? You don't like her, because she isn't on board with your program of blood sacrifice and eunuchs. Fine, I won't appoint Cathy."

The Lady Alena raised her chin. The gesture was haughty and triumphant, and it made Maltres want to punch her in the face. "Nor will you appoint any other child of Eve."

Sarah bobbled her head and then shrugged. "During my lifetime, I won't make any child of Eve a Lady of Tendance, including Catherine Filmer. Do we have a deal?"

The Lady Alena nodded.

"Then I reckon it's time for you to shut up and start anointin' giants."

"She travels the wrong direction."

———⋅❈⋅———

CHAPTER TWENTY-EIGHT

Ma'iingan awoke from a dream. In his dream, the healer Nathaniel was bound by writhing plants and calling for his help.

He sat up in the spot where he had lain sleeping, in a half-buried house that belonged to the queen, Nathaniel's sister. Rain drummed on the roof of the building, and the sound reminded him of Nathaniel's own drumming, which allowed him to leap into the sky.

Ma'iingan's manidoo had taken Nathaniel into the sky at first, and then later, Nathaniel had taken Ma'iingan. It was in the sky that Ma'iingan and Nathaniel had fought the mock battle that allowed Ma'iingan's son Giimoodaapi to become, finally, one of the people. Nathaniel had healed Giimoodaapi, allowing him finally to eat and sleep normally as a baby should.

And now Nathaniel called for Ma'iingan's help.

But all that Ma'iingan knew of Nathaniel's location was that he was somewhere far away. The young man had appeared to Ma'iingan in his dreams by approaching him across the starlit plain of the sky precisely because he was in some remote land. How could Ma'iingan find him now?

He could ask the queen for help, but she was dying. Besides, Nathaniel had called for him, and not for Nathaniel's sister.

Ma'iingan's manidoo could help. The manidoo could enter the sky and travel across it, and the manidoo had once before shown Ma'iingan where to find Nathaniel. But to meet his manidoo, Ma'iingan had always before fasted, journeyed into the wilderness, and then built a sweat lodge. Reducing his attachment to his physical body by those means, he had connected with his spirit self, and it was to that spirit self that the manidoo had come. When he had been unable to make such preparations, the manidoo had instead appeared to his son.

But Ma'iingan had no time for such measures.

He could attempt other methods, techniques he had not before tried, but which he had heard his father mention. Ma'iingan's father was a member of the Midewiwin, the spirit society of healers of Ma'iingan's people. Ma'iingan's father always carried dried leaves of the sacred herb asemaa, and he had taught Ma'iingan to do the same, from his earliest boyhood. Asemaa was excellent for offerings, and it had many other fine sacred and magical properties.

Asemaa could induce visions.

Ma'iingan examined the contents of his pouch and found four bundles of the dried leaves. The room in which he lay sleeping, on his blankets on the floor, was a bedroom, and its only furniture was a cot. Ma'iingan padded quietly into the kitchen and returned to his room with two chairs. Laying them on their backs beside the cot, and then throwing the blanket over the top, he created a small wiigiwaam-like space, into which he then burrowed and sat with his legs crossed. He shifted the blanket to allow just a tiny amount of air to flow under two of the corners, and then he used flint and steel to ignite the four bundles.

He closed his eyes and breathed deeply, inhaling the sacred smoke into his lungs. He listened to the sound of the rain and imagined in his mind's eye that the sound was caused by the hooves of many horses, tiny horses that raced across the rooftop of the sky, which was an infinite grassy plain. Those horses were also drums, and they called Ma'iingan to rise up and join them in the dance, in the running through tall grass.

He chanted wordlessly, finding the rhythm of the rain and then singing along with it.

Then, though his eyes were closed, he felt that he was not alone.

He opened his eyes and saw his manidoo. His personal spirit guide took the form of a man, but had the ears of a wolf and wings like a butterfly's. He wore a long white robe that was made of stars.

"Ma'iingan," the manidoo said. His voice was deep, like the shuddering of a remote earthquake, like the bellow of an angry bison. "Why have you come?"

"Why do you toy with me?" Ma'iingan asked. "You are much wiser than I am, spirit."

"If I am wiser than you are, why do you avoid my questions?"

"I come because I believe the healer Nathaniel is in danger. I need your help to save him."

"But why is the healer Nathaniel anything to you?"

"I owe him. He saved my son."

"He saved your son, but you saved his life first. If there is a tally to be kept in these matters, perhaps you are even."

"I would help him, even if there is no tally in his favor."

"Why?"

Ma'iingan considered the question. "Because I like him. Because I believe in him."

"You may die, Ma'iingan. The child the healer saved may grow to manhood without your guiding hand."

Ma'iingan nodded. He inhaled the asemaa smoke, and it steadied him. "Nathaniel is good. What he does in this world, there should be more of it. If my role in this world is to save the boy Nathaniel, then it is a noble role."

The spirit nodded. "Pick up your brands and come with me."

Ma'iingan looked at the ground on which he sat and saw that the bundles of asemaa were four long torches, burning bright and emitting rich, aromatic smoke. He gathered them up, two in each hand, and then he stood. As he stood and raised his head, the close walls of his blanket rose and changed hue, becoming the dark blue of the nighttime sky, sown with ten thousand stars.

"Step up to me." The manidoo extended his hand.

Ma'iingan reached to take the offered hand and stepped up—

finding himself still standing below the spirit, whose hand was still extended.

"Step up," the spirit said again.

Ma'iingan shifted the torches into his left hand so he could take the offered hand with his right. He stepped up, and again found himself one step below the spirit.

"Will I ever reach you?" he asked the spirit.

"There is always a higher step," the spirit said. "But take courage. Tonight, you have only a few more steps to rise."

Ma'iingan took the offered hand again, and then again, and then three more times—

And then he stood upon the starlit plain that he had ridden with Nathaniel. His manidoo stood beside him now and radiated a smile of peace and welcome.

A breeze blew, and it seemed to pass right through Ma'iingan. ~I am flesh and bone,~ he said, ~I do not belong here.~

~And you will not stay. But this is the way to rescue the healer.~

Ma'iingan looked about him. The plain seemed to stretch endlessly in all directions, and the stars overhead rotated backward, which threw his sense of direction into disorder. ~How will I find him? Nathaniel has a horse, and can run fast across these plains, and knows the way. I am on foot, and ignorant.~

~But he is calling for you. Listen, and you will hear.~

Ma'iingan listened, and he did hear. He heard Nathaniel's voice calling his name from the east. It seemed to come from over a low rise. He turned to thank the spirit, and to ask the spirit how to return, once he had rescued Nathaniel.

But his manidoo had disappeared.

Ma'iingan ran. The smoke of the burning asemaa billowed out before him and to the sides, leaving a trail and also creating a cloud of smoke through which he ran. The scent of it invigorated him, and it seemed to have a physicality, as if he could not only breathe the smoke, but could, if he wanted, jump up and stand upon it.

Beyond the rise he found Nathaniel. The healer lay tangled in a thick mass of plant stalks and tendrils, beside two Zhaaganaashii, a man and a woman, who danced close. The Zhaaganaashii were also covered with the dark green plants, but the plants didn't slow them down at all. On the contrary, the plants propped them up, and it seemed to Ma'iingan that perhaps even their movement was caused by the motion of the plants.

Two men stood to the side of the scene, one with the muzzle of a fox and the other with the tail of a beaver. Both men wore robes of stars—they were spirits, and they looked at Ma'iingan with pleading eyes. He had seen them before, accompanying God-Has-Given, but he thought he had seen one of them even earlier than that.

~*I know you,*~ he said to the one with the fox muzzle. ~*You are named Jacob Hop. I knew you as a man, before you were a beaver.*~

~*You sound like an Indian I know,*~ Hop the spirit said. ~*His name is Ma'iingan. But you are twenty feet tall, and you are holding fire in all your hands.*~

In *all* his hands?

~*I am called Wilkes,*~ the second spirit said.

~*The Franklin. I remember. Can you help me?*~ Ma'iingan asked. ~*Can you hold this fire?*~

The spirits nodded, and Ma'iingan handed each man an asemaa brand.

They advanced in a line, Ma'iingan in the center,

with a torch in each hand. They marched directly for Nathaniel, and as they approached, he began to thrash about.

No, it was the plants that writhed, but they slammed Nathaniel up and down, striking his head repeatedly on the ground.

~*How is he not dead?*~ Wilkes asked.

~*You should know by now that things in this realm do not always obey the same laws as things on earth,*~ Hop told him.

~*Iron bones!*~ Nathaniel grunted.

Ma'iingan knelt and put fire to the thickest plant fiber wrapped around Nathaniel. For an instant it pulled back, but then it relaxed. The flames scorched the dark green into a darker green color, but the plant continued to hold Nathaniel.

~*Watch out!*~ Wilkes leaped forward. A green tendril had been snaking its way beneath Ma'iingan's feet. The beaver-tailed spirit stomped on the stalk and put fire to it. The plant withdrew, back into the bubbling mass of vegetable matter.

~*Keep them off me.*~ Ma'iingan focused on the large tendril, and pressed both flames to it. Again, for a brief moment, the plant shuddered and pulled slightly back, but then the shuddering stopped and it did not let go.

Nathaniel screamed.

Ma'iingan looked up, his attention jerked away from the plant tendril, to look at the healer. A thin plant stalk was pressing its way into Nathaniel's face, drawing blood that crawled down his face in a sluggish trickle.

The male Zhaaganaàshii released his dance partner and turned to face Ma'iingan and the two spirits. He lurched forward, plants lifting each knee in turn and mechanically forcing him to walk toward Ma'iingan.

Wilkes got in the way and waved his brand. The Zhaaganaashii hesitated, his green eyes narrowing, and his arms raised to ward Wilkes off.

Ma'iingan looked down at his work and saw that the plant tendril had again pulled back. He pressed the flames to the green stalk—

and the plant relaxed.

He smelled a smell like scorched grass, but with the smell came the hint of an idea.

He pulled the asemaa brand back, but only slightly—

and the plant recoiled.

~It isn't the flame,~ he said. ~It is the smoke that wounds it.~

Wilkes the spirit inhaled a deep breath and blew. The smoke of the asemaa in his hands fanned out and smothered the face of the two Zhaaganaashii. The man's greenish complexion turned pale, and he began coughing. The woman tried to turn and take two steps, but the plants tripped her and she fell.

~Smoke!~ Ma'iingan cried.

He crouched low, holding his two brands close to the plant monster embracing Nathaniel. The smoke rose in a cone, and where it touched the plant tentacles, they withdrew. Ma'iingan inhaled, and blew the smoke directly onto the plants.

The plants shuddered. They tore at Nathaniel as if trying to rip him in half. A tendril shot out toward Ma'iingan and Wilkes intercepted it, weaving a defensive wreath of smoke that knocked back the plant as if it had been a physical shield. A second tentacle whipped from the plant mass and zigzagged back and forth, aiming for Ma'iingan's leg. Hop stomped on the tentacle and then waved smoke onto it, until the tentacle's spasms of pain and wrath tossed him to one side.

Ma'iingan kept blowing.

A third tendril of the plant crept forward, snaking through the tall grass, and Hop and Wilkes were both looking elsewhere. Ma'iingan tried to blow smoke at it, but it was too low to the ground. He was afraid that if he pulled back, the plant holding Nathaniel would recover, or would finally rip him in two.

Ma'iingan blew, and the plant turned pale green.

The tendril reached his chin.

Ma'iingan huffed and puffed, and the pale green faded to a sickly yellow.

The tendril reached up to Ma'iingan's lips.

He blew, dodging from side to side slightly with his head, and the yellow became gray.

The plant stalk shot forward suddenly, and into his mouth.

His two spirit allies didn't see, and suddenly Ma'iingan couldn't breathe. He couldn't call out, either, and he was desperately afraid to release the pressure of his asemaa smoke on the plant monster. He waved the brand, showering smoke on the plants.

The stalk in his mouth started forcing its way down his throat—

and he bit down on it.

The taste of the plant was like the taste of blood, though the sap that flowed through it was thick and cold. Ma'iingan's mouth filled instantly, and he spat and coughed, trying to free his mouth of the sticky ooze and the fibrous plant.

Wilkes saw him. Kneeling, the spirit reached into Ma'iingan's mouth with his fingers and pulled out the plant. It still writhed and shook, so Wilkes heaved it far away and out of sight. Then he dropped to the ground beside Ma'iingan, lay his own brand beside Ma'iingan's torches, and blew.

Ma'iingan blew.

Jacob Hop dropped to the ground, added his fire to the others' and blew.

Plant tendrils wrapped around Ma'iingan's shoulders and arms. From the corners of his eyes, he could see plants similarly engulfing the two spirits. He kept blowing, and then another plant stalk wrapped around his ankle and began to pull.

It hurt. He felt stretched, and he felt his muscles begin to tear. Whatever Nathaniel might be made of, Ma'iingan did not have iron bones. He screamed and blew, and he heard Wilkes and Hop both screaming, and he couldn't see Nathaniel for the thickness of the smoke—

And the plants suddenly let go.

Ma'iingan dropped one of his asemaa torches. He grabbed Nathaniel by the arm and stood, hoisting the healer up with him. Nathaniel bled from numerous small punctures in his skin, and immediately began to vomit thick green liquid.

The two Zhaaganaashii still wrapped in plants roared with rage and lunged toward Ma'iingan. The spirits Hop and Wilkes stepped into their path, waving their brands.

A thick green loop of plant flesh hurled itself forward onto the ground at the spirits' feet. It fell hard on top of the asemaa brand Ma'iingan had dropped—

snuffing it out instantly.

Ma'iingan ran. *~Nathaniel, wake up!~*

Nathaniel vomited. Within the green sludge that he spit onto Ma'iingan's chest, the Anishinaabe saw dark, spherical pods, like seeds. He held the brand close to his chest to smother the ooze in asemaa smoke; the seeds burst and the sludge fell away from his skin as if sluiced off by water.

He looked back over his shoulder and saw the two spirits following. The plant-wrapped Zhaaganaashii were following too, and not far behind. The motion meant that the asemaa smoke was too quickly dispersed to hurt them.

Ma'iingan could run no faster, and the Zhaaganaashii were catching up. *~Nathaniel!~*

The boy vomited again, but now what came up was clear water.

~Manidoo!~ Ma'iingan cried. *~Help!~*

Nothing. The pounding footsteps behind drew closer.

~If you will not help me, then help him!~

Nothing.

~Nathaniel!~ Ma'iingan was screaming now.

~I'm awake.~ Nathaniel's voice was weak, but clear. *~Set me down.~*

~We are being chased.~

~Set me down.~

Ma'iingan set the healer down, slowing from a run to a walk and trying to lay him on the ground rather than throw him, while also conscious that the plant monsters were close behind. He turned around just in time to stand shoulder to shoulder with Hop and Wilkes and raise his brand.

They waved the asemaa and they blew. Behind him,

Ma'iingan heard the sound of drumming—where did the drum come from? He had not seen Nathaniel holding his instrument, but the sound of drumming was also the sound of running horses and the sound of the rain and the sound of a rushing wind, and the asemaa brands seemed to exploding, tripling or quadrupling their smoke output from one instant to the next. The drum-wind rushed over Ma'iingan as sound, and also as air, and the wall of asemaa smoke knocked the two Zhaaganaashii to the ground.

Then Nathaniel was there, sitting astride his horse.

~*Ride behind me!*~

Ma'iingan leaped upon the horse, and so did Hop and Wilkes, and they all fit. Ma'iingan was no horseman, but he tried to look closely at his mount to understand how it worked, and he could not. It seemed to be a single horse with a very long saddle, and four horses with four saddles, and also four drums, upon which the four men were mounted, all at the same time.

The horse shot forward.

Plants lunged past them and around them, threatening to engulf the horse and its riders. The grass itself seemed to rise and become tentacle-like, groping, and even the stars overhead were blacked out, momentarily, by a darkness that looked like the shadow of weaving, grasping, intertwining, growing brambles.

But Nathaniel shouted a song and his horse raced forward, and they were over the hill and gone.

~*I dreamed I called you,*~ Nathaniel said.

~*I dreamed it too,*~ Ma'iingan said. ~*So I came.*~

~*How?*~ Nathaniel asked.

~*I had help.*~ Ma'iingan was reluctant to say too much about his manidoo, even to a person who already knew of its existence. ~*I believe there are powers in the world that are happy to assist healers.*~

~*Where are you?*~

Ma'iingan looked about him and chuckled. ~*Well, before I climbed to this place, I was in your sister's city. Cahokia.*~

Nathaniel nodded and his horse changed direction. They rode quickly over the endless plain, and soon Ma'iingan saw a cluster of mounds. Atop one of them, he saw Mesh and his Misaabe, standing in a circle and preparing to lift something. What that something might be, he had a hard time telling, because it shone so brightly.

~*That is my sister Sarah,*~ Nathaniel said.

~*Why do you sound sad?*~

~*She is weak,*~ Nathaniel said. ~*She stands so close to the spirit world, I wonder whether she even has a body at all. But she is preparing for a journey.*~

In the morning, Luman Walters emerged from the cave under a white flag.

He had slept, a little, huddled in the corner of the cave on sand and his stolen army coat. He was still tired, so he limited himself to a simple braucher prayer for eloquence, crossing himself at the appropriate moments.

They might be more formulaic and less powerful than gramarye, but braucher prayers worked. They also didn't drain him the way gramarye did.

The goal was delay and distraction, and specifically, he aimed to delay any process that might lead to an execution of Montserrat Ferrer i Quintana. Sarah had said she'd come to the cave, and Luman believed her.

On the other hand, he had no idea how much time that might really take.

Montse had acted, more or less, on Luman's direction, but he couldn't say so. Even if he were her military leader, a nighttime raid into an enemy camp, wearing the enemy's uniform, was the action of a spy or an assassin, not an army officer. Spies and assassins were hanged, under the laws of war.

But, since the goal was mere delay, there were other ways he could both use Montse and protect her. Maybe only for hours, but then, maybe hours was all he needed.

He waved the flag, which was an old white shirt fading to yellow, tied to the end of a spear, and marched down the scree. He carried no weapons, other than the tiny blade of his athame. He walked until he was fifty feet from where the scree petered out and the forest began, then stopped.

He waved the flag back and forth and shouted at the trees. "I've come to talk."

Beyond the trees, he saw the two wooden giants, stepping tirelessly back and forth, pacing somewhere behind the Imperial lines.

A soldier in Imperial blue emerged from the trees. He had dark hair, a hard face, and wary, skeptical eyes. "I'm Lieutenant Bridgwater, of the 4th Pennsylvania. Who are you?"

The longer he stood, the more Luman spotted musketeers crouched in the trees. None pointed his weapon at Luman, many pointed guns up at the cave mouth.

"My name is Walters," Luman said. "I don't have military rank. I'm a confidential advisor to Her Majesty,

Queen Sarah Elytharias Penn of Cahokia. Your force seems rather large, to be commanded by a lieutenant."

"I'm a really good lieutenant, and the captain is indisposed. Does 'confidential advisor' mean 'spy'?"

This was not the direction he wanted the discussion to go. On the other hand, in the short term, mystery and uncertainty could only help him, so Luman thought he was best served by not answering. "I am here on Her Majesty's errand, and I need to be on my way, so I have come under a flag of truce to make you an offer."

"We saw your flag. Do you have a passport?"

"Do I need one? Standing here, a free man under the open sky, do you think I need to show you a passport? And while I'm under a flag of truce, at that?"

"I guess that might be a question for the lawyers." Bridgwater frowned. "What offer do you think you can make us?"

"I have the King of Koweta with me in the cave."

"That raises all sorts of questions, but ... go on."

"I will give you the King of Koweta," Luman said. "Trussed like a pig, tied to a stake, rolled into a ball, pressed between the pages of a book, however you like him. I require two things from you in return."

"You cannot have free passage for the rest of the Kowetans," Bridgwater said. "I'll be taking them all under arrest. That's what I'm here for."

"You can have them," Luman said. He wasn't, after all, conducting a real negotiation. He was merely stalling. He didn't want the lieutenant either to reject his proposal out of hand, or to accept it. Delay was his friend. "I want free passage for everyone inside who is not a Kowetan."

"How many people is that?"

"Not many."

"Who are they?"

Luman shrugged. "Me. People like me. People in the service of the Queen of Cahokia."

"I would want to see a list," Bridgwater said. "Names, descriptions. Titles, if they have them."

"I can probably get you a list."

Bridgwater nodded, sucking his teeth. "So, maybe. What's the other thing you want, supplies?"

Luman shook his head. "We have supplies. You ought to know that, actually, it's important. We have months of supplies stashed away in the cave."

"Months?" Bridgwater looked skeptical.

"Apparently this has long been the personal pantry of the Kings of Koweta. If you and I can reach an agreement, we avoid a grinding, demoralizing siege."

Bridgwater squinted up at one of the wooden automatons as it rumbled past to his right. "Maybe. Or maybe I just save ten minutes of that big fellow there, pounding out the opening to the cave with his hand."

"If it was that easy, you would have taken Koweta in five minutes."

Bridgwater sighed. "What, then? Horses?"

"I think your sentries may have arrested a woman last night, who is also in my queen's service. She may not have been willing to tell you her name, but she is tall and wiry, with large hands, for a woman, and black hair."

"You saying you sent a spy into our camp?"

"I'm saying your sentries might have arrested someone of that description last night. If they did, she serves the queen as I do."

"You want this woman returned?"

"I do."

The lieutenant sucked his teeth and thought. "Some days, our sentries arrest more than one person. Tell me this woman's name, so I can figure out whether we're thinking of the same individual."

Should he share Montse's name? Luman wasn't sure how the Imperials would use that against her.

Unless, of course, they were aware of any of the various bounties on the head of the Catalan smuggler, in which case they might try to hold on to her for the money.

But wouldn't bickering over whether to claim a reward merely help bring about the delay Luman sought?

"She goes by various names," he said. "Montserrat Ferrer i Quintana is one of the best known."

Bridgwater frowned. "Catalan?"

Luman nodded.

"You'd have to leave your weapons."

"There are so few of us, our weapons would be no threat to you. We won't try to take any artillery."

"I'd need to see that list. How many people are we talking about?"

"Fewer than ten. I would need to count to be sure."

"There's ten of you, and you're going to turn in the whole village of Kowetans? What is that, five hundred people? They gonna let you turn 'em in? What's in it for them?"

"Peace. An end to the siege. They'll only surrender subject to your promise of good treatment."

"Ah." Lieutenant Bridgwater took a cigarette from his coat pocket and offered it to Luman, who shook his head no. The lieutenant lit the cigarette and thought briefly. "So that's a third thing, a promise of good treatment. You sure there ain't a fourth thing?"

"There isn't."

"So let me ponder my options. I could wait, get a list from you, debate over who's on that list and whether they're really who they say they are, given that your Catalan is obviously a spy or worse, and you as much as admitted that you're a spy. You know what that sounds like to me?"

"Prudence," Luman suggested.

"Time," the lieutenant said. "Time, time, time, time, time. During which maybe reinforcements are on their way, and here I am, way out in the Ohio and somewhat ahead of my supply chain."

Luman shook his head. "We can reach agreement on the list quickly."

"Another alternative," Bridgwater continued, "is that I could shoot you, hang the Catalan, and order the big wooden men to batter that mountain down. Finish up the whole thing in a couple of hours, and then when your reinforcements get here, they can sort through the rubble and figure out whose names they want to write on their own little list."

"You would violate all the laws of war."

"Some of them, maybe. But I don't see that I'd leave anyone alive who would complain."

Luman's mouth and throat were dry. He swallowed. "I'll go prepare a list."

"I don't think so," the lieutenant said. "I think you'll stay right here with me."

The muskets in the bushes swiveled and pointed at Luman.

❖   ❖   ❖

"How many such barricadoes have you erected, Madam Director?" Franklin asked.

He and Schmidt stood beneath a flap of canvas, drinking mugs of hot coffee and looking at the works the director had ordered upon the road. Fftwarik the badger-headed ambassador stood a few feet from them, exposed to the open sky. The wind that threatened to suck the hot black coffee from Franklin's cup and blew Schmidt's short hair sideways blew a smile onto the badger snout, and when lightning struck, Fftwarik laughed until he heard the following thunder.

The Imperial pike upon which the director had placed her constricting seal was wide enough, along most of its length, for carriages to pass each other going in opposite directions with no risk of touching. For the length of a hundred yards, in a section where the pike cut through thick woods, Schmidt had complicated the situation. Her Company men had erected a series of five staggered walls across the pike, each extending across two-thirds of the road and anchored on alternating sides. As a result, traffic that passed had to move in an extended S-like pattern, and was reduced to a single lane. Her men took the opportunity to pull travelers aside to inspect trustworthiness certificates, stamps, passports, and other devices of the Pacification.

The walls themselves were a kind of construction Franklin had never seen before, and which he promptly dubbed *Ohio casemate*. Two walls were built of planks, a foot apart, and four feet tall, the ends closed off by more planks. The interior space thus created was then filled with sand or earth, or, in the present case, mostly mud. The walls oozed, but they held, and they were thick.

There were now half a dozen traveling parties—wagons, coaches, travelers on foot—waiting at each end of the barricado to pass through. The director's tent, in which they stood, was at the eastern end of the barricado, a few steps to the side.

"Perhaps a dozen by now." She took a sip of her coffee. "More in the offing."

"The little Elytharias minx is cunning, though," Franklin pointed out. "She's evaded capture before, and it seems to me she's just as likely to travel through the forest or by river in a canoe as to travel on the highway."

"True," Schmidt agreed. "And then she'll be slower, especially in this rain and the mud and the flooding. With luck, she'll drown. And the woods are full of our Foresters. And in the meantime, we execute our mandate to impose the Pacification upon the upstarts of this flat, sodden land. And if we do not exactly swell My Lord Shareholder's coffers to bursting with the tariffs we impose, at least we defray some of the expense of keeping so many men in the field."

"And Cahokia?" Fftwarik rumbled. "I care nothing for this Pacification."

Fftwarik had a disconcerting habit of sometimes speaking as if he were the emissary, and sometimes speaking as if he were Simon Sword himself. Franklin pretended not to notice.

"Our armies come from the east," Schmidt said. "My reports tell me that we should see our numbers begin to swell as early as tomorrow, and that the reinforcing troops include the New Models and the Mockers and the draug."

"Mmm," Fftwarik rumbled.

Light flashed in the west. Fftwarik laughed, but then his laughter stopped, because the light did not fade. Nor was it following by thunder. Nor was it lightning at all, as Franklin looked at it. A single point on the horizon glowed a yellow that was fierce, warm, and persistent.

"That is no ordinary light," Fftwarik growled.

"Is that not at least in the general direction of the westward course of this pike?" Franklin asked. "Might that light not be emanating from something actually on the pike itself?"

"One of your grandfather's contraptions?" the director asked.

"We are a long way from the Lightning Cathedral," Franklin said, "and I am unaware that the late bishop ever devised a portable counterpart."

Director Schmidt squinted. "Schäfer!" she shouted. "Something comes!" She pointed at the western light, which was growing steadily in size and brightness. "Clear the barricado now and set the men out."

"The beam is so strong," Franklin murmured. "It seems almost like a...land-lighthouse. In weather such as this, it might even be a useful device."

"Weather such as this," Fftwarik said, "shall be the end of land and lighthouses alike."

"Hmm." Franklin drained the last of his coffee and set the empty mug on a table just inside the tent.

A horn blew. At the sound, Fftwarik cringed and covered his ears. The company men, who were now hustling to shove through all the travelers they could, looked around, baffled at the source of the sound. The horn's call began as a single note, but then was joined by other horns, blowing long, slow, rhythmic tones.

"That is not a hunting call." Schmidt pulled pistols from her coat and examined them. It took Franklin a moment to realize that she was checking the powder in her pans.

"Good heavens, are we being attacked?" he asked.

"We do not know yet," Schmidt said. "Perhaps a mobile land-lighthouse is coming this way. I prefer to be prepared, in either case."

The travelers had all been ushered through the barricado, or had taken shelter directly in the trees. Director Schmidt's Company men were lining up behind the wooden walls.

The light drew nearer. If it was indeed coming from the horizon, it was traveling at an astonishing speed. Franklin realized that he could hear other tones wrapped around and woven through the sound of horns. He heard chanting, in deep, male voices. He heard a bass line, but it was sung by voices that he would have sworn were feminine. He heard high-pitched singing, too, with an ethereal, ringing quality to it that *sounded* like light.

The Company men laid muskets along the top of the Ohio casemate walls. "Will their guns fire in the rain?" Franklin asked.

"Some will not," Schmidt acknowledged. "But if the men have been diligent with the beeswax, and careful with the oilcloth covers—see the yellowish patch on that nearest man's musket, over the lock and the firing hole? If the men have done their jobs, then most of the weapons will fire. Enough to give an unpleasant surprise to whatever Eldritch troop approaches."

As she spoke the word *approaches*, the barricado exploded.

Franklin didn't see the cause, but the effect allowed him to make inferences. The five walls did not explode instantly, but in such quick succession that a person who was not watching closely would have perceived a simultaneous wrecking. The walls shattered from west to east, all five within the space of a single heartbeat, so the thing that destroyed them was moving very fast.

None of the men were killed, but many were thrown aside as if struck by an invisible force, and the few that were not hurled away staggered back instead, so that the track of the barricado was transformed in the blink of an eye from a mud-filled, S-shaped trough packed with men into a lane filled with splinters.

Moments later, he would lose sight of this, but for a short period after the barricado was smashed, Franklin saw a ditch running down the center of the Imperial pike. The ditch was small, the size of a mere furrow, but the sight of it told Franklin that whatever had smashed the defensive walls on the pike had done so burrowing just beneath the surface of the earth.

Fftwarik roared and charged. In that same moment, the director raised one of her pistols and pointed it at the pike, muttering curses in Pennsland German.

Then the track where the barricado had been constructed was filled.

And then it was empty again.

Fftwarik was left snapping his teeth alone in the rain, but Franklin gasped at what he had seen. His vision swam and he groped within the director's tent until he found a stool and managed to wedge it beneath his posterior to prevent himself from fainting entirely.

He had seen a throne.

Not just any throne, he was certain, but the Serpent

Throne. In it sat a queen, tall and beautiful and full of light, and about her seven dancing salamanders. Standing upon the throne and about it, he had seen men and women. Crowned men, but also men who looked like trappers. Women who blew trumpets and who sang. And carrying it all, he had seen giants. Anakim, fifteen or twenty of them, also full of light, and also singing.

Light had sprung not only from the people and from the salamanders but from the throne itself, a dazzling white that was also every other color, a burning light that ignited the very air through which it shone, and that left Franklin's eyes struggling to find purchase even after the throne was gone.

He would have sworn that he saw it all, clear as crystal, and that he saw the giants take a single step. But in that single step, the throne and its bearers and all its passengers disappeared from view, and the light that had grown so rapidly nearer from the west now quickly faded into the east.

As the Serpent Throne disappeared, the fire that rode with it ignited the powder in every firing pan within fifty feet of the pike. A sudden, ragged racket of multiple muskets going off startled the company men. Men fell wounded and even killed, and they dropped their weapons as if they had suddenly become unbearably hot.

"She travels the wrong direction," Franklin murmured.

Schmidt looked at him, her mouth open. It was the most discomposed he had ever seen her. "What?"

"She is a sun," Franklin said, feeling dazed, "only she travels from west to east."

"She travels in exactly the correct direction," Imperial and Dutch Ohio Company Sole Director Schmidt said. "She travels away from her city, and she leaves it undefended."

Fftwarik laughed again. "Then it is time to shake the earth in earnest."

"The queen is dead."

———◆———

CHAPTER TWENTY-NINE

The soldiers threw Montse into a cage.

It was a strange thing for an army to be dragging around, resembling more an instrument of criminal justice. Having been, all of her life, various kinds of criminal, Montse had in fact experienced such cages before.

It measured two paces by two, and was large enough for even a tall man to stand. Iron bars rose vertically and other bars stretched horizontally, creating a lattice on all four sides and a lattice roof, as well. Shackles bolted into the lattice at shoulder height in two of the walls suggested that a prisoner could be made to stand spread-eagle within the cage, but the Imperials had shut the door on Montse and locked it without shackling her.

The entire apparatus was mounted on a cart, and stood in a small clearing.

From the moment when she had been thrown into the cage, well before sunrise, soldiers had begun to jeer and spit at Montse. Stripped not only of her weapons but also her coat, she could do nothing to defend herself. When the first man had yelled "Whore! Murderer!" at her, she had snarled back, but after that initial encounter, and her instinctive reaction, she had simply stood.

Back straight, head erect, looking toward the front of the cart as if willing the future to come to her. Men spit on her. They threw balls of mud. They shouted insults, and she ignored them.

Once, a dark-haired soldier with tiny eyes had shoved a stick through the bars to poke her, shortly after sunrise. Only then had she reacted, yanking the stick into the cage so quickly that she had barked the man's knuckles on the iron. As he stumbled back, surprise in his eyes, she had snapped the stick in two and dropped it to the floor of the cage.

That had bought her fifteen minutes of peace, and then the men had gone back to shouting and throwing mud.

She could ignore the men. The rain was cool, though, and she would die of a chill if she stood too long in it.

But surely, they would shoot her before it came to that.

Let this be her death, then. She had been unable to save Hannah, but she was proud in the knowledge that she had saved Hannah's daughter Margaret, hiding her for years from her mother's murderer as well as from Montse's enemies. And perhaps, with her death, she might have saved Hannah's other daughter, as well, might have permitted the Kings of Adena and Koweta to escape, so that Sarah could be blessed and healed.

And, if nothing else, she had taken many of the Imperials with her. They would remember.

Late in the morning, Montse stood shivering, with chattering teeth, and Luman Walters was hauled into the clearing. He looked furious, but also a little embarrassed.

"This is a violation!" the wizard shouted. "You are disrespecting a flag of truce!"

"You are not part of an organized military unit." Two soldiers dragged Luman, one holding each arm, but the man walking behind them, whose rank insignia marked him as a lieutenant, spoke. Luman still wore his stolen Imperial coat. "You are not in uniform, or, at least, you are not in *your* uniform. You are part of a company that sent assassins into my camp in the middle of the night. You are entitled to nothing, and your flag of truce is a lie."

"I am a counselor to a queen and Elector!"

"A queen who is an outlaw," the lieutenant said, "and who has never been seated in the Assembly."

The lieutenant himself had the key, on a string around his neck. He climbed onto the cart to unlock the door, and then the soldiers tossed Luman in.

The lieutenant locked the door. He stood on the cart and looked through the bars, eyes narrowed. "Many of my men would like to hang you right now. But I think I'll let you live, so you can watch us drag the King of Koweta right back out of the hole into which you stuffed him, and know that your heroic nighttime raid was a failure."

"Oh?" Montse stared with disdain, though her jaw rattled with cold.

"*Then* I'll hang you."

The officer stepped down from the cart and trudged into the trees. He shouted orders as he went, and the soldiers in the clearing followed him. Luman dragged himself to his feet, and moments later, the sounds of muskets and artillery broke the silence.

Luman inspected the cage. "This must have been sent to bring Aha Koweta back to Philadelphia in." He struck one of the shackle cuffs with a knuckle. "See? This is to force him to stand proudly, like a king, to emphasize how much greater is the dignity and the majesty of the emperor who humbled him."

Cold water ran down Montse's back. She nodded, afraid that if she tried to speak, her teeth would chatter uncontrollably.

"Let me try the lock." Luman looked around the clearing, but there were no Imperials in sight. "I'm tired, but I think this is a small thing." He knelt, wrapping his fingers around the block of iron in which the lock was set. *"Ianuam aperio"*—

He fell back with a cry, falling onto his posterior.

"What's wrong?" Montse knelt to steady the wizard. Her teeth began rattling, and she saw that the palms of his hands were crisscrossed with bright red welts.

Luman shook his head slowly. "I think...perhaps a countercharm, but more likely, there is simply silver wire inside the lock."

"They did, after all, send this cage to hold an Eldritch king."

"Well, I feel foolish." Luman rose to a crouch and looked closely at the lock. "But then, I still think like a braucher, or a Memphite. Those charms don't have the same strong negative reaction to the presence of silver."

Montse shuddered. "Do you have a door-opening braucher charm, then?"

"Yes," Montse said. "And it requires a disk of wax with a certain prayer imprinted on it. And I have such disks, but they are in my own coat. Which I gave to Ritter at Parkersburg. And I suppose Roland Gyanthes's Germans must have returned my coat to Cahokia by now."

He stood and examined the bars. "Could we knock these open?" He tested, pushing and prying without obvious effect.

Montse shook her head, and nearly fell down with the violent paroxysm of shivering that seized her.

"Oh, I am such an ass." Luman climbed out of his Imperial coat and wrapped it around her shoulders. Montse would have resisted, but she hadn't the strength.

"You should keep the coat," she told him. "I am so chilled, it is probably too late for me."

"I'll hold you," Luman said. "I'm still warm. Also, I have more belly fat than you do, so I'll resist the rain better. Don't stab me." He embraced Montse, pressing his belly against hers and drawing her face against his neck. The sudden warmth of his flesh was shocking.

"I would gut you like a fish," she murmured, "only the soldiers took away my weapons."

"For the first time in my memory, then, I am grateful to an Imperial soldier."

Montse shivered, but the warmth that began to trickle into her body made the shiver feel pleasurable. This reprieve, though, was temporary. The relentless rain would kill them both, eventually.

If the soldiers didn't hang them first.

Kinta Jane had never had religion of any meaningful kind. Others sacrificed to the mystères, or said prayers to Christian saints, or had gods she had never known or understood. For Kinta Jane's part, Franklin's vision had always given her enough meaning and direction in her life, and, until his death, René had given her all the help that she needed.

But the Queen of Cahokia, whom Kinta Jane had met as a witch, seemed to have religion in a way Kinta Jane had never even imagined. She seemed to see with that ice-blue eye directly into the world of the gods themselves. In the last blue darkness of night, the queen's priestesses had anointed Kinta Jane, and then she had been directed to stand as close to the Serpent Throne as she could, and to stay close.

Dockery was there also, and Ma'iingan, and Mesh and all his giants. Mesh leaned in to whisper to her, "Forgive the presumption of a lowly worm such as myself. I asked the queen to include you."

"Are we going to Kanawha?" Kinta Jane asked.

"No. I believe we are going to Koweta."

Others assembled; a corps of priestesses with horns and timbrels. The three kings of the Ohio clustered close beside Sarah. The Queen of Cahokia lay on the Serpent Throne, barely moving. She wore a simple linen shift and she held four objects on her lap: a smooth iron sphere like a cannonball; an iron crown with seven points; a black wooden staff with a horse's head in iron for its cap; and a golden object like a plowshare.

Each of the Eldritch kings bore something in his hands; their parcels, whatever they contained, were wrapped in linen. They looked reflective, and focused, and afraid.

As the first rays of dawn, dull and rain-grayed,

came through the eastern door of the Temple of the Sun—and this was not an equinox, not one of the days of alignment, so the light did not strike the Serpent Throne directly—the priestesses began to blow their horns. They blew strange tunes that Kinta Jane could not entirely hear, and other priestesses sang a high part, and then the seven lamp bowls of the Serpent Throne were suddenly filled with seven salamanders. The lizard-like creatures danced, and, opening their mouths, they sang as well. Their note was deep and resonant, and undeniably female. The giants took up a chant in their language, which Kinta Jane could not understand.

Sarah leaned forward and slightly to her right. She held the golden object in both hands and she stretched to reach past the flanks of the throne and hold it directly over the floor. One of the giants, and the Indian Ma'iingan, both stepped aside to make her room. Her eyes were shut, her breath came with effort, and her hands trembled.

"Terram sanctifico. Viam facio. Ohio deae eius consecro."

She threw the object to the ground.

The plowshare burrowed into the floor and lanced forward, and behind it, the tiles were not left shattered, but as whole as they had ever been. But to either side, as it raced ahead, the plowshare cast a skein of light that lingered upon the floor, making a pathway or a road that shot straight forward and out the temple door.

Sarah fell, exhaustion and pain on her face. The King of Tawa had tears in his eyes.

And fire exploded from the Serpent Throne.

Kinta Jane sucked air into her lungs, expecting for

one terrifying moment to be immolated. Instead, she felt the golden-white flames around her as warmth and love, and she heard them as a sound like tinkling bells and birdsong and the buzzing of bees.

Still chanting rhythmically, the giants bent at the knees and hoisted the Serpent Throne into the air. They stepped forward, the golden path dimpling under their feet, and began to run. The timing of their steps was governed by the rhythm of their music, like the keelboatmen of the Mississippi and the Ohio.

> *Heave and lift, the angels call*
> *The rising of the Serpent tide*
> *With chorus clear and bearers tall*
> *See the Throne of Wisdom ride*

Kinta Jane found herself humming along as she ran, and she heard Dockery's voice, and Ma'iingan's, and the voices of the kings, humming as well. The giants surely were chanting their own song, in their own tongue, and yet it harmonized with the horns of the priestesses and the singing of the salamanders, which was in a different language, and somehow Kinta Jane could understand the song.

> *Heave and lift, the angels sing*
> *Now the Serpent rides to war*
> *Rattle shake and timbrel ring*
> *See the Throne go on before*

The Serpent Throne flowed smoothly across the nave of the Temple of the Sun, borne on a river of music and light.

The throne passed out the open doorway and into the world, and time became honey, running slow and sweet. Was the plowshare immediately ahead of, or even underneath, the throne? Had it raced miles and miles ahead, leaving a golden ribbon cast across the sodden landscape? Was the entire world wrapped in filaments of golden light? All those things seemed to be true. She cast an eye over her shoulder and saw the sanctum, and also the temple doors, and also the Great Mound, and also the Treewall, and also a hundred miles of hammered brown forest.

She did not have the sensation that they were moving fast. Rather, she had the sensation that they were in all places at once. To her right as she ran, she saw the gates of New Orleans, and the fires of the mystères within it, and the chaparral of Texia and New Spain. She also saw leaping goats and swarming bees, and she saw creatures that she had never imagined, outside the confines of Franklin's vision: a bear that was also a duck; a stag with a third eye, in the center of its forehead; a fish that sat on a wooden throne carved of a living tree and called to her in incomprehensible words.

To her left, beyond the throne, Kinta Jane saw Ma'iingan, playing with two young boys, and the island of Quebec, and the wide highway of the Hudson River. Lions with long red beards prowled in a course parallel to that of the throne and looked on with curious eyes, and a creature that looked like a sloth but had six limbs raised its head and released a mournful howl that joined in the harmony of the caravan.

She thought she saw a young man riding on a drum. If she looked straight ahead, over the top of the plowshare that also seemed to be at her feet, Kinta Jane could see the Ohio. Rain, mud, trees blasted nearly to leafless nudity by a spring of relentless storm, and road. Looking into the storm gave her the sensation that they were moving into darkness, or perhaps that darkness was moving toward them. The plowshare struck objects, but it was difficult to tell what they were; Kinta Jane saw walls appear for a split second and then disappear. She saw the faces of determined men, soldiers, who stood in the way but then evaporated. Low hills flashed before her, and long ridges, and burning towns.

If she tried to place her feet carefully on the ground, panic washed over her. She couldn't see the ground, but only something that was either golden light or else a road whipping beneath her faster than any horse could run. If she tried to guide her feet by the images she saw flashing at her over the top of the plowshare, she felt similarly overwhelmed and off-balance.

So she focused on neither. She breathed and ran, breathed and ran, and let the world rush past her in a stream.

The sun was in her eye. And then it was overhead, without having appeared to move at all. And then suddenly, still without any apparent motion, it was behind her, and the images flashing in her direction over the top of the golden plowshare were themselves bathed with late afternoon gold.

The Serpent Throne shook.

"We are under attack!" the King of Talamatan cried.

What could attack a vessel and a procession such as this one?

Sarah cried out, arching her back in pain. Kinta Jane reached a hand up as if to steady her, but the King of Tawa frowned and shook his head at her. "Dangerous," he murmured.

The Serpent Throne shook again, and abruptly slowed.

The world about the throne regained a more ordinary appearance. Fire and light still cast a web about the throne, but rain now splashed through that light and struck Kinta Jane on her face and arms. A slate-blue storm cloud clamped a lid down above them, from horizon to horizon, lit by sporadic flashes of white lightning. A low knob of earth with one gray rock face stood before them; around three sides of the low hill, and all around as far as the eye could see, stretched gray-green Ohio forest.

Standing thirty, or maybe forty or fifty, feet tall, out in the forest, were two giants. Kinta Jane had to blink several times before she could see that the giants were made of wood, with painted features on them. One giant wore the coat of arms of Youngstown on its chest and had a ragged orange smile and two orange dots for eyes painted on its face; the other wore the arms of Akron, and its eyes and frown were bright green. The two giants pivoted on unseen legs and raised ball-like fists to shake them at the Serpent Throne and its occupants. Then they began to lumber toward Sarah and her entourage.

Of more immediate concern, several hundred Imperial troops lay behind trees or stood protected by rough breastworks, in an arc around the rock face. Kinta Jane now saw, looking at the rock, a crack in the stone, large enough to be the opening into a cave.

"*Pallottolas averto!*" Sarah shouted. She clutched the iron orb in her hand, and her forearms shook, as if the orb were immensely heavy, or perhaps very hot. "Toward the cave!"

As if responding to her verbal command, the plowshare turned and crashed into the forest. Striking a squad of Imperial soldiers, in the act of turning themselves and their small wheel-mounted gun about to face the Serpent Throne, the plowshare shattered both wheels of the cannon and threw soldiers in all directions.

From farther up the hill, though, came explosions and plumes of smoke.

A cannonball raced directly at Kinta Jane's head. In any other circumstance, she was sure, she would have been killed, beheaded and dead instantly. She saw the iron sphere hurtling toward her in disjointed steps, as she had seen the countryside on her journey to this place, the ball looming and swelling until it seemed about to block out the sun—

and the ball careened away at a right angle, flying into the forest.

"*Averto!*" Sarah shouted. "*Averto!*"

Was that blood on her lips and in her eyes?

A line of blue-clad soldiers with fixed bayonets stepped from the trees, facing the Serpent Throne. Mesh and his giants bellowed their song louder, the horns rose in volume and in pitch, and if anything, the throne rushed toward the soldiers faster—

fire struck the men just before the throne reached them.

Soldiers screamed as hair and coats burst into flame. Powder in firing pans and in powder horns and in cartridge belts exploded, sending musketballs and bullets flying in all directions. Men fell shot by their own firearms, or burning in the uniforms that were wrapped about them, or clawing out their own eyes in pain and madness. More bullets whizzed close to, and then past, Kinta Jane; she heard their buzz and shivered.

Sarah was weeping. Her back was arched and her arms clutched the iron orb on her lap as she shouted Latin phrases, but her voice grew weaker from moment to moment.

The bearers of the throne burst from the trees and began racing up the scree beneath the cave mouth. Kinta Jane could see faces in the cave, but not the face of anyone she recognized.

The two wooden giants were racing closer. Looking through the flames that engulfed her, Kinta Jane thought she saw something within the wooden constructs, something that had multiple arms like the long nose of a shu-shu, something that looked at Kinta Jane with a cold eye and wished to eat her.

Men of ordinary height would have stumbled and fallen, rushing up the boulder-strewn slope. Kinta Jane was hard pressed not to fall behind, and she carried no burden. The Anakim, though, took enormous strides, ignoring boulders that a man six feet tall would have had to walk around. Their song accelerated its tempo as Mesh began shouting out the words; the big giant looked over his shoulder and drove his followers forward.

What was he seeing? Kinta Jane turned, halfway up the scree; one of the wooden giants was closing in on them. Its grotesque, rounded wooden foot thudded to the ground just above the tree line, shattering stones and throwing squirts of mud in all directions.

Guns in the trees, muskets and small cannons alike, continued to fire. They struck invisible barriers, close to the Serpent Throne, and then whirled away into the rain. It seemed to Kinta Jane that the whining of the bullets and cannonballs grew louder, and that Sarah's screaming grew correspondingly more shrill.

The Serpent Throne was nearing the mouth of the cave. The wooden giant lurched forward.

"Sarah!" one of the kings cried.

"*Ignem convoco!*" Sarah screamed, and the tail of her words melted into an inarticulate shriek of pain.

Flame and light and music exploded from the Serpent Throne as the wooden giant swung its enormous fingerless hand. Fire scorched the ball-fist and the giant slipped, losing its balance and crashing onto the stones on its side. Through the film of fire and light surrounding the throne, Kinta Jane saw the thing inside the giant writhe and squirm.

And then she was stumbling down through the crack in the rock, into a cool, dry cave. The passage descended before her into the belly of the earth, and she saw the light of at least two fires ahead of her. Men with muskets pulled her through, along with the kings, the Anakim, the priestesses, and the others.

The golden plowshare pushed on into the second chamber of the cave, and there cut furrows around a rectangular space in flat, sandy soil, then finally came to a stop. Mesh urged his men on, and they carefully laid the throne down within the rectangle.

The fire around the throne fell away like a veil.

The caves were full of Firstborn, who stared with

wide eyes and open mouths. Kinta Jane found that her heart was racing and her breath came hard and fast in her lungs, leaving a bitter, acidic taste on the back of her tongue.

"Your Majesty?" the King of Tawa called, approaching the throne, still holding his linen parcel. "Sarah?"

There was no answer. The king crept up to the edge of the throne, and then his face fell.

"The queen is dead."

Cathy Filmer was watching through the trees when the sky suddenly burst into flame.

"That is Sarah," she said. "I would bet my life."

"If we move forward now," Jarom Atheles, the King of Oranbega, said, "you *will* bet your life, and the lives of several others."

They sat on horseback in the forest of Koweta, looking at a low hill with one face a bare cliff, cracked by a shadow that Atheles assured her was a cave opening. The king had brought four men with him as a bodyguard; they were hard-faced, lean Firstborn warriors, with scale mail corselets, lances, long straight swords, and long rifles. Together with Cathy, Zadok, and Yedera, that made a party of eight. They were too many to be inconspicuous, so they had come this far by sticking to small paths and riding fast.

The King of Oranbega knew the small roads. He was a hunter, and though his men carried firearms, he carried a long bow, taller than himself, and when he could, he regaled Cathy, in particular, with tales of the beasts he had slain. The pursuit of wild game was what had made him friends with Kyres Elytharias, when they had both been younger men, he had said more than once.

And once, his face falling into sober lines, he had observed that his friendship with Kyres was what had led his son to become a Sword of Wisdom.

Within moments, from the fire emerged a bolt of golden light. Cathy was so surprised at what she saw that at first her eyes would not admit it, but soon she recognized that the Serpent Throne itself raced up the small knob of hill, on the shoulders of a pack of running Anakim.

"My god," she murmured, "this was not the world as I expected it to be, as a young lady of Virginia, taking my first riding and dancing lessons."

Jarom chuckled. "This is not the world that existed, when you were taking your first dancing lessons. The world dies and is born anew every moment. Sometimes things that have lasted forever disappear and are gone. Sometimes," he pointed at the Serpent Throne, rushing up the scree toward the cliff face, "things that were believed dead and gone return. Sometimes they even return in glory."

"There are too many for us to break through," Cathy said. "Could we sneak past the soldiers?"

Jarom Atheles laughed. "The slope below the cliff is bare. Even with the cloud cover, and even under darkness, we would be seen."

The Serpent Throne slipped into the cave in the face of the cliff. At the last moment, one of the two wooden giants with the Imperial forces lurched forward, trying to smash the throne and its bearers. A burst of fire and light knocked the giant aside.

Once the throne had disappeared, though, the giant

stood again. It smashed its enormous fist against the cave opening several times, then stalked away into the forest.

"We could descend from above," Yedera said. "With ropes."

"We could probably obtain ropes," the king said. "Perhaps we could approach the back side of the hill without being seen. Do you know how to descend a rope quickly?"

"I have seen it done," Yedera said.

"I have not," Cathy admitted. "If we came down the ropes slowly, we would be easy targets for the soldiers, and terribly visible."

"There is an art," the king said. "It's an art I know. But you do not have to learn it; your presence is not required for the Serpent Daughter Anointing."

"I fear nothing." Yedera scowled.

"I am loath to let this anointing proceed without my presence," Zadok said.

"You do not trust the ways of the goddess?" Atheles asked.

"I . . . would be there to observe."

"I will not stay behind alone," Cathy said.

"You would not be alone." This was a new voice, and a man stepped from the trees. He was Firstborn, tall and dark, with thin limbs and a belly. He wore an Ohioan tunic and leggings, with no indication of any rank or other insignia, and his torso was wrapped in blood-stained lint bandages. Turning to face the king, he bowed slightly. "Your Majesty."

"Identify yourself," Jarom said. The four men of his bodyguard leveled their lances at the newcomer.

"My name is Ritter," the man said. "I knew your son. And I guess your errand. I recently helped a magician named Luman and a pirate named Montserrat sneak the King of Adena from his hall, and the entire population of Koweta from the Onandagos Lick." He tapped his bandage with a finger. "I was wounded in the action. You have come to anoint the queen."

"You speak as if you are our friend," the king said.

"I am a Sword of Wisdom," Ritter replied. "I left Montse to get reinforcements. Having found them, I have returned."

"Where are your men?" the king scanned the trees with his eyes. Cathy did too, and saw a string of men on foot slowly emerge from the trees. They wore no uniforms. They carried swords or spears and half had rifles, but they were on foot, and had no armor.

"There are eight, all told," Ritter said. "It was all I could gather from the nearby villages, and only two of them, properly speaking, are Swords. But the others hate the Pacification and are happy to fight for the Queen of Cahokia's life. But with you, our numbers are doubled." He smiled. "And we have rope."

Two of the king's bodyguards scouted the back side of the hill on horseback. They came back within twenty minutes, reporting that the Imperials didn't have so much as a single sentry on the far slope.

"They aim to keep those inside the cave from escaping," Jarom Atheles commented wryly. "They give no thought to preventing new arrivals. Because, of course, it would be an act of *madness* for anyone to try to enter the cave."

"An act of madness Sarah had already committed," Zadok pointed out. "Let us go quickly, before it occurs to the Imperial officers that where one person may be mad, so may a second."

Cathy and her companions rode up the hill. Ritter and his men kept pace by jogging. They had not only rope, but also a bundle of extra rifles, a bundle of blankets, and two bundles of food, but the way was not long, and they arrived with the horses.

At the peak of the hill, Cathy crept to the edge and looked over. Trees grew very near the crest, tall, thick-boled pines, so she crouched behind one to observe the Imperials. Soldiers in blue worked small wheeled artillery—no Pitchers—turning the pieces back around and aiming them at the hillside. Had they been aimed elsewhere before? Perhaps the Imperials had turned their guns to try to attack Sarah upon her arrival.

The cliff face was sheer. It wasn't an enormous fall—only thirty feet or so—but if she jumped from this spot, she'd land with a broken neck. The cave opening lay in a sort of vertical slot, so that a person who was a skilled climber might even be able to descend into the cave from here. In any case, the cliff face would give some shelter to someone sliding down a rope.

Cathy imagined a rope sliding through her palms, tearing off all the flesh, and she winced.

Yedera pulled her away, to where the King of Oranbega was explaining the technique.

"We have four lengths of rope," he said. "So we can descend four at a time, or four in quick succession. I should go first."

"I go with you," Cathy said.

"Fine," the king said. "And the Podebradan and the priest, let's all go together. Gods, I should go fourth, so if one of you slips, you don't fall on me." He sighed. "But no, it's first for me, in case only one gets through. My men will provide covering fire in the event that we are noticed."

Cathy saw that the Ophidians Ritter had brought with him were chopping down trees to erect a small defensive wall facing down the back side of the hill.

What the king had said was true; it was madness to enter a cave that was under siege. Cathy took a deep breath.

"Here is the technique," the king said. "The middle of the rope around a tree trunk, and then one length under each armpit, so. Forgive me, ladies, for using the word *armpit*, it is indelicate, but I will use even more shocking language anon."

"I will stand the shock," Cathy said.

"Very good." The king nodded. "Bring the two lengths in front of you, stepping over each length to the outside, so. Then run the two halves of the rope together under your groin."

"Shocking," Cathy said. "Be careful, I may swoon."

"I am glad that you are dressed in the Turkish fashion, Mrs. Filmer, as I do not believe this maneuver is compatible with the wearing of a skirt. You, Tarami, will have to hitch that robe up around your waist, so I hope you are wearing underdrawers. Collect the two ropes in your right hand. Wrap them around your forearm." The king demonstrated. "You will be able to walk backward down the face of the rock. If you pull your hand forward, your descent will stop. If you wish to speed up, move your hand back, and away from your body."

"The rope will abrade one's skin," Cathy observed.

"Wear your gloves," the king advised. "Do not let the rope run over exposed skin, if at all possible. Are you certain that you want to do this?"

"Yes," Cathy and Yedera said together.

"No," Zadok said. "But I will do it anyway."

"Try it once on the gentler slope," the king suggested.

Cathy followed his example closely, running the ropes behind her back and between her legs and up around her right arm. She found it reassuring that she could, in fact, walk backward down the gentle slope, leaning into the cradle of the ropes, and feel supported.

Her heart nevertheless beat like a hammer, and the pounding grew faster and harder as she selected a tree and passed the middle of her rope around its trunk, dropping the two ends over the cliff.

Jarom Atheles leaned over the cliff and called down in a stage whisper. "You there!"

Cathy was nervous that his whisper would carry to the Imperials, but she peered out over the cliff top and saw no motion among the soldiers.

Apparently, someone down below answered the King of Oranbega, because he whispered again, "Tell that dreamy-eyed nimbus-head Kodam Dolindas that the spirit of the Lord is coming."

Zadok frowned, presumably at the impiety of the king's words, but said nothing.

"I will go first," the king said. "You can run. You can descend very fast, by simply moving your arm away from your body. But unless you need to, I suggest walking at a measured pace, and staying in the groove of the rock."

Cathy nodded.

"And remember," the king said, "you are at all times just one bad decision away from a violent death. But that's no different from, say, riding a horse."

And with that, the king went down the cliff face. Cathy paid attention to how the king moved. Despite his paunch, the king moved down the rock like a cat, with movements that were short, quick, and confident, and then he was in the opening of the cave, and arms were pulling him into darkness.

Ritter hauled up the king's rope.

"You could just stay here," the Sword said. "We have brought the kings together. Was that not the quest?"

"Move aside," Yedera said.

The Podebradan's motions were not as smooth as the king's, nor as small. Where he had gone down moving from side to side, she raised her braking hand away from her body and plummeted down the cliff, falling in three long jumps directly into the cave mouth. She landed with a clatter of scale mail that made Cathy wince, but the Imperial line continued to be dark.

Ritter pulled up Yedera's rope, too.

"I will go next." Zadok Tarami shuffled forward, turning awkwardly to situate himself posterior first, as the king had shown them, and rucking up his robe to reveal knotted, muscular legs. One step from the edge, he tripped—

and Ritter caught him, wrapped an arm around the priest's narrow chest, and pulled him away from the cliff.

"Are you sure you want to do this?" the Sword asked.

"Whatever is happening down there," the priest said, his breathing fast and shallow, "I must be party to it."

If Yedera leaped down the cliff, then Zadok crawled. Halfway down, his feet slipped and he bumped against the cliff face in sitting position. Mercifully, he didn't let go of the rope, and he descended the last half of the drop scraping against the stone and whimpering.

Cathy checked her anchor as Ritter hauled up rope again. She wound the rope around her right forearm and turned her back to the soldiers, feigning a confidence she did not feel. "I will see you soon," she said to Ritter, and then she stepped over the cliff.

In the middle of the night, Nathaniel woke up. He sat up, looked around, and then looked Margaret in the eye. "I'm needed," he whispered. "I have to help Sarah. I know it's asking a lot, but can you wait here? Can you protect me?"

She nodded, he lay down again and drummed, and then he was unconscious.

But the boatmen would not continue oblivious to their presence forever, especially once the night ended. Before dawn, when Nathaniel had been in his sleep state for hours, Margaret dragged him off the coal boat and into a thicket overlooking the river. That involved wrestling Makwa again, who had been willing to fight at her side more than once when defending Nathaniel, but who also unhesitatingly attacked her when she tried to move her brother.

After the first scratch on her arm, though, she became angry. In her anger, she bowled the shadow bear backward into the water with the back of her hand and then leaped to the shore. By the time Makwa reached her again, Nathaniel was stretched out on green grass beneath a thin canopy of brambles, sheltered from view by a screen of trees and by the height of this small promontory above the Charles.

Sitting beside her brother, she waited.

He didn't seem to be in pain this time. But sitting beside him, doing nothing, bored Margaret, and led her inevitably to wonder what Nathaniel might be doing, and think of things she might be doing instead of watching him, and feel resentment.

At midday, she realized that a building a few minutes' walk down the road and across a hedged-in lane was an inn. She imagined that she could smell baking meat pies.

But if she was only imagining the smell, why not imagine something more familiar, like the smell of *pa amb tomaquet*, or *botifarra*? The meat pies she was increasingly convinced she could smell definitely gave off a Roundhead odor, but the odor was delicious.

She turned her back on the inn.

Throughout the day she sat watch, occasionally drifting into sleep beside Nathaniel, making up in catnaps some of what she'd missed during the night. She wondered about her experience the night before.

Where were Thomas and Julia now? How much of what Margaret had seen had been visible to them, also? Or rather, how had they experienced the fight on the starlit plain, with the creeping plants that had captured Nathaniel?

And then Nathaniel had somehow escaped. And she had no idea how, because he hadn't told her. He hadn't felt obligated to tell her.

Hadn't felt that she deserved to know.

But that wasn't fair to Nathaniel. He had taken her with him onto the starlit plain, and that had ended badly. Perhaps he left her now to protect her.

But he asked her to protect him.

He was perfectly willing to take the time to ask her to watch his sleeping body, which required her to fight his bear-shadow-self-creature, Makwa, and be physically injured. He could take the time to inflict injury on her, for his convenience, but he couldn't take the time to explain what he was up to, or help her understand what she had experienced.

She drifted off to sleep in the afternoon, with the cool spring breeze coming off the Charles ruffling her hair.

She awoke to screaming.

The sky was dark, and Margaret was momentarily disoriented. She had slept longer than she should have, but that was no wonder—she must have been very tired.

Nathaniel was the one screaming. "Sarah!"

"Shh," Margaret urged him, shaking him gently. "Shh." She felt her muscles tighten, and her nerves seem to sing to her like unseen banjo strings, plucked too fast and scraped against the frets to cause a painful buzz.

"Sarah! Don't go!"

"Shh."

But it was too late.

Two riders turned from the lane, pushing their horses through a gap in a hedge. Margaret stood to meet them. In the darkness, at least, they wouldn't see Nathaniel. She would simply say she was waiting here for her father and brother, who were due to return any minute, and claim that the scream had been hers. She had had a bad dream.

But when the two men reached her, she recognized them immediately. They were Stambo and Pottles, of the Philadelphia Blues. By their grins—triumphant and a little malicious—they recognized her, too.

"Why look," Stambo said, "the sweet little Dutch girl who ran away."

"Only it turns out she isn't Dutch," Pottles said. He dismounted easily, and put a hand on Margaret's shoulder. "Where's your brother?"

CHAPTER THIRTY

~*Sarah!*~ Nathaniel cried. ~*Don't go!*~

He stood on the starlit plan, on a spot that, moments earlier, had been a small rise, a mere knob of grassy earth. A tower of glass and gold had erupted from that knob, and then Sarah had emerged.

Sarah looked haggard. She wore a white linen shift, and golden light leaked from her skin. There was crusted blood in the corners of her eyes and her mouth, and she stared at the remote horizon.

Nathaniel heard speech. It sounded distant and fading, but it also seemed to emanate from the tower. ~*Her spirit is yet here. Do not call her dead yet.*~

Sarah took a faltering step. Her eyes and shoulders drooped, her entire body appearing to be on the verge of melting into the grass.

~*Don't go, Sarah,*~ he pleaded.

~*I'm tired,*~ she said, without raising her eyes. ~*I can be finished now.*~

~*You've earned rest,*~ Nathaniel said. ~*You saved me. You saved Margaret. You saved our father's city. If anyone has earned rest, it is you. But your work isn't done. The city needs to be saved still. Our uncle still seeks to murder us.~*

~You were going to heal him.~

~I failed.~

Sarah's shoulders straightened. *~You don't git to go puttin' that on me, Nathaniel. I can't always be the one as has to rescue everyone. No one e'er asked me to do that, and I ne'er offered.~*

Nathaniel's cheeks burned. *~You're right. But no one chooses to need to be rescued, either. Sometimes there are people in need, and there are people who can help. Be grateful that you're someone who can help, and not someone who needs saving.~*

~But I am in need. I need rest. And iffen I walk away, mebbe the Imperials'll leave, too. The people can all go back to their homes and have peace.~

~The people who are with you chose to help you,~ Nathaniel said. *~All of them. They risked their own lives, and their freedom, and their families, to help you. Because they need help. Because the Ohio is in need.~*

~It can be someone else as helps 'em.~ Sarah shrugged. *~It can be you.~*

~I don't think it can.~ Nathaniel took Sarah by the hand. She felt cold, and frail. He pressed his normal ear against hers. *~Listen.~*

He heard the voice of an old man, praying, and with it came the smell of incense. *~Father, there are many mysteries beyond my understanding. If it be in accordance with thy will, I beg thee to raise Sarah Elytharias from her sick bed. And . . . Mother . . . if it be proper to petition thee, I know not. Forgive the unworthiness of this petitioner, and help Sarah.~*

Sarah gasped at the words, and stood a little straighter. *~That's Zadok Tarami. The Metropolitan.~*

~He's your priest?~

~He's a priest, all right. I don't know whose he is. Maybe he doesn't, either.~

He heard two women, speaking softly within the tower. Their voices were undergirded by the sound of rasping metal. A blade being sharpened? *~What are you doing, Yedera?~*

~Preparing for my death.~

~I don't think we are condemned to die. The kings have not given up hope—see, they apply herbs and unctions. The King of Tawa is a healer, greater than any Harvite, and Sarah may yet rise.~

~If she does not, then I shall give her this final service. I shall kill as many Imperial soldiers as I can before they cut me down.~

Sarah sighed. *~That's Yedera. And Cathy. Dammit, I . . . I betrayed Cathy, and she doesn't even know it yet.~*

~I don't believe that.~

~But it's true. I had to make a bargain to come this far, and what I gave away was Cathy.~

~Then take her back.~

Sarah had a thoughtful expression on her face, but she took another step toward the far horizon.

Nathaniel stepped closer, pressed his ear to hers, and listened again.

He saw two people, outside the tower. Sarah saw them too, because she flinched, and then a tear of blood ran down each cheek. One of the people was Luman Walters; the other was a red-haired, raw-boned woman, and they stood locked in an embrace. They trembled, their skin was pale, and water streamed down their bodies, pouring from their own hair. Nathaniel smelled woodsmoke.

~*Can you help them?*~ Sarah asked.

Nathaniel considered. ~*I can try. Will you help the others?*~

~*I'm so tired, Nathaniel.*~

Nathaniel wrapped his arm around his sister and drew her close. She laid her head on his shoulder and he could feel her breath, a flutter against his neck. His horse stood beside him, and with his left hand he stroked the beast's flank. The horse stamped gently on the earth, drawing forth a steady rhythm.

> *I ride upon four horses, to heal I ride*
> *This queen, a mighty hero, by perils tried*
> *Her mortal frame exhausted, and enemies*
> *   outside*
> *I'll bear this hero's burden, to heal I ride*

An unseen weight crashed down upon Nathaniel's shoulders. It was so heavy he staggered sideways, losing his grip on his sister. Strength drained from his limbs, his blood felt cold and slow, and he lost sensation in his hands and feet.

Sarah caught him with one hand, but it wasn't enough to hold him up, and he fell to his knees.

~*Nathaniel, what did you do?*~

~*What I intended.*~ He smiled, trying to appear carefree. ~*How do you feel?*~

~*Better,*~ she said. ~*Lighter.*~

~*Where will you go?*~

Sarah turned and gazed at the tower of glass and gold. ~*Back. My work is not done. And you?*~

Nathaniel dragged himself to his feet. His horse approached, and he climbed into the saddle. Strength flowed from the animal into him, warming his blood, if not restoring him completely. ~*I'll help Luman and the woman.*~

~*Her name is Montserrat*,~ Sarah said. ~*Montse. I believe she was our mother's lover.*~

Nathaniel nodded. ~*Life is surprising.*~

~*Family even more so.*~ Sarah turned and entered the tower.

Montse wouldn't survive until morning. She had stopped trembling and lay cold against Luman's chest. Luman still shuddered. He felt his own heartbeat slowing; he might not last until sunrise, either.

The soldiers had left them alone through the night, busy at their guns and their fortifications, throwing up breastworks of felled trees. Luman and Montse had seen the fire explode around the cliff face, which must have signaled Sarah's arrival—but the trees had kept them from seeing details.

"Luman." His name came from Montse's lips, but it wasn't Montse's voice. It was a deep, mechanical sound, as if someone were using Montse's lungs as a bellows to make the noise, without Montse's cooperation.

He had heard such a voice before.

"Nathaniel?"

"Yes. I am here to help."

"Can you pick locks?" Luman's mind was foggy. "Or get me a pistol so I can shoot the lock off?"

There was a brief hesitation. "Do you have stiff wire, something you could use as a lockpick? Isaiah Wilkes says he might be able to talk you through the process of opening the lock on your cage, but I don't know how to...to take over a body, more than to make it speak. I can't make Montse do the work."

"We have no such wire, in any case." Luman trembled, and leaned against the bars of his cage. "Is Sarah...alive?"

"Yes," Nathaniel said. "The kings are helping her."

"Good." Luman pondered. "You don't have your sister's gifts, I understand. You could not, say, transform Montserrat and me into birds, so we could fly away."

"No," Nathaniel said. "But you have those gifts, do you not?"

"For my great gift of gramarye," Luman said, "I am drained. I used the last energy I had trying to open the lock, and failed. It's wired with silver. And since then, I've been struggling to stay alive."

"Could you exit the cage some other way, with your gramarye?" Nathaniel asked. "For instance, by shattering the wooden floor under you?"

"Opening a lock is a small thing," Luman said. "Breaking solid matter is much more difficult. I don't think I had the strength, earlier, even if it had occurred to me. I certainly don't have the strength now."

"This is our solution," Nathaniel said. "I am going to give you the strength. But I'm not certain I can help you and Montse both, so I'm going to give you power, and then I must ask you to aid her."

"I will place her life above my own," Luman said.

For a moment, there was silence. Luman chuckled softly. Had he, after all, imagined his conversation with Nathaniel? Was he now dying of the cold, and losing his rational faculties?

But then he realized that he felt warmer.

His heartbeat was accelerating.

Montse felt light in his arms.

His first impulse was to warm her, but he didn't know how long this sensation of vitality would last. If he warmed Montse and revived her, but they remained stuck in the cage, he only delayed their deaths.

But what was the most efficient way to escape the cage, the route out that would leave him the most power? He should use natural processes. Move the smallest thing possible, make the least unlikely thing come to pass.

Maybe even simply give a helping hand to something that was inevitable already.

Luman organized his thoughts. Letting Montse lie inert against him, held in place by mere gravity, he touched one finger each to the door's iron hinges. "*Rubiginem crescere facio,*" he said, willing his soul to the work. "*Pluviae labor accelero. Rubiginem invoco.*"

Rust. The iron of the cage must rust eventually, it wanted to rust all on its own, with no help from Luman. The rain and time, eventually, would destroy the iron.

So he would nudge that destruction forward, just a little. Speed it up.

"*Rubiginem invoco,*" he repeated.

The first spots appeared in moments, blotches of dull red-brown barely visible in the dim light. Luman kept his fingers in place and pressed with his will, forcing more energy through his arms and into the iron bars.

The blotches became a cancerous patch of rust that felt rough under his fingers. Luman felt his strength begin to slip, but he dared not let up. "*Rubiginem crescere facio.*"

The rust spread. It had engulfed both hinges, and now began racing up the bars to which the hinges were bolted. Luman carefully lay Montse in the corner; she sat crumpled like balled-up paper, the army coat draped over her as best Luman could manage.

He gripped the door with both hands and yanked.

With a mighty screech, the hinges snapped and the door bent inward. Luman yanked again and it came closer. Then he put his back against the iron bars on the opposite side of the cage and kicked, kicked, and kicked a third time, and finally the door snapped entirely free of its frame and fell out, rattled down the front of the cart, and splashed into the mud.

Luman lifted Montse and carried her out. His eyes picked out the shadowy forms of tents in the forest, and he headed for a cluster from which there came no sound, and where he saw no signs of motion. Finding an empty tent, he was tempted to simply occupy it, but the soldiers who slept inside might return, so instead, he stole two bedrolls. He found two dry coats, and dressed Montse and himself.

He carried Montse and the two bedrolls a quarter mile into the forest, away from the hill and the cave and probably Sarah, until he found a stand of trees knitted so thickly together that the ground beneath was merely wet, and not a pit of mud. There he stretched out one bedroll and laid Montse upon it. Sitting beside her, he covered them both with the second bedroll, and then he began chanting, willing all the strength he could through his limbs and into hers.

"*Vitam do,*" he chanted. "*Calorem do. Animam do.*"

❖   ❖   ❖

When Cathy had untangled herself from the ropes she had used to descend, she found herself staring at a strange scene.

Twenty Anakim stood about the cave in a loose ring, heads bowed and hands clasped before themselves in a gesture of humility. They hummed, a single, unified, low note.

Within the ring knelt the seven Ladies of Tendance. Cathy ground her teeth and managed to keep a look of disdain from leaping to her face at the sight of the Lady Alena, who bowed her head and shook a sistrum. She and the other priestesses also sang, and also without words, but a higher, more melodic line that didn't seem as if it should harmonize with what the giants were doing, but nevertheless did.

Beyond the two circles, she saw faces. People huddled against the walls of this cavern, and in a passage that led deeper underground, where she saw the lights of fires. She recognized Kinta Jane Embry and the two men who had accompanied her to Cahokia, but most of the faces were Ophidians and strangers.

Within the circle, two people stood apart from the others. One was Yedera, the oathbound Podebradan. She rested with one hand on the hilt of her scimitar, scowling as if she dared anyone to interrupt the proceedings. The second person was Zadok Tarami, who waited in the corner with arms folded and head bowed, murmuring.

In the center of the circle rested the Serpent Throne. The six kings of the Ohio stood, three to each side. Sarah lay on the throne, and she had been dressed in robes such as Cathy had never seen. They glittered, and were woven of multiple colors—blue, purple, crimson, and white—and the effect was that Sarah shone in an array of many colors, like a rainbow.

On her head she wore the Sevenfold Crown.

Sarah's face and her hands and bare feet looked pale to the point of being white. Cathy stared for long seconds before she saw Sarah's chest rise slightly, indicating life.

The seven lamp bowls of the Serpent Throne were filled, not with oil, but with burning incense. The smell was thick and resinous; Cathy instantly felt light-headed, and the edges of her vision faded into a golden glow.

She had walked in on the middle of a rite. Of *the* rite, it seemed, the Serpent Daughter Anointing.

Kodam Dolindas spoke, and his words had a melody to them. "And there shall come forth a rod out of the stem of Jesse, and a Branch shall grow out of his roots."

"And the spirit of the Lord shall rest upon him," Jarom Atheles added. He reached over to place a hand on Sarah's brow.

"The spirit of wisdom," sang another of the kings. Cathy didn't recognize him, so he must be from Adena or Koweta. He, too, placed his hand on Sarah's head.

"And understanding, which is her son." Kodam Dolindas added his hand.

"The spirit of counsel," Sarah herself croaked.

"And might, which is the great lady." This from the other king Cathy didn't recognize, and he put his hand in.

"The spirit of knowledge," Ordres Zondering said.

"And of the fear of the Lord," the King of Talamatan said. The last two kings added their hands in to the anointing.

The Lady Alena rose slowly to her feet, but the

King of Tawa looked at Cathy. "The spirit of counsel does not have the strength to hold the anointing cruse. She has asked that the Lady Cathy Filmer perform the physical act."

Cathy took a deep breath and exhaled slowly. She did not look at Alena, she did not let triumph touch her face, she tried not to let the sensation of victory or acceptance even touch her heart. She had been offered a chance to serve.

She must take it.

She stepped forward and was admitted into the circle. The King of Tawa reached toward her with his free hand, offering her a small, red clay cruse. He nodded toward a shelf at Cathy's knee height, formed by a flat space on the neck of one of the golden serpents. Cathy stepped up and held the cruse ready.

She did not look at the Lady Alena.

The King of Tawa continued. "And shall make him of quick understanding in the fear of the Lord: and he shall not judge after the sight of his eyes, neither reprove after the hearing of his ears."

Cathy watched the king closely, and saw him looking at Sarah. He was directing her with his eyes, and she followed his direction, anointing first Sarah's forehead, touching the first two fingers of her right hand to the oil and then to Sarah's face, just below the iron rim of her crown. Then she anointed each of Sarah's eyelids, and then each of her ears.

The assembled kings nodded and smiled warmly at Cathy.

"But with righteousness shall he judge the poor," the king said, "and reprove with equity for the meek of the earth."

Following the king's eyes, Cathy anointed the back of each of Sarah's hands.

Was Sarah's breathing coming more easily?

"And he shall smite the earth with the rod of his mouth, and with the breath of his lips shall he slay the wicked."

Cathy anointed Sarah's lips.

"And righteousness shall be the girdle of his loins, and faithfulness the girdle of his reins."

Cathy anointed Sarah's sternum, reaching in through a fold in her robe to do so, and then her navel.

"The wolf also shall dwell with the lamb, and the leopard shall lie down with the kid; and the calf and the young lion and the fatling together; and a little child shall lead them."

Sarah sat up. Light flashed from her robe.

Or did it flash from her skin?

Or from her Eye of Eden?

The King of Tawa nodded to Cathy. She set down the cruse, in a small niche formed by the coilings of a golden serpent, and then stepped back. With no prompt from anyone, she knelt.

The priestesses sang:

> And the cow and the bear shall feed
> Their young ones shall lie down together
> And the lion shall eat straw like the ox
> And the sucking child shall play on the hole
>   of the asp
> And the weaned child shall put his hand on
>   the cockatrice's den
> They shall not hurt nor destroy in all my
>   holy mountain

> *For the earth shall be full of the knowledge*
> *of the Lord*
> *As the waters cover the sea*

Sarah stood.

No, she *rose*, out of the seat of the Serpent Throne, turning and straightening her limbs and raising her arms to shoulder height. She radiated light and heat, and she smiled.

She smiled at Cathy.

More singing burst into the room, though it came from no visible singer:

> *For unto us a child is born*
> *Unto us a daughter is given*
> *And the government shall be upon her*
> *shoulder*
> *And her name shall be called*
> *The Angel of Great Counsel*
> *And I shall bring peace upon the princes*
> *And health to her*

And then a burst of light dazzled Cathy's eyes. The light seemed to bounce off the walls of the cave and yet linger, so the entire chamber was left glowing a soft, warm golden color, and in the burst of light, Sarah disappeared.

"Where is she?" Zadok cried, turning and looking, and then pointing out the cave opening. "There—is that the dawn?"

A brilliant golden light shone down upon the Imperial lines, which were beginning to crackle with the sound of gunfire.

"It's Sarah!" Yedera drew her scimitar and rushed up the short sandy slope, jumping out the cave mouth past the startled sentries and onto the scree below.

But was it?

Turning back to the Serpent Throne, Cathy saw that a figure still lay in the seat of the throne, and that figure was Sarah. For a moment, she thought Sarah was dead, and a wave of bottled-up emotion rushed from her heart and slammed against her face, leaving her cheeks burning and her eyes watering.

But then Sarah raised a hand and beckoned Cathy over. The kings stepped aside, and Cathy approached the throne.

"Sarah," she said.

"That is the Messenger of Great Counsel." Sarah's voice was an octave lower than usual. "The Angel of the Throne."

"And you?" Cathy asked.

Sarah smiled. "I am still me. I live. And I am the angel. And I am the queen. And I am the city of the goddess."

"Your Majesty." Cathy bowed her head. "How may I serve thee?"

"You can git these Anakim a-pickin' up my chariot," Sarah said. "I got a battle to fight."

Margaret grabbed Pottles by the wrist with both hands.

"Easy, now." Stambo had a long horse pistol resting across the bow of his saddle. "We've been warned about you, and we're ready. You come with us, nice and slow."

Margaret's breath came faster and her heartbeat

was loud in her ears. She looked back into the thicket
at Nathaniel, who continued to lie still. Where was
he now? Was he healing Sarah, or fighting a battle
with her?

Wherever he was, he had abandoned Margaret.

With his other hand, Pottles produced a pair of
manacles from his pocket. From the dull glint of
distant lantern light on the cuffs, Margaret guessed
they had silver worked into their construction. She
could not surrender, and she had no time to waste.

She ripped Pottles's arm from its socket.

He screamed and fell to his knees. Margaret struck
him in the face with his own arm, and when that
didn't stop the screaming, she hit him a second time
and then a third, and then finally he fell silent.

Bang!

Stambo fired his pistol. Margaret felt the ball strike
her underneath her right arm, but it didn't break her
skin. She turned and flung Pottles's arm. The bloody
shoulder joint of the severed limb struck Stambo in
the throat. He dropped his pistol, choked for breath,
and tried to get control of his horse, which had begun
to buck and leap in protest.

Margaret took a step closer. When the plunging
beast next touched earth, she shoved it violently with
both hands. The horse went over sideways, screaming,
and landed on its flank, trapping the leg of its rider
underneath it.

Stambo screamed, too, and dropped the empty pistol.

Margaret stooped to pick up the gun. It was long
and heavy, a large-caliber, accurate pistol that the
empire gave to its dragoons. A man on foot would be
weighed down, carrying two such guns.

She stepped around the horse, holding the empty pistol by its barrel and hefting it to feel its weight. The animal champed at the night air, lips flecked with foam, but she ignored it. Stambo waved his left hand vaguely at her as if trying to push her away, and with his right hand, he reached for a second pistol.

Margaret cracked his skull with a single blow.

The horse was having trouble rising; something was wrong with one of its legs. Margaret didn't wish the animal any ill, angry and hurt though she was. She tried to free the pistol that Pottles had been reaching for, but it was tied too tightly and her fingers shook.

Finally, she wrapped both arms around the horse's head, braced her feet against the ground, and snapped its neck.

Pottles's horse had bolted. Margaret stood staring at it as it galloped down the lane. Should she chase it? For a moment her body, strengthened and quickened by fear and anger, wished to run, but the feeling passed. She dragged Stambo's mount up to the top of the shoulder and threw it into the river. Then she did the same with Stambo.

When she returned to get Pottles, the dragoon was moving. With his one remaining arm, he was dragging himself away, toward the lane.

Margaret looked past the wounded dragoon and saw the inn. Men stood outside, talking with great energy and looking in all directions into the night. They must have heard the gunshot. And Pottles was trying to reach them, perhaps.

She didn't care if Pottles told anyone about her; she was leaving. But she would do Nathaniel this one last favor, and at least leave no witness to tell the local Roundheads that Nathaniel was wanted by the emperor, and was a dangerous Ophidian subversive, and brother of the witchy queen of the Ohio.

She broke Pottles's neck, too.

Then she walked to the lane. Men in front of the inn saw her and waved, but she ignored them. Turning right, which pointed her in the direction of Polaris, she walked briskly into the darkness.

The Messenger of Great Counsel flew into the air. She was aeons old, and she was newborn. An umbilicus of life and power tethered her to her mortal half, she could feel it. She saw and felt the throne supporting her body, and she heard the words of consolation and wry amusement spoken to Cathy Filmer by her own jaws and throat. She could also feel every blade of grass, every mortared brick, and every nailed plank of her domain Cahokia, many miles to the west.

And below her, she saw Imperial soldiers.

They began firing at her. She saw the plumes of smoke emitted by their weapons and heard the sharp cracks. She felt lead bullets strike her body, and they did not trouble her.

What did trouble her were the two wooden giants that circled in opposite directions and closed in. They had already stomped a broad circular path in tromping back and forth around the little hill. Trees lay splintered and ground to pulp, paths obscured, and meadows ground into muddy pits by the giant, ball-like wooden feet.

Now the giants closed on her, smashing new trails. A tree exploded, sending splinters flying into the backs of men in blue Imperial uniforms, who screamed in

pain and surprise, and then either fell dead in place
or fled. Two small cannons were trodden into the mud
under the crushing weight of one giant; when it lifted
its foot again, the guns were gone.

The Angel of the Throne pivoted. She did not fly
like a bird or a butterfly; she had no wings to flap,
or with which to glide. In flight, she moved like a
dancer, only a dancer who was not limited to two
dimensions of movement.

Although the giants were featureless carved pseudo-
men, with rough faces splattered on with paint, the
angel could see older enemies that lurked within.
The demons inhabiting the wooden giants had no
names in the tongues of men, but they were infernal
warriors, creatures endlessly born and endlessly dying
in the Pit. One might not be dangerous to the angel,
but two together, taking advantage of their beast-like
cunning, might.

She hurled herself toward the giant on her left.

The demon coiled about the automaton's neck and
chest fired three arms in her direction. They struck
her...

And she fell instantly into doubt. Was she the right
person to be doing this? She was the Messenger of
Great Counsel, but Great Counsel had had many
messengers over the centuries, and this particular
Messenger was new, untutored, and unskilled.

But she was all there was.

The words of someone far away echoed in her ear.
*There are people in need, and there are people who
can help. Be grateful that you're someone who can
help, and not someone who needs saving.*

She deflected the attack, moving beneath it. The

demon's maw, surrounded by its many arms, and full of as many tongues as it had teeth, gaped to receive her.

Below, she saw the Serpent Throne emerge from the mountain. It was borne by the Anakim, who shouted, and upon it rode the Queen of Cahokia. From here, she appeared tiny and frail.

Was she too frail? Would the angel's actions, and the wounds the angel must take, injure the brittle queen?

The mouth closed around the angel. She dodged the teeth, but the tongues lashed her. *You are no angel, no force for good. You are a destroyer of all you hold dear. You were forced to choose between two faithful priestesses, and you abused them both. You let your mentor, Thalanes, die. You let Sherem die, and in their deaths, you used both men. You are a vampire, no better than Oliver Cromwell. Sherem killed himself for you. You drove your general, William Lee, from your land, by neglecting him. You did not intervene to stop him from dosing himself on laudanum. You abandoned your city, your goddess's city, leaving it protected only by that ineffectual time-server, Maltres Korinn . . .*

The angel screamed.

The demon lied. The demon lied. The demon lied.

The tongues lashed her, tearing her golden skin from her flesh. How could she justify her presumption? How could she ascend to the throne of the goddess, sinner and vile wretch that she was? How could she think she was anything other than a repugnant sack of blood and bone, that had outlived its usefulness and was now fit only to cast aside?

Below her, she saw the Serpent Throne crashing into the ranks of the Imperial soldiers. Fire fell from her own body and rained down on the fighters in blue. Fire rocketed from the throne itself; consumed by fire, the Imperials held their line briefly, and then fled.

Sarah lay on the throne down there.

She directed her bearers, and through her—as also through the Angel of the Throne—the power of the Mississippi ley flowed and churned.

Behind her came the six Sister Kings of the Ohio, and behind them, people of Koweta. They brandished weapons, and a few of them worked gramarye, but mostly they sang. Their marching pushed forward the Misaabe, who carried forward the throne. All those people placed their faith in Sarah, mere flesh that she was. They chose her, and why? Because the goddess chose her.

And also because Sarah chose them.

The angel, too, chose, had chosen in the first great war before the worlds were and continued to choose from moment to moment, eternally. And she was chosen, a warrior on the side of light.

The demon's tongues wrapped around her and drew her into the monster's gullet. The demon had teeth not only at the opening of its mouth, but lining its cheeks and gullet; it appeared to be all teeth, all the way down, glistening and dripping with the venom of Abaddon.

The demon swallowed her—

and the angel refused.

By the power of her will, she stood her ground. By the same force with which she flew, she chose not to succumb, not to despise herself, and, above all, not to be sucked down into the demon's maw.

"You are not my master!" she cried.

The demon constricted around her, arms tightening and throat muscles contracting to swallow—

and then the monster exploded.

The wooden head of the giant automaton exploded along with the creature inside. Fire from the Messenger of Great Counsel licked along the ball joint of the machine's neck, scorching the splinters and leaving black streaks along the wood. Splinters hurled by the explosion burst into flame, and fiery wooden spears rained down.

The angel reached with her angelic hand and cupped it over the Serpent Throne and those who followed it. The fiery darts struck the back of her hand harmlessly, and she swept them aside.

They would be grateful to her, she knew. And they should be. She was the Angel of the Throne, the heavenly manifestation of the enthroned queen, and she had saved her people. They would worship her.

Pride?

The Messenger of Great Counsel looked down at her chest and saw a demonic tentacle wrapped around it. Pride. She turned, wrenching herself away from the second demon, but further tentacles struck her as she moved, winding themselves around her.

Foolish mistake, pride, but it was the mistake of the angels. It was so easy to say that one was superior to mankind when one was in fact superior. The angel could fly, and was impervious to physical harm. The angel was wise, remembering the mistakes as well as the successes of many centuries' worth of the children of Adam. The angel was both immortal, which was to say, undying, and eternal, which was to say, a member of the celestial court. The angel stood as a peer in the presence of gods and spirits. If Cahokia was to be saved, it was going to be saved by the Angel of the Throne, rather than by its sickly queen.

The tentacles drew her closer to the demon.

The children of men were callous brutes, incapable of thanking those who deserved it. Was it pride to admit a simple truth, that the men and women of Cahokia owed their lives, now and forever, to their angelic protector? They were fools and savages, circumcising each other and murdering sheep. At best, they acknowledged their goddess, but at worst they were infidels and ingrates who acknowledged no one.

The messenger should kill them.

The demons could wait. The demons were not truly the angel's enemies, but only co-immortal, co-eternal beings who came from a different court. The angel could battle the demons another day. First, it should punish the greedy, worthless followers of the Queen of Cahokia.

Punish them and take what they had.

They had been given an Eden. It was not the eternal, the perfect, Undying Eden, but it was a close shadow to it. Their land was fertile and creative and benevolent, and the only obligations imposed on them were the obligations to worship their goddess, and defend the land against the periodic return of Simon Sword.

They had done neither.

They did not deserve what they had. The angel deserved to have it instead.

The demon's mouth gaped, showing teeth and tongues. The Messenger of Great Counsel could smell the rotting venom inside the creature's mouth.

Anger, the angel told herself, naming the attack upon her. *Anger, envy, pride.*

The angel loved the goddess, and she loved the goddess's people, and the goddess's queen.

She moved down into the demon's tooth-filled throat, on purpose.

What cause did she have for pride? If she had greater capability than the children of Adam, it only meant she must bear a greater burden. And their failure was her failure, so where was her right to boast?

What cause did she have for anger? The children of Adam had taken nothing from her. And if they joined her in serving the same goddess, was that not a cause for celebration, rather than a pretext for requiring worship of her own self?

And what cause did she have for envy? She dwelt in Unfallen Eden, singing the song of the salamanders and drinking honey and fire from the goblets of heaven. She had no need of seventy years of bleeding, itching, sneezing, hunger, confusion, and slow decay to find her way into the presence of the goddess. She was there now.

She was always in the goddess's presence.

The Angel of the Throne flew down the demon's throat and through its stomach and exploded out its head. Fine, fine strings of spiritual matter that had been the beast's brain and stomach bile flew with her. The chest of the second wooden giant cracked into two halves and slowly fell apart. One half dropped like a stone, tumbling directly onto a sputtering campfire, within a circle of rain-beaten tents. That half of the chest threw the arm that had been attached to it, hurling the tree-trunk-sized length of wood deep into the forests of the Ohio.

The other half tilted, bent back, swayed in the storm winds, and finally fell.

It carried with it most of the automaton's head, now burning, and an entire arm, and fell toward the Serpent Throne.

Sarah, the child of Wisdom who sat on the throne, raised her hands to ward off the falling rubble—

her people stood firm, around her and behind her—

and the Messenger of Great Counsel swooped back around to intercept the falling wood. She struck it like lightning, like a meteorite, like fire from heaven, and shattered it into a thousand pieces, setting fire to each piece at the same time.

The Queen of Cahokia raised her tiny shield, and it was enough to deflect the burning splinters.

The bodies of both giants stopped moving, feet apart. One was reduced to legs and pelvis; the other retained its chest and arms, though the arms now hung limp at its sides. Both had lost the demon inside that had given them impetus, and both were now transformed into mere hunks of wood.

A cheer rose from the Anakim and from the assembled people of Koweta. The priestesses blew on their horns, an ancient melody of triumph and joy, and the procession turned. Clambering over wrecked Imperial artillery placements and wooden breastworks, they circled the remains of the two wooden giants once, twice, and then a third time before the Kowetans threw lines around the automatons' legs and dragged them to the ground.

"I shall make it with powder and ball!"

———◆———

CHAPTER THIRTY-ONE

Nathaniel descended the seven steps of heaven into his body with dragging feet. He felt ill, weary, and shattered, but also...

Hopeful.

Sarah had lived, he was sure of it. He didn't know quite what had happened that had caused her to assume two simultaneous forms, but he himself assumed simultaneous forms, whenever he left his body to travel on the starlit plain. He assumed three, in fact; his disembodied self, his sleeping body, and the shadow-bear Makwa, which seemed to be another part of Nathaniel.

And now Sarah had done something similar.

One day, he would sit down with Sarah and ask her ten thousand questions. His path was entwined with hers, and they regularly had contact, but he had yet to actually meet her in physical space, and he only felt that he knew half, or less, of the story of every encounter.

But he wouldn't meet her today. Today he was tired, and he would hide and sleep.

He stepped down into his body and sat up. The darkness of night was relieved by a little lantern light across a hedged lane. A swamp of fatigue sucked at his limbs, trying to draw him into sleep.

He hurt; he had been wounded in his chest and in one arm, he wasn't sure when. The wounds were bandaged, which must be Margaret's work.

He shook off the pain and fatigue and stood.

He was stiff and slow as he stretched, looking for his sister.

"Margaret!"

Silence.

On the starlit plain, he had a strong ability to find people by listening for them; could he do the same thing directly on earth, in the Covenant Tract? He strained his ear, but could not hear his sister.

He did hear two terrified voices, men's voices.

~*She's a monster!*~ one cried.

~*Kill her!*~ the second bellowed.

The voices sounded familiar, but Nathaniel couldn't instantly place them.

He picked up his drum and limped through the hedge toward the light. His limbs loosened as he moved, but the weight of what he carried from Sarah and from Luman Walters still slowed him. He shivered, wrapping his arms around himself.

As he approached the light, he saw that it was a lantern hanging outside a tavern. The signboard depicted a blind man in a soldier's uniform, holding a cup in one hand and a walking cane in the other. Men spilled out of the tavern door, puffing and slapping each other on the back.

"Here's another man, Constable!" one of them

bellowed, grabbing Nathaniel by the arm and shaking him. "Press him, too!"

Nathaniel smelled beer and sweat.

"You're not pressed, you idiot." The addressed man, who must be the constable, wore a yellow coat and a dirty neckcloth, and had two pistols stuck into his wide leather belt. "You're part of the *posse comitatus*."

"You get paid!" another shouted.

"I'm not armed," Nathaniel said. "I don't even have a knife." He did have the stone knife of his own creation in his pocket, but even mentioning that would only necessitate a lot of explanation.

"What kind of fool travels without a knife?" Nathaniel couldn't see the speaker.

"He's an idiot drummer boy, poor child," said a third man, who held a thick cudgel. "Clothes on backward and all."

Nathaniel didn't object. Whatever these men were up to, he wanted no part of it. Then a terrible thought struck him. "You're pursuing a criminal?"

"A murderer." The constable rubbed his jowls and neckcloth with a greasy hand. "Killed two men and threw them into the river. Imperial dragoons, and armed men, and it looks like she beat them to death. Even broke the neck of a horse."

"That kind of strength," one of the men muttered, "can only mean sorcery."

"She ambushed them!" a second said.

"I've seen madness that made a man terribly strong," offered a third.

"Eh," the constable said. "So you can see how we've got to do something."

"It was a woman?" Nathaniel asked.

"Witness said he thought so," the constable said. "And she headed north. Listen, come along. You can run errands, carry messages. Not everyone in the posse comitatus has to carry a weapon. If we catch her, there might be a copper penny or two in it for you."

He had failed Thomas, but he felt within himself a determination to try again to help his uncle.

But first, he must protect Margaret.

Nathaniel stepped aside, letting the *posse comitatus* pass him. They turned left in the lane and headed north, Nathaniel stumbling at the tail end of the half-drunk mob chasing after his sister.

The greatest earthquake Cahokia had yet experienced struck it in the early dawn light. Mounds were shaken, houses flattened, and the tremor tore great gaps in the Treewall. Despite the rain, fires broke out, especially in the parts of the city where refugees clustered, from Zomas or Missouri.

Maltres Korinn was organizing the wardens to respond to the fires when the city was hit from two sides. On the eastern side, the defenders resisted for nearly an hour, despite the parlous state of the wall, and despite the fact that the attackers included not only the shuffling draug but also fifty-foot-tall wooden men. On the west, though, beastkind swam in through the gaps en masse.

Maltres reorganized the wardens to fight, and led a street-by-street defense. The Missourians and Zomans joined him, battling fiercely, but they were driven back at a steady pace, leaving their dead stacked in burrows and on street corners. The city's few remaining mages helped, and an allied force consisting of riders from

Johnsland and Chicagoan warriors reinforced Maltres after the initial harrowing retreats. Most of the rest of Cahokia's allies had evaporated before the enemy reached the walls.

By the time the defenders of the eastern wall had retreated into the city, there was scarcely any city to retreat into.

Mercifully, Simon Sword's son Absalom did not emerge from the Temple of the Sun.

"We must withdraw." Arngrim Egilsson looked like a specter of death with his unadorned iron helmet, its nosepiece and cheek guards adding to the skull-like impression he made. The fact that his blue shirt was stained dark purple by the blood of beastkind and of his own men only added to the effect. "North. To your country and mine, Korinn." Egilsson was a landsknecht, holding land under the Duke of Chicago. "There is enough land to shelter the people."

The two men stood in a plaza at the north end of the city. The third man with them was Landon Chapel, who commanded the Cavalier allies stationed in the city; he held the bridle of his horse, but stood beside the others. The city's inhabitants were crushed shoulder to shoulder in that quarter, some standing under roofs but many exposed to the storm.

"But no buildings," Maltres said. "Would they huddle in the rain? Would they fight for the right to squat in my barn or yours?"

"There are no buildings left here to squat in," Egilsson said. "My men and I will retreat now. I hope you will come with us."

Maltres was grateful for the rain that hid his tears. He was abandoning the city of his goddess, and of his queen. Sarah had told him that she saw and heard and felt everything that happened in the city. What sense of betrayal must she feel now? What wounds must she be suffering?

He nodded. "The city has fallen."

"We will guard the rear." Landon Chapel had looked dashing upon his arrival at Cahokia, but the defense of the city and its lands had worn him haggard. His hair hung around his cheeks like bedraggled weeds on a riverbank, and his soaked purple coat looked black in the rain. He swung up onto his horse, a look of grim satisfaction on his face, and rode to join his men.

"We will guard the flanks," Egilsson said.

"It is death," Maltres told him. "You may better serve your lord by riding now to Chicago, to erect your shield wall there."

Egilsson smiled. "My lord is Odin. Death serves *him*."

Maltres gave orders to his wardens. Each man of them counted off twenty civilians, gathered them into a file, and began the march north. The Chicagoan berserks led the way and fought on their flanks, but mercifully, both the Imperial forces and the beastkind seemed more interested in taking the city than in pursuing its citizens.

Maltres and a small troop of his wardens fought with the Cavaliers, counting and sending on the escaping people of the city. The Cavaliers might have done poorly against defensive positions, but neither the Imperials nor the beastkind erected defenses. As they advanced into the city, Chapel's riders hit them from one side and then the other, and then retreated. In his months in the Ohio, the young Cavalier had learned not only the roads and rivers of the land, but the plazas and alleys of its capital, and he made use of that knowledge now. The wardens helped by setting ambushes, where they could, firing onto invading troops from rooftops before fading back toward the Chicago Gate.

And the only giant wooden man that was felled came down when Cavaliers led by Chapel tangled its ankles in rope and tied the rope to a low mound. Even the cannons, while their fire lasted, had no impact on the giants.

Maltres shuddered as he retreated out the Chicago Gate, just ahead of the last squads of Cavaliers, at the thought of what the invaders might do to the Temple of the Sun and its furnishings.

Though not the Serpent Throne.

How did Sarah fare? Had she even reached Koweta? The Serpent Throne hadn't left the Great Mound, to Maltres's knowledge, in thousands of years. The sight of it racing away across the rain-crushed Ohio had raised contradictory feelings in his breast; the unanswered question where it might be now, and whether it had fallen into Imperial hands, and whether Sarah Elytharias Penn, Queen of Cahokia and Beloved of its goddess, lived, caused Maltres to tremble.

If she lived, she was now also the Angel of the Throne. And what did *that* mean?

Beastkind emerged from the flooded Mississippi on the journey north. They were not soldiers, but frenzied, blood-lusting individuals, and Egilsson's berserks and Chapel's riders defended the caravan with ease.

On the first night, Maltres ordered a census. His wardens counted nearly twenty thousand people. That was nothing, he knew, compared to the population of

New Orleans, or New Amsterdam, or Philadelphia, but it was still a city's worth of people. As his wardens counted, Maltres walked from fire to fire, shaking hands with Missourians, and Firstborn, and Zomans, and allied warriors. Exhausted refugees wept on his shoulder, he was offered bread and thin soup and weak beer, and one Zoman woman, lying exhausted on a travois that one of the Cavaliers had pulled behind his horse and holding her newborn son in her arms, told him that the baby would be named *Malter*, after him.

After he had visited every campfire he could, Maltres sat alone on a slick boulder at the edge of the floodwaters and pondered. He nodded in and out of light sleep, trying to gather his thoughts, as well as his strength for the next day's push.

Had his goddess abandoned him? He was not an especially religious man, but he had done his best to accomplish Her will. He had faithfully administered the city, had tried to find it a ruler, and when the goddess had finally revealed Her choice to hold the Serpent Throne, he had promptly supported it.

Had She then abandoned him and the city?

Or did Her return, Her rise, necessarily accompany the rise of counterpart evils?

Or was it that She was rising in response to a world in crisis?

Before dawn, the rain had slowed to faint sprinkling in a thin mist, and Maltres thought he could see the stars of the northern sky.

Olanthes Kuta himself carried the message.

It was designed to be the second piece of information that the Youngstown garrison received. The first had been carefully planted with Logan Rupp; Charlie Donelsen and Olanthes had had a long conversation in the lawyer's presence, over a map of the Imperial pikes in the Ohio. They had agreed to an elaborate plan in which Olanthes and his fellow Swords of Wisdom would ambush Imperial supply trains. Since the Imperial army was stretched all across the Ohio, its supply lines were vulnerable to attack. The plan was spelled out in detail, with various contingencies and possible points of attack, all of which put the attacks south and west of Akron.

The plan was, of course, a complete fabrication.

To do this, Olanthes had had to reveal that he was a Sword of Wisdom. This was a sacrifice he was willing to make—he was under no categorical obligation to keep secrecy at all times, but merely subject to an injunction to be discreet. To exercise wisdom.

And this seemed wisdom to him. The time of open war had finally come.

Now he wore the uniform of an Imperial courier. He wore a blue stovepipe hat and blue cloak, and on the hat was the seal of the courier corps, an image of a man riding a galloping horse. He'd taken the uniform, and the horse, from a genuine Imperial courier that he and his allies had ambushed only hours earlier.

Now the courier and his real messages—missives about progress westward, including the depressing news that Cahokia itself had fallen to Imperial forces, together with unnamed "western allies"—lay in the basement of a burned-out farmhouse west of Youngstown, and Olanthes rode through the town's gates.

He bore the message himself. Impersonating a courier was a serious offense, as was interfering with the mails. If caught, the person carrying out this task was likely to be hanged, so Olanthes would impose the burden on no one else.

Others, over the preceding week, had carried out the other important task, here and at Cleveland and at Akron. One and two at a time, dressed as burghers and merchants and farmers coming to market, and bearing, where necessary, falsified passports and trustworthiness certificates, they had filtered into the Free Imperial Towns of the Ohio and taken refuge. Root cellars and warehouses and ostensibly empty rooms in certain hotels with dependable proprietors had filled up with reliable men. They were not all Firstborn: Charlie Donelsen had sent word into the mountains of western Pennsland and into the Kentuck, and several hundred Appalachee fighters had responded. They were Polks, Caldwells, and Bells, as well as Donelsens, and Olanthes found himself humming the Elector song.

> Look to Appalachee, what do you see?
> The great families of the Ascendancy
> Jackson, Donelsen, Polk, Caldwell
> Henry, Knox, Calhoun and Bell
> Alexander, Houston, Campbell, Clay
> And Graham, thirteen on Election Day

The goal had been to get a thousand fighting men into each of the three Imperial towns in the Ohio, and Olanthes and his allies had easily bested that target. Unseen to most people, the three towns were bursting at the seams.

Since the town watch controlled weapons coming through the gates, more armament had had to be smuggled in. Rifles, spears, and swords all fit nicely into chambers drilled into raw lumber or hollowed into the heavier timbers of large wagons. Weapons also rode into town concealed in new false bottoms beneath carriages, and in a few cases were even hoisted over the walls at night, with enterprising Polks climbing up the ramparts and lowering down baskets on ropes. The Polks who had engineered that particular route took to calling their rifles "Paulines," for reasons Olanthes could not quite fathom.

Olanthes galloped. He needed to deliver his message before anyone discovered that the real courier was missing, and he needed to communicate urgency.

Similar false couriers, bearing similar messages, would be riding into Akron and Cleveland, perhaps at this very same moment.

He rode to the hotel that had been commandeered by the Imperial army to act as its headquarters. The units headquartered here were part of the 2nd Pennsland, and their commander was a Colonel Mortensen. Olanthes had taken care to learn Mortensen's name, and had surveilled him to learn his habits and appearance, so that he could deliver the message at a time when Mortensen would certainly be at his desk, and he could hand the message to Mortensen in person.

He threw the reins of his horse into the hands of a waiting sentry and rushed past him into the building, thumping the messenger satchel that hung from his shoulder. "Urgent communiqué for the colonel!" he shouted.

A maid dusting in the hotel parlor bowed, exposing the top of her white bonnet. He brushed past her, and tried to push his way past the corporal at the bottom of the stairs leading up to the colonel's suite.

The corporal was a slab of beef with black boots and a small-brimmed blue cap, and he would not be moved. He pushed back, and nearly knocked Olanthes down.

"Message for the colonel." Olanthes panted, genuinely out of breath.

"You give me the message," the corporal said. "Then you go water your horse and wait for return messages. That's how this works."

"Yes, of course." Olanthes handed over the message. "Only I was told to wait for the reply. Top priority. A supply train has been attacked."

The corporal turned and marched up the stairs. "You want to ride back with a thirsty horse, that's on you."

The corporal was mouthy, but he was doing his job. Mortensen was also known as a man who did his job, and a man of action. That was why he had the position that he did. He was also thought to be a man who was firm, but not cruel. In better times, he might have been a good mayor of the town, or run some Imperial department with efficiency.

But today, he would efficiently respond to a threat.

A minute later, Mortensen came rattling down the stairs, thick white mustache bristling. He had no questions for Olanthes; the false message had been carefully crafted to contain answers to any question he might ask. The time of the attack—just yesterday. The location of the insurgents: south and west of Akron, precise coordinates supplied. The size of the army: enough to require that Mortensen mobilize his men and join the counterattack, to recover the stolen supplies.

The imaginary attack was described in a way to

match, in general and in some important details, the fictitious plan that had been fed to Logan Rupp. The same forger who had worked with Logan Rupp, now Olanthes's prisoner, had falsified appropriate signatures on all three messages.

Mortensen bellowed two captains from their quarters and began barking orders. Immediate mobilization. All furloughs canceled. March to commence within the hour.

Olanthes would wait. Once the 2nd Pennsland had left, he and his men would easily overpower the town watch and seize Youngstown. If all went well, the same thing would be happening in Akron and in Cleveland. His fellow Swords of Wisdom were already well experienced in smuggling men and materiel across the Ohio; the line of supply would come down from Oranbega, and across the seas. The Swords planned to hold the three towns.

"Is there a return message?" Olanthes asked, when the captains rushed from the hotel with their orders, and Mortensen spun on his heels to return to his office.

"There *is* a return," Mortensen barked, "but *I* shall make it, and I shall make it with powder and ball!"

Calvin Calhoun set a barrel on the ground along the side of Nashville's Market Street, a stone's throw from Town Hall, and climbed atop it. It was an empty barrel, which was the only reason he had been able to push it along, because it was big enough for any two men to stand on. Abraham Calhoun handed up his banner—Andy Calhoun's sleeve, pinned to a ten-foot pole—and Calvin hoisted it over his head.

The crowd surrounding Cal was handpicked. They weren't city people, but hill-folk like himself. They

were overwhelmingly Calhouns, but there was a sprinkling of men from other families of the Ascendancy,
as well as men who had no special family name, but
were on Calvin's side.

Men who were fed up, and ready to stand against
the emperor.

Cal thumped the butt of his standard on the barrel
and waved the banner back and forth.

He raised his voice in pitch and volume to what he
thought of as his preachin' voice, though he wasn't a
preacher; it was a sound that would carry, and, some
said, cut through hardwood.

"They's some of you here as knows me real well,"
he called. "My name's Calvin Calhoun, and I come
here tradin' tobacco and other necessaries on jest about
every market day since I's knee-high to my grandpa.
For some of you, I might a read o'er your corn."

"For some of us," one of Cal's own men yelled, "you
might a borrowed our cattle once or twice!"

The crowd laughed.

"Yessir," Cal said, "I reckon that might be true."

The men he'd brought with him moved subtly.
Some crowded around Cal as if he were a novelty,
staring in order to encourage others to stop and stare.
Others blocked traffic on Market Street, not by any
sort of organized blockade, but by merely standing in
clusters in the street. Frustrated carters and tradesmen
tried to fight their way through, but when they were
forced to give up they stood and watched the spectacle. Others still drifted to the edges of the crowd
and kept their eyes open.

A picked group stood by the door to the Town Hall.
"Iffen youins don't know me yet, that's all right,"

Cal said. "But youins'll git to know me soon enough. And you sure as *hell* knew my grandpa."

"Iron Andy!" Abraham shouted.

"Iron Andy." Cal nodded. He didn't have to falsify the wounded expression that came across his face. "Andrew Calhoun, same feller as signed the Compact, a feller as lived here man and boy. I bet they ain't a man here as ain't had his life touched by Iron Andy. Some of you traded with him. Others sold to him. Some were protected by him, when relations with the Indians got tricky, or when the Imperial hand got a little too heavy in your pocket. Some of you saw him at your children's weddin's, or got a good-luck shillin' from him when you baptized a child, or some of you might even a seen him dance."

A *whoop* came from the back of the crowd; that had not been planned, and it made Cal grin.

A captain of the Town Watch pushed his way to the front of the crowd. His cudgel hung from the side of his belt unthreateningly, but four of his men stood behind him. They had muskets, which rested on their shoulders at the moment, and they looked at the crowd closing in tightly about them with leery eyes.

"Here, what's this all about?" the captain demanded. "You a preacher?"

"No. I'm the Elector Calhoun." Cal thumped the butt of the standard on his barrel again, and looked up at the Elector's sleeve. A fortuitous breeze snapped the standard out to full length. "Here rememberin' my grandfather, and all the love he gave these people."

The watch captain looked left and right, took a deep breath, and nodded. "I was sorry to hear about your grandpa."

"Yeah?" Cal fixed the man with his eye. "How sorry *were* you?"

As he asked this question, his men were slipping into the Town Hall. In the corner of the hall stood the gaol, with its thicker stone walls and the iron bars in its windows. Cal listened for gunshots, and didn't hear any. Did that mean his men had overpowered the guards, or were they being thrown into cells themselves?

"I don't think you want a riot," the watch captain said. "Any more than I do." He spoke Penn's English, but with a twang. The captain might not be a high-lander, but he was no foreigner, either.

"I don't want a riot," Cal agreed.

"Why don't you step down, then, and you and I can have a drink?"

"That's an excellent idea." The crowd stretched up and down Market Street as far as Cal could see. People at the front of the throng passed back accounts of what they were seeing in whispers. "Abraham, can you fetch along a couple of beers?"

But Cal stayed on the barrel.

Abraham pushed his way toward a tavern called the *Tup and Ewe*. The sign was a little rowdy, but the owner served strong liquor and good beer.

Men of the town watch were appearing around the edges of the crowd and at various points within it. Cal's own men were carefully surrounding them, without appearing to. Having no uniform, they blended in among the townsfolk.

"I'd heard you Calhouns were New Light," said the watch captain.

"New Light," Cal agreed, "but not *unreasonable*."

The watch captain shifted from one foot to the other and hitched his thumbs into his belt. This brought one hand close to his cudgel, so Cal hooked his own right thumb into his belt and drummed the four fingers of his right hand on the metal head of his tomahawk.

"Look, I'm being friendly—" the captain began.

"Here's the beer," Cal said.

Cousin Abraham reached the front of the crowd with a foaming mug in each hand. He handed one to the watch captain, who took it warily, and the other to Cal.

"Say," Cal added, "might could we git a beer for Uncle David, too?"

"We keep David well fed," the watch captain said. "And we do give him beer, but only once a day, with his supper."

"That's as may be." Cal nodded amiably toward the door of the Town Hall. "But don't he look thirsty to you?"

Uncle David stood in the door of the Town Hall, holding his boots folded over his forearm. He stood beside Black Charlie; they were surrounded by Cal's men, and one of Cal's Calhoun cousins was already pushing toward them, with two mugs from the *Tup and Ewe*.

Other Calhoun men held the lawyer Logan Rupp in shackles, preparing to thrust him into the cell vacated by David and Black Charlie Calhoun.

"I don't want anyone to get hurt," the watch captain said.

"Hurt?" Cal smiled. "I's hopin' you'd join me in a toast."

"I reckon I can do that," the captain said slowly. "Providing the toast isn't too...incendiary."

Cal raised his mug. "Andrew Calhoun was a hell of a feller. He led, he provided, he defended, and he loved. We ain't ne'er seen his like afore, and we ain't gonna see it e'er again. To Iron Andy!"

"To Iron Andy!" the crowd shouted.

Cal drank.

"To Iron Andy!" Uncle David raised his glass and drank.

"To Iron Andy," the watch captain said, and drank.

Cal handed his mug, still three-quarters full, down into the crowd. "Now, listen. Your men are surrounded. We know who you are, and we got you three to one at least, on every man. We got guns on the mayor and the Town Council. They's still the artillery to deal with, but they ain't gonna turn their cannons around and start blastin' away at the town, now, are they? It's over."

"You think this is political, but it's not," the watch captain said. "You're just committing a crime."

"I'm committin' a whole passel of crimes," Cal said. "And I reckon Tommy Penn might be a-sendin' folks to come try to hang me for it. But since he's already tried to kill me, it ain't clear to me as I'm any worse off. Now, as you and I were both sayin', we don't want anyone to git hurt. How about you git up on this barrel with me and tell your men to lay down their weapons?"

The watch captain sighed and extended his hand to be pulled up.

Etienne stood upon the northern wall of New Orleans and looked down upon the Spanish army. How many hundreds had died, stung by basilisks, drowned in the Mississippi, sunk by the Lafitte brothers and the river forts, or blown to kingdom come by Eggbert Bailey and his engineers?

And still, on the other side of a moat that swarmed with the flying venomous snakes, they lay camped in their tens of thousands.

Lusipher Charpile murmured. The blind man continued to follow Etienne wherever he went. He moved like a man with his full sight.

Or better, Etienne thought, remembering the battle in the St. Vincent de Paul cemetery.

"You are murmuring because they are so many?" he asked his bodyguard in French.

"I am regretting my decision to try to kill the chevalier," the wrestler said. "If instead I had simply hidden among their ranks, I could have reduced their numbers considerably."

Etienne laughed. "You are ambitious, and I admire that. But you have always acted in my service as I hoped you would."

"You still seek the chevalier's death?"

"His destruction." Etienne mused on that thought. What amount of humbling, what punishments, were necessary before he would feel that the chevalier had had enough justice? Merely removing the man from office had given Etienne pleasure, but left him wanting more.

"He wants your destruction, as well."

"Excellent," Etienne said. "That makes our final meeting inevitable."

"He sends assassins."

"That seems fair." Etienne squinted at a crew that was dragging forward cannons, preparing to begin battering the wall. They moved slowly, half of their number pushing forward a thick wooden screen to shield them from the musketballs that Bailey's men hurled at them from the walls, as the other half dragged the long gun. "What does not seem fair is that his ally comes to battle with such bottomless numbers."

"Ah, but then, we have the serpents."

"Without them," Etienne agreed, "we would have fallen months ago. And do you know who sent the serpents?"

"Your gods?"

"In a manner of speaking. Or the deities of a thin, back-talking, strange-eyed girl from Nashville, who seems to live half in this world and half in the world of the angels. I did her a very small favor. In return, she and her goddess have protected New Orleans for months."

"What does that tell you, Eze-Nri?"

"Perhaps that I, too, live half in the world of the angels."

Charpile murmured again, an approving sound.

Eggbert Bailey and Onyinye Diokpo approached along the wall.

"Are your magicians arriving soon?" Etienne asked the hôtelière. "I fear that Eggbert has exhausted our supply."

"Magicians are rare in any people," Onyinye said.

"This is what is so vexatious about New Spain." Etienne nodded. "They have altogether too many peoples in their empire. It gives them an oversupply of battle wizards."

"The Franklin Gate is still open," Onyinye said. "And we are still able to get a few ships past the blockade, from time to time."

"For now," Etienne said, "provided they are small."

"Have you two come up with a plan?" Onyinye asked the two men.

"We have no allies and no money," Eggbert said. "Soon we shall be bottled in entirely, and then we will begin to run out of food and ammunition. I fear we have no alternative."

"No alternative to what?" Onyinye's eyes narrowed.

"We shall simply have to win."

Notwithstanding Schmidt stood once again within the nave of Cahokia's Temple of the Sun. The veil of the temple's sanctuary was drawn open, and the famous Serpent Throne was gone. This struck her as the strangest thing; stranger than the unending storm over the Ohio, stranger than the earthquakes that rattled her step daily, stranger than the flood that had submerged the roots of the western Treewall.

Thousands of years, the Eldritch said. For thousands of years, it had sat immobile, since the arrival on this spot of their legendary founder, the culture hero or demigod or myth Onandagos. Thousands of years of stationary rest, and now the Appalachee witch was riding it about the Ohio Valley as if it were a carriage.

"You have brought the Parlett," Fftwarik said, entering the nave through the door behind her. "Good."

Franklin was with him. The emperor's confidential advisor smiled faintly and nodded at Schmidt. She nodded back.

"I serve my shareholder in this," Schmidt said. Unspoken, but thought: *I do not serve your master, the monster of Missouri.*

Fftwarik nodded, a sly grin on his badger-like snout. Schäfer stepped forward, his hand on the shoulder of the Parlett boy in question. The Youngstown factor had stuck closer and closer to Schmidt since they had arrived in Cahokia, and she had permitted it. Was he nervous about their new allies?

She certainly was.

"My Lord Thomas," Schmidt said, addressing the Parlett.

"I AM HERE," the Parlett said, in an imitation of Thomas's voice.

"Are you enjoying your honeymoon, My Lord?" Franklin inquired.

"IT IS ENDING. WE SAIL UP THE DELAWARE NOW, AND SOON WILL BE HOME. BUT IT HAS BEEN A DELIGHT. IS THE AMBASSADOR WITH YOU?"

"I am," Fftwarik said.

"AND I AM HERE AS WELL." These words came from the Parlett's mouth, but they were not an imitation of Thomas's voice. The voice was deep and sonorous, but there was the shriek of a hunting bird's cry within it, as well.

"AND I." This was again the Parlett, but now he spoke with a voice like shattering glass.

Schmidt met Franklin's gaze and was surprised to see apprehension there. Were they here merely to be witnesses?

And I.

This voice sounded in Schmidt's mind, but it seemed to be a voice behind her. Turning, she saw the Yankee chaplain, Ezekiel Angleton. He had decayed since their last meeting, and was now a Lazar, or something similar. Black pus oozed from his eye sockets, around white, staring orbs, and his nails were long and curved.

"Oh, good," Schmidt said. She longed for Luman Walters's help, for the knowledge that she had a himmelsbrief stitched into the lining of her coat, or for any other magical aid.

Could Gottlieb's leather apron society give her the aid and strength she wanted?

"YOU ARE WITNESSES," the Parlett screeched in his birdlike voice. "SEVEN WITNESSES, IN HONOR OF OUR CAHOKIAN FOE. THREE PARLETTS, MY EMISSARY FFTWARIK, THE DEAD PRIEST, THE MERCHANT QUEEN, AND FRANKLIN."

"BUT NOT I?" shattering glass asked. This must be Cromwell.

"YOU ARE A PARTY TO THE COVENANT," the Heron King said.

The words were deadly serious, but Notwithstanding Schmidt nearly laughed out loud. Watching the hairless young man in blue standing and talking to himself in three different voices had a comical aspect. It was like watching a young thespian reciting all the parts of a play for practice.

We are ready, My Lords, the dead man rasped, and her urge to laugh vanished.

"WHAT IS THE TEXT OF THE COVENANT?" Thomas asked.

"I SHALL MAKE MY VOW FIRST," the Heron King said. "IT IS CONDITIONAL ON YOUR VOWS. THEN THE NECROMANCER. LAST YOU. DOES THAT SATISFY YOUR DESIRE TO CONSULT A LAWYER?"

The Parlett laughed in Thomas's voice. "IT WILL DO."

"IF YOU SWEAR TO ME AS I REQUIRE," the

Heron King continued, "I WILL BEND MY FORCES TO CRUSH YOUR FOES. I WILL OBLITERATE THE KINGDOMS OF THE OHIO AS FORCES OF RESISTANCE TO YOUR RULE."

"YOU WILL GIVE US FREE ACCESS TO THE TEMPLE OF THE SUN," Cromwell said. "AND WILL NOT INTERFERE WITH WHAT WE DO TO THE CAHOKIAN GODDESS."

"I WILL LEAVE THE TEMPLE OF THE SUN AND THE GODDESS TO YOU," the Heron King agreed. "YOU WILL CEASE TO WASTE YOUR TROOPS ON WAR IN THE OHIO, AND WILL INSTEAD USE THEM TO SECURE YOUR REALM ON ITS OTHER BORDERS."

"GLADLY," Thomas said.

"MY STORMS SHALL RIDE WITH YOU," the Heron King said. "MY LIGHTNING SHALL BE YOUR CHARIOT, AND MY QUAKES SHALL HURL YOUR DETRACTORS TO THEIR KNEES BEFORE YOU."

"THAT SOUNDS MORE LIKE POETRY THAN LIKE STRATEGY," Thomas said. "BUT IT IS A POETICS I CAN APPROVE."

"YOU WILL LEAVE THE QUEEN OF CAHOKIA TO ME," the Heron King said.

There was a brief silence.

"I WANT HER DEAD," Thomas said.

"I WILL KILL HER," the Heron King told him, "WHEN I AM THROUGH WITH HER."

"WHEN WILL THAT BE?"

"AS SOON AS POSSIBLE."

"DO YOU EVEN KNOW WHERE SHE IS? I UNDERSTAND SHE HAS BECOME . . . UNEXPECTEDLY MOBILE."

"SHE TAKES REFUGE ON THE SERPENT MOUND. IT IS A FOOLISH CHOICE. THE MOUND LIES VERY CLOSE TO MY REALM."

"VERY WELL," Thomas agreed. "ANYTHING ELSE?"

"THIS IS ALL. I SWEAR IT."

"I SWEAR IT," Cromwell said.

There was another brief pause. "I SWEAR IT," Thomas said at last.

A bolt of lightning crashed through the nave of the temple. It seemed to come from the Parlett, but at the same time it came from, or perhaps it struck, Fftwarik, and Angleton, and Franklin, and Schmidt herself. An arm of the lightning bolt forked into—or out from—the apse of the Temple of the Sun. It struck the back wall of the sanctum, and, for the seconds-long duration of the bolt, Schmidt thought she saw there an open door.

Then the sustained lightning ended, and everyone dropped to the floor.

Thomas rose, unsteady on his feet from the bolt of lightning that had arced from the body of the Parlett in which Oliver Cromwell was housed and had struck him. He extended a hand to help Cromwell rise, too, but the Necromancer ignored his offer and stood on his own.

Sailors raced about them, cursing.

The ship was one of Thomas's, not a yacht, but a three-masted warship, the *Majestic*.

"Philadelphia!" cried the sailor in the crow's nest.

Thomas looked upriver, and saw the splayed, scattered, living collection of buildings that comprised the edge of his capital. His city, the capital of his empire. The Heron King was real, and his efforts to forge an alliance with the elemental force of the god of the Mississippi River had succeeded. The pesky Appalachee, the defiant Cavaliers, the hesitant Roundheads, the bickering French, and above all, the verminous Firstborn, would come to heel.

The sky was only lightly overcast, but lightning cracked across the sky above Philadelphia. It raced in a straight line until it struck, Thomas fancied he could see, the Lightning Cathedral, and there it raced briefly in a circle before disappearing.

From the west came thicker, darker clouds.

> *"Gather close, so I may teach you
> the words you will say."*

CHAPTER THIRTY-TWO

You are with me, My Lord, Ezekiel Angleton said.

"YES." The voice came from the magical remote-talking Parlett boy.

Ezekiel disliked hearing his master's voice this way. It struck his ear as rough, as a crude imitation of the real thing, as this Cahokian temple was a crude caricature of the temple of God laid out in Kings and Chronicles. As the Cahokian bitch-demon was an obscene imitation of a divinity.

He stood in the Temple of the Sun, with the Parlett boy, who had remained there at the command of the Emperor Thomas. Cromwell was with Thomas physically, in another of the Parletts . . . although, since Cromwell lay inside the breasts of other men, could it not just as easily be said that the Lord Protector was with Ezekiel?

Would that Lucy could be with him.

A pang of yearning stabbed Ezekiel in the chest. The cold that numbed his entire body numbed the pain, too, but something else made the pain more vivid, sharper. Some sentiment drifted slowly through his limbs, something that felt almost like warmth.

Was it hope?

The others had all left the temple following the Heron King's lightning strike, as Thomas had directed, leaving Ezekiel Angleton and the Lord Protector.

The throne is gone.

"WE DO NOT NEED IT. IT SAT FOR CENTURIES IN THAT SPOT, SO IT MAY AS WELL BE THERE STILL, FOR OUR PURPOSES."

Ezekiel advanced up the nave. The mosaics were beautiful. He saw them as a landscape depicting the descent from Eden. That made them true, even if the Firstborn used them to tell monstrous lies. All heresy was thus, at its heart.

He hesitated at the steps leading up to the sanctum. Did he dare?

Cromwell pushed past him and entered. Ezekiel shook himself to be rid of the sense of foreboding that hung about his shoulders, and then stepped up into the cubical space.

The walls of the sanctum were of gold. The floor was tiled with precious stones and inlaid with gold as well.

Gold, he said, to exorcise the thought. *Like Aaron's calf.*

"LIKE THE HOLY OF HOLIES IN JERUSALEM," Cromwell said.

Ezekiel felt betrayed. *My Lord?*

"THERE IS SANCTITY HERE," Cromwell said. "DO NOT DESPISE IT. THERE IS SANCTITY, AND SANCTITY IS POWER, AND SANCTITY IS LIFE. IT IS BECAUSE THERE IS GREAT SANCTITY HERE THAT WE HAVE COME."

We have come to make a sacrifice of the Serpent.

Cromwell-Parlett grinned, clapping a hand on Ezekiel's arm. The boy wasn't tall enough to reach Ezekiel's shoulder. "GOD HAS GIVEN US THIS FIRSTBORN TO SACRIFICE."

That was correct, that was the truth on which Ezekiel needed to center. He was doing God's will.

We will bring life to millions.

"FOREVER."

And life to Lucy.

"FIRST OF ALL, MY GOOD AND FAITHFUL SERVANT. FIRST OF ALL, WE WILL RESTORE LIFE TO THY LUCY."

Cromwell stalked about the interior of the sanctum, examining its every corner. What was he seeing, that Ezekiel did not see? What details were revealed to his lore, what secrets opened up to his greater wisdom?

"WE SHALL NEED TIME," he finally said, "BUT NOT MUCH."

Henricia was at war, but it was unclear to Bill against whom.

In part, it was unclear because Bill didn't ask. He avoided the Henrician companies in yellow and orange as they rode along the Imperial pikes, and eventually abandoned the pikes altogether. He rode smaller roads southward, trekking from landmark to landmark on the list that Mary had given him.

In a signless, nameless tavern at a crossroads west of Charleston, a planter deep in his cups finally put a name to Henricia's enemy: Ferdinandia.

"It's the dons," the farmer pronounced in a slurred voice, gesturing grandly with his mug and sloshing beer onto the table. The man was bent and gray and his hand wobbled from liquor, but his eyes were keen. "They joined the emperor's new thing, new what is it?"

"Club?" Bill suggested. "Forum?"

"Alliance," said a second farmer. This must be the other man's son or nephew; they shared the same eyes, but this man was younger, with hair that was mouse-brown and long, coming down to his shoulder.

"Alliance, my arse," the old man said. "It's a new empire."

"You've been reading too many broadsheets," the younger man told him. "News-paper-men are all liars, don't you know that? They just want to sell papers."

"There was that letter from Honest Harry," the old man insisted.

"Honest Harry isn't a real man," the younger fellow said. "Honest Harry is what Chivers the news-paper-man calls himself when he wants you to read one of his essays, and not be angry about the fact that he owes you money."

"He *does* owe me money."

"He's a news-paper-man."

"What new empire?" Bill asked. "What alliance?"

"It's called the Shackamaxon League," the younger man explained. "Thomas—mind you, this is where it gets murky, and all the argument starts, because apparently Thomas Penn was quick enough to see a loophole in the work of old John Penn—Thomas *as the Penn land-holder*, and *not* as the emperor, has announced a new set of alliances. He calls it the Shackamaxon League."

Bill frowned. "He dissolved the empire?"

"No," the younger man said.

"The Appalachee think he did!" the old man snapped,

and then took a long drink. "They've taken back the Imperial towns."

"All of them?" Bill asked.

"Many." The younger man nodded. "Not Providence or Trenton, I don't think. And I'm not certain about the Ohio."

Bill's frown deepened. "So the Appalachee dissolved the empire, suh?"

"That's not what *they* say, either." The younger man shrugged. "Their leader is Calhoun, and he says Thomas has to be held accountable for . . . oh, I don't know. Murder. The Pacification. There's some business of blackmail, and the Chevalier of New Orleans."

Bill laughed. "The thought of Iron Andy Calhoun holding Thomas Penn accountable for his crimes does, I admit, lighten my heart."

"It ain't Iron Andy, though," the old man said. "It's the new one. His grandson."

"Calvin," the younger man said. "A whippersnapper, but a hell of a fellow, they say. Went off to the Ohio and met that sorcerer queen, come back full of fire."

"Yeah," the old man added, "only she's up and disappeared now."

"What?" Bill asked. "What do you mean?"

"I mean I read in the *Post and Courier* that the rebellion had been put down in Cahokia, except that the rebel queen was still at large. There's a reward, if you know where she might be."

"They say she was carried out on her throne," the younger man said. "Like some kind of pasha, I guess."

"The throne?" Bill reached into his coat pocket and wrapped his fingers around the flask of laudanum-laced brandy.

"Aren't you from Johnsland?" the younger man asked Bill. "The earl has men fighting in the Ohio, though I think he's also had some skirmishes with Imperials up along the Virginia border, and I've seen more than a few purple coats down here, fighting the dons."

Bill stared in astonishment. "Hell's bells. I walk away for a few weeks, and the world turns itself upside down."

"That's about the size of it." The old man drained his cup.

Bill produced another small coin, one of his last. "I'll buy you another drink, if you can tell me the way to the farm of a man named Bolger."

Both men gave him directions, and they were similar enough that Bill felt he could find the place.

He rode west deep in thought. He had no reason to believe his informants were especially reliable, but if they were reading the news-papers, then what they reckoned was likely what the men of Henricia in general thought. Had Calvin Calhoun become Elector, then?

And leader of a revolt against Thomas Penn?

But what of Sarah? If her city had fallen, wasn't it most likely that she had simply died, her body destroyed or lost among the dead?

Only that one queer detail niggled at Bill. *Carried out on her throne.* That rang true, because Sarah had been ill, and unable to leave the throne room. It was surprising that a news-paper in Charleston would publish a reference to it—unless Sarah had in fact been carried out of Cahokia on her throne.

And it also rang true because it was so strange. If a person were going to invent a story about the magician-queen of Cahokia, as a tall tale, or to guess at explanations of things he didn't understand, he'd tell a tale of a women who flew, or could escape from chains, or dodged bullets, or killed from miles away with Franklin bolts.

Heaven's footstool, some of that was even *true*.

But that the Serpent Throne, which had never moved in Bill's lifetime—or *ever*, that he had ever heard—should move, was an extravagant tale. It was as if he had heard that Thomas Penn, to evade capture, had picked up Horse Hall and carried it away with him to Acadia.

It had to be true.

But where would Sarah go, carried on her throne?

Bill imagined the bulky golden seat on the shoulders of fifty men. His platoon of beastkind could have done the lifting, when they were alive.

He wiped away a single tear at the thought of their heroic deaths.

Sarah would have to go somewhere safe. It seemed to him that she would go somewhere in the Ohio, but was that foolish? If the Serpent Throne could leave Cahokia, could it not just as easily board a ship for France?

But she would go somewhere that was high ground. The flooding Mississippi made that necessary. So her family estate of Irra-Zostim, for instance, was likely out, as it lay low and close to the river.

The Bolger farm stood in the center of a broad valley that, according to his tavern information, belonged entirely to Marcus Bolger. That was Caroline's husband. There was something fitting about his daughter Caroline coming to live in Henricia, which was still often called *Carolina*. That she should have married a man with land made Bill proud.

Marcus Bolger also appeared to be a man with horses. Bill counted several dozen head as he rode across the valley toward the farmhouse, and a hundred or more cattle. The land was watered by a large stream that flowed through it, and the house that stood back a hundred yards from the road was surrounded by well-tended gardens and trellises heavy with vines.

Caroline had made a home.

Bill stopped at the bridle path that led to the house and watched. Late afternoon sun splashed yellow over two small children playing at the edges of the garden: a boy and a girl. They hid, and ran, and shouted at each other, in some sort of mock war game, like those Bill himself had played as a young man. They were too young for the blood sports that so interested young Cavalier men as they approached adulthood: cockfighting and ganderpulls, racing dogs and bearbaiting.

Though perhaps Marcus Bolger was not a man who permitted such blood sports on his land. Mary had known little of him. Perhaps Bolger had the New Light, or was the devotee of some soft-hearted saint who did not permit bloodshed. Bill wanted a husband who would never touch his daughter with an angry hand, but then, he also hoped Bolger would be a man who was willing to load his guns and step into the night, when such was called for.

He could ride up to the house and find out.

But he didn't. He sat still on his horse, fingers clenched around the flask of brandy in his pocket.

What was holding him back?

"Good day, suh," piped a small voice to his side. Bill turned in the saddle and found himself looking at a boy, perhaps seven or eight years of age. "Have you business with my father?"

"Is your father Marcus Bolger?" Bill asked.

"Yes, suh." The boy had black hair, thick and long, almost to his chin, but he threw his head back proudly and the hair parted, revealing strong cheekbones, an aristocratic nose, and bright green eyes. "I am his oldest child. William Lee Bolger."

Bill tried to make a polite response, and found he had an enormous lump in his throat. Finally, he backed his horse away a step and bowed his head in acknowledgement, doffing his hat.

"Tell me," he managed to say, clearing his throat and sniffing, "what kind of man is your father?"

"He is shrewd," young William said. "He is the best judge of horseflesh in the county, and strikes a keen bargain. It is not for nothing that he is justice of the peace."

"Good God, is he that?" Bill looked again at the house and the garden and meadows surrounding it. "And your mother?"

"She is the most loyal woman alive," William said. "She is wise and hardworking, and if my father can birth the most tangled calf healthy, my mother can make beans grow from solid rock."

"And you, master William?" Bill asked. "You speak like an orator, or, God forbid, a preacher."

"God does not forbid preachers, suh," William said. "But I rather think my father might. He has suggested that I might one day consider studying for the bar. I told him that this seemed an exercise in contraries, Satan being notoriously a lawyer, but he has persisted in his opinion."

"Hell's bells!" Bill guffawed.

He looked one last time at the Bolger farm.

"What is the nature of your business with my father?" William asked.

"I have business with your father and your mother both," Bill said. "Only I see now that I have come too soon. I will be back to conduct our business another day."

"Shall I give them your regards?" William's face was a study in earnestness.

"Not this time." Bill smiled. "I shall give them my regards myself, when my other business is finished and I return. But in the meantime, I give *you* my regards, William Lee Bolger. I hope I shall always have attorneys as eloquent as you when I come myself to the bar."

He raised his hat and inclined his head again, and then Bill rode west.

He knew where he could find Sarah.

As soon as he was out of sight of young William, he opened his flask of cherry brandy, pouring its contents out onto the side of the road. Tossing the empty flask aside, he pulled the small glass bottle of straight laudanum, that he used to lace his brandy, from his pocket. He emptied and discarded that, as well.

His legs hurt him, and he welcomed the pain.

He rode north and west, bound for the Ohio and the storm.

The sky over the Serpent Mound was a brilliant summer-blue, though clouds roiled to the north and east, and muddy water surrounded the bluff on three sides. It was the first clear sky Cathy Filmer had seen in weeks.

"What does it mean?" she murmured to Zadok Tarami as they rode toward the bluff.

"Eh?" Zadok stumbled out of a deep reverie at her question. He had been trapped with his own thoughts since the battle at the Kowetan cave. Did he worry for the fate of his city, Cahokia? Was he simply deep in thought over what he had seen?

Cathy hadn't had the will to explore those thoughts, struggling as she was with her own fears. Where was Bill? Where was Landon? How did her son and her husband, both separated from her by walls of flood and fighting, fare?

But the sight of clear blue sky shook her out of those thoughts, and now Zadok looked up at the heavens with her.

"I do not know." The Metropolitan's voice sounded ten years younger. "But surely it must be a good thing. And you will have noticed that the ground here does not shake, either."

The long, slow incline that carried them to the base of the bluff, and the stone road that climbed to its peak, was now hedged in by floodwater on the right and left, turned thus into a causeway connecting the Serpent's Bluff, now the Serpent's Island, to the mainland.

In the flooded junction of the rivers, which now seemed an inland sea, a small sailing ship rode at anchor. Cathy didn't recognize it, but Montse's step acquired a new spring at the sight of it, and she began to whistle.

The darkness of night lay over the Serpent Mound like a blanket. The night made the storms over the

Ohio seem distant in space and time, notwithstanding the flood water surrounding the bluff.

Kinta Jane Embry stood with Ma'iingan, Tim Dockery and the giants Mesh and Udu. The rest of the giants stood slightly behind them, and they all faced the Serpent Throne. Mesh's dogs were with the giants—had they run with the Serpent Throne across the Ohio? But the shu-shu were nowhere to be seen.

The throne sat on the circular mound within the jaws of the long, winding mound of earth that was the serpent. The raised oval struck Kinta Jane as resembling a snake's egg, borne carefully within the jaws of the snake itself.

Sarah lay on the throne. She was awake, and her regalia, including the Earthshaker's Rod, lay across her lap. Their physicality, their concreteness, served to emphasize her frailty and her fading physical presence. Her breaths came with effort, and occasionally she was racked with coughing fits, at the termination of which she spat blood.

But about her and above her hovered a shimmering presence in the air, like a gossamer veil so thin it was barely visible. In moments when Sarah's words were most intense and her gaze hardened, the veil seemed to thicken, too, and become a personage that enveloped her, moving when she moved, speaking when she spoke.

That was the Angel of the Throne.

For the moment, the angel was quiet, but it gave off light, adding its glow to the illumination of the bonfires farther down the hill, around which huddled the refugee Kowetans. The six kings stood arrayed around Sarah's throne, looking variously somber, resolved, exhilarated, and exhausted.

"Seek your Kanawha," Sarah said. "I give you my blessing."

"We had hoped for more than a blessing," Udu said. "We had hoped for the gift of your vision. We had hoped for guidance."

"Though we are undeserving worms," Mesh added, bowing.

Sarah nodded. "I wish I could give you aid, but I have looked for your Kanawha and I cannot find it. Now all my force is bent to keeping this shattered form alive until I can accomplish the last task that is given to me."

Mesh and Udu both bowed. "We have had enough vision in your presence already, Your Majesty," Mesh said.

Sarah turned to the children of Adam. "You will go with the Anakim?"

Kinta Jane nodded. "We are sworn to oppose the Heron King, even if the Conventicle is shattered."

"Not the Heron King," Sarah said. "Simon Sword."

"Yes." Kinta Jane inclined her head in acknowledgement. "We would like to empower Mesh and his people as an ally."

"Henh," Ma'iingan said. "It seems the world of the spirits will not leave me alone."

Sarah nodded, and looked back to the giant. "How will you find the place?"

Kinta Jane had not known the witch queen long, but those words still pierced her heart.

"We will seek help," Mesh said. "We have some signs to follow."

Sarah looked a long time at the giant. The Angel of the Throne coalesced about her, giving golden color to her pale skin; seen through this veil, both of Sarah's eyes seemed to flash icy white. "I do not see the future, Mesh," she said slowly. "But I see in you determination and great strength. If any man can make his destiny, and the destiny of his people, then that man is you."

Mesh bowed his head. "Thanks from such a groveling creature as I, a mere varmint, as you might term me in the Appalachee, can scarcely mean anything to the mighty queen and magician that you are. Nevertheless, I give them to you with my whole heart."

"Mesh," Sarah said. "Shut up and go."

Luman stood with Cathy and Zadok, before Sarah and to her right. To each side of the throne stood three of the kings of the Ohio, and before Sarah and to her left stood the seven Ladies of Tendance, and the Lady Alena's eunuch mouthpiece.

Sarah had summoned Luman, Cathy, and Zadok first, and told them where to stand, so the staging was deliberate. That it was also a snub was evident from the look of shock and outrage on the Lady Alena's face.

"Say nothing," Sarah told the Lady Alena's eunuch. "I am not here to bargain or inquire, and you are not here to petition. You have come to the mountain, and you shall hear the law."

"But you swore—" the eunuch began.

Sarah suddenly flashed golden, and seemed to be twenty feet tall, with golden skin, six wings, and a retinue of flaming salamanders. "*Dormi!*" she shouted. The word rolled like thunder across the top of the bluff.

The eunuch collapsed.

The cloak of power that was the Messenger of Great Counsel faded again into a shimmer.

"I committed," Sarah continued, "that I would not, in my mortal life, appoint Cathy Filmer as a Lady of Tendance."

Luman gasped. Sarah's appearance was so frail that any reference to her mortality or death made him fear she was announcing her imminent demise. He found he was holding his breath, and forced himself to exhale.

The Ladies of Tendance bowed their heads. In the light cast by the distant bonfires and the angel itself, Luman could see the clenched jaw muscles of the Lady Alena.

"I will keep that vow," Sarah said. "As I will keep my promise to permit you your eunuchs. Understand this, though. In the future, there will be no bargaining. If I require something of you, Alena, you will give it. If you do not, I will replace all seven of you with women of my choosing, and you will be cast out of the presence of the goddess forever. Is that clear?"

Slowly, woodenly, the Lady Alena nodded.

"I have need of close counsel," Sarah said. The salamanders seemed to echo her words, giving them a deep bass, and yet feminine, undertone. As she spoke, the angel again coalesced about her. "Today I am constituting a new quorum of my priesthood."

Her priesthood? And Sarah threatened Alena with casting her out of the presence of the goddess—rather than out of Sarah's presence?

To what extent did Sarah see herself as one with her goddess?

Luman smiled and tried to look calm.

"My High Council shall contain as many counselors as I shall from time to time require," Sarah said. "They shall advise me, and they shall share in my powers of government. Today I appoint ten counselors. Each of the six Sister Kings of the Ohio is a counselor. I also appoint Cathy Filmer, Zadok Tarami, and Luman Walters."

The Lady Alena shrank visibly.

"The duties of the Ladies of Tendance shall not be in any way diminished," Sarah said. "Nor shall they be any further magnified. At this time, Alena, you and your quorum are dismissed."

The Lady Alena and her sisters bowed. The gathered up the fallen eunuch with some effort, and dragged him away down the hill.

"Ten counselors," Cathy said. Her voice was as cool and collected as ever. "Your Majesty, are you the tenth member of the High Council?"

"The tenth member of the High Council," Sarah said, "is my father, Kyres Elytharias."

An astonished mumur ripple through the six Sister Kings. Luman's knees wobbled, knocking together.

"I do not have the strength to rise from this seat to anoint you," Sarah continued, "but that is no barrier. You shall anoint each other. Gather close, so I may teach you the words you will say."

The kings left, some to sleep, with plans to travel the next morning, but Tawa and Koweta and Adena said their farewells, announcing they planned to leave together.

Sarah drifted in and out of sleep. Her goddess's salamanders sang to her, a deep, wordless song of soil and leaf and rain, and she felt, in her sleep, as if she were suspended in a vat of honey.

The Messenger of Great Counsel stood beside her

and above her. Her father stood beside her bed, and when she was awake, they spoke.

"You know that there remain two things to do," he said.

"And then I can rest?" she asked.

"I am not stopping you from resting."

"I know I have to marry Simon Sword," she said. "Ain't that ironic? The thing he rushed to offer me, marriage, is the only thing that can defeat him."

"Not marriage, exactly."

"His son," Sarah said. "His son has to be enthroned as Peter Plowshare. My son and his, because only I can give birth to Peter Plowshare. That is the pact Peter Plowshare made with Wisdom. All other pacts— John Penn, Onandagos, Ben Franklin—are secondary to that one."

"It's an ancient covenant," her father said. "It holds the world together."

"I have to bear his son, and that son has to be enthroned. That enthronement is the second thing I had in mind."

"I do not think it was a mistake for you to reject his offer," her father suggested. "You were not ready, then. Marriage to Simon Sword might have killed you, and two generations might have passed before the goddess could raise another Beloved Daughter. As bad as a year of the reign of Simon Sword has been, consider what forty years might result in."

"Can Simon Sword never win, then?" she asked. "If I fall, then eventually the goddess can raise another in my place to try again?"

"As long as the goddess lives."

These words should have been comforting. They

were not. "Oliver Cromwell and his minions are in Cahokia as we speak," she said. "Wisdom's death is exactly what they seek."

"Then there is a third thing that must be done," her father said. "Cromwell must be defeated."

"My path is clear." Sarah sighed, and the effort of exhaling rattled her frame. "I only wish it were easier."

"As do I," Kyres Elytharias said. "As do I."

DRAMATIS PERSONAE

A very brief description of a few of the personalities of the Witchy War.

Ahmed Abd al-Wahid. Prince-Capitaine of the mameluke order. Sent to the New World to kill the Abbé du Talleyrand and then stayed to assassinate Etienne Ukwu. Initially the leader of a band of mamelukes, who have since either been killed or abandoned Abd al-Wahid.

Absalom. Son of the Heron King and a New Orleans mambo named Adaku Marie Nwozuzu. Absalom was born among the Merciful of Chigozie Ukwu.

Shelem Adena. King of Adena.

The Lady Alena. A senior priestess of the goddess, one of the seven Ladies of Tendance. Alena keeps a vow of silence, speaking through a eunuch.

Ezekiel Angleton. A Martinite preacher and Thomas Penn's chaplain. Angleton is also a wizard, and tried to capture Sarah for his master when her location was discovered. Having made a pact to serve Oliver Cromwell, Angleton is now a more powerful magician, and is also undead.

Jarom Atheles. King of Oranbega.

Ayaabe. Ma'iingan's son, twin brother of Miigi-wewin.

Eggbert Bailey. Former soldier with Andrew Jackson in his invasion of New Orleans, then a gendarme. Recruited by Monsieur Bondí to lead the revolt of the gendarmes against the Chevalier of New Orleans.

Belladin. Companion of Auntie Bisha.

Auntie Bisha. A Zoman Ghostmaster recruited by Gazelem Zomas to help him find Zomas's Earthshaker's Rod.

Caroline Lee Bolger. Daughter of William and Sally Lee. Married and lives in Henricia.

Monsieur Bondí. Creole accountant and employee of Etienne Ukwu.

Parson Brown. Family priest to William Lee in Johnsland.

Yevgeny Bykov. New Muscovite gunrunner rescued from Absalom by Chigozie Ukwu and the Merciful.

Uris Byrenas. Counselor to Alzbieta Torias. Murdered by turncoat wardens.

Andrew "Iron Andy" Calhoun. One-armed war hero, signer of the Philadelphia Compact, and the Calhoun Elector. A prominent voice for restraining the powers of the emperor and a personal critic of Thomas Penn.

Andrew "Young Andy" Calhoun. A Calhoun young'un.

Calvin Calhoun. Iron Andy Calhoun's grandson. Cattle rustler and former corn reader. Cal accompanied Sarah in her flight from Nashville up to the night when the goddess selected Sarah as her Beloved. Having inadvertently shed blood on the Serpent Throne, Cal was not allowed to witness Sarah's selection, and he fled in grief.

David Calhoun. Son of Iron Andy Calhoun and father of Young Andy Calhoun.

Jedediah Calhoun. Also called Jet Calhoun. Calhoun cousin and cattleman, not from Calhoun Mountain.

Jeffrey Simmons Calhoun. Tyler of the Calhoun Mountain Lodge.

Landon Chapel. Illegitimate son of Earl Isham and Cathy Filmer. Charles Lee challenged him to a duel and Landon killed Charles before the duel could begin.

Achebe Chibundu. Igbo wrestler who performed under the name Lusipher Charpile. Part of Onyinye Diokpo's extended family, he is the bodyguard of Etienne Ukwu.

Granny Clay. Member of the Calhoun clan near Nashville. Dispenser of folklore and sometimes hexes.

Reuben Clay. Senior Hansard trader of Parkersburg. Was pressured by Notwithstanding Schmidt into a corrupt bargain, in which he would refuse to sell to the people of Adena, and would sell instead to Imperial agents, for a bribe.

Oliver Cromwell, the Necromancer. Undead secret patron of Thomas Penn who seeks to end death for all mankind, no matter how many Firstborn must be sacrificed to achieve that end.

Dadgayadoh. Haudenosaunee trader of the Imperial Ohio Company who was killed and then reanimated as a draug by Robert Hooke. He was destroyed at the Siege of Cahokia.

Josiah Dazarin. Cahokian priest who is promoting the reverence of Jock of Cripplegate as an Eldritch saint of martyrdom.

Koiles Delet. An Adenan shopkeeper and patriot, owner of the Giant of Adena dry goods store.

Timothy Dockery. A Pennslander frontiersman and member of the Conventicle.

Kodam Dolindas. The King of Tawa, a magician and healer.

Charlie Donelsen. The Donelsen Elector and friend of Iron Andy Calhoun.

Onyinye Diokpo. Igbo hôtelière with an extended family network of trade connections. A member of the New Orleans City Council, sided with Etienne Ukwu in provoking the tax rebellion that led to the revolt of the gendarmes.

Renan DuBois. Plantation owner, with lands on Louisiana's borders with the Cotton Princedoms. A member of the New Orleans City Council, sided with Etienne Ukwu in provoking the tax rebellion that led to the revolt of the gendarmes.

Kyres Elytharias. The Lion of Missouri. Military hero, King of Cahokia, and Imperial consort. Elytharias was murdered by a conspiracy led by his brother-in-law, Thomas Penn. With his dying blood, he anointed three acorns and sent them to his wife, Hannah Penn. After eating the acorns, Hannah conceived her three children.

Kinta Jane Embry. Choctaw conspirator, member of the Conventicle, which cut out her tongue. Sister of René du Plessis and a member of his cell. Watched the prison hulks of the Chevalier of New Orleans, and witnessed there the return of Simon Sword. Traveled north to warn the Conventicle, and was met by Isaiah Wilkes, who took her to bear witness of what she had seen to Thomas Penn, as Brother Onas. When Penn failed to respond, she and Wilkes headed toward Acadia to try to meet up with Brother Anak and Brother Odishkwa.

Ferpa. One of the leaders of the Merciful. A large, cow-headed woman married to Kort.

Fftwarik. Beastman emissary of Simon Sword.

Montserrat Ferrer i Quintana. Catalan smuggler and pirate, captain of the *Verge Caníbal*.

Intimate friend of Hannah Penn, took the infant Margaret Penn into her care and raised her as a niece.

Catherine Filmer. Studied to become a healer, one of the Sisters of St. William Harvey, then fled to the western powers of the empire. Serves the goddess as a priestess, and is betrothed to William Lee.

Temple Franklin. Grandson of the Lightning Bishop Benjamin Franklin, Temple is the confidential advisor, spymaster, and machiavel of Thomas Penn.

Fridrich. A captain of the Cahokian wardens.

James Goram. Adenan patriot who took the place of Shelem Adena in his confinement.

Roland Gyanthes. King of Talamatan. Wears a Tyrolean hat and has a great mustache.

Robert Hooke. Also called the Sorcerer. Chief of the Lazars of Oliver Cromwell, undead servants dating to the time of Cromwell's reign in England. Hooke pursued Sarah from Nashville to New Orleans and then was lured into a trap she set on the Mississippi River. Luman Walters inadvertently freed Hooke from that trap while attempting to summon a familiar for himself. Hooke participated in the Siege of Cahokia, and was destroyed when Sarah ascended the Serpent Throne.

Jacob Hop. Born a deaf-mute, Hop was inhabited for a brief time by Simon Sword. The experience left him with accelerated powers of learning, including learning languages. Hop was murdered by Temple Franklin, and is now one of Nathaniel Penn's familiar spirits.

Holahta Hopaii. Choctaw holy man. A member of the New Orleans City Council, sided with Etienne Ukwu in provoking the tax rebellion that led to the revolt of the gendarmes.

George Randolph Isham. Heir of the Earl of Johnsland. Nathaniel Penn was raised with George.

Noah Carter Isham. The Earl of Johnsland. Earl Isham was driven mad by the death of his son Richard, and believed himself to be a bird for some fifteen years. He was restored to health by Nathaniel Penn.

Richard Randolph Isham. Earl Isham's son, killed in a duel by William Lee.

Father Jean-Claude. Oranbegan priest.

Josep. Catalan smuggler and pirate. Mate of the *Verge Caníbal*.

Eoin Kennedie. Gangster and fence. A member of the New Orleans City Council, sided with Etienne Ukwu in provoking the tax rebellion that led to the revolt of the gendarmes.

Heron King. The god of the Mississippi and the Ohio, he exists in the alternating father-son dyad Peter Plowshare and Simon Sword.

Maltres Korinn. The Duke of Na'avu, former Regent-Minister of the Serpent Throne and, after Sarah's selection as the Beloved of the goddess, Vizier of Cahokia.

Kort. One of the leaders of the Merciful. A large, bison-headed man married to Ferpa.

Aha Koweta. King of Koweta, and a magician.

Olanthes Kuta. Firstborn warrior formerly in the service of Alzbieta Torias. During the Siege of Cahokia, Kuta was one of the riders who successfully broke through Imperial lines to carry a call for help to Appalachee. He is now in Philadelphia, supporting the effort to impeach Thomas Penn.

Charles Tazewell Lee. William Lee's son, a promising cavalry officer killed by Landon Chapel.

Mary Lee. Daughter of William and Sally Lee. Lives on the farm in Johnsland where William was a boy.

Sally Tazewell Lee. William Lee's former wife.

William Johnston Lee. Cavalier soldier, formerly captain of the Imperial House Light Dragoons. Lee hid Nathaniel Chapel in the household of the Earl of Johnsland and then spent fifteen years making a living as Bad Bill, a notorious thug, in New Orleans. General of Cahokia's armies.

Lieke. Body servant to Julia Stuyvesant.

Kimoni Machogu. The Prince of Shreveport. Since the return of Simon Sword, his lands are overrun by rampaging beastkind.

Ma'iingan. Ojibwe man. To save his son Miigiwewin, Ma'iingan rescued Nathaniel Penn when he was injured in the wilderness, and participated in Nathaniel's ascent into the starlit plain.

Chu-Roto-Sha-Meshu (Mesh). A prince of the Misaabe, the red-headed giants of the north. He seeks his people's legendary homeland, Kanawha.

Miigiwewin. Also called Giimoodaapi. Twin brother of Ayaabe. Born too late to be properly adopted into the People, he received the unorthodox name Giimoodaapi ("he laughs in secret") from his uncle. After Nathaniel Penn and his father Ma'iingan successfully adopted him into the People, Ma'iingan gave him the second name Miigiwewin ("gift").

Miquel. Josep's younger cousin. A sailor on the *Verge Caníbal*.

Onacona Mohuntubby. Cherokee Imperial army officer who escorted three of the five Parlett quintuplets to Notwithstanding Schmidt in the Ohio.

Gaspard Le Moyne. The Chevalier of New Orleans. Provoked an Imperial dragoon officer into murdering Chinwe Philippe Ukwu. After his gendarmes revolted, he withdrew from New Orleans and joined a besieging army from New Spain.

Adaku Marie Nwozuzu. New Orleans Vodun mambo who cooperated with the Chevalier of New Orleans in fighting Etienne Ukwu. Marie voluntarily had the child of Simon Sword, Absalom, and did not survive giving birth.

Elsa Nwozuzu. Mother of Adaku Marie Nwozuzu.

Solomon Nwozuzu. Cooper, and father of Adaku Marie Nwozuzu.

Ira Oldham. Imperial Ohio Company trader. Said to be good with a knife. Was left in Parkersburg by Notwithstanding Schmidt to keep an eye on Reuben Clay.

The Parlett quintuplets. Five identical brothers who share a single soul, and who are used as a communication device between Thomas Penn and his servants in the Ohio and elsewhere.

John Parshall. A soldier of Johnsland.

Hannah Penn. Empress and Sister Onas after her father. Married the King of Cahokia, Kyres Elytharias. Thomas successfully had Hannah sequestered as a madwoman after Kyres's murder. Hannah gave birth to triplets Margaret, Nathaniel, and Sarah, after eating three acorns smeared with Kyres's blood. Years later, when he learned of the birth of the children, Thomas tortured Hannah to death.

Margaret Penn. Daughter of Kyres Elytharias and Hannah Penn. Raised by the Catalan smuggler and pirate Montserrat Ferrer i Quintana as her niece, aboard her ship the *Verge Caníbal*. Margaret possesses great strength and can shrug off fearsome blows when she is angry or afraid.

Nathaniel Penn. Son of Kyres Elytharias and Hannah Penn. Raised by the Earl of Johnsland as a foster child, and tormented by voices and seizures until he ascended into the sky with the assistance of Ma'iingan and Ma'iingan's manidoo, upon which he gained powers of healing and of traveling in the spirit realm. Nathaniel is subject to taboos, including that he wears his hat backward and his coat inside out, he cannot ride horses, and he cannot use metal blades.

Sarah Penn. Daughter of Kyres Elytharias and Hannah Penn. Raised by Iron Andy Calhoun as his daughter. Queen of Cahokia. Sarah is magically powerful, and possesses the unusual gift of being able to see soul-energy, in living beings and also in ley lines.

Thomas Penn. Emperor. Son of John Penn and brother of Hannah Penn. A military hero as a younger man, he locked his sister away as a madwoman and ultimately killed her when he realized she had given birth to three children who could challenge his right to be the Penn Landholder, which is also the source of his political influence.

René du Plessis. The former Seneschal, or Intendant, of the Chevalier of New Orleans. A member of the Conventicle, senior member of the cell that included his half-sister, Kinta Jane Embry. Du Plessis was killed at the Serpent Mound in a battle with Sarah's companions, giving a Masonic cry for help.

Peter Plowshare. The benevolent, peaceful manifestation of the Heron King. Alternates with Simon Sword.

Ravi. A Jew with some arcane lore, and one of the mamelukes formerly under the command of Ahmed Abd al-Wahid. Ravi left the mameluke order to remain in the New World.

Ritter. A Sword of Wisdom who acts as guide and facilitator for Montserrat Ferrer i Quintana and Luman Walters when they try to bring the kings of Adena and Koweta to Cahokia.

Roppet. Beastkind, one of the Merciful.

Logan Rupp, aka Logan Huber. Former Philadelphia lawyer and bankrupt who fled creditors to practice law in Nashville. Represents Iron Andy Calhoun, and is now in Philadelphia supporting the impeachment effort.

Theophilus Sayle. Roundhead Imperial artillery commander, famous for his ten large cannons with Biblical verses inscribed upon them. Killed at the Siege of Cahokia, and his apostolic cannons were raised into the air by the sudden growth of new trees.

Schäfer. Imperial Ohio Company trader from Youngstown.

Notwithstanding Schmidt. Formerly one of five directors of the Imperial Ohio Company, now sole director. A key administrator in the Pacification of the Ohio, and leader of the forces besieging Cahokia.

Sthoat. Beastkind, one of the Merciful.

Naares Stoach. An outrider captain of Zomas. Participated in the raid into Simon Sword's realm to kidnap the pregnant mambo Adaku

Marie Nwozuzu and her unborn child, Absalom.

Adriaan Stuyvesant. Chairman and significant shareholder of the Dutch Ohio Company, and Elector of the Hudson River Republic. Member of the Conventicle. Against the urging of Isaiah Wilkes, agreed to marry his daughter to Thomas Penn in exchange for a merger between the two Ohio companies.

Julia Stuyvesant. Daughter of Adriaan Stuyvesant, and the betrothed of Thomas Penn. She carries the child of Timothy Dockery.

Simon Sword. The Heron King in his destructive, change-bringing aspect. Alternates with Peter Plowshare.

Zadok Tarami. Metropolitan of Cahokia. He became a priest in the reforming party, and Tarami at first opposed Sarah on the grounds that the serpent was an ancient demon rather than a goddess. Having witnessed various miracles, Tarami softened his position, and fought at the Siege of Cahokia on Sarah's side.

Sherem Tauridas. Magician and servant to Alzbieta Torias. After losing his magical abilities in a battle against Sarah, he gave his life as a martyr, egged on by Josiah Dazarin and his acolytes of St. Jock of Cripplegate.

Thalanes. Cetean monk and magician, former father confessor to Kyres Elytharias. Hid Sarah with Andrew Calhoun, and returned fifteen years later to save her from the Imperial officers who were coming to capture her. Killed on the rooftop of the St. Louis Cathedral in New Orleans.

Alzbieta Torias. Sarah's cousin, Firstborn priestess. Rival to Sarah for the throne of Cahokia and then ultimately her ally. Died in the Siege of Cahokia.

Benjamin Trumbull. A thief who is sacrificed by Oliver Cromwell to demonstrate his Mockers and New Models to Thomas Penn.

Udu. Anak warrior, follower of Mesh.

Chigozie Ukwu. Son of Chinwe Ukwu, and a priest. Left New Orleans when he learned that his brother had been anointed bishop, and found a ministry as the Shepherd of the Merciful, a congregation of penitent beastkind, in Missouri.

Chinwe Philippe Ukwu. The former Bishop of New Orleans, whose murder was provoked by the Chevalier of New Orleans.

Etienne Ukwu. Vodun houngan and mobster, son of Chinwe Philippe Ukwu. Swore to his mother on his deathbed that he would protect his father and avenge his death. Schemed to succeed his father as Bishop of New Orleans, and then drive his father's murderer, the Chevalier of New Orleans, out of the city.

Varem. Zoman general who acted briefly as regent for Turim Zomas III after the death of Turim Zomas II. Killed by Simon Sword in the wrecking of Zomas.

Father Vaudres. Father confessor of Jarom Atheles. Companion of Zadok Tarami in his pilgrimage along the Onandagos Road.

Gert Visser. Timothy Dockery's romantic rival for the affections of Julia Stuyvesant. Accompanied Isaiah Wilkes, Kinta Jane Embry, and Dockery to Acadia, and was killed by Mesh.

Gottlieb Voigt. Body servant to Thomas Penn. Member of the Conventicle.

Voldrich. Wealthy Cahokian landowner. Stood as a candidate for king in the presentation arranged by Maltres Korinn. Betrayed the city by spying on it for the besieging Imperials, and was killed in the Siege of Cahokia.

Waabigwan. Wife of Ma'iingan, mother of Miigiwewin and Ayaabe.

Luman Walters. Hedge magician and student of esoteric traditions. Walters was briefly magical aide to Notwithstanding Schmidt, before defecting to Sarah's cause. Walters was physically present at Sarah's ascent, and afterward had the gift of gramarye.

Isaiah Wilkes. Actor, master of disguise, former printer, and Franklin of the Conventicle. Wilkes attempted to remind Thomas Penn of his obligations to stand against Simon Sword as Brother Onas, but Thomas drove him out. En route to seek out Algonk and Anak allies, Wilkes drowned. He is now a familiar spirit allied with Nathaniel Penn.

Lucy Winthrop. Fiancée of Ezekiel Angleton, who died in a carriage accident before they could be wed.

Yedera. After being rescued from Comanche slavers by Kyres Elytharias, Yedera swore a Podebradan oath to serve her people, and the Elytharias family. She was bodyguard to Alzbieta Torias, and now serves Sarah.

Gazelem Zomas. Outcast prince of Zomas, the eighth kingdom of the Firstborn. An accomplished poisoner, and acquaintance of Kyres Elytharias.

Turim Zomas. Last kings of Zomas. Turim Zomas I was grandfather to Gazelem Zomas, and exiled him for his own safety. Turim Zomas III was a small child when his father died and he was crowned.

Ordres Zondering. King of Talega. Wears a flower crown, and is part Lenni Lenape.

Jaleta Zorales. Artillery commander who was one of seven candidates to become monarch of Cahokia, and who sided with Sarah in driving the Imperials from Cahokia.